A. FADEYEV

THE YOUNG GUARD

A Novel

University Press of the Pacific
Honolulu, Hawaii

The Young Guard
A Novel

by
Alexander Fadeyev

Translated from the Russian by
Volet Dutt

Edited by David Sevirsky

ISBN 089875-129-2

University Press of the Pacific
Honolulu, Hawaii

http://www.UniversityPressofthePacific.com

Forward, forward, comrades, to meet the rising sun!
We'll fight our way to Liberty with bayonet and gun.
Let crimson banners be unfurled
That working men should rule the world.
To battle, valiant young guard
From factory and farm!

Youth Song

Part ONE

Chapter 1

"Oh, look, Valya, how beautiful! Fascinating! Like a sculpture. It's not marble or alabaster, it's alive and yet how cold! And so fine and delicate: no human hand could ever have made anything like it. See how it rests on the water, so pure and austere and aloof. And look at the reflection: I don't know which is lovelier. And the colours! Look, look, not white, I mean it is white, but so many shades: yellow, pink, sky blue, and in the centre, where it is moist, like mother of pearl, it's simply enchanting. There just aren't any names for colours like that!"

The voice came from the willow bushes, where a girl bent over the creek. She had wavy black hair gathered in plaits emphasizing the whiteness of her blouse, and her lovely, dark eyes were so alight with sudden radiance that she herself was not unlike the water-lily reflected in the shadowed water.

"A fine time for going into raptures! You really are funny, Ulya!" came the answer as Valya, too, thrust her head through the branches. Despite the slightly prominent cheekbones and snub nose, the face, youthfully fresh and good-natured, was attractive.

Without a glance at the lily, her eyes worriedly searched the bank for the group of girls from whom they had strayed.

"Hello-o-o!" she cried.

"He-ere! He-e-ere!" came answering shouts from near by.

"Come over here! Ulya's found a water-lily," shouted Valya with a teasing, affectionate glance at her friend.

Just then, like the echo of distant thunder, came the rumble of gun-fire from the north-west, near Voroshilovgrad.

"Again!"

"Again," Ulya said tonelessly. The radiant light, which had sparkled a moment before, faded from her eyes.

"Will they break through this time?" Valya said. "My God! Remember how we worried last year? Yet everything turned out all right. But last year they never came so close. Listen, it's like thunder!"

They listened in silence.

"When I hear that," Ulya said in a low voice filled with emotion, "and see the clear sky and the trees in leaf, and feel the grass warm with the sun and smell the sweet smell of it, it hurts me, as if all this were lost for ever and ever. You think you've been hardened by the war, that you've learnt to crush everything that might soften you, and suddenly such a rush of love and pity breaks through! Of course, you know that you're the only person I can talk to about this sort of thing."

Their faces were so close, among the leaves, that their breath mingled, and they looked straight into each other's eyes: Valya's light, wide-set, kindly, filled with humble adoration; Ulya's large and dark, with long lashes, milky whites, and deep, mysterious pupils in which that intense radiance was glowing again.

The distant booming of the guns set the leaves rustling even here, down by the river, bringing a shadow to the girls' faces.

"Wasn't it lovely out in the steppe last night, Valya? Wasn't it?" Ulya asked softly.

"Oh, it was! That sunset. Remember?"

"Yes. Nobody likes our steppe; they say it's dreary and bleak: hills, endless hills—desolate they call it—but I love it. When Mother was still well, she used to take me with her to the melon patch. I was quite small then. While she worked I'd lie there on my back, looking up, up, as high as I could, trying to see to the very top of the sky.... Yesterday it hurt me when we watched the sunset and then all those sweating horses and the guns and the carts and the wounded.... The soldiers were so tired and dusty. And all of a sudden I realized that it wasn't a regrouping at all but a terrible, yes, a terrible retreat. That's why they won't look us straight in the face. Have you noticed?"

Valya nodded.

"I looked at the steppe where we've sung so many songs together, and at the setting sun, and I could hardly keep my tears back. You haven't often seen me cry, have you?... And when it grew dark, there they were, marching and marching in the twilight, and all the time that rumbling, the flashes on the horizon, the red glare—that must have been Rovenki—and the deep, crimson sunset.... I'm not afraid of anything on earth, you know that. I'm not afraid of hardship or fighting or suffering, but if only I knew what to do! Something terrible is hanging over us," Ulya said and a dismal look came into her eyes.

"And what a lovely time we had," Valya said with tears shining in her eyes.

"What a lovely time everyone in the world could have, if only they'd try, if only they'd understand!" Ulya said. "But what shall we do? What shall we do?" she ended, with a sudden change of mood, in a childish, lilting voice, her eyes sparkling mischievously, as she heard the other girls drawing near. Swiftly, kicking off her shoes and gathering up the hem of her dark skirt in one thin, sunburnt hand, she darted into the water.

"Look, a water-lily!" A slim, supple girl with reckless, tomboy eyes came crashing through the bushes. "I saw it first. It's mine!" she shouted and, snatching up her skirt in both hands, leapt into the water with a flash of bare, tanned legs, showering herself and Ulya with amber spray. "Ow! It's deep!" she laughed, as she caught one foot in the tangle of water-weeds, and drew back.

The other six girls came rushing to the bank, chattering noisily. Like Ulya, Valya and slender Sasha, who had just dashed into the water, they all wore short skirts and simple blouses. The burning Donets winds and the scorching sun had tanned each girl differently: arms, legs, faces, necks down to the shoulder-blades were here golden brown, there darkly bronzed, while those of another were fiery red, as though she had been through a furnace.

Like girls everywhere, when there are more than two together, they all talked at once at the top of their voices—without listening to each other—in high, shrill tones, as if each were imparting news of the utmost importance, which the rest had to know forthwith.

"... He parachuted right down, honest! Such a handsome, fair chap, with wavy hair. And eyes like little buttons!"

"I could never, never be a nurse; I'm horribly afraid of blood."

"Surely they won't leave us behind. How can you say such a thing? It'll never happen."

"Oh, what a beautiful lily...."

"But Maya, my little gypsy, suppose they do leave us behind?"

"Look at Sasha! Just look!"

"But to fall in love at first sight! I don't believe in that."

"Ulya, you idiot! Where are you off to?"

"You'll be drowned, you silly things!"

They spoke in the rather rough Donbas dialect, a mixture of Central Russian vernacular, Ukrainian idiom, Don Cossack dialect, and the colloquial speech of the Azov ports: Mariupol, Taganrog and Rostov-on-Don. But whatever language the world over girls speak, it sounds sweet on their lips.

"Ulya darling, do you really have to have it?" Valya called, with a worried look in her gentle, wide-set eyes as her friend's brown calves and then her white knees disappeared under the water.

Cautiously feeling her way with one foot through the weeds and hitching her skirts higher until the edge of her black panties showed, Ulya took another step. Her graceful, slender body bent forward, she seized the lily with her free hand. One of her thick, dark plaits slipped over her shoulder, the loose, curly end falling into the water. A last effort and her fingers pulled out the lily together with its long stem.

"Good for you, Ulya!" Sasha cried, fixing Ulya with her round, hazel, boyish eyes. "You deserve the title of Hero of the Union. Not of the whole Soviet Union, but, let's say, our little union of restless girls of Pervomaisky. Let's have it!" Standing up to her calves in the water Sasha caught her skirt between her knees, reached out for the lily and dexterously fastened it in Ulya's black, wavy hair. "Oh, that does suit you! I'm simply green with envy...." Suddenly she stopped, raised her head and listened. "Just a moment.... Do you hear that, girls? Those beasts!"

Sasha and Ulya scrambled to the bank.

All the girls stood listening to the intermittent hum, now high and waspishly thin, now a low rumbling drone. With upturned faces they strained to see the aircraft through the white heat-haze.

"There are at least three of them!"

"Where? Where? I can't see a thing."

"Neither can I, but I can tell by the sound."

Now the vibrating hum of the engines merged into a menacing roar; now it was broken into separate piercing or low rumbling sounds. The planes zoomed somewhere overhead. Though they could not be seen, it seemed that the dark shadows of their wings flitted over the girls' faces.

"They must be heading for Kamensk, to bomb the crossing."

"Or Millerovo."

"Millerovo? Rubbish! We've got out of Millerovo; didn't you hear the communiqué last night?"

"All the same there's fighting farther south."

"What shall we do, girls?"

They began to listen again to the distant thunder of artillery fire which seemed to have come closer.

Grim and cruel as war is, grievous as are the losses and sufferings of humanity, happy, healthy youth in its simple-hearted, good-natured egoism, its loves and its dreams of the future, will not and cannot recognize the threat of danger and suffering to itself in the common danger and suffering so long as its own joyful rhythm remains undisturbed.

Ulya Gromova, Valya Filatova, Sasha Bondareva and the rest of the girls had that spring finished their secondary schooling in the mining village of Pervomaisky.

Leaving school is always an important event in the life of a young person, but to leave school in time of war is very special indeed.

In the previous summer, after the outbreak of war, the pupils in the upper forms—people still called them boys and girls—had worked on the state and collective farms round Krasnodon, in the mines, or in the locomotive works at Voroshilovgrad. Some had even travelled as far as Stalingrad to work in the tractor plant, now producing tanks.

In the autumn the Germans had broken through into the Donbas and occupied Taganrog and Rostov. In the whole of the Ukraine, only Voroshilovgrad Region had remained untaken. The Ukrainian Government authorities, retreating from Kiev with the army, transferred to Voroshilovgrad, while the Voroshilovgrad and Stalino (formerly Yuzovka) regional administration moved to Krasnodon.

Late into the autumn, until the Southern Front was stabilized, an unending stream of people from the occupied areas of the Donbas passed through Krasnodon, churning up the rust-red mud of the streets which seemed to get muddier every day as the people brought it in on their boots from the steppe.

The school children were got ready by the school to evacuate to Saratov Region, but stayed on when the Germans were brought to a halt far beyond Voroshilovgrad. Rostov-on-Don was retaken and, in the winter, after the defeat of the Germans on the approaches to Moscow, the Red Army offensive began and everyone hoped that now things would take a turn for the better.

The school children had grown accustomed to having strange people living in their cosy homes—the stone houses of Krasnodon, the farm-houses of Pervomaisky, even the little clay-daubed cottages of the "Shanghai" neighbourhood—which had felt so empty in the first weeks of the war when fathers and brothers had left for the front. Now they held an everchanging stream of lodgers: men and women working in the evacuated administrative organizations, soldiers and officers passing through on their way to the front, or quartered as part of the garrison.

The youngsters soon learnt to distinguish between the different branches of the services, ranks and types of arms, the makes of motor cycles, lorries and other forms of motor transport, their own as well as those captured from the enemy. They were able to identify any type of tank at first glance, not only when they stood massively at rest in the shade of the poplars by the roadside, the heat-haze rising from their steaming armour, but also when they thundered over the dusty Voroshilovgrad Highway or rolled heavily westwards through the autumn mud or winter slush.

They learnt to distinguish, by sound as well as sight, every type of Soviet and German aircraft, recognizing them when the Donets sky was ablaze with sunlight, or red with dust, or spangled with stars, or inky-black in stormy weather.

"They're Lags (or Migs or Yaks)," they would say quietly.

"That was a Messer!"

"J-87s, heading for Rostov," they would say casually.

They had got used to night duty in the air-defence squads, standing watch with gas-masks over their shoulder at pit-heads or on the roofs of schools and hospitals. Their hearts no longer missed a beat when the earth shook with explosions and searchlight beams crossed like knitting-needles in the distant night sky over Voroshilovgrad, and the glare of fires leapt up here and there on the horizon; or when, in broad daylight, dive-bombers attacked the long columns of motor vehicles winding across the steppe and then rained cannon and machine-gun fire on the highway, scattering men and horses to left and right like a speed-boat cutting the water.

They had grown to love the long drive to the collective farms and the songs they sang at the top of their voices in the open lorries carrying them across the steppe; and the summer harvest time among the boundless stretches of heavy wheat; and the exchanges of confidences and sudden bursts of laughter in the stillness of the night on the oaten chaff.

They loved the long, sleepless nights on the roof, when a girl's warm hand rested motionless, hour after hour, in the rough palm of a boy; when the dawn rose over pale hills and the dew sparkled on the dull pink roof-tops and dripped into the front garden from the yellowing acacia leaves; when the air smelt of the decaying roots of withered flowers in the moist earth and of the smoke from distant fires, and the first cock crowed as though all was right with the world....

And then this spring they had left school and said fare-well to teachers and school clubs. And suddenly, as though it had been waiting for them, they had come face to face with the war.

On June 23, the Soviet troops retreated in the direction of Kharkov. And on July 3, like a bolt from the blue, came the radio announcement that, after an eight months' defence, Sevastopol had fallen.

Stary Oskol, Rossosh, Kantemirovka; fighting west of Voronezh; fighting on the approaches to Voronezh. July 12—on the approaches to Lisichansk. And all at once the retreating troops began pouring through Krasnodon.

Lisichansk, practically next door, meant tomorrow Voroshilovgrad and, the day after, Krasnodon and Pervomaisky; it meant the little streets, familiar down to the last stone, with the dusty jasmine and lilac bushes tumbling over the fences of the front gardens, Grandfather's apple orchard and the cool rooms, shuttered against the sun, where Father's pit jacket still hung on the hook, just as he had left it when he came from work the last time before going off to the war commissariat; it meant the home where Mother's warm, veined hands had scrubbed each floor board till it gleamed, had watered the China rose on the windowsill and spread a bright-coloured cloth of fresh-smelling unbleached linen on the table ... it meant that this could, this would be invaded by the German fascists.

During the lull at the front a number of commissary officers—all majors—had settled down comfortably as though for life. They were all clean-shaven, alert and cheerful, and exceptionally well-informed about everything. When they sat down to a game of cards with their hosts they made jokes all the time and were always willing to explain the situation at the front. They bought pickled water-melons in the market and occasionally made contributions of tinned food for the housewife's soup. At the Gorky Club of 1B Pit and the Lenin Club in the municipal park there was always a crowd of lieutenants: a jolly lot, fond of dancing, and well-mannered or full of tricks—there was no telling. Lieutenants came and went, but there were always new ones to replace the old and the girls got so accustomed to this succession of sunburnt, manly faces that they all seemed old friends.

Then suddenly they were all gone.

Verkhneduvannaya, the drowsy little wayside station which spelt home for Krasnodon people returning after an official trip, or a visit to relatives, or at the end of a year's study, Verkhneduvannaya, like all the other stations on the Likhaya-Morozovskaya-Stalingrad line, was jammed with people, shells, machines and grain.

Women and children could be heard weeping in the little houses shaded by acacia, poplar and maple. Here a mother was packing for a child who was to be evacuated with a kindergarten or school; there a son or a daughter was being seen off; elsewhere a husband and father was saying goodbye to his family as he prepared to leave the town with his factory. Other houses stood with shutters tightly closed in a silence more appalling than a mother's weeping. Some were empty; in others there remained, perhaps, an old grandmother, her work-blackened hands heavy in her lap, too tired for tears, with bitter anguish in her heart, sitting motionless in a room after seeing the whole family off.

In the morning the girls wakened to the sound of distant gun-fire. After the usual bickering with their parents—for they wanted their parents to evacuate at once and leave them behind, while the parents argued that they had lived their life and that it was the Komsomols who must be kept from harm—after the usual bickering, the girls ate a hasty breakfast and hurried away to join their friends and learn the latest news. They would flock together like birds and, drooping with heat and the lack of occupation, sit about for hours in some half-dark room, or under an apple-tree; or they would run down to the shady wooded gully by the river, filled with a secret premonition of disaster which was beyond their power to realize fully with either heart or mind.

And now disaster had come.

"I bet they've lost Voroshilovgrad by now, only they won't tell us," said one of the girls sharply. She was a small creature with a broad face and pointed nose. Her glossy hair, so smooth that it looked glued on, ended in two short pigtails which stuck out pertly.

Her name was Zina Vyrikova but nobody at school had ever called her by her first name. It was always "Vyrikova, Vyrikova."

"How can you talk like that, Vyrikova? If they haven't told us, then it isn't lost," said Maya Peglivanova, a beautiful dark-eyed girl with the complexion of a gypsy, stubbornly pursing her full proud lower lip.

Until she had left school that spring, Maya had been the secretary of the Komsomol organization in the school and had acquired the habit of correcting people and instructing them and, in general, wanting to put everything right.

"We all know what you're going to say: 'Girls, you don't understand the first thing about dialectics!'" Vyrikova retorted, mimicking Maya so aptly that everybody laughed. "As if they'd tell us the truth! We've believed them and believed them, and now that's worn thin," she went on, her close-set eyes flashing and her stiff little pigtails quivering aggressively, like the feelers of a beetle. "They've probably cleared out of Rostov again too and there's nowhere for us to go. But they're packing off themselves all right!" Vyrikova was obviously repeating an expression she had often heard.

"What a funny way to talk, Vyrikova," Maya said, making an effort to keep her voice calm. "How can you say things like that? You, a Komsomol, and you used to be a Young Pioneer leader."

"Oh, don't bother with her," murmured Shura Dubrovina, a silent girl, slightly older than the rest. She wore her hair cropped in a mannish way and her wildish pale eyes, under almost invisible eyebrows, gave her face a strange expression.

The daughter of a Krasnodon saddler and boot-maker, Shura Dubrovina had been studying at Kharkov University, but had returned to her father in Krasnodon the year before when the Germans advanced on Kharkov. Though she was about four years older than the other girls, she was always to be found in their company, drawn by a secret, girlish adoration of Maya Peglivanova whom she trailed after, as the girls put it, "like the thread after the needle."

"Don't bother with her. If she's got that bee in her bonnet, there's nothing to be done about it," Shura advised Maya.

"They made us dig trenches the whole summer," Vyrikova went on, taking no notice of Maya. "What a lot of energy was wasted! I was ill for a whole month as a result. And now look at those trenches! Grass growing all over them! Isn't that so?"

Sasha looked at her with mock surprise and shrugged her thin shoulders, letting out a long whistle.

It was the general state of uncertainty and not so much what Vyrikova said that made the girls listen to her with strained attention.

"After all, the situation's really dreadful, isn't it?" Tonya Ivanikhina, the youngest of them all, said, glancing timidly from Vyrikova to Maya. Tears welled up in her eyes. She was still a little more than a child, long-legged, with the large nose and heavy, chestnut hair brushed back behind her big ears.

Ever since her elder sister Lilya, whom she had loved dearly, had gone to the front as a feldsher and had been reported missing in the fighting round Kharkov, everything, everything in the world had seemed to Tonya irreparably lost, and the slightest thing brought her to the verge of tears.

Ulya was the only one who took no part in the conversation and did not seem to share her companions' perturbation. She undid the long, black plait that had fallen in the water, wrung it and replaited it. Then she stretched out first one leg then the other to dry in the sun, standing quietly with her head on one side—the white lily emphasizing the dark eyes and hair—as though she were listening to some inner voice. When her legs were dry, Ulya brushed the white soles of her feet, wiped the toes and heels and deftly slipped into her shoes.

"What a fool I was, not to join the special school when I had the chance!" Sasha said. "The Commissariat for Home Affairs invited me to go in for special training," she explained artlessly, looking round with boyish unconcern. "Then I'd stay and work behind the German lines and none of you would know anything about it. You'd all be in a great state and I wouldn't give a damn. 'What's the matter with Sasha?' you'd think. And all the time I'd be working for the Commissariat for Home Affairs! And as for those fat-heads of the Gestapo," she suddenly exploded with laughter, darting a sly glance at Vyrikova, "I'd just twist them round my little finger!"

Ulya lifted her head and turned serious, attentive eyes on Sasha. Something quivered: her lips or her delicate, finely-cut nostrils.

"I shall stay here, Commissariat or no Commissariat. So there!" Vyrikova retorted sullenly, with a shake of her pigtails. "As nobody cares what happens to me, I'll just stay behind and go on living the same way as before. Why not? I'm a schoolgirl, according to German ideas, a grammar-school pupil. After all, they're civilized people. What harm can they do me?"

"A grammar-school pupil?" Maya cried, her face growing scarlet.

"'I've just finished grammar-school, how d'you do!'" Sasha imitated Vyrikova so well that the girls laughed again.

Just then a deafening crash seemed to shake heaven and earth. Dry twigs and withered leaves fell from the trees and a ripple passed over the water.

The girls turned pale and stood silently staring at one another for a few moments.

"Could they have dropped something?" Maya asked.

"It's ages since they passed and we haven't heard any others," Tonya Ivanikhina said, her eyes wide with fright. She was always the first to sense disaster.

And then came two more explosions, almost simultaneous, one very near, the other a little farther away.

Without a word the girls made off home, their sunburnt legs flashing through the bushes.

Chapter 2

THEY RAN across the steppe, the sun-scorched Donets steppe, so trampled by sheep and goats that clouds of dust rose at every step. It was hard to believe that they had just emerged from cool, leafy shade. The gully through which the river flowed between narrow, wooded banks was so deep that three or four hundred paces away the girls could no longer see either trees or river or even the gully itself. The steppe had swallowed them up.

The steppe was not flat here, as round Astrakhan or Salsk, but full of hills and ravines, and far to the south and north the ground rose to meet the horizon, forming an enormous blue bowl holding the quivering, white-hot air.

This furrowed, parched steppe was dotted with mining villages and farms sprawling over the hill-sides and in the hollows and surrounded by green and yellow rectangles of wheat, maize, sunflowers and sugar-beet. Here and there loomed lonely engine-houses, marking the mine shafts, and beside them, overshadowing them, the deep blue cones of the coal-tips.

All the roads connecting mines and villages were thronged with refugees, hurrying towards the highways that led to Kamensk and Likhaya.

The noise of a distant, furious battle, or rather of many battles, large and small, to the west, the north-west, and even somewhere far to the north, could be heard quite clearly here, in the open steppe. Smoke of distant conflagrations rose slowly to the sky or hung in heavy clouds on the horizon.

The first thing that caught the girls' eyes as they came out of the wooded gully was three fresh columns of smoke—two quite close and one further away—in the vicinity of Krasnodon itself, which was hidden from view by the hills. The three thin grey columns of smoke were slowly dissolving in the hazy atmosphere. The girls might not have noticed them at all had it not been for the explosions and an acrid, garlic-like smell which grew stronger as they approached the town.

There was a low, round hill facing Pervomaisky. They climbed it and before their eyes lay the whole suburb straggling over mounds and hollows, and beyond it, the Voroshilovgrad Highway, crossing the ridge of the long hill which divided the suburb from the town of Krasnodon.

As far as the eye could see, the highway was crowded with military units and refugees. Motor transport of all types, overtaking the foot columns, raced past with a furious blaring of horns: ordinary civilian cars, and camouflaged military machines, dusty and battle-scarred; lorries, vans, ambulances. And the red dust, disturbed by these countless feet and wheels, hung like a canopy over the whole length of the highway.

And then the impossible, the incredible happened: the huge, concrete mass of the engine-house of 1B Pit, which alone of all the buildings in Krasnodon was visible from this side of the highway, suddenly swayed. Then a vast fan of torn-up earth concealed it from view for an instant, and again a tremendous subterranean shock, which sent a hollow rumble through the air and under the ground, startled the girls. The air cleared: there was no trace of the engine-house. The enormous dark cone of the tip glittered in the sunlight as before, but where the engine-house had stood there was only a cloud of dirty, yellow-grey smoke. And over the highway, over the stunned suburb of Pervomaisky, over the invisible town, over the whole countryside, hung a strange drawn-out sound, a moan in which faint human voices seemed to rise and fall, weeping, or cursing, or groaning in torment.

It had all come upon them at once: the sight of the people streaming along the highway, the speeding vehicles, the shock of the explosion, the disappearance of the engine-house. But through all the emotions which constricted their hearts, came one single feeling, stronger and deeper than any fear for themselves: the feeling that a yawning chasm had opened at their feet, marking the end of their world.

"They're blowing up the mines!"

Whose cry was that? It must have been Tonya. But this cry came from all their hearts. "They're blowing up the mines!..."

Not another word was said. They could not speak. The group broke up of its own accord, most of the girls running off to their homes in the suburb, while Maya, Ulya and Sasha, heading for the district Komsomol committee, followed the nearest footpath across the highway into the town.

But as the two groups separated, Valya Filatova suddenly seized her friend's hand.

"Ulya ... Ulya darling!" she said in a timid, pleading voice. "Ulya, where are you off to? Come home." She faltered and then added, "Anything might happen!"

Ulya turned abruptly and looked at her silently. No, she did not look at Valya, but through her, far, far into the distance; and the expression in her dark eyes was that of impetuous movement. So must be the expression in the eyes of a bird in flight.

"Wait," pleaded Valya, laying a hand on Ulya's arm. With her free hand she quickly pulled the lily from Ulya's dark, wavy hair and threw it on the ground. It was done so swiftly that, far from stopping to think why Valya had done this, Ulya did not even notice it. And now, for the first time in all their years of friendship, these two ran off in different directions, without a word.

Yes, it was difficult to believe that what they had seen was true. But when Maya, Ulya and Sasha had crossed the highway they could no longer doubt it: there stood the massive coal-tip and next to it—nothing! No trace of the impressive engine-house with its powerful winding wheels; only a billow of yellow-grey smoke rising slowly to the sky and filling the air with the unbearable stench of garlic.

Fresh explosions shook the earth, some very near, others more distant.

This part of the town where 1B Pit stood was cut off from the centre by a deep ravine which had a muddy, sedge-grown stream flowing at its bottom. Except for this ravine with clay-daubed dwellings clustering its slopes, the whole district, like the centre of the town, was built of single-storey stone houses, with tiled or slate roofs, designed for two or three families. Each house had its little front garden, with vegetable patches and flower-beds. Some people had planted cherry-trees, or lilac, or jasmine; others had set out rows of acacia or maple saplings along the low, neatly painted fences. And now, going past these tidy little houses and gardens, were columns of workers of every kind, men and women, and lorries laden with the equipment of the Krasnodon factories and offices.

The whole remaining population had come out of doors, and while some looked over their garden fences with sympathy, or mere curiosity, at the fleeing crowds, others came into the street, lugging bags and bundles and pushing handcarts loaded with household goods. Little children perched on top of the loads and many women carried babies in their arms.

Attracted by the explosion, crowds of youngsters had run towards 1B Pit, but there militiamen had formed a cordon, letting no one through. People were pressing in the opposite direction, from the pit. And into this confusion poured a multitude of collective farmers from a narrow street leading out of the market-place. There were old men, women and young people, with baskets and barrows full of vegetables and other produce, and horse-carts and bullock wagons.

The people in the columns walked in silence with sombre faces, concentrating on one thought which so preoccupied them as to make them quite unaware of what was going on round them. Only the leaders, striding beside the columns, hung back or ran ahead to help the foot and mounted militiamen bring order among the refugees whenever they blocked the roads or hampered the movement of the columns.

A woman in the crowd caught Maya by the arm and Sasha stopped to wait for her: but Ulya, who only wanted to get to the district committee as quickly as possible, hurried on, breasting like a bird the crowd that pressed from the opposite direction.

A green lorry roared up the ravine and round the corner. The crowd surged back and Ulya was forced against a fence, and if it had not been for the gate, she would have overturned a slight, fair girl who was standing between two dusty lilac bushes just inside it. The girl was very delicately built, with an upturned little nose and blue eyes screwed up against the sun.

Strange as it might seem in the circumstances, at the very instant when Ulya collided with the gate, almost knocking the girl down, she had a sudden mental picture of this girl swaying to the strains of a waltz. She could even hear the tune played by a brass band. The vision made her heart contract with sweet, sudden pain, as in a dream of happiness.

The girl danced and sang on the stage; she danced and sang in the hall; she danced till the small hours, tirelessly, danced with anyone and everyone. Her blue eyes and her even, little white teeth sparkled with happiness. When was it? It must have been before the war, in another life, in a dream.

Ulya did not know the girl's surname. Everyone called her Lyuba. Yes, this was Lyuba. "Lyuba the Actress" the little boys called her.

The astonishing thing was that Lyuba should be standing there calmly between the lilac bushes at her gate dressed as though she were on her way to a dance at the club. With her pink face, always carefully protected from the sun, her golden hair beautifully dressed, her small hands that seemed carved of ivory, and her bright nails, which looked as if she had just had a manicure, and her small, graceful feet in high-heeled, cream-coloured shoes, Lyuba might have been on the point of going on to the stage to sing and dance.

But what amazed Ulya even more was the extraordinarily provocative and, at the same time, open and intelligent expression on her rosy face with the slightly snub nose, the full, rouged lips, the mouth that was rather large for her face, and, above all, the narrowed, blue, uncommonly lively eyes.

She seemed to take it as perfectly natural that Ulya had nearly torn the garden gate off its hinges and, without a glance at her, continued to stand calmly, keeping a sharp eye on everything that happened in the street, and shouting whatever came into her head.

"Idiot!" she yelled at a lorry-driver, her nose in the air, her blue eyes flashing between their heavy lashes. "Who are you shoving? You must have a screw loose; can't you let people get out of the way? Hey, stop! Where do you think you're going, you fool?"

Actually, the driver had just brought his lorry to a stop opposite her gate and was waiting for the road to be cleared. It was loaded high with militia property and several militiamen to guard it.

"My word! What a lot of guardians of the law have managed to pile in!" Lyuba cried, well pleased to have found a new target. "Instead of reassuring people, you clear out as fast as you can!" She waved her small hand in an inimitable gesture and whistled like an urchin.

"What's the silly goose quacking about?" growled one of the men, a militia sergeant, riled by the obvious injustice.

But this was only asking for more trouble.

"Ah, Comrade Scrimshanker," Lyuba hailed him. "Wherever did you come from, my gallant knight?"

"Shut up before I make you!" the "gallant knight" exploded and made as if to jump off the lorry.

"You won't get off! Too frightened of being left behind!" taunted Lyuba with no change of voice and not the slightest sign of anger. "*Bon voyage*, Comrade Scrimshanker!" And with an indifferent gesture of her hand at the sergeant who, though crimson with rage, had, indeed, not jumped off the lorry, she waved them on.

Lyuba's comments, her elegant appearance, and the composure with which she stood there at a time when everyone else was in flight might have suggested that she was the worst enemy of the Soviet regime, waiting impatiently for the arrival of the Germans and mocking her unhappy countrymen; but this impression was belied by her open-hearted, childlike expression and the fact that her jibes were aimed mostly at people who really deserved them.

"Hey, you there, in the hat! Look at the load you've piled on your little wife, and your own hands empty!" she shouted. "Such a tiny little woman. And you've even stuck a hat on your head! Oh, you make me sick!"

And then, to an old woman on a cart:

"Aha, Grandma, gobbling collective-farm cucumbers while nobody's looking, eh? I suppose you think that if the Soviets are leaving, you've nobody to answer to. But what about God in His heaven, eh? Don't you think He sees you? He sees everything!"

Nobody paid the slightest attention to her and she was quite aware of it. She seemed to want justice done purely for her own personal entertainment. Ulya was fascinated by her calm fearless manner; she felt an instantaneous confidence in this girl and turned to her:

"Lyuba, I'm a Komsomol from Pervomaisky—Ulya Gromova. Tell me, what started all this?"

"Oh ... just the usual," Lyuba replied readily, giving Ulya a friendly look with her bright, audacious blue eyes. "Our troops left Voroshilovgrad early this morning. Orders were given for all organizations to evacuate right away."

"And the district Komsomol committee too?" Ulya asked bleakly.

"Don't you dare hit that kid, you lout, you good-for-nothing! Just you wait till I get at you, I'll teach you!" Lyuba screeched at a boy in the crowded street. "The district committee?" she said, turning back to Ulya. "The district committee left at dawn this morning, in the vanguard, as it ought to be.... What are you goggling at me like that for, my girl?" she spoke irritably. Then suddenly looking at Ulya and realizing what was going on inside her, she smiled and added: "I'm joking, of course.... They got orders, you see, and had to leave. They didn't run away. Understand?"

"But what about us?" Ulya demanded in a sudden rush of furious resentment.

"You leave too, of course. The instructions went out early this morning. Where've you been all day?"

"And what about you?" Ulya countered.

"Me?" Lyuba hesitated. Her intelligent face took on a distant and blank expression. "I'll wait and see," she said evasively.

"Aren't you a Komsomol?" Ulya persisted. For an instant her dark eyes, stern and penetrating, met Lyuba's watchful, narrowed ones.

"No," Lyuba said, slightly pursing her lips and turning away. Then all at once, with a shout of "Daddy!" she threw open the gate and ran to meet a group of people coming towards the house. They stood out sharply among the crowd, these people; and it made way for them with a sort of frightened and special reverence.

The group was led by Valko, director of 1B Pit, a thickset, clean-shaven man of about fifty, sombre and swarthy as a gypsy, in a jacket and high boots; and Grigory Ilyich Shevtsov, a coal-hewer from the same pit, known to the whole town for his output record.

Behind them came a few more miners and two men in uniform. They were followed at a respectful distance by a miscellaneous throng of the curious; for even in the most extraordinary and distressing times there are sure to be people who are there out of curiosity pure and simple.

Grigory and the other miners were in their working clothes, with the hoods thrown back. Their faces, hands and clothing were black with coal-dust. One of them had a heavy coil of electric cable on his shoulder; another carried a box of tools, while Shevtsov held some queer sort of metal appliance in his hands, with bits of wire protruding from it.

They were not talking. They seemed afraid to meet one another's eyes, or the eyes of the people in the crowd. Sweat rolled down their faces, making white furrows in the black coal-dust. They looked utterly worn out, as though they were carrying a weight beyond their strength.

And suddenly Ulya understood why the people in the street made way with a certain awe, leaving the whole road clear for these men. It was they who, with their own hands, had blown up 1B Pit, the pride of the Donets Basin.

Lyuba ran to Grigory, and put her hand in his. The dark, sinewy hand closed tightly on the small white one and Lyuba walked back towards the house at his side.

Just then the whole group with Valko and Shevtsov in the lead reached the gate. With evident relief, the miners threw their burdens over the fence—the heavy coil of cable and the box of tools and the strange metal appliance—straight on to the flower-beds. And it became clear that these flowers, planted with such loving care, had become things of the past, like the very way of life which had made these flowers and so many other things possible.

They dropped their burdens and stood about awkwardly for a while, avoiding each other's eyes.

"Well, Grigory Ilyich," Valko said at last, "get ready as fast as you can. The car's waiting. I'll collect the people, and we'll come for you and your things."

He did not look up at Shevtsov as he spoke, but kept his eyes, shadowed by thick, gypsy eyebrows, which met over his nose, fixed on the ground. Turning, he walked slowly down the street, accompanied by the miners and the two men in uniform.

One miner, an old man with long thin legs, whose straggling beard and moustache were stained yellow by tobacco, stayed beside Grigory, who was still standing at the gate with Lyuba, her hand in his. Ulya, too, remained where she was, as though here and only here could her problem be solved. The others paid no attention to her.

"Why don't you do as you're told, Lyuba?" Grigory said. He looked severely at his daughter but did not release her hand.

"I've told you, I'm not leaving," Lyuba answered sullenly.

"Stop playing the fool," Grigory said in a low voice with evident agitation. "How can you stay here? You're a Komsomol!"

Lyuba flushed, throwing a glance at Ulya; but at once her face assumed a rebellious, almost an insolent expression.

"I've hardly been any time at all in the Komsomol,"

she retorted. "I've never done anyone any harm and no harm will come to me." There was a pause. Then she added, softly: "I can't leave Mother."

"She's repudiated the Komsomol!" Ulya thought, horrified. But at the same time her heart was torn by the memory of her own ailing mother.

"Well, Grigory Ilyich," said the old miner in a voice so deep that one could hardly believe it issued from so dried-out a body, "it's time to say good-bye ... good luck to you." He looked straight at Shevtsov, who stood before him with bowed head.

Grigory silently bared his head. He had fair hair, blue eyes and a thin, deeply lined face. A man getting on in years, dressed in unbecoming overalls, his face and hands black with coal-dust, he nevertheless gave the impression of being well-built, strong and good-looking in an old Russian way.

"Maybe you'd take your chance with us after all ... eh, Kondratovich?" he asked without raising his eyes, obviously embarrassed.

"Now where could we go, me and the old woman? No, we'll wait for our children to come back with the Red Army to free us."

"What about your eldest?" Grigory asked.

"Him? No good talking about him!" the old man said gloomily. He gesticulated with his hand, and the expression on his face eloquently said: he's disgraced me, why bring him in? .

He offered his thin, sinewy hand to Shevtsov.

"Good-bye, Grigory Ilyich, good-bye!" he said sadly.

Shevtsov took his hand and for some moments they stood in silence. Something else had to be said.

"You see, my old woman ... and my daughter, too ... they're staying behind," he mumbled slowly. Then his voice broke. "How in the world did we bring ourselves to blow her up, Kondratovich? Our beauty... the country's bread and butter...." He heaved a great sigh and the tears, glistening like crystals, slowly ran down his coal-blackened cheeks.

With a hoarse sob the old miner lowered his head. Lyuba burst into tears.

Biting her lip but unable to hold back the tears of impotent rage Ulya dashed away towards her home in Pervomaisky.

Chapter 3

WHILE everything in the outskirts of the town was disturbed by the excitement of retreat and hurried evacuation, nearer the centre things were somewhat quieter and appeared more normal. The columns of refugees with their families had already dwindled and left the streets. Lines of carts and lorries were parked in the drives and courtyards of office buildings. People, but no more than were necessary for the job, were loading crates of office equipment and sacks stuffed with bundles of documents. Conversation in undertones seemed to be deliberately confined to the business in hand. From the open doors and windows could be heard the sound of hammering and occasionally the tapping of typewriters. The more meticulous office managers were making last-minute lists of the equipment being evacuated and what was being left behind. The only indication that the offices were not simply moving to new premises was the pounding of distant artillery and the earth tremors from bursting shells.

On a hill in the heart of the town stood a new single-storey building with sprawling wings. Rows of young trees grew along the whole length of the façade. The building could be seen by the people leaving from every part of the town. It housed the district Party committee and the executive committee of the District Soviet, and since the previous autumn the Voroshilovgrad Regional Committee of the Bolshevik Party had also had its offices there.

Officials from offices and factories were constantly driving up to the main doors and quickly leaving again. From its open windows came the sound of telephones ringing incessantly and telephone conversations, some deliberately restrained and others unnecessarily loud. A few cars, civilian and military, were parked in a semicircle near the main entrance. The last in the row was a very dusty jeep. Two soldiers in faded tunics sat in the rear seats: a major in need of a shave and an enormously tall young sergeant. The faces and bearing of the two soldiers and, indeed, of the drivers of all the cars wore the same indefinable expression—anticipation.

Meanwhile, in a large room in the right wing of the building a scene was being enacted, which in its intensity would have overshadowed the great tragedies of the ancients had it not been such a simple affair to all outward appearances. Leading figures from the region and district were taking their farewell of those of their colleagues whose business it was to remain to complete the evacuation and then, on the arrival of the Germans, to disappear without a trace, to merge with the population and work underground.

Nothing draws people closer together than partnership in hardship.

All the long months of war, from the first to the present day, had seemed to these people one single long working day of superhuman effort which only the toughest and most physically fit could endure.

They had selected and sent to the front all the strongest, healthiest, youngest. They had transferred to the east all the larger plants and factories which were in danger of destruction or seizure by the Germans. They had shifted to the east thousands of machine-tools, tens of thousands of workers, hundreds of thousands of families. And then, as if by a miracle, they had discovered yet more machine-tools, more workers, and had instilled new life into idle mines and abandoned factory buildings.

They had kept industry and the people in such a state of preparedness that it had become possible again, in the new emergency, to uproot still more and move it to the east. And all this time they had unfailingly performed tasks without which the life of the Soviet people would have been inconceivable: they had fed and clothed them, taught children, healed the sick; they had trained new engineers, teachers, agronomists; they had kept open the dining-rooms, canteens, shops, theatres, clubs, sports grounds, public baths, laundries and barbers' shops, and maintained the militia and the fire service.

They had worked through the months of the war as if all these months had been one single day. They had forgotten what it was to have a private life: their families were away in the east. They had lived, fed and slept, not in their homes, but in offices and factories. They could be found at their posts at any time of the day or night.

One part of the Donbas had fallen to the enemy, then

another, then a third. But they had worked on still more strenuously in the areas that remained. They had worked to the limit of their endurance in the last remaining part of the Donbas just because it was the last remaining part. But to the very end, they had upheld the people's titanic determination to face up to the burden that the war had placed upon their shoulders. And when nothing further could be wrung from the efforts of the people, they had squeezed out the last ounce, again and again, from their own spiritual and physical supplies. It had been impossible to gauge whether their efforts would run out, for there had been no limit to them.

The day finally came when this last part of the Donbas had to be abandoned. And then for several days they had again been mounting everything on wheels: thousands of machine-tools, tens of thousands of people and hundreds of thousands of tons of precious equipment. The last moment had now come. They could no longer stay behind.

They stood close together in the large office of the secretary of the Krasnodon District Party Committee. The red baize cloth had already been removed from the conference table. They faced each other, cracking jokes, slapping one another on the back, each hesitating to say the words of farewell. The minds of those who were leaving were heavy and troubled and in their hearts there was a searing pain.

It was only natural that Ivan Fyodorovich Protsenko, who worked at the regional committee, should be the central figure on this occasion. He had been chosen for underground work as long ago as the autumn of the previous year when the danger of occupation first threatened the region. But at that time the matter had of itself been postponed.

Ivan Protsenko was a small man of thirty-five, sturdy and well-knit. His fair hair, thinning at the temples, was brushed back; his ruddy face, formerly always clean-shaven, now had a soft, dark growth which no longer could be called a stubble, but it was not a beard either. He had been growing it for two weeks, from the time when events at the front had clearly shown that illegal existence would inevitably be his.

Cordially and respectfully he shook hands with a tall

elderly man wearing uniform without distinctive marks or flashes. His lean, strong face, wrinkled with the marks of years of strain and weariness, was remarkable for that expression of calm, simplicity and authority which is the hallmark of the truly great leader of men and arises out of profound knowledge and understanding of what takes place in the world.

This man was one of the leaders of the recently formed headquarters of the Ukrainian partisans and only the previous day had arrived in Krasnodon to establish relations between the partisan detachments in the region and units of the army.

At that time the extent of the retreat had not been foreseen. It had been hoped that the enemy would be held on the lower reaches of the Donets or the Don. Ivan Protsenko's instructions from the partisan headquarters were to establish contact between the partisan detachment which was to be his base and the army division which was being thrown into the Kamensk sector to support the covering detachments on the Northern Donets. This division, after sustaining heavy losses in the fighting round Voroshilovgrad, was only now nearing Krasnodon, and the divisional commander, a general of about forty, had arrived the previous day together with representatives of the partisan headquarters and of the Political Administration of the Southern Front. Now he awaited his turn to take his farewell of Ivan Protsenko.

Meanwhile, Protsenko was conversing with the partisan leader who had been his chief before the war, had often visited him in his home and was well acquainted with his wife.

"Many, many thanks for your help and guidance, Andrei Yefimovich," Protsenko was saying. "Carry our partisan thanks to Nikita Sergeyevich Khrushchov. Should you happen to visit Central Headquarters tell them that we've now got some pretty good partisans round Voroshilovgrad too. And if you're lucky enough to see the Commander-in-Chief Comrade Stalin, tell him we'll do our duty."

Protsenko spoke in Russian but from time to time involuntarily lapsed into his native Ukrainian.

"Do your duty and you may be sure people will hear about it. I don't doubt for a minute that you will do your duty," Andrei Yefimovich said, a serious smile lighting up his wrinkled face. Suddenly, he turned to the assembled company. "He's sly, this Protsenko," he said. "He hasn't even started fighting, yet he's already dropping hints about getting supplies direct from Central Headquarters."

Everybody laughed, except the general who had stood quietly throughout the whole conversation with a stern, sad look on his strong rounded face.

A cunning light flashed in Protsenko's clear blue eyes and a mischievous twinkle seemed to skip from one eye to the other.

"Oh, I've got enough supplies. And when they run out we'll get along without a quartermaster's stores; like that old Kovpak fellow: what we take from the enemy is ours. Still, if you feel like adding a thing or two, well...." Protsenko threw out his hands and everybody laughed. Then he turned to shake hands with an elderly army man, a regimental commissar.

"Please tell the workers of the Front-Line Political Administration how grateful we are to them. They've given us a great deal of help. As for you lads, what can I say?" And, deeply moved, he turned and embraced each of the young fellows of the People's Commissariat for Home Affairs in turn.

He was subtle and understood that one should never give offence to any worker, whether important or not, if he had shouldered his share of responsibility. And so he thanked every organization and every individual for the help they had given him in building up the partisan detachments and the underground network. Taking leave of his colleagues from the regional committee was a long, sad business. Friendship and destiny had bound them close together through all these long months of war which had passed like one day.

With misty eyes he broke away from his friends and glanced round to see whether he had overlooked anyone.

The general, a short, stocky figure, walked towards Protsenko with a swift strong movement of his whole body and put out his hand. There was something childlike in the expression of his simple Russian face.

"A thousand thanks," said Protsenko with feeling. "Thank you for troubling to come over in person. Now we're well and truly bound together, as though with a single rope." And he shook the general's firm hand.

The childlike expression left the general's face. He made an involuntary, almost irritable movement of the head. His small, clever eyes held the former stern expression as he looked at Protsenko. It was clear he had something of importance to say, yet he said nothing.

The decisive moment arrived.

"Look after yourself," Andrei Yefimovich said, with a change of countenance, and embraced Protsenko.

Everyone again shook hands with Protsenko, his assistant and the officials remaining behind and then left one by one, with just a trace of something like guilt on their faces. The general alone departed with his head held high, walking with his usual quick, easy gait which seemed so strange in one so stout. Protsenko did not accompany them to the door, he only heard the noise of the departing cars.

Meanwhile in the office the telephones had been busy and Protsenko's assistant had been lifting one receiver after another and requesting callers to ring back later. The last visitor had scarcely left when he handed Protsenko one of the receivers.

"The bakery. They've already phoned a dozen times."

Protsenko took the receiver in his small hand, perched himself on the corner of the desk and at once ceased to be the amiable, soft-hearted person, at times witty, at times merry, that had been only recently saying good-bye to his comrades. The way he grasped the receiver, the expression on his face and his tone of voice showed calm firmness and authority.

"Stop this drivel and listen to me!" he said, immediately silencing the voice at the other end. "I've told you there'll be transport. That means that there will be. Gortorg* will collect the bread from you and supply the population on the road. To destroy all that bread would be a crime. Why do you think you worked all night baking it? I can see, you're in a hurry. You'll start hurrying when I tell you. Is that clear?" He hung up and reached for another telephone, which was ringing shrilly beside him.

* City trading organization.

Army units and lorries leaving the town and columns of the evacuating population could be seen on the roads from an open window looking out towards 1B Pit. From the top of the hill three currents of movement were almost as clearly defined as on a map: the main stream moving towards the south in the direction of Novocherkassk and Rostov; a smaller one proceeding in the general direction of Likhaya in the south-east; the smallest making for Kamensk in the east. The cars which had just left the district committee were driving in single file towards Novocherkassk; only the general's dusty little jeep was heading towards the Voroshilovgrad Highway.

The thoughts of the general now returning to his division were far from Ivan Protsenko. The rays of the burning sun beat down slantwise on his face. Dust enveloped the car, the general and his chauffeur, and the silent unshaven major with the tall sergeant in the back seat. The sound of the distant gun-fire, the noise of the engine, the appearance of the population evacuating the town, everything pinned the minds of these soldiers—so different in age and rank—on the grim realities.

The general and the representative of the partisan headquarters had been the only military people among those who had taken their farewell of Ivan Protsenko. They alone therefore could fully appreciate the implication of the capture of Millerovo by German tanks and their subsequent thrust at Morozovsk, a town on the railway linking Stalingrad and the Donbas. This meant that the Southern Front was now isolated from the South-Eastern Front and that the whole of Voroshilovgrad Region and a large part of Rostov Region were cut off from the central areas; communication between Stalingrad and the Donbas was broken.

The assignment confronting the division was to hold back the German forces pushing southwards from Millerovo so that the armies of the Southern Front could complete their withdrawal towards Novocherkassk and Rostov. This meant that in a few days' time the division under the general's command would either cease to exist or be encircled by the enemy. His mind rebelled at the idea of encirclement. Neither did he wish to entertain the idea of his division ceasing to exist. On the other hand, whatever the outcome, he knew he would do his duty. His mind was grappling with this problem for which there seemed no solution.

The general's age did not place him with the older but with the middle generation of Soviet Army leaders, the generation which, as young, quite ordinary lads, had joined the army during, or soon after, the Civil War.

As a rank-and-file soldier he had tramped these same steppes through which his jeep was now rattling.

The son of a Kursk peasant, he had been a shepherd, and joined the army at the age of nineteen, when eternal glory had already been won by the Perekop victory. He became a soldier when the Makhno band was being wiped out in the Ukraine; this was the final feeble echo of the great battles against the enemies of the Revolution. He had fought under Frunze and in those early years had distinguished himself as a staunch and able soldier. But he was promoted not only for that: staunchness and ability are not rare qualities. Unassumingly, little by little, even slowly as it appeared, he had assimilated everything a Red Army soldier could learn from the company political instructors and the battalion and regimental political commissars—that countless, nameless army of workers from the political departments and Red Army Party groups, and may the memory of these people live on down the ages! He did not simply learn their science; he chewed it over and made it an integral part of himself. Then all at once he stood out among his fellows as a man with exceptional political gifts.

From then onwards his progress was direct and led to dizzy heights, as did that of any other army commander of his generation.

When the war broke out he was in command of a regiment. By then he had gained experience at the Frunze Military Academy, and in the fighting at Khalkhin-Gol and on the Mannerheim Line. This had been a great deal for a man of his age and background, yet how little it had seemed! The Patriotic War made him a leader of armies. He had developed but still more had events developed him. He was now being developed by the experiences of the war, just as he had been trained earlier at the army training-school, then at the Frunze Academy, and later by his experiences in two minor wars.

This new sensation, this consciousness of himself which became stronger during the war months in spite of all the bitterness of the retreat, was astounding. The Soviet soldier was better than that of the enemy, not only in the sense of moral superiority—what comparison can there be?— but simply in the military sense. Soviet commanders were immeasurably superior not only for their political consciousness but also their military training and their way of rapidly seizing on what was new, and making practical and wide use of their experience. Soviet weapons and equipment were no worse, and in certain respects even better, than those of the enemy. The military theory which had created all this and directed all this, derived from great historical experience, but at the same time it was new and bold, like the Revolution which engendered it, like the first Soviet state in history, like the genius of the people who shaped this theory and put it into practice. It soared on eagle's wings. And yet, they must now retreat. At the moment the enemy was gaining by means of numerical superiority, surprise attack, and cruelty which one could not, in all conscience, describe in normal terms; he was gaining each time by exerting every effort to the utmost, including his reserves.

Like many Soviet Army officers, the general had early realized that this war, more so than any in the past, was a war of reserves, both human and material. It had become necessary to know how to create these reserves during the course of the war itself. More complicated even than that was to know how to put them to use: to deploy them in time and to send them where they were needed. The rout of the enemy on the approaches to Moscow and the defeat in the south pointed not only to the superiority of Soviet military theory, Soviet soldiers, Soviet equipment, but in far greater measure to the fact that the great reserves of the population and the state were in thrifty hands, capable hands, skilful hands.

It hurt, it hurt very much to be retreating again, in full view of the population, when one felt that absolutely everything about the enemy and about oneself was common knowledge.

The general travelled in silence, plunged deep in his own thoughts. It was not without difficulty that his jeep made its way through the crowds of refugees.

Scarcely had it reached the Voroshilovgrad Highway than three German dive-bombers passed almost overhead, their engines screaming. They appeared so suddenly that none of the occupants of the car had time to leap clear. The stream of troops and refugees divided into two and cascaded down on each side of the road. Some threw themselves flat in the ditches, others took cover in the ruins of houses or pressed close to the walls of buildings.

And at that very instant, the general caught sight of a lone slip of a girl, in a white jacket and with long black plaits, standing by the side of the road. The road itself, as far as the eye could see, was abandoned, the girl stood completely alone. With a fearless, grim expression on her face, she watched the painted "birds" with their black swastikas on the wide-spread wings, as they flashed past, flying so low that they seemed to fan the girl's skirts.

A curious choking sound came from the general and his companions turned to him in alarm. With an angry jerk of his big, round head, ostensibly because his collar was too tight, he turned away: the sight of the solitary girl on the high road was more than he could endure. The jeep swerved sharply off the road, lurched across the ditch and drove on to the steppe parallel with the highway—not towards Kamensk but in the direction of Voroshilovgrad, from which the general's division was approaching Krasnodon.

Chapter 4

THE DIVE-BOMBERS, which had flashed by over Ulya Gromova's head, had already, some distance beyond the town, fired a few rounds at the highway from their machine-guns and then disappeared into the eye-searing glare of sunlight. Only after a few minutes was there the dull sound of distant explosions; no doubt the aircraft were bombing the crossing over the Donets.

In Pervomaisky everything that could move was in motion. Ulya met horse-drawn carts and whole families fleeing from the town. She knew all these people, just as they knew her, but no one looked at her or spoke to her.

Zinaida Vyrikova, the "grammar-school girl," surprised her most of all. With an indescribable terror in her eyes, she was seated in a cart between two women surrounded by boxes and bundles and sacks of flour. An old man in a cap was driving. His legs, in top boots covered with flour, dangled over the side of the cart and he was trying with all his might to get his old nag to gallop up the hill by lashing its back with the ends of the reins. Although it was incredibly hot, Vyrikova was wrapped in a thick brown coat, but wore no hat or shawl. Over the rough collar of the coat her pigtails stuck out in their usual aggressive manner.

Pervomaisky was the oldest of all the mining villages in this district, and the town of Krasnodon really started here. The name Pervomaisky was a fairly recent one. Before coal had been discovered in those parts, the whole area had been occupied by Cossack farmsteads, the largest of which had been the Sorokin farm.

Coal was found at the turn of the century. It was worked at first from drifts which followed the veins from outcrops. The pits were small, and the coal was brought to the surface along the sloping drifts by horse-driven or even hand-operated winding gear. The pits were owned by various people, but from earliest memory the whole area had been called the Sorokin Coal-Field.

The miners came originally from the Central Russian provinces and the Ukraine. They had lodged with the Cossacks on the farms and married into their families. The Cossacks themselves began to work in the pits. The families grew, split up and settled down alongside the others.

Other pits came into being beyond the long hill over the ridge of which runs the highway to Voroshilovgrad; and more still on the far side across the gorge which today divides the town of Krasnodon into two unequal parts. These new pits belonged to a lonely landowner called Yarmankin, also known as the Mad Squire. Consequently, the village which grew up round these pits was commonly called Yarmankin, or the Mad village. The squire himself lived in a grey stone single-storey house, half of which consisted of a greenhouse containing exotic plants and birds brought from overseas; it stood alone, exposed to the four winds on the high hill beyond the gorge, and was also called "mad."

Under Soviet rule new pits were sunk during the first and second five-year plans and the centre of the Sorokin Coal-Field shifted to this area. Modern dwellings went up, large buildings were built for the various offices, hospitals, schools and clubs. On the hill, by the side of the Mad Squire's house, the attractive winged building of the District Soviet was erected. The Mad Squire's house became the Designing Offices of the Krasnodon Coal Trust, the present staff of which knew nothing of the history of the building where they were spending one-third of their lives.

Thus the Sorokin Coal-Field became the town of Krasnodon.

Ulya and her school-friends had grown up with their town. As small school children they had joined in the Holiday of Trees and helped to plant trees and shrubs on the vacant plots covered with rubbish-heaps and overgrown with burdock which the Town Soviet had set aside for the park. The idea that there should be a park there had come from the early Komsomols, the generation which could remember the Mad Squire, Yarmankin village, the first German occupation, and the Civil War. Some of them were still working in Krasnodon, with their hair and Budyonny-style Cossack moustaches now touched with grey; but life had scattered most of them to all parts of the country, and some had been promoted to high positions. The planting had been supervised by Danilych, the gardener, who was already then an old man; although quite decrepit now, he still had the job of head gardener in the park.

And now the park had grown green and shady and had become a favourite haunt for recreation and leisure. The young people found it more than that: for them it was life itself in its youthful blossoming, for the park had grown up with them; like them it was young, yet its green treetops already murmured in the breeze, on sunny days there was already shade under its foliage and one could find mysterious, secluded nooks. But at night, under the moon, it was superb, and on rainy autumn evenings, when the wet yellow leaves circled and rustled in the darkness as they fluttered to the ground, it was even a little eerie.

So the children grew up with their park and their town and according to their fancy, as is the way of children, they had given names to the different districts, suburbs and streets.

When new flats of the wooden barrack type were built the whole site immediately became known as Noviye Baraki (New Barracks). These had long ago disappeared and been replaced by stone buildings, yet the name had persisted, outliving what had given it birth.

One of the suburbs is known to this day as Golubyatniki (Dove-Cots). At one time three wooden shacks stood there in isolation and small boys kept pigeons in them. But modern houses now took their place. Then there was Churilino, which at one time had been no more than a little house belonging to a miner named Churilin. Another place, Senyaki, had derived its name from the hayloft which at one time had been there. Derevyannaya, or Wooden, Street, which lay beyond the level crossing, isolated from the town by the park, still consisted of the wooden houses which had given it its name. Valya Borts lived there, a proud girl with dark grey eyes and two golden plaits who was not more than seventeen. Kamennaya (Brick) Street had been the first to have modern houses built of bricks. Now there were plenty of them everywhere, yet the street retained the name: after all, it had been the first. Vosmidomiki (Eight Houses) was the name of a whole administrative district of the town; it now consisted of several streets, but at one time there had been only eight brick houses.

People from all corners of the country pour into the Donbas. And their first question, of course, is, "Where can we live?"

A Chinese by the name of Li Fan-cha chose a vacant plot and made himself a home out of a mixture of clay and straw. Soon he added a second room, then a third, so that it was like a honeycomb. Then he began to let his rooms until new arrivals realized that there was no need to take rooms with Li Fan-cha, because it was simple enough for them to build their own. Thus an extensive new district came into being: a host of little huts clinging to each other which came to be called Shanghai. Later honeycomb huts of this kind began to spring up all along the side of the gorge which divides the town into two and also on the vacant plots round the town, and these little nests of dwellings were called Little Shanghais.

Since the day when work began at 1B Pit, the largest in the district and located exactly half-way between the Sorokin farm and what was formerly Yarmankin village, the town of Krasnodon had spread towards the Sorokin farm and almost merged with it. And so the Sorokin farm, which had long since joined up with the smaller neighbouring farmsteads, had developed into the village of Pervomaisky, which was now one of the districts of the town. It differed from the others only in that most of the dwellings there were the original Cossack farm-houses. No two houses were alike and all of them were privately owned. Among the population there were still many Cossacks who did not work in the mines but cultivated wheat on the steppeland and had formed into several collective farms.

The little house where Ulya Gromova lived was at the far end of the district, where the ground sloped down to the steppe. It had been the Gavrilov farm and was a real old Cossack cottage.

Matvei Maximovich Gromov was a Ukrainian from Poltava Gubernia; at an early age he had gone with his father to work at Yuzovka. As a lad he had been tall and strong, bold and handsome, his fair wavy hair falling in soft curls. He was much sought after by the girls and so it was not surprising that, having arrived in these parts to earn his living in the days which seemed to Ulya almost Biblical in their antiquity, when the first pits were opened, and having earned a reputation as a mighty hewer of coal, he should have captured the affections of Matryona Savelyevna, at that time just Matryosha, a little dark-eyed Cossack girl from the Gavrilov farmstead.

During the Russo-Japanese War he had served with the 8th Regiment of the Moscow Grenadiers and had been wounded six times, twice severely. He had been decorated several times, on the last occasion with the Order of St. George, for saving the regimental colours.

From then onwards his health had begun to fail. For some time he continued to work in the smaller pits, then became a carter for one of them and now, after a life of wandering, he had settled down to end his days at the Gavrilov farm which had been part of Matryona's dowry.

No sooner had Ulya reached the little front gate of her home than her resolution suddenly left her.

She loved her parents. She was young and like all young people she had never thought, nor could she imagine, that one day she would actually have to take a decision for herself, to decide her own destiny apart from the family. And now that moment had arrived.

She knew that her parents were too sick and old, too much attached to their home to leave it. Their son was in the army and Ulya was just a girl who had not determined what she would do in the future, who had no employment and could not provide for them. The other daughter was much older than Ulya and had married a clerk in the office of the pit administration, a man who was already elderly and who lodged with the Gromovs. She had children of her own and had also decided to stay behind. In fact, all of them long ago had quite made up their minds that come what may they would not leave their hearth and home.

Up to this very moment Ulya alone was without any definite plan; she alone had no firm goal before her. It had always seemed to her that it was for other people to tell her what to do. First she had wanted to enlist—in the Air Force, of course—and had written asking her brother, who was a mechanic in an Air Force unit, whether he would help her to get into an aviation school. Sometimes she felt the simplest way would be to go in for a nursing course, like some of the other Krasnodon girls. That way she might very soon find herself with the army at the front. At other times she was pursued by a secret dream of going underground with the partisans in enemy-occupied territory. And then there were the days when she was gripped suddenly by a craving to study more and more. For the war would not last for ever. One day it would end, and one would have to live and work. People who knew their job would be needed badly; why, she could very quickly become an engineer or a teacher.

But no one had decided her future for her, and now the time had come when she must open the gate and—.

Only then did she realize how terrifying life could be.

She must leave her mother and father at the mercy of the enemy and plunge by herself into this unknown, frightening world of hardships, wanderings, and struggle.... She felt so weak at the knees that she almost sank to the ground. Oh, if only she could crawl now into the cosy little cottage, close the shutters, throw herself down on her virgin bed and lie there quite quietly, without having to decide anything! Who cared about little black-haired Ulya anyhow! Just to climb into the bed, to curl up in a ball, just to go on living with the people she loved and take whatever came.... But what would come? And when? And would it come to stay, and for how long? Perhaps it would not be so terrible after all?

But at the same moment she shuddered with humiliation at the thought of being able to admit of such a solution. And it was already too late to choose: her mother was running out to meet her. What could have given her strength enough to leave her bed? She was followed by Ulya's father, her sister and her brother-in-law. The little ones came running, too. Extraordinary agitation was written on their faces; her little nephew was crying.

"Wherever have you been, child? We've been searching for you since daybreak," the mother cried, and the tears she made no attempt to wipe away coursed down her wan, brown, wrinkled cheeks. "Run as fast as you can to Anatoly, if he hasn't already gone! Oh, dear, oh, dear!"

The mother was old and her back was bent, but her hair was still black; her dark eyes were still beautiful and, although she was a little woman, made one think of some huge wild bird. She was wise and had strength of character. Old Matvei and the daughters were in the habit of heeding what she said. But now the time had come when the daughter had to make her own decision, for the mother's strength was failing.

"Who's been looking for me? Anatoly?" Ulya asked, speaking rapidly.

"Somebody from the district committee," her father replied. He was standing behind her mother, his large hands hanging heavily at his sides.

How old he looked now! thought Ulya. He was almost bald in front; only the back of his head and the temples showed traces of his former curls, but there was a great deal of grey in the once flaming Grenadier moustaches and his stubbly beard was quite grey, while his brick-coloured face—the face of the soldier—was heavily wrinkled, and the nose a bluish grey.

"Go on, child, run!" her mother urged again. "Oh no, wait, I'll give Anatoly a call!" The little old woman ran down the path between the rows of vegetables towards the house of the Popovs, whose son Anatoly had finished school with Ulya that year.

"Please go back and lie down, Mama, I can go myself," Ulya said, but her mother was already running among the cherry-trees at the bottom of the garden. The old woman and the young girl hurried forward together.

The gardens of the Gromovs and Popovs adjoined each other. Both sloped towards the dry bed of the stream which marked the boundary, where there was also a wattle-fence. Although Ulya and Anatoly had been neighbours all their lives they had never seen much of each other outside school and, of course, Komsomol meetings, where Anatoly often made speeches. As a child he had had his own boyish interests, and in the upper forms he had been teased because it was said he was afraid of girls. And it was a fact that when he encountered Ulya, or any other girl for that matter, in the street or in someone's home, he was so embarrassed that he forgot to greet her or, if he did remember, he turned as red as a lobster and caused the girl to blush too. Sometimes the girls talked about this and made fun of him among themselves. Still, Ulya had a high opinion of him: he was so well-read, clever, self-contained; he liked the same poems as she did and he collected beetles, butterflies, plants and specimens of rock.

"Taisya Prokofievna, Taisya Prokofievna!" the old mother shouted, leaning over the low wattle-fence into the neighbours' garden. "Anatoly, my dear, Ulya's come back!"

Anatoly's little sister piped up in reply from higher up the garden, though she was hidden from sight by the trees. And then out came Anatoly himself, running through the cherry-trees which were heavy with ripening fruit. He wore, open at the neck, a Ukrainian shirt with embroidery on hem and sleeves, and a little Uzbek cap on the back of his head to keep his well-combed, corn-coloured hair in place.

His lean, tanned, ever serious face, with its bleached eyebrows, was flushed with the heat, and he had sweated so much that there were round damp patches under his arms. Clearly he had completely forgotten to feel shy in Ulya's presence.

"Ulya," he panted, "you know I've been trying to find you since early this morning. I've been round to all the others and because of you I've made Victor Petrov postpone the departure; they're all here now and his father's swearing something terrible, so get your things at once!"

"But we didn't know a thing! Who gave the orders?"

"The district committee. Everybody's to get out. The Germans will be here any minute. I warned them all, but I couldn't find any of your crowd and I've been getting terribly anxious. And then Victor Petrov and his father came over from the Pogorely farm. His father was a partisan here against the Germans during the Civil War and he shouldn't be delayed for a minute, and just imagine Vitka coming specially to get me! There's a real pal for you! His father's a forester and he's got some marvellous horses from the forestry station. And I tried to get them to wait, of course. The father began to make a row, so I said, 'You're an old partisan yourself. You know you can't just leave a comrade behind like that, and besides, you're surely a brave man,' I said, and that's how it is we're waiting for you."

Anatoly had spoken rapidly, clearly anxious to share with Ulya everything he had experienced. The sudden sparkle in his grey-blue eyes had given a touch of charm to the face with its almost colourless eyebrows and hair.

How was it that until this moment she had not appreciated him? There was spiritual strength in his face, something about the shape of the full lips, the broadly cut nostrils.

"Anatoly..." Ulya began. "Anatoly, you—" Her voice trembled. She stretched her slim brown hand across to him over the wattle-fence.

Then, indeed, did he blush.

"Quick, quick," he said, avoiding her black eyes that seemed to bore right through him.

"I've got all your things together—drive round to the gates, both of you, go on! Quickly!" Ulya's mother urged them on while the tears rolled fast down her cheeks.

Until this very last moment the mother had not quite believed that her daughter would be starting out alone in this immense, crumbling world, but she knew it would be dangerous for her daughter to stay behind, and here were some good people to take charge of things, and with an adult accompanying them, so now it was all decided.

"But, Anatoly, have you warned Valya Filatova? She's my best friend and I can't go without her." Ulya spoke with determination.

Anatoly was so genuinely distressed that he could not conceal it on his face, nor did he try to.

"Well, they're not my horses, and there's already four of us.... I just don't know," he said at a loss.

"But don't you see I can't just go and leave Valya behind?"

"They're strong horses all right. But still ... five people...."

"All right then, Anatoly, thank you very much for everything. You go on ahead and I'll come on with Valya on foot," Ulya said resolutely. "Good-bye, Anatoly."

"Lord Almighty, child! You can't go on foot! I've already packed your dresses and underclothes in a case, and what about the bedding?" The mother's tears began to flow again. She sobbed piteously and rubbed her eyes with her knuckles, like a child.

Ulya's loyalty to her friend did not surprise Anatoly. It seemed quite natural to him. He would have been surprised if Ulya had acted differently. So he showed no irritation or impatience; he simply tried to find a way out of the situation.

"You might at least ask her," he suggested. "Perhaps she's gone away already, or isn't likely to be going at all. After all, she's not a Komsomol!"

"I'll run over for her," said Ulya's mother, suddenly animated. By now she no longer realized how weak she was.

"Please go and lie down, Mother, I'll see to everything," Ulya said. She was getting irritated.

"Anatoly! Are you coming?" Victor Petrov's loud, resonant voice called from the Popovs' cottage at the far end of the garden.

But Anatoly was continuing his train of thought aloud when he said, "They've got pretty strong horses, at a pinch we could take turns walking behind the cart."

There had been no need for Ulya to set out in search of her friend. By the time she and her mother reached home again there was Valya surrounded by Ulya's relations, crowded between the porch and two small outbuildings—the scullery and a cowshed. She looked pale in spite of her well-tanned face.

"Hurry and get your things, Valya! They've got horses and a cart and we'll get them to take us both!" Ulya said quickly.

"Wait, I must tell you something," Valya said, seizing her friend's hand and drawing her away towards the gate.

"Listen, Ulya," she said and looked straight at her. There was deep anguish in her clear, wide-set eyes. "Ulya, I'm not going anywhere, I ... I ... Ulya," she went on firmly, "you're somehow different from other people. Now don't contradict me ... there's something strong about you, something great. My mother says God gave you wings and she's right.... Ulya, we've been so happy together," she went on ardently, "you've been all my happiness in the world, but I ... I'm not going with you. I'm only an ordinary girl and all my dreams have always been about ordinary things.... That when I'd finished school I'd go to work and then meet a nice, kind chap and get married and have children—a boy and a girl—and our life would be happy and simple, and I've never wished for more than that. Ulya, I can't fight and I'm afraid to go out alone into the strange world.... Oh, I know, all that's finished now, all my dreams and everything, but I've got an old mother, and I've never done any harm to anybody. I'm just a nobody, and I'm ... I'm going to stay here and ... and ... I'm sorry!"

She began to cry into the handkerchief which she had been crumpling in her hand all this time. Ulya, suddenly embracing her, also burst into tears as she held the sweet-smelling, familiar head close to her breast.

They had been friends from earliest childhood; at school they had moved together from one class to the next, and had shared joys, sorrows and secrets. Ulya was usually reticent and only showed her feelings under great emotional stress, while Valya always burst out with everything. She did not always understand Ulya, but young people are not much concerned with mutual understanding. With them what matters is the feeling of trust, the being able to share. As it turned out, they were totally dissimilar.... But there had been so many sunny days behind their tender, devoted, girlish friendship that the misery of separation was breaking their hearts.

Valya felt she was giving up something that had been the greatest, brightest thing in her life, that ahead lay something very shadowy, wholly uncertain and terrifying.

Ulya was aware that she was now losing the only person to whom, whether in moments of happiness or of difficulty, she had always been able to reveal her real self. She had not cared whether her friend understood her; all she knew was that Valya would always respond with kindness or acquiescence, with affection or at least sympathy.

So Ulya wept because this meant the end of her childhood; she was now grown-up. She must now go out into the world and go alone.

Only now did Ulya recall how Valya had torn the water-lily from her hair and thrown it to the ground. Now she understood the meaning of her action. In that moment of terrible shock Valya had realized how absurd Ulya would look with a water-lily in her hair against the background of exploding coal-mines. No, she was not quite the ordinary person she said she was; she could understand many things.

They each had a sort of presentiment that there was something final in what was taking place between them. They not only felt, but knew, that in some special sort of spiritual sense they were parting for ever. And so they wept and their tears flowed freely and neither was ashamed of them or tried to check them.

Many tears were shed in those years, not only in the Donbas but throughout the whole of the ravaged, scorched, blood-drenched Soviet Land. Among those tears were tears of impotence, horror and sheer unendurable physical pain. But how many tears were there of the loftiest, most sacred and noblest that ever mankind has shed!

A long farm wagon, drawn by two strong bay horses, rattled towards the gate. It had been built out of a cart to form a roomy, four-wheeled vehicle. It was piled high with bundles and suitcases and was driven by a heavy man, well on in years, whose fleshy face yet had strong features. He wore a leather cap and a jacket of military cut.

Ulya broke away from her friend. She wiped away her tears with the long, cushiony palm of her slim hand and her face assumed its natural expression.

"Good-bye, Valya!"

"Good-bye, Ulya!" Valya replied in a choking voice.

The girls kissed.

The wagon pulled up at the gate. Behind it came Anatoly's little sister Natasha with her mother, a tall, fleshy Cossack woman with bright eyes and fair hair. The father had been at the front from the first days of the war. Mother and daughter were in tears and their faces were flushed and sweating from the exertion of running.

Anatoly was already seated on the wagon. Beside him sat Victor Petrov, dark-haired, handsome and with a melancholy look in his bold eyes. He wore an open-neck sports shirt; a guitar, which he had wrapped in something soft and tied with string, was tucked under his arm.

Ulya turned and moved woodenly towards her family. Her case, bundle and shawl had been brought out from the house. The little old mother with the dark eyes of a big bird ran to her.

"Oh, Mother!" Ulya cried.

The old woman flung up her shrivelled arms and fell to the ground in a dead faint.

Chapter 5

NOT SINCE the days of the great popular migration had the Donets steppe witnessed such a movement of people as took place in July 1942.

Along highways and country lanes, over the open steppe, with the scorching sun beating down, retreating Red Army troops marched endlessly with their supplies, artillery and tanks; following them came children from children's homes and kindergartens, carts and lorries and herds of cattle, columns of refugees in small groups or singly, pushing wheelbarrows with bundles and cases of personal belongings and children perched on top.

As they went they trampled the ripe and ripening corn and no one grieved, neither he that trampled it down nor he who had sown it, for now it belonged to no one, it had to be left behind for the Germans. The fields of potatoes and vegetables which were state- or collective-farm property had been thrown open to all. Refugees dug up potatoes and baked them in the ashes of the fires made from straw and fencing. Whether walking or riding they all carried cucumbers or tomatoes or juicy slices of water-melon or muskmelon.

The air was so filled with dust that you could look at the sun without squinting.

To the man who had been sucked like a grain of sand into the stream of the retreat, this movement might have seemed accidental and senseless, for he was more occupied with what was on his mind than with what was taking place around him. In effect, it was an unprecedented evacuation of masses of people and valuable equipment directed by means of a highly organized state machinery of war mechanism operating by the will of hundreds and thousands of people, great and small.

However, since of necessity the retreat was taking place at a forced pace, in addition to the large main columns of troops and civilians whose progress, though difficult, was planned, there were other refugees moving in an easterly and south-easterly direction along all the roads and over the open steppe; these were the clerical staffs and manual workers from the smaller offices and factories; groups of soldiers and baggage trains which had lost contact with their headquarters after their units had been broken up in battle, straggling groups of sick and wounded who had fallen behind or been left through lack of transport. Because these refugee groups, large and small, had no idea of the situation at the front they could only select what appeared to them the right and suitable direction. But they clogged the pores and choked the arteries of the main retreat; more than this, they blocked the crossings over the Donets, for day and night the camps by the pontoon bridges and ferries were full of milling crowds of people, lorries, carts and wagons, all fully exposed to bombardment from the air.

Senseless though it was for civilians to proceed towards Kamensk at a time when German units had already pushed far across the Donets into the Morozovsk area, it was precisely this direction that a large number of the Krasnodon refugees had chosen, because it was the route taken by the advance detachments of the army division which had just left Krasnodon on its way to reinforce the Soviet defences on the Donets, south of Millerovo. It so chanced that this was the column of refugees in which Ulya Gromova, Anatoly Popov, Victor Petrov and his father found themselves as they rode on the farm wagon drawn by the two powerful bays.

The last farm buildings had disappeared from sight and the wagon with the caravan of other carts and lorries had begun to descend the slope of a hill when without warning a frenzied screech of engines filled the blue sky, and German raiders again dived, hiding the sun and raking the highway with machine-gun fire.

The colour suddenly went from the fleshy face of Victor's father, a big energetic man.

"Get down flat on the ground!" he roared in his powerful voice.

The boys had already jumped off the wagon and thrown themselves among the corn. Victor's father dropped the reins, leapt down and in a trice had vanished into thin air as if he had been a ghost, and not a big forester in heavy boots. Ulya alone remained on the wagon: she did not know why she had not run for cover. At the same moment the terrified horses plunged forward and she was almost thrown out.

Ulya tried to grab the reins but could not reach them. The horses, which had almost collided with a light carriage in front, reared again and swerved aside, almost snapping their traces. The long, heavy, capacious cart nearly overturned, but righted itself and became steady on its wheels again. Ulya gripped the side with one hand and clung to a heavy object inside the cart with the other, straining hard not to be thrown out, for otherwise she would have been crushed instantly beneath the maddened horses of the other carts.

The big bays, flecked with foam, dashed wildly among people and carts in the trampled wheat, rearing and snorting. At that moment a tall fair youth with broad shoulders and bare head leapt from the carriage in front and seemed to throw himself under the horses' hoofs.

Ulya did not immediately take in what was happening but a second later she saw, in the midst of the flying manes and bared teeth, an extremely young, face with cheeks flushed, eyes sparkling and an expression of extraordinary tenseness and strength.

Seizing the reins close to the bit of one of the snorting bays with one hand, he placed himself between the horse and the middle shaft, leaning heavily against the animal to avoid being bruised by the shaft. There he stood, tall and unruffled, in a well-pressed grey suit and dark red tie, with the white, ivory end of a fountain-pen protruding from his breast pocket. With the other hand he was straining over the middle shaft, endeavouring to grasp the reins of the second horse. Only the muscles bulging through the sleeves of his jacket and the veins standing out at the brown wrists showed the strain he was putting on himself.

"Whoa, there, whoa!" he was saying in a voice that was soft, but peremptory.

As soon as he had managed to grasp the reins of the second horse both animals began to quieten under his control. They still tossed their manes and rolled their wild eyes in his direction, but the youth kept his hold on the reins until they were perfectly calm. Then he let fall the reins and, to Ulya's great astonishment, began with his big hands to smooth his sleek fair hair, the side parting of which had scarcely been disturbed. Then he raised his sweaty, boyish face with its prominent cheek-bones, large eyes and long dark lashes and beamed broadly.

"Strong horses! They m-might have c-carried me off!" he said with a slight stutter as he grinned at Ulya. The girl, her nostrils slightly distended, was still gripping the side of the cart and a piece of the baggage. Her dark eyes were full of respect as she returned his gaze.

People were flocking to the road again, seeking out their

carts and lorries. From here and there came groans and cries as the womenfolk crowded round the dead and injured.

"I was afraid they would push you on to the shaft!" Ulya said, her nostrils still trembling

"That's what I was afraid of too. But the horses aren't spiteful, they're geldings," he said simply. His large, brown hand carelessly smoothed the shining, sweaty neck of the horse nearest him.

In the distance, from somewhere across the Donets, came the dull yet jarring sound of bombing.

"It's terrible for the people," said Ulya, looking round her.

People and carts were already passing on either side in a great noisy torrent.

"Yes, terrible. Especially for the mothers. What they've had to go through! And what they still have ahead of them!" the lad said. His face immediately became serious, and deep horizontal lines, not usual in one of his age, showed on his brow.

"Yes, of course." Ulya's voice was flat as the picture rose before her of her own little mother, lying prostrate on the sun-baked ground.

Victor Petrov's father appeared beside the horses as suddenly as he had vanished and with exaggerated attention began to examine traces, belly-bands and reins. After him came Anatoly Popov in his little Uzbek cap. He was laughing to himself and wagging his head from side to side and looked a little guilty, but his usual serious expression was still there. Then came Victor, also somewhat shamefaced.

"Is my guitar all right?" Victor hastened to ask and cast an anxious eye at the load on the cart. As soon as he saw it among the bundles, still wrapped in the blanket, he turned his sad, bold eyes to Ulya and burst into laughter.

The youth, who until then had been standing with the horses, ducked under the middle shaft and the horse's head and came up to the wagon, his large fair head held easily above the broad shoulders.

"Anatoly!" he exclaimed happily.

"Oleg!"

They linked arms like old friends and Oleg glanced towards Ulya.

"I'm Koshevoi," he said by way of introduction and shook hands with her.

His left shoulder was slightly higher than the other. He was very young, still quite a boy, yet his tanned face, his tall, light frame, the well-pressed suit, the red tie, the white tip of the pen, the slight stutter and his every movement breathed such an air of vigour and strength, of kindliness and mental alertness that Ulya at once felt she could trust him.

For his part, the lad had instantly, with the spontaneous scrutiny of youth, taken in the graceful figure in the white blouse and dark knee-length skirt, the firm supple waist of the village girl accustomed to harvest work in the fields, the dark eyes which rested on him, the long plaits, the curious cut of the nostrils, the long shapely brown legs. He flushed crimson, turned quickly towards Victor and offered his hand to him.

Oleg Koshevoi had been a pupil at the Gorky School, the largest in Krasnodon, situated in the central park. He had never met Ulya and Victor before but he knew Anatoly. Between them there existed that casual sort of friendship often to be found among active Komsomols—a friendship growing from one Komsomol meeting to the next.

"What a place to meet in," Anatoly said, "and d'you remember it was only three days ago that the whole lot of us went back home with you for a drink of water and you introduced us all ... to your granny!" He laughed. "Is she travelling with you now, by the way?"

"No, my g-granny stayed behind. Mother too." The brow wrinkled again. "There are five of us: Kolya—that's Mother's brother, but somehow I can never call him uncle," he smiled, "and his wife and their little boy and the old man, who's driving." With a nod he indicated the *britzka* in front, from which someone had already called him several times.

The *britzka*, drawn by a small, high-stepping, dun-coloured horse, rolled forward just ahead of the cart. The bay horses kept so close behind it that their hot breath could be felt on the necks and ears of its occupants.

Oleg Koshevoi's uncle—Nikolai Korostylev, a geologist with the Krasnodon Coal Trust—was a handsome, phlegmatic young man with brown eyes and black eyebrows, wearing a blue suit. He was only seven years older than his nephew and they were more like brothers. He began to tease his nephew.

"Don't miss your chance, old chap," he muttered in a monotonous tone of voice, without looking at Oleg. "It's no joke saving a girl like that almost from death! It'll end up with a wedding, I reckon. Eh, Marina?"

"Stop your nonsense! I'm quite shaken up!"

"But she is lovely, isn't she?" Oleg said to his young aunt. "She's really wonderful!"

"And what about your Lena?" the aunt asked, fixing her black eyes on him. "Oh, what a lad you are, Oleg!"

Aunt Marina was one of those charming, doll-like aunts who seem to have jumped straight out of a picture-book: embroidered Ukrainian blouse and strings of beads, gleaming white teeth, luxuriant black hair like a soft cloud round her head. And sudden and hurried though the preparations for the journey had been, she had managed to adorn herself in a way that became her.

She held by the hand a fat little boy of about three years old, who was responding in an unusually lively way to everything around him and had no suspicion of the terrible world he had come into.

"No, what I say is that Lena is a good match for our Oleg, while this one, though she's quite a good girl, wouldn't love our Oleg because he's still a boy, and she's already, as you can see, a young woman." Aunt Marina spoke very fast, her eyes roving restlessly about and every now and then looking watchfully skywards. "It's when a woman is getting on that she likes the young men, but when she's young herself she never falls in love with a lad younger than herself, and I'm one who should know." The words tumbled out in a torrent, which showed that Aunt Marina had indeed been seriously shaken up.

Lena Pozdnysheva had stayed behind in Krasnodon. She had been in the same form as Oleg and he was in love with her. Many pages of his diary were devoted to her. Perhaps he behaved badly towards her in going into raptures over Ulya? But what harm could there be in it? Lena would always be in his heart, he would never forget her, while Ulya—

In his mind's eye he saw her again and the horses, too; again he felt the breath of the horse on the left. And was it possible, after all that, that Aunt Marina could be right and that this girl could not love him because he was still a boy? "Oh, Oleg, you're a lad!" He was a susceptible lad, and deep down he knew it.

Both the *britzka* and the cart manoeuvred their way for a long time across the steppe in their attempt to overtake the column, but there were hundreds and thousands of other people also trying to forge ahead, and everywhere was a moving throng of pedestrians, cars and carts.

Gradually the images of Ulya and Lena faded from Oleg's mind, and everything was shut out by this endless stream of people in which the carriage with the dun-coloured horse and the cart drawn by the two bays bobbed about like two light rowing boats on the ocean.

There was no end to the steppe. It seemed to stretch to all the ends of the earth. Thick smoke hung everywhere over the horizon. Only far, far away in the eastern sky there was a wreath of billowing clouds looking strangely pure and bright; and if angels with silver trumpets had come gliding out of them it would have caused no surprise.

Oleg recalled his mother and her soft, gentle hands....

... I remember your hands, mother mine, from the first moment I was conscious of being alive in the world; always tanned by the sun in the summer, and in the winter the tan never faded altogether, they were such soft, smooth hands, just a little dark along the veins. Perhaps they were a little rough sometimes, those hands, because so much work came their way; but to me they were always tender hands, and I loved to kiss those dark veins.

Yes, from the first moment that I was conscious of living in the world to the moment I left you behind, when you were so tired and gently laid your head on my breast as you saw me off on the hard road of life, your hands, I remember, were everlastingly at work. I remember them dipping in and out of the soap suds, rubbing my sheets clean, those sheets that were so small they were like swaddling clothes; in the winter, in your sheepskin jacket you would carry pails of water with the yoke across your shoulders, and your very small hand in its mitten, resting on the yoke, and yourself as small and fluffy as your mitten. I can still see your finger, the joints slightly thickened, following the letters which I repeated after you. And I can see the sickle gripped in one strong hand swinging into the handful of corn held firmly by the other, the tiny flash of the sickle blade, the quick feminine movement as the bundle of cut corn was tossed aside, carefully so as not to break the stalks.

I remember your hands getting stiff and cold, red and chapped from the water in the ice-hole where you rinsed the linen when we lived all alone, alone in the big world, as it seemed to me; yet how gently they could remove a splinter, how nimbly they could thread cotton through a needle. Then when you were sewing you used to sing, and always you sang only for us two. There was nothing in the world your hands could not do, nothing in the world was too much for them. I have seen them mixing manure and clay and coating the outside walls of the cottage; I have seen your hand peeping from silken sleeves, with a ring on the finger, raising a glass of red Moldavian wine. And with what submissive tenderness you would twine your arms, so white and full above the elbows, round my stepfather's neck, as he playfully lifted you in his arms; the stepfather whom you taught to love me and whom I accepted as my real father simply because you loved him.

But more than anything else I always remember how your hands, a little rough perhaps but warm and yet so cooling, would tenderly caress my hair, cheeks and chest when I lay semiconscious in bed. And whenever I opened my eyes you were always near; the night-light was burning in the room and you looked at me with your tired, drooping eyes out of the darkness, as it were; and you yourself were all still and bright, just like an icon. I salute those pure, sacred hands of yours!

You have seen your sons off to the war, or if not you, then some other mother like you. Some of your sons you will never see again. And if that bitter cup has passed you by, there is yet some other mother who has not been spared. Yet if, in times of war, the people have bread to eat, clothes to wear, if the hayricks are standing in the fields, the trains are running, if the cherry-trees are in bloom and fires are roaring in the blast furnaces, if some unseen agent is lifting the soldier from the ground or raising him on his sick-bed, it is all being done by the hands of my mother, someone else's mother, your mother.

You, too, look back, my young friend, look back as I do and say if there is anyone in your life whose feelings you have wounded more than those of your mother. Is it not because of me, of you, of all of us, because of our misfortunes, our errors, our sorrows, that her hair has turned white? And will not the day arrive when at our mother's grave our hearts will be tormented with misgivings?

Oh, Mother! Forgive me because of all people you alone can forgive; lay your hands on my head as you did in my childhood and forgive me....

These thoughts and feelings were crowding into Oleg's mind. He was quite unable to forget that his mother had remained "back there"; and Grandma Vera, who was also a mother, the mother of his mother and of Uncle Kolya, had remained "back there," too.

Oleg's face had grown serious and still; the large eyes in the dark golden eyelashes were damp with unshed tears. He sat hunched up, legs dangling, the fingers of his large hands interlocked. There were deep furrows on his brow.

Silent, too, were Uncle Kolya and Marina and even their little son; and quiet had also descended on the cart following in their rear. Soon the dun-coloured horse and the two bays wearied of the pressing throng and the terrible heat and, without realizing it, the drivers of the two vehicles found themselves again on the highway along which the people, carts and lorries continued to roll forward in an endless stream.

And no matter what the people were doing or thinking or saying in that great tempest of human sorrow, whether joking or dozing or providing for their children, whether getting to know each other or watering their horses at the infrequent wells, beyond all this and over all spread a black, invisible shadow, moving up from behind them, its wings extended and reaching to the north and to the south, covering the steppe more rapidly than the human stream could flow.

The realization that they had been compelled to leave their hearths and homes, to travel into the unknown, and that the force which cast this shadow could overtake and crush them, lay heavy on the heart of each of them.

Chapter 6

BOTH *britzka* AND CART reached the highway along the edge of which moved the long procession of refugees and motor vehicles.

Among them was the lorry from 1B Pit carrying the office staff and equipment, Valko the director, and Grigory Shevtsov at whose garden gate Ulya had stood only a few hours previously.

There, on foot, were children from a war orphanage which had stood in Vosmidomiki. The boys and girls, from five to eight, were in the care of two young nurses and the matron, an elderly woman with piercing eyes, a red scarf tied over her head after the fashion of harvest workers and dusty rubber overshoes worn without shoes, straight over her stockings.

Several carts carried the property of the orphanage and, as they grew tired, the children took turns to ride on them.

As soon as the miners' lorry overtook the orphans, all its occupants jumped down and placed the children on it.

Grigory Shevtsov took such a liking to one fair-haired, blue-eyed little girl with a small serious face and fat cheeks— cream-puff cheeks, he called them—that he carried her almost all the time, talking to her, planting kisses on her small hands and cream-puff cheeks, himself just as fair and blue-eyed as she.

Behind the *britzka* and the cart which now followed the orphanage carts marched an army unit which straggled a long way down the road with its field kitchens, machine-guns and artillery. An experienced army man would have seen at once that the unit was strongly equipped with anti-tank rifles and guns. The Guards' minethrowers presented a strange sight against the background of the steppe sky; the lorries on which they were mounted were invisible in the distance and the strange weapons seemed to float unsupported above the miles of soldiers and civilians, as they bobbed gently like banners in a church procession.

Rust-coloured dust had accumulated in a thick layer on the boots of soldiers and officers alike. They had been on the march for several days. At the head of the detachment, directly behind the carts and bulging round on either side of them whenever the carts slackened speed, marched a company of tommy-gunners. The sun had burnt their faces a dark brick colour. They supported their guns on their chests as they might an infant, using one arm, an arm worn out and sometimes wounded and bandaged.

As though by some unwritten command, Ulya's cart was somehow appropriated by the company of tommy-gunners and became almost part of the company itself; whether proceeding forward or at a halt, the cart always seemed to find itself in the centre of the company, and wherever Ulya looked her eyes met the casual glance, sometimes the frank stare, of young soldiers in forage-caps and dusty boots, their tunics faded and worn by countless soakings in rain and sweat and camping on rough ground, sand, pine-needles and swamps.

In spite of the retreat, the soldiers were in the cheerful, lively, playful mood which the presence of girls inspires. Like any army company on the march or at rest, this group of tommy-gunners had their own pet buffoon.

"Here, where're you off to, with no orders issued," he shouted at Victor's father whenever he urged on the horses as an opportunity arose of pressing a little ahead. "Oh no, my dear friend, you're not going anywhere without us! You're attached to our company for keeps, old chap, you're in the army now. We've put you down for rations and kit and soap and extras; and the girl—may God and the whole Church of the True Faith preserve her beauty— she's going to get a cup of coffee every morning! With sugar!"

"That's the ticket, Kayutkin, don't let the company down!" laughed the gunners merrily with a glance at Ulya.

"All right! Let's get it confirmed right away. Comrade Sergeant-Major! Fedya! Asleep, is he? You've lost your soles!"

"And have you lost your head?"

"Yes, the stupid one, and it's found its way to your shoulders somehow. I've kept the clever one. They are screw-on heads, take a look."

And suiting the action to the words, Kayutkin, with a neat movement, grasped his own small head, one hand under the chin, the other at the nape of the neck below the forage-cap which he had shoved carelessly over one eyebrow, made his eyes bulge and cunningly turned his head as if unscrewing it at the neck. The illusion of head leaving body was perfect and the whole company and everyone near him burst into peals of laughter. Ulya's reserve broke down and she joined in the merriment, laughing aloud like a child. Then she suddenly felt embarrassed. All the gunners threw merry glances in her direction as if they knew Kayutkin had only been performing for her benefit.

Kayutkin the buffoon was a small man, neat in his movements. His face was covered with tiny wrinkles but so lively was it that it was impossible to guess his age: he might have been over thirty, or barely twenty; judging by his build and behaviour he was not more than a lad. His large blue eyes had crow's feet at the corners. When he was still, intense perpetual weariness showed in the depths of his eyes, but he seemed not to want people to see it, and so was almost never still.

"Where are you from, young men?" he inquired of Ulya's companions. "There, you see! From Krasnodon," he added with satisfaction. "And the girl, I suppose, is somebody's sister? Or, excuse me, Pa, perhaps she's your daughter? What's all this, then? A girl at a loose end, nobody's daughter or sister or wedded wife? In Kamensk, she'll be called up, for sure. Called up and put on traffic control. In heavy road traffic!" With an inimitable gesture, Kayutkin indicated everything that was taking place along the highway and over the steppe. "She'd do better with us in a tommy-gunners' unit! Honest, you chaps will soon be reaching Russia and there are hosts of girls there, while we haven't one in our unit. And we need a girl like that, believe me, to teach us to speak properly and improve our manners...."

"Well, she'll do as she pleases," said Anatoly with a smile and a shy glance at Ulya, who tried hard to keep a straight face and did not quite succeed but looked the other way to avoid Kayutkin's eyes.

"But we'll soon talk her round!" Kayutkin exclaimed. "Our company's got just the right sort of lads for that. They'll talk any girl over!"

"And suppose I do go with them, suppose I just jump off the wagon and go?" Ulya thought suddenly, her heart nearly missing a beat.

Oleg Koshevoi, meanwhile, was walking by the side of the wagon and, as though hypnotized, never for a moment took his eyes off Kayutkin. He fascinated him and Oleg wanted everyone else to be fascinated by him. Kayutkin had only to open his mouth and Oleg would burst into laughter, his head thrown back and his teeth gleaming. He had taken such a liking to Kayutkin that he was rubbing his hands with glee. But Kayutkin seemed completely unaware of it, never once looking at Oleg any more than at Ulya or anyone else he was trying to amuse.

At a moment when Kayutkin had just said something quite outrageous and the soldiers were laughing uproariously, a jeep, moving over the steppe parallel with the road and covered with a thick layer of dust, drew abreast of the company.

" 'Ten-shun!"

A captain with a long, sinewy neck emerged from the midst of the company and, holding down his swinging revolver holster with one hand, ran hurriedly on his thin legs to the jeep where a corpulent general with a new peaked cap on his big round head was looking around him.

"There's no need," the general said. "As you were!"

He climbed out, shook the saluting captain's hand and at the same time cast a quick glance along the ranks of tommy-gunners marching on the road in a cloud of dust. His small eyes twinkled in his otherwise stern, ordinary face.

"Well, I'll be damned, they're our Kursk people and— Kayutkin!" he suddenly interjected with obvious pleasure. He motioned to the jeep to follow and, with a step surprisingly light for one of his build, marched along with the tommy-gunners.

"Kayutkin ... that's splendid! While Kayutkin is alive,

the spirit of the troops is invincible!" he said and looked at Kayutkin with a twinkle in his eye, though clearly the words were meant for all the soldiers thronging round him as they marched.

"I serve the Soviet Union!" Kayutkin said, not in the artificially elated, bantering tone he had been using, but very seriously.

The general turned to the company commander who was keeping pace with him a step or two in the rear.

"Comrade Captain, do the soldiers know where we're going and why?"

"They do, Comrade General!"

"They put up a fine showing at the water-tower ... remember?" the general said, with a rapid glance at the soldiers pressing round him. "And most important of all, they preserved their skins.... Yes, that's just the point," he stressed, as though someone had offered an objection. "It's not difficult to get killed!"

They all knew that the general was not so much praising them for past events as preparing them for what lay ahead. The smiles left their faces and gave way to meaningful expressions that had something indefinably in common.

"You're young people," the general continued, "but do you realize how experienced you are? Is there any comparison with, say, my early years? There was a time when I marched along this road. But the enemy then was different, and so were his arms and equipment! Compared with the school I went through, you've graduated from university...."

The general made a movement with his large head which could have meant either that he wanted to drive something out of his mind or confirm something. It was his way, in certain circumstances, of expressing displeasure or, in other cases, of showing that he was satisfied. In this case he was showing satisfaction: evidently, he derived pleasure from recalling his youth, and the sight of the tommy-gunners, with the military bearing which had become natural to them, pleased him.

"Excuse me," Kayutkin said, "but have they got very far?"

"Far enough, the fiends!" the general replied. "So far that you and I are finding it a bit awkward."

"Will they get any farther?"

The general walked in silence for some moments.

"It depends on you and me.... Since the thrashing we gave them last winter, their strength has been sapped. They collected arms and equipment from all over Europe and then pounded away at one spot ... at you and me! But they have no reserves! There, that's the point!..."

His glance fell on the cart in front and among its occupants he suddenly recognized the lone girl he had seen on the highway, when the German dive-bombers had attacked. He pictured to himself all that might have happened to the girl, all that might have passed through her mind, in the short time during which he had managed, in his jeep, to call on the second echelon of his division and then overtake the leading units which had bypassed Krasnodon. His face bore an expression more of gloomy concern than of pity, and suddenly he quickened his pace.

"Well, good luck to you!" he cried out. Then motioning to the jeep to slow down, he walked briskly towards it with the light step which was so surprising in view of his corpulence.

While the general was with the gunners, Kayutkin's questions and behaviour had been quite serious. Evidently he considered it unnecessary to display before the general that side of him which made him conspicuous among the soldiers and for which they loved him. But as soon as the jeep had disappeared from sight the former spirit of cheerful jocularity took possession of him.

An infantryman of tremendous size with hands as big and black as frying-pans fell out from the rear of the column. He was carrying some heavy objects wrapped in a greasy rag and was panting with the effort.

"Comrades! Where's the miners' lorry?" he asked. "I was told it's moving somewhere here."

"There it is, only it's not moving!" Kayutkin joked and pointed to the lorry full of children.

The column had in fact come to a halt because of a hold-up ahead.

The infantryman approached Valko and Grigory Shevtsov, who carefully put down the little fair-haired girl. "Excuse me, Comrades," he said, "I want to turn in some tools. You're skilled men and you'll probably find them handy. To me they're only so much extra weight." He began to unfold the greasy rag.

Valko and Shevtsov bent over to watch.

"See?" the soldier said gravely. Spread out on the cloth in his big hands lay a new set of fitter's tools.

"I don't follow you—are you trying to sell them?" asked Valko with an unfriendly look in his gypsy eyes under the bushy eyebrows.

"How your tongue does wag," the infantryman retorted. His brick-coloured face had turned dark red and little beads of sweat had broken out on it. "I picked them up on the steppe. I was just passing and there they were, wrapped up in the rag. Somebody must've dropped them."

"Perhaps someone threw them away, the better to make a run for it," Valko laughed.

"A skilled worker doesn't throw his tools away. He dropped them," the soldier said coldly, speaking only to Shevtsov.

"Well, thank you very much, my friend!" Shevtsov said and hurriedly assisted the soldier to wrap up the tools.

"Well, that's settled then. It would've been a pity, such good tools. You've got a lorry but I'm marching in full kit. Where'd I find room for them?" the soldier said more cheerfully. "Good luck to you!" He shook only Shevtsov's hand, then hurried back and was soon lost in the column.

Valko followed him for some time with his eyes, an expression of strong approval on his face. "He's one of the right sort," he said in a husky voice.

As he held the bundle of tools in one hand and stroked the little girl's hair with the other, Shevtsov realized that his director had doubted the soldier not because he was hard-hearted, but rather because as manager of an enterprise employing thousands of people and producing thousands of tons of coal a day he was accustomed to the idea of someone cheating him sometimes. The mine was now destroyed, blown up by his own hand; some of the people had been evacuated, but others had remained to face the Germans. And the thought struck Shevtsov for the first time that the director's heart must now be heavy indeed.

Towards evening gun-fire was heard ahead of the column.

It came nearer during the night and even the rounds of machine-gun fire could be distinguished. All night long from the direction of Kamensk fires were breaking out, sometimes so large that they lit up the whole column. The glow from them made broad wine-coloured streaks in the sky and shed a dark purple light on the ridges of the burial-mounds, making them stand out clearly in the dark steppe.

"Common graves," Victor's father said. He had been sitting silently in the cart, the glow of his hand-rolled cigarette intermittently lighting up his fleshy face. "They aren't ancient barrows, but our own graves," he said thickly. "We broke through here with Parkhomenko and Voroshilov, and it was here we buried our dead...."

Anatoly, Victor, Oleg and Ulya gazed in silence at the graves flooded with the glow from the fires.

"How many were the compositions we wrote at school about that war, how we dreamed about it and envied our fathers! And now war has come to us, another war, as though on purpose to show what stuff we're made of, and yet we're running away from it!" Oleg said and sighed heavily.

During the night there had been changes in the movement of the column. The cars, lorries and carts belonging to offices, factories and private individuals and the throng of refugees had halted. It had been said that the army units were moving in front. The turn of the tommy-gunners had come, and they were shifting about in the darkness, their weapons clanking faintly. The whole unit moved up in their wake. Cars with engines revved up crowded together to make way for the unit to pass. Cheroots glowed in the dark, and seemed like tiny stars against the sky.

Someone touched Ulya's elbow. She turned. Kayutkin was standing on the side of the cart opposite to that where Victor's father sat and the boys were standing.

"Listen a minute!" he whispered, his voice scarcely audible. The note of urgency made her slip off the cart and go to him. They moved away.

"Forgive me for troubling you," he began softly, "but you mustn't go to Kamensk. Any moment now the Germans will take it; and they've pushed a long way down that side of the Donets. Don't tell anyone what I've told you, I've no right to, anyway, but we can trust each other, and I'd be sorry if anything happened to you. You must swerve much farther south and may God grant that you're not too late."

Kayutkin spoke with bated breath as though he held a little light in his hand which he feared he might blow out. His face could hardly be seen in the dark but it was serious and gentle; now there was no fatigue in his eyes, they shone in the darkness.

It was more the way he spoke than what he said that had an effect on Ulya. She regarded him in silence.

"What's your name?" Kayutkin asked softly.

"Ulyana Gromova."

"You haven't got a photograph of yourself?"

"No"

"I might have known." His voice was sad as he spoke.

A wave of compassion and at the same time something like audacity swept over Ulya. She lowered her face quite close to his.

"I haven't got a photo," she whispered, "but if you look at me closely, very closely..." she paused and looked him straight in the face for a moment or two with her dark eyes, "you won't forget me...."

He was quite still for some moments, only his large eyes showed a sad light in them through the darkness.

"I won't forget you. Because you can't be forgotten. Good-bye," he whispered, and could hardly be heard.

There was a crunching of heavy army boots as he left in the darkness to join the unit, which was marching farther and farther away into the dark night, cheroots glowing to form an endless sort of Milky Way.

Ulya considered whether she should tell anyone what he had told her, but it was soon obvious that others knew besides him; word had gone right down the caravan of vehicles.

When she returned to the cart she found that a number of cars, lorries and carts had swung off into the steppe towards the south-east. A long trail of refugees was making off in the same direction.

"We'll have to head for Likhaya," Valko said huskily.

Victor's father asked him something.

"Why separate? Let's keep together now that fate has joined us," Valko said.

By daybreak they were in the steppe and far from any road.

Dawn came to the open steppe and it was very beautiful. Slowly the sky cleared and brightened over the immense expanses of wheat, almost undamaged in these parts. The soft light of the sun threw its horizontal rays on the stream of human beings and slid between the hillocks, making silvery reflections in the tiny dewdrops lying on the new pale green grass.

But in the light of the early morning sun how much sadder was the sight of the sleepy, exhausted, drawn faces of the children and the grim, worried, apprehensive faces of the adults.

Ulya caught sight of the orphanage matron in the now dust-covered rubber overshoes that she wore over her stockings. Her face was dark with grief. She had walked the whole way and only at night had seated herself on one of the carts. The Donets sun seemed to have dried and burnt her up completely. She had obviously had no sleep that night, and now she said nothing at all and her every action seemed mechanical. Her piercing, vacant eyes held an expression not of this world, but of the world beyond.

Since early morning there had been a constant noise of engines in the air. There were no planes in sight but in front and a little to the left came the reverberating crashes of exploding bombs and sometimes far away in the distant sky there were bursts of machine-gun fire.

There, over the Donets and Kamensk, out of sight but within hearing, dog-fights were being fought. Only once did they see ahead of them a German raider flying low after dropping his load of bombs.

Oleg suddenly jumped from the *britzka* and waited until the cart came abreast. Then he walked at its side holding on to it and looking at his friends with large moist eyes.

"Just imagine, just think," he said, "if the Germans have really crossed the Donets and if this unit we've just left is to hold them up at Kamensk, it will have no outlet, and those tommy-gunners, that grand little chap who was amusing us all, that general, all of them will have no way of escape! And they knew it, of course, when they went off, they knew it!" Oleg said in great agitation.

The thought that Kayutkin had come to her to say farewell before facing death cut Ulya to the quick. She blushed with shame when she recalled what she had said to him. But then a clear inner voice told her that she had said nothing that would distress Kayutkin, if he remembered her when the hour came for him to die.

Chapter 7

REFUGEES were still passing through Krasnodon. Dark brown dust hung in a heavy cloud over the town, enveloping clothing, flowers, and the leaves of burdock and pumpkin.

From the railway sidings beyond the park came the rumbling and clanging of railway trucks and shunting engines as they went back and forth collecting from each mine in turn all the equipment that could possibly be moved out; engines snorted, whistles blew, the horns of the switch-men blared. At the level crossing near by there were excited voices, the shuffling of countless feet, the hum of car and lorry engines, the crunch of heavy gun-carriage wheels: army units were still making their way out of the town. Here and there beyond the distant hills, like an enormous empty barrel being trundled over the boundless steppe beyond, the hollow pounding of artillery fire could be heard.

A lorry still stood on the wide street outside the double-storey building of the Krasnodon Coal Trust, opposite the park gates. Through the open doors men and women were carrying out the last remaining property of the Trust and piling it on to the lorry.

They worked calmly, efficiently and in complete silence. Sullen preoccupation was expressed in their faces; their hands, heavy and swollen with the strain of moving the heavy bales and cases, were dirty and sweaty.

A few feet away and directly under the windows of the building stood a youth and girl engaged in eager, lively conversation: obviously neither the lorry nor the people sweating on the job nor anything of what was going on round them could possibly be as important to them as the subject of their conversation.

The girl was in a pink blouse and wore yellow slippers on her bare feet. She was tall and plump and had flaxen hair. Her almond-shaped eyes were dark with a soft light in them. She had a slight squint, and as she looked at the youth she held her finely chiselled head high and a little to the side on the smooth, full, white neck.

He was a lanky youth, loose-jointed and a little round-shouldered. His faded blue shirt was drawn in by a narrow belt, and the sleeves were too short for his long arms. He wore a pair of grey brown-striped trousers, also too short for him, and his feet were in unlined leather slippers. Long strands of dark straight hair fell over his forehead and ears as he talked and from time to time he tossed them back with a quick movement of the head. His pale face was of the kind which rarely tans in the sun. The youth was obviously bashful. On his face was so much natural humour and a latent enthusiasm ready at any moment to break through that it excited the girl; she kept her eyes fixed on his face.

They seemed not to care whether they were overheard or watched. But they were being observed.

On the opposite side of the street, near the gate of a small prefabricated house, stood a badly battered, highly sprung black car of a very old make: its chassis was rusty and here and there its sides had been scraped to a tinny sort of shine, so that one involuntarily thought of the skinned flanks of the Biblical camel after passing through the eye of a needle. This was the Soviet motor industry's first-born; the Gazik was its popular name and it is almost non-existent nowadays.

Yes, this was one of those Gaziks which had travelled tens of thousands of miles across the Don and Kazakhstan steppes, and the tundras of the North; it had almost clambered up the goat tracks in the mountains of the Caucasus and the Pamirs; it had penetrated the taiga of the Altai and Sikhote-Alin; it had served in the building of the Dnieper Dam, the Stalingrad Tractor Plant and the Magnitogorsk Iron and Steel Plant; it was one of those cars which had taken Chukhnovsky and his comrades to the northern aerodrome to rescue the Nobile Expedition and had forged its way through blizzards and over ice barriers down the frozen

Amur to help the first builders of Komsomolsk. In short, it was one of those Gaziks whose strenuous efforts had carried through the first five-year plan and then become obsolete and given way to the modern cars, the products of those very factories they had helped to bring into existence.

The Gazik parked outside the prefabricated house was of the closed type, a limousine. Inside it a heavy box stood on the floor in front of the back seat; across the box and back seat lay two suitcases, one on top of the other, and on them, squeezed to the top of the car, were two tightly packed haversacks with a couple of tommy-guns leaning against them. The magazines were fixed to the guns and spare magazines lay beside the guns. On what was left vacant of the seat sat a fair-haired, sun-tanned woman with stern features, attired in a thick travelling suit, the colour of which had become nondescript through frequent exposure to sun and rain. She had nowhere to put her legs and had them crossed one over the other and cramped in the space between the box and the door.

The woman was restlessly watching through the frame of the door, which had been without glass for a long time, her eyes moving from the porch to the opposite side of the street, where the lorry was being loaded. She was obviously waiting for someone, had been waiting for a long time and was finding it unpleasant that the people loading the lorry should be able to see the solitary car and herself sitting in it. A worried expression kept passing over her stern features like a shadow, then she threw herself back in the seat and gazed intently and thoughtfully at the youth and girl talking under the windows of the Trust. Gradually her features softened. The hint of a kind, sad smile stole impulsively into the grey eyes and touched the sharp line of her firm lips.

She was a woman of thirty; and she was unaware that this kindly sympathy and sadness which showed on her face as she watched the young man and girl was merely an expression of the fact that she was thirty and could never again be like them.

The young man and girl, completely oblivious of everything round them and of the world in general, were declaring their love for each other. They could not do otherwise for soon they would separate. And they declared their love as only young people do, by resolutely talking of everything except love.

"I'm so glad you came, Vanya, it's a load off my mind," she said, looking at him with eyes sparkling and her head on one side, a habit which the youth thought was the most lovable thing on earth. "I thought we would leave and I wouldn't see you."

"But you understand why I haven't been round these last few days?" he asked in a husky bass, looking down at her short-sightedly. The light of enthusiasm in the youth's eyes seemed like an ember ready to burst into flame. "But I know you understand absolutely everything.... I should have left three days ago. I had everything packed and had even smartened up to come and say good-bye, when I got a sudden call from the district Komsomol committee. They had just received the evacuation order and after that everything went wrong. I'm annoyed that the course I was attending has evacuated and I'm left behind. And the lads want help and I can see for myself that I must help.... Oleg offered me a seat in their *britzka* today to go to Kamensk ... you know what friends we are ... but I felt awkward about leaving...."

"You know, it's such a weight off my mind," she said again, her eyes, glowing with a soft, dark light, fixed on him.

"Frankly I was glad too," he said, "because, as I said to myself, I thought I'd be able to see you again and again. The hell I can!" He could not tear his eyes away from hers; he was enthralled by the tender warmth from her flushed face and full neck, from the whole of her palpable self, under the pink blouse. "Can you imagine it," he continued, "the Voroshilov School, the Gorky School, the Lenin Club, the children's hospital, they're all my responsibility now! Lucky for me I've got a good assistant: Zhora Arutyuniants. Remember him from school? Wonderful fellow! Volunteered himself. We can't remember when last we slept! On our feet day and night: carts and motorcars, loading lorries, fodder for the horses, then a blinking tyre has to burst, then a *britzka* has to go to the smithy .... It's a positive nightmare. But I knew you hadn't gone.

Dad told me," he said with a shy smile. "I went past your house last night—my heart was thumping, and I wanted to knock." He laughed aloud. "Then I remembered your father. No, Vanya, I said to myself, wait a bit...."

"You know it's a weight off ..." she began, but he was carried away and gave her no chance to finish.

"I made up my mind to chuck everything for today, because I was afraid you'd be gone and I wouldn't see you. And what do you think happens? It turned out that the children's home hadn't been evacuated, you know, the orphanage we set up last winter in Vosmidomiki. The matron, she lives in our house, comes to me almost in tears. 'Comrade Zemnukhov,' she said, 'you must help us! You might still manage to get transport through the Komsomol committee.' I said, 'The Komsomol committee's gone, try the education department.' She said, 'I've kept in touch with the education department all these days. They've promised to get us away any time now. This morning I ran round to them again: they have no transport for themselves! By the time I'd run back and forth and here and there, the education department no longer existed!' I said, 'Where had it got to, if it had no transport?' She said, 'I don't know. It's just melted away!' The education department just melted away!" Vanya Zemnukhov suddenly laughed so heartily that his long unruly hair fell over his forehead and ears, but he tossed it back at once with a quick jerk of the head. "Cranks!" he chuckled. "Well, that does it for you, Vanya, I said to myself. You'll no more see Klava again than your own ears! And d'you know what? Zhora and I got down to the job and rounded up five carts! D'you know from where? From the army! The matron thanked us and nearly drowned us in tears. But there was more to come! I said to Zhora, 'You run home and pack your things; I'll do the same.' And I gave him a hint that I had to go somewhere first, to you of course, and I said, 'Hang back a bit, don't rush, just in case.' I gave him the general idea.... I'd just finished packing when who d'you think rushes in? Tolya Orlov! D'you know him? He's got a nickname—the Thunderer...."

"It's like a weight off my mind," she finally interjected into the torrent of words. "I was so afraid you wouldn't

come. For, of course, I couldn't go and see you ..." she added, her voice low and velvety, and a passionate glint in
her eyes.

"Why not?" he asked, suddenly surprised at this idea.

"Oh, can't you understand!" She became embarrassed.
"What would I say to Dad?"

That was perhaps as far as she could go in the conversation: she had to make him understand that their relationship was not an ordinary one, that there was something
secret about it. She had, somehow, to remind him of the
fact, if he refused to speak of it himself.

He fell silent and looked at her in such a way that her
big face and full neck down to the edge of her pink blouse
suddenly turned the same colour as the blouse.

"It isn't that he doesn't like you, don't think that!"
she said quickly, her almond-shaped eyes flashing. "Time
and again he's said, 'What a clever chap that Zemnukhov is!'
And you know"—here she again used her irresistible, velvety tone of voice,—"if you wanted to you could come
with us!"

The thought had never entered his head that he might
evacuate together with the girl he loved; and this sudden
opportunity was so tempting that he found himself quite
at a loss and looked at her with an awkward smile. Suddenly
his face became serious and he gazed absent-mindedly down
the street. He was standing with his back to the park;
before him, running to the south, lay the long street, bright
in the hot glare of the sun shining in his face. Where it
sloped down towards the second level crossing the street
seemed to end abruptly, and far away in the distance were
the blue hills of the steppe, and columns of smoke from
fires hung in the sky beyond the hills. But he saw nothing
of all this for he was very short-sighted. He only heard the
roll of distant gun-fire, the whistling of the railway engines
behind the park, and the familiar note of the switch-man's
horn, sounding clear and crisp and peaceful under the
steppeland sky.

"I haven't got my things with me, Klava," he said sadly, and absently waved his arms about as if to indicate the
bare head with the long, unruly hair, the faded shirt with
the short sleeves, the worn brown-striped trousers, and the

leather gym slippers on his bare feet. "I've even forgotten my glasses and can't see you properly!" he bantered, wistfully.

"We'll ask Dad, and drive over for your things," she said softly and passionately. She threw a sidelong glance at him and made as if to take his hand, but hesitated.

As though on purpose, Klava's father, in cap and high boots and a worn grey jacket, and the sweat pouring down his face, appeared from behind the lorry. He looked about to see where he could find room on the lorry for the two suitcases he was carrying, but the lorry was already overloaded.

A worker standing on the lorry among the bales and boxes bent down on one knee and leaned over the side.

"Let's have them, Comrade Kovalyov, I'll find room!" he called and hauled up the cases one after the other.

Meanwhile Vanya's father, too, had appeared from behind the lorry. He came up with what looked like a bundle of laundry, probably household linen, in his sinewy brown arms. He was having great difficulty with it; his feet dragged along the ground and his long legs were almost doubled up under him. His drawn, wrinkled face was pale in spite of the tan, and sweating freely; against the pallor and exhaustion in his face, his agonizingly stern eyes, faded and with an unhealthy glint in them, were very prominent.

Alexander Zemnukhov, Vanya's father, was a watchman in the Coal Trust offices; Klava's father, Kovalyov, who was the stores manager of the Trust, was his immediate superior.

Kovalyov was one of those innumerable stores managers who, in normal times, quietly bear the burden of human indignation, ridicule and contempt, which is the lot of all stores managers in retaliation for the evil caused to mankind by certain of their dishonest colleagues. He was one of those stores managers who, in difficult times, demonstrate what it means to be a really good stores manager.

During the past few days, from the moment he had received instructions from the director to evacuate the property of the Trust, he had packed and loaded and sent off everything that might be of the slightest value in his customary, unruffled, swift and steady fashion, despite the entreaties and complaints of the other employees and the flattering assurances of friendship from those of his chiefs who ordinarily took no more notice of him than of the broom in front of the tiled stove. At sunrise this very morning he had received orders from the person responsible for the evacuation of the Trust not to delay a minute longer, to destroy all documents which could not be evacuated and then immediately to leave for the east.

Having received his orders Kovalyov just as calmly and quickly dispatched, first of all, the person responsible for the evacuation of the Trust together with his belongings, and then, having obtained every form of transport from no one knew where and in some unknown fashion, he continued to send away what remained of the Trust's property because his conscience forbade him to act in any other way. He was afraid of nothing so much as that he might even on this tragic day be accused, as always, of looking after his own interests first, and therefore he had firmly made up his mind that he and his family would leave on the very last car which he had, all the same, reserved for that purpose.

Old Zemnukhov, the Trust's watchman, had made no preparations because his illness and age prevented him from going away. Like the rest of the employees who were staying behind he had, some days previously, received his final pay, together with a two weeks' bonus. That meant that all his connections with the Trust were ended. But during all these days and nights he had shuffled back and forth, dragging about his rheumatic legs and helping Kovalyov to pack, load and dispatch, for the old man had come to regard the property of the Trust as his own.

Alexander Zemnukhov was an old Donets miner, a marvellously skilled carpenter. When just a lad he had come from Tambov Gubernia to make a living down the mines. Deep in the bowels of the Donets earth he had timbered and reinforced the workings, climbing and crawling about while his wondrous axe played and crowed in his hand as though it were the Golden Cockerel. He had worked in permanent dampness from his early youth and contracted acute rheumatism. He had been pensioned off and became a watchman with the Coal Trust and he had done his work as watchman there just as though he was still a carpenter.

"Come, Klava, get busy! Go and help Mother!" Kovalyov

barked, using the back of a dirty hand to wipe the sweat from his brow under the battered peak of his cap. "Hello, Vanya," he said casually. "See what's going on?" He shook his head angrily, at the same time seizing the bundle old Zemnukhov was carrying and helping him to lift it on to the lorry. "To think we've lived to see this!" he continued, panting. "Blast you!" he cursed, and made a grimace as a terrible resounding clatter rolled calamitously along the horizon. "How about you, aren't you going? And what about the lad, Alexander Fyodorovich?"

Alexander Zemnukhov neither replied nor so much as glanced at his son, but went off to fetch another bundle: he was afraid for his son and also annoyed with him for not having left days ago for Saratov to catch up with the Voroshilovgrad Law Courses where he had studied during the summer.

When Klava heard her father's words she signalled furtively to Vanya with her eyes, even touched his cuff and was about to say something to her father herself. But Vanya anticipated her.

"No," he said, "I can't go just now. I've still to find transport for Volodya Osmukhin who's not yet up after an appendix operation."

Klava's father looked at him and whistled.

"You're likely to get transport, I don't think!" he said in a tone that was tragic and derisive at the same time.

"Besides, I'm not alone," Vanya continued, avoiding Klava's eyes, his lips suddenly growing pale. "Zhora Arutyuniants and I have been working together all the time and we've sworn to keep together and evacuate on foot when we've cleared up everything here."

So Vanya burnt his boats. He looked at Klava and saw that her dark eyes were clouded over.

"I see," Kovalyov said, completely indifferent to Vanya, Zhora, and their pact. "Well, good-bye for now, then." He stepped towards Vanya, jumped as another artillery salvo rent the air and offered him a big sweaty palm.

"Are you making for Kamensk or Likhaya?" Vanya asked in a very deep bass.

"Kamensk?" Kovalyov roared. "With the Germans there any moment now? We're making for Likhaya and nowhere else! Heading for Belokalitvenskaya, across the Donets. Try and catch us after that...."

Something clattered and softly tinkled above them and a shower of dust and dry putty fell on their heads. They looked up and saw that a window had been flung open on the first floor in the room occupied by the Trust Planning Department. A large, red, bald head was thrust out, sweat literally pouring off it and all but dripping on the people below.

"You don't mean you're still here, Comrade Statsenko?" Kovalyov called out, surprised. He had recognized the chief of the department.

"Yes, I'm still sorting out papers so that nothing important is left for the Germans." Statsenko's deep voice was quiet and polite as always.

"Well, it's lucky we now know!" Kovalyov exclaimed. "We should have been gone in another ten minutes."

"But you go right ahead. I'll find means of getting away," Statsenko said, unassumingly. "Tell me, Kovalyov, d'you know whose car that is, parked over there?"

Kovalyov, his daughter, Vanya, and the worker on the lorry looked towards the Gazik. The woman inside immediately changed her position to avoid being seen through the door.

"He won't take you, Comrade Statsenko. He's already got his hands full!" Kovalyov exclaimed.

He knew as well as Statsenko that Ivan Protsenko of the regional Party committee lived in that house. He had rented a room there the previous autumn just for himself; his wife worked in Voroshilovgrad.

"But I don't need favours from him!" said Statsenko and looked at Kovalyov with eyes small and bloodshot, which showed that he liked to drink.

Kovalyov was taken aback and threw a quick glance at the worker on the lorry, hoping he had not noticed the malice behind Statsenko's words.

"Well, in all innocence I had imagined that they'd all made off long ago. Then suddenly I saw the car and wondered whose it might be!" Statsenko explained with a good-natured smile.

They continued to look at the Gazik for a moment or two.

"You can see now they're not all gone," Kovalyov said, frowning.

"Ah, Kovalyov, Kovalyov!" Statsenko said sadly. "It's no good being a more faithful believer than the Pope of Rome himself!" he added, misquoting a proverb which meant nothing at all to Kovalyov.

"Comrade Statsenko, I'm nobody in particular," Kovalyov said hoarsely, straightening his back and looking at the worker on the lorry, not at the window above him. "I'm only an ordinary chap and don't understand your insinuations...."

"Why take offence? I've said nothing to annoy you.... Well, a pleasant journey, Kovalyov! We'll hardly meet again this side of Saratov," Statsenko said, and the window was banged shut.

Kovalyov, with unseeing eyes, and Vanya, in bewilderment, looked at each other. Kovalyov suddenly flushed a deep purple as though he had been offended.

"Get a move on, Klava!" he shouted, walking round the lorry and into the Trust building.

Kovalyov had indeed taken offence, but not for himself. He was offended that a man like Statsenko, not an ordinary chap like himself who not being aware of the circumstances might have the right to grumble and complain, but a man high up in authority, who was on familiar terms with government representatives and who, in happier days, had used flowery, flattering words to them, should now censure the same people when they could no longer speak up for themselves.

Now finally annoyed by the attention paid her, and red with embarrassment and anger, the woman in the Gazik turned and fixed her angry gaze on the door of the prefabricated house.

Chapter 8

Ivan Protsenko, with two other men, sat in one of the rooms facing the back yard. The windows were open to let the draught blow away the smoke from the burnt documents. The owners of the flat had left a few days previously. The room, like the rest of the building, was dismal, comfortless and bare. Life had departed from the building. Only the shell remained. Objects had been moved out of their places. Protsenko and his colleagues were not sitting at the table but on chairs in the middle of the room. They were outlining the work ahead and exchanging secret addresses.

Protsenko had now to leave for the partisan base; his assistant had started off for the same destination some hours earlier. As one of the leaders of the regional underground his place would be with a detachment based in a forest near Mityakinskaya, a Cossack village on the border between Voroshilovgrad and Rostov regions. His two comrades would remain here in Krasnodon. Both were local men, Donets miners who had fought in the Civil War during that other German occupation and the Denikin White Guard campaign.

Filipp Petrovich Lyutikov who would remain as secretary of the underground district committee was a man in his fifties and slightly older than his comrade. He had streaks of grey in his thick hair, particularly in front and at the temples. His short bristling moustache was also grey. One felt that he had been a man of great physical strength but with the years he had grown stout and his face had filled out so that his naturally heavy chin appeared still more ponderous. Lyutikov was a man of tidy habits and even in the present circumstances he was dressed in a neat black suit, which fitted well on his stout figure, a clean white shirt and a well knotted necktie.

He was an old factory worker and had become a Hero of Labour in the early years of the period of restoration after the Civil War. He proved to be an able industrial executive, first as director of small enterprises and later of increasingly larger ones. He had worked in Krasnodon for fifteen years, during the past few of which he had been chief of the mechanical department at the central repair shops of the Krasnodon Coal Trust.

Matvei Shulga, his underground comrade-in-arms, had been among the first group of industrial workers to respond to the appeal for workers to assist agriculture. Born in Krasnodon, he had spent his life working in various parts of the Donets Basin on mechanical jobs connected with agriculture. At the outbreak of the war he had become deputy chairman of the executive committee of a northern district of Voroshilovgrad Region.

Unlike Lyutikov, who, at the first threat of occupation, had known that he would work underground, Shulga had received his appointment only two days previously, at his own request, as soon as the Germans had occupied the district in which he was working. It had been determined that Krasnodon would be the most convenient and favourable locality for his underground work, because, on the one hand, he was a local man, and, on the other, he had been away for so long that there were few people here who knew him.

Matvei Shulga was about forty-five with powerful rounded shoulders, a strong, tanned, sharp-featured face with bluish flecks here and there—the marks of his basic trade, marks which all who have worked long as miners or foundrymen carry with them.

He had pushed his cap to the back of his head revealing a close-cropped head, the top of which was unusually broad. His eyes were serene and large.

In the whole town of Krasnodon there were none as collected and yet as elated as these three.

"There'll be some good people, real people you might say, left behind under your command. With people like that great things can be done," Protsenko said. "Where d'you plan to live?"

"Where I've always lived, at Pelagea Ilyinichna's," Lyutikov replied.

Protsenko's face did not express astonishment, but just a certain doubt.

"I don't think I heard you right!" he said.

"Why should I hide, Protsenko? Judge for yourself," Lyutikov said. "I'm so well known here that it's not possible for me to go under cover. The same with Barakov." This was the name of a third, absent leader of the underground. "The Germans would immediately discover us; what's more we'd arouse their suspicions if we tried to hide. We've no reason for hiding. The Germans badly need our workshops, and we'll be right there! We'll say: 'The Trust director has run away, the engineers and mechanics have been forcibly evacuated by the Bolsheviks; but we're here, we've stayed behind to work for you. The workers have run out on us, but we'll collect them up. No engineers? Here's Nikolai Petrovich Barakov for you: a mechanical engineer. What's more, he speaks German!' Oh, we'll work for them all right!" Lyutikov said, without a trace of humour in his face.

His eyes, stern and alert, with that expression of sagacity peculiar to people who take nothing on trust, but think everything out for themselves, were fixed firmly on Protsenko.

"How about Barakov?" Protsenko asked.

"It's our joint plan."

"And do you know what your immediate danger will be?" Protsenko asked. He was one of those people who can see all sides of the matter and judge how things might turn out.

"I know: Communists," Lyutikov replied.

"Not at all. What could be better for the Germans than that Communists have gone over to work for them. But the Germans may be slow in realizing their good fortune: while you're still giving whatever explanations you like, they'll fly into a rage and bump you off," Protsenko indicated the ceiling.

"We'll disappear for the first few days, and turn up when we're wanted."

"That's the whole point! And I'm interested in where you're going to disappear to!"

"Pelagea Ilyinichna will know where to hide me." Lyutikov smiled for the first time since the conversation had begun, and his heavy, drooping face brightened because of the smile.

All doubt vanished from Protsenko's face. He was satisfied with Lyutikov.

"Now, Shulga, how about you?"

"He's not Shulga, he's Yevdokim Ostapchuk. That's the name in the work-book issued by the railway repair shop. He began as fitter in the machine-room the other day. It's quite simple: he used to work in Voroshilovgrad; when fighting broke out, and having no family, he made his way to Krasnodon. The minute the repair shops start up we'll get fitter Ostapchuk to work for the Germans. We'll work for them all right!" Lyutikov said.

Protsenko turned to Shulga and, without noticing it, began to talk to him not in Russian, as he had done with Lyutikov, but in a mixture of Russian and Ukrainian. That was how Shulga himself always talked.

"Tell me, Shulga: d'you know anyone personally at the addresses you've been given as hiding-places? In other words, d'you know anything about anybody there, their families, their background?"

"Well, you might say I do," Shulga replied slowly, and fixed his serene, large eyes on Protsenko. "At one of the addresses, in Golubyatniki, there's Gnatenko, Ivan Kondratovich Gnatenko. He was a partisan in 1918, and a good one, too. And at the second address, in Shanghai district, there's Ignat Fomin. I don't know him personally, he's new in Krasnodon, but you've most likely heard of him as a Stakhanovite in Pit No. 4. They say he can be trusted and has given his consent. It's convenient that he's non-Party, and although well known, they say he's never been active publicly, never spoken at meetings. An inconspicuous sort of chap."

"Ever been to either of these places?" Protsenko persisted.

"The last time I called on Kondratovich, I mean Ivan Gnatenko, was some twelve years ago. I've never been to Fomin's place. How could I, Protsenko? You know yourself that I only arrived yesterday and only yesterday got permission to stay and was handed the addresses. But whoever chose these people must know something about them," he said, half replying, half questioning.

"Now listen here." Protsenko lifted a finger and looked first at Lyutikov, then at Shulga. "Don't believe what's in writing or what's said to you or what you are instructed to do. Verify everything and everybody yourselves again and again. The people who organized your underground are no longer here—you know that. According to the rules of conspiracy—golden rules—they have gone! They are miles and miles away. Possibly they are in Novocherkassk by now," Protsenko said with a subtle smile, while a twinkle skipped from one blue eye to the other. "What's the point in what

I'm saying?" he continued. "The point is that the underground was organized while we still had Soviet power here; but now the Germans are going to be here. The real test of people is coming, a life and death test...."

He was interrupted before he could develop his idea. The street door slammed; steps were heard approaching and the woman from the Gazik entered the room. The anxiety she had just experienced was clearly written in her face.

"Tired of waiting, Katya? Just coming!" Protsenko said with a broad guilty grin and stood up. The others also rose. "Let me introduce you to my wife. She's a teacher," he said with sudden pride.

Lyutikov respectfully shook her strong hand. She already knew Shulga and smiled at him:

"And what about your wife?"

"Er ... all my—" Shulga began.

"Oh, I'm sorry, forgive me," she blurted and quickly covered her face with a hand which did not, however, conceal the flushed face.

Shulga's family had remained behind in German-occupied territory and that was one of the reasons why he had asked to be left in the region to work underground. His people had not been able to get away when the Germans had made a sudden break-through. At the time Shulga had been away in the outlying villages, organizing the round-up of cattle to be driven to the east.

Like himself, his family were just ordinary folk. When the families of the local officials had been evacuated to the east, the Shulgas—his wife, a daughter at school and his seven-year-old son—had not wanted to leave, nor had Shulga himself insisted that they should. During the Civil War, when he had been a young partisan in those parts, his wife had stayed at his side. Their first son, now a Red Army officer, had been born just at that time and the memory of those days had instilled in the family the conviction that they should stick together, that even when life became difficult they should all share the burden. They had brought up their children in that spirit too. Shulga was now feeling that it was his fault that his wife and children were in German hands and he lived for the day when he would be able to rescue them if they were still among the living.

"Forgive me!" reiterated Protsenko's wife. She removed the hand from her face and looked apologetically and sympathetically at Shulga.

"Well, what about it, my dear comrades..." Protsenko began but immediately fell silent.

The time had come to go. But all four felt very much that they did not wish to separate.

Only a few hours had passed since their comrades had gone, had gone to their own people to travel across the land that was theirs, but these four would remain here and were about to start a new life—an illegal existence—an existence which seemed uncertain and strange to them after living freely in their native land for twenty-four years. It was only a little while since they had seen their comrades; they were not so far away and it would still be possible to hurry and join them—yet it was not to be. And so, these four were now so close to each other, closer than the members of any family. Hence the difficulty they found in parting.

They stood a long time shaking hands with each other.

"Now we shall see what those Germans are like, what sort of masters and rulers they are," Protsenko said.

"You take care of yourself, Ivan Protsenko!" Lyutikov said, very seriously.

"Ho, I'm as tough as weed. Look after yourself, Filipp Lyutikov, and you, Shulga!"

"I'm immortal," Shulga said and smiled sadly.

Lyutikov looked sternly at him but said nothing.

In turn they embraced, avoiding each other's eyes.

"Good-bye!" Protsenko's wife said. She did not smile. She said the words solemnly even, and her eyes filled with tears.

Lyutikov went first, Shulga followed. They left as they had come: secretly through the back door. There were several small outhouses in the yard. From behind them each went separately and unnoticed to a side street, which ran parallel with the main road.

Ivan Protsenko and his wife left together, passing through the front door on to the main street, which began at the gates of the park and was called Sadovaya. The hot rays of the afternoon sun beat down on their faces.

Seeing the loaded lorry on the opposite side of the street, the worker on top of it and the youth and girl saying good-bye, Ivan Protsenko understood why his wife had been so worried.

He spent a long time cranking up the engine, but the Gazik only shuddered, the engine refused to start.

"Katya, you try while I give her some juice," Protsenko said sheepishly and jumped into the car.

His wife gripped the handle in her slim brown hand and, with surprising force, gave it a few sharp turns. The engine ticked over. She wiped the sweat from her forehead with the back of her hand, flung the crank handle under the driver's seat and took her place beside Protsenko. The Gazik back-fired, shot out blasts of dirty-blue smoke, moved jerkily down the road, bucking like a lively foal; then it settled down and was soon out of sight, as it descended to the level crossing.

"So, you see, in comes this Tolya Orlov—d'you know him?" Vanya was saying in a low, husky voice, at just about the same time.

"I don't. He's probably from the Voroshilov School," Klava replied tonelessly.

"Anyway, he says to me, 'Comrade Zemnukhov, just a few doors away from you lives Volodya Osmukhin, a very active Komsomol; he's had an appendix operation and they took him home too soon and now his wound's opened and gone septic. Can't you get him transport?' I know Volodya well— one of the very best! See the fix I'm in now? So I said, 'You go on to Volodya, I've got to go somewhere else first, then I'll try to find something and come along, too.' Then I hurried to you here. Now d'you see why I can't leave with you?" Vanya said guiltily and tried to look into her eyes which were filling with tears. "But Zhora and I—" he began again.

"Vanya," she interrupted him and brought her face very close, so that her breath was warm on his face. "Vanya, I'm proud of you, so very proud of you! I—" She let out a low moan more like that of a woman than of a girl. In an equally ungirlish, motherly fashion she wound both her large, cool arms round his neck and, throwing caution to the winds, kissed him passionately on the lips. Then she tore herself away and ran off through the garden gate.

For a moment or two Vanya did not move. Then he turned his head towards the sun and, with dishevelled hair, which he no longer bothered to smooth down, and long arms swinging, walked quickly down the street leaving the park gates behind him.

The enthusiasm which always smouldered in his heart seemed to burn brightly in his uncommon face. But neither Klava nor anyone else was there to see how handsome it made him look. Alone he strode down the street, long arms swinging idly. Somewhere in the neighbourhood they were still blowing up the mines, somewhere people were still fleeing and weeping and cursing; soldiers were still retreating, the roar of guns still thundered and the formidable buzzing of aircraft engines filled the sky; there was smoke and dust in the air and the sun scorched down mercilessly. But for Vanya Zemnukhov nothing of all this existed. There were only those full, cool, soft arms round his neck and that roughly passionate, tear-soaked kiss on his lips.

Nothing could frighten him now because there was nothing he could not achieve. He could have evacuated not only Volodya but the whole town now: women, children and old men, together with all their possessions.

"I'm so proud of you ... so proud ..." she had said in her low, velvety voice, and for the moment he had no thought for anything else.

He was only nineteen.

Chapter 9

No ONE could tell what life would be like under the Germans.

Lyutikov and Shulga had in good time agreed on the method of contacting each other: it was only to be after a pre-arranged signal and through a third person, someone whose flat was to be the central meeting-place in Krasnodon.

They left separately and each went his way. Could they guess then that they would never meet again?

Lyutikov did what he had told Protsenko he would do: he vanished.

And Shulga too should have hidden humbly at one of the addresses he had been given, preferably at the home of Ivan Gnatenko, or Kondratovich, as he was usually called; he was an old partisan and his close crony. But it was twelve years since Shulga had seen him, and he felt that in the present circumstances he had not the slightest desire to visit Ivan Gnatenko.

Though outwardly calm, he felt sick in heart and mind. He needed the company of someone very close to him now. And he tried to remember whether there was anyone left in Krasnodon with whom he had been particularly intimate during that other underground period in 1918 and 1919.

A childlike smile spread over his large coal-pitted face as he remembered Liza, the sister of Leonid Rybalov, his old comrade. He recalled her as she used to be in those years: with her shapely figure, fair hair, fearless nature, lively eyes, abrupt movements and curt voice. He called to mind how she would bring food to him and Leonid in Senyaki, how her white teeth had flashed in a smile when he had jokingly said what a pity it was that he already had a wife. And she knew his wife well, too.

Ten or twelve years ago he had met her in the street and once at a women's meeting. If he remembered correctly, she had been married by then. Yes, she had married somebody by the name of Osmukhin right after the Civil War. This Osmukhin had later got a job with the Trust, and Shulga remembered that he had been on the housing commission when Osmukhin was given a flat in a new residential building somewhere on the street leading to Pit No. 5.

A picture rose before him of Liza as he had known her when they were young; memories of those days rushed in on him, he felt young again and those memories of his youth shed a brighter light on everything that he would have to face. She can't have changed much, he thought, and her husband seemed like one of us, too.... Oh, I don't care what happens, I'm going to see Liza Rybalova first. Maybe they haven't yet left and fate is leading me to them. Or perhaps she's living alone now ....

So his thoughts raced on as he went down the sloping road towards the level crossing.

During the ten years of his absence the whole neighbourhood had been rebuilt with modern brick houses and it was difficult now to determine in which of them the Osmukhins lived. He walked a long time through the now silent streets, past the shuttered houses, hesitating to knock and ask. Finally he hit on the idea of using the tower of No. 5 engine-house as a landmark. It stood out clearly across the steppe and when he followed a road leading straight towards it he found the Osmukhins' house at once.

The windows were wide open and flowers stood on the sills; he could hear young voices in the rooms inside, and when he knocked on the door his pulse quickened, as in his youth. There was no answer. They probably hadn't heard him. He knocked again. Muffled footsteps could be heard approaching.

Liza stood before him: Yelizaveta Alexeyevna Rybalova, in her slippers, her face angry yet full of grief, with eyes puffy and red with weeping. "How life has knocked you about," thought Shulga.

But he recognized her immediately. She had always in her younger days had this rather grim expression, something between irritability and anger, but Shulga knew that she really had a kind heart. She still had a good figure, there was no grey in her fair hair, but deep, long wrinkles, which told of grave suffering and hard work, lined her face. And she was somehow slovenly in her dress—formerly she would never have let herself go like this.

There was hostility and interrogation in the look she gave the stranger in her doorway. But suddenly an expression of surprise leapt to her face and an echo of past happiness showed in her eyes behind the tears.

"Matvei Konstantinovich ... Comrade Shulga!" she said. Her hand dropped helplessly from the door handle. "What wind's blown you this way? And at a time like this!"

"Excuse me, Liza ... or, I don't know, should I say Yelizaveta Alexeyevna.... I'm off to the east, getting evacuated, and I came to pay a visit...."

"So it's that; you're off to the east! Everything and everybody is off to the east! And what about us? And our children?" she said, immediately flaring up. She straightened her hair with a nervous hand and looked at him with eyes which were both angry and terribly tortured. "You are going off to the east, Comrade Shulga, and my son's in bed after an operation! And you're off to the east!" she repeated as though she had warned him that this very thing would happen, that it had happened and that it was all his fault.

"I'm sorry. Don't be angry," Shulga said, very calmly and in a conciliatory voice, although he suddenly felt distressed and a very faint voice spoke up in his mind: "So that's what you've turned into, Liza Rybalova," it said, "that's how you welcome me, my dear Liza!"

But he had seen a great deal in his life and he restrained himself.

"Tell me straight what's been happening to you?"

"Oh, you must forgive me." Her manner was still abrupt, but the shadow of their former good relations again showed in her face. "Come in. Only things are in an awful state here!" She waved her hand in a hopeless gesture and her swollen, red-rimmed eyes again filled with tears.

She stepped back and motioned him to enter. He followed her into the dim passage. Through an open door he had a fleeting glimpse of a sunlit room on the right of him. Three or four young people stood round a bed on which lay a lad in his teens, propped up with a pillow. The sheet was smoothed down and his arms lay on the coverlet. He wore a white sports shirt with an open collar. His eyes were dark in a face from which the sunburn had faded.

"They've come to say good-bye to my son. Come in here," she said, and showed him into the room opposite. It was on the shady side of the house, cool and somewhat dark.

"Well, first of all: how d'you do?" Shulga said. He took his cap off, revealing his close-cropped, powerful head. "I don't quite know how to address you now," he said, offering his hand, "is it Liza or Yelizaveta Alexeyevna?"

"Call me what you like. I'm not one to stand on ceremony or give myself airs, only what's left of Liza now? I was Liza once, but now—" She made a quick movement with her hand as though dismissing the subject and looked straight at him, an apologetic, tortured and, at the same time, very womanly expression in her light, swollen eyes.

"For me you'll always be Liza though I'm old myself," said Shulga with a smile, and sat down.

She sat down opposite him.

"And since I'm an old man you'll forgive me if I start by giving you a talking-to," Shulga continued, still smiling but with a very serious undertone in his voice. "You should not be angry because I'm going east and some more of our people are going east. The damned Germans allowed us no time.... Once upon a time you were my comrade so there's no harm in telling you that they have cut deep into the rear."

"Does that make it easier for us?" she said wearily. "You're going, but we have to stay behind...."

"Well, whose fault is that?" he said, frowning. "Since the war started we've been evacuating families like yours," here he recalled his own people, "and have given them help and transport. Families? We've taken tens of thousands of workers' families to the Urals and Siberia. Why didn't you leave when you had the opportunity?" Shulga asked, while a feeling of bitterness rose up in him.

She made no reply and he knew, by the way she sat, motionless and erect, as though listening to what was going on in the room across the passage, that she was hardly listening to him. He, too, involuntarily began to listen to what was taking place in the other room.

Only now and then could low voices be heard from the other room, but it was impossible to gather what was going on.

For all his insistence and cool-headedness, which had become almost proverbial among his comrades, Vanya Zemnukhov had not managed to secure either a cart or a seat in a car for Volodya Osmukhin and had returned home, where he had found Zhora Arutyuniants impatiently waiting. His father had also returned home and so Vanya knew that the Kovalyovs had gone.

Zhora was very tall but even so he was half a head shorter than Vanya. Seventeen years of age, with a naturally dark complexion made darker by the sun, he had handsome, curly eyelashes, black Armenian eyes and full lips. There was something of the Negro about him.

Despite the difference in their ages they had become fast friends during the last few days: they were both passionately fond of books.

At school Vanya's friends had even called him the Professor. He possessed only one good suit, the grey one with brown stripes, which he put on for all important occasions and which, like everything else Vanya wore, was too small. But when he had it on with a white, turned-down-collar shirt, brown necktie and his horn-rimmed glasses, and appeared in the school corridor, his pockets stuffed with papers, carrying a book tucked under his arm or clapped against his shoulder absent-mindedly from time to time, when he walked down the corridor, invariably calm, silent, with that restrained enthusiasm, which burned so steadily and clearly in his heart, giving a kind of reflected warmth to his pale face, all his comrades, and especially the pupils of the junior classes, Young Pioneers all, stood aside for him instinctively just as though he really were a professor.

Zhora Arutyuniants kept a special ruled notebook in which he entered the author's name and the title of every book he read together with his own brief remarks. For instance:

"N. Ostrovsky. *How the Steel Was Tempered*. First-rate.

"A. Blok. *Verses on a Beautiful Woman*. Hosts of nebulous words.

"Byron. *Childe Harold*. It is inconceivable why this work so stirred people's minds. It is so boring to read.

"V. Mayakovsky. *Good!* (No comment.)

"A. Tolstoi. *Peter I*. Excellent. It shows that Peter was a progressive man."

And much more could be read in that ruled notebook. In general, Zhora was very neat and tidy. He liked order and discipline and was persistent in his convictions.

During the days and nights when they were busy evacuating the schools, clubs and children's homes they were not at all silent for a minute. They had heated arguments about the Second Front, the poem *Wait For Me*, the Northern Sea Route, the strange behaviour of the Sikorski Government in London, the film *A Great Life*, Academician Lysenko's works and the shortcomings of the Young Pioneer movement; they discussed Shchipachov the poet, Levitan the radio announcer, Roosevelt and Churchill. And on only one point did they really disagree: Zhora thought it far more useful to read newspapers and books than to go chasing after girls in the park, while Vanya said that as far as he was concerned, he would certainly chase them if he were not so short-sighted.

While Vanya was bidding farewell to his weeping mother, elder sister and father who was angrily snorting, snuffling and sighing while endeavouring not to look at his son, though at the last moment he suddenly pressed his dry lips to Vanya's forehead and blessed him with the sign of the cross, Zhora was trying to convince him that since he had failed to get transport there was no sense in calling on the Osmukhins. But Vanya said that he had given his word to Anatoly Orlov and would have to go and explain everything.

They had put a few personal belongings into haversacks and these they now swung over their shoulders. For the last time Vanya glanced at his own particular corner by his bed: on the wall there was a print of Pushkin's portrait by Karpov; there was the shelf with his books, and the *Collected Works* of Pushkin and some smaller volumes by Pushkin's contemporaries occupying the place of honour. Vanya looked at it all, pulled his cap down over his eyes with an exaggerated, abrupt gesture and went off with Zhora to Volodya Osmukhin.

Volodya, in a white singlet, sat propped up in bed, the sheet drawn up to his waist. Beside him lay a book, *Protective Relays*. It was open at the place where he had put it down that morning.

In the corner between bed and window, obviously pushed there so that it would not interfere with the cleaning of the room, lay a variety of tools, coils of wire, a home-made film projector, radio parts: Volodya loved inventing things and dreamed of becoming an aircraft designer.

Tolya Orlov, or the Thunderer, as he was called, was an orphan and Volodya's closest friend; he was sitting on a low stool near the bed. He was nicknamed the Thunderer because summer and winter alike he was afflicted with a loud reverberating cough which sounded as though it came from inside a barrel. He sat hunched up, his huge knees very prominent. All his joints—elbows, wrists, knees and ankles—were abnormally developed and were very bony. His thick, coarse, mousy hair stuck out in all directions from his round head. There was a mournful expression in his eyes.

"You can't walk at all then?" Vanya asked.

"Walk? The doctor says if I try to the wound will burst open and my intestines will fall out!" Volodya said gloomily.

He was dejected not only because he would have to be left behind but because his mother and sister would have to stay with him.

"Show us the stitches!" Zhora demanded.

"Nonsense, it's all bandaged up!" Lyudmila interjected, alarmed. She was Volodya's sister and was leaning on her elbows which rested on the foot of the bed.

"Don't get excited, everything will be all right," Zhora said, smiling courteously. His pleasant Armenian accent seemed to give special meaning to his words. "I've completed the first-aid course and I know how to remove and put on bandages."

"But it's unhygienic!" Lyudmila protested.

"The latest in army medicine," Zhora said peremptorily, "which is called upon to work under intolerable conditions on the battle-field has proved what you say to be prejudice."

"You're thinking of something else you've been reading," said Lyudmila haughtily. But she glanced at this dark lad with rising interest.

"Lay off, Lyudmila! I can understand Mama, she's a nervous woman, but why must you interfere in things that don't concern you? Go away, go on!" Volodya said angrily to his sister. He threw the bedclothes back and uncovered a pair of legs which were so sunburnt and muscular that no amount of illness and lying in hospital could wear off the tan or destroy the hard muscles. Lyudmila turned away.

Tolya and Vanya supported Volodya while Zhora pulled down the blue shorts and began to undo the bandages. The wound was septic and in an appalling state, and Volodya, who had to make an effort in order not to screw up his face with pain, turned pale.

"Nasty business, isn't it?" Zhora said, frowning.

"None too good," agreed Vanya.

Silently, and trying not to look at Volodya, whose narrow, brown eyes, always bright with boldness and cunning, were now sad and searching to catch the eyes of his comrades, they bandaged him up again.

The most difficult part had now come: they really had to abandon their comrade, knowing the danger he was in.

"Where's your husband, Liza?" Shulga said, meanwhile, changing the subject.

"Dead," Yelizaveta Alexeyevna replied harshly. "He died last year, just before the war. He was ill for a long time, then he died." She repeated the words several times, in angry reproach, it seemed to Shulga. "Ah, Matvei Konstantinovich!" she continued in an agonized voice. "You've become somebody important now too and perhaps you don't see everything. If you only knew how hard it is for us now! You hold authority on behalf of us ordinary people. I know the class of people you come from, you're the same as us. I remember how my brother and you fought for the life we have now, and I have nothing at all to blame you for. I know you mustn't stay here and get killed. But can't you see that besides you people who are taking nothing with you, there are others who are taking furniture and lorry-loads of junk, and they don't care in the least about us ordinary folk, yet we, the ordinary people, built up all this with our own hands. Ah, Matvei Konstantinovich, can't you see that this scum, forgive the word, consider their belongings more precious than us, the ordinary people?" she cried, her lips twisted in anguish. "And then you're surprised when other people are offended by you! You only have to experience this sort of thing once in a lifetime, and you lose faith in everything."

Subsequently Shulga frequently recalled this part of their conversation with pain and grief. The most irreparable thing was that in his heart he had understood the woman's feelings and in his strong broad-mindedness he had known the right words to use to her. But the trouble had been that while she was saying all those things with such anguish and, as he thought, rancour bursting out of her, her whole appearance, every word she had said, had been so unlike the picture of Liza as he had known her years ago, had been so strikingly at variance with what he had expected! So it suddenly seemed an insult to him that, when he himself was remaining behind and his whole family were in German hands and possibly already dead, this woman should speak of nothing but herself, should have not even asked after his family and particularly his wife, with whom she had been friends when they were young. And so Shulga, too, had let fall words which he later recalled with regret.

"You've let your thoughts run away with you, Yelizaveta Alexeyevna," he said coldly. "They've gone a very long way! It's very convenient, isn't it, to lose faith in your own government just when German rule is at your gates. D'you hear that?" Sternly he raised his hand with its stubby, hairy fingers and the sounds of distant gun-fire seemed to burst into the room. "Have you given a thought to how many of the flower of our people are meeting death out there—ordinary people who have 'gained power' as you would put it; but I would call them ordinary people who have reached understanding, the flower of the people, the Communists. And if you have ceased to have confidence in those people at a time when the Germans are trampling on us, then I am deeply offended. I am offended and I pity you very much indeed!" He said the words gravely and his lips trembled like those of a child.

"What are you suggesting? What's this? Are you accusing me of only waiting for the Germans to come?" the woman stammered, almost choking with rage at his interpretation of her words. She screamed at him, "How could you ... what about my son, I'm a mother! And you—"

"Can you have forgotten the time, Yelizaveta Alexeyevna, when we were all ordinary working people, as you say, and we faced danger from the Germans and the White Guards; did we think of ourselves first then?" he said bitterly, not listening to her. "No, we didn't think of ourselves but of the best of our people—our leaders, they were the ones we were always thinking about! You remember your brother? That's how we always thought and acted, we working people! To conceal them, to shield our leaders, the flower of the people, while we ourselves stood four-square against the enemy. That's how the working man has always argued and still argues and he would consider it a disgrace to think otherwise. Can you really have changed so much since those days, Yelizaveta Alexeyevna?"

"Wait!" she said suddenly and sat up erect, trying to interpret the sounds in the room across the passage.

Shulga listened, too.

No sound came from that room and her mother instinct told her that something was afoot there. Momentarily she forgot Shulga, rose and opened the door sharply and crossed the passage to her son. Dissatisfied with himself, Shulga followed gloomily, crumpling his cap in his big hairy hands.

Yelizaveta Alexeyevna's son, still propped up on his bed, was saying good-bye to his comrades. Silently, he took his time shaking hands with each of them. His neck and head, on which the dark, usually close-cropped hair was beginning to grow long, twitched nervously. He was agitated, yet, strange as it might seem in the circumstances, his face was cheerfully animated and his narrow, dark eyes sparkled. One of his comrades, tousle-haired, ungainly and muscular, stood at the head of the bed. His face was averted and was visible only in profile and he was gazing through the open window into the sunshine, his eyes wide, and a bright, hopeful expression on his face.

The girl still stood smiling at the patient from the foot of the bed. Shulga's heart was suddenly pained as he recognized in the girl something of the old Liza Rybalova. Yes, she was just like the Liza he had known, only more softened than Liza, the working woman with the rather large hands and jerky movements, whom he had known and loved over twenty years ago.

Yes, it's high time I went, he thought. There was sadness in his heart as, still twisting and turning his cap, he stepped clumsily across the creaking floor boards.

"Are you going?" Yelizaveta Alexeyevna asked loudly and hurried towards him.

"It seems so. Don't be angry. It's time to go." He put his cap on.

"Already?" she said. It was neither a question nor an exclamation, yet it seemed that he heard something of pity as well as bitterness. "Well, don't you be angry either.... God grant, if he exists, that you get there safely, and spare us a thought—don't forget us!" Her hands dropped helplessly. There was something so kind and maternal in her voice that he suddenly felt a lump rising in his throat.

"Good-bye," Shulga said, frowning, and stepped out into the street.

Why, oh, why did you go, Comrade Shulga? Why did you forsake Yelizaveta Alexeyevna and the girl who was so much like the Liza Rybalova of earlier days; why did you not think or even sense what was taking place before your eyes among those young people, why did you not even try to find out who those youngsters were?

If Matvei Shulga had acted differently the whole course of his life would have altered. But not only was he at the time unable to understand, he had felt offended and insulted. And there had been nothing for him to do but set out for that distant part of the town formerly known as Golubyatniki to seek the little house of Ivan Gnatenko, his old comrade of partisan days whom he had not seen for twelve years. How could he know that at the same time he was taking the first step along the road which was to lead to his death?

Now this is what took place only a moment before Shulga had followed Yelizaveta Alexeyevna into the passage. This is what took place in the room where Yelizaveta's son was lying.

There was an oppressive silence. Then Tolya Orlov rose from the small stool on which he had been sitting, that same Tolya who was nicknamed the Thunderer. He rose from the little stool and said that since Volodya, his best friend, was unable to leave then he, Tolya, would stay behind with him.

For a moment nobody knew what to say. Then Volodya had burst into tears and embraced Tolya and a second later they were all filled with happy excitement. Lyudmila threw her arms round the Thunderer's neck and kissed him on his cheeks, nose and eyes—he could not remember a happier moment. Then she scowled at Zhora Arutyuniants. She very much wanted this neat, handsome dark lad to remain with them as well.

"Good for you, Tolya, that's a real pal! You're grand, Tolya!" Vanya Zemnukhov said in a deep bass voice. "I'm proud of you." Then he corrected himself: "I mean Zhora and I are both proud of you," and he shook Tolya's hand.

"But d'you think we're just going to live here and do nothing?" Volodya said, his eyes sparkling. "No, we're going to fight, aren't we, Tolya? And the regional Party committee is bound to have left people here to work underground. We'll find 'em! D'you think we can't make ourselves useful?"

Chapter 10

VANYA AND ZHORA had said good-bye to Volodya Osmukhin and joined the stream of refugees following the railway line to Likhaya.

Their initial plan had been to make for Novocherkassk
where Zhora had, as he put it, influential relations who
would be able to help them to continue their journey: one
of his uncles worked as a shoemaker at the railway station.

Vanya, however, who knew that the Kovalyovs were on
their way to Likhaya had suggested the other route at the last
moment after giving vague reasons to the effect that his route
had certain advantages.

Zhora was quite used to leaving the initiative to his older
friend and, since it was completely immaterial to him
where he went, he had readily given up his clearly defined
route for Vanya's doubtful one.

At a halt on the road they were joined by an army major
in cracked, ill-shapen boots and a badly crumpled uniform
with Guards' flashes. He was small with bow legs and incredibly long, shaggy whiskers. His uniform and boots in particular were in such a woeful state, he explained, because
they had been in the hospital store-room for five months
while his wounds had been healing.

The military hospital had recently been housed in part
of the Krasnodon Municipal Hospital and was now evacuated. Because of the lack of transport it had been suggested
that all walking cases should proceed on foot, while over a
hundred of the more seriously wounded had been left in Krasnodon with no hope of getting away.

Apart from his detailed account of the fate of the hospital
and his own position the major said nothing during the whole
of the journey. He remained extremely taciturn, he was stubbornly and quite hopelessly uncommunicative. In addition
he limped, but in spite of that he managed to get along
briskly in his misshapen boots and never lagged behind the
boys. He quickly inspired so much respect that whatever
the subject of their conversation they turned to him as to
some mute authority.

While the great multitude of people, old and young, and

not only women but men, too, with weapons in their hands, suffered torment in this unending tide of retreat, Vanya and Zhora, sleeves rolled up, caps dangling in their hands, and haversacks slung over their shoulders, strode over the steppe full of vigour and rainbow hopes. They had an advantage over the others in that they were very young, quite alone, had no knowledge of the whereabouts of the enemy, or, for that matter, of their own troops, and refused to believe any rumours. And they felt that in this boundless, hot, sun-scorched steppe with the smoke from the fires and the clouds of dust hanging over the roads which were being bombed and machine-gunned intermittently by the Germans, the whole world was opening out before them.

And they talked of things which had no connection whatever with what was happening round them.

"Why d'you think it's not interesting to be a lawyer nowadays?" Vanya asked in his deep bass.

"Because while the war's on you have to be a soldier and when the war's finished you have to be an engineer so that industry can be restored. It isn't so important now to be a lawyer," Zhora replied with the customary clarity and defined judgement which was part of him, despite his being only seventeen years old.

"Yes, of course, while the war's on I'd want to be a soldier, but they won't take me because of my eyes. When you move away from me a bit I can only see you as something vague and dark and lanky," Vanya said with a grin. "Engineers are most useful, of course, but you've got to have a bent in that direction and my leanings are all towards poetry, as you know."

"Well, then you'll have to go to some literary college," Zhora pronounced clearly and laconically, with a side glance at the major as if to say that here was the man who alone could understand how right Zhora was. But the major did not respond.

"That's exactly what I don't want to do," Vanya said. "Neither Pushkin nor Tyutchev went to a literary college—there weren't any then, of course—and in any case one can't learn to be a poet that way."

"One can learn anything," Zhora replied.

"No, to try and learn to be a poet in a college is just

plain nonsense. Everyone should study something and start life with some ordinary trade or profession and then, if he has a natural talent for the Muses, then it will develop of itself and I think that's the only way to become a professional writer. For example, Tyutchev was a diplomat, Garin an engineer, Chekhov a doctor, Tolstoi a landlord...."

"Comfortable profession that!" Zhora said, his black Armenian eyes looking slyly at Vanya.

Both laughed and the major, too, smiled into his whiskers.

"Was there a lawyer among them?" Zhora asked in a business-like tone. If there had, Zhora would have been quite willing to concede Vanya a point.

"I don't know, but the training a lawyer gets is the kind which provides knowledge of all the sciences a writer needs: general science, history, law, literature."

"I would say," Zhora said a trifle pretentiously, "that courses in those subjects might best be obtained in a teachers' college."

"But I shouldn't want to be a teacher even if you have always called me Professor."

"Still, it would be silly to become, say, a defence lawyer," said Zhora. "Remember the trial of that gang of saboteurs, for example? I'm always thinking about the defence counsels. Stupid position they're in, aren't they?" Zhora laughed and showed his dazzling white teeth.

"Well, of course, a defence lawyer's job isn't very interesting, because we've got People's Courts, but I think it would be interesting to be an examining magistrate; you'd meet all sorts of people."

"Prosecutor is the best job. Remember Vyshinsky? Marvellous! All the same, I shouldn't dream of becoming a lawyer myself."

"Lenin was a lawyer," Vanya said.

"Things were different then."

"I wouldn't mind going on with this discussion about our future careers if it weren't so plain to me that the subject is futile and stupid," Vanya said with a smile. "You've got to be educated, to know your job and like your work, and if you've got a gift for poetry it'll show itself."

"You know, Vanya, I've always liked reading your poems

in the wall newspaper and in *Parus*, which you and Ko-shevoi put out."

"So you read our magazine?" Vanya asked, brightening.

"Yes," Zhora replied gravely. "I also read our school *Krokodil*. I kept in touch with everything that was pub-lished at school," he continued complacently, "and I can tell you that you've definitely got talent!"

"Talent!" Vanya was embarrassed. He threw a sidelong glance at the major and tossed back his long straggling hair with a jerk of his head. "It doesn't take talent to scribble a few verses. Pushkin now—he's my God!"

"No, you're really good, Vanya. I remember how you pulled Lena Pozdnysheva up for always making faces in front of the mirror." He chuckled loudly. "It was fine, really!" His Armenian accent was becoming very pronounced. "How did it go again? 'Her charming little mouth she opened '" And he chuckled gleefully again.

"What nonsense," Vanya growled, embarrassed.

"Have you written any love-poems?" Zhora asked with a mysterious air. "Go on, recite us something about love, eh?" Zhora winked at the major.

"What d'you mean—love-poems! Really!" Vanya was completely put out of countenance by now.

He had written poems to Klava entitled in the Pushkin manner: "K..." Just like that. A capital K and a row of dots. And again he recalled all that had taken place between him and Klava, and all their dreams. He was happy. Yes, happy amidst all this universal misery. But could he be ex-pected to share all this with Zhora?

"Well, you've probably got some all right. I say, recite something, come on!" Zhora's boyish Armenian eyes sparkled mischievously.

"Stop talking rubbish!"

"Do you really mean you don't write love-poems, then?" Zhora suddenly became serious. The schoolmaster note was again manifest in his voice. "Well, you're quite right not to! After all, is it the time to be writing love-poems, like that Simonov? When the people have to be educated in the spirit of uncompromising hatred of the enemy! You need to write political poems now. Like Mayakovsky, eh? And Surkov. They're splendid!"

"That's not the point. You can write about anything," Vanya said meditatively. "Since we have been born on this earth and are living lives about which, perhaps, generations of the finest people have only dreamed and struggled for, we can write about all aspects of our lives, and we have a right to do so, for all of it is important and unprecedented."

"Come on, for heaven's sake, recite something!" Zhora begged.

The heat was intolerably oppressive. They strode along laughing and shouting and sometimes dropping their voices for intimate, trustful confidences; they gesticulated as they walked, their backs were wet under the bundles of belongings, thick dust had settled on their faces and as they wiped away the sweat they left muddy streaks all over their faces. Zhora, dark-complexioned at best, Vanya with his long pale face and the bearded major, all looked like chimney-sweeps. But the whole world, just at that moment, was for them, including the major they were sure, centred on what they were talking about.

"All right then, I'll recite something."

Unflustered and in a deep, calm voice Vanya declaimed:

> *Ahead of us the road through life.*
> *We have no fear or qualm!*
> *No passions of a nameless strife*
> *Assail our conscience calm.*
>
> *Impatient youth—and fortunate—*
> *Runs through its years in play;*
> *Hearts dream of future's open gate*
> *And of a coming day!*
>
> *Let's breast life's storm through to the end!*
> *We'll never meet distress,*
> *Nor doubts of youthful days misspent,*
> *Nor mental emptiness!*
>
> *We march into the future bright*
> *Fearless and joyful all;*
> *And from a hill-top within sight*
> *Tomorrow's Communes call!*

"Jolly good! You've definitely got talent!" Zhora exclaimed and looked at his older comrade with genuine admiration.

At that moment the major made a strange noise in his throat and both Vanya and Zhora turned to him.

"Er, boys, you've no idea at all what sort of people you are!" he said hoarsely, his feelings touched, his eyes, set deep under beetling brows, swimming. "I say a country like ours has stood firm and will go on standing firm!" he continued and fiercely wagged his stubby, blackened finger as if threatening someone in space.

"He thinks he's put an end to our kind of life here!" he scoffed. "Oh no, my fine fellow, you're just playing the fool! Life goes on here and our young people regard you as the plague or cholera. You've come and you'll get out, and our kind of life will go on, and people will study and work as before. But what did he think?" the major jeered. "Our life will go on for ever, but what is he? Just an abnormal growth on a healthy body: cut it out and it's gone! Nothing is left! In that damned hospital I almost lost heart myself, the enemy seemed so strong and I was so weak, but I no sooner joined forces with you chaps than my spirits rose again. Lots of people must be cursing us soldiers now, but why? True enough, we're having to retreat, but what a mailed fist he aimed at us! And only think what strength of will we've shown. My God! It's a wonderful thing, I can tell you, to stand four-square, not to retreat an inch, and to sacrifice your life. Believe me, I'd have considered it an honour to lay down my life for lads like you!" the major concluded, his small shrunken body trembling with emotion.

Vanya and Zhora said nothing but looked at him very kindly, feeling a little perplexed.

The major had said his say; he blinked his eyes, wiped his moustache with a dirty handkerchief and remained silent until nightfall. But during the night, with a sudden display of energy and fury, he rushed forward to "resolve," as he put it, a gigantic traffic-jam of cars, lorries, guns and carts, and Vanya and Zhora lost sight of him for ever and promptly forgot about him.

It took them two full days to reach Likhaya. By that time it had become known that the fighting in the south had reached the outskirts of Novocherkassk and that German tanks and motorized forces were in operation east of the Donets, in the wide expanse of steppe between the Donets and the Don.

Rumour had it that some unit or other was stubbornly fighting at the approaches to Kamensk and preventing the Germans from reaching Likhaya. Even the name of the general in command was being whispered from ear to ear. People owed it to him and his troops that the crossings over the Lower Donets were still in our hands and that it was still possible to travel unhindered over the steppe cart-tracks to the Don and take the ferry across it.

That night, exhausted by two days' march in blinding sunshine, Vanya and Zhora threw themselves down on the hay in a barn. They were so tired that their legs were numbed. They awoke to the dull explosions of bombs which were so near that the barn shook.

The sun was still low over the steppe but already the vast expanse of waving corn lay behind a blue-gold heat-mist by the time Vanya and Zhora reached a huge encampment of cars, human beings and carts stretching along the bank of the Donets, a little below a big Cossack settlement on the opposite side of the river, with its green orchards and stone buildings housing government offices, trading establishments and schools, many of which had been bombed and reduced to still smoking ruins.

This gigantic encampment had come into being about two weeks previously, but it was already living a life of its own. The transient population, which already included some old-timers, was being continuously replenished as more and more people came up to the river on foot, in lorries or carts.

It was an inconceivable mixture of the remnants of army units, office staffs and factory employees, transport vehicles of all kinds, refugees representing all sections of the population, all ages. And the whole effort, the whole attention, the whole activity of all these people was directed towards getting as close as possible to the river, to the narrow strip of the pontoon bridge across the Donets.

But while the people crowding together in the encampment were doing their utmost to get on to the bridge, the army people controlling the crossing were concentrating on keeping them off, and giving priority to the military units on their way to the new defence lines between the Donets and the Don.

In this conflict between individual, personal desires and efforts and the urgent requirements of the army and the state, at a time when at any moment the enemy might suddenly appear on either side of the Donets and when rumours, each more monstrous than the last, fanned the conflicting passions and efforts to white heat, life went on in the camp from one day to the next.

Some organized groups had been awaiting their turn for so long that they had found time to dig shelters for themselves. Others had put up tents and built makeshift fireplaces where they cooked their food. The camp was teeming with children. Day and night a narrow, unending line of lorries, carts and people crossed the Donets, while on both sides of it people ferried themselves over on rowing-boats and rafts. Thousands of sheep and cattle crowded on the river-bank, lowing and bleating, and eventually swam across.

Several times each day German aircraft bombed and machine-gunned the crossing and the AA guns, defending it, pounded back at them, while the entire camp immediately scattered into the steppe. But no sooner would the planes pass over than life would go on as usual in the camp.

From the moment he set foot in the camp, Vanya's sole aim was to find the Kovalyovs' lorry. Two feelings struggled inside him: he had begun to realize how great the danger was and he would have liked Klava and her parents to have been not merely across the Donets, but on the far side of the Don as well; yet at the same time he would have been happy to have met Klava again here, in the camp.

Vanya and Zhora were roaming through the camp together, on the look-out for people from Krasnodon, when suddenly they heard their names shouted from one of the carts and, in a matter of seconds, they were being embraced by the powerful long arms of Oleg Koshevoi, their school-mate, tanned by the sun, clean and neat as always, with an air of bustling activity about his slim, broad-shouldered person and with eyes that sparkled under the fair lashes.

They had stumbled on the lorry from 1B Pit, carrying Valko and Shevtsov; they had found the carts with Ulya and Oleg Koshevoi's family and that very same orphanage which had got away from Krasnodon through their efforts, though the matron no longer recognized them.

Chapter 11

ORDER REIGNED throughout the part of the camp at which Vanya and Zhora had now arrived, for the swarthy, iron hand of Valko, director of 1B Pit, held sway there: lorries and carts had been parked in rows to one side, slit trenches had been dug. A pile of firewood, fencing from the farms, lay near the miners' lorry. Aunt Marina and Ulya were cooking a thick soup with fresh cabbage and pork fat.

Old, gypsy-faced Valko was a thoroughgoing organizer. Taking with him his own workers and half a dozen Komsomols and glaring fiercely from under beetling, black eyebrows which caused people to fall back before him, he marched heavily to the edge of the river, hoping to take charge of the crossing.

From the moment Valko began introducing order Oleg Koshevoi was as fascinated by him as, just a short while before, he had been fascinated by Kayutkin and, earlier still, by Ulya.

Oleg had an inordinate thirst for action, a desire to show his worth, to share in the life of the people, in their activities, so that he could contribute something of himself, something more complete, more versatile and full of new content, a spiritual force, not yet fully understood, but embracing the whole of his being and forming the basis of his very nature.

"Oh, but it's g-g-grand, Vanya, that we're together now," he said gaily, as they followed close behind Valko. "I was beginning to miss you. See what's b-b-been happening? And you with your poems!..." With his eyes and one finger

Oleg respectfully indicated Valko, who was striding ahead of them. "Yes, old chap," he said, "there's nothing like a good organizer!" His eyes sparkled. "Without organization the best and most urgent undertaking falls to pieces, just as knitted material when it gets torn. But if you go at it with a will—"

"And before you know it you'll get your face bashed for your pains," Valko put in without turning round.

The boys gave this pointless remark no more attention than it was worth.

From the depths of the army's second line defences it is difficult to gauge the extent and ferocity of a front-line battle. Similarly, with this crossing, it was impossible to assess the real dimensions of the calamity from the tail end of those waiting to cross.

The nearer they approached the pontoon bridge the more confused and hopeless became the situation and the more intense the general atmosphere of acrimony which had become of such long standing and had reached such fever-heat that no power on earth seemed capable of relieving it. Anxious to get as close as possible to the bridge and because the vehicles behind were pressing hard on those in front, milling crowds of people were mixed up among the cars, carts and lorries. They had become so tightly and irrevocably entangled and wedged into such impossible positions that there was no longer any chance of marshalling them except by gradual movement in a forward direction.

In the unbearable heat, which was intensified by the congestion, the sweating people were so very hot that they felt that if they as much as touched each other they would blow up.

The army officers controlling the crossing had not slept for many days and their fatigued faces were black from exposure to the sun in which they were roasted from sunrise to sunset, and from the dust thrown up continuously by thousands of feet and wheels. Their voices were hoarse from shouting and cursing, their eyelids inflamed, and their black and sweaty hands had reached that stage of nervous exhaustion where they failed to grip anything. But they continued to perform their superhuman task.

It was quite obvious that they were doing everything that could be done, but Valko nevertheless pushed his way to the ramp of the bridge where his raucous voice was lost among all the other voices and the roar of lorry-engines.

With the close attention of a child and an expression of surprise and disappointment on his face Oleg, followed by his friends, watched the heavily laden lorries and carts crawling in the dust and heat one after the other down the gradually sloping river-bank which was churned up into an inconceivable mush, while the sweaty, dirty, angry and humiliated people pushed on and on and on.

Only the river itself, the beloved Donets, wide and serene in its middle reaches where, as young school children, they had so often come to swim or fish, continued as before to roll along carrying its tranquil, warm, muddy waters.

"Just the same I'd gladly bash someone's face for him," Victor Petrov said suddenly. A melancholy expression in his eyes, he was gazing into the water away from the bridge. He was from the Pogorely farm, born and bred by the river.

"That someone's most likely across by now!" Vanya joked.

The boys chuckled.

"The place to do the bashing is over there, not here!" Anatoly said coldly, nodding his head in the little Uzbek cap in the direction of the west.

"Quite right!" Zhora agreed.

And just as he said it a shout went up:

"Air raid!"

At once the anti-aircraft batteries opened fire, the machine-guns spluttered and the sky became filled with the roar of engines and the penetrating, rising screech of falling bombs.

The boys threw themselves to the ground. Explosions close by and more distant shook the area, lumps of earth and bomb-splinters flew up all round and following on the heels of the first came a second wave of aircraft, then a third. The screeching, whining and crash of exploding bombs and the pounding of AA batteries and machine-guns seemed to fill the air between steppe and sky.

The aircraft had gone and the people had begun to get up from the ground when suddenly the roar of artillery came from somewhere in the neighbourhood of the farm where Vanya and Zhora had spent the night; and in another moment shells crashed and exploded in the camp, raising columns

113

of earth and chips. Some threw themselves flat again, others turned to watch the bursting shells, keeping one eye on the bridge. And the faces and the behaviour of the soldiers by the bridge told the people that something untoward had happened.

The men controlling the crossing exchanged glances and stood for a moment as if listening; then one of them suddenly dashed into a shelter close to the ramp of the pontoon bridge, while another yelled out along the bank, summoning the commanding officers.

A moment later the soldier came running out of the shelter carrying two greatcoats and dragging some kit-bags by their straps, and the whole unit, officers and men, ran at the double, their ranks broken, across the pontoon bridge, overtaking the lorries and cars which had already again begun to move down to the bridge and across the river.

What took place after that happened so quickly that no one was able to say how it all started. Shrieking as they went some of the people pelted off on the heels of the soldiers. There was sudden confusion among the cars and lorries at the bridge ramp: several of them made a simultaneous dash for the pontoon, crashed and became locked together, and though it was plain that they now blocked the road, other lorries, those behind pressing hard on those in front, continued, with a terrible roar of engines, to converge upon this jumble of cars on the bridge; one lorry fell off into the water, then another, and a third was about to roll over, but the driver managed with a great effort to jam on the brakes.

With amazement in his myopic eyes, Vanya watched all this and then suddenly shouted, "Klava!" and flew down to the ramp.

Yes, the third lorry which had all but plunged into the river was Kovalyov's lorry, and he, his wife, daughter and a number of other people were sitting on top of the load.

"Klava!" Vanya shouted again and somehow managed to push his way close to the lorry.

The passengers scrambled off it. Vanya held out his hand and Klava jumped down to him.

"It's all up! Blast and to hell with it!" Kovalyov said in a voice which almost froze Vanya's blood in his veins.

Klava, whose hands Vanya felt he should not hold in

his any longer, looked sideways at Vanya, too stunned to take him in, and began trembling all over.

"D'you think you can walk? Tell me, can you?" Kovalyov asked his wife, his voice almost tearful, as she pressed a hand to her heart and gasped open-mouthed like a fish.

"Leave us, leave us here. Run, they'll kill you," she gasped.

"But whatever's happened?" Vanya asked.

"The Germans!" Kovalyov cried.

"Run, run and leave us!" Klava's mother repeated.

Kovalyov seized Vanya's hand. Tears were streaming down his face.

"Vanya!" he cried, in tears. "Save them, don't desert them! If you live through it, get them to Nizhny Alexandrovsky. We've got relations there. Vanya! I'm relying on you...."

With a crash a shell exploded on the ramp of the bridge, in the thick of the melee of cars and lorries.

The people on the river-bank, soldiers and civilians alike, rushed in an avalanche to the pontoon.

Kovalyov released Vanya's hand, took a jerky step towards his wife and daughter as if to say good-bye, then suddenly flung up his arms in a despairing gesture and rushed away to the floating bridge with the rest of the people.

Oleg called Vanya from the bank but Vanya did not hear him.

"Come on, let's go while we're still unharmed," he said to Klava's mother, his voice stern and calm, as he supported her with his arm. "Let's get into this shelter. D'you hear? Klava, you come too." His voice was stern, but gentle.

Before he entered the shelter he had caught sight of the AA gunners feverishly dismantling the heavier parts of the gun-barrels, carrying them a short distance along the bridge and then dropping them into the water. Along the whole length of the river, above and below the bridge, people and cattle were swimming across. But Vanya no longer saw this.

Vanya's comrades, having lost sight of both him and Valko, began running back to where they had left their carts, struggling the while to avoid being pushed back by the torrent of people rushing in the opposite direction.

"Keep together ... we must keep together!" Oleg was

shouting, while with his broad shoulders he cut a way ahead of the others through the crowd, and constantly looked back at them, his eyes aflame with burning anger.

The whole camp had been swarming, but was now beginning to break up; lorries and cars were moving forward, their engines roaring, and those which succeeded in breaking out rolled slowly downstream along the river-bank.

When the first wave of aircraft had come over, Aunt Marina had been squatting on her haunches feeding the fire with sticks from a fence which Uncle Kolya was chopping up with a gunner's dagger. And Ulya had been sitting beside her on the grass so deep in thought that something in her features, in the lines at the corners of the mouth and the dilated nostrils showed signs of a grim strength. She had been watching Grigory Shevtsov as he sat on the running-board of the lorry giving some milk to the little blue-eyed girl in his arms and whispering something in her ear that made her laugh. Watched by their nurses the orphans had been playing round the lorry, which stood parked about thirty yards from the fire. The matron had been sitting near the lorry taking no part in what was going on. The orphanage carts and those of Koshevoi and the Petrovs had been drawn up in line with the other transport.

The aircraft had appeared so suddenly that no one had had time to rush to the slit trenches and people had fallen flat where they were. As Ulya threw herself on her face, the swish of a falling bomb filled her ears—a scream mounting in intensity as the bomb hurtled downwards. At the same instant it seemed to her that a sharp blow hit her like lightning and went through her body. A rush of air whistled overhead and a shower of earth fell on her back. She heard the roar of engines in the sky and again the scream, more distant now, but she remained where she was and hugged the ground more closely.

She could not remember when she stood up and what had urged her to try to stand up. But suddenly she felt everything spinning before her eyes and a wail of horror like the cry of a wild animal broke from her innermost being.

No longer was there any lorry from 1B Pit, nor was there any Grigory Shevtsov and the little girl with the blue eyes. They were gone; they were nowhere to be seen. Nothing where the lorry had stood but a round, hollow funnel of black churned-up earth, round the edge of which lay charred bits of lorry and the mutilated bodies of children. A few paces from Ulya a strange stump in a red scarf was moving slightly on the ground. Ulya recognized in it the upper part of the body of the orphanage matron. The lower part with the rubber boots worn straight over the stockings had vanished. It no longer existed.

A boy of eight, his head pressed against the earth, his arms bent back as though he were preparing to jump, was writhing and screaming, his little legs kicking the ground.

Almost beside herself Ulya rushed to him, wanting to take him in her arms. But the boy wriggled away with a shriek. She lifted his head and saw that his whole face was puffed up into a large watery blister and the whites of his eyes were standing out of the sockets.

Ulya slumped to the ground and sobbed bitterly.

There was frantic movement all round her but she saw and heard nothing. All she felt was that Oleg had appeared at her side. He was saying something and his large hands were smoothing her hair: he even tried to raise her but she continued to sob and cover her face with her hands. She heard the thunder of gun-fire, bursting shells and the distant hammering of machine-guns but she remained indifferent to it all.

Then suddenly she heard Oleg say in a very young, musical, trembling voice:

"The Germans!"

This reached her brain. She stopped crying and straightened up. In an instant she recognized Oleg, and all her friends—Victor's father, Uncle Kolya, Aunt Marina with a child in her arms—standing near her. Even the old man who had driven Oleg and his relatives was there. Vanya and Valko alone were missing.

All these people were staring intently in one direction and there was a strange expression on their faces. Ulya's eyes followed their gaze. There was nothing at all left of the camp over there. Before them in a hazy white glare under a blazing sky lay the open steppe and across the bright steppe out of the hazy glare German tanks painted a tree-frog green were coming straight towards them.

Chapter 12

THE GERMANS captured Voroshilovgrad at two o'clock in the afternoon of July 17, after a fierce battle fought on the fields of the experimental farms. One of the armies of the Southern Front had been deployed there as a covering force and was destroyed in this battle against the superior strength of the enemy. Fighting every inch of the way, the survivors fell back along the railway lines towards Verkhneduvannaya. They fought until the last of them lay dead or wounded on the Donets earth.

By this time all of the inhabitants of Krasnodon and the surrounding areas who had wanted to evacuate and had been able to go had left for the east. Only in the distant Belovodsk District a large group of eighth- and ninth-class pupils from the Gorky School doing farm work in that area had so far not made a move, owing to ignorance of the situation and lack of transport.

The education department had sent Maria Andreyevna Borts, who taught Russian literature at the school, instructions to evacuate the children. She was an energetic woman, a native of the Donets Basin and familiar with local conditions. She was, in addition, personally interested in the success of the undertaking because among the children was her own daughter Valya. Only one lorry would have been needed to take the group, but Maria Borts had received her instructions when it was no longer possible to get any sort of transport. By various means she managed to make her way to the state farm, losing more than one day in the process. Despite the incredible strain put on all his means of transport, engaged as it was in the evacuation of the farm property, the director of the state farm, whom she found hoarse from shouting orders, unshaven, and lacking several days' sleep, unhesitatingly put his last lorry at her disposal. Exhausted by the long journey and anxiety about the fate of her Komsomol daughter and the other children, Maria Borts' pent-up emotions and deep gratitude found relief in a flood of tears.

Although the gravity of the position at the front was known in Belovodsk District, the children—until the arrival of Maria Borts—had been undismayed and confident, in the manner of youth, that the adults would make arrangements for them in good time. They were happy and exuberant as always when young people are gathered together freely in beautiful natural surroundings, and romantic friendships sprang up as is only natural among the young.

Maria Borts did not want to upset the children earlier than was necessary and kept the facts about the actual state of affairs from them. But they gathered that something was seriously wrong from the nervous concern and hurry with which she made them get ready to go home. Their spirits suddenly fell and each of them thought of home and what the future might hold for them.

Valya Borts was rather over-developed for her age but there was something still childlike in her brown arms and legs covered with golden down. The eyes under the black lashes were dark grey and had an independent, rather cold expression. She had golden plaits and there was something haughty about the shape of her full bright lips. While working in the state-farm fields she had become friendly with Styopa Safonov, a short, fair-headed, freckled lad from the same school, who had a snub nose and lively, intelligent eyes.

Valya was in the ninth form and Styopa in the eighth. This might have been an obstacle to their friendship, if Valya had been on a friendly footing with the girls, but she was not, or if there had been one among the boys whom she liked, but there was not. She was well-read and a good pianist. She was conscious that her development was different from that of the other girls and had become used to receiving homage from young people of her own age. She felt drawn to Styopa not so much because he liked her, but because he amused her. He was a clever, sincere lad, but he concealed the fact beneath a surface of boyish mischief. He was also a true comrade, but a terrible chatterbox. And just because Valya was not a chatterbox, trusted no one with her secrets, except her diary, dreamed of great deeds—like all the rest she wanted to be a pilot—and in her mind's eye saw her hero as a man of prowess, she found Styopa amusing with his chatter and his inexhaustible store of pranks.

For the first time Valya ventured on a serious conversation with him and asked him outright what he would do if the Germans came to Krasnodon.

She had gazed at him very seriously and searchingly with her cold, uncommunicative, dark grey eyes, and carefree Styopa, who was deeply interested in zoology and botany and forever thinking about becoming a famous scientist and who never gave a thought to what he would do if the Germans came, had said, also without a moment's thought, that he would carry on a relentless underground struggle against the enemy.

"Is that just talk? Or the truth?" Valya coldly asked.

"Why should it be just talk? Of course it's the truth," Styopa said without thinking.

"Swear...."

"All right, I swear. Of course I swear. What else should we do? We're Komsomols, aren't we?" As he raised his eyebrows in surprise fair-haired Styopa suddenly did give a thought to what he had been asked. "And you?" he asked, his curiosity aroused.

She put her lips close to his ear and whispered darkly: "I s-s-swear...."

Then she pressed her lips against his ear and suddenly snorted into it like a foal, nearly bursting his ear-drum.

"Anyway, you're a fool, Styopa! A fool and a gas-bag!" she said, and ran off.

They left at night. A dappled patch of light from the dimmed head lamps streaked the steppe in front of the lorry. A starry sky stretched dark and immense over their heads and a freshness breathed from the steppe—a smell of hay, of ripening corn, of honey and wormwood. A warm breeze fanned their faces and it was hard to believe that in their homes the Germans might be waiting for them.

Here was a lorry-load of young people. At any other time they would have sung all night and yelled into the steppe and laughed and kissed in secluded corners. But now they rode along, turned in on themselves and silent; only rarely did they exchange casual remarks in an undertone. Soon most of them had drowsed off sitting on their packs pressed close to each other, their heads lolling from side to side with the bumps in the road.

Valya and Styopa remained awake to keep watch and sat at the back end of the lorry. Styopa was beginning to doze. Valya sat on her rucksack and continued to gaze into the darkness of the steppe before her. The suggestion of haughtiness in her full lips had now. with no one to observe her, changed to a childlike expression of sadness and offence.

They had not accepted her at the aviation school, How many times had she applied and each time they had turned her down, the idiots! Life was a failure. What could the future hold for her now? Styopa was a chatterbox. She would work in the underground, of course, but how does one go about it and who would direct the work? And what would happen to Dad?—Valya's father was Jewish—and what about school? For all her brains she had not even managed to fall in love. And this was all that life amounted to! Life was definitely not a success. Valya would never amount to anything in people's eyes, she would never excel in anything, never become famous or enjoy the admiration of others. Tears of wounded pride gathered in her eyes; yet they were commendable tears for she was seventeen and her dreams were not self-seeking and callous, but were only the disinterested, lofty dreams of a young girl possessed of a strong character.

She suddenly sensed a strange sound at her back, as though a cat had jumped on to the back of the lorry and was clinging to it with its claws.

Quickly she turned round—and drew back with a start.

A young fellow, almost a boy, lean, in an army cap, was gripping the edge of the lorry with both hands and had already drawn himself up. He was raising a leg to swing himself over and inside, at the same time casting a quick glance round.

Had he come to steal? What could he want? Valya made an instinctive movement to push him off but on second thoughts decided to rouse Styopa in order to avoid trouble.

But the lad was unusually quick and agile; he was already inside the lorry, had already sat down by Valya's side and bringing his mocking eyes close to hers had placed a finger on his lips. He obviously had no notion of whom he was dealing with. Another moment and he was going to feel very sorry for himself. Only in that moment Valya managed to take a look at him: a lad of her own age in a cap pushed to the back of his head, with a face that had not been washed for a long time but was full of boyish courage, with laughing eyes which shone in the darkness. And this moment during which Valya had been scrutinizing him decided matters in his favour.

Valya did not stir or utter a word. She looked at him with that detached and rather chilly expression which her face invariably wore when she was not alone.

"What lorry's this?" he asked in a whisper close to her face.

She could see him better now. He had curly hair which was probably wiry; the line of his lips was strong and rather heavy, the lips themselves were thin and protruded slightly; there seemed to be a swelling inside.

"Why? Haven't they sent the one you expected?" asked Valya in a frigid whisper.

He smiled.

"My own car's laid up for an overhaul and I'm so tired that—" He waved his hand as if to say: "It's all the same to me."

"Sorry, but all the sleepers have been taken," Valya said.

"I haven't had a wink for six days and nights—another hour won't kill me." He was not offended and spoke with amiable frankness. At the same time his eyes quickly searched their field of vision, trying to discern faces in the darkness.

The lorry jolted and now and again they had to grasp the sides. Once her hand fell on his and she quickly withdrew it. He raised his head and looked at her closely.

"Who's this sleeping here?" he asked and looked down at Styopa's nodding fair head. "Styopa Safonov!" he said, suddenly no longer in a whisper but in his normal voice. "I know now what lorry this is. The Gorky School? You're from Belovodsk District?"

"How d'you know Styopa Safonov?"

"We met at the creek in the hollow."

Valya waited, expecting to be told more; but the lad was silent.

"What were you doing at the creek in the hollow?"

"Catching frogs."

"Frogs?"

"Exactly."

"What for?"

"I thought he'd use them as bait for catfish but he only wanted them for dissecting!" The lad laughed in obvious mockery of the singular doings of Styopa Safonov.

"And then what?" Valya asked.

"I talked him over to come and fish for catfish. We went one night and I caught two, one about a pound and the other a little better. Styopa didn't catch a thing."

"And then?"

"I got him to go for a swim at dawn. He came out all blue and said, 'I'm cold and stiff like a plucked rooster, and my ears are full of water!'" The lad snorted. "So I showed him how to get the water out of his ears and get warm at the same time."

"How?"

"You press a hand over your ear and jump up and down on one leg and shout, 'Katerina, little dear, get the water out of my ear.' Then the other ear and you shout again."

"Now I know how you come to know each other," Valya said with a slight twitch of the eyebrows.

The sarcasm in her words escaped him. He suddenly became serious and gazed straight ahead into the darkness.

"You're rather late," he said.

"Why?"

"The Germans'll be in Krasnodon tonight or tomorrow morning, I think."

"And if they are?" asked Valya.

Perhaps she wanted to test him or just show him that she wasn't afraid of the Germans; anyhow she could not say herself why she had made that remark.

He surveyed her quickly with a frank, bold glance, then dropped his light-coloured eyes without saying anything.

Valya felt suddenly hostile to him. And strangely enough, the lad sensed it.

"No chance of getting away," he said, as though to restore harmony.

"Why get away?" she said, to spite him.

But he firmly declined to quarrel with her. "True enough," he said, again in a conciliatory tone.

All he had to do was give his name to satisfy her curiosity and things would immediately have been put right between them. But he either did not think of it or else did not want her to know his name.

Valya maintained a proud silence. He began to doze, but with every jolt of the lorry and every voluntary or involuntary movement Valya made, his head jerked up.

The buildings on the outskirts of Krasnodon loomed through the darkness. The lorry slowed down for the level crossing near the park. No one was on duty there, the barriers were raised and the signal lamp was out. The lorry lumbered over the sleepers and the faintly clattering rails.

The lad shook himself and ran his hand along his waist as though feeling for something under his jacket which he had flung carelessly over his dirty tunic.

"I'll walk from here. Thanks for your kindness," he said.

He stood up and his pockets seemed to Valya to be bulging with some heavy objects.

"I didn't want to wake Styopa," he said and once more brought his laughing bold eyes close to Valya's. "But when he wakes up say that Sergei Tyulenin asked him to come and see him."

"I'm not a post-office nor a telephone exchange," Valya said.

Genuine disappointment showed on his face and he was so chagrined he did not know what reply to make. His lips seemed more swollen than ever and, without a word, he leapt down from the lorry and disappeared into the darkness.

Valya immediately felt miserable, because she had upset him. The most vexing thing was that having spoken to him in that way she couldn't possibly tell Styopa about it and so remedy her unfair behaviour towards this courageous, suddenly-appearing, suddenly-disappearing young man. And so he remained in her mind, with his thin, swollen lips and bold laughing eyes which had become so sad after her rude words.

The whole town lay in darkness. There was not so much as a glimmer of a light anywhere, neither in the windows nor in the watchmen's huts at the pit gates nor at the level crossings. It was getting cool and there was a distinct smell of smouldering coal from the still smoking mines. Not a single person was to be seen in the streets and it was strange not to hear the usual noise of work coming from the pits and the railway sidings. There was only the barking of dogs.

With a quick, cat-like gait Sergei Tyulenin walked along the siding past a huge vacant lot where normally the market was held, went round it and slipped past the dark Li Fancha clay huts clinging together like a honeycomb amidst cherry-trees; soundlessly he approached his father's whitewashed cottage. It stood out clearly among the dark, thatched barns.

Closing the gate carefully behind him, he looked round, then ran into the sheds and, after a few seconds, emerged with a spade in his hand. Although it was dark, he found his way with ease and in a few moments stood near some acacia bushes which made a black outline against the wattle-fence in the vegetable garden.

He dug a fairly deep hole in the loose ground between two of the bushes and, at the bottom, placed the contents of his jacket and trouser pockets: several hand-grenades and two Brownings with ammunition. Each of these objects was wrapped separately in a piece of cloth and he laid them in the hole without unwrapping them. Then he filled the hole with earth and levelled the ground with his hands so that the drying rays of the morning sun would obliterate all trace of his labours. He neatly wiped the spade clean with a corner of his jacket, returned to the yard, replaced the spade and softly rapped on the door of the cottage.

The door latch from the room leading into the passage clicked and his mother, he recognized her heavy tread, shuffled barefoot over the earthen floor to the door.

"Who's there?" she asked sleepily, alarm in her voice.

"Open the door," he called softly.

"Good God Almighty!" she whispered in a trembling voice. There were sounds of shaking, fumbling hands groping feverishly for the latch and at last the door opened.

He stepped over the threshold into the darkness and caught the familiar odour of his mother's warm, sleepy body. He embraced her, pressing his head against her shoulder. Silently they stood for a few moments in the passage.

"Where have you been? We thought you'd been evacuated or even killed! Everybody's come back but you weren't there. The least you could have done was to have told some-body what had happened," she grumbled softly.

A few weeks previously, Sergei Tyulenin, together with some other youngsters and women, had been sent from Krasnodon, just as similar groups had been sent from other districts of the region, to dig trenches and build defences at the approaches to Voroshilovgrad.

"I was held up in Voroshilovgrad," he said in his normal voice.

"Quiet! You'll wake Grandpa," she said angrily. Grandpa was her husband. They had eleven children and some of the grandchildren were as old as Sergei. "He'll give you what for!"

The threat went in at one ear and out of the other: Sergei knew his father wasn't ever likely to give him "what for." He was an old hewer who had been mangled almost to death by a runaway wagon-load of coal in the Annensky Pit at Almaznaya station. Being very tough in those days, the old man had survived and had worked later at surface jobs. Now he was quite doubled up and could hardly get about. Even when seated he had to support himself under one arm by means of a crutch which was padded in soft leather; his spine was too weak to keep him upright.

"D'you want something to eat?" asked Sergei's mother.

"Yes, but I'm too tired, I'm falling asleep."

He tiptoed through the first room past his snoring father into the adjoining one where his two elder sisters slept: Dasha with her eighteen-month-old baby (her husband was at the front), and Nadya, the younger of the two and his favourite.

There was another sister, Fenya, in Krasnodon, who with her children lived separately from the family; her husband was also on active service. Gavril and Alexandra Tyulenin's other children were scattered all over the country.

Sergei passed through the stuffy room where his sisters slept, found his way to his bed, quickly flung off his clothes and lay down outside the counterpane, in only his shorts, not at all concerned that he had not washed for a week.

His mother, her bare feet shuffling over the earthen floor, followed him into the room. With one hand she groped and found his curly head, with the other she thrust a large delicious-smelling morsel of fresh, home-baked bread under his nose. He quickly took it, kissed her hand and, exhausted as he was, began, gazing ecstatically into the dark, to devour the wonderful hunk of bread.

What an unusual girl that had been on the lorry! What character! And the eyes! But she hadn't liked him, that was obvious. If only she had known what he had been through during the past few days! If only it had been possible to share it all with just one human being in the whole wide world! But how good it felt to be home with the family, how grand to lie in bed in the cosy room and to enjoy this wonderful-smelling piece of bread that Mum had baked. One would have thought that the moment he lay on his back he would have been dead to the world and have slept at least twice round the clock, but it was impossible to get to sleep without letting someone hear something of his experiences. If only that girl with the pigtails had known! No, he had been quite right not to say anything. God knows who and what she was! Maybe he'd tell Styopa Safonov all about it tomorrow and, incidentally, learn who the girl was too. But Styopa was a chatterbox. No, he would only tell Vitya Lukyanchenko, if he had not gone yet. But why wait till tomorrow when everything, absolutely everything could be told at once to his sister Nadya!

Sergei slipped noiselessly from his bed and groped his way to Nadya, carrying the piece of bread with him.

He squatted down and touched her shoulder with a finger.

"Nadya, Nadya," he called softly.

"What? What is it?" she said in alarm, only half awake.

"Sh-h-h!" He touched her lips with unwashed fingers.

But she had recognized him and, sitting up, quickly took him into her hot bare arms and kissed him somewhere on the ear.

"Sergei! My dear, dear.... You've come home!" she whispered happily.

Sergei could not see her but he could imagine the happy smile on her face and her cheeks, flushed with sleep.

"Nadya! I haven't slept since the thirteenth of the month! Since the morning of the thirteenth and until this evening I've been fighting all the time," he said excitedly, and took a bite of bread.

"Oh, goodness!" Nadya exclaimed in a whisper, touching his hand; she drew up her knees and tucked her feet up under her nightdress.

"Our men were all killed and I came away.... Actually when I went there were about fifteen of them left, but the colonel said, 'Go away, no need for you to be killed.' He was wounded himself, in face, hands, legs, back; bandages and blood all over him. He said, 'We'll get killed all the same, but why should you?' And so I went.... And I don't suppose one of them is left alive now."

"How horrible!" the girl whispered.

"Before I left I took a sapper's spade and carried some rifles from the dead men into the trenches the other side of Verkhneduvannaya, the place can be recognized again by its landmarks, two hills and a clump of trees on the left. I took rifles, hand-grenades, revolvers and ammunition and buried everything, and then I came away. The colonel embraced me and said, 'Remember my name: Nikolai Pavlovich Somov. When the Germans withdraw, or if you get back to our people, write to the Gorky Army Commissariat so that they can inform my people and whom it concerns that I did my duty.' I told him I would."

Sergei fell silent as he gulped down his tears and munched the bread, now damp and salty.

"Oh, my dear!" Nadya breathed with a stifled sob.

Her brother must have endured a great deal. She could not remember when she had last seen him cry, certainly not since he was seven at least—he was as hard as nails.

"How did you come to be with them?" she asked.

"This is how it happened," he said, brightening again. He swung his feet on to the foot of the bed. "We finished the work on the defence fortifications and our troops fell back and occupied them. Then all the Krasnodon people were packed off home, but I went up to a company lieutenant and asked him to enlist me, but he said he couldn't without the permission of the regimental commander. I said, 'Help me get permission.' I implored him, and a sergeant-major backed me up. The soldiers all laughed and the lieutenant would have none of it. There we were arguing when suddenly the Germans opened up with artillery. I jumped into the dug-out with the other soldiers and they wouldn't let me go until it was dark. They felt sorry for me, but when it got dark they told me to go. I climbed out of the dug-out, but lay down again just behind the trenches. In the morning the Germans attacked, so I jumped back into the dug-out and snatched a rifle from one of the dead, and fired away with the others. For several days we beat off all attacks, and, of course, nobody tried to chase me away. Then the colonel recognized me. 'If we had any chance at all of coming out of this I'd enlist you,' he said, 'but you've got your life before you.' Then he laughed and said, 'Consider yourself a sort of partisan.' So I stayed with them and we fell back almost as far as Verkhneduvannaya station and I saw the Fritzes as close as I'm seeing you now," he said in a sibilant whisper. "I killed two of them myself, maybe more, but two I saw I killed myself." His thin lips curled. "And now I'll kill them everywhere I see them, the filthy reptiles. You mark my words."

Nadya knew that Sergei was speaking the truth, that he had killed two Fritzes and that he would go on killing them.

"But they'll kill you!" she said, terrified.

"Better die than lick their boots or just sit round doing nothing."

"Oh, my God, what's going to happen to us?" she said in desperation as with greater force than ever she visualized what tomorrow might bring, or this night even. "There are still over a hundred wounded left in the hospital. They're so weak they can't walk. The doctor, Fyodor Fyodorovich, has stayed behind with them, too. Every time we go past there we shudder at the thought that the Germans may murder them all!" she said in an agonized voice.

"How can you say things like that! The people must take them in, singly!" Sergei was agitated.

"The people! There's no telling who's who nowadays! They say there's somebody no one knows hiding in Ignat Fomin's place in Shanghai district. Who is he? He might have been sent in by the Germans to take a look round before they arrive. Fomin's not likely to hide a good man."

Ignat Fomin was a miner, who had been granted a bonus and mentioned in the papers several times for good work. He had appeared here in the village in the early thirties at a time when numerous strangers came not only to Krasnodon but to the rest of the Donbas as well. He had made himself a home in Shanghai district and there were rumours current about him. To this Nadya was now referring.

Sergei yawned. Now that he had got things off his chest and eaten the bread, he felt he was really and truly home and all he wanted was to go to sleep.

"Lie down now, Nadya...."

"Oh, I couldn't sleep now."

"I could," said Sergei and groped his way back to bed.

No sooner had his head touched the pillow than he saw the eyes of the girl on the lorry. "Never mind, I shall find you," he said and smiled, as everything around him and inside him faded away.

Chapter 13

How WOULD YOU conduct yourself, dear reader, if you had an eagle's heart full of courage and daring and a burning desire to perform heroic deeds, yet you were still a small boy running about with bare feet with scratches on your legs, and everything, absolutely everything your spirit cried out for was misunderstood by the rest of mankind?

Sergei Tyulenin was the youngest of the family and had grown up like the steppe grasses. His father, as a youngster, had come from Tula to the Donbas in search of work. In his forty years as a miner he had acquired that naïve, self-respecting despotic pride which is more marked in sailors and miners than in men of any other calling. Even after he had ceased to be a worker in any sense of the word, Gavril Petrovich had persisted in considering himself the most important person in the house. By force of habit, as when he had worked in the mines, he would get up before dawn; then he would rouse everyone else in the house, because he felt bored by himself. Even if he had not felt bored he would still have wakened the rest of the family, because his loud hacking cough would start up. He would go on coughing for at least an hour after he left his bed. His cough would nearly choke him, then he would expectorate heavily, and then a shocking wheezing, whistling and whining would follow, like the sounds from a broken-down harmonium.

After that he would sit all day long, resting his lean, emaciated frame on his padded crutch. He had a prominent hooked nose which had once been large and fleshy, but was now sharp and thin enough to cut the pages of a book. His sunken cheeks were covered with a hard, grey stubble and he had an enormously aggressive moustache; from its magnificent base under the nose, it gradually tapered away to the infinite fineness of a single hair sticking out straight on each side of his face. Thus he would sit quite alone on his bed or at the cottage door or on the chopping block by the woodshed looking about him from faded eyes under thick bushy brows, ordering everyone about, shouting curt instructions to all and sundry in a stern, sharp voice and occasionally breaking into a fit of coughing. The snorting, wheezing and whining would then be heard all over Shanghai district.

Assume that you lose more than half your capacity for work before you are so very old, then, some time later, become altogether disabled and finally are confronted with the job of bringing up, educating and starting off in life three boys and eight girls—eleven people! Try it!

Most likely it would have been beyond the strength of Gavril Tyulenin had it not been for his wife, Alexandra, a strong woman of Orel peasant stock, a real Amazon, in fact, a second Marfa Posadnitsa.* She was still robust and seemed immortal and never knew a day's illness. Neither did she know how to read and write but when necessary she knew how to be severe, sly, taciturn, talkative, malicious, kind, flattering, witty, or sarcastic; and if anybody, through lack of experience, started picking a quarrel with her, he would very quickly feel the rough side of her tongue.

Ten children were already earning their living. Sergei, the youngest, was still at school and growing up like the steppe grasses: he never really had clothes or shoes of his own, they had been patched and made over a dozen times before ever he got them. The sun and wind, the rain and frost had toughened him; the soles of his feet were as hard as a camel's and whatever wounds and bruises life inflicted on him they healed in a twinkling, as with the giant in the fairy-tale.

* A famous mayoress of the ancient free town of Novgorod.

And his father, who would snort and wheeze and whine at him more than at any of his children, also loved him more than any of the others.

"What a lad, eh?" he would say with satisfaction and stroke his awe-inspiring moustache. "Eh, Shurka?" This was his name for sixty-year-old Alexandra, his life companion. "Just take a look at him! Never afraid of a fight anywhere, at any time! Just like me as a boy, eh?" And he would be seized by a coughing fit which nearly drove him mad.

The heart of an eagle, yet only a small boy, poorly dressed, with chapped legs. How would he play his part in life? First of all, of course, he'd try to perform some great and heroic deed. But who does not, in childhood, dream of heroic deeds? But to attempt to perform them does not always bring success.

Suppose yourself a schoolboy in the fourth class releasing a sparrow from your desk during an arithmetic lesson; this cannot possibly bring you glory. The head master sends word to your parents to call on him, and not for the first time by any means. This only concerns your sixty-year-old mother. Grandpa—all the children address their father in this way, just as their mother does—Grandpa snorts and wheezes and would be happy to box your ears but cannot reach you, so he angrily bangs the floor with his crutch, which he cannot even hurl at you, because it is holding his weak body upright. But Mother comes back from school and gives you such a clout that your ears and cheeks sting for days. Mother's hand seems to grow heavier with the years.

And your friends? Friends indeed! As the saying goes, fame is like smoke. By the following morning the exploit with the sparrow is forgotten.

In the summer you can put your whole heart into getting more sunburnt than the others, swimming and diving better and snatching carp from under the rocks more skilfully than the rest. Or when you see a bevy of girls promenading on the bank of the creek you can race along the edge and catch up with them, jump off from the overhanging bank and swallow-dive into the water and then, while the girls are feigning complete indifference but are really waiting with interest for the moment when you will appear above water again, you can quickly slip off your trunks under water and suddenly push into view your rosy-white backside, the only part of your body not tanned by the sun.

It gives you momentary satisfaction to see the flashing pink heels and fluttering skirts of the girls scuttling away as though blown by the wind, one hand pressed to their mouths to choke back the giggles. While sun-bathing later on with your friends you are able, with a casual air, to acknowledge their delight in your exploit, for you have won for all time the great admiration of some very small boys who will henceforth follow you in droves, ape you in everything and obey your every word and gesture. It is a long, long time since the days of the Roman Caesars but the small boys will make a god of you.

But this does not mean much to you, of course. And one day, no different from any other in your life, you suddenly jump from a first-floor schoolroom window into the yard where all the children are having their break and engaging in the usual, harmless amusements. And as you hurtle through the air you experience a brief flash of thrilling delight: the flight itself, the sensation of wild, complete terror, the passion to have the whole world at your feet, the screams of all the girls, from the first class to the tenth. But the rest brings you only disenchantment and suffering.

The interview with the head master is a very serious one. Things are clearly moving towards your expulsion. Because you know you are guilty, you are discourteous to him and, for the first time, he comes in person to your parents' cottage in Shanghai district.

"I've got to know something about this boy's home conditions. I've got to try and unearth, at long last, the cause of all this," he says in a grave, polite tone. But there is a trace of reproach for your parents in it.

And the parents—Mother with her soft, plump hands which she doesn't know where to hide because she has just cleaned the grate and they are black with soot, and she is not wearing an apron; Father, completely at a loss and without the vaguest idea of what is expected of him, leans silently on his stick trying to stand up before the head master. And both of them look guiltily at him as though everything actually were their fault.

And when the head master leaves, for the very first time you are not scolded, but everybody seems to avoid you deliberately. Grandpa just sits there and never looks at you; he only occasionally heaves a sigh and his moustache is no longer at all aggressive, but is just the dejected-looking moustache of a man whom life has badly knocked about. Mother bustles round the house, her feet shuffling over the earthen floor. She clatters the pots and pans and, suddenly, as she bends over the range, you see her furtively wiping away a tear with her beautiful, plump, sooty hand. And it is as though their whole appearance is saying to you: "Look, just look at us, this is what we are really like!"

You notice for the first time that your old parents have for a long time now had nothing to wear on high days and holidays. Practically all their lives they have not eaten at the same table as their children, but have taken their meals alone, so that the children should not see that they had nothing but black bread and potatoes and buckwheat porridge, because then the children, one after another, could grow up and stand on their own feet, because then you, the youngest, would be educated and find a place in the world.

Your mother's tears cut you to the quick, and you see for the first time that your father's face is grave and sad, that his choking and wheezing is not at all funny, but something tragic.

Your sisters' nostrils quiver with anger and contempt as, first one, then the other, flings you a glance over her knitting. And you are sullen towards your parents and sisters and cannot sleep that night. There's a gnawing feeling that you have been injured in some way and a realization that you have behaved like a criminal, and without making a sound your dirty hand wipes away two miserable little tears rolling down over your small hard cheek-bones.

And after that night you seem to have grown up a little.

During the unhappy days which follow—days of general silence and condemnation—a whole new world opens up before your fascinated eyes, a world of inconceivably fabulous exploits.

People travel under water over a distance of 20,000 leagues and discover new worlds; they land on uninhabited islands and make everything with their own hands; they scale the highest mountains in the world; people even reach the moon. They battle with terrifying storms on the seas, climb to the top of masts swaying in the gale and take their ships over jagged reefs by pouring oil on the raging sea; they cross the ocean on a raft and suffer from thirst so that the dry, swollen tongue feels like a ball of lead in the mouth; they survive sand-storms in the desert, fight boa constrictors, jaguars, crocodiles, lions and elephants, and overcome them. Some people accomplish these things for gain, or to further their careers, or out of a passion for adventure, or because of a desire for comradeship, or for the sake of true friendship, or to save the beloved from danger; others accomplish them for no personal reason but for the good of mankind, for the glory of their country and in order that the light of science may shine on earth for ever: Livingstone, Amundsen, Sedov, Nevelskoi....

And the great deeds people perform in times of war! For thousands of years people have fought wars and thousands of people have made their names glorious in war. What hard luck that you are born at a time when there is no war. You live in parts where the dusty grass grows over the graves of soldiers who gave their lives so that yours might be happy, and the fame of the generals of those great years is fresh in our minds to this day. Something courageous and inspired, like a marching song, sounds in your heart as you scan the pages of their biographies, oblivious to the fact that the hour is very late. You feel you want to turn to them again and again and to impress the features of those people on your mind, and you draw their pictures—no, why lie?—you trace their portraits with the aid of a piece of glass and then shade them, as you best know how, with a soft pencil which you lick now and again to give better definition to your picture; and when the job is done your tongue is so black that even pumice-stone will not get it clean. And the pictures of those people still hang over your bed.

The heroic deeds and exploits of those people ensured life to your generation and will remain for ever in the memory of man. Among their names are those of ordinary people like yourself: Mikhail Frunze, Klim Voroshilov, Sergo Orjonikidze, Sergei Kirov, Sergei Tyulenin ... yes, his own name, too. The name of a rank-and-file Komsomol might yet find a place among them if only he succeeded in showing his worth. How attractive and extraordinary were the lives of those people! They knew underground existence in tsarist days; they were tracked down, imprisoned and exiled to the North or Siberia, but again and again they escaped to take up the struggle once more. Sergo Orjonikidze escaped from exile, Mikhail Frunze escaped twice. Stalin—six times. At first, their followers were few in number, then they became hundreds, then hundreds of thousands, and finally millions of people.

When Sergei was born there was no reason for any underground existence. He did not have to escape from anywhere or to anywhere. He had jumped from the first-floor window at school but now it was clear to him that it had been a stupid thing to do. And the only supporter he now had was Vitka Lukyanchenko.

But one must never lose hope. The mighty ice-floes of the Arctic Ocean crushed the hull of the *Chelyuskin*. There was a terrible, crashing, rending noise in the night and it was echoed throughout the land. But the people did not perish, they moved on to the ice. The whole world watched the course of events and wondered whether rescue would be possible. And then all of them were saved. There were people in the world with eagle's hearts. They were ordinary people like yourself. Through snow-storm and frost they made their way to the men in distress and brought them to safety lashed to the wings of their aircraft. They became the first Heroes of the Soviet Union.

Chkalov! He was just an ordinary chap like yourself, but his name now sounds throughout the world like a fanfare. The flight to America across the North Pole—the dream of mankind! Chkalov. Gromov. And the Papanin Expedition on the ice-floe.

Life goes on and is full of dreams and ordinary, day-to-day work.

All over the Soviet Land—and here in Krasnodon—there are quite a number of ordinary people like yourself who are noted for their exploits and the fame they have achieved, people of a kind about whom no books were ever written in the past. Throughout the Donbas—and beyond it—everyone knows the names of Nikita Izotov and Stakhanov; and any Young Pioneer can tell you about Pasha Angelina and Krivonos and Makar Mazai. Everyone has great respect for these people, and Grandpa is forever asking to be read those parts of the newspapers where they are mentioned, and then goes off into a lengthy and unintelligible snorting and wheezing and it is obvious that he feels bitter about his age and being smashed up by the coal-truck. Yes, Grandpa Gavril Tyulenin has gone through a great deal of hard toil in his life and Sergei can well understand how he must feel now that he no longer has a chance of joining the ranks of these famous people.

The glory of these people is a very real glory. But Sergei is still small and has to go to school. All that will come later, some time when he is grown-up. Yet he feels in his heart that he is grown-up enough for exploits like those of Gromov and Chkalov. The trouble is that he is the only one in the whole world who understands it—there is no one else. He alone of all mankind understands!

Thus the war found him. Time and again he tried to get into the special army school—he felt he had to become a pilot. But they would not accept him.

All the school children had gone out on farm work, but he, wounded to the heart, got himself a job in the mines. Within two weeks he was working with the hewers and cutting coal as efficiently as the adults.

He did not realize how much he had gained in the eyes of people. He would emerge from the cage dirty, with bright eyes and small white teeth gleaming out of his black face; he would walk along with the adult workers aping their sturdy, slightly rolling gait; he would go under the shower and snort and spit like his father, and then turn homewards, leisurely, barefoot, for his working boots were on loan from the pit stores.

He would arrive home late, after everyone had finished dinner. He would get a separate meal, for he was grown-up, a man, a miner.

With a cloth in each hand Alexandra Tyulenina took the cast-iron soup pot from the oven and poured him out a bowl, full to the brim. Steam curled up from the *borshch*, and the white, home-made bread had never tasted better.

Gavril regarded his son from under his bushy eyebrows, beaming at him with piercing, faded eyes. His moustache stirred slightly. He did not cough or wheeze, but conversed quietly with his son as he might have done with a fellow-worker. Everything was of interest to him: how things were going in the pit, how much coal each miner had cut. He asked questions about the tools and the special protective clothing. He spoke about galleries and drifts and faces and blind shafts as though they were the rooms, corners and larder of his own home. Actually the old man had worked in almost all the pits in the district and, although no longer able to work, he kept in touch with everything through his former mates. He knew in which direction and at what rate the cutting was being done. He could trace in the air with one finger the plan of the mine workings and everything that was being done down there in the bowels of the earth, and he could explain it all to anyone.

In the winter, Sergei would hurry off straight from school, without even stopping for a bite, to meet some friend of his in the Air Force or with the gunners or sappers. He would do his homework at midnight with drooping eyelids and at five in the morning would be at the firing-range, where his friend, the sergeant on duty, taught him, side by side with the soldiers, how to fire a rifle and a tommy-gun. And it was a fact that he was almost as good a shot as anyone with the service rifle, the Nagant, the Mauser, the Degtyarev tommy-gun, the Maxim, and all the rest. He threw hand-grenades and incendiary bottles and could dig himself in and set the fuses of mortar shells and knew how to lay and clear mines; he was familiar with the construction details of the aircraft of every nation in the world, and he knew how to cope with the fuse of a bomb.

And with him all the time would be Vitka Lukyanchenko whom he took in tow wherever he went and who had roughly the same respect for him as Sergei himself had for Sergo Orjonikidze or Sergei Kirov.

This autumn he had made another most desperate attempt to be accepted into the real, adult aviation school, not the special one for young people; and he had again suffered a set-back. They had told him he was too young, and should apply again the following year.

It had indeed been a terrible set-back to have to build defence works outside Voroshilovgrad instead of going to the aviation school. He had decided that he would not come back from there.

How he had schemed and manoeuvred to get enlisted into that unit! He had not told Nadya even the hundredth part of the ruses he had employed and the humiliations he had suffered. And now he knew what it was like to be in the thick of a battle, to taste the meaning of fear and of death.

Sergei slept so heavily that even his father's morning coughing fit failed to wake him. He awoke when the sun was high in the sky; the shutters of his windows were closed but he could always tell the time by the angle of the golden rays stealing in through the chinks and the flecks of sunshine on the floor and furniture. He rose and at once realized that the Germans had not yet arrived.

He went into the yard to wash. Grandpa was sitting on the doorstep and a short distance away sat Vitka Lukyanchenko. Mother was in the kitchen garden and both sisters had left for work long ago.

"Aha, there's my fine warrior! Let's look at you," Grandpa greeted him and fell to coughing. "So you're alive, eh? That's the most important thing these days. He-he! Your pal's been waiting for you to get up since sunrise." He threw a kindly glance in the direction of Vitka who, motionless and with a resigned air, surveyed with soft, grave, dark, velvety eyes the features of his crony, whose face, despite the sleep on it, seemed already full of restless energy.

"That's what I call a real pal," Grandpa continued. "Every morning at daybreak he's here: 'Has Sergei come in yet?' 'Is Sergei back?' Sergei to him is like the guiding light in the window," he said contentedly.

Grandpa's speech showed that Vitka had remained loyal to their friendship.

They had both been digging defences at Voroshilovgrad and Vitka, completely under the spell of his friend, had wanted to stay with him and enlist as well. But Sergei had made him return home, not so much out of solicitude for Vitka or even his parents, but because he felt sure that they would never both succeed in enlisting and Vitka's presence might therefore be an obstacle to his being accepted. So, extremely upset and hurt by his despotic friend, Vitka had had to leave and not only that: he had had to swear that he would not divulge Sergei's plans either to his own or Sergei's parents or to anyone in the world. Sergei's pride insisted on this in view of possible failure.

From what Grandpa said, it was clear that Vitka had kept his word.

The two friends went behind the cottage and seated themselves by the side of the dirty reed-grown creek beyond which lay a stretch of pasture-land. A large isolated building loomed in the distance: it was a miners' bath-house, newly erected but not yet in use.

They sat on the bank, smoked, and exchanged news. Of their schoolmates—both had attended the Voroshilov School—Tolya Orlov, Volodya Osmukhin and Lyuba Shevtsova had remained in the town. The last-named, according to Vitka, had adopted a way of life most unusual for her: she never left home and was never to be seen anywhere.

Lyuba Shevtsova had spent seven years at the Voroshilov School and had left it before war broke out, when she had made up her mind to go on the stage. Later, she had begun to sing and dance in the theatres and clubs in the district. The fact that she had remained here was particularly pleasing to Sergei, she was a daredevil and his equal in every way. In fact, she was a Sergei Tyulenin in petticoats.

Vitka whispered some news items into Sergei's ear, the first of which Sergei already knew, namely, that an unknown man was in hiding at Ignat Fomin's place and that everyone in Shanghai district was puzzling his brain concerning his identity, and everyone was afraid of him.

The other news was that several dozen incendiary bottles, which had apparently been tossed aside in the hurry, were lying about quite openly in a cellar in Senyaki district, where there had been several munition dumps.

Vitka suggested timidly that it might perhaps be a good idea to find a hiding-place for the bottles. Sergei made no reply. Then suddenly he seemed to remember something and announced tersely that there was urgent business for them at the army hospital and they would have to go there without delay.

Chapter 14

WHEN THE FRONT crept closer to the Donbas and the first wounded began to arrive in Krasnodon, Nadya Tyulenina had volunteered for a course in nursing. She was now in her second year at the army hospital, which occupied the whole of the ground floor of the municipal hospital.

The staff of the army hospital had been evacuated and there remained only one doctor, Fyodor Fyodorovich. Most of the nurses and doctors, including the house surgeon of the municipal hospital, had also left for the east. Nevertheless, life went on as usual, and Sergei and Vitka were at once filled with respect for the institution when they were stopped at the door by the reception nurse, made to wipe their feet on a damp cloth, and instructed to wait in the hall while she went to fetch Nadya.

Some moments later the reception nurse returned with Nadya. But she seemed a changed Nadya, not the same sister with whom he had chatted that night, seated on her bed: there was a strange, grave expression on her face with the high cheek-bones, and her fine eyebrows were raised inquiringly. There was a similar expression of gravity on the wrinkled kindly features of the nurse.

"Nadya," Sergei began in a whisper; the new expression on her face intimidated him a little. "Nadya, they've got to be taken away, can't you see.... Vitka and I could call at every house.... Tell Fyodor Fyodorovich."

For some moments she looked at him thoughtfully and said nothing. Then she shook her head, slowly and doubtfully.

"Go on, call him, or take us to him," Sergei insisted, and frowned.

"Lusha, give the lads overalls," Nadya said.

The reception nurse brought out two white overalls from a high cupboard and helped the boys into the sleeves.

"The lad is right all the same," she burst out, and looked at Nadya with a gentle, indulgent expression in her eyes. Her soft, sunken lips worked as though she were chewing something. "People would take them in, to be sure. I could take one myself. Who wouldn't feel sorry for them? I'm all alone, my boys are fighting at the front; there's only the little girl with me now. We live in the village. If the Germans come I'll say he's my son. And we must tell everyone else to say the same."

"You don't know the Germans," Nadya said.

"I don't, that's true, but I know our own people," Lusha returned, her mouth still chewing on something. "I could let you know of some very good people in the village."

Nadya led the boys down a bright corridor, the windows of which overlooked the town. A heavy, pungent smell of neglected, suppurating wounds and unwashed linen, which even the antiseptics and medicines could not disperse, was wafted in their direction every time they passed the open door of a ward. And suddenly the town outside the windows seemed to them to look brighter and more peaceful and pleasing than ever before.

All the wounded left in the hospital were bed cases and only a few of them could hobble about on crutches along the corridor. On all their faces, young or old, clean-shaven or bristly with the stubble of many days, was the same intense, grave expression as the boys had seen on Nadya's and Lusha's.

The men in the beds could hear the boys passing down the corridor and as they passed lifted their heads with interrogation and hope in their eyes; the men on crutches silently followed them with their eyes and a vague and troubled animation showed momentarily on their faces as their own, stern-faced nurse Nadya led the two lads down the corridor.

The trio stopped outside a closed door at the end of the corridor. Nadya opened it without knocking or hesitating.

"For you, Fyodor Fyodorovich," she said and pushed the boys inside in front of her.

Both lads rather reluctantly stepped into the room. A broad-shouldered, elderly man with white hair got up from a table and went forward to meet them. He was clean-shaven and had strong features, an aquiline nose, square chin and long, sharply defined lines on his brown face. He gave the impression of being cast in bronze. There were no books or papers on his desk, no bottles of medicine anywhere; the room was bare. The boys realized that Fyodor Fyodorovich did not work in this office; he simply sat at his desk alone with his thoughts, sad and depressing as they must be. They could see, too, that he was not in uniform but wore a civilian suit: grey trousers and jacket, the collar of which protruded over the top of the overalls where the tapes were tied at the back of the neck; and he wore boots which had not been cleaned and were probably not his own.

He too had a grave expression on his face and there was no surprise in the look he gave the boys.

"Fyodor Fyodorovich, we've come to help you find homes among the people for your wounded," Sergei began. He knew instinctively that more than that need not be said to this man.

"Will they take them?" the doctor asked.

"People to take them will certainly be found," Nadya said in her melodious voice. "Lusha, a nurse from the municipal hospital, has agreed to take one and has promised to tell others, and the boys can go round inquiring, and in that I can help them. The Krasnodon population won't refuse help. We should like to take one as well only we haven't any room ..." Nadya said and blushed. Sergei's face also suddenly flushed up even though Nadya had spoken the truth.

"Ask Natalya Alexeyevna to come here," the doctor said.

Natalya Alexeyevna was a young surgeon attached to the municipal hospital. When the hospital staff was evacuated she had decided to remain, because of the ill health of her mother, who lived in the mining village some ten miles from Krasnodon. As some patients, hospital property, medicines and instruments were left behind, and as Natalya Alexeyevna felt a little ashamed before her colleagues for choosing to remain under the Germans, she had voluntarily assumed the duties of head surgeon.

Nadya left the room. The doctor resumed his seat at the desk. With an energetic movement he slipped his hand through the back slit of his overalls and brought out of his pocket a tobacco pouch and a folded newspaper; he tore off a strip of paper and with a rapid combined movement of fingers and lips rolled a small tapering tube which he filled with *makhorka** and then lit.

---

* A very strong tobacco of coarse cut.

"Yes, that would be the solution," he said and without a trace of a smile looked at the boys sitting side by side on a couch.

First he looked at Sergei, then at Vitka, then at Sergei again, as though he could see that Sergei had initiated the plan. Vitka understood the meaning of that second glance but was not in the least offended. He would have agreed that Sergei was the leader. He wanted it to be so and was proud of Sergei.

Nadya returned with a little woman in her late twenties. She looked younger than she was because there was a softness and chubbiness about her small face and hands and legs which produced the impression of a child, and this frequently led to mistaken assumptions of a like character. When her father had opposed her medical training, those small feet had carried Natalya Alexeyevna all the way from Krasnodon to Kharkov; with those small, chubby hands she had earned enough by sewing and washing to enable her to continue her studies, and when her father died she had taken into those hands the care of the whole family of eight souls. Now some of her family were fighting, others were at work in various towns, the remainder were studying. With those hands she fearlessly performed operations which older and more experienced male surgeons hesitated to undertake; and in Natalya Alexeyevna's chubby, childish face were a pair of eyes whose frank, strong, inflexible, business-like expression might be the envy of the managing director of any establishment of an all-Union scale.

Fyodor Fyodorovich rose to meet her.

"Don't bother, I know all about it," she said and folded her arms across her breast in a gesture which somehow seemed to contrast with the matter-of-fact expression of her eyes and her precise, rather dry manner of speaking. "I know all about it. It's a wise plan," she said. She looked at the boys, showing no personal interest in them but rather as if she were making a cool assessment of their ability to be useful. Then she turned inquiringly to the doctor. "And you?" she asked.

He understood her.

"It would be best for me, as the local doctor, to remain attached to your hospital. I could then give the men assistance, no matter what the circumstances." They knew that he was alluding to the wounded Red Army men. "Could that be arranged?"

"Yes, that could be done," she replied.

"In your hospital I would not be betrayed?" he asked.

"No one in our hospital will give you away," she said, crossing her plump arms over her breast.

For the first time a trace of a smile played in the doctor's eyes. "Thank you both very much," he said and offered his large hand with the strong fingers, first to Sergei, then to Vitka Lukyanchenko.

"Fyodor Fyodorovich," Sergei began, looking straight into the doctor's face with steady, bright eyes which seemed to say: "You, and everybody else here for that matter, can think what you like about what I'm going to say, but I'll say it just the same, because I consider it my duty to do so." "Fyodor Fyodorovich, please bear in mind that you can always count on me and my friend Vitka Lukyanchenko—always. You can keep in touch with us through Nadya. And, furthermore, I want to tell you, for myself and my friend Vitka Lukyanchenko, that we think your staying behind with the wounded at a time like this ... that we consider it to be a great and heroic deed," he concluded and sweat broke out on his forehead.

"Thank you," the doctor said. He was very grave. "Since you have broached the subject I want to tell you this: no matter what the profession, no matter what the calling of a man may be, a situation may arise in his life which would not only permit him, but would oblige him to abandon the people who depend on him, people whom he has led and who rely on him. Yes, such a situation may arise when it is more expedient to abandon them and go away. Expediency may require it. I repeat: this applies definitely to people in all professions, even to generals and political leaders, but not to the medical profession, and particularly not to the army doctor. The army doctor must remain with the wounded. No matter what happens. Expediency can never be greater than this duty. Even military orders and discipline may be violated if they conflict with it. Even if the general commanding the front instructed me to abandon these wounded and leave my post I should not carry out the order. But he would never issue instructions like that.... Thank you both very much." His grey head nodded.

Natalya Alexeyevna continued to stand with her plump arms crossed over her breast looking at the doctor with a solemn expression in her matter-of-fact eyes.

At a brief conference that took place in the hall between Sergei, Nadya, Lusha, and Vitka, the shortest in the past quarter of a century, because it lasted just long enough for the boys to remove the overalls, a plan of action was outlined. No longer able to restrain themselves, the boys at last darted out of the hospital into the dazzling sunlight of a July noon. An inexplicable delight, a feeling of pride in themselves and mankind in general, an extraordinary thirst for action filled them to overflowing.

"Isn't he a grand chap?" Sergei said excitedly.

"Not half!" Vitka said with a wink.

"And I'm going to find out now who's lurking in Ignat Fomin's house," Sergei said suddenly; this had no apparent connection with what they had been saying or experiencing.

"How'll you find out?"

"I'm going to ask Fomin to take one of the wounded men into his house."

"But he'd give him away," Vitka said with great conviction.

"Then I'll tell him the truth about himself! All I want is to get into his cottage!" Sergei smiled cunningly and merrily, his eyes and teeth gleaming. The idea so possessed him that he knew he would certainly act upon it.

Under the windows of Ignat Fomin's cottage beyond the market-place in Shanghai district, the sunflowers bowed their thick heavy heads, which were large as frying-pans.

For a long time Sergei's knock remained unanswered. He guessed that he was being watched from a window and purposely stood close against the door so that he could not be seen. At last the door opened: Fomin appeared and, leaning on his arm against the lintel, kept his hand on the door latch. He was long and thin like a centipede and bent his head to look down at Sergei with genuine curiosity in his small grey eyes, set deep in the various and numerous folds of his wrinkled skin.

"Oh, thanks very much," Sergei said and ducked under Fomin's arm as nonchalantly as though the door had been opened for him for that express purpose. He had not only entered the passage but was already opening the door to the living-room before Ignat Fomin, with no time to be surprised, had rushed after him.

"Forgive me, Citizen," Sergei said—already inside the room—and inclined his head. Fomin stood in all his height before him, attired in a check jacket and waistcoat with a heavy gold-plated chain across his stomach. His trousers were tucked into shiny leather riding-boots. On his long, fine-looking face of a eunuch was an expression of surprise mixed with anger.

"What do you want?" he asked, raising his eyebrows, and the numerous wrinkles round his eyes moved about as if to get themselves into the right position again.

"Citizen!" Sergei said pathetically, and, quite unexpectedly, assumed the pose of a member of the Convention at the time of the French Revolution. "Citizen! Save a wounded soldier!"

The wrinkles round Fomin's eyes instantly stopped moving while his eyes stared puppet-like at Sergei.

"No, I'm not wounded," Sergei explained, realizing what had astonished Fomin. "The troops have fallen back and left a wounded man out in the street, right by the market-place. The boys and I found him and so I came straight to you."

The signs of many conflicting emotions appeared on Fomin's large face and he involuntarily threw a glance at the closed door leading to another room.

"But why did you come straight to me?" he asked, in a low hissing voice, pinning angry eyes on Sergei. The wrinkles round his eyes had resumed their ceaseless movement.

"Who to, if not to you, Citizen Fomin? The whole town knows you're our leading Stakhanovite," Sergei said and his eyes were as innocent as a baby's as he mercilessly launched this poisoned dart at Fomin.

"And who are you?" Fomin asked, more and more at a loss and becoming increasingly bewildered.

"I'm the son of Prokhor Lyubeznov who's also a Stakhanovite and most likely well known to you," Sergei replied with all the more decisiveness, since he knew, with just as much certainty, that no such person as Prokhor Lyubeznov existed.

"I don't know Prokhor Lyubeznov. And what's more, my fine fellow," Fomin said (he was himself again, and was waving his long arms about futilely and generally fussing about), "I've got no room for your soldier because my wife is sick and as for you, my friend—" and his hand described movements which—not very clearly perhaps—indicated the direction of the street door.

"You're acting rather strangely, Citizen, when everybody knows you've got a spare room," Sergei said reproachfully, looking straight at Fomin with his limpid, childish, bold eyes.

Before Fomin could make a move or open his mouth Sergei had not at all hurriedly walked across to the closed door, opened it and passed through.

The shutters at the windows were half closed. In the room was some furniture, tropical plants in pots and seated at the table a powerful-looking man with close-cropped head and dark flecks in the skin of his face. He was neatly dressed in working clothes. He raised his head and calmly faced Sergei.

In a flash, Sergei realized that he was face to face with just an honest man, strong and calm. And in that same instant all his courage deserted him—wildly improbable as it might seem. Not an ounce of courage remained in the eagle heart! He was in such a blue funk that he could neither move nor utter a sound, and then Ignat Fomin's infuriated, scared face appeared at the door.

"Hold your horses, friend," the stranger said, calmly, restraining Ignat Fomin, who was making for Sergei. "Now, tell me, why you didn't take that wounded soldier into your own home?" he asked Sergei.

Sergei said nothing.

"Is your father here or evacuated?"

"Evacuated," Sergei lied, and blushed to the roots of his hair.

"And your mother?"

"Mother's at home."

"Why didn't you go to her first?"

Sergei did not answer.

"Is she the kind who wouldn't take him?"

With a ghastly feeling inside him, Sergei nodded. The moment the game was up the words "Father" and "Mother" summoned up the picture of his parents and he was agonizingly ashamed of having told such a mean lie about them.

But the man evidently believed him.

"So that's it," he said, examining Sergei. "Fomin told you the truth when he said he couldn't take the soldier in," he continued slowly. "But I'm sure you'll find someone who will. It's a fine thing you're doing. You're a good lad, I can see that. Keep searching and you're sure to find someone. Only be careful—don't just go to anyone. And if no one takes him in, then come back to me. If you find a place for him don't come back, but, best of all, leave me your address so that I can find you if I need you."

And now Sergei had to pay for his mischief in a manner most painful and distressing. Now, when he would so gladly have given his real address, he had instead to give the first address that came to his mind and, because of the lie he had told, to give up any opportunity of ever meeting this man again.

Sergei found himself in the street, perplexed and perturbed. There could be no doubt whatever that the man hiding in Fomin's cottage was a good, important person. There was hardly a shadow of doubt, on the other hand, that Ignat Fomin was at best not a very nice person. That there was some kind of connection between them was certain, and this was something he could not explain.

Chapter 15

THE DAY Matvei Shulga left the little cottage of the Osmukhins, he had set out for the Krasnodon suburb known as Golubyatniki district, intending to find Ivan Kondratovich Gnatenko, a comrade of his early partisan days,

Like many of the districts of Krasnodon, Golubyatniki now mainly consisted of modern stone houses. However, Shulga knew that Gnatenko still lived in a small wooden cottage, his own property. It was one of those cottages which had given the district its name.

A tap on the window brought a young woman to the door. She had the features of a gypsy, was very fat and generally slovenly in appearance, though she was not poorly dressed. Shulga told her he was just passing by, but that as he had business with Gnatenko, perhaps the old man would come out and discuss it with him.

And thus they came together again, Matvei Shulga and Ivan Gnatenko, in a little hollow in the steppe behind the cottage so as not to attract attention. Their conversation was punctuated by the sound of distant artillery fire, which that day was still audible.

Ivan Gnatenko, or Kondratovich, as he was more often called, was one of the generation of miners who could rightly claim to be the founders of the Donets mines. His father and grandfather, both Ukrainian by birth, had also been miners to the bone, and it was men like them who had developed the Donbas, were the guardians of its glory and traditions and had, in 1918-19, formed the Miners' Guard, on which the German invaders and the White Guards in the Donbas had broken their teeth.

This was the same Kondratovich who, with Andrei Valko, the mines director, and Grigory Shevtsov had blown up 1B Pit.

The sun was sinking in the western horizon as he stood facing Shulga in the hollow behind the cottage.

"You know why I've come, Kondratovich?"

"I don't, Matvei, but I can guess," Kondratovich said gloomily, his eyes averted.

A puff of wind from the steppe blew through the hollow and fluttered the old man's jacket which, judging by its style and numerous patches, had been passed down from his grandfather's day. It hung on his shrunken frame as though draped over a cross.

"I've been left behind here to do the same work as in '18 and that's why I've come to you," Shulga said.

"I'll do anything you wish. My life is yours. You know that, Matvei," Kondratovich said, his eyes still on the ground. He spoke in a low, rasping voice. "But I can't take you into my house."

The old miner's statement was so contrary to what Shulga had expected, so incredible, that he was at a loss for words. He remained silent for a few moments and Kondratovich, too, said no more.

"Do I understand you right, Kondratovich?" Shulga asked at last, softly. "You refuse to take me into your home?" Neither looked at the other now.

"I'm not refusing, I can't," the old man said mournfully.

For some time both stood with averted gaze.

"Didn't you give your word?" Shulga asked, anger boiling up in his heart.

The old man's head drooped.

"You knew what it would mean?"

Kondratovich made no reply.

"You know that this is almost betrayal?"

"Matvei Shulga," the old man said in a deep, hoarse voice. "Don't say anything you'll be sorry for!" There was a threatening note in the way he barked it out.

"Why should I be afraid?" Shulga demanded angrily. His eyes flashed with rage as he looked straight into Kondratovich's wizened face with its nicotine-stained, wispy little beard. "Why should I be afraid now? There can't be anything more terrifying than what I've just heard you say!"

"Wait a minute." Kondratovich raised his head; his scrawny hand with its black, broken finger-nails grasped Shulga's elbow. "You believe me?" he said, his deep voice dropping to its lowest pitch.

Shulga wanted to speak but the old man tightened his grip on his elbow, and fixing on Shulga his piercing eyes under the drooping eyelids, he whispered almost pleadingly:

"Wait ... listen to me...."

They were now looking each other straight in the face.

"I can't take you into my home because of my eldest son. I'd be afraid he'd give you away!" he whispered hoarsely and brought his face close to Shulga's. "You remember you were here in 1929? It was when the old woman and I celebrated our silver wedding. I don't suppose you remember all our children, why should you...." The old man smiled a little bitterly. "But you should remember my eldest son, even as far back as 1918."

Shulga said nothing.

"Well, he's turned out a bad lot," Kondratovich said huskily. "You remember he'd already lost his arm, back in '29?"

Shulga vaguely remembered seeing a scowling, slow-moving, sullen youth at Kondratovich's home in 1918. But he could not remember which of the young people he had seen in the house in 1929 had at one time been that youth and was without an arm. In fact, he was surprised to find that he remembered very little of that evening. That was probably because he had had to call on Kondratovich partly as a duty, and that particular evening was only one of many spent with other people out of a sense of duty.

"He had his arm mangled in machinery at a factory in Lugansk." The old man was using the old name for Voroshilovgrad, and because of this Shulga realized that the accident had happened a long time ago. "He came straight home and became dependent on us. It was too late for him to start studying, neither did we think of it at the time, and because of his disability he couldn't get work in his own line. So he went to the bad. He took to drinking, on my money of course. And I was soft with him. No girl wanted to marry him and because of it he drank more and more. And then, in 1930, that fancy piece you saw at the door threw herself at him, twisted him round her finger, and they went in for one shady bit of business after another. She ran a secret drinking-place, then they took to profiteering and—I'm trusting you with this confession—they're not above dealing in stolen goods. At first I was sorry for him, then I began to dread the disgrace. The old woman and me, we decided to keep quiet. And we did. We never said a word about it, not even to our children. And we'll go on saying nothing. He's been in court twice. It should've been that baggage, but he shouldered the blame each time. Well, you know... the judges know that I'm an old partisan and a leading miner, and well known in general, so he got off with a warning the first time; the second time he was given a suspended sentence. But he gets worse from year to year. You do believe me? How can I take you into my home! He could even betray us old people so's to get his hands on the house!" Kondratovich turned away from Shulga, ashamed.

"But how could you have given your consent, when you knew all this?" Shulga asked. He was perturbed. He looked at the old man's face, as sharp as a blade, and could not decide whether to believe all this or not. He suddenly realized in desperation that in the circumstances in which he found himself he seemed to have lost his power to judge which people he could or could not trust.

"How could I refuse, Matvei?" Kondratovich said in anguish. "Just think of me, Ivan Gnatenko, suddenly refusing! What a disgrace it would have been! It's a long time since the matter was discussed. It was put like this: 'It may never happen but if it does will you agree?' It was like a test of my loyalty—how could I mention my son? It would have looked as though I was trying to get out of it—and my son would have had to go to prison. He's still my son!" the old man cried suddenly, on the verge of despair. "You can do what you like with me! You know me—I can keep my mouth shut to the very grave, and I'm not afraid of death. Use me any way you need. I'll find a safe place for you, I know some people; I can find people you can trust, believe me. In the district committee that time I thought to myself, I'm ready for anything, but as far as my son's concerned, I'm a non-Party man and I didn't have to mention him there at the district committee. And my conscience will still be clear. The most important thing to me now is that you should believe me. I'll find you somewhere to live all right," Kondratovich said, unaware that an ingratiating note had crept into his voice.

"I believe you," Shulga said, not quite truthfully. He believed the old man and yet somehow he did not. He had doubts. He had replied in the affirmative only because it suited him to do so.

A complete change suddenly came over the face of Kondratovich. His whole appearance seemed to soften, he let his head droop and snivelled quietly for some moments.

Shulga watched him and mentally summed up everything the old man had said, weighing each item on each side of the scales. Of course he knew that Kondratovich could be trusted. But what he did not know was what kind of life Kondratovich had lived for the past twelve years. And what eventful years they had been for the whole country! Furthermore, there was the fact that Kondratovich, on the most responsible occasion in his life, had drawn the veil of secrecy over the affairs of his son, that he had lied in connection with so vital a matter as the possibility of his house being used for underground work against the Germans.... All that weighed the scales down against Kondratovich's being completely trustworthy.

"You sit down here for a while or lie down. I'll fetch you something to eat," Kondratovich said in his hoarse whisper. "Then I'll hurry along to a place I know and everything will be arranged."

For a second Shulga was about to comply with this suggestion. But that same instant an inner voice which he recognized as not that of mere caution but of practical experience, prompted him not to follow this inclination.

"See here, don't trouble yourself, I've more than one place where I can go. I'll find something," he said. "And I'm in no hurry to eat. I'd rather wait than arouse the suspicions of that woman or your son."

"You know best," Kondratovich said dejectedly. "But don't strike me off, I'll be of some use yet."

"I know that, Kondratovich," Shulga said, to cheer the old man up.

"And since you trust me you can tell me where you're going. I'll tell you whether the person is any good, whether you are right to go there; besides, I'll know where to find you just in case...."

"Tell you where I'm going? I have no right to do that. You're an old underground fighter yourself—you know the rules!" Shulga said with a crafty smile. "What's more, the person I'm going to is someone I know."

Kondratovich wanted to say, "I'm also a man you know and just look how little you knew about me! It would be better if you consulted me now." But he was too conscious of his shame to talk to Shulga in that manner.

"You know best," he said gloomily, realizing at last that Shulga did not trust him.

"Oh, well, Kondratovich, it's time to get going!" Shulga said with exaggerated cheerfulness.

"You know best," the old man repeated slowly with averted eyes.

He began to lead the way back to the street past his cottage. Shulga stopped and said:

"You'd better take me through the garden so that I'm not seen by ... by that baggage, as you call her." He smiled wryly.

Kondratovich wanted to say, "Since you know the rules you ought to know that you should leave the same way you came. Nobody would then suspect you of coming to old Gnatenko in connection with underground matters." But he could see that he was not trusted and that it would be useless to say anything. He took Shulga through the garden to a side street. They stopped when they came to a small coalshed near the corner.

"Good-bye, Kondratovich," Shulga said, thoroughly despondent. "I'll find you again."

"That's up to you," the old man replied.

Shulga walked away down the street and Kondratovich remained standing at the shed, following Shulga with his eyes. He looked shrunken and gaunt in his ancient jacket.

So Shulga took the second step towards his death.

Chapter 16

SERGEI TYULENIN, his sister Nadya, his friend Vitka and old Nurse Lusha had managed within a few hours to find homes for over seventy of the wounded soldiers in various parts of the town. However, that left about forty of them still unplaced, and neither Sergei, nor Nadya, nor Vitka, nor Lusha, nor, for that matter, any of the people who had helped them could think of other families who might be approached without jeopardizing the whole undertaking.

It had been a peculiar day—like something out of a dream. The remote sounds of army units moving through the streets and the rumbling of gun-fire in the steppe had ceased the day before. There was a strange hush over the town and the steppe around it and an air of expectancy—the Germans might arrive at any moment now. But there was no sign of them. Office buildings and shops stood open, no one entered or left. The factories were silent and deserted. A wisp of smoke hung over the destroyed mines. There was no authority whatever in the town; no militia; no work being done and no trade—there was nothing. The streets were empty. A solitary woman might be seen running to the well or tap for water, or into the garden for some cucumbers—then silence again and no one anywhere. No smoke rose from the chimneys of the houses because no dinners were being cooked. Even the dogs were quiet—there was no passer-by to disturb their sleep. Occasionally a cat might run across the street, then all was deserted once more.

The wounded were removed during the night of July 19. Sergei and Vitka did not take part in this but used the dark hours to transfer the incendiary bottles from Senyaki to Shanghai district. They buried most of them among the bushes in the ravine but each took a few bottles home and hid them in his vegetable garden in order to have them at hand.

But what had happened to the Germans?

Dawn found Sergei outside the town in the steppe. The sun rose big and round behind a pink-grey haze and one could look into it. Then its edge pushed itself above the haze and seemed to cascade over it; millions of dew-drops began to sparkle everywhere, each with a colour of its own, and the dark cones of the pit-head tips jutting out here and there began to glow with a pink hue. Everything round Sergei became radiant and imbued with life, and he felt light and buoyant like a rubber ball bouncing.

The road and the railway ran parallel here, separating for a short stretch and then converging again. Both were on high ground and on each side smaller ridges with hollows between them branched off dipping towards the steppe and then gradually merging with it. These ridges and hollows were grown over with shrubbery and trees and the whole area was known as the Verkhneduvannaya Grove.

The sun was already beginning to burn fiercely and rose quickly over the steppe. Sergei gazed round, and before him almost the whole town lay scattered irregularly over hill and dale, clustering more densely near the pit-heads with their distinctive structures and round the buildings of the Krasnodon Coal Trust and the district committee. The crowns of the trees on the ridges became vivid in the sun but the depths of the thickly wooded hollows still lay in the cool half-light of the early morning. The rails glinted in the rays of the sun and ran off into the distance to disappear behind a hill where, in the direction of Verkhneduvannaya station, a little round white cloud of smoke rose slowly and peacefully into the sky.

Then suddenly on the crest of that hill, at the point where the road disappeared, a dark smudge emerged and began to stretch rapidly forward until it looked like a narrow dark band. In a few seconds the band had detached itself from the horizon and was quickly moving up from the distance towards Sergei in a compact, dark, elongated mass, leaving a cloud of reddish-brown dust behind. But before he could actually see what it was, the strident whirring sound which came across the steppe told him that a motor-cycle detachment was approaching.

He dived into the bushes below the roadway, lay flat on his belly and waited. In less than fifteen minutes the crescendo din of the engines filled the air round him and twenty or more German tommy-gunners on motor cycles shot past. From where he lay he could only see the upper part of their figures: they wore the forage-caps and usual dirty-grey uniforms of the German army but their eyes, foreheads and the top half of their noses were hidden by enormous dark goggles which lent a fantastic appearance to these people who had so suddenly appeared here in the Donets steppe.

They drove up to the houses on the edge of the town, stopped their cycles, dismounted and then dispersed into the side streets. Three or four of them remained near the motor cycles. Within less than ten minutes all of them had returned, mounted their machines and raced away into the town itself.

Sergei lost sight of them behind some low-lying houses, but he knew that if they were making for the centre of the town and the park they would have to pass over a rise in the road behind the second level crossing. He could see that rise quite well and began to keep it under observation. Four or five of them soon fanned out over it; they did not, however, drive on towards the park but swung off towards the hill where the district committee building and the Mad Squire's house stood among others. After a few minutes they raced back to the crossing and then Sergei could see the whole of the detachment again moving past the houses on the outskirts and taking the direction towards Verkhneduvannaya. He threw himself flat again and did not even raise his head until the whole unit had sped past. Then he made his way across to the top of a thickly wooded ridge opening out towards Verkhneduvannaya and giving a view of the whole area. He lay there for several hours under a tree. The sun in its path across the heavens again and again picked him out and began to bake him so that he had to keep on crawling away from it, describing a circle round the tree in order to remain in its shade.

Bees and bumble-bees hummed in the bushes collecting the July nectar from the late summer flowers and the clear sticky honey dew left on the underside of the leaves of trees and shrubs by plant-lice. A freshness breathed from the grass and foliage which grew luxuriantly here, while over the expanse of the steppe everything had faded and withered. Now and again a light puff of wind rustled through the leaves. High up in the sky and bright in the sunshine drifted little crisp plumes of cloud.

A lassitude crept over Sergei's limbs and settled on his mind making him forget momentarily why he was here. Calm and pure sensations from childhood days stole into his memory—he used to lie just like this in the grass somewhere in the steppe, with his eyes closed and the warm sun on his body, and the bees used to hum just like this and the hot grass had the same smell as now and the world had seemed dear and transparent and eternal. He thought he could hear the whirr of the cycle-engines again and see the riders in their absurdly large goggles racing across the blue sky and he suddenly knew that the calm pure feelings of youth, those early, precious moments of happiness, would never, never come back again. Now a sweet pang shot through his heart, now his whole being was suffused afresh with the savage urge for battle mounting in his blood.

The sun had passed the meridian when, once again, a long dark arrow thrust forth over the distant hill-top and at the same moment dust began to rise thickly on the horizon. Motor cyclists again—a large number of them in a long, seemingly endless column. And behind them came lorries, hundreds and thousands of lorries in columns, and, in the spaces between the columns, the jeeps of the officers. Without end the lorries kept coming over the hill; like a long fat green dragon, writhing and twisting, with its scales glittering in the sun, they crawled on and on from beyond the horizon. The dragon's head approached nearer and nearer to where Sergei was lying and still its tail was not in sight. Dust lay in a billow over the road and the roar of the engines seemed to fill the whole space between the earth and the sky.

The Germans were coming to Krasnodon. Sergei had been the first to see them.

With a stealthy, cat-like movement he half slipped and crawled, half dashed in a run across the road and over the railway tracks and then raced down into the hollow and along it and over the rising ground on the other side where he could no longer be seen from the direction of the German column beyond the railway embankment.

He had planned the whole manoeuvre in order to reach the town before the Germans and occupy the most advantageous observation post in the town itself: the roof of the Gorky School in the park.

By running across the empty space round an abandoned mine, he reached the back of the street behind the park known as Derevyannaya Street, isolated from the town and unchanged in appearance since the old days. And here he came upon a sight so startling that he stopped in his tracks. Noiselessly he slipped further along the fences of the back gardens of the houses on Derevyannaya Street and here in one of these gardens he saw the girl with whom fate had linked him when he encountered her on the lorry in the steppe two nights previously.

There, not more than five yards away from him she was lying on a dark striped rug spread on the grass under an acacia-tree. He could see her face in profile; her head lay on a cushion, her brown legs with the feet in slippers were crossed one over the other and she was reading a book oblivious of everything round her. One of her thick, golden plaits lay across the cushion, its colour setting off the sunburn of her face with its dark lashes and the proud tilt of the full upper lip.... Yes, at a moment when thousands of lorries—the whole German army—were moving down on Krasnodon with a roar of engines and a stench of petrol fumes filling the whole atmosphere between steppe and sky, the girl lay there on a rug in the garden with a book in her brown fluff-covered hands, reading.

Sergei tried to hold his breath which was bursting with a whistling sound from his chest; he grasped the fence with both hands and, dazed and happy, watched the girl for several moments. There was something artless and beautiful like life itself about this girl, lying in a garden with an open book in her hands on one of the most terrible days since the world began.

With desperate courage Sergei vaulted the fence and stood there at the feet of the girl. She put the book aside and her eyes behind their dark lashes rested on him without alarm, in pleased surprise.

Maria Andreyevna Borts had brought the children back to Krasnodon; the whole of the Borts family—Maria herself, her husband, seventeen-year-old Valya and her sister Lyusia, who was twelve—sat up the remainder of that night until the break of day.

They huddled round the table by the light of a paraffin lamp—the power station supplying the town had been shut down on the 17th. They sat face to face as though they were visiting somebody. The news they had exchanged was straightforward but so terrifying that they found it impossible to talk about it aloud in the stillness reigning in the house, the street, and the whole town. It was too late to go away. Yet the thought of remaining here was horrifying. All of them, even Lyusia, her big eyes serious in the pale face and her hair golden like Valya's but lighter, felt that something so irremediable had taken place that the mind was unable to fathom the full extent of the disaster.

The father was a pitiable sight. He just sat there rolling cigarettes of cheap tobacco and smoking. The children already found it difficult to picture to themselves the days when he had been the embodiment of strength, the bulwark and defender of the family. There he sat, small and thin. His sight had always been poor but during the past few years he had been gradually losing it more and more and already found it hard to prepare for his lessons. Like Maria Andreyevna he taught literature and his wife frequently corrected the exercise books of his pupils. His eyes, which looked Egyptian, were quite sightless in lamp light and just stared without blinking.

Everything about them was as usual and familiar from childhood days, yet everything was different. The dinner table with its coloured cloth; the piano on which Valya played her pieces every day; the sideboard with the glass doors behind which the simple but tastefully chosen plates and dishes were arranged symmetrically; the open bookcase— all this was as it had always been and yet it was strange. Valya's many admirers said that her home was comfortable and romantic and Valya knew that it was she, the girl who lived in this house, who lent romance to everything that surrounded her. And now it all lay before her naked and shorn of romance.

They were afraid to put the lamp out, afraid to separate, go to bed and be left alone with their thoughts and feelings. So they sat there in silence until dawn—the ticking of the clock was the only sound. Not until they heard the neighbours go to the tap at the water-tower opposite the house did they extinguish the lamp and open the shutters. Valya undressed, deliberately making as much noise as possible, and then lay down with her head under the blanket. She was soon asleep. Lyusia also went to sleep. But Maria and her husband did not even then go to bed.

Valya woke up to the faint tinkle of cups as her parents were getting tea ready in the dining-room. Maria was setting up the samovar. Sunshine poured in through the window. With a sudden feeling of disgust Valya recalled the night session. How terrible and degrading to give way to one's feelings in that way! After all, what did the Germans matter to her? She still had a mental life of her own. Let those who want to pine away with suspense and fear but she— oh no!

She washed her hair in hot water and enjoyed it. She drank a leisurely cup of tea, then took a volume of Stevenson with *Kidnapped* and *Catriona* from the bookcase, spread a rug under the acacia-tree in the garden and was soon engrossed in her reading.

It was quiet round her. The neglected flower-bed and the patch of grass lay bathed in sunshine. A cinnamon-coloured butterfly perched on a blossom, closing and opening its wings. Bumble-bees, dark and hairy, with broad, white, downy stripes round their middle, hummed sweetly, roaming from flower to flower. It was shady under the old, luxuriant acacia with its many trunks and countless branches. Patches of aquamarine sky peeped through its foliage which was beginning to turn yellow here and there.

And this enchanting world of sky and sun, of green foliage and bees and butterflies wove itself curiously into the imaginary world of the book, the world of adventure and wild nature, of human courage and nobleness, of loyal friendship and pure love.

Now and again Valya put the book aside and gazed long and dreamily into the sky between the branches of the acacia. What did she dream of? She could not have said. But, Lord, how good it was to lie all by herself with a book here in this wonderful garden!

"They've all probably gone away," she thought as she recalled her schoolmates. "Oleg's most likely gone too." She knew the Koshevois well, as did her parents. "Yes, they've all forgotten Valya. Oleg's gone. And Styopka— why hadn't he shown up? A friend he called himself. 'I swear!' What a gas-bag! If it had been that chap who jumped on the lorry last night ... what was his name again—Tyulenin—Sergei Tyulenin ... he'd have kept his word...."

And then she imagined herself in Catriona's place and the lad who had climbed on the lorry as the hero, daring and chivalrous. His hair was probably coarse to the touch, she thought, and she very much wanted to touch it. "And what sort of boy would he be with soft hair like a girl's, a boy's hair should be coarse.... Oh, if they'd only never come, those Germans!" she thought with longing. She again became absorbed in the fabulous world of the book and the sun-drenched garden with the hairy bees and the cinnamon butterfly.

Thus she spent the whole of that day and, on the following morning, she again took rug and cushion and the volume of Stevenson and went out into the garden. And no matter what might happen in the world, that was how she'd go on living—here in the garden under the acacia-tree....

Her parents were unfortunately not able to follow a similar mode of life. Moreover, Maria Andreyevna had reached the end of her tether. She was a noisy woman, healthy and lively, with full lips, big teeth and a loud voice. No, this was no way to carry on! She got herself ready before the mirror and went off to find out whether the Koshevois were in town or had left.

The Koshevois lived on Sadovaya Street which started at the main gates of the park. They occupied one half of a prefabricated stone house which the Coal Trust had allotted to Oleg's uncle—Nikolai Nikolayevich Korostylev. The other half was taken up by a teacher and his family, a colleague of Maria Andreyevna's.

The lonely ring of an axe carried down along Sadovaya Street. Maria thought it came from the Koshevois' yard and her heart started thumping. Before entering the yard she looked round to see whether anybody was watching, just as though she were doing something dangerous and illegal.

A dog, black and shaggy, was lying on the porch with his red tongue lolling out from the heat. He made a move to stand up when he heard Maria's heels clicking along the street but then he recognized her and sank to the ground again with an apologetic glance which seemed to say: "Forgive me, it's the heat. I haven't the strength even to wag my tail for you."

Grandma Vera Vasilyevna, thin, tall, sinewy, was cutting wood, swinging the axe high with her bony hands and bringing it down with such force that her breath came grunting and whistling from the aged chest. She had evidently never yet suffered from back trouble, or perhaps she thought that one ill drives out another. Her lean face was tanned a deep brown; it was thin, with a sharp nose, the nostrils of which quivered. In profile she always reminded Maria of Dante whose picture she had seen in a pre-revolutionary edition of the *Divine Comedy*. Her hair, dark chestnut streaked with grey, framed the swarthy face in curls which twined and fell to her shoulders. Usually she wore black horn-rimmed spectacles which she had acquired so long ago that one of the arms had broken off from old age and had been tied on to the frame with black cotton. But for the moment Grandma Vera was without her glasses.

She seemed to be working with special energy, with doubled, even trebled energy, so that the logs flew clattering in all directions. The expression of her face and her whole figure seemed to be saying something like: I wish the devil would come and take those Germans and I wish he'd take the lot of you too if you're afraid of them! I'd rather get on with these logs here ... crash ... bang ... and what if they do fly in all directions—to hell with 'em! I'd rather bash these logs about than sink to your humiliating state. And if I'm fated to die because of it then the devil take me. I'm old and not afraid of death ... crash ... bang....

The axe stuck fast in a knot. Grandma Vera lifted axe and log, swung them over and behind her back and crashed them down so hard on the chopping block that the log flew away in two pieces, one of which all but hit Maria's leg.

Owing to this circumstance Grandma Vera noticed her, screwed up her eyes, recognized her and, tossing the axe aside, called out in a voice which was probably heard all the way up and down the street:

"Ah, Maria Andreyevna ... that's good, glad you came and glad that you're not afraid to come! As for my daughter Yelena, she's had her head in the pillow for three days now bawling like a baby. I said to her, 'When *are* you going to run out of tears?' Come in, won't you, be so kind."

Maria flinched at the loud voice but at the same time found it reassuring somehow; after all, she liked to talk in a loud voice herself. Nevertheless, hers was quiet and timid when she asked:

"Have our friends gone?" She pointed to the teacher's flat.

"He's gone off somewhere but his family's here and they're bawling too. Maybe you'll have a bite of food with me, will you? I've made such a good *borshch* and now nobody wants to eat it."

As always, Grandma Vera was equal to the situation. She was a widow, daughter of a village carpenter from Poltava Gubernia. Her husband was from Kiev and had worked at the Putilov Works. He had been badly wounded in the First World War and had settled in Grandma Vera's village. Although a married woman, Grandma Vera had taken her own road, had been a delegate to the Village Soviet, had worked in the peasant-aid committee and later in a hospital. Her husband's death had not broken her, but rather given fresh impetus to her independent nature. True, she was now retired and lived on her pension, but she could still let her powerful voice be heard when the need arose. Grandma Vera was a member of the Party, which she had joined some twelve years ago.

Yelena Nikolayevna, Oleg's mother, lay on the bed with her face hidden in the pillow. Her legs were bare and she wore a flowered dress which was now quite crumpled. Her luxuriant fair plaits, usually wound round her head in an elaborate style, had been allowed to fall loose and her hair, reaching almost to her heels, covered the whole of her small body which was beautifully developed, young and strong.

When Grandma Vera and Maria Borts entered the room, Yelena raised a tearful face with swollen eyes, which held a kindly, intelligent, soft expression. With a cry she flew into Maria's arms. They clung to each other, they kissed and wept and then burst into laughter: they were happy to have each other during these terrifying days, to understand and share their common grief. They wept and laughed and Grandma Vera, with her sinewy arms akimbo, wagged her curly Dantesque head from side to side.

"Silly things, oh the silly things! One minute they cry, the next they laugh! There isn't much to laugh about, I'd say, and we'll all manage to have a good cry yet...."

As she spoke a strange sound struck their ears; it seemed to come towards them down the street and was like the roar of countless engines; it was accompanied by the ferocious, high-pitched barking of dogs—all the dogs in the town seemed suddenly to have gone mad.

The noise was steadily getting louder.

Yelena and Maria moved away from each other. Grandma Vera let her hands drop, the colour had drained from her lean, dark face. Thus they stood for a moment, not daring to accept the significance of that sound.... But they knew. Then suddenly the three of them, with Grandma in the lead, then Maria, and Yelena last, dashed out into the garden, silently and with an intuitive knowledge of the right course to adopt, running not to the garden gate but between the flower-beds and through the sunflowers into the jasmine bushes by the garden fence.

The noise of a large number of lorry-engines was carried across from the lower part of the town and was coming nearer and nearer all the time. The lorry wheels were already thundering over what sounded like the sleepers of the second level crossing, out of sight from here. And suddenly a grey army car appeared over the rise at the end of the street. Its hood was down and the rays of the sun were reflected in blinding flashes from the windscreen. It rolled leisurely up the street towards the women in the jasmine bushes. In it, straight, stern and immobile, sat several grey-clad officers wearing peaked caps with the front part of the crown pushed up high.

The grey car was followed by a number of similar small cars. They came down the rise in the street and slowly trundled along towards the park.

With a sudden feverish movement of her small hands with the slightly thickened finger joints Yelena Nikolayevna seized her plaits, each in turn, and began to wind them round her head without taking her eyes off the cars. She did this quickly and quite mechanically and when she discovered that she had no hairpins she continued to stand there and gaze out on the street holding her plaits to her head with both hands.

With a low cry Maria Andreyevna rushed out from the jasmine bushes, not to the front gate, however, but back to the house. She ran round it on the side where the teacher lived and out through another gate into a street parallel with the one in which the Germans were arriving. This street was empty and Maria flew along it towards her home.

"Forgive me, I've no strength left to prepare you for it. Be brave. You must go into hiding right away ... at any moment now they may come pouring into our street!" Maria said to her husband.

She stood panting, a hand pressed to her heart, and, like all healthy people, she was so red and sweating from having run that the outward signs of her agitation failed to reflect the terrible meaning of her words.

"The Germans?" Lyusia asked quietly with an expression of terror in her voice so unlike that of a child that Maria fell silent, looked at her daughter and then gazed about with a lost expression in her eyes.

"Where's Valya?" she asked.

Her husband remained silent. His lips were white.

"I can tell you—I saw everything," Lyusia said in an unusually low and serious voice. "She was reading in the garden when some boy or other—almost grown-up he was— came jumping over the fence. She was lying down, then she sat up and they talked for a while. Then she jumped up and they climbed over the fence and ran off."

"Where to?" Maria asked, wide-eyed.

"Towards the park. She left the rug and the cushion in the garden and her book too. I thought she might be back in a little while so I went out to watch her things but she didn't come back and I brought everything inside."

"Oh, my God..." Maria said and fell heavily to the floor.

Chapter 17

GRANDMA VERA and Yelena had remained standing in the jasmine bushes and watched huge, long, high lorries emerge, one after another, over the rise and come crawling down the street. The lorries were beginning to fill the whole street and the noise they made was everywhere. Rows of sweating sunburnt German soldiers sat in them. Their grey uniforms and forage-caps were covered with dust, their rifles were held between their legs. Angry dogs rushed at the lorries from all directions and, yapping fiercely, began to leap round them in the thick red-brown dust.

The leading cars with the officers had come level with the Koshevois' front garden when the two women suddenly heard a ferocious barking behind them. Like a streak of lightning the black shaggy dog came flying through the sun-flowers, jumped over the low garden fence and with throaty howls and resonant barking started to dance round the car in front.

Horror-struck, the women exchanged glances. They felt that something terrible was about to take place. But nothing happened. The car drove on towards the park and stopped at the building of the Krasnodon Coal Trust. It was followed by the other cars. By now the whole street was crowded with lorries full of soldiers. They leapt down from the vehicles, stretched their arms and legs and, talking noisily and harshly in a manner strange to Russian ears, began to spread about through the gardens and yards and knock on the doors of the houses. The black dog, perplexed and uncertain now, stood at the gate and barked at random in all directions.

The officers stood smoking in front of the Trust; batmen were carrying suitcases into the building. A short officer with a paunch and wearing a peaked cap with a crown so high that it dwarfed the head under it, had taken charge of the unloading of the jeeps. Another, a young fellow with absurdly long legs and accompanied by an uncouth-looking soldier of towering build, in coarse boots and a forage-cap on his straw-coloured hair, ran quickly across the street and into the house where Protsenko had lived. In a moment they came out again and hurried to the house next door. In this house, too, regional committee workers had had rooms but had left several days previously, taking with them the people who permanently resided there. The officer and the soldier came out of the garden and directed their steps towards the front gate of the Koshevois.

Now at last the shaggy black dog saw an enemy, real and in the flesh, coming straight towards him, and with a bark he flew at the young officer. The officer halted, his long legs apart, and his face assumed a boyish expression. Then, with a curse, he pulled his pistol from its holster and fired point-blank at the dog. The dog's nose ploughed into the ground; with a howl he crawled a short distance towards the officer, then stretched out.

"They've killed the dog—what will they do next!" Grandma Vera cried.

The officers and soldiers at the Trust building and along the street looked round as the shot rang out; when they saw the dead dog they resumed their activities. Single shots could be heard coming from other parts.

The officer, accompanied by the huge batman with the straw-coloured hair, opened the gate of the Koshevois' front garden. Grandma Vera walked towards him holding her Dantesque head high and rigid. Yelena remained in the jasmine and continued to support her fair plaits round her head with both hands.

The officer planted himself on his long legs opposite Grandma Vera. Grandma was also tall but the cold colourless eyes of the German looked down at her.

"Who will show your house?" he asked.

He seemed to think that he spoke very correct Russian. His glance travelled from Grandma to Yelena who was still in the jasmine bushes with her hands up. He looked back at Grandma.

"Well, hm ... Yelena! You show him," Grandma said in a hoarse voice. She seemed confused.

Still holding the plaits up, Yelena picked her way between the flower-beds towards the house. Surprised, the officer looked at her for a moment, then back at Grandma.

"Well?" he said, raising his pale eyebrows. A capricious look came into his young, smooth face, the face of a son of the gentry.

Tripping along in a manner most unusual for her, Grandma almost ran to the house. The officer and his batman followed.

The Koshevois' flat consisted of three rooms and a kitchen. From the kitchen you came into a large room with two windows facing a street which ran parallel with Sadovaya Street. It served as a dining-room and also contained Yelena's bed and a divan on which Oleg usually slept. A door on the left led to a room which had been occupied by Nikolai Korostylev with his wife and child. Another on the right opened into a very small room where Grandma slept. It adjoined the kitchen and as the kitchen stove stood against the wall common to both rooms the heat in the small room when the stove was lit was almost unbearable, especially in the summer. But like all old countrywomen Grandma loved heat. When it did bother her she would open the window looking out on the lilac bushes in the front garden.

The officer entered the kitchen. After a rapid glance round he passed into the dining-room; he had to duck at the door to avoid knocking his head against the lintel. He looked round the room and it was clear that he liked it. The whitewash on the walls was spotless, the whole place gleamed with cleanliness. Home-made mats, simple and fresh, covered the painted floor; the table had a snow-white cloth on it, a white counterpane covered Yelena's bed; the pillows, the top one smaller than the other, were puffed up high and covered with something airy made of lace. There were flowers in the windows.

Again stooping in the doorway the officer quickly walked into the Korostylevs' room. Yelena remained in the dining-room. She had pinned up her luxuriant crown of fair hair—how or when she hardly knew—and with her head thrown back stood leaning with her back against the door-post. Grandma Vera followed the German. This room, with its small desk and the writing materials neatly arranged on it, with a T-square, set-square and graph rule hanging on their hooks by the side of the desk, also pleased him.

"*Schön,*" he said in a satisfied tone.

Suddenly his eyes fell on the rumpled bed where Yelena had been lying when Maria entered the room. He walked across to it with quick steps, turned the blankets and sheets back and felt the mattress with two fastidious fingers. He stooped and sniffed the air, then turned to Grandma.

"No bugs?" he asked, frowning.

"No bugs—no!" Grandma said with an offended shake of her head. To make it as clear as possible to the German she deliberately used Ukrainian slang.

"*Schön,*" the German said. He ducked his head and re-entered the dining-room. He cast a brief glance into Grandma's room, then turned to Yelena.

"Here will live the General Baron von Wentzel," he said; "these two rooms to be vacated." He indicated the dining-room and the Korostylevs' room. Then he pointed to Grandma's little room. "You are permitted to live here. What you want from these two rooms take out now. Remove this, and this." With two fingers he daintily flicked back the snowy counterpane, quilt and sheets on Yelena's bed. "In that room also ... remove, quick!" He walked out of the room past Yelena Nikolayevna. She recoiled from him.

"Bugs, eh? A barbarian, if I ever saw one! That Grandma Vera should live to hear *that* in her old days!" Grandma said in her loud sharp voice. "Yelena! Are you paralyzed, or what?" she called, exasperated. "Come on, we've got to clear all this out for the baron—may his eyes fester! Rouse yourself, will you! It may be our good fortune to have this baron, perhaps he's not as mad as all the rest."

Yelena silently rolled up her bedding, took it into Grandma's room and did not come back again. Grandma Vera removed the bedding from the room of her son and daughter-in-law. Then she took her son's and Oleg's photos from the wall and table and placed them in the dresser: "So we don't get questions about who's who." Next she collected her own and her daughter's clothing and took it into her room: "So we don't have to push past 'em—may the palsy strike 'em down!" Then, unable to remain still because curiosity was plaguing her, she again went out into the garden.

The huge batman with the straw-coloured hair and yellow freckles on his fleshy face appeared at the gate. With both hands he was carrying several long flat suitcases with suède dust-covers. Following him came another soldier with three tommy-guns, two Mausers and a sabre in a silver scabbard. He in turn was followed by two more soldiers carrying another suitcase and a radio receiver which was not large but seemed very heavy. They entered the house without a glance at Grandma.

And then, courteously conducted by the long-legged officer, the general himself passed through the gate. He was very lean and tall, in high, shiny, but slightly dusty boots, and wore a peaked cap with a tall crown propped straight up in front. His clean-shaven face and Adam's apple were old and wrinkled. The officer walked a step behind his superior, his head inclined.

There were double stripes down the side of the general's grey trousers, his service tunic had dull gilt buttons and a black collar with gilt palm leaves on red tabs. There was grey at his temples and his long narrow head was held high on the long neck. He spoke curtly and the officer behind him hung politely on every word.

The general had entered the garden. He halted and looked round, turning his head slowly on the raspberry-coloured neck which gave him the appearance of a goose, the more so because the peak of his cap stuck out such a long way. The general cast his eyes about, while the immobile face remained expressionless. Then he described an arc with his arm and shrivelled fingers on the narrow wrist as though damning everything in sight and mumbled something. The officer inclined his head still more deferentially.

A mixture of perfume and other odours wafted towards Grandma as the general walked past giving her a momentary glance from his pale, tired, watery eyes. He entered the house, stooping to avoid the beam over the door. The long-legged officer signalled to the soldiers to remain where they stood at attention at the porch, then followed the general. Grandma Vera remained in the garden.

A few minutes later the officer came out again, gave the soldiers a brief order and at the same time waved his arm over the garden, exactly repeating the general's gesture. With a click of their heels the soldiers faced about and marched out of the garden in single file. The officer re-entered the house.

By this time the sunflowers in the kitchen garden had their golden heads well inclined towards the west and long heavy shadows lay across the flower-beds. Laughter and an animated buzz of strange voices came from the street beyond the jasmine. Lorry-engines were still roaring in the direction of the level crossing to the right. Single shots rang out here and there; now and again a dog barked, a hen cackled.

Two soldiers already familiar to Grandma again appeared at the gate. They carried broadswords in their hands. Before Grandma had had time to wonder what they were to be used for, the soldiers, one on each side of the gate, began to hack down the jasmine bushes along the fence.

Unable to restrain herself Grandma rushed at them with skirts flying. "What're you doing that for—chopping the bushes down! They're not in your way!" She darted angrily from one to the other scarce able to keep from pulling them away by the hair. "They're flowers, they're lovely flowers! They're not in your way, are they?" Puffing and sniffing the soldiers went on silently hacking at the jasmine bushes without a glance at her. Then one of them made a remark and both laughed.

"They think it's funny," Grandma said contemptuously.

One of the soldiers straightened his back, wiped the sweat off his forehead and looked at Grandma with a smile.

"This is an order from higher up," he said in German. "Military necessity. It's being done everywhere—look!" With his sword he indicated the garden next door.

Grandma did not understand what he said but turned round in the direction indicated and saw that in her neighbour's garden, and beyond it, and in the gardens behind her, everywhere, German soldiers were hacking down trees and bushes.

"*Partisanen*—bang, bang!" The soldier tried to explain. He stopped behind a bush, stuck out his dirty, thick-nailed index finger and demonstrated how the partisans acted.

Suddenly feeling faint, Grandma brushed the proceedings away with a movement of her arm, left the soldiers, and seated herself on the porch.

A soldier appeared at the gate wearing a chef's cap and a white overall, below which the legs of grey trousers and dirty, wooden-soled boots were visible. In one hand he carried a large aluminium pot, in the other a closely woven basket in which dishes could be heard tinkling. He was followed by another soldier in a greasy tunic carrying something in a large earthenware bowl which he held with both hands. They passed Grandma and entered the kitchen.

Then abruptly, like something bursting in from another world, scraps of music came from the house, intermingled with crackling and hissing noises, snatches of German speech, then crackling and hissing again and more music.

Everywhere along the street soldiers were hacking down bushes and trees in the front gardens and soon the view was unobstructed and one could look down the whole length of the street to the right and to the left, from the level crossing to the park. Everywhere soldiers were hurrying to and fro and motor cycles were rushing about.

Then, from a room inside at Grandma's back soft distant music suddenly sounded. Somewhere very far from Krasnodon life was going on in its calm, measured course, a life alien to everything that was taking place here at this moment. The people for whom this music was intended lived an existence apart from the war, from these soldiers running up and down the streets destroying front gardens, and far removed from Grandma Vera. That life was probably far removed, too, from the soldiers who were at work on the jasmine bushes in the garden, and alien to them, because they did not raise their heads; nor did they pause to listen, nor did they exchange a single word about the music coming from the house.

They hacked down every tree and every bush in the garden up to the very window of Grandma's room where Yelena sat alone and silent. And then they turned on the sunflowers, whose golden heads were bowing towards the setting sun, cutting them down close to the ground. And when that was done a clean sweep had been made and there was nowhere for the partisans to do their "bang, bang."

Chapter 18

As THE EVENING wore on German soldiers and officers from the various service branches penetrated into all parts of the town with the exception of the Shanghais and the outlying Golubyatniki and Derevyannaya Street districts, where Valya Borts lived. For the present these areas remained free of them.

The townsfolk kept off the streets. The town seemed to be packed full of dirty-grey uniforms and forage-caps with the German silver eagle on them. They spilled over into kitchen gardens and yards and appeared in the doorways of the houses, shops, sheds and barns.

The street in which the Osmukhins and Zemnukhovs lived had been one of the first to be taken over by the infantry arriving on the lorries. The street was wide enough to provide parking space for these lorries but, fearful of attracting the attention of Soviet bombers, orders had come to pull up all vehicles under cover of the houses and sheds, and everywhere soldiers were breaking down the low fences of the front gardens to make a free passage for them.

With its engine roaring, a long, high lorry, from which the soldiers had already dropped off, backed into the Osmukhins' front garden, the solid tyres of its huge twin wheels splintering and then crushing the fence. Flattening the flower-beds and crushing the flowers, filling the air with its roar and petrol fumes, the lorry moved backwards across the garden and stopped close against the wall of the house.

A dashing lance-corporal with a small black moustache bristling from his swarthy face stepped up to the entrance of the house. His forage-cap was tilted over his eyes, his temples and the back of his head were covered with coarse, black hair which looked like felt. He kicked the door open and with several other soldiers burst through the porch into the passage of the Osmukhins' home.

Yelizaveta Alexeyevna and Lyudmila, who resembled each other, sat at Volodya's bed, both in unnaturally tense attitudes. Volodya lay on the bed, covered to the chin with a sheet. His narrowed brown eyes gazed gloomily straight ahead trying not to betray his agitation to the rest of the family. They heard the noise at the front door and when the sweating dirty faces of the corporal and his men appeared through the open door in the passage Yelizaveta stood up briskly with characteristic determination on her features. Erect and with quick movements she went into the passage to confront the Germans.

"Fery gut," the corporal said with a good-humoured laugh and looked straight at her with impudent cheery frankness. "Here will live our soldiers. Only two or three nights. *Nur zwei oder drei Nächte.* Fery gut."

The soldiers standing behind him were silent and looked unsmilingly at Yelizaveta. She opened the door of the room usually occupied by herself and Lyudmila. Some time before the Germans arrived she had decided that if German troops were to be billeted in her house she would move into Volodya's room so that they would all be together. But the corporal did not enter the room nor even look at it. Through the open door of Volodya's room his glance had fallen on Lyudmila, who sat straight and immobile at Volodya's bed.

"Oh!" he exclaimed with a gay laugh and saluted. "Your brother?" Coolly he thrust a black finger at Volodya. "Wounded?"

"No, he's sick," Lyudmila replied. Her face had become fiery-red.

"She speaks German!" the corporal said with a laugh, turning to the unsmiling soldiers behind him. He grinned at Lyudmila, his black eyes glittered. "What you're trying to do is conceal the fact that your brother's a wounded Red soldier or a partisan. But we can always check that."

"No, no, he's only a schoolboy, he's seventeen. He's had an operation," Lyudmila said anxiously.

"Don't worry, we're not going to touch your brother," the corporal said, grinning. He saluted again and then turned to inspect the room which Yelizaveta had pointed out to him. "Fery gut. And this door where?" Without awaiting a reply he opened the kitchen door. "Excellent! Make a fire now, quick. You have chickens? Eggs, eggs!' He laughed amicably, with a stupid frankness.

It was really astonishing that he should have said the very thing which during all the months of the war had been the subject of jokes about the Germans and eyewitness stories, which had been commented on in dispatches to the press and used in the captions of cartoons. But that was what he did say.

"Friedrich, get some food for us!" And he entered the room Yelizaveta had indicated to him. The soldiers followed him and the whole house began to resound to their talk and laughter.

"Mama, did you hear him? They want eggs and they want the kitchen stove lit," Lyudmila said in a whisper.

Yelizaveta remained standing in the passage without replying.

"You hear, Mama? Shall I get some wood?"

"I heard all right," her mother said, standing in the same attitude. She seemed somehow too tranquil.

A middle-aged soldier with a square jaw came out of the room. A scar ran down his forehead under the forage-cap.

"You're Friedrich, I expect. Are you?" Yelizaveta asked in a quiet voice.

"Friedrich? Yes, that's me ... Friedrich," he replied in a lugubrious tone.

"Come then, you can help me to get some wood in. I'll give you the eggs myself."

"What?" He did not understand Russian.

She motioned to him and left the passage. The soldier followed her.

"Well now," Volodya said without looking at Lyudmila. "Shut the door, will you?"

She closed the door and returned to his bed under the impression that he wanted to talk to her. But he continued to lie in silence with his eyes closed. Then, without knocking, the corporal appeared at the door. His black hairy chest was naked to the waist; in his hand was a soap-dish and a towel was flung over his shoulder.

"Where's your wash-hand basin?" he asked.

"We've got no wash-hand basin. We use the jug in the yard," Lyudmila replied. "We pour the water over each other's hands."

"What barbarism!" With feet apart the corporal stood in the door in his thick-soled brownish boots and looked at Lyudmila with a cheerful grin.

"What's your name?"

"Lyudmila."

"What?"

"Lyudmila."

"I don't understand ... Lu— Lu—?"

"Lyudmila—Lyusia."

"Oh, Luise!" he exclaimed, satisfied. "You speak German but you wash from a jug," he said with disgust. "Very bad."

Lyudmila was silent.

"And in the winter?" the corporal asked. "Ha-hah! What barbarism! Well, the least you can do then is to come and pour the water over me."

She rose and walked to the door. He continued to stand there—feet apart, hairy. He grinned and gave her a frank, direct stare.

She stopped before him, blushing, her head bowed.

"Ha-hah!" He continued to stand there for a moment, then stepped aside for her.

They went out to the porch.

Volodya had been able to follow the conversation. He had kept his eyes closed and felt the thumping of his heart through his body. If he had not been ill he, instead of Lyudmila, would be pouring the water over the German. He felt ashamed when he realized the humiliating position he and the whole family were in, and which they would have to continue to be in. He lay there with his heart pounding away and he kept his eyes closed to conceal the state of his mind.

He could hear the Germans in their hobnailed boots as they walked through the passage to the yard and back again. His mother's incisive voice came to him from the porch; he heard her slippers shuffling towards the kitchen, then back to the porch. Then Lyudmila quietly entered the room and closed the door behind her: her mother had taken her place.

"Volodya, how awful!" she said rapidly in a whisper. "All the fences everywhere have been knocked down. All the flower-beds have been trampled on, the gardens are packed with soldiers. They've got their shirts off, shaking the lice out of them, and right outside our porch they're pouring water over themselves from pails—they're standing there quite naked! I was nearly sick."

Volodya lay still without opening his eyes.

From the yard came the wild cackling of a hen.

"Friedrich's killing our chickens," she said, a sudden mocking note in her voice.

The corporal walked past their door towards his room. He was snorting and emitting strange noises; evidently he was towelling himself as he walked through the passage. For some moments they could hear his loud voice, the hearty voice of a very healthy man, then their mother made some reply. In a few minutes she came into the room carrying a roll of bedding, which she placed in a corner.

Something was being cooked or baked in the kitchen; the smell of it came to them even though the door was closed. Their whole home had become like a busy corridor: somebody was for ever coming or going. Laughter and German speech reached them from the kitchen, the yard, and from the room of the corporal and his soldiers.

Lyudmila had a gift for languages and after finishing school—the first year of the war—had concentrated on German, French and English. It had been her plan to enter the Institute of Foreign Languages in Moscow in order to qualify for diplomatic work at a future date. Now willynilly she both heard and understood much of what the soldiers were saying, peppered as it was with coarse words and jokes.

"Hello, Adam, old fellow! Good! What've you got there?"

"Pork fat, Ukrainian style. You can have some."

"Great! Got any brandy? No? Oh well, *hol's der Teufel*, let's have Russian vodka then."

"Someone told me there's an old man living at the end of the street who's got honey."

"I'll send little Hans after it. Let's make hay while the sun shines. The devil only knows how long we're here for and what's ahead of us."

"What's ahead of us? The Don's ahead, and the Kuban! And maybe the Volga too. We shan't be worse off there, I can tell you that!"

"While we're here we're at least alive."

"Oh, to hell with these damned coal-fields. Nothing but wind and dust and dirt, and everyone looks at you with the eyes of wolves."

"And where did they look at you with the eyes of friends? What makes you think you're bringing 'em happiness? Ha-ha-hah!"

Somebody entered the hall. A throaty, effeminate voice called out:

"*Heil Hitler!*"

"Hell, that's Peter Fehnbong! *Heil Hitler!* First time we've seen you in those black togs, *verdammt noch mal.* Come on in, show yourself! Look, fellows, this's Peter Fehnbong! To think that we haven't met since we crossed the frontier!"

"One'd think that you'd actually missed me!" the effeminate voice said and chuckled.

"Peter Fehnbong! Where on earth have you sprung from?"

"Better ask where I'm going! We've got orders to stop in this god-forsaken hole."

"What's that flash on your chest?"

"Been promoted to *Rottenführer*."

"Oho! No wonder you're getting fat! Probably the SS feeds better than we do!"

"But I'd say that he still sleeps in his clothes and never washes. I can tell by the smell of him!"

"Never make a joke you might be sorry for later!" the effeminate voice said.

"Oh, sorry, Peter, but we're old friends, aren't we? And what's a soldier got left when he can't make a joke! What brings you here?"

"I'm looking for a billet."

"Looking for a billet? You people always get the best places!"

"We've taken over the hospital, that's a huge place, but I need a billet just the same."

"There's seven of us here."

"So I see! *Wie die Heringe!*"

"Yes, you've risen in life all right! Still, don't forget your old friends. Look us up while we're here."

The effeminate voice hooted something in reply, there was laughter all round, then his hobnailed boots were heard stumping down the passage and he left.

"Queer fellow, that Peter Fehnbong."

"Queer? He's only making a career for himself and I can't blame him."

"But have you ever seen him in his undershirt, let alone stripped? He never washes!"

"I suspect he's got scabies and is ashamed to show it. Grub ready soon, Friedrich?"

"I need laurel leaves," Friedrich said dolefully.

"You think the end is coming and want to get yourself a laurel wreath ready in time, eh?"

"There'll be no end because we're fighting against the whole world," Friedrich said morosely.

Leaning her elbow on the sill, Yelizaveta sat at the window, deep in thought. Before her, bright in the evening

sun, lay a large vacant lot. At its far side, nearly opposite her cottage, she could see the two isolated white stone
buildings; the larger of these was the Voroshilov School
and the smaller—the children's hospital. Both the school
and the hospital had been evacuated and the buildings
stood empty.

"Lyudmila, look, what's that?" she said suddenly and
pressed her forehead against the pane.

Lyudmila hurried to the window. Along the dusty road
entering the square from the left and leading past the two
buildings came a long snake-like column of people. At
first Lyudmila could not even imagine who they were.
Bare-headed and wrapped in dark dressing-gowns, the men
and women dragged themselves along the road; some hobbled
painfully on crutches, others laboriously carried stretchers
with sick or wounded. Nurses in white caps and gowns and
men and women in everyday clothing carried heavy bundles
on their shoulders. These people had come along the road
running from a section of the town which could not be seen
from the window. They began to crowd round the main
entrance of the children's hospital where two women were
trying to open the big front doors.

"They're the patients from the municipal hospital! They've
simply been thrown out!" Lyudmila said. She turned towards her brother. "You hear? You know what that means?"

"Yes ... yes, but not only the patients, surely! I was in
one of the wards and we had wounded there too, you know!"
Volodya said, worried.

For some minutes Lyudmila and her mother watched the
patients being transferred and continued whispering their
observations to Volodya until the noisy talk of the German
soldiers distracted them. Judging by the voices there were
about ten or twelve people in the corporal's room; and
there was a ceaseless coming and going of others. They had
started to eat at about seven; now it was getting dark and
they were still eating, while in the kitchen cooking was
still in progress.

Heavy army boots tramped back and forth in the passage.
Toasts, the clinking of mugs and loud bursts of laughter
sounded across the passage. The conversation became animated, then ebbed again as more food was brought in. The

voices were gradually getting more drunken, more abandoned.

The heat and the fumes of cooking seeped into the room where the masters of the house were sitting; it was stuffy but they still hesitated to open the window. And, as though by tacit agreement, they did not light the lamp although it was getting quite dark now.

On the square outside nothing more could be distinguished; only to the right the long dark hill with the district committee offices and the house of the Mad Squire jutting out above it stood vaguely silhouetted against the lighter background of the sky. The dark July night was falling fast but their beds were still not made up, nor did they feel they wanted to go to bed.

The Germans had started to sing. They did not sing like ordinary drunks but like drunken Germans: in completely identical deep voices and with awful intensity, and being anxious to sing their deepest and loudest at the same time, they sounded hoarse and raucous. Then they clinked their mugs and there was more singing and after that it was quiet for a time because they were eating again.

Suddenly heavy boots clumped down the passage. They stopped at the door of the Osmukhins as though someone were trying to listen.

Then came a loud knock. Yelizaveta made a sign to Lyudmila to ignore it and pretend that they were all in bed. There w   another knock. Then a fist pounded on the door; it swuas open and a dark head was thrust into the room.

"Who there?" the corporal demanded in Russian. "Landlady!"

Yelizaveta rose from her chair and went to the door.

"What do you want?" she asked quietly.

"Me and my soldiers, we ask you a little with us to eat. You and Luise. A little. And the boy! Him you can also something bring. A little."

"We've eaten, we don't want anything now," Yelizaveta said.

"Where is Luise?" He had not understood her reply. He sniffed and belched and reeked of vodka. "Luise, I can see you!" he said with a broad grin. "Me and my soldiers invite you to come and eat with us. And have a little drink too if you don't mind."

"My brother isn't well and I can't leave him," Lyudmila replied.

"I expect you'll want the table cleared now," Yelizaveta said and with great courage seized his hand. "Come now, I'll help you." She took him out into the passage and closed the door.

The kitchen, the hall and the room in which the banquet was taking place were full of yellow-blue fumes which made her eyes water. Through this haze came the faint yellow flicker of lights burning in small round tins, filled with a substance similar to candle wax. These candle tins were everywhere: on the kitchen table and the window-sill, on the shelf of the coat-hanger in the passage and everywhere in the room full of German soldiers which Yelizaveta now entered with the corporal.

The Germans were sitting round the table which had been pushed close to the bed. They sat close together on the bed and on chairs and stools, and gloomy Friedrich with his scar was seated on the log, which usually served as a chopping block. Several vodka bottles stood on the table; many were empty and more stood under the table and on the window-sill. The table was covered with dirty dishes and lamb and chicken bones, bits of vegetables and crusts of bread. The Germans sat about in their grimy undershirts unbuttoned at the neck. They were sweaty and dirty and their hands and forearms were greasy from finger-tips to elbow.

"Friedrich!" the corporal yelled. "What's the idea—sitting there? Don't you know how to fuss over the mothers of pretty girls?" And his laugh was more boisterous than when he was sober, and everyone joined in.

Yelizaveta could feel that they were laughing at her and she suspected worse than what the corporal had actually said. Pale with anger and silent, she swept the remains of the food into an empty dirty bowl.

"Where's your daughter Luise? Have a drink with us!" called a young soldier, his face flushed from drinking. His unsteady hand reached for a bottle and he looked round for a clean mug. Not finding one he filled his own. "Ask her to come here. German soldiers are inviting her. Somebody said she speaks German. Let her come and teach us Russian songs."

With the bottle in his hand he waved his arm in the air, puffed himself up and with bulging eyes intoned in a terrible, deep voice:

Wolga, Wolga, Mutter Wolga,
Wolga, Wolga, Russlands Fluss....

He stood while he sang and kept time with the bottle so that the vodka splashed over soldiers, table and bed. The dark corporal burst out laughing and took up the song. Then the remainder joined them in voices as deep as they could make them.

"Yes, we'll reach the Volga!" shouted a very fat soldier with sweat pouring from his forehead. "Volga—*Deutschlands Fluss*! German river! That's what we've got to sing!" His voice rose above the singing and to reinforce his words and reassure himself he seized a fork and drove it into the table so that the prongs bent.

They were so engrossed in their singing that Yelizaveta was able, unnoticed by anybody, to remove the bowl with the scraps of food and take it to the kitchen. She wanted to swill the bowl out but did not find the kettle with boiling water on the stove.

"Well," she thought, "it's not tea they're drinking!"

Friedrich was busy at the stove. With a cloth in his hand he removed a frying-pan filled with pieces of mutton floating in grease. "Probably the Slonovs' sheep," she thought. The strains of the old Volga song sung by discordant drunken German voices still reached her ears. But she was indifferent to it as she was to everything taking place around her. The yardstick of human feelings and human behaviour which she and her children were accustomed to in their daily life could not be applied to this life which they now had to live. Not only outwardly, but also in their inner selves, they were now living in a world which had so little in common with the world of ordinary human relationships that everything seemed unreal to them. It felt as if one had only to open one's eyes and all this would disappear.

Quietly, she went into Volodya's room. The children were talking in a whisper and fell silent as Yelizaveta appeared at the door.

"Perhaps it would be best for you to make up the bed and lie down, you really should get some sleep," she said.

"I'm afraid to go to bed!" Lyudmila said softly.

"If that swine tries it just once more," Volodya said suddenly, raising himself up on his elbows, "if he just tries it again, I'll kill him, and I don't care what happens, I'll kill him!" His eyes flashed in the semi-darkness.

There was another knock and the door opened slowly. The corporal appeared at the door in his undershirt tucked into his trousers; the flickering light of the candle in his hand fell on his full, dark face. He craned his neck and for a moment regarded Volodya sitting up in bed and Lyudmila on her stool at Volodya's feet.

"Luise!" he began solemnly. "You shouldn't disdain soldiers who may have to face death any day, any time! We'll do you no harm. German soldiers are high-minded people—I'd say that they're gentlemen. We're inviting you to share our company, that's all."

Volodya glared at him with hate.

"Get out of here!" he said.

"Oh, you're a fine fellow, only unfortunately you're struck down by illness!" the corporal said amicably. He had not understood Volodya and could not see his face in the semi-darkness.

There was no telling what might have happened in that instant had Yelizaveta not quickly stepped to the bed, grasped her son in both arms and, pressing his head to her breast, firmly laid him down.

"Quiet—quiet now!" her hot dry lips whispered in his ear.

"The soldiers of the Führer are awaiting your reply," the drunken corporal said solemnly. Candle tin in hand, the open undershirt revealing the black hair on his chest, he swayed drunkenly at the door.

Lyudmila's face had paled. She remained seated, unable to think of a reply.

"Good, very good! Good," Yelizaveta said in a sharp voice and nodding her head went up to the corporal. "She'll come in a minute, understand? *Verstehte?* She'll change her clothes and come." She indicated in mime the changing of a dress.

"Mother!" Lyudmila said, her voice trembling.

"Shut up, if God gave you no sense at all!" her mother said, nodding to the corporal while she steered him through the door. He went out. From across the hall came shouts and guffaws, the clinking of mugs and then again the deep voices singing in unison with renewed vigour:

Wolga, Wolga, Mutter Wolga....

Yelizaveta quickly stepped to the wardrobe and unlocked it. "Get inside. I'll lock it after you," she whispered.

"But—"

"We'll tell them that you've gone to the yard."

Lyudmila vanished into the wardrobe, her mother locked the door and placed the key on top of the wardrobe.

The Germans sang furiously. It was late. Outside, the school and the hospital and the long hill with the district committee and the house of the Mad Squire were no longer visible. Only a narrow chink of light penetrated beneath the door into the room. "My God," thought Yelizaveta, "can all this really be true?"

The Germans stopped singing and a bantering, drunken argument broke out among them. There was laughter and they all pounced on the corporal who retaliated in the husky, cheerful voice of the bold soldier, who is never despondent.

And then, again he appeared in the door with a light in his hand.

"Luise?"

"She's gone out into the yard ... the yard!" Yelizaveta pointed with her hand.

Swaying, the corporal clumped back into the passage, carrying the candle before him, and then his heavy boots stumbled down the steps of the porch.

For some moments the soldiers continued their talk and laughter. Then they also trooped along the passage and down the steps of the porch into the yard. All at once it grew quiet. Across the passage someone, probably Friedrich, was clattering the dishes. Outside, close to the porch, the soldiers could be heard urinating. Some of them soon returned into the house, with their loud drunken talk.

The corporal was not among them, but at long last his steps were heard coming up the porch and into the passage. The door was pushed open and, carrying no light this time, the corporal appeared in it framed against the spectral light and smoke at the open door of the kitchen.

"Luise " he whispered.

Yelizaveta rose up like a shadow before him.

"What? Haven't you found her? She hasn't come back in here!" She shook her head and made a negative sign with her hands.

His bleary eyes swept round the room.

"Oh, you—" he bellowed suddenly, drunkenly and offended, fixing his clouded, black eyes on her. At the same time he placed his huge, greasy hand on her face, drew his fingers close together almost scratching her eyes out, and shoved her from him. Then he tottered, and stumbled out of the room. She quickly turned the key in the lock.

There was more noise from the Germans and drunken muttering. Finally they fell asleep without extinguishing the light.

Yelizaveta sat in silence at Volodya's bed. He was still awake. Unbearable mental weariness overpowered them but they did not want to sleep. Yelizaveta waited a little longer and then let Lyudmila out of the wardrobe.

"I'm almost suffocated. My back's all wet, and even my hair," Lyudmila said in an excited whisper. The adventure had somehow stimulated her. "I'll open the window quietly. I'm stifled."

Noiselessly she opened the window nearest to Volodya's bed and leaned out. The night was close but after the stuffy atmosphere of the room and everything that had happened in the house a balmy freshness was wafted in from the square outside. The town was so still that there seemed to be nothing out there—no town at all, only this cottage all by itself with the sleeping Germans in it. Suddenly a bright glare over the park beyond the crossing lit up the sky for an instant and threw its light over the square, the long hill, the school and the hospital. Then another sudden glow shot up, more intense, and again everything seemed to step out of the darkness; even the room was lit up for a brief instant. There followed the sound of explosions from across the square, or rather a repeated, noise-less convulsion of the air as though caused by distant ex-plosions. Then the darkness closed in again.

"What's that? What's that?" Yelizaveta asked in a frightened voice.

Volodya raised himself on the bed.

With a strange fear in her heart Lyudmila gazed into the darkness, in the direction where the flares glowed in the sky. Subsiding, then becoming bright again, the glare from invisible flames now began to flicker in the sky over the hill and to cast its intermittent light over the roofs of the district committee and the house of the Mad Squire. Suddenly a tongue of flame soared high up into the sky over the place where the strange light originated and a purple glare spread wider and wider over the sky illuminating the whole square and the town with a bright light. Faces and objects in the room grew visible.

"It's a fire!" Lyudmila said. Her voice was strangely triumphant. She turned round towards the room, then again towards the high tongue of flame.

Yelizaveta felt frightened. "Close the window!" she cried.

"It doesn't matter—no one can see us," Lyudmila said and shuddered, as though she were cold.

She had no idea what sort of fire it was or how it had started. But there was something soul-cleansing in that high, raging, victorious flame; something strangely elevat-ing and terrible. Her face lit up by the fire, Lyudmila con-tinued to gaze at it.

The glare had now spread not only over the centre of the town but far beyond it. Not only were the school and the hospital clearly visible but, beyond the square, the distant sections of the town round 1B Pit could also be seen now. The purple sky and the glow from the fire on the roofs and the hills presented a picture that was ghostly and fantastic and at the same time magnificent.

The whole town seemed now to be awake. People were moving across the square, isolated shouts could be heard; somewhere lorry-engines began to roar. The Germans had been roused and they swarmed about in the streets and the Osmukhins' garden. Apparently, not all the dogs had been shot and, forgetting the terrors of yesterday, they barked furiously at the fire. Only the drunken Germans in the room across the passage heard nothing and continued to sleep.

The fire raged for about two hours, then began to peter out. The distant districts of the town and the hills were again wrapped in darkness. Only now and then, when the fire flared up momentarily, did the curve of a hill or a group of house-tops or the dark cone of a pit-head tip stand out in the darkness. The purple reflection hung in the sky over the park and the buildings of the district committee and the Mad Squire were visible on and off for a long time. Then they too began to grow dim and when they finally vanished, darkness more intense than ever descended upon the square outside the window.

Lyudmila had remained at the window all the time, her excited gaze fixed on the blaze. Yelizaveta and Volodya, too, kept awake.

Suddenly Lyudmila thought she saw a cat darting across the square to the left, then there was a rustling by the foundations of the house. Someone was creeping up to the window. The girl instinctively drew back and was about to slam down the window, when she heard her name whispered.

"Lyudmila, Lyudmila!"

Her blood froze in her veins.

"Don't be frightened ... it's me, Tyulenin," came the whisper again, and Sergei's curly head rose to the level of the window-sill. "Any Germans in your house?"

"Yes," Lyudmila whispered, and looked with fear and happiness into Sergei's laughing, desperate eyes. "What about your house?"

"Not yet."

"Who's that?" Yelizaveta asked, terrified.

Then the reflection of the distant fire lit Sergei's face for a moment and both Volodya and Yelizaveta recognized him.

"Where's Volodya?" Sergei asked, resting his chest on the sill.

"Here."

"Who else has stayed behind?"

"Tolya Orlov. I don't know of any others, I haven't been out at all.... I've got appendicitis."

"Vitka Lukyanchenko's here and so's Lyuba Shevtsova," Sergei said. "And I've seen Styopa Safonov from the Gorky School."

"What're you doing here, at this time of night?"

"Was watching the fire. From the park. Then I started to go home across the Shanghais and noticed your open window from the gully.

"What was the fire?"

"The Trust."

"You don't say!"

"Their staff's moved in there. They came running out in their underpants!" Sergei chuckled softly.

"Someone did it, d'you think?" Volodya asked.

Sergei did not immediately reply. His eyes shone in the dark like a cat's.

"Well, the chances are it didn't start on its own," he said and again laughed quietly. "How d'you plan to live?" he asked Volodya suddenly.

"And you?"

"As if you don't know!"

"Same here," Volodya said, relieved. "Oh, I'm so glad you're here. I'm so glad...."

"So am I," Sergei said reluctantly. He could not stand effusiveness. "Are they a bad lot, the Germans in your place?"

"They boozed all night. Killed all our hens. Burst into the room several times," Volodya said casually and not without a slight feeling of pride at having personally experienced what the Germans were like. He said nothing about the corporal having worried Lyudmila.

"Oh well, then so far it's not so bad!" Sergei said calmly. "The SS have taken over the hospital; there were some forty of the wounded still left there; they took them to the Verkhneduvannaya Grove and ... machine-gunned them. When they started to move them out it was more than Doctor Fyodor Fyodorovich could stand and he spoke up for them. So they shot him right there in the corridor."

"Good God! And he was such a good man!" Volodya cried, scowling. "Why, I was operated on there!"

"Yes, he was one in a million," Sergei said.

"My God! What's going to happen?" Yelizaveta moaned softly.

"I'll run off now, before it gets light," Sergei said. "We'll keep in touch." He looked at Lyudmila and with a flourish of his hand said jauntily, "*Auf Wiedersehen!*" He knew that she planned to study foreign languages.

Then his slender agile form slipped away into the darkness and nothing more could be seen or heard of him. It was as though he had vanished into thin air.

Chapter 19

Most astonishing of all was how quickly they arrived at an understanding.

"What a time to be reading a book! The Germans are marching into Krasnodon!" Sergei said as he stood at her feet and tried hard to get his breath. "Can't you hear their lorries roaring down from Verkhneduvannaya?"

Valya continued to gaze at him in silence, an expression of calm, happy surprise in her face. Then she asked:

"Where were you running to?"

For a moment he was taken aback. Surely he couldn't have been wrong about this girl?

"I was on my way to your school to see if they'll—"

"How'll you get in? Have you ever been there?"

Sergei said that he'd been to a literary evening there a year or two ago. "I'll get in somehow," he said with a laugh.

"What if the Germans take over the school before anything else?"

"If I see them coming I'll go straight to the park," Sergei replied.

"I'll tell you, the best place to watch from is the attic— you can see everything from there without being seen," Valya said, sitting up. She quickly tidied her hair and straightened her blouse. "I know how to get up there. I'll show you."

Sergei suddenly showed indecision.

"Look ... it's like this..." he said. "If the Germans do suddenly make for the school it might mean a jump from a first-floor window."

"Well, and what of it?" Valya said.

"Could you do it?"

"What a question!"

He looked at her strong, brown legs with the golden down on them. A wave of warmth filled his heart. Of course a girl like her could jump from a first-floor window!

Soon they were both running across the park towards the school.

The large two-storey building was just inside the main gate of the park opposite the Krasnodon Coal Trust; of red brick with bright class-rooms and a large gymnasium, it now stood empty and locked. And in view of their lofty aims, Sergei saw nothing shameful in breaking a branch from a tree and smashing one of the windows on the ground floor which overlooked the park.

Their hearts were full of reverent awe as they tiptoed over the floor of one of the class-rooms to the corridor. There was a hush over the whole spacious building and the slightest rustle or tap produced a hollow echo all round.

Within the past few days much had been dislocated in the world; like people, many buildings had lost their purpose and calling, and had not yet found a new one. Even so, this was still a school in which children had been taught, the school in which Valya had spent many bright days of her life.

They passed the door with a small name-plate: Staff Room; another with the words Head Master on it. Others bore inscriptions such as: First-Aid Room, Physics Laboratory, Chemistry Laboratory, Library. Yes, this was a school. Here adult people had taught children how to live in this world.

And from the empty class-rooms with their bare desks, rooms which still retained the peculiar smell of school, there suddenly came to both Sergei and Valya a fresh breath of the world in which they had grown up, a world which was inalienably theirs and which had now seemingly receded for ever out of their reach. There had been a time when that world had appeared ordinary and commonplace, even boring. And now it rose before them so uniquely wonderful and free, full of frank, direct and pure relationships between those who taught and those who learned. Where were they—where had the wind of fate blown them all now? And for a moment a great love welled up in the hearts of Sergei and Valya; a love for that receding world, an undefined awe in the face of the supreme dignity and splendour of that world, which in the past they had been unable to appreciate.

They each experienced the same emotions—they knew this without exchanging a word; and in those few minutes they became extraordinarily close to each other.

Valya led the way up a narrow back staircase to the first floor, then still higher to a small door opening to the attic. The door was locked but that did not discourage Sergei. He rummaged in his trouser pocket and brought out a penknife which combined many useful tools, among them a screwdriver. With it he loosened the grub-screw of the door handle, which he then removed, so that he was able to get at the lock.

"That's first-class work—easy to see that you're a professional cracksman," Valya said with a laugh.

"Besides cracksmen there are people in the world called locksmiths," Sergei replied. He turned round to her and grinned.

With the chisel from his penknife he poked about in the lock and opened the door, and, from under the sun-baked iron roof, the hot attic smell of sand and dust and cobwebs was wafted into their faces.

Ducking to avoid the rafters they made their way to one of the windows. It was thickly coated with dust but they did not wipe it—they did not want to risk being seen from the street below. With their cheeks almost touching they pressed their faces close to the pane.

Below them they could see Sadovaya Street running off from the park gate; they had a good view of the side with the houses of the regional Party committee staff, and directly opposite them on a corner was the two-storey building of the Trust.

Between the time when Sergei had left the Verkhneduvannaya Grove and the present moment, when he and Valya were pressing their faces to the attic window, the German units had entered the town: their lorries were crowding each other all along Sadovaya Street and here and there German soldiers could be seen.

"Germans! So that's what they look like! Germans in our Krasnodon!" Valya thought. Her heart thumped in her breast.

Sergei was more concerned with the external, practical aspect of the matter. His keen eyes took in everything that lay within his field of vision from the attic window and automatically committed every detail to memory.

The school was no more than ten yards from the Trust building and was the higher of the two; Sergei looked down upon the iron roof of the Trust and could see into the first-floor rooms and the floor boards near the windows of the ground-floor rooms. In addition to Sadovaya Street Sergei could also discern others although his view of them was partly obstructed by the houses. He could see how the German soldiers were lording it in the gardens and yards and he began to comment to Valya on what he saw.

"The bushes, they're hacking down all the bushes," he said. "They're even cutting down the sunflowers! It looks as though they're making the Trust their headquarters. Look how they're spreading themselves!"

German officers and soldiers—clerical staff apparently—were settling themselves in on both floors of the Trust building. All were in a gay mood; they flung the windows open and wandered about inspecting the rooms they had been allocated; they rummaged through the drawers of the desks, smoking and tossing their cigarette ends out into the deserted lane which separated the Trust building from the school. After a time several Russian women, young and old, appeared in one or other of the rooms and, with skirts tucked up, began to wash the floor. The neat, clean German clerks exchanged witticisms at their expense.

All this took place so close to Valya and Sergei that all at once an idea began to steal into Sergei's mind. It was as yet vague and incomplete, cruel and tormenting, but it gave him pleasure. He went so far as to take note of the fact that the attic windows could be removed with ease: their light sashes were held in the window-frames by thin nails driven at an angle into the frames.

Sergei and Valya had been sitting in the attic for some time now and they began to talk of irrelevant matters.

"You never saw Styopa Safonov again, did you?" Sergei asked.

"No."

That means that she hasn't had a chance to say anything to him yet, thought Sergei with satisfaction.

"He'll show up all right—he's a good lad," he said. "How d'you plan to live now?"

Valya shrugged her shoulders with a haughty air.

"How can one say? No one knows yet what things'll be like."

"That's true," Sergei said. "Is it all right to come and see you some time? Parents won't mind?"

"Parents? Come tomorrow if you like. I'll get Styopa to come as well."

"What's your name?"

"Valya Borts."

At that moment they suddenly heard several long bursts from tommy-guns, then a few shorter ones. They came from the direction of the Verkhneduvannaya Grove.

"Firing—hear it?" Valya asked.

"God knows what's happening in the town while we're sitting here," Sergei said gravely. "For all we know the Germans may have planted themselves in our own homes by now."

It was only then that Valya realized how she had gone off from home; it struck her that Sergei might be right and that her parents would be worried about her. But pride would not allow her to be the first to say that it was time for her to go home. Sergei, however, had never been concerned with what other people might think of him.

"It's time we went home," he said.

They left the building as they had entered it.

For a few moments they stood by the fence in the front garden. They felt slightly embarrassed after sitting together up in the attic.

"See you tomorrow then," Sergei said.

When he arrived home Sergei heard the news which he later passed on to Volodya Osmukhin: that the wounded left in the hospital had been taken out of it and that Doctor

Fyodor Fyodorovich had been killed. He had been told by his sister Nadya, who had witnessed it all.

Two cars and several lorries full of SS troops had pulled up at the hospital. Natalya Alexeyevna went outside and was given orders to clear the premises within half an hour. She at once instructed all who could move to transfer to the children's hospital. At the same time she requested an extension of the time limit giving as a reason the fact that she had numerous bed cases and no transport for them.

The officers had already resumed their seats in the cars.

"Fehnbong! What does that woman want?" shouted a senior officer to a tall, hulking N.C.O. with gold teeth and light horn-rimmed glasses. Then the cars drove off.

Although the horn-rimmed glasses did not give the N.C.O. the appearance of a scientist, they did at least make him look an intellectual. But when Natalya Alexeyevna approached him with her request and even tried to speak to him in German his eyes stared through the glasses and seemed to look past her. In an almost effeminate voice he proceeded to summon his men, who started to herd the patients out into the yard without waiting for the allotted half-hour to pass.

They dragged them out on their mattresses or simply seized hold of them under the arms and flung them on the lawn outside the entrance.

And then they discovered that there were wounded soldiers in the hospital.

Fyodor Fyodorovich came forward as a surgeon of the municipal hospital and tried to explain that these were all extremely serious cases none of whom would ever be able to fight again; that they had been placed under civilian care. The N.C.O. maintained that since they were soldiers they had become prisoners of war and would have to be taken to the proper place. And the wounded were then dragged out of their beds in their underclothing and flung just as they fell, one on top of the other, into the lorries.

Knowing Fyodor Fyodorovich's quick temper, Natalya Alexeyevna suggested to him to go away, but he remained standing in the corridor between two windows. His dark sunburnt face had turned ashen. His lips were rolling round what was left of a hand-rolled cigarette; his knees were trembling so much that he bent over now and again to rub them with his hand. Natalya Alexeyevna was afraid to leave him alone and asked Nadya not to go away either until everything was over. It was pitiful and terrible to watch the half-dressed wounded men in their blood-stained bandages being dragged through the corridor—simply dragged at times along the floor. Nadya did not dare to weep, though tears rolled down her face without her noticing; but at the same time she did not go away, because she was so much more afraid for the doctor.

Two Germans were dragging along a wounded man who had had one of his kidneys, damaged by a mortar shell splinter, removed by Fyodor Fyodorovich some two weeks previously. His condition had much improved in the past few days and the doctor was very proud of the operation. As the Germans dragged this man along the corridor one of them was called away by N.C.O. Fehnbong. The soldier let go his hold on the feet of the wounded man and ran off into the ward. The second soldier began unaided to pull the wounded man over the floor.

Fyodor Fyodorovich suddenly detached himself from the wall and darted over to the wounded man before anyone knew what was happening. Like most of the others this man had not uttered a sound despite the agony he was suffering. When he saw the doctor he said:

"Look, Fyodor Fyodorovich—look what they're doing! Are they human?"

And he burst into tears.

The doctor said something in German. Probably he said that that was not the way to do it. And it was probable too that he added, "I'll give you a hand with him." But the German soldier laughed and continued to drag the wounded man over the floor. At that moment Fehnbong came out of the ward and Fyodor Fyodorovich walked straight up to him. The doctor's face was ashen and he trembled all over. He almost brushed against the N.C.O. and said something to him in a sharp voice. The N.C.O., in a black uniform which was creased over his bulky frame, a shining metal badge with the skull and cross-bones on his chest, grunted something in reply and thrust a pistol into the doctor's face.

Fyodor Fyodorovich fell back and again said something— probably something very offensive. And then, with his eyes bulging terribly behind the spectacles, the N.C.O. shot Fyodor Fyodorovich straight between the eyes. Nadya had seen his forehead fall away while the blood spurted out and Fyodor Fyodorovich fell to the ground. Natalya Alexeyevna and Nadya had run out of the hospital and Nadya could not remember how she had got home.

Nadya was sitting there in her cap and white overalls just as she had run out of the hospital and again and again told the story. She did not cry, she was very white, her small cheek-bones were a flaming red and her shining eyes did not see the people to whom she told all this.

"Hear that, you!... Loafer!" Coughing angrily the father rounded on Sergei. "By God, I've a good mind to thrash the hide off you! Germans in the town and he's loafing about all over the place! It's enough to bring your mother to her grave."

Mother began to weep.

"I was worried to death about you. I thought they'd killed you!"

"Killed me!" Sergei said with sudden rancour. "No, they didn't kill me. They killed the wounded though. In the grove. I heard it."

He passed through to the living-room and threw himself on the bed, burying his face in the pillow. His whole body was filled with a violent craving for vengeance. His breath was laboured. The thought which had worried and tortured him up in the school attic now found an outlet. "Just you wait till it gets dark!" he thought, tossing about on his bed. No force in the world could now restrain him; he would carry out his plan.

They did not light the lamp and went to bed at an early hour. They were all so keyed up, however, that they were unable to get to sleep. There was not the slightest chance of getting out of the house unnoticed—he went out openly as though he was not going further than the yard. Then he darted into the kitchen garden. With his bare hands he dug open one of the pits in which he had hidden the incendiary bottles—it was risky to use a spade at night. He heard the cottage door open, heard Nadya come out a few steps and call softly twice:

"Sergei!"

She waited a moment, called again, then went back into the house and he heard the door close.

He pushed a bottle into each of his trouser pockets, a third inside his shirt. Then under cover of the dark, close July night he set out for the park once more; he made a detour over by Shanghai districts in order to avoid the centre of the town.

The park was still and deserted. And it was particularly quiet inside the school building once he had found his way in through the window forced open earlier in the day. It was so silent there that each step he took seemed to be audible not only to him but all over the town. A dim light from outside filled the tall windows of the staircase and when Sergei climbed past them he felt that anyone hiding in a dark corner could see him against the background of the windows and make a grab at him. He fought down this momentary panic and soon found himself at his observation post in the attic.

For some minutes he sat at the window, although he could see nothing at all now. He simply wanted to get his breath.

Next he felt for the small thin nails which held the window in its frame, gently bent them back and noiselessly removed the window. Fresh cool air blew into his face, for it had been still very hot and stuffy in the attic. After the darkness of the school, and especially of the loft, he was now able to make out what was going on in the street below. He could hear lorries driving through the town and see their moving, dimmed headlights. The ceaseless movement of troops from Verkhneduvannaya continued well into the night. Along the whole road over there he could see the lights shining through the darkness. The headlights of some of the lorries were full on—suddenly from over the hill they would cut across the sky like searchlights or light up a section of the steppe, showing the white undersides of the leaves in the grove.

The army's night activities continued outside the main gates of the Trust. Lorries and motor cycles kept driving up. Soldiers and officers were continually coming and going and there was a perpetual clicking of heels and clattering of weapons. Harsh, alien speech could be heard. But the windows of the Trust building were blacked out.

Sergei's senses were so much on the alert, his mind was so concentrated on his single purpose that the unforeseen circumstance of the blacked-out windows did not make him alter his decision. He remained seated at the window for at least two hours. The town had grown quite silent. All movement outside the Trust had also ceased but inside they were not yet asleep. Sergei knew that much because of the narrow chinks of light along the edges of the black-out paper. Then the light went out in two of the windows on the first floor, and first one window, then the other was pushed open from the inside. Sergei sensed that somebody invisible to him against the dark interior of the room was standing at the window. More lights were put out on the ground floor and those windows also opened.

"*Wer ist da?*" suddenly came an authoritative voice from a first-floor window and Sergei could vaguely discern a figure leaning out over the sill. "Who's there?" repeated the voice.

"*Leutnant* Meyer, *Herr Oberst*," replied a youthful voice from below.

"I shouldn't advise you to open the windows on the ground floor," said the voice above.

"It's terribly close inside, *Herr Oberst*. But of course if you forbid it—"

"Oh, all right—there's no need to be stewed alive. *Sie brauchen nicht zum Schmorbraten werden*," the authoritative voice on the upper floor said with a laugh.

Sergei listened with a beating heart, not understanding a word of German.

Lights were being extinguished everywhere now, blinds were rolled up and windows opened. Here and there snatches of speech came from them. Somebody started whistling. Now and again a match was struck and momentarily lit up a face, cigarette and fingers; then the glowing end of the burning cigarette gleamed for a long time from the depths of the room.

"What an immense country—there seems to be no end to

it. *Da ist ja kein Ende abzusehen,*" said someone at a window, speaking no doubt to a comrade inside the room.

The Germans were going to bed. Silence descended on the building of the Trust and the whole town. Only on the Verkhneduvannaya road were there lorries still rolling along, slashing the sky with the beams from their headlights.

Sergei listened to his heart beating and it seemed to resound all through the attic. It was still very close up there and Sergei was sweating.

Outlined vaguely before him was the Trust building with its windows open, plunged in darkness and sleep. He made out the darkly yawning apertures of the open windows of both floors—yes, the time for action had come.... He made one or two trial swings with his arm, to measure the distance and take his aim.

As soon as he had reached the attic, he had removed the bottles from his pockets and shirt and they now stood beside him. He felt for one of them, grasped it firmly by the neck, took aim and, with all his strength, hurled it through an open ground-floor window. A blinding flash lit up the whole window and even part of the lane between the Trust and the school. In the same instant there was a sound of shattering glass and a small explosion as though a light bulb had burst. Flames burst out of the window. A moment later Sergei flung a second bottle through the window; with a loud crash it burst in the flames. Flames were already raging inside the room, the window-frames were burning, and tongues of fire were licking the wall almost to the first floor. Someone was screaming frantically inside the room, and shouting burst out through the whole building. Sergei seized the third bottle and launched it on its way into the first-floor window directly opposite.

He heard the crash as it exploded and saw the flash which was so powerful that it showed up the whole interior of the attic. But by that time Sergei was far from the window, darting through the door to the dark staircase; down he rushed headlong, with no time to look for the classroom with the open window, and burst into the first room he came to. It was the Staff Room and there he quickly pushed open a window, jumped out and ran as fast as he could into the thicket in the park.

From the moment he hurled the third bottle until he suddenly realized he was running through the park, Sergei had acted quite instinctively and scarcely remembered how everything had happened. But now he knew that he must throw himself flat and lie still for a moment to listen.

He could hear a mouse rustling through the grass near him. From where he lay he could not see the fire, but the shouting and the sounds of people running along the street reached him. He jumped up and ran to the edge of the park near the tip of the disused mine. In the event of the park being surrounded he could get away from there whatever happened.

He could now see a huge red glare spreading wider and wider in the sky, throwing its purple reflection on the gigantic ancient cone of the tip, which was some distance from the fire, and over the tree-tops throughout the park. He felt his heart swelling and almost taking wing. His whole body trembled, he had to keep a firm grip on himself in order not to burst out laughing.

"That'll hold you for a bit, you ... *setzen sie Sich! Sprechen sie Deutsch! Haben sie etwas!*" With indescribable elation in his heart he repeated phrases remembered from his German grammar at school.

The glow from the fire increased still more, tinting the sky over the park, and even here the noise and confusion in the centre of the town reached him. He must get away. He felt an overpowering desire to visit again the garden where earlier in the day he had seen the girl, Valya Borts; yes, now he knew her name.

Noiselessly, he crawled through the darkness and made his way to the back of the Derevyannaya Street houses. He found the garden, climbed over the low fence and was about to pass through the gate to reach the street, when he heard a murmur of soft voices near the gate itself. The Germans had not yet taken over Derevyannaya Street and so the people who lived there had ventured out of their cottages to watch the fire. Sergei ran noiselessly round to the other side of the house, quietly slipped over the garden fence and then approached the gate from the street. A group of women stood there illuminated by the glare from the fire. He recognized Valya among them.

"What's on fire there?" he asked in order to make his presence known to her.

"Must be somewhere in Sadovaya Street ... possibly the school," an agitated woman's voice replied.

"It's the Trust on fire," Valya said sharply, almost provocatively. "I'm going to bed, Mama," she added, pretended to yawn and went through the gate.

Sergei was about to follow her but heard her heels on the steps of the porch and the door shut behind her with a bang.

Chapter 20

KRASNODON and the neighbouring towns and villages lay along the route of the advancing German Army and through them for many days in succession the columns of its main forces rolled ceaselessly: tank formations and motorized infantry, heavy guns and howitzers, communication units and supply trains, medical and engineering units, as well as the commanding staffs of greater and lesser army groupings. A constant drone of engines hovered in the air and rumbled over the ground, and great clouds of dust hung over town and steppe.

In this ponderous, rhythmic movement of countless troops and weapons of war there was a ruthless system— "*die Ordnung.*" There seemed to be no power on earth strong enough to withstand this force with its inexorable iron system—its "*Ordnung.*"

Immense lorries loaded with supplies and munitions and standing as high as railway trucks and flattened elliptical petrol tanks rolled along smoothly and heavily, churning the ground with their huge wheels. The uniforms of the troops seemed of good quality and well-fitting. The officers were even elegant. With the Germans came Rumanians, Italians, Hungarians. The guns, tanks and aircraft of this army bore factory trade-marks from all over Europe. The trade-marks on the lorries and cars alone were enough to stagger the imagination of anyone able to read languages other than Russian and to strike terror into his heart at the thought that the productive forces of most of the countries of Europe were supplying this German Army, which was now moving across the Donets steppe to the accompaniment of roaring engines and through a cloud of dust so enormous that it shut out the sky like a blanket of black fog.

The most insignificant human being versed in the smallest degree in military affairs could feel and see that it was inevitable that before the impact of this force the Soviet armies should be recoiling—some people thought irrevocably—farther and farther to the east and southeast, towards Novocherkassk and Rostov, and across the quiet Don towards the Volga and into the Kuban. And who could truthfully claim to know where they were at this moment? It was only possible from the German communiqués and from the talk of German soldiers to hazard a guess as to where, in what strange parts your son, your father, your husband or brother might now be fighting or already lying dead in the earth of his beloved land.

While German units continued to move through Krasnodon, devouring like locusts everything that had not been devoured by others passing through before them, the administrative sections of the advancing German armies—staff headquarters, supply departments, reserve units—began to billet themselves on the town as securely and efficiently as though they were in their own homes.

For the first few days of life under the rule of the Germans none of the local people could make out which of the German authorities were temporary rulers and which permanent, or what authority had been established in the town and what was expected from its inhabitants, apart from what they had to do in their own homes to suit the whims and desires of passing soldiers and officers. Each family lived for itself and, with an ever increasing realization of their helplessness and the horror of their position, each tried to cope in his own fashion with the new and terrifying situation.

What was new and terrifying in the life of Grandma Vera and Yelena Nikolayevna was the fact that their home had been put at the disposal of one of the German headquarters headed by General Baron von Wentzel, his adjutant and the batman with the straw-coloured hair and pale freckles. There was always a German sentry at the entrance to their house now. It was always full of generals and officers, coming and going as freely as in their own homes, holding conferences or simply eating and drinking, and there was always the sound of their German talk, and of German marches and speeches broadcast from their radio. Grandma Vera and Yelena, the owners of this house, had been pushed into a small, unbearably stuffy room, which was incessantly warmed from the kitchen range adjoining it, and from early morning to late at night they had to wait upon their lordships, the German generals and officers.

Only the day before, Grandma Vera, who had made a name for herself through her work in the countryside and was now an old-age pensioner and the mother of a geologist in one of the largest coal trusts of the Donbas, and Yelena Nikolayevna, the widow of a prominent figure, who had been the manager of the Kanevo Agricultural Department, and mother of the best pupil of one of the Krasnodon schools, had been well-known, respected local personalities. Today they were the complete and absolute subordinates of a German batman with yellow freckles.

General Baron von Wentzel was so much absorbed in military matters that he ignored Grandma Vera and Yelena. He would sit for hours over a map, read and write and sign the papers which his adjutant put before him and drink brandy with other generals. Sometimes he became angry and then he would yell as though he was shouting orders on a parade ground and the other generals would stand before him with their hands to the red stripes of their trousers. It was obvious to Grandma Vera and Yelena that the movement of German troops, with their tanks and guns and planes, through Krasnodon and far into the country, was being carried out by the will of General von Wentzel, and that it was important for the general that they should move and arrive exactly at the time and the place which had been stipulated. But what they did in the places through which they passed was of no interest to General von Wentzel any more than the fact that he was living in the house of Grandma Vera and Yelena Nikolayevna.

Hundreds and thousands of vile, mean actions were committed either by order of General von Wentzel or else with his cold, tacit consent. Something was purloined from every home—lard and honey and butter from Grandma Vera and Yelena. But that did not prevent the general from carrying high and stiff-necked the head with the red Adam's apple, resting so confidently between the palm leaves; it would appear that nothing vile or mean could possibly have ever entered the mind of the general.

The general was very clean about his person: he washed in hot water from head to foot twice daily—in the morning and at night. His narrow wrinkled face and Adam's apple were always clean-shaven, washed and scented. A special lavatory had been built for him which Grandma Vera had to clean out every day; thus the general could do the necessary without sitting on his haunches. He went to the lavatory at exactly the same time every morning and the batman would stand guard near by and listen for the general to cough, when he would hand him the special soft paper. But for all his cleanliness the general would belch loudly after meals, unashamed by the presence of Grandma Vera and Yelena, and when alone in his room he would break wind, without any thought for Grandma Vera or Yelena in the next room.

The long-legged adjutant did his best to ape the general in everything. He seemed to have grown to his height for the express purpose of being as tall as his tall general. And, like him, he endeavoured to avoid noticing Grandma Vera and Yelena.

For the general and his adjutant Grandma Vera and Yelena did not exist, either as people or as objects. The batman was now their sovereign lord and master.

In trying to adjust herself to this new and terrible state of affairs Grandma, within the first few days, had discovered that she was not prepared to reconcile herself to it. Shrewd Grandma Vera had guessed that the batman had not sufficient authority to dare, in the presence of his superiors, to kill her. And with a boldness that increased with each new day, she picked quarrels with him and, when he shouted at her, she shouted back at him. On one occasion, when in a fury he kicked her with his huge boot, she retaliated by hitting him with all her might over the head with a frying-pan, and the flushed and infuriated batman, strange though it may appear, merely choked back his anger. Thus an unusual and complex relationship grew up between Grandma Vera and the freckle-faced batman. Yelena, on the other hand, was still in a state of complete mental torpidity, and holding high her head with the luxuriant crown of fair hair, she would do what was demanded of her mechanically.

One day when Yelena had gone to the back street for water, she suddenly saw driving towards her a small, familiar carriage drawn by a small dun-coloured horse; her son Oleg was walking by the side of the carriage.

She looked round helplessly, dropped the yoke and pails and, with arms outstretched, ran to him.

"My little Oleg ... my boy!" she repeated over and over, first laying her head on his breast and then smoothing his hair, glistening golden in the sun, and patting his shoulders, his chest and his back.

He was the taller of the two, and in the past few days he had become very sunburnt and his face had thinned—somehow he seemed more adult. Yet behind this grown-up appearance, and clearer than ever before, there were the features of her son as she had always known them since before he lisped his first words and took the first bold steps on his little brown legs, when, strong and round though they were, they carried him sideways as though the wind was pushing him off course. He was only a big child, really. With his long firm arms he embraced her, and his eyes shone under the broad light eyebrows with the same clear, pure filial light as they had shone for his mother for the past sixteen and a half years.

"Mama ... Mama!" he reiterated again and again.

In those few moments nothing and nobody mattered to them, neither the two German soldiers watching from a door near by to see whether there was anything in all this that might violate *die Ordnung*, nor the relatives who stood round the carriage and each with different emotions watched the reunion of mother and son. Nikolai Nikolayevich was indifferent and dismal, Aunt Marina had tears in her dark, beautiful, tired eyes, the three-year-old was surprised and annoyed because Aunt Yelena had not first picked him up and kissed him; and Grandpa, the driver, wore the tactful expression of old age which seemed to say, "Well ... the things that do happen in this world!" And all the kind folk who behind their windows were secretly watching this union of two people who were so much alike—he with the bare head and sunburnt brown face and she a very young-looking woman with lovely plaits twined round her head—might easily have assumed that this was a meeting of brother and sister. Only they knew that this was Oleg Koshevoi returning to his mother just as hundreds and thousands of other Krasnodon townsfolk were returning after their unsuccessful efforts to leave calamity behind them; all were now returning to their families, to their cottages where the Germans were now in possession.

These were hard times for the people who had left their hearth and home and their dear ones. But those who had succeeded in getting away from the Germans were now walking in their own, their Soviet Land. How much harder was the position of those who had strained every effort to escape from the Germans only to find their efforts had been in vain, to see death staring them in the face and to be wandering now over the land of their birth which only yesterday had been theirs but now had become German; to be wandering about without food and shelter, alone in their despondency, thrown on the mercy of the first German conqueror they chanced to meet and regarded by him as criminals!

When Oleg and his comrades saw the German tanks coming straight at them out of the misty, white glare over the open sunlit steppe, their hearts quaked; it was the first time they had come face to face with death. But death was in no hurry.

German motor cyclists had rounded up all the people who had failed to get across the Donets and herded them in one spot near the river. And so Oleg and his comrades had again encountered Vanya Zemnukhov, with Klava and her mother and Valko, the director of 1B Pit. Valko had been soaked to the skin. His jacket and trousers were dripping into his calf-leather knee boots.

During the general commotion no one had paid much attention to anyone else, but when Valko came into view, everyone thought: "Even he hadn't managed to swim across the river!" Valko himself, with an expression of concentrated anger on his unshaven, swarthy, gypsy face, had seated himself on the ground, pulled off his sturdy boots and poured the water out of them. Then he had wrung out his socks, put both socks and boots on his feet again, turned his lugubrious face towards the young people and suddenly all but winked at them: it was the tiniest of flickers of the lid of one of his dark eyes, as if to say, "Courage! I'm here with you!"

A German tank officer with an angry, smoke-begrimed face, wearing a black beret, had shouted an order in broken Russian to the effect that all army men were to step out from the crowd. Soldiers, already unarmed, had stepped out singly or in groups. The Germans had led them away, pushing them on with their rifle-butts, and soon they formed a separate smaller group exclusively of army men, standing a short distance from the larger civilian group. There was something strikingly sad in the faces and glances of these men as they stood close to one another in their soiled battle-worn tunics and dusty boots, in the middle of the bright sunlit steppe.

They were formed into one column and driven off upstream along the river. All the civilians had been allowed to disperse to their homes.

Gradually, the people had begun to move off in all directions, leaving the Donets behind them. The majority strung out along the road to the west, towards Likhaya and past the farm where Zhora and Vanya had found shelter during the night.

When Victor Petrov's father and Grandpa, who was driving the Koshevois' *britzka*, saw the German tanks coming over the steppe, they had immediately joined up with their own people, and so it came about that the whole of this group, which now included Klava and her mother, fell in with the stream of people going off to the west along the road to Likhaya.

For a time none of them believed that things were what they seemed—that they had been let off like this without there being some hidden trick. Consequently, they cast apprehensive glances at the columns of German troops moving along the road in the opposite direction. But the weary, sweating soldiers with their dust-smeared faces and their thoughts on what lay ahead of them scarcely so much as looked at the Russian refugees.

Then, when the initial shock had worn off, someone surmised doubtfully:

"There must be an order from the German command not to hurt the local people...."

Valko, steaming in the heat of the sun like a horse, emitted a short mirthless laugh. He jerked his head towards the ill-tempered Germans with faces as black as devils'.

"Can't you see they're in a hurry? Or they'd stop and give you a taste of the river-bottom!" he said.

"You've already had a taste—by the look of you!" called one of those irrepressible voices which unfailingly make themselves heard, even under the most alarming circumstances, when Russians are gathered together.

"I've had my taste, yes," Valko agreed ruefully. Then pensively he added, "But I haven't drained the cup yet."

This is what had actually happened when Valko left the boys standing on the river-bank and pushed his way through to the crossing.

His fierce appearance helped him to get one of the soldiers in charge of the bridge to answer his questions and he learned from him that the officers in command of the crossing were on the other side of the river. "I'm going to see to it that he with his good-for-nothings gets some sort of order into this mess here!" was Valko's enraged thought as he leapt from pontoon to pontoon by the side of the line of lorries rolling over the bridge. Just then the German raiders came over and together with other pontoon-jumpers he had to lie down flat. Then the German artillery opened fire and panic broke out on the pontoon bridge. That was when he began to have second thoughts.

Because of his position he not only had the right but was in duty bound to avail himself of the last chance to get across the river. But as often happens in the life of even the strongest and most sober-minded types, with hot blood coursing at boiling-point through their veins, personal duty, less important but closer to them, prevails over social duty, which is more important, but farther removed from them.

Valko pictured to himself what his workers would think of him, and his friend Grigory Shevtsov and the young Komsomols standing on the river-bank—and hardly had he done so than the blood rushed to his swarthy face and he turned round to go back. By that time an avalanche of people covering the width of the bridge was rushing towards him. So forthwith, in his clothes, Valko dived into the river and swam back to the shore.

While the Germans were shelling the stretch of river-bank and surrounding it, people from that river-bank were making a frantic rush over the pontoons towards the other bank and a struggle had broken out on the bridge ramp; in tens and hundreds they tried to swim their way across to the other side—Valko, cleaving the waves with his strong arms, did swim over to the river-bank. He knew he would be one of the first to be dealt with by the Germans, but he had kept on swimming because his conscience would not allow him to act otherwise.

Unfortunately for them, the Germans could not anticipate events and so they did not kill Valko but let him go with the others. Here he was then in the west-bound stream of refugees instead of on his way to the east, to Saratov, where he was supposed to report for work and where his wife and children were awaiting him.

The whole, mixed column of refugees began to disperse before reaching Likhaya. Valko suggested that the group of Krasnodon people should split off, bypass Likhaya and proceed to Krasnodon, not along the main roads, but by country roads and even over the open countryside.

Always during difficult periods in the life of a nation or a state the thoughts of even the most ordinary people about their own fate are always closely intertwined with concern for the whole nation.

During the first days after their recent experiences, both adults and children were in a dejected mood and hardly spoke to one another. Their minds were not only troubled by thoughts of their own immediate future; it seemed to them that the fate of their Soviet Land was in the balance. And each brooded over these problems in his own particular way.

Marina's baby boy—Oleg's cousin—was, however, in a state of perfect mental equilibrium. He had not the slightest doubt about the permanence of the world he lived in— were not his Mama and Papa constantly in sight? True, he had experienced one terrible moment when something in the sky started to roar and thunder, and all the people round him began to run and there were crashing noises all around.

But he lived at a time when there were a great many crashing noises everywhere and people were always running; so he just cried a little and then was quiet again. And now everything was good, he felt, except that the journey seemed rather too long. This feeling came over him around midday which was when he always began to feel bored with it, and then he would start to whimper; how long would it be before he would be home with Grandma? But then they all stopped to rest, and he got his porridge; and after that he enjoyed himself poking a twig into the molehills and cautiously circling round the two bay horses, each of which was almost twice as big as the little dun-coloured pony; then came the sweetness of a sleep in Mama's lap, and everything was in complete order again and the whole world was filled anew with wonders and delight.

Grandpa thought that a little old man like himself could hardly be in danger from the Germans. But he was afraid that the Germans might take his horse away from him before they reached home. Then they might deprive him of the pension he was getting after forty years' work as colliery carter; and he would not only lose the allowances for his three sons in the army, but would most likely suffer precisely because he had three sons in the Red Army. And would Russia win the war? That worried him considerably, for judging by what he had seen he was very much afraid that Russia would not win the war. The little old man with the straggling fringe of grey hair at the back of his head, making him somehow look like a sparrow, began to regret very much that he had not died last winter when, as the doctor had said, he had had an "attack." But sometimes he thought of his past life, and he recalled the wars he had fought in himself and remembered how great and rich Russia was and how much richer she was now, after the past ten years. Surely the Germans weren't strong enough to conquer Russia? And when that thought struck Grandpa he became lively in a nervous sort of way and scratched his sun-blackened ankles. Then he pursed his lips like a child and started to make encouraging noises to the little dun-coloured pony and slap the reins across its back.

Oleg's uncle, Nikolai Nikolayevich, was a young geologist who, after working only a few years at the Trust, had already done some remarkably successful research work. To him the most galling thing was the fact that after making such a good start, it had all come to such an unexpected, wretched halt. He thought the Germans would most certainly kill him, and if they did not, then he would have to muster considerable resourcefulness to avoid working for them. He knew that under no condition would he work for them because he would find that as distasteful and unnatural as walking on all fours.

Young Aunt Marina was reckoning up their joint source of income before the arrival of the Germans. And she found that they had been living on Nikolai Nikolayevich's salary plus the pension of Yelena Nikolayevna, which she had been receiving since the death of her husband, Oleg's stepfather, plus Grandma Vera's pension, plus the house supplied by the Trust, plus the kitchen garden which they worked themselves. With the arrival of the Germans, they lost first three sources of income and would possibly lose the others as well. Often she thought of all the children at the bridge who had been killed and while grieving for them she thought of her own small boy and began to weep. She recalled the stories she had heard about how the Germans molested and raped the women and, horror-struck, she realized that she was attractive and could expect to be pestered by them, but her fears were allayed by the thought that she would dress simply and change her hair style and then, perhaps, everything would be all right.

Victor Petrov's father, the forester, knew that on their return he and his son would be in mortal danger for he was a well-known figure in the district, because he had fought the Germans in 1918, and his son was a Komsomol. Yet try as he might, he was unable to plan what steps he should take. He had no doubt that some of the Party people had stayed behind in order to organize underground work and the partisan struggle. But as far as he was concerned he was already middle-aged; all his life he had carried out his work as an ordinary forester to the best of his ability and had come to think that he would remain a forester to the end of his days. He had planned to give his son and daughter a good education and set them on their feet. But when the thought now stole into his mind that his past life could remain undisclosed and that he would be able to continue working as a forester under the Germans, he became filled with such longing and at the same time disgust that, big strong man that he was, he naturally wanted to fight.

His son meanwhile was feeling extremely hurt and insulted on behalf of the Red Army. From his childhood he had worshipped the Red Army and its commanders and since the outbreak of the war he had been preparing himself to take part in it as a Red Army commander. At school he had run a military circle and, rain or shine, had held the classes on military subjects and conducted the physical training, just as Suvorov had done. In Victor's eyes the Red Army retreat could not, of course, harm its prestige. But it hurt that he had not been able to join up from the outset as a commander. He was sure that if he had been a Red Army commander in these days, the Army would never have got itself into such a difficult and distressing situation. As for his own fate under the Germans, Victor had not given it a thought. He relied entirely on his father and on his friend Anatoly Popov, who always found surprising, yet perfectly correct solutions to life's most difficult situations.

Meanwhile, his friend Anatoly was deeply worried about his Motherland. Biting his finger-nails and not saying a word he had spent the whole journey wondering what course of action he should take now. Since the war began he had made numerous speeches about the defence of the Motherland at Komsomol meetings but in none of them had he been able to convey his conception of the Motherland as something great and throbbing with life and song, something like Taisya Prokofievna, his own mother, with her tall, plump figure, her kind rosy face and her beautiful old Cossack songs which he could remember her singing since he was in his cradle. This conception of his Motherland was always in his heart and brought tears to his eyes when he heard his favourite songs or saw the trampled wheat or a burnt-out cottage. And now calamity had come to the Motherland, calamity so great that the mere thought stabbed him to the heart. He must act, and act immediately, but how, where, and with whom?

Thoughts like these agitated all his comrades to a greater or lesser degree.

Ulya was the only one who had no strength left to think

about her own fate or that of her country. Everything she had experienced since she had witnessed the tottering engine-house tower of 1B Pit: the parting from her mother and her dearest friend, the journey in the broiling sun over the trampled steppe and, finally, the river crossing where the sight of the blood-stained upper half of the woman with the red kerchief still on the head and the boy with eyes bursting from their sockets, all this again and again revolved in her bleeding heart, sometimes keen as a knife, sometimes heavy as a millstone. She walked the whole journey in silence, apparently at ease, by the side of the wagon; only the outlines of a hidden strength to be seen in her eyes, her nostrils, her lips, revealed the storm that was raging in her heart.

To Zhora, on the other hand, it was perfectly obvious how he would exist under the Germans. With great authority he argued aloud:

"Cannibals! Is it possible, d'you think, for our people to put up with them? They'll most certainly take up arms, just as they have where the Germans have already taken over. My father is a quiet sort of chap, but I've no doubt he'll take up arms. And my mother? With her character, she's sure to take up arms, too. And if that's how our old people will behave, then how should we young ones act? We, the youth, must make a list, that is, we must find them first and then make a list," he corrected himself, "of all the young people who have not evacuated and then, without delay, get in touch with the underground organization. I know, for one, that Volodya Osmukhin and Tolya Orlov are left in Krasnodon—d'you think they'll sit there with folded arms? And Volodya's sister Lyudmila, what a fine girl she is!" he interjected with feeling. "She'll most certainly not sit about doing nothing!"

Choosing a moment when no one but Klava was within earshot, Vanya Zemnukhov said to Zhora:

"Look here, *abrek!** Nobody's contradicting you, I assure you. But hold your tongue! In the first place, this is a matter of conscience and, secondly, you can't vouch for everybody. Suppose one of them were to fail us? Then what would happen to you and to all of us?"

* Mounted irregular of the Caucasian tribes resisting the Russian conquest early in the 19th century.

"Why did you call me an *Abrek*?" Zhora asked and in his dark eyes appeared an expression of inspired self-satisfaction.

"Because you're so swarthy and behave like a wild horseman."

"You know what, Vanya? When I go underground I'll most certainly adopt the nickname *Abrek*," Zhora said, dropping his voice to a whisper.

Vanya shared Zhora's thoughts and moods. Only intruding into every thought that occupied Vanya's mind was the happiness of Klava's proximity and the pride he felt when he remembered his behaviour at the bridge and again heard Kovalyov saying, "Vanya ... save them...." He felt that he had, indeed, rescued Klava. The feeling of happiness was all the more complete since Klava shared it. Had it not been for her anxiety about her father and the mournful lamentations of her mother, Klava would have been frankly and openly happy here, with her dearest friend, in the sunlit Donets steppe, in spite of the fact that the turrets of German tanks and the barrels of AA guns and helmets, helmets and more helmets of German soldiers racing through the golden wheat to the roar of engines and in clouds of dust could be seen here and there on the horizon.

Yet among all these people engrossed in their various thoughts about their own fate and that of all the population, there were two who, although greatly differing in age and character, were surprisingly alike in that both were in a state of extraordinary enthusiasm and full of spirited activity. One of these was Valko, the other Oleg.

Valko was a man of few words and no one could ever tell what went on behind his outward gypsy appearance. It seemed that everything had gone wrong for him, yet never had he appeared so lively and gay. He made the whole journey on foot, did what he could to take care of everybody, willingly chatted with the boys, each of them in turn, as though sounding them, and joked with them more and more.

And Oleg too was unable to remain still in the carriage. He expressed his impatience aloud, wanting to know how long it would be before he at last saw his mother and Grandma. He would rub his finger-tips pleasurably while listening to Zhora Arutyuniants, then suddenly start jeering at Vanya and Klava or, stuttering timidly, would try to comfort Ulya, or nurse his little cousin, or make love to Aunt Marina, or enter into long political discussions with the old man. Sometimes he would walk by the side of the *britzka* silently, with deep furrows on his brow, his stubborn, full lips still like a child's touched by a smile, his eyes straining into the distance with a stern, tender, pensive expression in them.

When they were less than a day's journey from Krasnodon they encountered a stray unit of German soldiers. In a business-like manner—even without being very rough, but just in a business-like manner—the soldiers ransacked both vehicles, took away every silk article from Marina's and Ulya's cases, pulled the boots from the feet of Victor's father and Valko and, in addition, relieved Valko of a very old gold watch which, despite the plunge into the river, was going very well.

The strain they experienced during this first direct clash with the Germans, from whom all of them had expected worse, gave way to general embarrassment all round and then to an unnatural animation: they all imitated the German soldiers looting the carts, they teased Marina who was very distressed at losing her silk stockings and they did not spare Valko or Victor's father who, in breeches and with their feet in slippers, were more disconcerted than anyone else.

Oleg alone did not participate in this false merriment and for a long time his face wore an expression of intense anger.

They reached the outskirts of Krasnodon after dark and on Valko's advice, since he assumed that all movement by night was prohibited, they did not enter the town but camped in a ravine near by. It was a bright moonlit night. They were excited and no one could sleep for a long time.

Valko went off by himself to explore the ravine. Suddenly he heard footsteps following him. He stopped abruptly, turned round and, by the light of the moon shining on the dew, recognized Oleg.

"Comrade Valko! I have to talk to you on a very urgent matter. Very urgent," Oleg said, stuttering slightly, his voice very soft.

"All right. Only we'll have to do it standing. It's very damp," Valko said, and laughed.

"Help me to find someone of our underground people in the town," Oleg said, looking searchingly into Valko's downcast eyes beneath their bushy eyebrows.

Valko looked up quickly and for some moments studied Oleg's face closely.

Before him stood a representative of the new, the very young generation.

Character traits which on the surface seemed quite irreconcilable—dreaminess and the urge for action, flights of fancy and sound common sense, ruthlessness and a love of everything good, generosity and sober calculation, self-control and delight in the earthly pleasures—all these apparently contradictory traits together made up the unique mould of this new generation.

And Valko knew it well, this new generation, for to a great extent it was a chip off himself.

"I would say you've already found one," he said and smiled. "We can now go on to discuss what next."

Oleg waited in silence.

"You've been thinking about this for some time, I can see that," Valko said.

He was right. Without disclosing his intention to his mother for the first time, Oleg had gone to the district Komsomol committee as soon as the immediate threat to Voroshilovgrad had become apparent and put forward a request to be made use of in organizing underground groups.

He had been very hurt when, without explanations of any sort, he had been told something like this:

"Look here, young fellow, get your things together and clear out of town if you know what's good for you! And look sharp about it!"

He had not known that the district Komsomol committee was not setting up its own independent groups and that those of the Komsomols who were to remain behind at the disposal of the underground network had been selected much earlier. Therefore the reply he had received, far from being unkind, had even in a certain sense been an expression of solicitude for a comrade. And so he had had to leave.

The moment the initial shock of the events at the bridge had passed, Oleg realized that he had failed to get out and the thought actually cheered him, for now his dream would come true. All the hardships of the flight, the parting from his mother, the uncertainty of his fate simply slipped from his mind. All his mental powers, all his passions, dreams and hopes, all the ardour and urge of youth rushed to the surface.

"And because your mind is made up, you are so collected," Valko continued. "I'm just like that myself. Only yesterday I was marching along there and I couldn't get it all out of my mind: how we blew up the pits and the way the Red Army's retreating, the tragedy of the children and the refugees. My thoughts were so black," he said with unusual candour. "I should have been happy because I was soon to be with my family again, I haven't seen any of them since the war started. Yet deep in here something kept saying, 'And then— what?' That was yesterday. And what about today? Our army has withdrawn. The Germans have got us in their clutches. I shall not see my family, maybe I shall never see them again. But my mind is easy. Why? Because now the road before me is clear. And that's the most important thing for people like us."

Oleg felt that now, in this ravine outside Krasnodon, here in the moonlight shining beautifully in the dew, this stern, reticent man with the eyebrows that met in the middle had spoken to him, Oleg, with greater frankness than he had ever shown to anyone before.

"Now listen! Don't you lose contact with the other boys, they're good fellows," Valko said. "Don't give yourself away but keep in touch with them. And seek out some more and study them to see whether they'll suit. They must be as solid as rock. But don't you do anything without my knowledge—you'll only make a mess of it. I'll tell you what to do and when."

"Do you know who's stayed behind in town?" Oleg asked.

"I don't," Valko admitted frankly. "I don't, but I'll find out."

"And how shall I find you?"

"It won't be necessary for you to find me. And if I had a home I shouldn't tell you where it was. But so far I haven't got one, to tell the truth."

Sad as the task would be to bring news of the death of husband and father, Valko had nevertheless made up his mind to take shelter for the time being with the Shevtsovs, who knew him well and liked him. With the help of a keen lass like Lyuba he hoped to establish contacts and find a place to live somewhere in an out-of-the-way area.

"Better let me have your address so that I can find you."

Valko repeated Oleg's address several times in order to commit it to memory.

"Don't worry, I shall look you up," Valko said quietly. "And if you don't hear from me soon, just sit tight. Better go now." His big hand gently pushed Oleg's shoulder.

"Thank you," Oleg's voice was barely audible.

With unaccountable elation which seemed to carry him along over the dewy grass he walked back towards the camp. The horses were still grazing, but everyone was asleep, except Vanya Zemnukhov, who was sitting by the heads of Klava and her mother with his hands clasped round his bony knee.

"Good old Vanya," thought Oleg with a tenderness which he now felt for all the people. He walked up to his comrade and sat down beside him on the damp grass, excitement in his heart.

Vanya raised his face, which was pale in the light of the moon.

"Well? What did he say?" he asked breezily in his deep voice.

"What are you talking about?" Oleg said, taken aback and disturbed at the same time.

"What did Valko say? Does he know anything?"

Oleg looked at him hesitantly.

Vanya showed annoyance. "Look, don't let's play hide-and-seek—surely we're not children!"

Oleg looked at him in growing bewilderment. "How d-d-did you know?" he whispered, wide-eyed.

"There's nothing clever about recognizing your underground contacts," Vanya smiled. "They're the same as mine! Can you possibly imagine I hadn't thought about it all?"

"Vanya!" Oleg's large hands firmly gripped Zemnukhov's slim one and received an energetic handshake in return. "Then we're together!"

"Of course."

"Always?"

"Yes, always!" Vanya said very softly and gravely. "As long as the blood flows in my veins."

They looked at each other, their eyes shining.

"See here, he knows nothing at all yet. But he says he'll find out. And he will, too!" There was a ring of pride in Oleg's voice. "You see to it that you don't get stuck in Nizhny Alexandrovsky."

"I shan't, don't worry," Vanya said with a determined shake of the head. He showed some embarrassment. "I shall only see them settled in there."

"D'you love her?" Oleg asked in a whisper and bent close to Vanya's face.

"One doesn't talk about that sort of thing, you know."

"Oh, don't be shy about it. It's good, it's a very good thing! She's such a w-w-wonderful person and y-y-you are too!" Oleg said with a naïve, happy expression in his face and in his voice.

"Yes, with all we and all the rest have to go through, life still remains wonderful," Vanya said.

"That's t-t-true," Oleg stuttered and the tears came to his eyes.

Little more than a week had passed since fate had led all these different people, adults and children, out on to the steppe. And now the sun rose and shone on all of them together for the last time. It was as though a lifetime lay behind them, so warm and sad and moving were their farewells when the time came to part.

Valko, in breeches and slippers, stood by himself in the middle of the ravine. "Well then, lads and lasses ..." he began, then made a helpless gesture with his swarthy hand and fell silent.

The boys exchanged addresses, promised to keep in touch and said good-bye. A long time after they had separated and gone off in different directions they could still see each other and someone waved a handkerchief here, an arm there. Then the first disappeared over a hill, then a second, just as though they had never made the journey together through those frightful days under the blazing sun.

Thus Oleg crossed the threshold of his own dear home, where Germans had now taken up their abode.

Chapter 21

MARINA with her little son moved into the tiny room by the kitchen, where Grandma Vera and Yelena Nikolayevna were living; Nikolai Nikolayevich and Oleg knocked up two trestle-beds out of planks and settled themselves in the wood-shed.

Grandma Vera who had become bored without an audience—she could not very well regard the freckled batman as someone to talk to—immediately heaped on them a spate of news about the town.

Two days previously hand-written Bolshevik leaflets had been found posted on the walls of the gatemen's huts at the larger pits, of the Gorky and Voroshilov schools, the district committee and a few other buildings. The leaflets were signed: "Krasnodon District Committee of the Communist Party of the Soviet Union (Bolsheviks)." The surprising thing was that back numbers of *Pravda* with pictures of Lenin and Stalin had been pasted up by the side of the leaflets. And rumour had it that conversations overheard between the German soldiers revealed that attacks had been made by partisans on German transport and troop units in various parts of the region, especially along the Donets, along the border between the Voroshilovgrad and Rostov regions and in the Bokovo-Antratsit and Kremensk districts.

Not a single Communist or Komsomol had so far reported to the German Commandant for special registration ("What? Go and put my head into their noose? I'll see 'em in hell first!" was Grandma Vera's comment), but many of them had already been discovered and arrested. Not a single factory or office was working, yet the Commandant's orders were that the people were to report at their jobs and sit out the prescribed hours. Grandma said that Barakov, an engineer-mechanic, and Filipp Petrovich Lyutikov had reported for work at the Central Electrical Machine Workshops of the Krasnodon Coal Trust. According to rumours, far from harming them the Germans had made Barakov manager of the workshops and Lyutikov superintendent of the machine-shop, which had been his former post.

"And who'd have expected it from people like that? They're old Party members! Barakov's seen active service, been wounded. And Lyutikov! He's a public figure. Everybody knows him! Have they gone mad—working for the Germans?" Grandma was puzzled and indignant.

She also told them that the Germans were hunting out the Jewish townsfolk and taking them to Voroshilovgrad where a ghetto was said to have been set up. But many people maintained that in actual fact they were only taken as far as the Verkhneduvannaya Grove where they were killed and buried. And Maria Borts was terribly worried for fear someone might betray her husband.

The moment Oleg arrived home the stupor which had lain on Yelena since he had left, and especially since the arrival of the Germans, vanished as though by magic. She was now in the perpetual state of mental tension and energetic activity which was typical of her nature. Like a mother eagle with an eaglet fallen from the nest she hovered round her boy. And he would frequently catch her strained, anxious glance resting on him: "How is it, my son? Will you be strong enough to bear it all, my son?"

He, on the other hand, had lost the moral enthusiasm of the journey; his feelings had become numbed. Things had not turned out as he had imagined they would.

To the youth about to enter into battle, it appears in dreams like an uninterrupted series of heroic exploits against violence and evil. But the evil proved to be elusive and unbearably, abominably prosaic.

Oleg had spent much of his time with the shaggy good-natured black dog, but now it was dead. The street looked bare now that the trees and bushes had been hacked down in the backyards and front gardens. And the Germans strolling along the bare street seemed paltry, insignificant.

General Baron von Wentzel took no more notice of Oleg, Marina and Nikolai Nikolayevich than he did of Grandma Vera and Yelena. And it was true to say that Grandma Vera found nothing offensive in the general's attitude towards herself.

"It's just that 'new order' of theirs," she said. "I'm an old woman and from what my grandfather told me I can tell that it's an old order and no different from the order we had under serfdom—there were Germans here then, too; landlords they were and just as hard and stuck-up as this baron here—

may his eyes drop out! Why should I feel offended by him? He'd be just the same, until the day our troops come back and tear the gizzard out of him."

But in Oleg's eyes it was the general with his narrow shining boots and the well-washed Adam's apple who was chiefly to blame for the insupportable humiliation of Oleg and his family and everyone else in the neighbourhood, and the only way to get rid of this feeling of degradation seemed to be to kill the general. But there would only be another general in his place, and he would probably be exactly like this one, shining polished boots, well-washed Adam's apple and all.

The long-legged adjutant began to pay a great deal of polite cool attention to Marina and made increasing demands that she wait on the general and himself. When he looked at her with his pale eyes they had a disdainful expression mixed with a schoolboy curiosity as though he were looking at some exotic animal which could be the source of much amusement if one knew how to handle it.

One of the adjutant's favourite pastimes was to entice Marina's little boy with a sweet and, when the child stretched his podgy hand out for it, to pop it quickly into his own mouth. He would do it two or three times until the child began to cry. He would then squat down on his heels in front of the child and poke out the red tip of his tongue with the sweet on it, then suck and chew it demonstratively and laugh long and uproariously, rolling his colourless eyes the while.

Marina found him thoroughly repulsive from his long legs to his unnaturally white finger-nails. To her he was not only inhuman but something below a brute beast—as loathsome as a toad, lizard or any other reptile. And when he compelled her to wait upon him the realization that she was in the power of this creature filled her with revulsion and horror.

But if anyone made the life of the young people truly unbearable it was the freckled batman. He had a surprising amount of free time, for he was chief of all the other orderlies and cooks and soldiers in the personal service of the general; and all his free time was spent in endlessly and repeatedly questioning the young people as to why they had wanted to get away from the Germans and how it was that they had failed, and in giving them, for the umpteenth time, his opinion that only stupid, savage people could want to get away from the Germans.

He pursued the young people into the wood-shed where they now sat most of the time, and into the yard when they went out for a breath of fresh air, and inside the house, when the general was away. Only the arrival of Grandma freed them from the batman's attentions.

Strange though it was, the big, beefy-handed batman was rather afraid of Grandma Vera, though outwardly his attitude to her was as insolent as it was to all the others. He and Grandma conversed with each other in a monstrous mixture of Russian and German reinforced by gestures and facial expressions, always very precise and venomous on Grandma's side, always very rude, brutal, malicious and stupid on the part of the batman. But they understood one another perfectly.

The whole family now took their meals in the shed, breakfast, dinner and supper, and they always took them as it were by stealth. They lived on meatless *borshch*, salads, boiled potatoes and, to take the place of bread, the unleavened wheat cakes which Grandma made. She had a hidden store of all kinds of things, and when the Germans had eaten up everything that was not well concealed, Grandma cooked very scanty meals in an endeavour to show the Germans that there was nothing else for them. But at night, when the Germans were asleep, Grandma would surreptitiously produce a bit of pork fat or some eggs, and in this too there was something humiliating—this eating in stealth away from the light of day.

There was no news from Valko. And Vanya kept away. It was difficult to think of a way they could meet with Germans in possession of every house watchfully scrutinizing every arrival with suspicion. Even a casual encounter or chat in the street aroused suspicion.

Oleg would lie stretched out on the trestle-bed with his hands under his head when everybody was asleep and the fragrant air of the steppe blew softly in through the open door of the shed. The moon, almost full, shed its grey-blue light across the sky and a shining square of light lay on the earth at his feet. At such times Oleg would derive excruciating delight from the thought that Lena Pozdnysheva was still here in the town. Her image, indistinct, shadowy, incomplete, would float before him, her eyes like black cherries in the night with golden flecks of moonlight in them (yes, he had seen them like that in the park in springtime or perhaps he had only dreamed of them), her laughter coming to him from far away like a string of little silvery notes which sounded almost artificial because each note was separate from the others, like spoons being rattled in the next room. The knowledge that she was near and the fact that he was separated from her filled him with the longing that only youth experiences, without passion, without pangs of conscience, the longing for her to appear, for the joy of seeing her.

At times, when neither the general nor the adjutant were about, Oleg and Nikolai Nikolayevich went into their own dear home. Their noses sensed a mixture of perfumes: scent, the smell of foreign tobacco and that peculiar odour that attaches to the bachelor which neither perfume nor tobacco smoke can mask and which is equally peculiar to the habitations of generals and privates, when they live away from their families.

At such an hour, Oleg chanced to go inside his home to see his mother. At the kitchen range the German cook and Grandma Vera were both silently engaged in cooking each for their own. In the large room which served as the dining-room, the batman lay stretched out on the divan in boots and forage-cap, smoking and obviously very bored. It was the divan which had once done duty as Oleg's bed. The batman's sluggish bored eyes fell on Oleg as soon as he entered the room.

"*Halt!*" he shouted. "It seems to me that you're beginning to put on airs—oh yes, I've been noticing it more and more," he said and sat up, dropping his huge feet in their thick-soled boots to the floor. "Hands to your trouser seams and keep your heels together, you're talking to someone older than yourself!" He tried to work himself up into a temper or at least to show annoyance, but the oppressive heat had so exhausted him that he could not muster enough strength for his purpose. "Do as you're told! Hear me? You!..."

Oleg had understood. Silently he gazed at the batman's pale freckles for a moment, then suddenly assumed a terrified expression, squatted quickly on his haunches and beating his knees shouted, "The general's coming!"

In an instant the batman had jumped to his feet, torn the cigarette from his lips and crushed it in his fist. His torpid features assumed a servile, vacant expression, he clicked his heels and stood rigid with his hands pressed to his trouser seams.

"Flunkey! Lolling about on the divan while the master's away! You just stay there like that now," Oleg said without raising his voice, revelling at the thought of being able to say it all without fear of being understood; then went to his mother's room.

She stood in the doorway, pale, with her head thrown back and her sewing in her hand. She had heard everything.

"How could you, Oleg?" she began, but that instant the batman rushed in to them.

"Come back! Come here!" he roared, beside himself. His face was so purple with rage that even the freckles had become invisible.

"Don't p-pay any attention, Mother, to that idiot," Oleg said with a slight tremor in his voice and ignoring the batman as though he were not there.

"Come here! You swine!" the batman screamed.

He made a sudden dive at Oleg, seized his jacket lapels with both hands and began to shake him furiously, in a blind rage, his eyes completely white in the purple face.

"Don't, don't do it! Oleg dear, let him have his way. Why must you—?" Yelena said, trying with her small hands to tear the batman's huge hands from her son's jacket.

Oleg, who had also flushed a deep red, seized the batman by the belt under his tunic with both hands and his blazing eyes bored into those of the batman with such fierce hatred that the latter was thrown momentarily off his balance.

"L-let me go, d'you hear?" Oleg hissed in a terrifying whisper, dragging the batman towards him and getting more and more furious because the batman's face wore an expression not so much of fear as of doubt that he had acted sufficiently to his own advantage.

The batman released his hold. They stood facing each other, breathing heavily.

"Run outside, my son! Run outside!" Yelena pleaded.

"You savage, worse than savage!" the batman muttered between his teeth, trying to make the words sound contemptuous. "The only way to train you people is with a whip, like dogs!"

"It's you who is worse than savage, because you're the flunkey of savages. All you can do is steal chickens, rummage in women's suitcases and pull boots off passers-by," Oleg growled with loathing in his voice, and he looked straight into the batman's white eyes.

The batman had spoken in German, Oleg in Russian, but the expression on both their faces and the attitudes they struck were so clear that they understood each other admirably. As Oleg said the last words, the batman's heavy hand slapped him on the cheek with such force that Oleg almost fell over.

Never before in his sixteen and a half years had anyone's hand been raised against him, either in anger or by way of punishment. The very air he had breathed from childhood, both in the family circle and at his school, had been the pure air of friendly emulation, where brutal physical force had been as impossible as theft, murder or perjury. A wave of furious passion went to Oleg's head. He flew at the batman. The batman leapt back to the door. The mother clung to her son's shoulder.

"Oleg! Think what you're doing! He'll kill you!" she said, while her eyes flashed and she clung harder to the boy.

The noise brought Grandma Vera, Nikolai Nikolayevich, the German cook with his white hat and the overalls over his uniform rushing to the spot. The batman was braying like a donkey. Grandma Vera, her thin arms outstretched and her brightly-coloured sleeves flapping about them, shrieked and flapped about the batman like a hen, trying to force him into the dining-room.

"Oleg! My boy! Please.... The window's open, run away, please!" Yelena whispered ardently into his ear.

"The window? I'm not jumping out of any window in my own house!" Oleg said, his nostrils and lips quivering proudly. But he had already calmed down. "Don't be afraid, Mother, let go of me. I'll go myself, anyway. I'm going to Lena," he added abruptly.

He walked resolutely into the dining-room. They all stood aside for him.

"And as for you, you're just a swine!" Oleg said over his shoulder to the batman. "You hit when you know you can't be hit back." With unhurried steps he walked out of the house.

His cheek was burning, but he felt he had won a moral victory: not only had he stood his ground against the German, but he had frightened him. He had no desire to think about the consequences of his action. What difference would it make? Grandma was right: have any truck with their "new order"? not on your life! He would do what had to be done. He would show them who had the upper hand!

He passed through the gate into the street parallel with Sadovaya Street and immediately ran into Styopa Safonov.

"Where are you off to? I was just coming to you," little fair-haired Styopa said, gleefully shaking Oleg's big fist with both his own.

Oleg felt embarrassed.

"Oh, I'm just going ... er ... somewhere."

He had wanted to add "on family business," but the words would not come out.

"What's made your cheek so red?" Styopa asked, surprised, and dropped Oleg's hand. It was almost as though he were being paid to ask awkward questions, Oleg thought.

"I had a fight with a German," he said, and smiled.

"Not really? Oh, good work!" Styopa looked with new respect at the red cheek. "So much the better, then. Because actually I was just on my way to see you on the same sort of business."

"What sort of business?" Oleg laughed.

"Let's move on, I'll go with you, because if we stand here one of the Fritzes may poke his nose in." Styopa took Oleg's arm.

"It would be b-best for me to walk a little way with you," Oleg stammered.

"Perhaps you could put off your business for a bit and come with me, couldn't you?"

"Where to?"

"To Valya Borts."

"Valya?" Oleg's conscience pricked him for not having gone to see her earlier. "Are there any Germans in her house?"

"No, that's the whole point. Actually Valya asked me to fetch you."

What luck, suddenly to find he could enter a house where there were no Germans; he could stand in that old familiar garden with its flower-beds that seemed to be trimmed with fur like Monomakh's hat,* with the old acacia-tree and its several trunks and its pale green foliage so still that it seemed to be stitched like embroidery on the blue sky of the steppe!

To Maria Borts all the pupils from her school were still small boys and girls. She seized Oleg in her arms and kissed and petted him.

"So you've been forgetting your old friends, have you? Comes back, he does, but not a whisper—he forgets all about us! And who loves you more than we do, tell me? Who was it that spent hours with us, his forehead puckered up, while someone played the piano for him? And whose books did you browse over just as though they were your own? I see you've quite forgotten! Ah, dear little Oleg! Well here, at home ..." and she grasped her head in her two hands, "he's in hiding, of course!" Her eyes were round with terror as she spoke in a whisper which burst from her like steam from a railway engine and was audible the length of the street. "Yes, and I shan't tell even you where.... Isn't it humiliating and terrible to have to hide in one's own house? And I think he'll have to go to another town. He doesn't really look very Jewish—don't you agree? Here he might simply be betrayed by someone, but in Stalino we've some good friends—they're relations of mine, Russians.... Yes, he'll have to go away," Maria Borts said, with a sad, almost aggrieved expression on her face. However, because of her extraordinary health, her aggrieved feelings did not register properly in her features: although she was perfectly sincere in what she said, Maria Borts seemed to be pretending.

Oleg freed himself from her embrace.

"It's quite right, you're a pig," Valya said, her full upper

* Gold headgear of the tsars. Legend has it that Prince Vladimir Monomakh of Kiev (1053-1125) received it as a present from the Byzantine Emperor Constantine.

lip curled in a pout. "You've come back and yet you never came to see us!"

"You c-c-could have come to see me!" said Oleg with an abashed grin.

"If you're calculating on girls coming to see you, you'll spend a lonely old age!" Maria Borts said boisterously.

Oleg threw a merry glance at her, and they laughed.

"You know, he's already had a fight with a Fritz. Look at his cheek!" Styopa said with great satisfaction.

"Seriously? Did you fight?" Valya asked and looked with curiosity at Oleg. "Mother," she said over her shoulder, "I think they're waiting for you inside."

"Good Lord, these conspirators!" Maria Borts cried and appealed to the heavens with plump outstretched arms. "I'm going, I'm going!"

"Was it an officer? Or a private?" Valya questioned Oleg.

Besides Valya and Styopa there was someone in the garden whom Oleg did not know: a lean barefoot young fellow with coarse, fair, wavy hair parted on the side and with slightly protruding lips. He was sitting quietly in a fork of the acacia-tree and had not taken his stern searching eyes off Oleg since the latter had entered the garden. There was something in the way he was looking and in his whole bearing that commanded respect, and Oleg involuntarily glanced in his direction.

"Oleg," Valya began with a determined expression in her face and a firm intonation as soon as her mother had disappeared into the house. "Help us to get in touch with the underground organization. No, wait..." she said, noticing the absent look on his face. The next moment he smiled broadly. "You probably know how it can be done. Your house was always full of Party members and I know that you're more friendly with adults than with the boys."

"No, I've lost all my c-contacts unfortunately," Oleg said, still smiling.

"Tell that to someone else—we're all friends here! Oh, perhaps you're afraid to talk because of him? That's Sergei Tyulenin," Valya exclaimed, throwing a quick glance at the young fellow in the fork of the tree.

Valya added nothing more by way of recommendation; what she had said was sufficient.

"I was speaking the truth," Oleg said, addressing Sergei because he had no doubt that he had in fact initiated the conversation. "I know that the underground organization exists because, in the first place, they put out the leaflets. Secondly, I have no doubt that the burning down of the Trust and the pit-head baths was also their work," and he did not notice when he said it the lively little spark which leapt into Valya's eyes or the faint smile on her full crimson lips. "And I've heard," he continued, "that we Komsomols will very shortly get instructions about what we have to do."

"Time flies and our fingers are itching!" Sergei said.

They began to discuss the boys and girls who might possibly be left in the town. Styopa Safonov, who got about a great deal and had friends throughout the town, made them all out to be such desperate characters that he had Valya, Oleg and Sergei rocking with laughter and quite forgetting all about the Germans and why they had started their conversation.

"And where's Lena Pozdnysheva?" Valya asked suddenly.

"She's here!" Styopa exclaimed. "I met her in the street. She was walking along all dressed up, with her head held like this," and with his freckled snub nose high in the air Styopa made an attempt at floating gracefully down the garden path. "I called to her, 'Hello, Lena!' But she only nodded—like this," and again he suited the action to the word.

"That's nothing like her!" Valya chuckled with a sly glance at Oleg.

"You remember the wonderful singsongs we had at her home? Three weeks ago—only three weeks ago, just think!" Oleg said and looked at Valya with a sad smile. And then he was suddenly in a hurry to leave.

He went off with Sergei.

"Valya's told me a lot about you, Oleg, and when I saw you I felt I could trust you," Sergei said, quickly glancing once or twice at Oleg. "I'm telling you this so that you know—and I won't talk of it again. This is the position: no underground organization of any sort burnt down the Trust or the pit-head baths. I did it...."

"W-what? By yourself?" Oleg looked at Sergei, his eyes shining.

"Yes."

For a few moments they walked along in silence.

"It was a b-bad thing, that, to act the lone wolf. Brave and clever, but by yourself, that's b-bad," Oleg said. His face showed signs of good-natured anxiety.

"That there *is* an underground organization I know, and not only because of the leaflets," Sergei continued, ignoring Oleg's remark. "I almost tracked it down but I couldn't get hold of it." A gesture of Sergei's hand indicated his chagrin.

He told Oleg how he had called on Ignat Fomin, and all the circumstances of the visit, without concealing the fact that he had been compelled to give a false address to the man hiding in Fomin's home.

"Have you told Valya all this?" Oleg asked suddenly.

"No," Sergei replied calmly.

"G-good ... very g-good!" Oleg took Sergei's arm. "Now that you've had a talk with that man you can go and see him again, can't you?" he said excitedly.

"The whole trouble is that I can't," Sergei replied. A harsh line appeared on his rather pouting lips. "Ignat Fomin has turned him over to the Germans. He didn't do it right away but waited for five or six days after the Germans had arrived. There is a lot of talk in Shanghai district about Fomin having planned to use him to blow the gaff on the whole organization, but that chap was careful. Fomin waited and waited and then in the end gave him away and got himself a job in the police."

"What police?" Oleg exclaimed in astonishment; to think that while he'd been sitting in the wood-shed such things had been going on!

"You know the barracks down there, beyond the district committee, where our militia used to be? German army police have taken them over now and they're forming a police force of Russians. It is said that they've found some scoundrel or other to act as police chief, a fellow called Solikovsky; he used to be foreman in a small pit somewhere in the neighbourhood. He's helping them to collect all sorts of riff-raff and they're making policemen out of them."

"What have they done with him? They haven't killed him, have they?" Oleg asked.

"Not unless they're a lot of idiots," Sergei said. "I think

they're still holding him somewhere. They'll want to get all the information they can out of him, but he's not the kind to talk. They've probably got him down in those barracks and are slowly torturing him to death. Besides him there are others there they've arrested but I can't find out who they are."

A horrible thought set Oleg's heart thumping: while he was still waiting for news from Valko that immensely courageous man with the gypsy eyes might already be imprisoned in a dark cramped cell in those barracks and also being slowly tortured to death, as Sergei put it.

"Thanks for telling me all this," he said thickly.

Then, without stopping to consider that he might be violating his promise to Valko, he proceeded, for reasons of expediency, to tell Sergei about the conversation he had had with Valko and, later, with Vanya Zemnukhov.

They walked slowly down Derevyannaya Street, Sergei barefoot and with a slight swagger, Oleg stepping lightly and firmly through the dust in his neat, polished boots. Oleg gave his comrade an outline of his plan of action. They were to proceed carefully and guardedly, so as not to endanger the scheme, and make a thorough search for the Bolshevik underground; at the same time, they should closely examine all the young people, make a mental note of those who were most trustworthy, staunch and fit for the job, then discover who in the town and the district had been arrested, and where they were being held; and then find ways and means of helping them. They should also do all they could to gather information among the German soldiers about all the military and civilian measures of the commanding authorities.

Sergei immediately became animated and suggested organizing a collection of weapons: after the battles and the retreat large quantities had been left lying about everywhere, even in the steppe.

They both realized fully how much of this would be humdrum activity, but it was a job they were capable of carrying out, and the voice of reality had asserted itself in both of them.

Oleg looked straight ahead, his eyes wide and bright. "No one, no matter how close they are to us or how friendly we are with them, must know anything about what we find out or what we are doing," he said. "Friendship is one thing, but there's a smell of blood in all this," he continued emphatically. "You, Vanya and myself ... that's all! Once we've established contact, then they'll tell us what to do."

Sergei remained silent: he disliked verbal pledges and assurances.

"What's happening in the park now?" Oleg asked.

"It's a German lorry park. The whole place is ringed with AA guns. They've dug up all the ground, like swine!"

"Poor old park! And have you any Germans in your house?"

"They give us a look in; they don't like our quarters," Sergei said, laughing. "But we can't meet there, too many people about," he added, understanding the reason behind Oleg's question.

"We'll keep in touch through Valya."

"Right," Sergei replied, satisfied.

They went on as far as the cross-roads, then parted with a firm handshake. They were almost the same age, and had been drawn close together during the course of their short conversation. Their mood was one of courageous elation.

The Pozdnyshevs lived in Senyaki district. Like the Koshevois and the Korostylevs they occupied one half of a prefabricated house. While still some distance away, Oleg saw their open windows with the old-fashioned lace curtains and heard the sound of the piano being played and the silvery disconnected notes of Lena's affected laughter. Somebody with strong fingers was energetically playing the introductory chords of a ballad familiar to Oleg, and then Lena began to sing. However, the accompanyist made a mistake and Lena first laughed and then sang a few notes to show him where he had gone wrong, and then they went through the whole thing again.

The sound of her voice and the notes of the piano so agitated Oleg that for some moments he could not make himself enter the house. All this had again reminded him of the happy evenings spent here in Lena's home with friends of whom there had seemed to be so many! Valya would play the accompaniment and Lena would sing while Oleg would watch Lena's face which showed a little nervousness; he had watched her, charmed and happy because of her nervousness, and her voice and the piano chords which had made a lasting imprint on his heart and filled the whole world of his youth.

If only he had never again stepped over the threshold of that house! If only this blend of impressions, music, youth, the vague stirring of first love, had remained for ever in his heart!

But he had already entered the passage and from there he went to the dimly-lit kitchen which was on the shady side of the house; and there calmly and at ease and not as though for the first time sat Lena's mother dressed in an old-fashioned dark dress, her hair in old-fashioned curls, and with her a German soldier with straw-coloured hair, just like the batman Oleg had quarrelled with, only this one was short and fat and had no freckles. Judging by his manner he was also a batman. They sat on stools opposite one another and the German batman with a smug polite smile on his lips and something like flirtatiousness in his eye took something from the rucksack on his knees and passed it to Lena's mother. She for her part, with her shrivelled face and ringlets and with an expression on her face of a genteel old lady who knew she was being bribed, accepted what was offered with a cunning, servile smile and trembling hands and dropped it in her lap. They were so engrossed in this simple operation which so fully occupied them both that they did not notice Oleg when he entered. Thus he was able to see what lay in the lap of Lena's mother: a flat tin of sardines, a bar of chocolate and a tall, flat-sided half-quart tin with a screw-top and a bright yellow and blue label. Oleg had seen the Germans in his own home with similar tins, which contained olive oil.

Lena's mother caught sight of Oleg and she involuntarily shifted her hands as though to hide what was in her lap; then the batman also saw Oleg and, the rucksack still in his hands, fixed his eyes on him indifferently.

That same instant the piano stopped playing in the next room and Lena's singing broke off, and there was laughter from her and the men in the room and snatches of sentences in German. Then, each little silvery note pronounced separately, Lena said:

"No, no, I repeat, *ich wiederhole*, there's a pause here, then a repeat and then immediately—" and her slim fingers ran over the keys.

"Oh, it's you, Oleg dear! You haven't left then?" Lena's mother said, raising her eyebrows in surprise, a false, caressing note in her voice. "Do you want to see Lena?"

With surprising swiftness she hid the objects from her lap in the lower shelf of the kitchen table, patted her ringlets to feel whether they were tidy and, with her head drawn into her shoulders and her nose and chin in the air, passed into the room from where the sound of the piano and Lena's voice were coming.

The blood had drained from Oleg's face and his large hands hung limply by his side. Suddenly he felt clumsy and awkward standing there in the middle of the kitchen under the indifferent eye of the German batman.

He heard Lena's expression of surprise and embarrassment. She was saying something in a low voice to the men in the room and seemed to be excusing herself. Then came the click of her heels as she ran across the room; she appeared at the kitchen door in a grey dark-patterned dress which hung heavily on her frail figure with the slender sunburnt neck, and her bare brown hands gripped the frame of the door.

"Oleg!" she said, her small sunburnt face flushing with confusion. "We were just—"

But she seemed totally unprepared to explain what they were "just doing." With the inconsistency of a woman and an unnatural smile on her lips she ran towards Oleg, took his hand to draw him towards her, then dropped it, to call out, "We're just coming." At the door she turned, tilted her head to one side and again invited Oleg to follow her.

As Oleg followed her into the room he almost collided with her mother who was just slipping out of it Two German officers in identical grey uniforms, one seated on a stool with his body half turned towards the open piano, the other standing between window and piano, looked at Oleg without curiosity and without annoyance but just as though he was a nuisance they willy-nilly had to put up with.

"This is a school-friend of mine," Lena said in her little silvery voice. "Find a seat, Oleg.... You know this ballad, don't you? I've spent an hour now teaching it to them. We'll repeat the whole song now, gentlemen! Sit down, Oleg."

Oleg raised his eyes, almost covered by the golden lashes, and clearly articulating his words one by one so that each of them truly found its mark he said:

"W-what are they paying you with? Olive oil? You're selling yourself too cheap!"

He turned on his heel, walked past Lena's mother, past the stout batman with the "regulation" yellow hair and went out into the street.

Chapter 22

So FILIPP PETROVICH LYUTIKOV had vanished and reappeared—in his new capacity.

What had happened to him in the meantime?

We remember that he had been selected for underground work as far back as the previous autumn. At the time he had kept it from his wife and had been very glad of his foresight, for the threat of occupation had receded.

But Lyutikov bore it in mind—constantly. What was more, Ivan Protsenko, a prudent man, supported him in this state of permanent mental preparedness.

"Who can tell how things will turn out! We've got to be like the Young Pioneers now: 'Be prepared!'—'Always prepared!'"

Among the people selected during the previous autumn, there was also Polina Georgievna Sokolova, a housewife, not a member of the Party but well known throughout the town for her active work among women, and she remained firmly at her post. She had been appointed to act as Lyutikov's contact during his underground period. Being too well known to the people of Krasnodon as a deputy to the Town Soviet, he would have been hampered both in moving about and in associating with people while working underground, so Polina Sokolova was to be his eyes, hands and feet.

From the moment Polina had agreed to stay behind and do this work she had, on Lyutikov's advice, completely withdrawn from public work. Among her women friends in the town this at first caused consternation and then called forth reproaches. How was it that such an active woman should withdraw from public work when the country was going through such difficult days? But, then, nobody had ever appointed or nominated her for work. She had worked voluntarily, when it pleased her. All sorts of strange things happen to people! She could, of course, have decided to devote herself entirely to the home. It might be that the difficulties of war-time life had urged her to do so. Gradually everyone forgot about Polina Sokolova.

She bought a cow which happened to be offered cheaply by someone evacuating to the east and began to make the rounds selling milk. Lyutikov's family did not require much milk—there were only three of them: his wife Yevdokia, his twelve-year-old daughter Raya and himself. But Pelagea Ilyinichna, his landlady, had three children of her own and her old mother living with her and so she too began to buy her milk from Polina Sokolova. And all the neighbours soon grew used to the sight of the woman with the kindly Russian face, in her simple dress and a white scarf tied village fashion over her head, walking unhurriedly up to Pelagea Ilyinichna's cottage each morning at the first gleam of daylight. She would slip her long thin fingers between the slats of the gate to lift the latch and let herself through the gate. then tap softly at the window by the side of the porch. The door would be opened by Pelagea's mother, who was always up before anyone else, and Polina would bid her a friendly "good morning," enter the cottage and, after a time, emerge with her milk-can empty.

The Lyutikovs had lived in this cottage for many years. Yevdokia and Pelagea were very good friends. Yevdokia's Raya and Pelagea's eldest daughter Liza were of the same age and in the same class at school. Pelagea's husband—an artillery officer of the reserve who had been on active service since the first days of the war—was fifteen years younger than Lyutikov. He was a joiner by trade and his attitude towards Lyutikov was that of pupil to teacher.

As far back as the previous autumn Lyutikov had learned from Pelagea that, because of her large family and her husband's absence, she was determined not to abandon her home if the Germans came. It was then, too, that Lyutikov had begun to make plans to send his people to the east, should the necessity arise, and remain living in the old home himself.

His landlady was one of the many simple, honest women to be found in our country. Lyutikov knew that she would ask no questions and would even deliberately pretend that she knew nothing, even if she knew something. Her conscience would be quieter and easier that way for, if she gave no undertakings, then no demands would be put on her. But she would not talk, she would shield him and never betray him even under torture, because she profoundly trusted him, her sympathies were with his cause and, simply, she was a kind and compassionate woman by nature.

Another thing was that her home was convenient for Lyutikov. It was one of the first wooden cottages to be built near the solitary shanty of the miner Churilin and the whole district still bore the name Churilino. Behind Pelagea's cottage lay a deep ravine which stretched away into the steppe and this was called the Churilino Gorge. The whole area was considered rather out of the way, which in fact it was.

Then came the menacing July days when Lyutikov finally had to explain the position to his wife.

"You're an old man and ailing," she had said, weeping. "Go to the district committee and have a talk with them, they may let you off. We'll go to the Kuzbas," she added, her eyes suddenly lighting up in a way he knew so well. It was always the same, as soon as she began recalling the early years, or thought of kind friends or something close to her heart. During the war a number of Donets miners and their families had been evacuated to the Kuzbas, and among them were many friends whom Lyutikov and his wife had known since childhood. "Yes, we'll go to the Kuzbas," she had said, as though they could now, in the Kuzbas, recapture the good times which had once been theirs here, in their native land, when they were both young.

Poor woman—as though she did not know her Filipp!

"Let's not talk about it any more. The question's settled," he said, looking sternly into her imploring eyes, so that it was plain that he would tolerate neither her pleading nor her tears. "But you and the girl can't remain here, you would hamper me. And it nearly breaks my heart when I look at you two...." And he kissed his wife and pressed his little daughter, his only child, to his heart for a long time.

Like many others, his family had delayed their departure too long and had to turn back before they even reached the Donets. Lyutikov, however, did not allow them to stay with him and made arrangements for them to live on a farm, some distance from the town.

During the three weeks which changed the position on the front in the Germans' favour, the regional Party committee and the Krasnodon District Committee were busy selecting additional people for the underground organization and the partisan detachments. A large group of officials from the Krasnodon and other districts was put at Lyutikov's disposal.

On the memorable day when Lyutikov had said farewell to Protsenko, he had gone home at the usual time: the hour he generally arrived home from the factory. The children were playing in the street and the old woman had taken refuge from the heat in the semi-darkness of a room which had the shutters closed. Pelagea sat in the kitchen with her sun-browned hands folded in her lap, and the expression on her still young, attractive face showed that she was in such deep thought that even Lyutikov's arrival did not stir her. For some moments she looked at him without seeing him.

"In all the years I've lived here this is the first time I've seen you sitting like that doing nothing," he said to her. "Are you grieving about something? You shouldn't."

She made no reply. She silently lifted one thickly-veined hand and again laid it on the other.

Lyutikov stood before her a moment, then walked through to the inner room with slow, heavy steps. In a short time he came back without cap and tie and in slippers but still wearing the new black jacket and white open-necked shirt. He was combing back his thick greying hair with a large green comb.

"I want to ask you something, Pelagea Ilyinichna," he began while he quickly ran the comb over each half of his short bristling moustache. "Since 1924 when I was accepted in the Party at the time of the Lenin Enrolment I've been a subscriber to our *Pravda* and I've saved every issue. I found I always needed them very much: for lectures, for teaching in political study groups and so on. Now that trunk I have in my room—you probably thought it was full of rubbish. Well ... that's where I keep my newspapers," Lyutikov said and smiled. He did not smile very often and perhaps for that reason the smile at once changed his face, giving it an unusual expression of tenderness. "What shall I do with them now? I've been saving them for seventeen years—I'd be sorry to burn them." He looked questioningly at Pelagea.

For a few moments neither spoke.

"Where could one hide them?" Pelagea asked as though talking to herself. "They could be buried. We might dig a hole in the vegetable garden after dark and bury them as they are, in that trunk," she went on, her eyes averted.

"What if I wanted any of them? They may be needed," Lyutikov said.

Just as he had expected she did not ask for what purpose he might want Soviet newspapers while the Germans were here; her face retained its detached expression. She remained silent for a moment, then said:

"Filipp Petrovich, you've lived with us for a long time now and you've got accustomed to everything but now I want to ask you: supposing you came into the house, came for the purpose of finding something — would you notice anything special about our kitchen?"

Very carefully and attentively Lyutikov looked round the kitchen: a small tidy kitchen in a small provincial cottage. Being a skilled worker he merely noted the fact that the painted wooden floor consisted not of continuous boards but of wide, short, solid boards laid side by side between the supporting beams and fitted into them. The man who built this cottage had known his job: the solid floor had been made to last and would not sag under the weight of the Russian stove, would remain free of rot longer than usual for a room used so many times a day and therefore scrubbed very frequently.

"I don't see anything special, Pelagea Ilyinichna," he said.

"There's an old cellar under the kitchen here." She rose from the stool, stooped and felt in a barely discernible dark spot on one of the boards. "There used to be a ring here. And the little staircase is here."

"Could I have a look at it?" Lyutikov asked.

Pelagea closed the outside door and fastened it with its hook. Then she reached under the stove and brought out an axe, but Lyutikov refused to use it for fear of leaving traces on the floor. He took a kitchen knife instead, while she took an ordinary table knife, and with these they neatly cleaned out the cracks round the square trapdoor. Then, finally, with some difficulty, they lifted three short heavy boards joined together.

Four steps led down into the cellar. Lyutikov climbed down and lit a match: the cellar was dry. At this stage it was difficult to foresee how useful this surprising little cellar would be to him one day.

He climbed out and carefully closed the trapdoor.

"Don't be angry with me, but I've something else I want to ask you," he said. "Later, of course, I shall fix myself up somewhere and the Germans won't touch me. But if they come during the first few days I'm afraid they may kill me in the heat of the moment. So if anything should happen, I'll pop in there." He pointed at the floor.

"And if they billet soldiers on me?"

"They won't do that: this is Churilino. I'm not too proud to stay down there. Now don't you feel nervous about it," Lyutikov said, slightly disconcerted himself by the indifferent expression on Pelagea Ilyinichna's face.

"I'm not nervous. It's no business of mine."

"If the Germans ask about a man called Lyutikov just tell them he's gone into the village to buy food, and will soon be back. Liza and Petka'll help me to stay hidden. I'll get them to keep watch during the day," Lyutikov said and smiled.

Pelagea cast a sidelong glance at him, shook her head as young people do and laughed. Forbidding as his appearance was Lyutikov was a born teacher of children. He understood and loved them, and knew how to win their affection. They always flocked to him. He treated them as though they were grown-ups. He could do things with his hands—they knew that he could make anything from toys to useful articles for the house, and make them out of almost nothing. A man like that gets to be known as an all-round handy man.

He made no distinction in any way between the children of his landlady and his own daughter and all of them were happy to do any sort of job he might have for them. He had only to beckon with one finger.

"You'd better have the lot of them for yourself, Uncle Filipp; they're so used to you that they look to you more than to their own father," Pelagea's husband would say. "You'd like to go and live with Uncle Filipp all the time, wouldn't you?" he would ask the children, looking sternly at them.

"No, we wouldn't!" they would shout together and rush at Uncle Filipp from all sides and cling to him.

In all the varied fields of activity one can meet with Party leaders who differ considerably in character, but who have a special trait of their own. And among them the Party leader who has a flair for teaching is likely to be the most frequent type. This refers not merely and not so much to Party leaders whose main activity is Party education proper and political instruction, but to the Party member who knows how to teach no matter what his field of activity— industry, the army, or administrative or cultural work. To this type of Party teacher Filipp Petrovich Lyutikov belonged.

It was not merely that he liked to teach people and could see the need for it; for him it was a natural requirement and necessity: to him it was second nature to teach and to train, to pass on his own knowledge and experience.

True, because of this much of what he said sounded didactic. But Lyutikov was not overbearingly didactic, nor did he force his teachings on people, for they were the fruits of his own experience and thought, and people accepted them in that way.

Typical of Lyutikov, and of this type of leader generally, was his combination of word and deed. He could translate everything he said into action; he could rally the most varied types of people for some special form of activity and inspire them with the full meaning of the work in hand. It was this chief attribute which made of Lyutikov a teacher of an entirely new type. He was a good teacher precisely because he was a man who knew how to organize, a man who had mastered the true art of living.

His lectures did not leave one indifferent; nor, indeed, did they repel. They made an appeal to the heart, and particularly to the hearts of young people, because young people are fired with an idea more readily when the idea is reinforced by example.

Sometimes he had only to say a word or simply give a look. By nature he was a man of few words, habitually silent. At first sight he seemed to be rather slow, even dull to some people, but actually he was in a state of quiet, rational, well-organized activity. When not at work in industry, he divided his free time between social activity, manual work, reading and entertainment, and was never behindhand in anything.

When with other people Lyutikov was even-tempered and never got excited. In conversation he knew how to listen, a quality few people possess. That was why he had the reputation of being a good conversationalist, a sincere man. Many people shared with him social and personal matters which they would never have discussed even with their closest relations.

Yet with all this, he was not what is called a kind man, far less a soft-hearted man. He was incorruptible, stern and, when necessary, merciless.

Some people respected him, others loved him. And there were those who were afraid of him. It would be truer to say that everyone who had dealings with him, including his wife and friends, entertained all these feelings, depending on the character of the person: in some the first feeling was dominant, in others—the second; in yet others—the third. If these people were separated into age groups, then one could say that the adults respected, loved and feared him, young people respected and loved him, while children simply loved him.

That was why Pelagea laughed when Lyutikov said, "Liza and Petka will help me."

And for the first few days after the arrival of the Germans the children did in fact take turns to keep watch in the street and so protect Lyutikov while he was in hiding.

Luck was with him. No German soldier moved into Pelagea Ilyinichna's home, for roomier and better houses could be found in the town, even close by. The Germans were frightened off by the gorge behind the cottage—they were afraid of partisans. German soldiers did occasionally enter the house to look at the living-quarters and to pick up anything lying about. Each time Lyutikov was hidden under the kitchen floor. But no one ever asked about him.

Every morning Polina would arrive, quiet and unassuming in her clean, white peasant kerchief, pour the milk into two earthenware jugs and then carry her milk-can in to Lyutikov. While she was with him Pelagea and her mother would remain in the kitchen. The children would be still asleep. Polina would come out of Lyutikov's room and spend some moments gossiping with the women in the kitchen before she left.

So a week passed, or possibly a little longer. Then one morning, before giving Lyutikov the local news, Polina said softly, "They want you to go to work, Filipp Petrovich."

In a flash he was a changed man: the expression of tranquillity and indifference, the slow way he had of moving, which was almost immobility at times, and which Lyutikov had assumed while living here in concealment, all of this slipped away from him in an instant.

One stride took him to the door. He looked into the adjoining room, but it was empty as it always was.

"Is everybody being called out?" he asked.

"Everybody."

"Nikolai Petrovich too?"

"Yes."

"Was he there?" Lyutikov asked and looked searchingly into Polina's eyes.

There was no need for him to explain to her where Barakov went. She was aware of all that, everything had been arranged beforehand between herself and Lyutikov.

"Yes," she replied almost inaudibly.

Lyutikov did not begin to fuss about or to raise his voice, but his large, heavy frame, his lowered head, his eyes, his voice, seemed suddenly to be flooded with energy as though a tightly wound spring within him was uncoiling.

He pushed two fingers, the straight, sure fingers of the skilled workman, into one of his jacket pockets and pulled out a tiny scrap of paper covered with close writing. He handed it to Polina.

"By tomorrow morning ... and run off as many as possible!"

Polina immediately tucked the paper down her blouse.

"Wait a few moments in the dining-room. I'll send the women to you."

Pelagea and her mother entered the adjoining room and found Polina already there, with her milk-can. They remained standing while they exchanged the local news. After a short time Lyutikov called Polina out into the kitchen.

He held a packet of rolled-up newspapers in his hand and she was surprised when she saw that it consisted of a number of folded, tightly rolled copies of *Pravda*.

ᴿ "Shove them into the milk-can," Lyutikov said. "And tell them to stick them up in the most conspicuous places."

Polina's heart began to thump. It seemed to her for a moment, incredible though it was, that Lyutikov had received the latest issue of *Pravda*. Unable to contain herself she looked at the date before pushing the roll of newspapers into the milk-can.

"Old ones," she said, unable to conceal her disappointment.

"They're not old. Bolshevik truth* doesn't age," Lyutikov said.

She quickly glanced through a few copies. Most of them were special celebration editions from various years, with photographs of Lenin and Stalin. Lyutikov's plan became clear to her. She rolled the papers up tightly again and pushed them into the milk-can.

"Before I forget," Lyutikov said, "let Ostapchuk start work too. Tomorrow."

Polina nodded, but said nothing. She did not know that Ostapchuk and Matvei Shulga were one and the same person, nor did she know where he was in hiding. She only knew the address where she had to pass on Lyutikov's instructions: it was one of the addresses on her milk round.

"Thank you. That will be all." His big hand grasped hers for a moment. Then he returned to his room.

He dropped heavily into a chair, placed his hands with the fingers widespread on his knees and remained in the same

---

Pravda, i.e., truth.

position for some moments. He looked at the clock: it was a little past seven. With slow, steady movements he pulled off his worn shirt and put on a fresh, white one, put on a tie and combed his hair which was greying, particularly in front and at the temples, slipped on his jacket and went into the kitchen. Polina had left, and Pelagea and her mother were both going about their business.

"Well, Pelagea, I could do with some milk from the crazy cow,* and some bread, if there is any. I'm going out to work," he said.

Within ten minutes he was on his way, his clothing clean and neat, and a black cap on his head, walking openly along the familiar route through the streets of the town in the direction of the Central Workshops of the Krasnodon Coal Trust.

Chapter 23

AMONG THE NUMEROUS RANKS of the German army and "New Order" administration which came on the heels of the army, a certain Lieutenant Schweide had arrived in Krasnodon. He was an elderly, very thin grey-haired German, technician in a mining battalion. None of the Krasnodon townsfolk could recall the day he first appeared: like other ranks he wore the standard army uniform with its unintelligible insignia.

He appropriated for his personal use a large house of four flats, each with its own kitchen, and from the moment *Herr* Schweide arrived all four kitchens were kept busy. He had brought with him a large retinue of German officials, who found themselves living-quarters elsewhere. Several German chefs, a German woman housekeeper and his batman were, however, accommodated in the house which he had requisitioned. Soon the list of his retinue was increased by the addition of a number of *russische Frauen*, the collective term he indifferently applied to maidservants, a washerwoman, a needlewoman and an interpreter whom the labour exchange sent him. Shortly there came also a woman to look after his cows, one for his pigs and a third for the chickens. Cows and

*Vodka is meant here.

pigs came into his possession almost as though by the wave of a wand, but for poultry *Herr* Schweide had a special personal passion.

But that would not have marked the lieutenant of the mining battalion out among other German officials. Yet he was much talked about in town.

Herr Schweide, together with the other officials who had arrived with him, took over the premises of the Gorky School in the park and in its place there sprang up a new institution: *Direktion* No. 10.

This militarized institution, it transpired, was the chief industrial administration, which controlled all the mines and similar undertakings in Krasnodon District, including the property and equipment which had not been taken away or blown up, and all their work-people who had failed, or been unable, to evacuate. It was only one of a large number of branch institutions of the great stock company, which bore the long, pretentious title of "The Eastern Company for the Exploitation of Coal and Metallurgical Undertakings." The board of this company was centred in the town of Stalino to which the old name of Yuzovka had been restored. This "Eastern Company" controlled the "Territorial Boards of the Mining and Metallurgical Undertakings." *Direktion* No. 10 was one of several others subordinated to the territorial management established in the town of Shakhty.

All this had been so well organized and still better planned that all that remained was for the coal and metals of the Soviet Donbas to flow in a wide stream into the coffers of the German "Eastern Company." And *Herr* Schweide had issued instructions that all workers, office staff, engineers and technicians of the mines and factories of the former Krasnodon Coal Trust should start work immediately.

How many serious doubts were entertained by each working man before he was finally compelled to make up his mind to work in his own pits and workshops, which had now become the property of the enemies of the Motherland, at a time when sons and brothers, husbands and fathers were giving their lives on the battle-fields in the struggle against these enemies! Surly and shame-faced they were as they walked to their jobs in the central workshops, these people who avoided each other's eyes and scarcely exchanged a word.

All the workshops had been standing wide open since the days of the final evacuation. No one had shut their gates or watched over them, because no one had any longer been interested in seeing that what had been left inside the workshops remained safe and sound. The workshops stood open, yet no one entered them. The workers sat about, not in groups but singly or, only rarely, in pairs, among the scrap-iron and debris in the yard, silently awaiting the management.

Then Engineer Barakov appeared on the scene — strong and well built, looking younger than his thirty-five years. His clothing was not just neat, but a little flamboyant and he had a self-confident expression on his face. He was wearing a black bow-tie, carried a hat in his hand, and his shiny shaved head shone in the sun. He approached the scattered group of workers standing about in the yard, greeted them politely, hesitated a moment, and then marched resolutely into the main building. The workers did not reply to his greeting, but silently they watched him pass through the wide-open door of the machine-shop, walk through it and enter the small office.

The German management was in no hurry. It was already hot when, through the watchman's hut, and into the yard, came *Herr* Feldner, Schweide's deputy, and a Russian woman interpreter with her hair done loosely.

As often happens in life, *Herr* Feldner was the direct opposite of his chief in physical qualities and temperament. Lieutenant Schweide was thin, suspicious and taciturn. Feldner was short and round, loud-spoken and talkative. His voice, which was always pitched fairly high, could be heard a long way off and always sounded as though not one, but several Germans were approaching, all arguing with each other. *Herr* Feldner wore army uniform with leggings and the grey officer's cap with the crown pushed up high in front.

Accompanied by a woman interpreter he approached the workers, who one by one rose to their feet. That afforded him a certain amount of satisfaction. He made a remark to the interpreter and without pausing proceeded to tell the workers immediately what he wanted, pouring out the words in one long sentence in German, or it might have been in several short sentences. And all the time the woman was translating he continued to shout. Probably the state of being silent was unknown to him. One might have supposed that from the moment he uttered his first cry when he emerged from his mother's womb he had never stopped yelling and, during his whole subsequent life, had remained in a constant state of bawling in some degree or other.

First he was interested to know whether anyone present had worked in the old administrative office. Then he instructed the workers to accompany him into the workshops. The bawling German walked ahead with the interpreter and several workers followed him as far as the machine-shop office which Barakov had entered earlier. Feldner threw back his head, puffed himself out as large as he could, then pushed the office door open with his plump fist and went in. The woman followed him and closed the door. The workers remained outside, listening.

At first they could hear only Feldner's shouting, which sounded as though several Germans were quarrelling. They waited for the interpreter's voice to say what the shouting had been about when, to everyone's surprise, Barakov's voice was heard to reply in German. He spoke politely and calmly and, as far as the workers outside could judge, spoke in the foreign tongue with ease.

Either because Barakov had spoken in German or because what he had said had been satisfactory, Feldner's voice gradually dropped to a quieter note and finally the miracle happened: he stopped talking. Barakov also ceased. In a few moments the German was shouting again, but now in quite a pacific tone. They came out of the office: first Feldner, then Barakov and the interpreter bringing up the rear. Barakov gave the workers a cold, gloomy look, then told them that they were not to disperse but to wait until he returned. In the same order as before the three walked through the workshop to the door: handsome powerful Barakov trailing behind the short round caricature of a German and showing him the most convenient way to get through the shop. It was a horrible sight to watch!

It was not long before Barakov was sitting in the staff room of the Gorky School, now the private office of *Herr* Schweide, chief of *Direktion* No. 10. Feldner and an unknown woman interpreter remained during the conversation, though the woman had no opportunity to show off her knowledge of the German language.

As mentioned earlier, Lieutenant Schweide, unlike the loquacious and expansive Feldner, was a man of few words. Because he found it difficult to express himself he gave the impression of being surly, though in fact he was far from that and loved gaiety and all life's pleasures. He was uncommonly thin yet ate a great deal. It was difficult to understand where he put the vast amount of food he swallowed and how it managed to make its way through his organism. He was passionately fond of *Mädchen* and *Frauen*, and, in the existing circumstances, *russische Mädchen und russische Frauen* in particular. The weaker of them were lured into his four-flat private residence every night by means of noisy parties with plenty of roast food and confectionery, not to mention various kinds of wine. He would say to his cooks: "Cook plenty! *Kocht reichlich Essen!* See that the *russische Frauen* can eat and drink their fill!"

And it was a fact that, since he was so reticent in speech, this was the only way he could entice into his home those *russische Frauen* who were at all likely to find their way into it.

The inability to form sentences out of words had made *Herr* Schweide distrustful of all those who could do it with ease. He did not even trust Feldner, his deputy. One can imagine how little he trusted people of other nations.

In this sense Barakov was in an awkward position. But first of all *Herr* Schweide was struck by the ease with which Barakov was able to form words into sentences, not in Russian, but in German. And, secondly, Barakov flattered *Herr* Schweide and there was nothing left for *Herr* Schweide to do but to accept it.

"I am one of the few representatives of the privileged classes of old Russia still alive," Barakov said, looking straight at Schweide without batting an eyelid. "From earliest childhood I have loved German genius, especially in the field of economy and particularly so in industry. My father was the director of one of the largest enterprises in tsarist Russia, a branch of the Siemens-Schuckert Concern. German was our second language in the family. I was brought up on German technical literature. And now I shall have the good fortune to work here under the supervision of an outstanding specialist like yourself, *Herr* Schweide. I shall do everything you instruct me to."

Barakov suddenly noticed that the interpreter was looking at him with surprise which she could not conceal. Where the hell had the Germans found the frowzy old fossil? If she was a local one she could not help knowing that he was not one of the surviving representatives of the privileged classes of old Russia but the hereditary and honoured representative of a whole dynasty of Donets miners by the name of Barakov. Sweat began to break out on the top of his smooth-shaven head.

While he was speaking *Herr* Schweide did some brain work which, however, was not reflected in his face.

Then, half questioning and half stating a fact, he said: "You are a Communist...."

Barakov made a gesture with his hand. It could have meant, taken with the expression on his face, that of course he was not or else that of course he was, because everyone had to be a Communist or, even, that he certainly was a Communist and therefore it would be so much the better for *Herr* Schweide if he agreed to work for him.

The gesture apparently satisfied the German for the time being. It was now necessary to explain to this Russian engineer how important it was to get the central workshops operating in order to restore the mining equipment. *Herr* Schweide put this complicated idea into the form of a negative statement:

"There is nothing. *Es ist nichts da*," he said and looked poignantly at Feldner.

Feldner, who had been suffering untold agonies from his enforced silence in the presence of his chief, automatically shouted in support of his chief's ideas.

"No machinery! No transport! No tools! No pit props! No workers!" he yelled. He was sorry to be unable to think of any more.

Satisfied, Schweide inclined his head, thought for a moment and then, making a great effort, repeated in Russian:

"There is nothing—and so no coal!"

He leaned back in his chair and looked first at Barakov, then at Feldner. This glance Feldner took to be a signal for action and he began to enumerate in his loud voice all the things the "Eastern Company" expected of Barakov.

Barakov was hard put to it to find a slight pause in this roaring torrent into which he could get a word in edgeways to the effect that he would do everything in his power.

Then again *Herr* Schweide became overwhelmed with a feeling of distrust.

"You are a Communist," he said again.

Barakov smiled wryly and repeated the former gesture.

On returning to the workshop Barakov put up a long announcement at the gates stating that he, the director of the central workshops of *Direktion* No. 10, called upon all workers, office staff, engineers and technicians to return to their jobs and that there were jobs open in various trades for people who wished to take them.

Even the most politically ignorant among those who had made a deal with their consciences and had decided to go to work had misgivings at the thought that Barakov, a skilled engineer and veteran of the Finnish Campaign and the Patriotic War, should have voluntarily agreed to become director of an enterprise of the greatest importance to the Germans. The ink on the announcement had not dried when none other than Filipp Petrovich Lyutikov turned up at the workshops, the selfsame Lyutikov who, not only in the workshop, but all over the town, had been known as the very conscience of communism.

He had come that morning quite openly, cleanly shaven and neatly dressed in a white shirt, black jacket and the necktie he reserved for holidays. And he was immediately put back on his old job of chief of the machine-shop.

The appearance of the first leaflets from the underground district Party committee coincided with the beginning of work in the shops. The leaflets had been pasted up in the most conspicuous places, side by side with old issues of *Pravda*. The Bolsheviks had not left little Krasnodon to its fate, they were continuing the struggle and calling to the struggle the whole population; that was the gist of the statement in the leaflets. And many who had known Barakov and Lyutikov in better times more than once thought: how will they ever dare to look into the conscience-clear eyes of their comrades when they return to us!

True, there was actually no work of any kind to be done in the workshops. Barakov spent most of his time with the German managers and displayed little interest in what went on in the shops. The workers arrived late, strolled about from lathe to lathe without anything to do, spent hours on end smoking on the grass in a shady corner of the yard. Lyutikov, presumably to placate the workers, encouraged them to make trips to the villages and issued them passes as though they were going on business for the central workshops. The workers did odd jobs for the townsfolk in order to increase their earnings. Cigarette lighters were what they turned out in particularly large numbers for matches had become scarce everywhere, while petrol could always be had from German soldiers in exchange for food.

Several times each day officers' batmen would come running to the shop with tins full of butter or honey to be soldered up for dispatch to Germany.

Some of the workers tried to get in conversation with Lyutikov—there was no chance at all of getting at Barakov—to find out how he had come to be working for the Germans and what this sort of life could hold for them. The conversation would start with other things and although they might get close to the subject which worried them, they never succeeded in broaching it. Lyutikov at once, however, saw what they were getting at and would say sternly:

"Never you mind—we'll go on working for them...."

Or he would say roughly:

"It's none of your business, old chap. You came to work here yourself, didn't you? Right. Are you my boss or am I yours? I'm yours! So it follows that I'll put demands on you and not the other way round! And you'll do as I tell you. You understand?"

Every morning Lyutikov would walk to work, passing through the length of the town with the slow, heavy step of an elderly man, short of wind, and every evening he would return the same way home. No one could have imagined with what energy and dispatch, and with what calculation he developed his main activity—an activity which was later to bring world fame to the outlying little mining town of Krasnodon.

What must he have experienced when, at the very outset of his activities, he suddenly learned that Matvei Shulga, one of his closest assistants, had inexplicably vanished!

As secretary of the underground district Party committee Lyutikov knew all the hide-outs and contact addresses throughout the town and the district. He knew of Ivan Kondratovich and Ignat Fomin, whose homes Shulga should presumably have used. But Lyutikov had no right to send one of his district committee contacts to these addresses, least of all Polina Sokolova. If he had done so, and if Shulga had in fact been betrayed at one of these two places, then it would have been enough for one of the householders to get a sight of the contact, to follow her and so discover Lyutikov and the other members of the district committee.

If everything had been well with Shulga he would have inquired long ago at the central contact address as to whether he should seek work in the central workshops. He had not to call in person at this address but merely to walk past it. The day Polina had passed on to this address Lyutikov's instructions, a pot of geraniums had been placed on the sill of the window by the street door. But Yevdokim Ostapchuk, that is Shulga, had not presented himself for work.

Some time elapsed before Lyutikov, who gathered together all the information concerning the traitors who had entered the service of the German police, learned about Ignat Fomin. In all probability Fomin had betrayed Shulga. But how had it happened and what had been Shulga's fate?

At the time of the evacuation, the district Party committee, acting on Protsenko's instructions, had buried all the type of the district printing works in the park and at the last moment Lyutikov had been handed a plan containing precise information as to how to find the spot. He was now very worried by the thought that German soldiers in the lorry park or the AA gunners might have found the type. Whatever the cost, the type had to be recovered and whisked away from under the noses of the German sentries. Who was capable of doing such a thing?

Chapter 24

During the first winter of the war, after the death of his father, Volodya Osmukhin had been a fitter in the machine-shop of the Central Workshops of the Krasnodon Coal Trust instead of doing his tenth and last year in the Voroshilov School. There he had worked under the guidance of Lyutikov, who knew his mother's family, the Rybalovs, intimately, and Volodya as well; he had remained at work there until the day he was taken to hospital with acute appendicitis.

He had had no intention, of course, of returning to work after the Germans arrived. But then came Barakov's order, and there was a rumour abroad that all dodgers would be driven off to Germany. There followed heart-searchings and discussions between Volodya and his bosom friend Tolya Orlov, particularly after Lyutikov had gone back to his job.

Whether to go to work or not, with the Germans in power, was for them, as for all Soviet people, one of the most difficult questions to put to their consciences. Work was an easy way of getting something to keep alive and at the same time of evading the repression which fell upon Soviet citizens who refused to work for the Germans. Besides that, the experience of many had shown that it was quite possible to go through the motions of working without really doing anything at all. But like all Soviet people, Volodya and Tolya had been morally trained to behave so that one should do no work at all for the enemy, neither much nor little; on the contrary, with his arrival all work should cease and a struggle should be launched against him with all available means, either by fighting underground or by joining the partisans. But where now were those underground fighters and partisans? How did one set about finding them and how, and on what, was one to live in the meantime?

Volodya could now walk about, and he and Tolya would lie out in the steppe in the sunshine, discussing over and over again the question as to what should they do now?

One day towards evening Lyutikov went to see the Osmukhins. The house was full of Germans—not those which included the bold lance-corporal who had taken a fancy to

Lyudmila but a second lot, or perhaps a third, for the main stream of the German troop movement passed through the district where the Osmukhins lived. Lyutikov climbed the steps to the porch with the slow, heavy tread of a man of position, removed his cap, politely greeted the soldier in the kitchen, and knocked on the door of the room which still remained the only living accommodation of three people, Yelizaveta, Lyudmila and Volodya.

"Filipp Petrovich! Well, I never!" Yelizaveta rushed impetuously towards him and took both his hands in her hot dry palms.

She was one of the Krasnodon people who had not condemned Lyutikov for returning to his job in the workshops. She knew him so well that she did not even think it necessary to ascertain the reason for his action. If Lyutikov had acted in that way it was because there had been no other way out or else because it had been necessary.

Lyutikov was the first intimate friend to call on the Osmukhins since the arrival of the Germans and all Yelizaveta's joy at seeing him was expressed in that impulsive rush towards him. He understood it and was grateful to her.

"I've come to drag that son of yours out to work," he said with his customary sternness. "You and Lyudmila come and sit with us for a bit for appearances' sake and later leave the room as if to go about your business outside, and I'll have a little talk with him." He smiled at all three and in that instant his expression softened.

From the moment Lyutikov had entered Volodya had not taken his eyes off him. In his talks with Tolya he had often hazarded a guess that it had not been compelling necessity and far less cowardice that had caused Lyutikov to go back to the job in the workshops—he wasn't that kind! His reasons had probably been deeper than that—reasons which, for all one knew, might not really have been so far removed from those which had more than once entered the thoughts of Volodya and Tolya. Anyway, he was a man with whom one could safely share one's intentions.

Volodya was the first to speak, as soon as Yelizaveta and Lyudmila had left the room.

"'Go to work'! You said—'go to work'! It's all the same to me whether I work or not—my aim remains the same in either case. And that is to fight the Germans, fight them mercilessly. And if I do go to work, then it'll only be to mask my intentions," Volodya said, with something of defiance in his voice.

His youthful courage, his candour and fervour, scarce restrained by the presence of German soldiers in the next room, did not cause Lyutikov to feel afraid for him, to feel annoyance or to want to ridicule. He merely felt he wanted to smile. But he did not reveal what he felt. Not a muscle moved on his face.

"Fine!" he said. "You tell that to everyone who happens to drop in, like I did. Or better still, go out in the street and say to everyone you meet, 'Look here, I'm fighting the Germans and I want to mask my intentions, help me, will you?'"

Volodya flushed crimson.

"But you're not just anyone," he said, crest-fallen.

"Maybe I'm not, but in these times you can never tell," Lyutikov replied.

Volodya could see that Lyutikov was about to lecture him. And Lyutikov did, indeed, lecture him.

"To be too trusting in these matters can cost lives; times have changed. And there's a saying about walls having ears. And don't imagine they're such simpletons, they're crafty in their own way," he said, nodding towards the door. "So it's lucky for you I'm well known and have been given the job of getting everyone back to the workshops, and that's why I'm here. And that's what you'll tell your mother and sister, and those other people," again he nodded towards the door. "We're going to work for 'em," he concluded. With that he fixed his stern eyes on Volodya. Volodya understood at once and turned pale.

"Who of the friends you can depend on are still in town?" Lyutikov asked.

Volodya named three: Tolya Orlov, Zhora Arutyuniants and Vanya Zemnukhov.

"And we'll find more," he added.

"First contact those you think can be completely relied on, see each of them individually, not when they're all together. When you've convinced yourself that they're all right...."

"They are, Filipp Petrovich."

"... When you've convinced yourself that they're all right," Lyutikov continued as though he had not heard Volodya's remark, "drop a direct hint that there are possibilities and so, would they be prepared, etc."

"They're prepared and each of them is wondering what he ought to do!"

"Tell them that you'll have a job for them. And as for you, here's work for you at once." Lyutikov proceeded to tell Volodya about the type buried in the park and gave him details as to its position. "Find out whether it's possible to dig it up. Report to me if it's not."

Volodya thought for a moment. Lyutikov did not press him for a reply. He realized that Volodya was not wavering but was simply considering the matter as one in earnest would be expected to do. Volodya's thoughts however were not on what Lyutikov had just proposed to him.

"I'll be completely frank with you," Volodya said. "You told me I should speak to the boys individually—I can see the reason for that. But even so, when I talk to each of them in turn, I ought to make it clear to them on whose behalf I'm speaking. It's one thing if I act as though I'm on my own, but quite another if I say that I've been given the task by someone connected with the organization. I'm not going to mention your name and none of the fellows'll ask—they'll understand." Volodya's intention was to forestall any objections Lyutikov might raise. But Lyutikov made no objections, he only waited for Volodya to go on. "If I spoke to the fellows simply as Osmukhin they'd still believe me of course.... But they'd go on looking just the same for contact with the underground organization—I can't lay down the law to them ... some of them are older than me and—" He almost said "and wiser." "What I mean is that some of the fellows take more interest in politics and understand them better. That's why it'd make it easier to tell them that I'm not acting on my own initiative, but on behalf of the organization. That's one point. The other point is, several of the fellows will be needed to recover the type and these fellows will have to be told that the job is a serious one and that the instructions come from somewhere underground. And in this connection I want to ask you a question: I've got three friends; one of them, Tolya, is an old friend, the others are new but

I've known them for some time; they're both fellows who've proved themselves when things have gone wrong and I trust them like myself—they're Vanya Zemnukhov and Zhora Arutyuniants. Can I bring them all together for consultation?"

Lyutikov remained silent for some moments, studying his boots. Then he looked at Volodya with a trace of a smile on his lips but his expression immediately became severe again.

"Right—get them together and tell them openly on whose authority you're acting—without names, of course."

Hardly able to control his excitement, Volodya merely nodded.

"Your reasoning's very sound: it has to be made clear to everyone that the Party is with us in everything we undertake," Lyutikov continued, as though deliberating with himself. His wise, stern eyes seemed to look steadily, calmly into Volodya's innermost heart. "And then you've understood correctly that our Party organization could well do with a youth group attached to it. That's really what I came to see you about. And now as we've already reached agreement on that point here's some advice for you, or an order if you like: take no action without consulting me—otherwise you might get killed and spoil things for us. I myself am not working on my own initiative, I take advice, too. I ask my comrades for advice or else the people who are supervising our work; we've got them right here with us in Voroshilovgrad Region. You can tell your three friends this and you too must ask each other's advice. That seems to be all." He smiled and stood up. "And come to work tomorrow!"

"Well—the day after tomorrow," Volodya said with a grin. "Can I bring Tolya Orlov with me?"

Lyutikov laughed. "I wanted to win one man over to come and work for the Germans and I've got two at once," he said. "Bring him along. All the better!"

He went into the kitchen, exchanged a few jocular remarks with Yelizaveta, Lyudmila and the German soldier and soon left. Volodya knew that his family must not be let into the secret with which he had been entrusted. But he had great difficulty in concealing his elation from the fond eyes of his mother and sister.

Volodya simulated a yawn, said he was getting up early the next day and that anyway he was sleepy and wanted to go to bed. Yelizaveta did not question him and that was a bad sign. Volodya suspected that his mother had guessed that he and Lyutikov had discussed more than just his job in the workshops. But Lyudmila questioned him point-blank:

"What were you talking about all that time?"

"What were we talking about? You know very well what we were talking about!" Volodya said, irritably.

"And you're going?"

"What can I do?"

"Going to work for the Germans!" There was so much shocked indignation in Lyudmila's voice that Volodya was unable to think of a reply.

"We'll work for them all right..." he sullenly repeated Lyutikov's words and, without a glance at her, began to undress.

Chapter 25

ON HIS RETURN from the unsuccessful evacuation, Zhora at once entered into frank and friendly relations with Volodya and Tolya Orlov. With Lyudmila, however, his relations were stiff and formal. He lived in a small house in a district which had not found favour with the Germans and so the friends usually met in Zhora's home.

The day after Volodya had been given the job of looking into the matter of the type the three of them met in Zhora's room, which was so small that there was scarcely room for the bed and his small writing-desk. Still, it was his own room. And this was where Vanya Zemnukhov found them. Just back from Nizhny Alexandrovsky, he was leaner than ever, his clothing had become threadbare and he was covered in dust, for he had not yet been to his own home. He was in very high spirits and full of energy.

"Will you have an opportunity of seeing the man again?" he asked Volodya.

"Why?"

"Because we ought to get his permission to include Oleg Koshevoi in our group at once."

"He said there was no need to include anyone else for the time being, but only to select likely people."

"That's why I said that we should ask his permission," Vanya said. "Can't you get to see him today—before tonight?"

"I don't see why there's such a hurry," Volodya said a trifle resentfully.

"This is why: in the first place, Oleg's a real comrade; secondly he's my best friend which means he's reliable; thirdly he knows the fellows in the seventh, eighth and ninth forms of the Gorky School better than Zhora does and there are more of them left in town than any of the others."

Zhora at once fixed his fiery black eyes on Volodya and said:

"After the failure of the evacuation I gave you a full account of Oleg's character. You must also take into account the fact that he lives very near the park and for that reason is in a better position than anyone else to assist in the task allotted to us."

Zhora's gift for selecting the correct phrases in which to describe his thoughts had made his idea sound so official that it was almost like an instruction.

Volodya wavered but, with Lyutikov's warning fresh in his mind, he refused to give in.

"All right then," Vanya said, "I can put forward yet another argument, but only in private." He adjusted his spectacles and, with a smile that was both bashful and audacious, turned to Zhora and Tolya: "You won't mind?"

"When it is a question of conspiracy there cannot be, nor must there be, any question of minding. The most important thing is expediency," Zhora said and left the room with Tolya Orlov.

"I'm going to prove to you that I trust you more than you trust me," Vanya said with a smile which was no longer bashful but the courageous smile of the determined, brave young man that Vanya, indeed, was. "Did Zhora tell you that Valko returned with us?"

"He did."

"But you didn't say anything about it to that comrade?"

"No."

"Now then—look: Oleg's in touch with Valko, and Valko's trying to establish contact with the Bolshevik underground!

You tell that to your comrade. And at the same time pass our request on to him. Tell him that we vouch for Oleg."

Thus fate decided that Volodya should present himself at the central workshops earlier than he had promised Lyutikov.

During his absence Vanya took Tolya the Thunderer aside and asked him to find out quietly whether there were any Germans in the Koshevoi's home and whether it was possible to reach Oleg.

As the Thunderer approached the house from Sadovaya Street, he noted the German sentry at the door and then saw a pretty woman suddenly run barefoot out of the house, the tears streaming down her face. She wore shabby clothing but had luxuriant black hair. She dashed into the wood-shed and Tolya could hear her weeping and a male voice trying to console her. Then a thin, sunburnt old woman came darting from the house with a pail in her bony hand, scooped it full of water from the butt outside and quickly went back into the cottage. Some sort of commotion was taking place inside the cottage, the lordly voice of a young German could be heard expressing displeasure about something, then women's voices with an apologetic note in them. Tolya could not hang about any longer without attracting attention, so he went along the side of the park to bypass the whole area, then approached the cottage from the back street which ran parallel to Sadovaya Street. But from there he was unable to see or hear anything. He noted then that, like the Koshevois' garden, the neighbouring one also had a back gate, so he went through it and a moment later was standing by the back wall of the Koshevois' wood-shed, which looked out on to the kitchen garden.

He could now distinguish four voices inside the shed, three female and one male. The voice of one of the women was young and she was sobbing as she said, "I won't go back to the house, not if they kill me for it!"

The man's voice was grimly persuasive: "Come now, come! Where'll Oleg go then? And what about the child?"

"Mercenary creature! All for a bottle of olive oil! The mercenary creature!... You haven't heard the last of me, not by a long chalk! You'll regret this yet!" Oleg was saying, meanwhile. On the way home from Lena Pozdnysheva he was torn between fits of jealousy and the torments of pride. The red, hot sun was dipping towards the western horizon and shone straight in his eyes. Again and again in the red, lowering circles of light there floated the thin, brown face of Lena and the heavy, darkly patterned dress she was wearing, the grey Germans at the piano. He kept repeating over and over again, "Mercenary creature! Mercenary creature!" And he choked with grief, almost like a child.

In the wood-shed he found Marina. She was sitting with her face in her hands, her head bent, her fluffy black hair falling round her shoulders. Crowded round her was the family.

In the absence of the general, the long-legged adjutant had decided he would like to freshen up and have a cold rub-down. He had ordered Marina to bring him a wash-basin and a pail of water. When she returned with them and opened the door she had found the adjutant standing before her stark naked. Marina had through her tears related that he looked long and white like a tapeworm. He had been in the far corner near the divan and she had not at first noticed him as she entered the room. But suddenly he had been there almost at her side and had looked at her with contemptuous, insolent curiosity. She had dropped the bucket of water and the basin, she had been so frightened and disgusted. The water had spilt over the whole floor and Marina had fled to the wood-shed.

The assembled family was now awaiting the consequences of Marina's carelessness.

"What a thing to howl about!" Oleg remarked rudely. "You thought he wanted to do something to you, I suppose. If he were the boss here, he would have, and he'd have called the batman in to help him. But all he wanted was to have a wash, you found him naked because it hadn't entered his head to be embarrassed by you. After all, to those brutes, we're worse than savages. Be thankful that they don't relieve themselves in front of you—that's what the SS soldiers and officers are doing in their billets. They relieve themselves in front of our people and reckon it's quite in the order of things. Ugh, how I can see through the filthy breed of swaggering fascists! They're worse than animals; they're degenerates, that's what they are!" he said fiercely. "And the fact that you're crying your eyes out and we're all gathered round you—what an occasion, indeed!—is degrading and shameful! We ought to despise these degenerate monsters if for the time being we can't defeat and annihilate them. Yes, treat them with contempt instead of degrading ourselves and crying and moaning like old women! They'll get what's coming to them!"

He went outside, exasperated. And then he thought how revolting it was always to be confronted with those bare front gardens—the whole length of the street from the park to the level crossing literally stripped—and German soldiers walking about everywhere.

Yelena Nikolayevna followed him.

"I was so worried. Where have you been all this time? How's Lena?" she asked, looking closely and searchingly at Oleg's gloomy face.

His lips began to quiver like a great baby's. "Mercenary creature! Don't ever mention her to me again."

And then, as usual, and scarcely aware of doing so, he told his mother everything: what he had seen in Lena's home and how he had behaved.

"What else could I have done?" he exclaimed.

"Don't pity her," his mother said softly. "You're worried about it because you feel sorry for her; but don't pity her. If she could behave like that, then she's always been like that and not what ... we thought." She almost said "you thought," but decided otherwise. "And that shows how bad she is, and not us."

The big steppe moon hung low over the southern horizon. Nikolai Nikolayevich and Oleg sat at the open door of the wood-shed looking at the sky.

Oleg gazed wide-eyed at the full moon with a halo round it, the light from it falling on the German sentry at the porch, and the leaves of the pumpkins in the garden. Oleg gazed at the moon and he felt he was really seeing it for the first time. He was used to life in the small steppe town where everything that took place on the ground and in the sky was straightforward and familiar; but now things were happening without his noticing them. He had ceased to notice how the new moon was born, how it grew larger and how it finally came to be this full moon in the deep blue sky. And who could tell whether he would live to see again those happy carefree times when he would be in complete harmony with all that is simple and good and wonderful in the world?

General Baron von Wentzel and his adjutant, both in crisp uniforms, arrived and entered the house in silence. Everything was quiet, only the sentry walked up and down by the house. Nikolai Nikolayevich had sat long enough and went to lie down. Oleg, bathed in moonlight and with big round childlike eyes, remained sitting at the open door of the shed.

Suddenly he heard something rustling at his back, behind the planks of the shed wall facing the neighbours' garden.

"Oleg ... you asleep? Wake up!" came a whisper close to a chink in the boards.

In a flash Oleg was at the wall.

"Who is it?" he whispered.

"It's me ... Vanya.... Is your door open?"

"I'm not alone. There's a sentry."

"I'm not alone either. Can you come out to us?"

"Of course."

Oleg waited until the sentry walked towards the gate in the other street, then, hugging the wall, went round the outside of the shed. In the wormwood shrubs of the next-door garden close to the back wall of the shed and hidden in its dense shadow, three boys lay, in a fan, flat on their stomachs: Vanya Zemnukhov, Zhora Arutyuniants and a third, as lanky as they were but with his face thrown into shadow by his cap.

"It's the very devil, these bright moonlight nights! We hardly managed to get through to you!" Zhora said, his eyes and teeth gleaming. "Meet Volodya Osmukhin, of the Voroshilov School. You can have the same absolute confidence in him as in me," he said, convinced that there was no higher recommendation for his comrade.

Oleg stretched out between Zhora and Vanya.

"I must admit I didn't expect you at this prohibited hour," he whispered to Vanya, and grinned.

Vanya smiled. "If you observe all their regulations you'll die of boredom."

"You're a fine chap, you are!" Oleg laughed and put his big hand on Vanya's shoulder. "Did you get them settled in?" he whispered into his ear.

"Can I stay in your shed until daybreak?" Vanya asked. "I haven't been home yet, because the house is full of Germans."

"I've already told you you can spend the night with us!" Zhora interjected indignantly.

"It's much too far to your house. The night maybe bright for you and Volodya, but I'd probably fall into a swampy hole and disappear for ever!"

Oleg could see that Vanya wanted to have a private chat with him.

"You can stay till daybreak," he said, and pressed his shoulder.

"We've got some exceptional news," Vanya whispered almost inaudibly. "Volodya's made contact with one of the underground comrades and has already been given a job.... Tell him yourself, Volodya."

Nothing could have aroused Oleg's active nature as much as this sudden nocturnal appearance of the lads and particularly Volodya's story. For a moment he even thought that none other than Valko could have given Volodya a task of that kind. With his face close to Volodya's he looked into his narrow dark eyes and began to question him.

"How did you spot him? Who is he?"

"I haven't the right to give you his name," Volodya said, beginning to feel slightly embarrassed. "D'you know anything about the disposition of the Germans in the park?"

"No."

"Zhora and I want to go now and do a bit of reconnoitring, but it'll be difficult with just the two of us. Tolya Orlov wanted to come, but he coughs too much," Volodya said with a laugh.

For some moments Oleg's gaze wandered past Vanya.

"I shouldn't advise you to do it tonight," he said. "Anyone approaching the park'll be seen right away, yet you can't see what's going on inside. Much simpler to do it all quite openly in broad daylight."

The park was surrounded by a slatted fence and streets ran along each of its four sides. Oleg, with the practical common sense he always showed, suggested that at different times during the following day one of them should walk leisurely along each of these streets and note and remember the position of the AA guns, shelters and lorries.

The enthusiasm for action with which the lads had come to Oleg cooled slightly. But they could not help agreeing with Oleg's simple arguments.

Have you ever, dear reader, strayed at night in the depth of a forest, or found yourself alone in a strange land, or faced danger alone? Or have you ever been in adversity so grievous that even your closest friends have turned their backs on you? Or have you ever searched long for something new, something unknown to mankind, and spent long years being misunderstood and disowned by everyone? If one of these misfortunes or difficulties in life has ever assailed you, then you will understand what radiant, courageous happiness, what inexpressible, heartfelt gratitude, what a torrent of mighty strength fills the heart of a man when he meets a friend whose word, whose faith, whose courage and devotion have remained unchanged! You are no longer alone in the world, side by side with yours another heart beats. A flood of emotions such as these filled Oleg's breast when, alone with Vanya, in the light of the steppe moon moving slowly across the sky, he saw those short-sighted eyes that were aglow with kindliness and strength, saw his friend's calm, humorous, inspired expression.

"Vanya!" Oleg put his long arms round Vanya and hugged him, laughing softly with happiness. "It's been a long time! I m-missed you so much, you d-devil," he stuttered and hugged Vanya again.

"Let go, you'll break my ribs! I'm not a girl!" said Vanya, chuckling, and he wriggled himself free.

"I didn't think she'd hook you like that!" Oleg said, grinning slyly.

"You really ought to be ashamed," Vanya said, ill at ease. "After what happened I couldn't very well just leave them, without seeing them settled in, without being sure they were out of danger. And then she is an unusual sort of girl! So crystal-clear, so broad-minded!"

As a matter of fact, during the few days which Vanya had spent at Nizhny Alexandrovsk, he had succeeded in explaining to Klava all he had thought and felt and put into verse in the nineteen years of his life. And Klava, who was a very kind-hearted girl and in love with him, had silently and patiently listened to him. And whenever he had asked a question, she had nodded and readily agreed with everything he said. So it was not surprising that the longer Vanya had remained with Klava the more broad-minded she had seemed to him.

"Yes, I can see you've been c-caught, all right," Oleg said and looked at his friend with laughing eyes. "Don't get angry," he added, suddenly becoming serious when he saw that his banter was annoying Vanya. "I was only fooling. I'm glad you're so happy. Truly, I'm glad," he said with sincerity and for some moments he looked past Vanya with far-away eyes, while deep lines appeared on his brow.

"Tell me frankly," he said after an interval, "wasn't it Valko who gave Osmukhin that job?"

"No, it wasn't. He told Volodya to find out from you how to find Valko. And that's really why I wanted to stay the night with you."

"That's the whole trouble, I don't know where to find him. I'm getting worried about him," Oleg said. "But let's get inside the shed."

They closed the door behind them and, without undressing, settled themselves on the wooden cot and kept up a long whispered conversation in the dark. It seemed as though there were no German sentry near by, no Germans anywhere. Several times one or the other said, "That's enough now, we've got to get some sleep." Then they started whispering again.

Oleg awoke when Nikolai Nikolayevich shook him. Vanya Zemnukhov had already gone.

"What's the matter with you—sleeping in your clothes?" Nikolai Nikolayevich asked with a barely perceptible smile on his lips and in his eyes.

"Sleep felled the warrior," Oleg said and stretched.

"Warrior, indeed! I heard the whole session in the weeds behind the shed. And the twaddle you talked with Zemnukhov!"

"Y-you heard it all?" Oleg sat up on his cot, a sleepy, perplexed expression on his face. "Why didn't you let us know you weren't asleep?"

"Didn't want to disturb you."

"I didn't expect this from you!"

"There's plenty more you didn't expect from me," Nikolai Nikolayevich said in his slow manner of speaking. "For instance, you didn't know I'd got a wireless set, did you? Right there under the floor, under the Germans."

Oleg was stunned. A foolish stare came into his eyes.

"You ... w-what? Didn't you hand it in?"

"I did not."

"You mean you concealed it from the Soviet authorities?"

"I did."

"But, K-K-Kolya, really ... I had no idea you c-could be as crafty as that," Oleg said, undecided whether to laugh or to be annoyed.

"Well, in the first place it's a set that was awarded to me for my good work and secondly it's a foreign-made, seven-valve receiver."

"But they promised you would have them returned!"

"Promised! And by now it would have been in the hands of the Germans! Instead of that it's under the floor boards and when I heard you talking last night I realized it'd come in very handy! So it means I've done the right thing from all points of view," Nikolai Nikolayevich said without a smile.

"Certainly a smart piece of work, Uncle Kolya! Let's have a wash and kill time till breakfast with a game of chess. We've got nobody to work for, now the Germans are here," Oleg said. He was in excellent spirits.

In that instant a girlish ringing voice was heard asking loud enough for the whole yard to hear:

"Listen you, half-wit: doesn't Oleg Koshevoi live in this house?"

"*Was sagst du? Ich verstehe nicht,*" came the reply from the sentry at the porch.

"Did you ever see the like of it, Nina? He doesn't know a word of Russian! Well, at least let us pass or call a real man, a Russian," the girlish ringing voice said.

Nikolai Nikolayevich and Oleg looked at each other and then poked their heads out of the shed door.

Two girls confronted the somewhat perplexed German sentry. The girl who had addressed the sentry was dressed in such bright colours that Oleg and Kolya noticed her first.

This impression of brightness was produced by the exceptionally gay and striking dress she was wearing, a bright blue crepe de Chine heavily dotted with red cherries, and green spots, and splashes of something yellow and lilac. The morning sun shone on her hair with its high, golden wave in front and the soft curls, no doubt carefully arranged in front of two mirrors, which fell on her neck and shoulders. The bright dress fitted so neatly at the waist and fell in such graceful folds to the shapely legs in their self-coloured stockings and smart, beige shoes on high heels that the girl gave an impression of being unusually lively, light, airy and natural.

Oleg and Nikolai Nikolayevich watched her through the shed door as she made an attempt to reach the steps of the porch, while the sentry, holding his tommy-gun in one hand, barred her way with the other.

Without a moment's hesitation the small white hand slapped his grimy hand aside and the girl ran up the steps of the porch, turning to call back over her shoulder to her friend.

"Nina, come on, now!"

Nina hesitated; the sentry had leapt to the porch and had planted himself in front of the door, arms outstretched, tommy-gun dangling by its strap from his thick neck. On his face was a fixed grin that was stupidly self-satisfied, because he had done his duty, and ingratiating, because he knew that only a young woman who had the right to do so would have treated him in this fashion.

"I'm Koshevoi, will you come this way!" Oleg said, emerging from the wood-shed.

The girl quickly turned her head, screwed up her eyes and quizzed him for an instant, then came running from the porch, her heels clicking on the wooden steps.

Tall, with his arms dangling by his sides, Oleg awaited her, his eyes holding a candidly interrogatory, kindly expression, as if to say: "I'm Oleg Koshevoi, only just tell me what you want of me? If it's for a good purpose, then I'm at your service, if not, then why pick on me?"

The girl came up to him, looked at him for a moment as though comparing his appearance with some photograph; her friend, whom Oleg had hardly noticed, had followed and stood a little to one side.

"It's Oleg all right," the girl said as though confirming it to herself. "We need to talk to you alone," she said, and winked a blue eye at him. Puzzled and a little embarrassed, Oleg let both girls into the shed. The girl in the gay dress looked hard at Nikolai Nikolayevich with narrowed eyes, then turned to Oleg with a surprised, questioning glance.

"Whatever you have to say to me you can say in front of him," Oleg said.

"Oh no, we can't. We want to talk about our love affairs, don't we, Nina?" she said and with a light-hearted laugh turned to her friend.

Both Oleg and Nikolai Nikolayevich looked at the second girl.

Her face was large-featured, and deeply tanned; her arms, large and well-formed, were bare to the elbows and almost blackened by the sun. An unusual wealth of dark hair framed her face, waving heavily as though cast in bronze to her firm rounded shoulders. The full lips, the soft chin, the broad face and the softened lines of her very ordinary nose produced an impression of unusual simplicity; yet the prominent bones over her eyebrows, the lines of the eyebrows, the frank courageous glance from wide-set brown eyes spoke of strength and defiance, passion and enthusiasm.

Oleg's eyes involuntarily rested on this girl; he was conscious of her presence during the whole ensuing conversation and it made him stutter.

The girl with the blue eyes waited until Nikolai Nikolayevich's footsteps had faded across the yard, then she peered into Oleg's face and said, "I've come from Uncle Andrei."

"That was courageous of you! And the w-way you handled that sentry!" Oleg said with a grin.

"Never mind, the louts like to be thrashed!" She laughed.

"Wh-who are you?"

"Lyuba," the girl in the gay, perfumed crepe de Chine said.

Chapter 26

LYUBOV SHEVTSOVA was a member of the group of Komsomol youths and girls who, as early as the previous autumn, had been selected for service under the partisan headquarters in the rear of the enemy.

She was finishing her army nursing courses in Voroshilovgrad and was about to be sent to the front when, instead, she was kept in Voroshilovgrad and put through a course of wireless telegraphy.

On the instructions of the partisan headquarters she had concealed all this from her family and friends; she wrote home and told all her acquaintances that she was still at the military nursing school. The fact that her life was now shrouded in secrecy pleased her; she had always been fond of play-acting—not for nothing was she "that artful vixen, Lyuba the Actress."

When she was a very little girl she had always been a doctor. She tossed all her toys out of the window and went about with a first-aid pouch with a red cross on it stuffed with cotton wool, gauze and bandages. She had been a plump little girl with blue eyes and dimples, for ever wanting to bandage up her Mummy, her Daddy, everybody, children and adults, cats and dogs.

One day an older boy had jumped barefoot off a fence and cut his sole on a piece of glass from a broken wine bottle. The boy came from some distant household and Lyuba did not know him, there were no grown-ups about to give first aid. Little Lyuba, six years old, washed his foot, dabbed the wound with iodine and bandaged it. The boy—his name was Sergei Levashov—showed no interest in Lyuba nor gratitude. He despised girls in general, and was never again seen in the Shevtsovs' garden.

When she began to go to school she learned as easily and happily as though it were all a game. But by that time she no longer wanted to be a doctor, nor a teacher, nor an engineer—no, she wanted to become a housewife and whatever task she undertook to do at home, from scrubbing floors to making dumplings, the work in her hands was performed more skilfully and with a better will than when her mother did it. True, she wanted to be a second Chapayev, not Anka, the girl who was his machine-gunner, but Chapayev himself, because it turned out that Lyuba too despised the girls. With a piece of burnt cork she would make herself Chapayev moustaches and fight with the boys to a victorious conclusion. When she was a little older she began to love dancing, Russian and foreign ball-room dancing, Ukrainian and Caucasian folk dancing, and when she discovered she had a good voice, it became quite clear that she would go on the stage. She began to perform in clubs and on the open-air stage in the park and when war broke out she took great pleasure in performing for the troops. But she was really no actress, she merely played at being one; she could not seem to find her level. There was something in her spirit, sparkling and colourful, which played and sang and sometimes surged up in her like a flame. Some sort of imp gave her no peace; she was plagued by a thirst for fame and a terrifying capacity for self-sacrifice. Her reckless courage and her feeling of childlike playfulness and deep happiness continually urged her onwards so that there should always be something new and always something to strive for. Now she dreamed of achieving great exploits at the front: she would be an Air Force pilot or, if the worst came to the worst, an army doctor. But it all ended with her becoming an intelligence radio operator working in the rear of the enemy—which was best of all, of course!

It was strange and amusing that of all the Krasnodon Komsomols sent for wireless training, her own group should include that same Sergei Levashov to whom she had given first aid in their childhood and who had so completely ignored her. Now she had a chance to turn the tables on him, because he fell in love with her at once whilst she, of course, did not reciprocate although he had a handsome mouth and handsome ears and was altogether a sensible lad. He had no idea how to court a girl, he could only sit, broad-shouldered and silent, and gaze at her submissively while she laughed at him and tormented him as much as she pleased.

While they were undergoing training it would sometimes happen that one of the trainees ceased to attend the lectures. Everyone knew what that meant: he had become proficient before the allotted time, and had been sent behind the German lines.

There had been a sultry evening in May. The town gardens had seemed to droop for lack of air, the acacias flooded with moonlight were in full bloom and their fragrant perfume was intoxicating. Lyuba loved being in crowds and wanted Sergei to take her to the pictures or for a stroll down Lenin Avenue. But he said:

"But see how lovely it is here. Surely you must feel good here?" And in the half-light of the park avenue his eyes would shine with a strange light.

They walked round and round the park and Lyuba began to feel very bored with Sergei's silence and his refusal to fall in with her wishes.

Suddenly a crowd of young fellows and girls swooped down on the park with squeals and laughter. Among them was Borka Dubinsky, a Voroshilovgrad boy who was also training at the wireless school and was also not indifferent to Lyuba. Lyuba liked him because he always sent her into fits of laughter with his nonsensical demand that one should judge from "the viewpoint of the tram traffic."

"Borka!" she shouted.

He recognized her voice, and came running towards her and Sergei and at once launched into a flow of words which it seemed impossible to stop.

"Who are you with?" Lyuba asked.

"Oh, they're from the print-shop. Want to meet them?"

"Of course!" she said.

After introductions all round Lyuba suggested a stroll along Lenin Avenue. Sergei backed out and Lyuba imagined he was sulking. So to teach him a lesson, she ostentatiously took Borka's arm and ran from the park, their four feet making impossible figures on the ground and her skirt flashing through the trees.

After breakfast the next morning she did not see Sergei in the hostel, nor did he turn up at the lectures. He was absent from dinner and from supper and it would have been useless to inquire into his whereabouts. She had, of course, dismissed the previous evening's events in the park from her mind. "Why should I think about it!" But, towards evening, she suddenly felt a longing for home; she thought of her father and mother and it seemed to her that she might never see them again. She lay quietly on her bed in the hostel room which she shared with five other girls. They were all asleep, the black-out had been removed from the windows. The light of the moon flooded the room and Lyuba felt very sad.

But the next day she forgot Sergei Levashov, just as though he had never existed.

On July 6th, the principal of the wireless school sent for Lyuba and told her that things were not going well at the front; the school was evacuating, and Lyuba was being put at the disposal of the regional partisan headquarters; she would return to her home in Krasnodon and await further instructions. If the Germans came she was to behave in such a way as not to arouse suspicion. She was then given an address in the Kamenny Brod where she was to call and make herself known to the landlady before leaving Voroshilovgrad. Lyuba had done as she had been told, had then packed her suitcase, and gone to the nearest cross-roads, and thumbed a lift. The very first lorry which came along had been passing through Krasnodon and the driver had found room for impertinent, fair-haired Lyuba.

After Valko had separated from the group, he had spent the remainder of that day lying out in the steppe. When darkness came he walked along the ravine until he arrived at the far end of Shanghai district. He had known the lay-out of the town from his earliest childhood and so he was able to reach 1B Pit by way of narrow lanes and twisting back streets.

He was afraid that there might be Germans billeted in the Shevtsovs' home; he therefore approached it stealthily from the back, climbed over the fence into the yard and concealed himself behind the outhouses in the hope that someone might soon come out into the yard. He had stood thus for a long time and his patience was beginning to run out when a door banged shut and a woman carrying a pail walked softly past him. It was Shevtsov's wife, Yevfrosinya Mironovna, and Valko moved towards her.

"Merciful Lord!" she exclaimed softly. "Who's that?"

Valko brought his face, black and stubbly with a few days' beard, close to hers and she recognized him.

"It's you! But where—?" she began. The half-light, with the moon clouded over, did not show Valko how the colour had drained from the woman's face.

"Wait a minute; and forget my name," he interrupted her in a hoarse voice. "Call me Uncle Andrei. Any Germans in your house? No? Let's go inside." He was depressed by the thought of what he would have to say to her.

Lyuba was sitting on the bed sewing when he entered; she rose to greet him but it was not the Lyuba in a gay frock and high-heeled shoes he had so often seen on the stage at the club; here was a simple, domesticated Lyuba, barefoot and in a cheap blouse and short skirt. Her golden hair hung loosely over her neck and shoulders. Her eyes appeared dark now as she screwed them up to look at him in the light of the miners' lamp hanging over the table; they betrayed no surprise.

Valko's eyes fell before hers, then looked absently round the room which still preserved traces of its owners' former prosperity and came to rest on a postcard tacked to the wall over the head of the bed. It was a picture postcard of Hitler.

"Don't think bad of us, Comrade Valko," Lyuba's mother said.

"Uncle Andrei," Valko corrected her.

"Er ... I mean Uncle Andrei," she said without smiling.

Lyuba calmly turned towards the postcard of Hitler and shrugged her shoulders contemptuously.

"A German officer put it there," Yevfrosinya Mironovna explained. "We've had two German officers here all the time; only yesterday they left for Novocherkassk. As soon as they came they started on her: 'Russian girl beautiful, nice, blonde,' and they laughed and gave her chocolate and biscuits. I saw her take it all, the little devil, and then she turns up her nose and is rude to them. Laughing one minute and insulting them the next—that's the sort of game she played," the mother said, gently condemning her daughter and completely confident that Valko would understand. "I said to her, 'Don't you play with fire.' So she says, 'It's got to be done.' Got to be done—I ask you! Playing round with 'em like that! And can you imagine, Comrade Valko...."

"Uncle Andrei," he again corrected her.

"... Uncle Andrei. And she ordered me to keep quiet about being her mother and she passed me off as her housekeeper and said she was an actress. She said, 'Oh, my parents were industrialists—they owned mines and the Soviet Government exiled them to Siberia.' Did you ever hear the like?"

"Can't say I did," Valko said calmly with a keen look at Lyuba who stood in front of him with her sewing in her hand gazing at him with a vague smile on her lips.

"The officer that slept in this bed—it's hers, but we both slept in the other room—well, he started to rummage in his bag for linen or something and brought out this postcard and stuck it up on the wall. And—can you imagine this, Comrade Valko—she makes a bee-line for it and woof!—the postcard's gone! 'That's my bed,' she says, 'and I don't want Hitler hanging over it!' I was sure she'd be killed on the spot. The officer took her wrist and twisted it, took the postcard and stuck it back on the wall and the other officer was there too and they laughed fit to make the windows rattle. 'Now, then,' they said, 'Russian girl *schlecht!*' I could see that she was angry. She was getting red in the face and clenching her fists—I nearly died, I was so frightened! And either because they were amused by her or because they were the very latest thing in half-wits, they just stood there and laughed. And she stamped her feet and shouted, 'Your Hitler, he's a monster, a vampire, he should be thrown down a watercloset!' And she went on like that, and I thought any moment he'd whip out his revolver and shoot her.... And when they left she wouldn't let me take Hitler down. 'No,' she said, 'let him hang there, it's necessary.'"

Lyuba's mother was not old but, like many other ordinary middle-aged women who had had a miscarriage in their younger days, she had grown very heavy round the hips and waist and her ankles had swollen. She had related her tale to Valko in a low tone of voice and had looked at him all the time with questioning, timid, imploring eyes. But he had evaded her glance. She had gone on talking and talking as though trying to postpone the moment when he would say what she dreaded to hear. But now she had come to the end of her story and she looked at him, anxiety and fear in her eyes.

"Have you any of your husband's old clothing here, Yevfrosinya Mironovna," he began in a husky voice. "I don't feel very comfortable dressed in a jacket, riding-breeches and slippers; that would draw suspicion immediately." He laughed grimly and there was something in his voice which caused Yevfrosinya to turn pale again and Lyuba to let fall her sewing.

"What's happened to him?" the mother asked, her voice barely audible.

"Yevfrosinya and you, Lyuba," Valko began in a quiet, firm voice, "I never thought I'd have to come to you with bad news, but I can't deceive you, nor have I anything with which to console you. Your husband, and your father, Lyuba, and the best friend I have ever had, is dead. Grigory Ilyich was killed when the damned butchers dropped a bomb on the evacuating civilians. Eternal remembrance and glory be his, and may he live on in the hearts of our people!"

Yevfrosinya did not cry out. She pressed the corner of her kerchief to her eyes and wept softly. As for Lyuba, the colour drained from her face. She stood for a moment stupefied, then crumpled up and fell senseless to the floor.

Valko lifted her and laid her on the bed.

He had expected a burst of grief from Lyuba, and tears, which would perhaps have helped her to overcome that grief. But she lay on the bed motionless and still, her face white and vacant, deep, bitter lines like her mother's imprinted on the turned-down corners of her large mouth.

The mother, simple Russian woman that she was, gave vent to her grief naturally, quietly and simply and with all her heart. The tears flowed freely, she wiped them away with the corner of her kerchief or flicked them away with her hand, or, as they trickled down to the lips and chin, she wiped them off with her open hand. And because her grief was so natural, she went about her business doing all the things a housewife normally does when a guest is in the house. She poured out water for him to wash, lit an oil-lamp for him and produced from a trunk an old shirt, jacket and trousers which her husband had been in the habit of wearing at home.

Valko took the oil-lamp, went into the other room and changed. The clothing was a little too tight for him, but he nevertheless breathed more freely, for now he looked like any other skilled worker.

He began to tell them the details of how Grigory Shevtsov had met his death. He knew that no matter how horrible the details, they alone could now give wife and daughter some comfort, even though it was cold comfort and painful enough in its bitterness. Despite his grief and anxiety, he sat long over the meal, eating his fill and drinking a whole carafe of vodka. He had been without food the whole day and was very tired, but he was determined to talk matters over with Lyuba. He helped her to rise from the bed, and they went into the next room.

"I guessed at once that you have been left here to do some sort of work for our people," he began, pretending not to notice how she suddenly started back and her face changed its expression.

"Don't try to explain," he went on, and raised his large hand as she tried to make objections. "I'm not asking who gave you the job or what it is and you needn't confirm or deny anything. I'm asking you to help me. I may be of some use to you."

He asked her to hide him for a day and to get him in touch with Kondratovich, who had helped him to blow up 1B Pit.

Lyuba looked with surprise at Valko's swarthy face. She had always known that he was a big-hearted, wise man; friendship between him and her father had been one of equals, yet she had always felt that he was a man who stood high above her, that she, Lyuba, was only a small person. She was taken aback now by his insight.

She fixed Valko up in the hayloft of the neighbours' barn. They had kept goats but they were evacuated now and the Germans had eaten the goats. Valko slept soundly.

Meanwhile, once alone, Lyuba and her mother mourned almost till the break of day, lying on the mother's bed.

Yevfrosinya grieved that this was the end of her life—a life which from its early years had been linked with Grigory Ilyich. And now she recalled this life, from the time when she had been a maid servant in Tsaritsyn and he a young sailor cruising down the Volga on a steamer and they had met on the sunny landing-stage or in the park, while the ship was taking on cargo. Times had been hard for them after they were married and he had been unable to find shore employment. They had moved here to the Donbas and still things had not been easy at first. But later Grigory began to get on a little and soon he had become famous and the newspapers had written about him. He had been given this three-roomed home and they had begun to live very comfortably and it had been a great pleasure, bringing Lyuba up like a princess.

And now it was all over. Grigory Ilyich was no more and here they were, two helpless women, one old and one young, left in the hands of the Germans. The tears flowed freely, unendingly.

Meanwhile, Lyuba whispered intimate, tender words to comfort her mother.

"Don't cry, Mummy. I'm qualified now. The Germans will be driven out and the war will end and I'll get a job at a radio station and become a famous wireless operator and they'll make me the chief of the station. I know you don't like noise so you'll come and live with me in a little flat at the radio station. It's always very, very quiet and still there; everything is softly upholstered, and not a sound can get through the walls and there are never many people about. Our little home will be clean and cosy and we'll live there together, just the two of us. We'll have a little lawn in the yard outside and when we've saved a little I'll build a chicken run, and you can keep hens, Leghorns and Cochin Chinas...." On and on she whispered softly through the night, pressing her mother to her breast, while her small white hand with the beautiful nails gesticulated unseen in the darkness of the room.

Suddenly they were startled by a soft tapping on the window-pane. They each heard it at the same time; they unclasped their hands, stopped crying and listened.

"Not the Germans again!" the mother said in a resigned whisper.

Lyuba knew that the Germans would not have knocked in that fashion. She ran barefoot to the window and lifted a corner of the counterpane which served as a black-out curtain. The moon had gone but from the dark room she was able to distinguish three figures in the front garden—a man close to the window and two women a short distance away.

"What d'you want?" she cried through the window.

The man put his face close to the window and Lyuba recognized him and the blood rushed to her face. To think that he had come here just now, at such a time, at the most difficult moment in her life!

She could not remember how she ran across the room and rushed like the wind from the porch, how, with all her grateful, unhappy heart, she had flung her strong, nimble arms round the lad's neck and pressed close to him, her face tear-stained, her half-dressed body warm from her mother's embrace.

"Quick, quick!" she said, drawing away from him and leading him into the doorway. Then she remembered his companions. "Who's with you?" she asked, and looked closely at the girls. "Olga! Nina! ... why, you darlings!" She took them both into her strong arms and showered kisses on them each in turn. "In here, in here, quickly," she breathed in a feverish whisper.

Chapter 27

THEY STOPPED on the threshold hesitating to enter, they were so dirty and covered in dust: Sergei Levashov, unshaven, in clothing that might have been worn by a lorry-driver or a mechanic; Olga and Nina, two strongly-built girls, Nina being the taller of the two, both with bronzed faces and dark hair literally powdered with grey dust, both dressed in identical dark dresses and carrying rucksacks on their backs.

They were the Ivantsova cousins and because of the similarity in the surnames they were often confused with the two Ivanikhina sisters, Lilya and Tonya, from Pervomaisky district. There was in fact a saying that if you see the two Ivantsovas and one of them is fair, then it's the Ivanikhinas. (Lilya Ivanikhina was the girl who had served as a feldsher at the front from the beginning of the war and had been posted as missing. She had been the fair one.)

The home of Olga and Nina Ivantsova was not far from the Shevtsovs and their fathers had worked in the same pit as Grigory Ilyich.

"My darlings! Where have you come from?" Lyuba asked, clasping her white hands; she assumed that they were on their way back from Novocherkassk where the elder cousin, Olga, was a student at an industrial institute. But what had Sergei Levashov been doing in Novocherkassk?

"Well—we're no longer where we were," Olga said discreetly, twisting her parched lips into a" smile, which caused her whole face with its dusty eyebrows and lashes to appear crooked. "D'you know whether there are Germans billeted in our home?" she asked while her eyes cast a rapid glance round the room, a habit which she had developed during her wanderings.

"There were, just as there were here. They left this morning," Lyuba said.

Olga's glance fell on the portrait of Hitler on the wall; her features became still further distorted into a grimace of derision and contempt.

"What's that for? For safety?"

"Oh, let him hang there," Lyuba said. "You probably want something to eat."

"No, thanks—we're going home if the house is free of Germans."

"And if it's not, you've nothing to fear, have you? Any number of people are arriving home again now after being turned back by the Germans at the Don and the Donets. And just say outright that you've been visiting in Novocherkassk and you've just come home," Lyuba said rapidly.

"We're not afraid. We'll say what you suggest," Olga said in a restrained tone.

Throughout this conversation Nina had remained silent and her eyes had wandered with an expression of defiance to and from Lyuba and Olga. Sergei, who had tossed his faded rucksack to the floor, stood leaning against the stove, his hands behind his back, watching Lyuba with a scarcely perceptible smile in his eyes.

"It's not Novocherkassk they've been to," Lyuba mused.

The Ivantsova cousins left. Lyuba removed the black-out curtain from the window and extinguished the miners' lamp hanging over the table. Everything became grey in the room, faces, furniture, the window.

"Would you like to wash?"

"You don't happen to know whether there are Germans in our house, do you?" Sergei asked, while she bustled back and forth between the room and the back door, bringing in a pail of water, wash-basin, mug and soap.

"I'm afraid I don't. They keep going and coming. Take your jacket off, don't be shy!"

He was so dirty that the water streaming into the basin from his hands and face was quite black. But Lyuba enjoyed watching his broad, strong hands and the energetic masculine movements as he soaped his hands and rinsed them, holding out his cupped hands for more water. His neck was sunburnt, he had rather large but well-shaped ears, and a strong, attractive mouth. His eyebrows were thick at the bridge of the nose, there were even hairs on the bridge itself, but they were thinner and arched upwards at the ends by the temples, and deep wrinkles furrowed his forehead. Lyuba enjoyed, too, watching him as he washed his face with those large hands, occasionally throwing a glance in her direction and smiling at her.

"Where did you pick up the Ivantsovas?" she asked.

He splashed water on his face, snorted and said nothing.

"You've come to me now, which means that you trust me. What are you holding back? We're leaves off the same tree, you know," she said softly, ingratiatingly.

"Give me a towel," he said. "Thanks."

Lyuba said no more and asked no further questions. Her blue eyes took on a cold expression. But she continued to see to Sergei's wants: lit the kerosene stove, put the kettle on it, placed food on the table and poured vodka into a carafe.

"It's months since I've had anything like this," he said and grinned at her. He tossed off some vodka and began to eat greedily.

It was already light. Beyond the faint, grey mist on the eastern horizon the rosy glow was gradually becoming brighter and turning golden.

"I didn't expect to find you here. Came on the off-chance—and this is how things are," he said slowly, thinking aloud.

His words held the question as to how it was that she, a fellow-trainee at the wireless school, should be here, at home? But Lyuba gave him no reply. She was hurt that when she was actually suffering so much and everything was so painful Sergei should imagine she was the flighty girl, full of whims, he had known earlier.

"Are you alone here? Where are your mother and father?" he questioned her.

"Is it anything to you, where they are?" she replied coldly.

"Has anything happened?"

"Go on, eat!" she said.

For a few moments he regarded her. Then he poured out another glass of vodka, tossed it off and continued to eat in silence.

"Thank you," he said, when he had finished, and drew his sleeve across his mouth. She noticed how coarse he had become during his journeyings; but it was not his coarseness that hurt her, but the fact that he did not trust her.

"You'll have nothing to smoke about the house, I suppose?" he asked.

"I'll find you something." She went to the kitchen and returned with some leaf tobacco from last year's crop. Her father had regularly planted tobacco and got several crops a year; he dried it and cut up a pipeful with a razor, as he wanted it.

They sat at the table in silence: Sergei, enveloped in tobacco smoke, and Lyuba. All was quiet as before in the room where the girl had left her mother. But Lyuba knew she was not asleep, that she was still weeping.

"You've trouble in the home, I can see it in your face. You've never looked like this before," Sergei said slowly. The look he gave her was full of warmth and tenderness, strange in his rather coarse, handsome face.

"There's grief in every home now," Lyuba said.

"If you only knew how much blood I've seen!" Sergei said with anguish, blowing clouds of tobacco smoke. "We'd been parachuted into Stalino Region. By that time so many people had been arrested that we were surprised our contact addresses were still of any use. People were being arrested not because they had been betrayed, but because the Germans were using a fine-meshed drag-net to catch thousands at a time, guilty or innocent, anyone who aroused the slightest suspicion was caught in it. The pit shafts are piled high with dead bodies," Sergei said, with deep emotion. "We worked separately and maintained contact for a time, but then lost all trace of one another. My mate was caught. They broke his arms and cut out his tongue, and it would have been all up with me if I hadn't accidentally run into Nina in Stalino and received orders to get out. She and Olga had been selected as scouts when the Stalino Regional Committee was still in Krasnodon—this was the second time they'd got through to Stalino. Then the news came that the Germans had reached the Don and it was clear to the girls that the people who'd sent them there were no longer in Krasnodon. In accordance with my instructions I handed my transmitter in to the operator of the underground regional committee and the three of us decided to go home together. And so we did. How I've worried about you!" he said suddenly, and a sigh burst from the depths of his heart. "I thought: supposing you'd also been dropped behind the lines and were now left all alone? Or suppose you'd been caught and the Germans were torturing your body and soul." He spoke softly, restraining himself. The look he now gave her was no longer warm and gentle but full of passion.

"Sergei! Oh, Sergei!" She laid her golden head on her arms on the table.

His large hand with the swollen veins passed gently over her head and arms.

"I've been left here—you understand what for. I was told to await instructions; it's almost a month now and there's been nobody and nothing," Lyuba said softly without raising her head. "German officers keep buzzing round like flies round honey; for the first time in my life I've been passing myself off as something I'm not. I've had to play the fool and dodge them all the time; it's disgusting and my heart aches for myself. Then yesterday some people came back from the evacuation and told us that my father had been killed in an air raid on the bank of the Donets," Lyuba said, and bit her bright red lips.

The sun was rising over the steppe, its blinding rays finding reflection in the dew-touched roof-tops. Lyuba tossed her head and shook back her curls.

"You'll have to go. How d'you plan to carry on?"

"Same as you. You said yourself we were leaves off the same tree, didn't you?" Sergei said and grinned.

She saw him off, through the yard and down the back streets. Then she quickly washed and dressed herself as simply as possible. Her road lay in the direction of Golubyatniki district and old Ivan Kondratovich.

She had left just in time. There was a fierce battering on the door. The house was near the Voroshilovgrad Highway: Germans were arriving to take up their billets.

Valko spent the whole day in the hayloft without food, for there had been no opportunity to reach him. When night fell, Lyuba climbed through the window of her mother's room and led him to Senyaki district where he was to meet Kondratovich at the home of a friend, a widow.

There Valko heard the whole story of the meeting between Kondratovich and Shulga. He had known Shulga in his youth, for they were both from Krasnodon; he had known him well in recent years when they had met in connection with the work of the region. No doubt was left in Valko's mind. He was sure that Shulga was one of the people left behind to work underground in Krasnodon. But the question now was how to find him.

"He certainly didn't trust you, did he?" Valko said with a gruff laugh. He could not understand why Shulga should have acted in that manner. "It was foolish of him! And you don't know anyone else in the underground?"

"No."

"What's your son going to do?" Valko blinked, frowning.

"Who can tell with him?" Kondratovich said and cast his eyes to the ground. "I asked him outright, 'Are you going to work for the Germans? I'm your father, so tell me the truth so that I know where I stand with you.' He said, 'Do I look a fool? Work?' he said. 'I can get along just as well without.'"

"Easy to see that he's a sharp one—not like his father," Valko laughed. "You can use him: shout it out from all the street corners that he's been up before a Soviet court; it won't hurt him and you'll be left in peace by the Germans."

"Ugh, Andrei, I never thought you'd ever try to teach me nonsense of that kind!" Kondratovich said, annoyance in his deep voice.

"Listen, brother ... you're old enough to know that you can't defeat the Germans with kid gloves on! ... Have you started work yet?"

"What work? The pit's blown up!"

"Well, but did you report at the job as they ordered?"

"I don't exactly understand you, Comrade Director...." Kondratovich was perplexed because everything Valko said seemed to run counter to the way he, Kondratovich, had intended to live under the Germans.

"That means you didn't. Now you go and report," Valko said quietly. "There's more ways than one of working. And it's important that we keep our people alive."

Valko remained in the widow's home for the day. On the following night, however, he moved elsewhere. The only one to know his new address was Kondratovich, whom Valko trusted implicitly.

Valko spent the next few days in nosing out what the Germans were doing in the town and in making contact with several Party members and some non-Party people he knew well. He was helped in all this by Kondratovich and Lyuba as well as Sergei Levashov and the Ivantsova cousins, who had been recommended to him by Lyuba. But he could find no trace of Shulga or any other of the people who had been left behind underground. It appeared to him that the only thread which could lead him to the local organization was Lyuba. But her behaviour and her nature had brought him to the realization that she was working for the intelligence, and that she would disclose nothing to him, until the proper time. He decided to act independently hoping that all roads leading towards one point would sooner or later converge; and sent Lyuba to get in touch with Oleg Koshevoi, who could now be useful to him.

"C-can I see Uncle Andrei in person?" Oleg asked, trying to hide his excitement.

"No, you won't be able to see him in person," Lyuba said with an enigmatic smile. "You see, our business truly concerns a love affair. Nina, come here and meet the young man."

Oleg and Nina shook hands awkwardly and both felt rather embarrassed.

"Never mind, you'll soon get to know one another," Lyuba said. "I must leave you now. You go for a walk somewhere arm-in-arm and have a heart-to-heart talk about how you're going to live ... and I hope you'll enjoy yourselves!" With a sly twinkle in her eyes she darted out of the shed, her bright dress flashing in the sunlight.

They stood facing one another—Oleg shy and embarrassed, Nina with a defiant expression in her face.

"We can't stay here," she said calmly but emphatically. "Let's stroll off somewhere; and I suppose you'll have to take my arm."

When Nikolai Nikolayevich, who was pacing up and down outside, saw his nephew leaving the garden with a strange girl on his arm, his usually impassive face expressed extreme astonishment.

Both Oleg and Nina were so young and inexperienced that for a long time they were unable to rid themselves of the feeling of awkwardness. Every time they bumped into each other they seemed to lose the gift of speech. Their linked arms felt like red-hot iron.

According to the plan agreed on by the boys the previous night, Oleg was to scout along Sadovaya Street edge of the park, and so he led Nina in that direction. The moment they were through the gate, Nina began to talk business despite the fact that all the houses in Sadovaya Street and bordering the park were full of Germans. She spoke softly as though discussing something very intimate.

"You mustn't meet Uncle Andrei yourself—you'll keep in touch with him through me. But don't feel hurt about it. I have not seen him either. Uncle Andrei wants to know whether any of your crowd can find out which of our people have been arrested and are kept in prison here."

"We've a fellow, a really smart one, on the job already," Oleg cut in quickly.

"Uncle Andrei wants you to tell me everything you know, both about our people and about the Germans."

Oleg reported what Tyulenin had told him about a member of the underground having been betrayed to the Germans by Ignat Fomin. Then he gave her an account of everything Volodya Osmukhin had told him that night and added what Zemnukhov had said about the underground workers trying to find Valko. He then gave her the address of Zhora Arutyuniants.

"Uncle Andrei can entrust Zhora perfectly with his whereabouts. He knows Zhora, anyway! And, through Volodya Osmukhin, Zhora will pass on the information to whom it concerns. While we've been talking," Oleg said, grinning, "I've c-counted three AA guns, in the distance, to the right of the school, and a shelter alongside, b-but there are no lorries in sight."

"And the powerful machine-gun and the two Germans on the school roof?" she asked suddenly.

"I didn't notice them," Oleg said, surprised.

"Yet from that roof the whole of the park can be kept under observation," she said, a little reproachfully.

"Then you've been taking note of things too! Were you also instructed to do so?" Oleg's eyes glistened as he tried to draw her out.

"No, it's just a habit I have," she checked herself and cast a quick challenging glance at him from under the heavy, arched eyebrows. Had she perhaps been too open, she wondered. But he was too inexperienced to suspect anything.

"Aha! There are the lorries, a whole string of them!" Oleg said gleefully, "they're in dug-outs up to their noses, only the tops showing. And there's one of their field-kitchens, smoking away. See it? Only don't stare in that direction."

"There's no point in looking; so long as that observation post is on the roof there's no way of getting at the type," she said calmly.

"T-true enough ..." Oleg gave her a pleased look and burst out laughing.

They had already grown used to one another. They walked leisurely along, Nina's full, round arm resting trustingly in his. The park was behind them now. To their right, all along the prefabricated houses, stood lines of German lorries and cars of all types, a mobile wireless station, a first-aid bus, and German soldiers swarmed everywhere. To their left lay a vacant plot and in the distance stood a barrack-like stone building and near it a German sergeant with blue shoulder-straps piped with white was drilling a small group of Russian civilians armed with German rifles. They fell into line, broke ranks, crawled over the ground and engaged in mock hand-to-hand fighting. All were middle-aged. They wore swastika arm-bands.

"Jerry gendarmes. They're training policemen to catch people like us," Nina said. There was a hard glint in her eyes.

"How d'you know?" he asked, recalling what Tyulenin had told him.

"I've come across them before."

"What scum they are!" Oleg said squeamishly and with loathing. "They should be strangled piecemeal."

"They deserve it!"

"Would you like to be a partisan?" he asked suddenly.

"Yes."

"But d'you realize what it means to be a partisan? His work is never spectacular but how noble it is! He kills one fascist, another, then the hundredth—but the hundred and first might kill him! He carries out one job, then another, and a tenth; then with the eleventh he may come to grief. You've no idea how much self-sacrifice the work demands. His own life means nothing to him, the Motherland always comes first. He doesn't grudge his life when there's work to be done for the Motherland. And he never sells or betrays a comrade. Oh, I should like to be a partisan!" Oleg said. His enthusiasm was so profound and genuine and simple that Nina raised her eyes to him and the expression in them was very simple and trusting.

"Listen, are we only going to meet when there's business to be discussed?" he asked suddenly.

"No, why? We can meet when we've nothing else to do," Nina said, slightly taken aback.

"Where do you live?"

"You could take me home if you're not doing anything now—will you? I'd like you to meet my cousin Olga," she said, but was not at all sure that that was quite what she wanted.

The two cousins lived in Vosmidomiki district, where their parents shared a prefabricated house, each family occupying one half of it. Nina took Oleg inside and left him in her mother's care.

Brought up in his Ukrainian family circle to respect his elders, Oleg, who had been much among grown people, easily drew the talkative youthful-looking Varvara Dmitrievna into conversation. He very much wanted Nina's mother to like him.

By the time Nina returned he knew all about the Ivantsov families. Nina's and Olga's fathers were brothers, had been miners and at present were both on active service. Both had worked as labourers for wealthy peasants in their native Orel Gubernia, and had later drifted to the Donbas and married Ukrainian girls. Olga's mother came from Chernigov but Varvara Dmitrievna had been a local girl, from the village of Rassypnoye. When she was younger she too had worked at the pits and this had left its mark on her. She was somewhat different from the ordinary housewife, a fearless, independent woman with considerable insight. Realizing at a glance that the lad had not come without some purpose, she watched him closely through eyes full of cunning perspicacity and found out everything about him, without in the slightest degree arousing his suspicions.

They got on very well. When Nina returned she found them sitting side by side on a bench in the kitchen, both in high spirits. Swinging his legs happily, Oleg rubbed the tips of his fingers together and laughed so infectiously that Varvara Dmitrievna could not help joining in. Nina looked at them, clapped her hands and laughed too; all three felt gay and light-hearted just as though they had been good friends for years.

Nina remarked that Olga was busy at the moment but was very anxious that Oleg should wait for her. Two hours went by and Olga did not appear; two hours which slipped by unnoticed while Oleg was engaged in carefree chatter. Yet they were decisive hours indeed, during which all the links of the Krasnodon underground were finally welded together. In that time Olga had managed to make her way to one of the Little Shanghais, far from the Vosmidomiki; she had spoken to Valko in his new home and given him all the information Nina had obtained from Oleg.

When Olga came to her cousin's home, the merriment which had reigned there abated slightly. It was true to say that her manner towards Oleg contained a degree of warmness rare for her; a broad, kindly smile enlivened her face which was always a little reserved, and which had striking, irregular features; she even sat beside him on the bench, usurping Nina's place. But she found it difficult to break into the confused, turbulent flow of their conversation which, to the outsider, appeared devoid of all sense. Having only just returned from seeing Valko, her heart and mind were filled with emotions of an entirely different order. She was the more serious of the two—not in the sense of being able to feel deeply, but in being able to translate thoughts and feelings into practical and vital action. Moreover, being the elder, she had been better informed about the essence of their cause, from the outset of their work as messengers of the Stalino Regional Committee.

She seated herself silently by Oleg's side and pulled off her kerchief, disclosing her dark hair looped heavily at the nape of her neck. Try as she would to be gay and smiling, her eyes gave her away. She appeared to be the eldest present, older even than Nina's mother.

Varvara Dmitrievna, however, was both subtle and tactful.

"Why are we sitting in the kitchen?" she said. "Let's go inside and play cards!"

They adjourned to the dining-room. Varvara slipped into the next room, where she and Nina slept, and returned with a pack of playing-cards, worn and dirty from much handling.

"Oleg will be Nina's partner, of course?" Olga said casually.

"No, I'm playing with Mother!" Nina retorted and threw a defiant glance at Olga. She very much wanted to be Oleg's partner but could not very well disclose her feelings at this stage.

All this had escaped Oleg but he was aware that as an old mining-hand Nina's mother should be an experienced player.

"N-no, I'm playing with M-mother!" he cried.

Because of his stutter he did not shout it but rather bellowed it softly like a calf and the effect was so amusing that everyone, even Olga, burst out laughing.

"The old one and the young one—you just watch out, girls!" Varvara said.

Everybody's spirits again soared.

The woman who had once worked in the mines was, indeed, an expert at the game but Oleg, as always when playing, was such a gambler that he began to get excited and at first they lost. Completely self-possessed, Olga kept baiting him slyly. Varvara, who did not mind losing, slyly watched him from the corner of her eye: she liked the boy very much.

With great difficulty they finally won the fourth game. It was Olga's turn to deal. Oleg glanced at his hand and saw it was a very poor one. Then a crafty look came into his eyes and he raised them trying to catch Varvara's glance. Their eyes met and for a second Oleg protruded his lips into the shape of a diamond as though for a kiss. Varvara's young eyes, set in a network of small wrinkles, began to dance; and without the flicker of an eyelid she immediately led diamonds: as Oleg had expected, the miner woman had perfectly understood his lip sign.

He was seized by an irrepressible gaiety. Now they could be sure of winning every time. "The old and the young" merrily went on signalling to one another, raising their eyes to heaven for clubs—"crosses" as they were called locally— squinting sideways for spades, placing a forefinger to their chins for hearts. The unsuspecting girls played with increasing care, yet lost all the time and were quite unable to resign themselves to the fact that victory continued to evade them. Nina was flushed with excitement. After each win Oleg broke into uproarious laughter rubbing his fingertips together. Finally Olga, being more experienced, tumbled to the fact that something was wrong and with characteristic restraint and skill began without betraying herself to watch her opponents. Before long she had seen through everything and, choosing a moment when Oleg was signalling with his lips, she clapped her fan-shaped hand of cards on his mouth and then flung the cards across the table, scattering them.

"Ugh, you cheats!" she said in her level, calm voice.

Varvara Dmitrievna laughed good-naturedly. Nina jumped up indignantly from the table. Oleg followed her, grasped her soft sunburnt hand in both of his and with his forehead against her shoulder begged forgiveness. It ended with them all laughing heartily together.

Oleg felt no desire whatever to go home but evening was approaching and a curfew was imposed on the town after six o'clock. Olga said that he had better leave at once and to prevent any possibility of going back on her word, she said good-bye and withdrew to her own part of the house.

Nina took Oleg out into the evening sunlight on the porch.

"I d-don't want to go a bit!" Oleg confessed frankly.

They remained standing on the porch for some moments.

"Is that your garden there?" Oleg asked, gloomily.

Silently she took his hand and led him round the house to where it was shady among jasmine bushes so luxuriant that they could almost be called trees.

"It's n-nice here! At our place the Germans have chopped down everything."

Nina said nothing.

"Nina," he said in a childish, pleading voice. "Nina, may I kiss you? Only on the cheek, you know, j-just on the cheek."

He made no move towards her, he had simply asked, yet she drew back from him and became so flustered that she could find no words to reply.

He did not notice her confusion but continued to regard her with an unaffected, childish expression.

"No, you might be late, you know," Nina said.

That he might be late because he had stopped to kiss her once on the cheek did not seem absurd to Oleg either. Nina was right in everything, of course. He sighed, grinned and offered her his hand.

"But you must certainly come and see us again," Nina said feeling guilty and holding his large hand caressingly between her own.

Happy because he had made new friends and because of the turn his life had taken, but very hungry, Oleg returned home. But he was destined to get no meal that day. Nikolai Nikolayevich came through the gate to meet him.

"I've been on the look-out for you for a long time: Tow Head (their name for the batman) is hunting for you."

"Oh, to hell with him!" Oleg said, negligently.

"All the same, you'd better keep out of his reach for a bit. Victor Bystrinov's here—he came last night. The Germans turned him back at the Don. Let's go to his place. It's a blessing his landlady's got no Germans billeted on her," Nikolai Nikolayevich said.

Victor Bystrinov, a young engineer and Nikolai Nikolayevich's colleague and friend, had some extraordinary news for them.

"Have you heard? Statsenko's been appointed Burgomaster!" he called out. He sneered angrily.

"Which Statsenko? Chief of the Planning Department?" Even Nikolai Nikolayevich was surprised.

"That's him!"

"You must be joking."

"There's nothing funny about it."

"But it can't be! Such a quiet, industrious fellow—never hurt a soul in his life."

"Yes, it is that very same Statsenko—quiet, never hurt a soul, no drinking-party or card-game was ever without him, the man about whom everyone said: he's one of us, he's a grand chap, a decent fellow, a tactful man. Yes, that very same Statsenko is now the Burgomaster!" Victor Bystrinov said. Thin, piercing, sharp as a bayonet, he was boiling over with fury and spluttering at the mouth.

"Here wait, give me time to think," Nikolai Nikolayevich said, still unable to believe it. "There was never a single party among the engineers to which he wasn't invited! The times I've sat and drunk vodka with him! And never once did I hear him utter a single disloyal word or even raise his voice about anything. And if there'd been anything in his past—well, everybody knows all about him: his father was a minor official, and he himself has never been mixed up in anything."

"Yes, I've had drinks with him too. And now just for old times' sake we'll be the first he'll grab by the throat: work for us or else—!" and Bystrinov's slim fingers made an eloquent noose-like gesture under the ceiling. "So much for your nice, popular friend."

Ignoring Oleg, who had so far said nothing, they went on for a long time discussing how it could have happened that a man whom they had known for years and who had been universally popular, should have found it in him to become Burgomaster under the Germans. The simplest explanation was that Statsenko had been induced to take on the job under pain of death—yet why had the enemy's choice fallen on Statsenko? And then the clear inner voice of conscience which determines people's actions in the most critical, terrible moments of life told them that if they, ordinary, rank-and-file Soviet engineers, had been faced with that choice, they would have preferred death to such degradation.

No, it was obviously not just a simple case of Statsenko accepting the Burgomaster's job on pain of death. And, faced with the incomprehensible situation, they could only repeat again and again:

"Statsenko! Would you believe it! Can you imagine it! Who, then, can we trust?" And with that they shrugged their shoulders and gesticulated with their arms.

Chapter 28

STATSENKO, chief of the Planning Department of the Krasnodon Coal Trust, was not an old man—somewhere between forty-five and fifty. He was, indeed, the son of a small official, who had served in the excise department before the Revolution, and it was true that he had never been "mixed up in anything." He was an expert in the economics of engineering and had always worked in the planning departments of various industrial organizations.

It cannot be said that he had climbed the promotion ladder very fast, but neither had he remained stationary: one might say that he climbed it rung by rung rather than in leaps and bounds. But he was never satisfied with the place he occupied in life.

He was not dissatisfied because his industry, energy and knowledge, shall we say, were insufficiently employed and therefore he failed to get out of life all the things he deserved. No, he was dissatisfied because he did not get all the blessings of life without spending labour, energy and knowledge. That it was possible to lead such a life and that such a life was pleasant, he had observed for himself when he was young, in the old days, and now he loved to read about it in books—about the old days or about life abroad.

It cannot be said either that he wanted to be a fabulously rich man, a big industrialist or a merchant or banker: that would have required energy and worry, eternal struggle, rivals, strikes and those damned crises! But there was the nice steady income, interest on some form of capital, rent or simply a good salary in a quiet respectable position—there was such a thing everywhere except "in our country." And the entire trend of life "in our country" showed Statsenko that he was getting older each year but was all the time becoming farther and farther removed from his life's ideal. And that was why he hated the society he lived in.

Yet, though dissatisfied with the structure of society and his lot, Statsenko had never done anything to change either, because he lived in fear. He was too afraid even to gossip on a grand scale; he was the most ordinary, commonplace gossip, never going beyond tales about how much people drank or who they were living with. He never criticized people by name, whether of his immediate circle or not, but he loved to talk in general terms about bureaucratic methods in offices, about the lack of individual initiative in the trading organizations, about the shortcomings in the training of young engineers compared with the position in "his day," and about the slovenly service in restaurants and public baths. He was never surprised at anything and was inclined to expect almost anything from anybody. If anyone mentioned a case of large-scale embezzlement or a mysterious murder or simply some domestic unpleasantness he would remark:

"I'm not surprised myself. One can expect anything. I lived with a lady once, very cultured she was and married, too, by the way—and, d'you know, she robbed me."

As was the case with most people, everything he wore, everything in his home, everything he used for washing himself or cleaning his teeth was produced in the Soviet Union and out of the country's own raw materials, and when in the company of engineers who had been on assignments abroad, Statsenko, from behind a glass of vodka, was fond of emphasizing the fact, with simplicity and cunning.

"Ours—Soviet-made!" he would say and with a plump hand that was extraordinarily small for his heavy build, he would finger the cuff of his striped jacket. But one could never tell whether he said it proudly or contemptuously. And secretly he so envied them their foreign ties and toothbrushes that the sweat broke out on his pink bald head.

"What a lovely little thing!" he would say. "Just imagine, cigarette lighter, penknife, scent spray, all in one! No, we don't know how to make things like that," said this citizen of a country where hundreds and thousands of ordinary peasant women had learned to work as skilled tractor-drivers and harvester-combine operators on the fields of the collective farms.

He praised foreign films although he had never seen any and would spend hours every day poring over foreign magazines—not the technical mining journals which occasionally arrived at the Trust, for they could be of no interest to him as he knew no languages and did not try to learn any, but magazines which his colleagues sometimes brought back with them, fashion magazines and others which contained numerous pictures of women in elegant attire or others in almost none at all.

But in the things he said, in his tastes, habits and inclinations there was nothing conspicuous enough to mark him out among other people. For many, very many people with interests and occupations, thoughts and passions of an entirely different order would now and again in conversation with Statsenko reveal tastes and opinions similar to his without being aware that, while in their own lives they occupied the tenth or the last place or were simply a casual phenomenon, in Statsenko's life they were an expression of his entire nature.

And thus he would have gone on living, this heavy-set, slow-moving man with the pink face and bald head, this inoffensive, rather pompous, inconspicuous man with the low, chesty voice and the small red eyes of the elderly, inveterate drinker; he would have gone on living to the end of his days without any intimate friends but accepted by all without exception, putting in the hours of work he loathed by day or by night as required, attending the sessions of the local works committee of which he was invariably a member, showing up at card- and drinking-parties, climbing slowly the ladder of promotion step by step without any effort of will on his own part. He would have gone on living in this way, if—

That the country in which this inconspicuous individual was living would be unable to stand up to Germany had been obvious to Statsenko from the outset. This was not because he was fully acquainted with the resources of both countries and had considerable understanding of foreign relations. Actually he knew nothing at all, nor did he want to know anything about either. It was because the country which did not conform to his life's ideal could not possibly hold its own against a country which, in his opinion, fully conformed to his ideal of what life should be like. And as long ago as that Sunday in June when he had listened to Molotov's broadcast he had begun to be aware of a certain restlessness inside him, a sort of excitement which arose out of the necessity facing him of changing his place of residence.

With every report that came in of the Red Army's retreat from yet another town, still further removed from the frontier, he realized with increasing clarity that he would have to change to a new home. The day Kiev fell Statsenko was practically on the road towards a new residence with grandiose plans for its lay-out and furnishings.

And so, when the Germans entered Krasnodon Statsenko in his mind covered roughly the same road as Napoleon did when he fled from the Elba and travelled to Paris.

For a long time, and very rudely, Statsenko was prevented from gaining admittance to General von Wentzel first by the sentry and then by the batman. Unfortunately Grandma Vera had also come out of the house, and Statsenko had always dreaded her, so, without knowing quite why he did so, he hastily pulled off his hat, bowed low to her and made it all look as though he was merely passing through the garden to get from one street to the other. Grandma Vera had seen nothing unusual in that. Meanwhile Statsenko had posted himself outside the garden gate to await the appearance of the young adjutant.

Fat and bare-headed Statsenko had trotted by the side of and a little behind the German officer. The adjutant had not looked at Statsenko nor had he understood what he said but he pointed a finger to the German *Kommandantur*.

SS *Sturmführer* Stobbe, Kommandant of the town, was one of those elderly Prussian gendarmes, all cast in the same mould, whom Statsenko had frequently seen in his youth in photographs of gatherings of the crowned heads, published in the *Niva*. *Sturmführer* Stobbe was apoplectic, the ends of his grey moustache were twirled tightly like the tail of a sea-horse; his puffy, beer-sodden face was covered with a fine network of tiny yellow-bluish veins and his protruding eyes were of that muddy bottle-colour, which makes it impossible to distinguish the whites from the pupil.

"You want to serve in the police?" *Sturmführer* Stobbe rasped, brushing aside the unessentials.

Statsenko stood modestly with his head inclined to one side and his small fat hands, with fingers the colour and shape of tinned frankfurters, pressed close to the seams of his trousers.

"I'm an expert in the economics of engineering and I might suggest ..." he began.

"To *Meister* Brückner!" Stobbe croaked, without waiting for more. His watery eyes glared so hard at Statsenko, that he drew back from him in zigzagging steps and passed through the door backwards.

The German police headquarters was in a long barrack on one floor, which had not been whitewashed for a long time. The old whitewash was peeling off. The building hugged the hill-side just below the offices of the District Soviet and was separated by vacant land from the area known as Vosmidomiki district. This building had formerly been the premises of the town and district militia and Statsenko had frequently been there before the war in connection with a theft which had occurred at his home.

Accompanied by a German soldier armed with a rifle, he entered the dim, familiar corridor and suddenly recoiled in terror: he had almost bumped into a tall man, head and shoulders taller than himself, and on raising his eyes had recognized Ignat Fomin, the famous Krasnodon miner, in his old-fashioned peaked cap. Fomin had no escort. He wore freshly cleaned boots and a suit which was just as respectable as Statsenko's. Both well-dressed gentlemen blinked their eyes, and walked past each other as though they were entirely unacquainted.

In the waiting-room of the very office in which, at one time, the chief of the Krasnodon Militia had officiated, Statsenko came face to face with Shurka Reiband, dispatcher of the bread factory wearing the familiar black Kuban hat with the red crown on his small brown head, which appeared to have been chiselled in bone. Shurka Reiband was a descendant of the Germans who years ago had settled in these parts and he was well known throughout the town because his job had been to deliver bread to the canteens at all the municipal offices, bread kiosks and shops. Nobody ever called him anything but Shurka Reiband.

"Vasily Illarionovich!" he exclaimed softly with amazement, and then stopped short when he spied the soldier behind Statsenko.

Statsenko cocked his bald head sideways and inclined it a little.

"Ah, Mr. Reiband!" he said, "I'd like to be of service here." He said "be of service," not "enter the service."

Mr. Reiband rose to his toes, hesitated a moment and then, without knocking, plunged into the chief's office. It was clear that Shurka Reiband was an integral part of the *Neue Ordnung*.

He remained in the room rather a long time. Then the chief's bell rang in the waiting-room. A German clerk straightened his mouse-coloured uniform and took Statsenko into the office.

Meister Brückner was not a *Meister* in the true sense of the word, but a *Wachtmeister* which means a sergeant of gendarmes. And this was not the German police headquarters at all but merely the Krasnodon German police station. The area police headquarters was situated in the town of Rovenki. However, *Meister* Brückner was not just *Wachtmeister* but *Hauptwachtmeister*—a sergeant-major of gendarmes.

Statsenko entered the office—*Meister* Brückner was not seated, but standing with his hands clasped behind his back. He was tall, not very stout but with a heavy, bulging paunch. He had flabby, wrinkled dark bags under his eyes, and if the origin of them had been investigated one might have discovered why *Hauptwachtmeister* Brückner spent so many of his waking hours standing instead of sitting.

"I'm experienced in the economics of engineering and I might suggest—" Statsenko said with modestly inclined head, sausage fingers pressed tightly to his striped trouser legs.

Brückner turned his head towards Reiband and said fastidiously in German:

"Tell him that I appoint him Burgomaster in the name of the Führer."

In that second Statsenko made a mental note of all those among the people he knew, who had formerly ignored him, who had treated him with familiarity, and who would now be his inferiors. He bowed his bald head which was beginning to sweat again. He felt he was thanking *Meister* Brückner cordially and thoroughly, but actually his lips moved soundlessly and he bowed.

Meister Brückner slipped his hand under the flap of his army jacket thus disclosing his ponderous belly, round as a water-melon and closely confined in his tight-fitting trousers, and produced a gold cigarette case. He took a cigarette and placed it between his lips with a swift, precise movement of his large yellow hand. On second thoughts, he took another cigarette from the case and offered it to Statsenko. Statsenko dared not refuse it.

Then, without looking down, *Meister* Brückner groped about on the table, found a narrow bar of chocolate, and, still not looking, he broke off a few squares and silently passed them to Statsenko.

Afterwards Statsenko said to his wife, "He's not human, he's perfection."

Reiband dispatched Statsenko to *Herr* Balder, the sergeant-major deputy and a mere sergeant who, in build and mannerisms and even as regards the deep, chesty voice, was so like Statsenko, that if the latter had worn German uniform it would have been difficult to distinguish them. From him Statsenko received instructions to form a town council, and acquainted himself with the structure of local government under the *Neue Ordnung*. Within this structure, the Krasnodon Town Council, with the Burgomaster at its head, was nothing more than one of the departments of the office of the German police station in Krasnodon.

Thus Statsenko had become Burgomaster.

Meanwhile Victor Bystrinov faced Nikolai Nikolayevich and both were gesticulating with their hands.

"Is there anybody now that we can trust?" they asked.

The evening Matvei Shulga took leave of Kondratovich he was left with no choice but to find his way to the Shanghai and call on Ignat Fomin.

Judged by outward appearances, Fomin made a good impression on him and it was only by outward appearances that Shulga could obtain his first impressions. He had been pleased, when he gave Ignat Fomin the password, that Fomin had shown no agitation or undue haste, but had regarded him closely, cast a glance round, showed him into the house and only then had given the reply. Fomin had said very little; he had asked no questions, had listened attentively and to all the instructions had replied, "It'll be done." Shulga was additionally pleased to see that Fomin, even at home, wore a jacket and waistcoat, a tie, and a watch and chain—all this was to him the mark of a cultured, intellectual working man, brought up in Soviet times.

True, there were a few trifles which, though Shulga did not exactly find them unpleasant at the time—they were too trifling, indeed, for him to pay much attention to them—nevertheless did strike him as being unpleasant. Fomin's wife, for instance, was a massive, powerful woman with wide-set, narrow, squinting eyes and a disagreeable smile which revealed large, yellow teeth with gaps between them and Shulga felt that from the moment they met she had behaved towards him in a manner most flattering and obsequious. On the very first evening too it forced itself on his unwilling notice that Fomin, or Ignat Semyonovich as Shulga had immediately begun to call him, was a bit of a miser: when Shulga frankly admitted that he was half-starved, Fomin said that as far as food was concerned it would probably be rather difficult. And in view of the fact that they appeared to have sufficient, it could not be said, indeed, that they fed him very well. But Shulga saw that they ate exactly the same as he did and he thought that he could not possibly know all the circumstances of their private life.

These trifles could not destroy the all-round favourable impression that Fomin made on Shulga. Yet if, without making any choice and by pure chance, Shulga had turned up at the home of the worst person on earth, it would have been better than going to Ignat Fomin. Because of all the people living in Krasnodon Ignat Fomin was the most abominable—for the very reason that he had long ago ceased to be a human being.

Before 1930, Ignat Fomin, whose name had been different then, was reputed to be the richest and most powerful man in his native Ostrogozhsk in Voronezh Region. He was the owner, either openly or through agents, of three farmsteads and two flour-mills. He owned two horse-drawn mowing-machines, a large number of ploughs, two winnowers, a threshing-machine, a dozen or so horses, six cows, many acres of orchard lands and nearly a hundred beehives. In addition to employing his own four regular farm-labourers, he could call on the labour of peasants in several districts because in all of them he had many people who were materially dependent on him.

He had been a rich man even before the Revolution and his two elder brothers had been still more prosperous, particularly the brother who had inherited his father's property. Ignat Fomin was the youngest and when, some time before the 1914-1918 war, he had married, his father had given him the smallest portion. On his return from the German front after the Revolution, Fomin had very craftily alleged that he was a poor peasant and hostile to the old regime. He had declared that he had no property and was an implacable foe of the enemies of the Revolution. In this way he had wormed his way into Soviet administrative organs and the various social organizations in the village, beginning with the peasant-aid committee. He made use of these organs of power and of the fact that his brothers were wealthy people and hated the Soviet Government. He succeeded in getting first the eldest brother prosecuted and exiled and later the other brother Next he took possession of their property and evicted their families, including a number of young children for whom he felt no pity, chiefly because he had no children of his own, nor could he have any. This was how he had become what he was in the district. And right up to 1930, despite his riches, there were many representatives of governing bodies who regarded him as something unique on Soviet soil, a rich man completely loyal to the Soviet Government, what was known as a progressive farmer.

But the peasants in a number of districts where his power was felt knew him to be a ruthless kulak blood-sucker, and terrible man. When, in 1930, collective farms began to be set up and the people with the support of the authorities began to strip the rich, Ignat Fomin, at that time living under his own name, was swallowed up in the wave of popular vengeance. He was deprived of his property and sentenced to be exiled to the North. But as he was well known and appeared to be a peaceable man, he was not taken into custody by the local authorities. So one night Ignat Fomin, aided by his wife, killed the chairman of the Village Soviet and the secretary of the village Party committee, who in those days did not live with their families but on the premises of the Village Soviet and were returning from a party somewhat the worse for drink on the night Fomin lay in wait for them. He killed them and fled with his wife, first to Liski, then to Rostov-on-Don, where he knew people he could trust.

In Rostov he bought identity papers in the name of Ignat Semyonovich Fomin, railway-shop worker, which described him as having been a working man for many years. He also obtained suitable documents for his wife. Finally he appeared in the Donbas knowing that workers were needed there and that no questions would be asked about who he was and where he had come from.

He firmly believed that sooner or later his time would come, but in the meantime, he followed a clear and definite line of conduct. Above all, he knew he would have to work conscientiously: in the first place because that would help him to hide his identity, secondly because conscientious work, with his skill and intelligence, would provide him with the means to live in prosperity, and, thirdly, because although he had been a rich man in the past, it was his nature to be industrious. Moreover, he decided never to push himself forward very much, never to poke his nose into public affairs, to submit to authority and, God forbid, never to indulge in criticism.

In the course of time this inconspicuous fellow had become respected by authorities, not only as a diligent and honest worker, but as a man of great modesty and discipline. He restrained himself sufficiently to avoid altering his behaviour in any way even when the Germans were at the gates of Voroshilovgrad. He did not doubt that the Germans would occupy Krasnodon. And only when he was asked whether he would agree to have his home used by the underground organization did he almost betray himself by the feeling of malicious delight and pleasure which overwhelmed him.

The explanation of the fact that Fomin went about at home in a suit, collar and tie and watch-chain, which had so pleased Shulga, was not that he liked to be so careful of his appearance for, like other workers, he was clean about his person but usually wore ordinary, everyday clothes, but that he expected the Germans to arrive any minute and, wishing them to like him, he had turned out from his trunk the finest clothing he possessed.

And so, while Statsenko was interviewing first Sergeant-Major Brückner and then Sergeant Balder, Matvei Shulga was lying beaten and bleeding in a small dark cell in the other half of the same barracks.

Formerly this part of the barracks, consisting of a few cells and a narrow passage which was the continuation of the corridor in the service quarters of the militia, had been the only place of confinement in Krasnodon. Under the *Neue Ordnung*, however, the large cells and the smaller, solitary confinement cells of the police station were crammed full of men and women, young and old. There were people here from the town and the Cossack villages and farmsteads, detained because they were suspected of being Soviet officials, partisans, Communists or Komsomols, people who, by word or deed, had insulted the German uniform, people who had concealed their Jewish origin, people detained for having no papers, or simply because they were people.

They were given hardly any food at all and were not let out for exercise or for their natural requirements. There was an intolerable stench in all the cells, the old floors long since rotten with fungus were covered with excrements and drenched with urine and blood.

Although all the cells were overcrowded Shulga, or Yevdokim Ostapchuk, the name under which he had been arrested, was given a cell to himself.

He had been badly beaten at the time of arrest. He had offered resistance and had proved to be so strong that it was a long time before they could overpower him. Later he had been beaten up again in the prison first by Sergeant-Major Brückner and Sergeant Balder, then by SS *Rottenführer* Fehnbong, who had arrested him, Police Chief

Solikovsky and German police officer Ignat Fomin—all in an attempt to break his will before he had time to recover. But if it had not been possible to get information out of Shulga when he was his normal self, it was still more impossible to do so when he was in the heat of battle.

He was so strong that even now, beaten and bleeding, he was lying down not from exhaustion but because he was forcing himself to lie down to get some rest. If he had been taken for interrogation again he would still have been capable of fighting as much as the situation required. His face was covered with bruises and one eye was swollen. One of his arms had been badly fractured above the wrist where Fehnbong had struck it with an iron bar. And Shulga was distraught at the thought that somewhere the Germans were similarly torturing his dear wife, his children, torturing them because of him, and that there was now no hope that he would ever be able to rescue them.

But more agonizing even than the physical pain or the mental anguish was Shulga's realization that he had fallen into the enemy's hands without having carried out his duty, and that it had been through his own fault.

The natural justification he had in the circumstances, namely, that the guilt lay not with him but with the people who had given him an untrustworthy contact had crossed his mind at first, but he had immediately cast it out as being false consolation for weaker types.

His experience of life had taught him that the success of any social undertaking cannot fail to depend on many people, among whom there were always some who carried out their part unsatisfactorily, or who simply made mistakes. But, having been chosen for an emergency job in an emergency situation and having failed in it, he would have been a miserable creature of feeble spirit to have complained that the fault lay not with him but with others. The clear inner voice of conscience told him that he was a very special person who had had experience of underground struggle in the past and had for that reason been chosen for this emergency job in an emergency situation, in order that he would be able, with his will-power, his experience and organizational skill, to overcome every hardship and danger, all privations and obstacles, the errors committed by other people on whom the job depended. That was why Shulga could not and would not blame anyone else for his failure. But the realization that he had not only fallen into a trap, but had failed in his duty tormented him more terribly and bitterly than anything else.

The constant, truthful voice of conscience prompted him in the belief that at some point, somehow he had acted wrongly. Over and over again he painstakingly analysed in his mind the minutest details of what he had done and said since the moment he parted with Protsenko and Lyutikov, yet nowhere could he discover when or in what he had acted incorrectly.

Before all this Shulga had not been acquainted with Lyutikov, but now he was endlessly concerned about him, particularly because it now depended entirely on Lyutikov whether the work entrusted to them both would be carried out. And still more frequently did his mind in great torment and unbearable anguish turn to Protsenko, their leader and his own personal friend:

"Ivan Fyodorovich, where are you now? What's become of you? Are you alive? Are you hitting back at the accursed enemy, are you getting the better of them and outwitting them? Or are they torturing your mind and body, like they are torturing mine? Or are you lying somewhere out in the steppe with the ravens pecking out your merry eyes?"

Chapter 29

AFTER PARTING with Lyutikov and Shulga, Protsenko and his wife had set out on the road to his detachment which was based in the Mityakinskaya Forest on the far side of the Northern Donets. They had had to make a considerable detour in order to skirt the territory already occupied by the Germans. They had succeeded in getting their old Gazik across the river and by night slipped into the partisan base just when German tanks were already entering the Cossack stanitsa from which the forest derived its name.

Forest ...? Was it really worthy of the name? Could this thicket of bushes covering only a small area be compared with the forests of Byelorussia or of Bryansk—the native home of partisan glory? Here, in the Mityakinskaya Forest it was difficult merely to conceal a large detachment, let alone open military hostilities.

Fortunately for Protsenko and his wife, they arrived when the partisans were not at the base but were fighting the Germans along the roads leading towards the west.

How Protsenko later regretted that on that first day he had not drawn and had been unable to draw all the conclusions from the simple, obvious thought that had entered his head, namely, that the detachment which was almost the largest in the region had no base where it could conceal itself!

Voroshilovgrad Region fell into several territorial areas each of which had as its leader one of the secretaries of the underground regional Party committee. Ivan Fyodorovich Protsenko was one of these. He was in charge of several district committees, with numerous underground groups subordinated to them. In addition the districts also had special sabotage groups some of which received their instructions from the local underground district Party committee, others directly from the regional Party committee and yet others from the Ukrainian or even the Central Partisan Headquarters.

This ramified underground network operated in conjunction with a still more highly conspiratorial system of contact addresses, hide-outs, food caches, arms dumps, and means of communication, both technical and through special scouts. In addition to the ordinary contact addresses throughout the districts, Protsenko and other leaders of the regional underground had at their disposal special addresses, which they alone knew. Some of these served as links with the Ukrainian Partisan Headquarters; others as liaison centres between the leaders of the region; others again as liaison centres for contacting district leaders or detachment commanders.

Several small partisan detachments were operating in each area. In addition, each area had a fairly large detachment in which, according to the original scheme, there was to be a secretary of the regional Party committee, acting as leader of the underground in the area. It was assumed that the secretary of the regional Party committee would be relatively safe with a large partisan detachment and consequently enjoy greater freedom of action.

The medical dispensary at Orekhovo, a large village in Uspensk District, was the chief contact address which linked the leaders of the Voroshilovgrad underground. Valentina Krotova, a local doctor and sister of Protsenko's scout Xenia Krotova, had been put in charge of the house by Protsenko himself. While Protsenko had been in Krasnodon Xenia had been staying with her doctor sister, and it was from her that Protsenko was to get the first news about the state of affairs in the other areas since the arrival of the Germans.

Protsenko now left his assistant in charge of the partisans' arms and supplies in the Mityakinskaya Forest and of the entire work of liaison with the other areas and set out to join his detachment. He had to start out on foot for the whole area was swarming with German troops. Much as he had relished the idea of travelling everywhere in his long-suffering Gazik—he had enough petrol to last at least a year—the time had now come to drive it into a cave in one of the clay quarries and block up the entrance. His wife, Katya, who was also one of his scouts, had a good laugh at him and together they set out for the detachment on foot.

Only a few days had passed since Protsenko had sat in the building of the Krasnodon District Party Committee arranging liaison problems with the general commanding the division, but how everything had changed since then! There was, of course, no question now of any sort of coordinated action with the division. It had held out at Kamensk on the Donets for just as long as it was ordered to, losing over three-quarters of its far from complete composition, and had then left its position and gone away. Losses had been so heavy that the division no longer really existed but no one would say in general conversation that it had been "routed," no one ever said it had been "surrounded" or had "retreated"—no, the division had "gone away" they said. And it had, in fact, gone away, and at a time when large German formations had already gone into action over those vast expanses between the Northern Donets and the Don.

The division had gone away over enemy-occupied territory, across rivers and over the steppe; it had fought battles all the way, using for defences the steep banks of the steppe rivers; it had vanished only to appear again in another place. During the early days when it was still not very far away, popular rumours of the division's battles had filtered through to these parts. But the division moved farther and farther to the east, striving to reach the appointed limit and so remote was this that all trace of a rumour of the division had faded and only the memory of it, its fame, the legend, remained in the hearts of the people.

Protsenko's partisan detachment had been operating alone and not at all badly. During the first few days it had routed in open battle several minor enemy units. The partisans annihilated the remaining German officers and men, set fire to petrol tanks, captured transport units, ambushed and caught German officials in the villages and executed them. News of the activities of other detachments had not yet come in but Protsenko estimated that the other partisan detachments had also made a good start, judging by rumours. Popular rumour exaggerated the exploits of the partisans, but that only meant that their struggle enjoyed the support of the people.

The enemy began to throw in large forces against the detachment; Protsenko, however, turned down the suggestion of the partisan headquarters that the detachment should return to its base, and, under cover of darkness, he moved it across to the right bank of the Donets. There no one expected the partisans and they created unprecedented havoc deep in the German rear.

However, with every passing day it became more and more difficult to maintain freedom of movement in a restricted area of the steppe which, in addition, was so densely populated that the mining villages, farms and hamlets almost merged into each other. The detachment was perpetually on the move. Only Protsenko's cunning manoeuvring, his excellent knowledge of local topography, and their first-class equipment, enabled the detachment for the time being to avoid heavy losses. But for how long could they keep up this perpetual circling in one spot, with the enemy on their tail?

Large partisan detachments of the type which had been formed in areas with extensive forests and in the vastness of the uninhabited steppeland were unsuitable for the thickly populated Donbas. This was the conclusion Protsenko had reached, but by that time disaster was already knocking at the door.

The news reaching him from Xenia Krotova cut deep into his heart: a large partisan detachment in action in the immediate vicinity of Voroshilovgrad had been encircled and broken up; Yakovenko, the regional committee secretary with this detachment, had been killed. Of the Kadievka detachment, formed on the same lines as the Yakovenko and Protsenko detachments, only nine partisans and the commander remained. In scattering the detachment the enemy had suffered losses three times as heavy, but what enemy losses could be considered payment for the loss of the famous Kadievka Miners' Guard? The detachment commander notified Protsenko that he was recruiting more men, but that henceforth they would be operating in small groups. The Bokovo-Anthracite detachment had managed to break out of encirclement without heavy casualties and had then and there split into several small groups, operating under one command. Small detachments in the Rubezhansky, Kremensky, Ivanovsky and other districts had been operating successfully and almost without losses. The Popasnyansky District detachment had from the very beginning fought in small groups under one command. The local people called it "The Redoubtables" in appreciation of its battle successes. In all districts new partisan detachments were springing up like mushrooms, consisting of the local people and straggling Red Army officers and men, and all of them had originated as small partisan groups.

This was dictated by experience.

Protsenko received this information and now he required only a very few hours to split his detachment into small groups, but fate did not allow him those few hours.

The Germans had closed the ring round them at dawn and now the sun was dipping towards the western horizon.

Once there had been a creek here which had flowed into the Northern Donets. It had dried up so long ago that the villagers of Makarov Yar, a Cossack hamlet near by, no longer remembered when they had last seen water in the wooded ravine which was all that was left now. Narrow at its upper end and widening towards its mouth it was triangular-shaped and the broad band of the forest extended to the river's edge.

Protsenko lay among some low bushes at the top end which from the point of view of defence was the most difficult sector of the whole ravine. His chin had sprouted a soft, light-brown peasant-style beard; a German bullet had grazed his right temple. removing skin and hair and covering the temple with drying blood, but he had barely noticed it. He lay prone under the bush working his tommy-gun, with a spare one cooling by his side.

Katya, pale and stern, lay a short distance away from her husband, also firing a tommy-gun. All her movements were sparing, accurate, full of latent energy and unconscious grace—she seemed to handle her gun with her fingers alone. To her right was Narezhny, an old collective farmer from Makarov Yar and "machine-gunner of the old German war" as he described himself. His thirteen year-old grandson, surrounded with cases of ammunition, was refilling the spare drums. In a small hollow behind the ammunition boxes was the commander's adjutant, never for a moment removing the hot earphones of the field telephone. The commander had not been with Protsenko, but on the river-bank. The adjutant kept repeating again and again in his regulation language:

"Mama calling ... Mama calling ... What's that? How are you, Auntie! Out of plums? Get some from the nephew ... Mama calling, Mama calling ... everything O. K. here.... How about you? Well, turn the heat on him! Sister! Sister! Sister! You asleep? Brother wants supporting fire on the left...."

Protsenko's mind was tormented not by the thought of possible death for himself or his wife, not even by the weight of responsibility for other people's lives, but by the realization that all this could have been foreseen and the grave situation in which they now found themselves averted.

He had, indeed, split the detachment into several groups and appointed a commander for each of them with a deputy for the political section. Each of them had been told of a place they could subsequently use as a base. The former commander with his deputy and partisan headquarters chief was in command of one of these newly-formed smaller detachments. At the same time they had to take charge of all the other groups, and as their number would not now be large, they would continue to use the Mityakinskaya Forest as their base.

Protsenko had prepared commanders and men for the idea that they would remain in the ravine until nightfall, then he would lead them and they would break through enemy encirclement and reach the open steppe. In order to facilitate their progress after the break-through, he had subdivided each detachment into still smaller groups of three to five, who would save themselves by getting away along whatever roads they chose. He and his wife would temporarily be concealed in a reliable hide-out by old Narezhny.

Protsenko knew that a number of them would be killed during the break-through; that others would be captured; and that some would get through safely but would then weaken and not turn up at the place appointed, the base. And all this lay a heavy moral burden on his mind. Yet far from sharing these distressing thoughts with anyone, the expression on his face, his gestures, his whole behaviour, were quite the opposite of what he was experiencing inside. As he lay there in the undergrowth, small, well-knit, his ruddy face almost covered by his peasant beard, he exchanged jokes with old Narezhny while keeping up his accurate fire at the enemy.

There was something Moldavian, even Turkish, in Narezhny's face: a pitch black, curling beard, black, darting eyes with a spark smouldering in them. He was shrivelled up, like a flower stalk in the sun, with broad, strong, bony shoulders and arms. Though his movements were slow, he was full of latent enthusiasm.

Despite the gravity of their position both of them seemed content in each other's company and conversation, which could not be said to be very profound. Approximately every half hour or so Protsenko, with a cunning twinkle in his eye, would call across:

"Well, how is it, Kornei Tikhonovich, pretty hot?"

And Kornei Tikhonovich would retort:

"Can't say it's cool but it's not really warm yet, Ivan Fyodorovich."

And when the Germans pressed them particularly hard Protsenko would say:

"Now if they had mortars and started to heave cucumbers at us it'd soon get good and warm—eh, Kornei Tikhonovich?"

To which the calm reply came:

"They'd need to be rich in cucumbers to bring them down on this forest, Ivan Fyodorovich."

Suddenly they both caught the sound of motor cycle engines rising above the rattle of tommy-gun fire and increasing to a crescendo from the direction of Makarov Yar.

For a moment they even stopped firing.

"Hear it, Kornei Tikhonovich?"

"Yes."

Protsenko turned warning eyes in his wife's direction and with his lips gave the sign to be silent.

A detachment of motor cyclists, German reinforcements, was moving along a road which was out of sight, but the noise they made had probably been heard all over the ravine. The telephone began to work feverishly.

The sun had set and the moon had not yet risen. There were no more long shadows, and yet it was not yet dusk. Many soft, pale colours still lingered in the sky melting into one another, and this strange, dim light that the darkness would soon engulf lay upon everything, the ground, people's faces, the guns and rifles and the empty cartridges strewn on the grass. This twilight, neither day nor night, remained only a few moments, then suddenly, like a fine mist or dew, began to disperse into the air and to settle on the bushes and ground and to become denser.

The noise of the motor cycles increased from the direction of Makarov Yar and soon spread over the whole area. Sporadic firing broke out again, particularly along the river-bank.

Protsenko looked at his watch.

"Time to be moving ... Teryokhin! At twenty-one hours sharp!" he said over his shoulder to the adjutant at the telephone.

Protsenko had agreed with the commanders of the partisan groups scattered over the ravine that, at a signal from him, the groups should all concentrate round an old hornbeam at the foot of a gorge leading upwards and out on the steppe. That was to be the starting point for the breakthrough. The time for it had now arrived.

In order to divert the Germans' attention, the two partisan groups defending the wood on the bank of the Donets were to remain at their posts a little longer than the rest and to appear to be making a last desperate attempt to get across the river. Protsenko cast a rapid glance round in search of someone to send down to them.

Among the partisans defending the top end of the ravine was a young lad from Krasnodon, a Komsomol by the name of Yevgeny Stakhovich. He had been attending an air raid defence course in Voroshilovgrad until the town fell to the Germans. He stood out among the partisans for his cultural development, restrained manners and for the fact that he had early shown signs of being public-spirited and interested in social problems. Protsenko had tested him on various assignments, planning to use him for liaison work with the Krasnodon underground. His glance fell on the youth's pale face and his damp, straggling fair hair which at other times lay in thick, careless waves on the proudly erect head. The lad was in a state of agitation but his pride had not allowed him to take shelter in the depths of the ravine. That had pleased Protsenko. He sent him off with the message.

With a forced smile Stakhovich bent close to the earth and ran down towards the river-bank.

"And you, Kornei Tikhonovich ... see to it that you don't stay longer than you have to!" Protsenko said to the courageous old man who was remaining behind with the partisan group to cover the break-through.

The moment the partisans at the river's edge began their feint preparations for crossing the Donets, the attention of the main forces of the Germans became concentrated on them and the enemy directed all his fire on that sector of the woods and the river. The whining of the bullets and the thudding noise as they dropped in the undergrowth merged into one continuous, ear-splitting sound; it was as though the bullets were splitting into fractions in mid air and the people were breathing hot lead dust.

The detachment commander at the river's edge had been given Protsenko's instructions by Yevgeny Stakhovich. He had sent the bulk of his partisans to the assembly point in the gorge and remained behind with twelve men to cover the withdrawal. Yevgeny Stakhovich thought it a dreadful place and he would very much have liked to set off with the majority, but he felt it was awkward to do so and utilizing the fact that no one was paying attention to him he lay down among the bushes and turned up the collar of his jacket in order to shut out at least some of the racket.

During the brief lulls in the deafening concentration of firing they could hear the Germans shouting orders. Small enemy groups had already infiltrated into the forest from the direction of Makarov Yar.

"Time, fellows!" came the sudden cry from the detachment commander. "At the double, now!"

The partisans ceased firing at once and rushed after their commander. Despite the fact that, far from reducing his fire, the enemy if anything had intensified it, the partisans felt they were running through the forest in complete silence. They ran for all they were worth and could hear one another's breathing. Then they were able to distinguish the dark figures of their comrades lying close together in the undergrowth. Dropping to the ground they crawled close up to them.

"Well, you can thank God for that!" Protsenko said, approvingly. He was standing by the old hornbeam. "Is Stakhovich here?"

"Yes," the commander said, quickly.

The partisans exchanged glances and saw that Stakhovich was missing.

"Stakhovich!" the commander called softly, searching the faces of the partisans round him. Stakhovich was not there.

"How could you be so mad as to lose your heads and not see whether he's been hit? We may have left him lying there wounded!" Protsenko cried. He was very angry.

"D'you take me for a schoolboy, Ivan Fyodorovich?" The commander was offended. "When we left our positions he was with us unhurt, and we ran close together keeping each other in sight."

Just then Protsenko spotted the supple though aged figure of Narezhny followed by his grandson and several more partisans, all of whom had silently crept up.

"Good old pal!" Protsenko exclaimed, overjoyed, unable to conceal his feelings.

Then he swung round.

"Get ready now," he called softly, and every partisan caught his words.

They hugged the ground, but adopted attitudes ready to spring up.

"Katya!" Protsenko said softly. "Keep close to me, but if I ... if anything should—" He gesticulated with his arm as though throwing off the thought. "Forgive me!"

"And me," she said, her head slightly bowed. "But if you get through and I—" He did not allow her to finish: "The same with me ... and you'll tell the children...."

They had no time to say more than that. Protsenko shouted softly:

"Fire! Forward!"

He was the first to dart out from the ravine.

They were unable to say how many they were or how long they had been running. It was as though they had no breath and no hearts. They ran in silence, some of them firing as they ran. Looking back Protsenko could see his wife and Narezhny and the grandson, and the sight of them gave him strength.

Suddenly the roar of the motor cycles came to them, carried far through the night air. Then they heard the sound of engines ahead of them; they seemed to have surrounded the runners on all sides.

Protsenko gave a signal and the partisans split up, hugged the ground and began to glide over the ground noiselessly like snakes, utilizing the uncertain light of the moon and the irregular contours of the locality. In an instant they had vanished from sight.

Within a few minutes Protsenko, Katya, Narezhny and his grandson were left alone in the moonlit steppe. They were now in the middle of the melon fields of a collective farm, which sloped upwards from them for several acres and probably went over the crest of the hill which lay clear against the sky.

"Wait a bit, Kornei Tikhonovich—I've no breath left in me!" Protsenko said and threw himself flat on the ground.

"Come on now, Ivan Fyodorovich," Narezhny said, rushing to bend over him, his breath coming hot against Protsenko's face. "We've no time to rest! The village is just over the hill. They will hide us there."

So they continued to crawl through the melon fields after Narezhny who now and again turned his face with its curling black beard and piercing eyes to look back at Protsenko and Katya.

They crept to the hill-top and spied the village with its white cottages and dark windows, the nearest of which were not more than two hundred yards distant. The melon fields stretched as far as the road leading past the wattle-fences of the nearest row of cottages. But just as they reached the crest of the hill several German motor cyclists raced along the road and turned into the heart of the village.

There was again the sound of sporadic tommy-gun fire. There seemed to be some return shots and the firing in the night echoed with anguish and gloom in Protsenko's heart. From time to time Narezhny's fair-headed grandson, who had no resemblance at all to his grandfather, raised his timid, questioning, young eyes to Protsenko, and it was hard to look into those eyes.

From the village they could hear cursing in German and the sound of rifle-butts thumping on doors. Now all was quiet, now there came the wail of a child, a woman's scream which changed to weeping only to rise again in loud cries of entreaty breaking the night stillness. Sometimes from the village itself or just outside it came the noise of one motor cycle or several or, it seemed, of a whole detachment. The full moon shone brightly in the sky. Protsenko, Katya whose legs had been chafed sore by her boots, Narezhny and his grandson lay flat on the ground, wet and shivering with the cold.

So they lay waiting until all was still in the steppe and village.

"Now's the time, it's almost daybreak," Narezhny whispered. "We'll crawl one behind the other."

The footfall of German patrols came to them from the village. Occasionally the light from a match or lighter flared up. Protsenko and Katya remained lying in the tall weeds at the back of some cottages in the centre of the village while Narezhny and his grandson swung their legs over the wattle-fence. For some time they heard no more of them.

The first cocks began to crow. Protsenko chuckled.

"What's the joke?" Katya whispered.

"Two or three cocks for the whole village! The Germans must've slaughtered the lot!"

They looked at each other for the first time, closely, appraisingly, and only their eyes smiled.

"Where are you? Come to the house now," came the whispered words from the other side of the fence.

A tall, thin, large-boned woman, with a white kerchief knotted under her chin, examined them across the fence. Her black eyes glistened in the moonlight.

"Come, don't be afraid, there's no one about," she said.

She helped Katya over the fence.

"What's your name?" Katya asked softly.

"Marfa," the woman replied.

"Well, how's the New Order?" Protsenko asked with a grim laugh, when they were all finally seated round the table inside the cottage dimly lit by a tiny oil-lamp.

"This is what it's like: a German comes along to us from the *Kommandantur* and demands six quarts of milk from each cow and nine eggs a month from each hen," Marfa said shyly, but looking sideways at Protsenko, an expression of natural womanliness in her black eyes.

She was in her late forties, but her movements as she placed food on the table and cleared away the dishes were those of a young, graceful woman. The clean, whitewashed cottage with colourful embroideries everywhere was full of children of all ages. A son and daughter, fourteen and twelve respectively, had been roused from their beds and were keeping a look-out in the street.

"He's back with more demands after every two or three days. You can see yourself, our village isn't large, only about a hundred households, but they've been twice now and each time demanded twenty cattle. That's your new order for you," Marfa said.

"Don't you worry now, Aunt Marfa! We know them from back in 1918. Quick as they may come, they'll leave quicker!" Narezhny said, and roared with laughter, displaying his strong teeth. The oriental eyes in his sunburnt face of flint gleamed with cunning and courage.

It was difficult to realize that the man who spoke had so recently stared death in the face.

Protsenko looked at his wife from the corner of his eye: her stern features had softened into a kindly smile. After many days fighting and their terrifying break-through they felt the breath of youthful freshness which emanated from these people who were no longer young.

"They've certainly fleeced you, Aunt Marfa, but I see they've still left you with a bit of something," Protsenko said, winking at Narezhny and indicating, with a nod of his head, the table which Marfa had generously loaded with curds and sour cream, butter, fried eggs and pork fat.

"Maybe you don't know that in a well-managed Ukrainian cottage you can take your fill of what you like, but you'll never eat, or steal, everything, unless you murder the housewife!" Marfa joked, blushing in confusion like a girl, yet speaking with such rough candour that Protsenko and Narezhny chuckled behind their hands and Katya had to smile. "I've hidden everything away!" Marfa said, now laughing herself.

"You're a wise little woman!" Protsenko said and wagged his head. "What are you now then—collective farmer or individual peasant?"

"I'm a collective farmer on holiday, you might say, until the Germans move out," Marfa said. "We're just nobodies to them, they consider our collective-farm lands are part of the German, what d'you call it again, the Reich, is it? Is that what they call it, Kornei Tikhonovich?"

"Yes, the Reich, may it be damned!" the old man said with a sneer.

"When they call us to a meeting they read us some kind of paper by, what's his name, again? Rosenberg? Is that what they call that thief, Kornei Tikhonovich?"

"Ye-es, Rosenberg, curse him!" Narezhny replied.

"This Rosenberg says he'll give us land for ourselves, but not all of us, mind, only those that work well for the German Reich, and own cattle and machines. And just tell me what machines he means when all they give us to cut the wheat and get the corn harvested for their Reich is sickles! We women have forgotten how to use sickles for harvesting! We go out in the fields, lie down in the shade of the wheat and have a snooze."

"And the village Elder?" Protsenko asked.

"Oh, he's on our side," Marfa replied.

"Wise little woman!" Protsenko repeated and again wagged his head. "Where's your man?"

"Where would he be? At the front. Yes ... my Gordei Kornienko's at the front," she said gravely.

"But tell me frankly," Protsenko said. "You've got all these children here, and now you're hiding us, aren't you afraid for yourself and the children?"

"No," she replied, her youthful black eyes looking him squarely in the face. "Let them chop my head off! I'm not afraid. I'll know what I'm going to my death for. Now you tell me: are you in touch with our people at the front there?"

"Yes," Protsenko replied.

"Then tell our men to fight to the end. Our husbands mustn't spare themselves," she said with the conviction of a simple, honest woman. "This is what I say: maybe our Dad"—she said "our Dad" as though speaking on behalf of the children—"maybe our Dad won't come back, maybe he'll die in battle, but we'll know what he died for! And when Soviet power comes back again, it will be like a father to my children."

"Wise little woman!" Protsenko said for the third time very tenderly. He looked down and did not raise his eyes for some time.

Marfa arranged for Narezhny and his grandson to sleep in the cottage and concealed their rifles. She had no fear for them. But she took Protsenko and Katya to a disused, underground cellar outside, which was overgrown with tall weeds and cold as a vault.

"It's damp in there so I've taken a couple of sheepskin

jackets," she said shyly. "This way, there's plenty of straw here."

They were alone, and sat for a time on the straw in the pitch-black darkness and said nothing.

Suddenly Katya put her warm arms round Protsenko's head and pressed it to her breast. His heart filled with tenderness.

"Katya," he said. "Katya, this partisan work will be different from now on. We'll organize it in quite a different way!" he said with agitation in his voice and freed himself from her embrace. "Oh, how my heart aches, aches for those who have died, died because of our inability. But surely not all of them were killed, were they? Most of them got out, didn't they?" he asked as though seeking moral support. "Never mind, Katya, never mind! We'll find thousands more like them—people like Narezhny, like Marfa, there are millions more like them! No! This Hitler fellow can fool the whole German nation if he likes, but I can't believe he can have outwitted Ivan Protsenko, oh no, he couldn't have done that!" he declared angrily, unaware that he had slipped into Ukrainian, though his wife was Russian.

Chapter 30

As subterranean waters, unseen by the human eye, silently and unceasingly seep in all directions under the roots of trees and grasses, through cracks and along capillary vessels, so under German rule millions of men, women, children and the aged from all the nationalities to be found in our land moved over the steppe, along forest tracks, mountain paths, gullies, by the steep cliffs overhanging rivers, along streets and lanes in towns and villages, through populous market-places and lonely, dark ravines.

On and on they trekked, innumerable as the sands, the partisans, underground fighters, saboteurs, agitators, scouts in the enemy rear, scouts of the great retreating army of a great people, people driven from their homes, returning to them again, seeking places where they would be unknown, breaking through front-line positions to get into free, Soviet soil, fighting their way out of encirclement, fleeing from German captivity and concentration camps, forced by necessity into the search for food and clothing, raising their weapons against the oppressors.

A short ruddy-complexioned fellow was making his way from the Donets River along a steppe road. He had a soft, light-brown peasant beard and wore simple peasant clothing; a rough linen sack was slung across his shoulder. Thousands upon thousands like him were on the move. Who could tell who he was? He had blue eyes, but can one peer into the eyes of all these people and do eyes reveal all that is going on in people's hearts? Perhaps there was an impish little sparkle in these particular eyes, but if they had to look at a *Herr Wachtmeister* or even a *Hauptwachtmeister*, they would become the eyes of the most ordinary man in the world.

The man in simple peasant clothing entered the town of Voroshilovgrad and was soon lost among the crowds in the streets. But why had he come? To take his linen bag to market with butter in it, or curds, or a duck, and to trade them for nails, or salt, or a piece of coarse calico? Or perhaps this man was Protsenko, that dangerous fellow who was capable of undermining the power even of Doctor Schultz, Counsellor of Department 7 of the *Feldkommandantur*?

In a little wooden house on the outskirts of a small mining town at the upper end of a dark narrow valley that runs away into the steppe, in a tiny room with only one window blacked out with a blanket, a flickering candle was shedding its dim light on two people seated at the table: an elderly man with a grave, drooping expression on his face, and a well-built youth with large round eyes and light-brown lashes.

A youth and an elderly man, yet they had something very much in common, for even at a late hour like this, during the grim days of German occupation, both were almost ostentatiously attired in clean, neat clothing and both of them were wearing collar and tie.

"Learn to take a pride in our native Donbas," the elderly man was saying and his stern eyes seemed not to reflect the dim light of the candle, but the glory of battles long ago. "You've heard of the struggles of our old comrades: Artem, Klim Voroshilov, Parkhomenko? I'm sure you've heard of them, but will you be able to tell the other lads all about them?"

The youth was sitting with his head inclined attentively towards the left shoulder which was slightly higher than the right.

"Yes, I've h-heard, I'll know h-how to tell them," he replied, stuttering slightly.

"What is it that makes our Donbas glorious?" the elderly man continued. "However great our difficulties, in the years of civil war and afterwards, during the first five-year plan and the second, and now in these days of war, we have always performed our duty honourably. Mind you bring that home to the fellows...."

The elderly man paused. The youth regarded him respectfully and said nothing, waiting for him to continue.

"And remember," the man warned, "vigilance is the guardian of underground work. Did you ever see the film *Chapayev*?" he asked, solemnly.

"Yes."

"Then why was Vasily Ivanovich Chapayev killed? He was killed because his sentries fell asleep and let the enemy get close. Always be on the alert, day and night, and always be cautious. D'you know Polina Sokolova?"

"Yes."

"How do you come to know her?"

"She used to work among the women with Mother. They still see a l-lot of one another, even now."

"Right. Now, everything that only you and I know about you'll pass on to Polina Sokolova. The usual contact'll be through Osmukhin, as it was today. You and I must not meet again," and as if wanting to forestall any feeling of hurt or chagrin, Lyutikov gave the youth a cheerful smile.

But there was no sign of either in Oleg's face. The fact that he had been trusted to the point of being allowed to come to Lyutikov's house, during curfew hours at that, filled his heart with pride and boundless devotion. A wide boyish grin spread over his face.

"Thank you," he said gaily, feeling very happy.

Curled up in a hollow in the steppe a young stranger lay sleeping. The sun shone on him and steam began to rise from his clothing. The sun had dried the wet track he had left, when he crawled up there from the river. He must indeed have been exhausted from his swim in the river to fall asleep in wet clothing out in the steppe at night!

When the sun became hot the youth woke and continued on his way. His fair hair had dried and lay picturesquely in waves on his head. The following night he spent in a small mining village with people who gave him shelter because he is almost a fellow-villager: his own home was in neighbouring Krasnodon and he was returning from Voroshilovgrad where he had been pursuing his studies. And the next day, quite openly and in broad daylight, he entered Krasnodon.

He did not know what might have happened to his parents or whether they had had German soldiers billeted on them and so first of all he called at the home of his school-friend, Volodya Osmukhin.

There had been Germans in the Osmukhins' home but now they had gone.

"Yevgeny! Where d'you spring from?"

And Volodya's friend replied in his usual rather haughty, official manner:

"You first tell me the kind of life you are living now."

Komsomol Yevgeny Stakhovich was Volodya's old comrade and there could be no secrets between them, apart of course from matters concerning the organization, and so Volodya proceeded to give Stakhovich a full account of everything that concerned himself.

"I see," Stakhovich said. "That's fine. I had not expected anything else from you."

There was a shade of condescension in his voice as he said it. But probably there was some justification for it. Like Volodya he was anxious to join the underground struggle—for bound by secrecy, Volodya had told him that he was still only anxious to do so—but he had already done some fighting in a partisan detachment and, as he explained, had now been sent officially by the partisan headquarters to organize the partisans in Krasnodon as well.

"That's excellent!..." Volodya said respectfully. "We must go and see Oleg immediately...."

"And who is this Oleg?" Stakhovich asked haughtily, because Volodya pronounced Oleg's name with great respect.

"Oh, he's a grand fellow!" Volodya said vaguely.

No, Stakhovich did not know Oleg. But if he was such a treasure, why not go and see him?

A man of military bearing dressed in civilian clothing with a grave expression in his face knocked softly on the door of the Borts' home.

Only little Lyusia was in. Mama had gone to the market to exchange some article or other for food, while Valya— Papa was at home too, but that was just what was most dreadful! Papa, in his dark glasses, had at once concealed himself in the wardrobe. With beating heart Lyusia put on her grown-up expression, went to the door and asked as unconcerned as she could;

"Who's there?"

"Is Valya in?" a male voice asked in a bashful, pleasing tenor from the other side of the door.

"No, she isn't." Lyusia waited expectantly.

"Open the door please, don't be afraid," the voice said.

"Who's that speaking?"

"Lyusia."

"Lyusia? Valya's little sister? Open the door, don't be frightened."

Lyusia opened the door. On the porch stood a stranger, a tall, handsome, modest-looking young man. Lyusia took him for a grown-up man. He had kind eyes and a courageous expression on his very serious face. He looked at Lyusia with a twinkle in his eyes and saluted like a soldier. Lyusia accepted the token of respect favourably.

"Will she be home soon?" he asked politely.

"Don't know," she said with an upward glance at the man's face. There was disappointment in it. He stood in silence for some moments, saluted again and with a smart about-turn prepared to go. Quickly she said:

"What message shall I give her?"

A humorous expression flitted across his face.

"Tell her that her *fiancé* called," he said, and ran down the steps of the porch.

"And you're not going to wait for her? How'll she know where to find you?" she hastily called after him in great agitation. But her voice was too timid and she had spoken too late: he was already a long way down Derevyannaya Street on his way to the level crossing.

Valya had a *fiancé*! Lyusia found this exciting. Of course she couldn't say anything about it to Papa. Nor must she mention it to Mama. "None of us at home know him. But perhaps they won't get married yet," Lyusia thought, trying to comfort herself.

A group of young people were taking a stroll in the steppe. Two youths and two girls. How was it that in these frightful times, when no one ever went for a stroll, there were two youths and two girls strolling about in the steppe? They were a long way from town, it was a week-day and they were strolling about in working hours. On the other hand, no one had been forbidden to go for a stroll.

They were paired off. One of the youths was barefoot, had slightly curly hair and was quick and agile in his movements; the girl with him was sunburnt, there was a slight down on her bare legs and arms and she had fair, golden plaits. The other youth was small, freckled, and very fair and the girl with him was quietly dressed, had quiet manners and intelligent eyes, and her name was Tosya Mashchenko. The two couples strolled off in different directions over very long distances, then came together again and always to the same place. Tirelessly they walked about from morning to nightfall, suffering from thirst under the blinding sun—in consequence of which the freckles on the fair-haired boy's face trebled in number. Each time they returned to their meeting-place they carried something in their hands or pockets: cartridges, hand-grenades, sometimes a German rifle, a revolver, a Russian service rifle. There was nothing startling in this for they were strolling not far from Verkhneduvannaya station, the area where the retreating Red Army fought its last battles. But instead of taking all these weapons to the German commandant they were collecting them into a hiding-place in a grove and burying them. And no one saw them doing it.

Then, on one occasion, the youth who was quick and agile in his movements and appeared to be the captain of the team found a live mine and, before the eyes of the girl with the golden plaits, proceeded to render it harmless, with unusual skill in his expert fingers.

Undoubtedly there should be a large number of mines in the area, so he would teach the rest of the group how to remove the fuse from them. Mines, too, would come in useful later.

The girl with the golden plaits came home badly sunburnt, tired out, but full of elation. This was not the first evening she had returned home in this state. Lyusia managed to detain her for a moment in the garden and with her eyes glistening in the dark told her in an excited whisper about the *fiancé*.

"What *fiancé*? What *are* you chattering about?" Valya said angrily, but somewhat disconcerted for all that.

It may have been a German spy or, on the other hand, someone from the Bolshevik underground organization who, having learnt of her activities, was trying to locate her. But both assumptions quickly faded away. Valya could be as stuffed with book adventures as a mine with explosives, but she really had a realistic, practical turn of mind like all her generation. She made a mental survey of all her acquaintances and suddenly it dawned on her: in the spring last year, the farewell performance of the Lenin Club Dramatic Circle, seeing Vanya Turkenich off to the Sevastopol AA Artillery School. In the play he was the suitor and she his bride. *The Fiancé*, of course!

Vanya Turkenich! Usually he acted the part of a comic old man. This was nothing like the Moscow Art Theatre, of course, but he always said: "It's my aim to have the whole audience from the first row to the last rolling, splitting their sides and laughing till the tears stream down their cheeks." And he always succeeded. Whatever he played in, from *An Unhappy Woman* to *The First Date*, he invariably wore the make-up of Danilych, the old gardener. But he was at the front, how did he come to be in Krasnodon? He was a lieutenant in the Red Army! He passed through the town last winter on his way to Stalingrad where he was to undergo training in the use of anti-tank guns.

"Don't go on and on about it, Mother, what difference does it make to you? I just don't want any supper." And Valya dashed off to find Oleg.

Turkenich in Krasnodon!

A small, fair-haired girl walked across the wide world. She had walked through the whole of Poland and then through the whole of the Ukraine, a tiny grain lost in the vast mass of human sand, a stray seed. And so she came into Pervomaisky and tapped softly on the window of a little house.

"If you think you see the two Ivantsova girls and one of them is fair then it's the Ivanikhina girls...."

Lilya Ivanikhina, reported missing at the front, had returned to the home in which she was born.

Ulya received the news from Maya Peglivanova and Sasha Bondareva. Lilya had returned—warm-hearted, merry Lilya, the life and soul of their little company, the first of them to be torn from family and friends, the first to be plunged into the frightful world of battle, missing without a trace, already buried and now resurrected from the dead!

And all three friends—slim, boyish Sasha Bondareva; dark, gypsy-like Maya with her proud, protruding lower lip, always busy and still, even under German rule, retaining her habit of always correcting and instructing everyone; and Ulya with her wavy black plaits hanging down in front over her simple dark-blue dress with the white polka-dots, almost the only one left to her since German soldiers had lived in her home—all of them hurried now to the Ivanikhinas, whose home was near the centre of Pervomaisky not far from the school.

How strange it felt to be running through the streets without a single German soldier in sight! The girls were filled with a sense of freedom and they had come alive again without noticing it. Ulya's black eyes sparkled and a gay mischievous smile, so rare for her, spread over her features and at once found a ready response in the faces of her friends and, seemingly, in everything within sight.

As they came level with the school building their eyes fell on a brightly-coloured poster stuck on one of the large doors of the school. As though by agreement the three girls ran together up the steps to the entrance.

The poster depicted a German family. A smiling elderly German in cap, working apron, striped shirt and bow-tie with a cigar in his hand. A plump, fair-haired woman, young-looking and also smiling, in house cap and pink dress, surrounded by children of all ages, from a fat baby boy with round cheeks to a blonde young woman with blue eyes. They were standing at the door of a farm-house with a high tiled roof over which strutted pouter pigeons. The man, the woman and all the children, the youngest of whom had his arms outstretched, were smilingly welcoming a girl approaching with a white, enamel bucket in her hand. She was wearing a gaily-embroidered Ukrainian dress, white lace apron, a house cap like the woman's and smart red shoes. She was plump, had a snub nose and unnaturally rosy cheeks. She, too, was smiling, displaying her large white teeth. In the background of the poster was a threshing-barn and cattle-shed with high, tiled roofs and more pouter pigeons strutting about on them, a strip of blue sky, a strip of a field with waving corn and some large brindled cows.

At the bottom of the poster was the Russian inscription: "I have found a home and a family here." And a little lower to the right: "*Katya.*"

Ulya, Maya and Sasha had become particularly good friends during the period of German occupation. They even used to spend nights in each other's houses when Germans were billeted on one or other of them and the home of another had remained free of them. But during all that time as though tacitly agreeing that they were not yet ready for it, they had refrained from discussing the greatest, the most important problem in their lives, the question as to how they ought to spend their lives under German rule. And so, even now they merely exchanged glances and silently descended the school steps and, avoiding each other's eyes, made their way to the Ivanikhinas.

Radiant with happiness, long-legged Tonya, the younger of the sisters, no longer a child, not yet a young woman, with her thick locks of dark chestnut hair and her large nose, came running out of the house to meet them.

"Girls! Have you heard? My God I'm so happy" she cried, and promptly burst into tears.

The house was full of girls and among them were Olga and Nina, the recently-returned Ivantsova cousins whom Ulya had not seen for many months.

But Lilya! What had happened to her! With her light hair and gentle, kind, laughing eyes she had always been so fair, so wholesome, so soft and round, like a currant bun. And now, standing in front of Ulya, she let her arms hang helplessly by the sides of her stooping, shrunken body. Her large thin nose stood out sharply from the small pale face, covered with an unhealthy sunburn. Only the eyes regarded Ulya with their former kind expression. But now, even they were different now!

Silently and impulsively, Ulya embraced Lilya and pressed her face close. And when Lilya raised her face and looked at Ulya, it held no expression of tenderness and emotion. Lilya's soft eyes looked at Ulya from far away, there was an estrangement in them, as though all that she had gone through had so cut her off from her childhood friends that she could no longer even share their ordinary, everyday feelings, no matter how sincerely and boisterously they were expressed.

Sasha Bondareva seized Lilya and spun her round.

"Lilya! Is it really you! Lilya darling! How thin you are! But never mind—don't you worry! We'll soon fatten you! If you only knew how happy we all are to have found you again!" she said expressing her feelings in her own spontaneous, impetuous way and whirling Lilya round through the room.

"Oh, leave her alone now!" Maya laughed, and pushed out her full, proud, lower lip. Then she in turn embraced Lilya and kissed her. "Come on now, your story!" she said.

And, there and then, seated on a chair in the midst of the girls crowding round her Lilya continued her narrative in calm, low voice:

"True, it was a bit difficult to be alone among all the men, but I was glad, no, I was really happy that they hadn't separated me from the fellows of my battalion. We'd stayed together during the whole retreat and had lost so many.... It's always terrible when your own people get killed. But when you're part of a unit of only seven or eight men, and you know each of them by name, you feel as though a part of your own heart is torn away when anyone of them is killed. Last year when I was wounded, they took me to Kharkov and put me in a nice hospital and my thoughts kept going back to the battalion and I wondered how they were getting on without me. I wrote a letter to them every day and they wrote to me, sometimes just one of them and sometimes all of them together and all I could think of was: when, oh when will I see them again? Then I went on leave and after that I was to join a different unit, but I put in a request to the commanding officer and got sent back to my old battalion. In Kharkov I always walked, because I took a tram once and it was so embarrassing. There were people there who pushed and insulted one another; I was upset—crying too, in uniform, mind—but not because of myself. I was hurt because of them. I was sorry for all those people. I thought, if they only knew how our people are dying at the front day after day, quietly, without unnecessary words, and how they look after each other and think of the other fellow first all the time. And they are your husbands and your fathers and sons! If you had given that a thought instead of pushing and shoving and using bad language, you'd be ready to make way for someone else, you'd exchange tender words, and if someone got accidentally offended, you'd console him."

She narrated all this in a flat, low voice; her eyes seemed to look past her friends into the distance. They kept quite silent, pressed close round her and listened without taking their shining eyes off her.

"In the camp we lived under the open sky. When it rained, we shivered in the rain; they fed us on bran soup and potato peelings and the work was very hard, digging roads, and our fellows burned away like candles. One day some of them would be gone and the next day more, and so it went on, day after day. We women"—Lilya said "women," not "girls"—"we women held on longer than the men. There was one of the fellows from the battalion, a Sergeant Fedya; I was very, very good friends with him," Lilya said softly, "and he was always joking about us women. 'You girls have nine lives,' he'd say. And when they started to herd us to

335

another camp, he was too weak and an escort shot him. But he didn't die at once, and he looked at me as I was going past, yet I couldn't take him in my arms and kiss him. I'd have been killed on the spot."

Lilya went on to relate how they had been driven to another camp and in the women's section there was a German overseer, Gertrude Göbbech, and this she-wolf almost tortured the women to death. Lilya described how the women decided to kill her or die in the attempt. One evening while returning from work in the forest they succeeded in deceiving the guards, ambushed Gertrude Göbbech, threw a greatcoat over her and strangled her. And then they ran away—there were several women and girls. But they separated, because they knew they would not be able to make their way together through the whole of Poland and the Ukraine. Lilya had come all those hundreds and hundreds of miles by herself and had been concealed and fed first by Polish people and then by her own Ukrainians.

It was Lilya who related all this, Lilya who at one time had been just an ordinary Krasnodon girl like any of them, plump and fair-haired and kind-hearted. It was difficult to realize that it was this same Lilya who had helped to strangle Gertrude Göbbech, and, on those small feet with the swollen veins, had walked all the way through German-occupied Poland and the Ukraine. And the thought entered the girls' minds: If all this had happened to me could I have lived through it? How would I have behaved?

It was the same Lilya of old, but she was somehow different. It could not be said that she had been embittered by her experiences; she did not spend her time talking about them, nor did she put on airs in front of her friends. No, it was just that she had come to understand a great many things about life. In a sense, she had become even more kind-hearted towards people as though she had come to realize their value. Though she seemed to have become shrivelled up both physically and mentally, this great human light of kindness lit up her thin, wan face.

The girls drew closer to Lilya again, everyone wanted to embrace her or at least touch her. Only Shura Dubrovina, a student and older than the others, was more reserved than the rest because she was jealous of the attention Maya Peglivanova was devoting to Lilya.

"Now come, what's all this? What a lot of cry-babies you are, really!" Sasha Bondareva exclaimed. "Let's have a singsong!"

She was about to start singing *Darkly Still the Hills Are Sleeping* but the girls shut her up—all sorts of people lived in the neighbourhood and one of the policemen might happen to stroll past. They began to cast about for one of the old Ukrainian folk songs and Tonya suggested *The Dug-Out*.

"It's one of ours and nobody could object to it, could they?" she said timidly.

But they all felt that they were miserable enough already and that this song would only make them burst into tears. Then Sasha, who sang better than anyone in Pervomaisky, began to sing:

> *Every day as evening's falling*
> *Stands a young man at my door—*
> *There he stands and sighs with longing;*
> *Stands and sighs, and nothing more.*

They all joined in. There was nothing in this song that could offend the ear of a policeman. It was a song the girls had often heard the Pyatnitsky Choir sing over the radio; it used to come over the air all the way from Moscow, and now they felt they were sending the song on its homeward journey from Pervomaisky to Moscow again.

The life in which the girls had grown up, a life which had been for them as natural as the life of the lark in the open fields, came back into the room as they sang their song.

Ulya sat by the Ivantsova cousins but, carried away by the singing, Olga, the elder girl, simply pressed Ulya's arm. There seemed to be a blue flame in her eyes, which gave beauty to her irregular features.

Nina's eyes roved provocatively round the room from under the heavy, arched eyebrows, and she suddenly bent over to Ulya and whispered earnestly into her ear:

"Kashuk sends his regards!"

"Who's Kashuk?" Ulya whispered back.

"Oleg. To us," Nina said, with emphasis, "he'll always be Kashuk from now on."

Ulya stared in front of her, puzzled.

The girls grew animated with their singing, their faces were flushed. How hard they were trying to forget, if only for a few moments, everything around them, the Germans, the policemen; to forget that they had to register at the German labour exchange; to forget the sufferings Lilya had undergone and forget that at home their mothers must be beginning to be worried by the long absence of their daughters! They sang song after song and wished that things were as they used to be.

"The times I used to think of our Pervomaisky!" Lilya said suddenly in her quiet, pathetic voice. "Sitting in the camp or walking at night barefoot and hungry through Poland, how often I used to remember our school and all of you and the way we used to get together and go out into the steppe and sing. Oh, why must all this be broken and trampled down? Why did they have to do it? What is it that people in the world want?... Ulya dear!" she said suddenly, "do recite us some good verses. You know, the way you used to...."

"Which one, then?" Ulya asked.

The girls began to cry out the titles of all Ulya's favourite poems, those they had often heard her recite.

"*The Demon*," Lilya said.

"All right then. Which part of it?"

"Whatever you like."

"Let her recite all of it!"

Ulya stood up. She slowly dropped her arms to her sides and without embarrassment, in the natural way that is typical of people who neither write poetry nor declaim it from the stage, began in her steady, deep, melodious voice:

> *The exiled Demon, Spirit of Despair,** *
> *Was flying o'er earth's sinful climes;*
> *While in his weary brain rose, dark and bare,*
> *Remembrances of happier times,—*
> *When, pure and holy, in the realms of light*

---

* M. Y. Lermontov, *The Demon*, tr. by A. C. Stephen.

He shone amid God's cherubim;
When, coursing in its golden tracks at night,
The fleeting Comet ever would delight
To interchange a smile with him;
When, through the circling ether's vast extent,
Thirsting some knowledge to achieve,
He watched the movements of the firmament
And all its wonders could perceive;
When he could love and still believe,
First of creation, happy and devout,
Guiltless of sin and ignorant of doubt....

It was a strange thing that as with all the songs the girls had sung, so Ulya's recitation instantly acquired a living, vital significance. It was as though the life to which the girls were now doomed stood out in irreconcilable contradiction to everything of beauty that had been created on earth, no matter how or when it had been created. And everything in the poem that was in favour of the Demon and everything that condemned him applied equally to all that the girls were now experiencing and stirred them to an equal degree.

What are the sorrows of which men complain,
What mortals' past or present care,
To one short minute of my endless pain,
Of my unrecognized despair?...

declaimed Ulya.

And to the girls it seemed that indeed there could be no greater suffering than that which they were experiencing.

And then the angel flies away on his golden wings, carrying with him the sinful spirit of Tamara, and the infernal ghost soars up to them from the abyss:

'Avaunt!' The Messenger of Heaven replied,
'Avaunt! Grim Potentate of Hell ...'

Ulya recited, her arms hanging loosely at her sides.

'Thy power has had sufficient spell.
No longer is thy victim clothed in clay,
Her chains of sin have all been cast away;

The hour of pain and trial is past....
Her tender soul was one of those whose life
Is but one moment of heart-rending strife,
Of longed-for, but untasted bliss....
Avaunt! Though dear thy victims purchased grace,
Yet hark! they wait for her above.
She lived, she grieved, she loved—and heaven's embrace
Is open to the child of love!' ...

Lilya buried her head in her hands and wept loudly, like
a child. Deeply moved, the girls flocked to comfort her.
And the hideous world in which they now lived again entered the room and seemed to poison the heart of each one of
them.

Chapter 31

ANATOLY POPOV had not been living at home but had
been hiding at the Petrovs' on the Pogorely Farm ever since,
together with Ulya, Victor and Victor's father, he had returned from the unsuccessful evacuation. The German administration had not yet penetrated to the farm and the Petrovs could move about freely.

As soon as the German soldiers moved out of Pervomaisky
district he returned to his own home.

Nina Ivantsova had instructions for him and Ulya, preferably the latter because she was less known in the town, to
get in touch with Koshevoi immediately for the purpose of
organizing a group of reliable Pervomaisky youths and girls
willing to take up the struggle against the Germans. Nina
hinted that Oleg was not simply working on his own initiative and passed on to them a few of his recommendations:
to talk to each young person singly, not to let any of them
know the names of any of the others, never to mention Oleg's
name, of course, and to give them to understand that all
this was something more than just a form of activity they
were engaged in by themselves.

Nina then left. Anatoly and Ulya walked down the slope
into the little hollow separating the Popovs' and the Gromovs' gardens and sat down under an apple-tree.

The shades of night were falling over steppe and gardens.

The Popovs' orchard had been badly damaged by the Germans, particularly the cherry-trees, many of the branches of which had been broken off to get at the fruit more easily; but still the garden was just as pleasant and tidy as when the father and son had been able to tend it.

Anatoly's natural-sciences teacher, who had been very keen on his subject, had at the end of his school year in the eighth class presented him with a book on insects, entitled *Pear-Tree Insects.* The book was so old that the first few pages were missing and there was no means of knowing the author's name.

Near the entrance to the Popovs' garden stood an ancient pear-tree, much older than the book, and Anatoly was very fond of both the tree and the book.

In the autumn, when the apples were ripening—the apple-trees were the Popovs' pride—Anatoly used to sleep in a camp-bed in the garden to prevent small boys from stealing the apples. If the weather was bad and he had to sleep in his room, he used a system of alarm-signals: he would weave string among the branches of the tree and attach the ends to a rope which ran through to his window. The slightest contact with one of the apple-trees would bring a cluster of empty tins clattering down at the foot of the bed and Anatoly would dash out into the garden in nothing but his running pants.

Now he and Ulya were sitting in this garden in serious thought, very conscious of the fact that since their conversation with Nina they had embarked on a new kind of life.

"We've never really spoken our minds to each other, Ulya," Anatoly said, a little abashed by her nearness, "but I've had a very high opinion of you for a long while. I feel it's time we had a frank talk, and spoke out about everything. I don't think that it would be exaggerating our position in all this, I don't think it would be conceited or whatever you like to call it, to say that you and I are just the right people to organize the young people of Pervomaisky. To begin with, of course, we must decide how we are going to live ourselves. There's this registering with the labour exchange to start with. Personally I'm not going to do it. I don't want to work for the Germans and I won't. I swear, and you're my witness, that I'll never do that!" he said, his voice restrained and emphatic. "I'll go into hiding if necessary, or disguise myself, or go underground, but I will not work for the Germans!"

"Tolya, you remember that time the German corporal rummaged about in our cases? His hands were so grimy and calloused and grasping, I keep seeing them all the time," Ulya said in a low voice. "I started seeing them again as soon as I got back home, grubbing about in our bedding and in the trunk and cutting up our dresses for kerchiefs; they even searched through the soiled linen, and now they're trying to get at our minds. Tolya, I've spent more than one sleepless night sitting up in our kitchen—it's an outhouse kitchen, you know—and I've sat there in the dark listening to the Germans bawling about the house and trying to get my sick mother to wait on them. Sitting there like that helped me to sort things out for myself. I wondered whether I had the strength, whether I had the right, to follow that road and then I suddenly saw that for me there is no other road. No, if I can't take that road, then I can't go on at all. For me there can be no other road. And I swear by my mother that I won't turn aside from this road until my dying breath!" Ulya's dark eyes looked into Anatoly's.

They were both deeply moved. For some moments they said nothing.

"Let's go through their names and see who should be approached first," Anatoly said, regaining his composure. His voice was hoarse. "Let's start with the girls, eh?"

"Maya Peglivanova and Sasha Bondareva, naturally," Ulya began. "And there's Lilya Ivanikhina of course, and Tonya will follow her. Lina Samoshina too, I think, and Nina Gerasimova."

"How about that Young Pioneer leader of ours—what's her name again?"

"Vyrikova?" A cold expression spread over Ulya's face. "You know, I'll tell you something: there used to be painful occasions when we strongly expressed our opinions on one thing or another. But everyone should have something in their make-up that is absolutely sacred, something that, like one's mother, must never be ridiculed or treated with disrespect or jeered at. As for Vyrikova — You can't tell what she's like. I wouldn't trust her, anyhow."

"Let's leave her out for now; we'll see later," Anatoly said.

"I'd rather suggest Nina Minaeva," Ulya said.

"That little blonde who's so timid?"

"Don't you imagine that she's timid. She's a bit shy, that's all. But she has very firm convictions."

"And Shura Dubrovina?"

Ulya smiled. "We'll ask Maya about her."

"I say, why haven't you mentioned your best friend, Valya Filatova?" Anatoly asked in sudden surprise.

Ulya did not answer at once. Anatoly could not see the expression on her face.

"Yes, she was my best friend and I still love her very much, and I know her kind heart better than anyone, but she can't take our road, she just hasn't the strength. I'm afraid she can only be one of the victims," Ulya said, and a faint tremor passed over her lips and nostrils. "And what about the boys?" she asked, as though deliberately changing the subject.

"Well, of the boys there's Victor; I've already had a chat with him. And since you've mentioned Sasha Bondareva, and quite rightly, then we also want her brother, Vasya. Zhenya Shepelyov, of course, and Volodya Ragozin. And Borya Glavan, too, I think; you know him, don't you? The Moldavian chap who was evacuated from Bessarabia."

Thus, they picked out all their friends and comrades in turn. With its reddish glow, the waning moon, still large, hung beyond the trees. Dark, sharply cut shadows lay across the garden, a disturbing weirdness lay over the whole of nature.

"How fortunate that both our houses are free of Germans! I simply couldn't bear to see any of them, especially now," Ulya said.

Since her return Ulya had lived alone in the tiny lean-to kitchen built against the wall of one of the outhouses in the yard. She lit the oil-lamp standing on the stove, and sat for a while on the bed, gazing into space. She was alone with her thoughts and the life ahead of her, in the state of infinite honesty with oneself, which comes to one in moments of grave mental fulfilment.

She knelt down beside the bed, dragged her suitcase from under it and among her clothing found a well-thumbed school exercise book with an oilcloth cover. She had not looked at it since the day she left home.

A half-obliterated inscription in pencil on the first page, a sort of motto for all that followed, indicated Ulya's purpose in keeping the notes in it and the date when she had begun to do so:

"There comes a time in the life of every man when his moral destiny is decided, when a turning-point is reached in his moral development. It is said that this turning-point comes only in youth. That is not true: for many it comes in the days of rose-coloured childhood." (*Pomyalovsky*.)

With a feeling of sadness, pleasure and astonishment at the thought that she, while almost a child, had written something which corresponded so nearly to her present state of mind, she read a few lines at random:

"In battle one must know how to utilize each moment and possess the ability to think quickly."

"What can withstand man's great will-power? The will embraces the whole mind; to will means to hate, to love, to pity, to rejoice, to live; in a word, the will is the moral force of every being, the free endeavour to create or to destroy, the creative power which out of nothing performs miracles!" (*Lermontov*.)

"I want to sink into the ground with shame. It is shameful, no, more than that, it is disgraceful to ridicule those who are poorly dressed! I cannot remember when I began to make a habit of that sort of thing. Yet today, with Nina M.— No, I can't bring myself to write of it. Everything I recall about it makes me blush and burn with shame. I have even become friendly with Lizka U. because together we jeered at everyone who was badly dressed and yet her parents ... but there is no need to write about it, she's a thoroughly nasty girl. And today, it was arrogant, yes, downright arrogant of me to ridicule Nina. I even tugged the blouse out of her skirt, and Nina said—No, I can't repeat her words. I have never had these horrid thoughts. It all really began because I wanted everything in life to be beautiful, but it all turned out differently. I simply had not thought that many people still live in want, and particularly Nina M., who is so defenceless.... I swear, Nina dear, I shall never, never do it again!"

There followed a pencilled postscript, evidently written the next day: "And you shall apologize to her—yes, you shall!..."

Two pages further there were these words:

"Man's dearest possession is life. It is given to him only once and he should live it in a manner which will cause no agonizing grief over aimlessly spent years and burning shame for a mean and petty past." (*N. Ostrovsky.*)

"A funny chap, really, this M. N.! I do not deny, of course, that I like his company (sometimes). And he dances well. But how he loves to parade his title and show off his decorations, yet these things mean very little to me. Last night he spoke of something I had been expecting him to speak of for a long time but had not wanted to hear. I laughed at him and I am not sorry. And when he said he would kill himself, he did not mean it and it was a beastly thing to say. He is so fat, he should be at the front doing a lot of marching, with rifle and pack. Never, never, never!"

"The bravest of all our modest commanders and the most modest of the brave, that is how I remember Comrade Kotovsky. May his memory and glory be everlasting!" (*Stalin.*)

Ulya sat engrossed over her school exercise book until she heard the garden gate bang to and light steps running across the yard to the kitchen door.

The door opened softly and Valentina Filatova ran blindly towards Ulya. She fell on her knees on the ground and buried her face in Ulya's lap.

For some moments neither spoke. Ulya felt the girl's heaving breast and beating heart.

"What is it, Valya dear?" she asked softly.

Valya raised her face, her mouth slightly open.

"Ulya! They're driving me off to Germany!"

With her deep loathing of the Germans and everything they were doing in the town, she was in mortal fear of them. Since the day the Germans arrived she had been expecting something dreadful to happen any moment to herself or her mother.

Since the order came to register at the labour exchange and Valentina had not complied with it, she had lived in constant fear of being arrested, for she regarded herself as a criminal for taking the path of conflict against the German authorities.

On her way to the market that morning she had met several people who had already been to the labour exchange. They were now on their way to work on the restoration of one of the numerous smaller pits, of which there were several in Pervomaisky area. And then Valentina too had gone to register—without a word to Ulya, ashamed to let her know that she had weakened.

The labour exchange was in a white single-storey house on a hill not far from the building of the District Soviet. Several dozen people, young and old, but mainly women and girls, had been waiting in a queue at the entrance. In the distance Valentina had seen among them a girl who had been in the same class with her at Pervomaisky school. She was Zinaida Vyrikova and she had recognized her by her short figure and the smooth, almost glued-down hair with the short pigtails sticking out aggressively in front of her. She had walked up to her in order to be near the front of the queue.

No, this was not one of those many war-time queues, in which people had waited their turn to buy bread and other rationed foods or to get ration-cards or even to join in the mobilization for work on the home labour front. In those, everybody had wanted to be as near the front as possible, and if anyone had tried to jump the queue, because they knew somebody or felt that their position entitled them to do so, there would have been trouble. No, this was the queue for the German labour exchange and no one had tried to get there ahead of anyone else. Vyrikova had silently gazed at Valentina from her close-set, unkind eyes and had allowed her to stand in front.

The queue had moved rather quickly because two people were allowed in at a time. Valentina's sweaty hand clutched her passport, wrapped in a handkerchief and pressed close to her breast as she entered the building with Vyrikova.

Directly opposite the door of the registration office stood a long table. Behind it sat a fat German corporal and a Russian woman with a very delicate rosy complexion and an exceptionally long chin. Valentina and Vyrikova both knew her: she had been the German teacher in several of the Krasnodon schools, including that in Pervomaisky. Her name, strangely enough, was Nemchinova.* The two girls said "Good-morning" to her.

"Ah... two pupils of mine!" Nemchinova had said, with a flutter of long dark eyelashes and an affected smile.

There was a tapping of typewriters in the room. There were two short queues to the doors on the right and the left.

Nemchinova had asked Valentina's age, her parents' names and her address and added them to a long list, at the same time translating the information to the German corporal, who added it in German to another list.

While Nemchinova was questioning her someone had come out of the room on the right and another person had entered it. Suddenly Valya had caught sight of a young woman with dishevelled hair, flushed face and tears in her eyes. She had passed quickly through the room one hand buttoning up the front of her blouse. At that moment Nemchinova had asked the girl another question.

"What did you say?" Valentina had asked, her eyes following the young woman.

"Are you in good health? Have you anything wrong with you?"

"No, I'm quite well," she had said.

Vyrikova, behind her, had suddenly given her blouse a tug. She had turned round, but Vyrikova had looked past her with eyes devoid of all expression.

"To the director!" Nemchinova had said.

The girl had moved mechanically across to the queue on the right and turned to look at Vyrikova who was replying to the same questions as she had been asked.

It had been quiet in the director's office, only from time to time curt phrases in German had been audible through the door. While Vyrikova was being questioned a youth of seventeen had come out of the director's office. He had been pale and covered with confusion, and he too had been buttoning his shirt as he came out.

Meanwhile Valentina had heard Vyrikova's strident voice saying:

* *Nemchinova*—from the word *nemets*, meaning German.

"You know very well that I'm tubercular, Olga Konstantinovna. Listen!" And Vyrikova had breathed demonstratively at Nemchinova and the fat German corporal. The corporal had drawn back in his chair and gaped at her in amazement as a wheezing noise came from her chest.

"I have to be taken care of in my home," she had continued shamelessly, glaring first at Nemchinova, then at the corporal, and back again at the woman. "But should there be anything for me in the town, here, I'd be delighted, simply delighted! Only please, Olga Konstantinovna—something in an intellectual, cultured profession! I will work with pleasure for the New Order, with great pleasure!"

"My God! What's she saying?" Valentina had thought, as she entered the director's office with a pounding heart.

She had stood in front of a well-fed German with sleek, greying, ginger hair parted in the middle. He wore an army jacket and incongruous yellow leather shorts and brown stockings. The hair on his knees was as thick as fur. He had cast a cursory, indifferent glance at the girl.

"Strip!" he had shouted.

She had looked helplessly round her. The only other person in the room was a German clerk seated behind the desk with piles of old passports beside him.

"Strip, can't you hear?" the German clerk had said in Ukrainian.

"How?..." The blood had rushed to Valentina's face.

"How, how!" mimicked the clerk. "Take off your clothes!"

"*Schneller, schneller!*" snapped the officer with the hairy knees, then had suddenly stretched out his arm and with his well-washed knotty fingers also covered with ginger hairs, pushed her teeth apart and looked into her mouth. Then he had begun to unbutton her blouse.

Bursting into tears with fright and humiliation, the girl had quickly begun to undress, fumbling with her underclothes.

The officer had helped her. She was left standing in nothing but her shoes. The German had surveyed her coldly, fastidiously, felt her shoulders, thighs and knees, then turning to the clerk had said brusquely as though he had been examining a soldier:

*"Tauglich!"**

"Passport!" the clerk had yelled and stretched out his arm without looking up.

Sobbing, and trying to cover herself with her clothing, Valentina had handed him the document.

"Address!"

She had told him.

"Put your clothes on," the clerk morosely said in a low voice, and tossed her passport on the pile with the others. "You'll be informed when to report at the assembly point."

Only when she was in the street again had the girl come to her senses. The hot midday sun lay on the houses, on the dusty road and the scorched grass. There had been no rain for over a month, everything was burnt and shrivelled and the air shimmered in the heat.

She had suddenly slumped down with a moan in the middle of the road where she had been standing up to her ankles in dust. Her skirt had billowed out round her like a balloon and then subsided. She had buried her face in her hands.

Vyrikova had helped her to recover her self-control. Together they had walked down the hill on which stood the District Soviet building and the militia barracks, through Vosmidomiki district towards their homes in Pervomaisky. Valya had shivered feverishly and then broken into a hot sweat.

"What a fool you are! What an idiot!" Vyrikova had said. "You deserve all you got! These are Germans," she had said with respect and even servility in her voice. "And you've got to know how to adapt yourself to them."

Valentina had walked by her side, not hearing what she said.

"What a crazy thing to do!" Vyrikova had continued, virulently. "I tipped you off. You should have told them you wanted to be of use to them here; they appreciate that. And you should have said your health is bad. You should have gone to the commission first, to Doctor Natalya Alexeyevna of the town hospital. Everyone who wants it gets a certificate of exemption from her or at least one that says they're not fit; that German in there is only a feldsher

* "Fit!"

and doesn't know a damned thing. You're a fool, a silly fool! I've been given a job in what used to be our cattle supply office and I'll be given rations, too."

Ulya's first impulse was to feel tremendously sorry for Valentina. She took her head between her hands and showered kisses on her hair and eyes. Her next thoughts were to plan her escape.

"You've got to run away," she said, "yes, just that, run for it!"

"My God, how can I!" Valentina said helplessly, and even petulantly. "I haven't got a single identity paper now!"

"Valya darling," Ulya said, in a tender persuasive tone. "I know we're surrounded by Germans, but it's still our country, you know. It's a big country and it's full of our own people and we've always lived among them. You'll see, we'll find a way out of this! I'm going to help you and all the lads and girls will help you."

"And Mother? How can you talk like that, Ulya. They'll torture her to death!" Her eyes filled with tears.

"Now don't start crying again, please," Ulya implored. "Do you think that if they ship you off to Germany it'll be easier for her? Will she survive that?"

"Oh Ulya! Ulya! Why do you torment me still more!"

"It's disgusting, the way you talk! It's ... it's vile and disgraceful— I despise you!" Ulya said, a feeling of terrible cruelty getting the better of her. "Yes, I've nothing but contempt for your helplessness and tears. There's so much grief everywhere, so many people, healthy, strong, beautiful people, dying at the front and in fascist concentration camps and torture-chambers! Do you realize what their wives must be suffering, and their mothers? Yet they go on working and struggling just the same and here you are, a young girl, with everything before you, and you're being offered help, and yet you sit there snivelling and expecting to be pitied. I'm not a bit sorry for you, not one bit!" Ulya declared.

She rose abruptly, went to the door and stood leaning against it with her hands behind her, staring out into space, anger flashing from her dark eyes. With her face pressed down on Ulya's bed, Valentina remained on her knees without uttering a sound.

"Valya! Valya dear! Think of how we always used to spend all our time together! Darling!" Ulya began. "Listen, dear!"

The girl sobbed.

"Can you say that I've ever given you bad advice about anything? There was the business with the plums, remember? And that time when you screamed you'd never manage to swim back to the bank, and I said I'd drown you with my own hands if you didn't? Valya dear! Please!"

"No! No! You've forsaken me! You pushed me out of your heart when you evacuated with the others and since then there has been nothing between us. Do you think I didn't feel it then?" Valentina sobbed, quite beside herself. "And now, now I'm all alone in the wide world!"

Ulya made no reply.

Valya got up and dried her tears with her handkerchief.

"Valya, I'm asking you for the last time," Ulya said coldly, in a steady voice. "Either you listen to me now and we go straight away and call Anatoly out to take you to Victor in the Pogorely Farm or—Valya, don't break my heart!"

"Good-bye, Ulya dear! Good-bye for ever!" Holding back her tears, she ran out of the kitchen into the moonlit yard.

Ulya found it hard not to follow her and take her in her arms and cover her unhappy tear-stained face with kisses.

She put out the light, opened the window and lay on her bed without undressing. She listened to the vague noises of the night coming to her from the steppe and from the mining settlement. Sleep eluded her. She imagined that while she was lying here, the Germans had come to Valentina's home and seized her and that there was no one to say a kind or encouraging word of farewell to her.

Suddenly she thought she heard footsteps on the soft ground and leaves rustling in the vegetable garden. The steps came nearer; it sounded like more than one person! She should have locked the door and quickly closed the window but the shuffling footsteps were close to the window and already a head had popped over the sill and she saw fair hair and a little Uzbek cap.

"Ulya, are you asleep?" Anatoly whispered.

In a flash she was at the window.

"Something terrible's happened," Anatoly said. "They've taken Victor's father!"

Ulya saw Victor's face, as he came closer to the window; the moonlight shone directly on it. His eyes were sombre, his face pale but full of determination.

"When did it happen?"

"This evening. An SS man came, in black uniform; he was fat, with gold teeth and he stank," Victor said with hatred in his voice. "He had another soldier with him and a Russian policeman.... They beat him. Then they took him to the office of the Forestry Station, where there was a lorry full of people they'd arrested and they brought them all here. I followed the lorry for twelve miles. If you hadn't left there the day before yesterday they'd have arrested you too," Victor said to Anatoly.

Chapter 32

MANY DAYS AND NIGHTS had passed since Matvei Shulga had been thrown into prison and he had lost all count of time. His cell was in almost perpetual darkness; the narrow chink close under the ceiling allowed only a little daylight to enter because it had barbed wire drawn across it on the outside and was almost obscured by the overhanging roof.

Shulga felt alone and abandoned by everyone.

Now and again a woman, a wife or a mother, succeeded in imploring one of the German gendarmerie soldiers or someone of the Russian policemen to pass in to the imprisoned husband or son some food or an article of clothing. But Shulga had no relatives in Krasnodon. Apart from Lyutikov and old Kondratovich, none of his friends knew that he had been left in Krasnodon to do underground work, that the stranger known as Yevdokim Ostapchuk languishing in this dark cell was really Matvei Shulga. He realized that Lyutikov might still be in ignorance concerning what had happened to him, and that if he had discovered something he might find it difficult to get in touch with him. So he expected no help from Lyutikov.

The only people he had any dealings with were his torturers, the German gendarmes. Among these only two spoke Russian: the German interpreter who wore a Cossack hat on his small, dark head, and the Police Chief Solikovsky, in his wide old-fashioned Cossack riding-breeches with the yellow stripe down the sides. With fists like horse's hoofs, he could be said to be worse than any of the German gendarmes—if anybody could be worse than they were.

From the first moment of his arrest Shulga had made no secret of the fact that he was a Party member, a Communist, because it would have been useless to do so and because to be honest and truthful gave him additional strength for the struggle against those who tortured him. He did, however, suggest that he was just an ordinary rank-and-file Communist. But stupid though his torturers were, they could see by his appearance and conduct that this was not the truth. They wanted him to name his accomplices and therefore did not wish to nor could kill him straight off. *Hauptwachtmeister* Brückner or his deputy *Wachtmeister* Balder would question him twice every day in the hope of ferreting out, through him, the Krasnodon Communist Organization and thereby earning the praise of Major-General Klehr, the chief regional *Feldkommandant*.

They would question Matvei and beat him when he exhausted their patience. More often, however, he would be beaten on their orders by SS *Rottenführer* Fehnbong, the corpulent non-commissioned officer with the gold teeth, the effeminate voice and the light horn-rimmed glasses. He was so evil-smelling that even *Wachtmeister* Balder and *Hauptwachtmeister* Brückner wrinkled their noses when he came too close and threw scornful remarks at him. N.C.O. Fehnbong would beat and torture Shulga, trussed up and in addition held down by several soldiers, methodically, indifferently and with perfect knowledge of what he was doing. This was his profession, his everyday work. When Shulga was not being questioned but alone in his cell, Fehnbong would not touch him, because he was afraid of Shulga when he was not bound and held down by soldiers and also because it was out of working hours and he was off duty and he would spend his free time in the prison gatehouse set aside specially for him and his soldiers.

Yet no matter how and for what length of time they tortured Shulga, he never changed his attitude. He was as remote, obstinate and ungovernable as always and wearied everyone and altogether he caused nothing but annoyance.

While outwardly Shulga's life dragged on in this utterly hopeless and agonizingly monotonous manner, his mind became increasingly active and his thoughts more profound. As with all people whose consciences are clear in the face of death he now saw himself and his whole life with infinite limpid clarity, with the extraordinary force of truth.

By sheer effort of will he had expunged from his mind all thought of his wife and children in order that such thoughts would not weaken him, and greater, in consequence, were the warmth and love with which he thought of the friends of his youth still living not far away from him in the town — Liza Rybalova and Kondratovich. It grieved him that even his death, which might have acquitted him in their eyes, would remain unknown to them. Yes, he knew how he came to be here in this dark cell and he suffered from the knowledge that he could no longer set things right, that he could not explain to people where he had been at fault, and so relieve his mind and also save others from making the same mistakes.

One day while resting in his cell after the morning interrogation he caught the sound of glib voices. The door was flung open, making a plaintive noise, and into the cell stalked a man with a policeman arm-band and a heavy revolver holster with a yellow cord dangling from it, hanging from his belt. The moustached German gendarme on guard in the corridor remained standing in the doorway.

Accustomed as he was to the darkness, Shulga immediately recognized the policeman who was still very young, almost a boy in fact. His hair was dark and his uniform black. He could not at first see Shulga properly, he seemed embarrassed and yet tried to appear at ease. His lively eyes darted round the cell and he rocked to and fro on his heels.

"Here you are! In the cage of the wild beast! Let's shut the door and see how you'll feel! In you go!" the moustached soldier said in German and laughed boisterously as he shut the door behind the young policeman.

Shulga raised himself on the dark floor and the policeman

quickly bent over him, his black penetrating eyes seeming to burn into Shulga's.

"Your friends are awaiting their chance," he whispered. "One night next week ... I'll give you the signal."

Then in a flash he was upright again, and with an insolent expression on his face he shouted in an unsteady voice:

"You can't frighten me. Not with a fellow like this, you damned Germans!"

With a loud laugh the German soldier opened the cell door and shouted something gleefully.

"Satisfied now, eh?" the young policeman said, his lank body reeling against Shulga. "You're lucky I'm an honest man and don't know you ... oh, you!" he shouted suddenly, and with a quick swing of his thin arm gave Shulga a light push on the shoulder and for a second pressed his fingers on it, and in that light pressure Shulga again sensed something friendly.

The policeman left the cell, the door was banged to and the key scraped in the lock.

Of course this could be a piece of provocation. But why should there be occasion for it now that he was in their hands and they could kill him any time they liked? It may have been a kite flown in the hope that, given the right circumstances, Shulga would open up to this policeman as he would before one of his friends. But could they really think he was as simple as that?

Hope rushed into Shulga's heart and drove the blood throbbing in waves through his tormented, warrior's body. It meant, then, that Lyutikov was alive and active! It meant that he was in their minds! How could he have thought otherwise?...

A feeling of gratitude to his friends for their concern for him; a newly-kindled hope of being able to save his family; the joy of possible release from physical torture and unendurable brooding—all this welled up in his mind in one mighty call to battle and to life. Tears of happiness surged up in the heart of this huge, elderly, conscience-stricken man at the thought that he might still live, that he yet might be able to do his duty.

Through boarded door and the walls the whole life of the prison was audible to him day and night. He heard people being taken in and out; he heard them being tortured; he heard them being shot outside the wall of the prison yard. One night he was awakened by noises, conversation and the tramp of feet in the cells and the corridors, by shouting in German and Russian from gendarmes and policemen; by the clatter of rifles and the weeping of women and children. He got the impression that people were being taken out of the prison. Then came a roar of engines as one lorry after another left the prison-yard.

When Shulga was taken along the corridor for the morning interrogation he did in fact sense that the prison was empty.

During the following night he was not awakened—for the first time. He heard a lorry drive up to the gate, then the muffled swearing of gendarmes and policemen as they hurriedly, as though each were ashamed of what he was doing, led the prisoners into the cells. He could hear heavy feet dragging along the corridor. All night long the prisoners were being brought in.

Long before morning came Shulga was again taken away to be questioned. But as he was not bound he guessed that he was not to be tortured; and, indeed, he was not escorted to the cell specially equipped for that purpose and located in the same wing as the other cells, but to *Meister* Brückner's office. Brückner was in his shirt-sleeves—it was unbearably hot in the office and he had hung his army jacket over a chair; *Wachtmeister* Balder was present, in full uniform, and the interpreter Shurka Reiband as well as three German soldiers in their mouse-coloured uniforms.

Then a heavy step was heard on the other side of the door, which opened to admit Chief of Police Solikovsky in his antiquated Cossack hat, who stooped to avoid the door beam; behind him Shulga saw his tormentor Fehnbong and several SS men who were holding a tall, half-dressed, elderly man with a strong fleshy face. He had nothing on his feet and his arms were bound behind his back. Shulga recognized Petrov, an old partisan in the 1918 Civil War, a fellow-Ukrainian whom he had not seen for fifteen years. It was clearly a long time since Petrov had walked barefoot and his foot was injured; he found it painful even to walk on the floor. His fleshy face was bruised and bleeding. Except that his shoulders had broadened and he had put on weight, he seemed to have aged little since Shulga had seen him last. His face was sullen but his manner dignified.

"D'you recognize him?" *Meister* Brückner asked.

Shurka Reiband translated the question to Shulga.

Petrov and Shulga both made it appear as though they were meeting for the first time. They maintained this attitude throughout the interrogation.

Meister Brückner bellowed at Petrov, standing before him barefoot and sullen:

"You liar! You lying old rat!" He stamped the floor so hard with his polished boots that his pendulous belly shook.

Then Solikovsky pitched into Petrov with his huge fists until he got him on the floor. Shulga was about to rush at Solikovsky but an inner voice warned him that it would only make matters worse for Petrov. Moreover, he felt that the time had come for him to keep his hands free. So he kept a hold on himself and, with quivering nostrils, silently watched them knock Petrov about.

Both men were then taken away.

Although Shulga had not on this occasion been beaten himself he was so shaken by what he had witnessed that after this second interrogation in one day, his mighty physique gave way under the strain. He never remembered being escorted back to his cell and becoming completely unconscious.

He regained consciousness when the key scraped in the door. He heard a commotion at the door but was unable to rouse himself fully. Then he felt vaguely that the door was opened and somebody was pushed into his cell. With an effort he opened his eyes. Bending over him stood a man with black eyebrows that met over the bridge of his nose and a black gypsy beard, trying to scan Shulga's face. The man could not see Shulga's features, either because coming into the cell from the daylight outside his eyes had not become accustomed to the darkness or else because Shulga no longer resembled his former self. But Shulga recognized him at once: it was his fellow-Ukrainian, who had also fought in the 1918 Civil War; it was Valko, director of 1B Pit.

"Andrei," Shulga called softly.

"Matvei? This must be fate!" Quickly, impetuously Valko embraced Shulga who had raised himself from the floor.

"We did everything we could to get you out, but it is my fate to join you here...." He paused, then went on in a curt, husky voice, "Let's look at you—what have they done to you!" He released Shulga and paced the cell.

His natural gypsy temperament seemed to have awakened and the cell was so small that he was truly like a tiger in a cage.

"So they've given it to you too," Shulga said calmly and sat down, his arms round his knees.

Valko's clothing was covered in dust, a jacket sleeve was half torn off, one trouser leg was torn at the knee, the other ripped at the seam and his forehead was bruised. He still wore his boots, however.

"It seems you fought. So did I," Shulga said with a note of satisfaction in his voice as he pictured what must have taken place. "Never mind, don't let it worry you. Sit down and tell me how things are outside."

Valko seated himself on the floor opposite Shulga, crossed his legs under him and winced when his hand touched the slimy floor.

"A man of position.... Not used to this!" he said and laughed at himself. "What's there to tell? Our affairs are going normally. Only ... I—"

Suddenly the features of this burly man became so contorted with anguish that a shudder went down Shulga's back. With a hopeless gesture Valko buried his dusky face in his hands.

Chapter 33

On the day Valko established contact with Lyutikov, all the secret strings controlling sabotage operations and subversive work were placed in his hands, because he was the man most familiar with all the mines of the Krasnodon Coal Trust.

The fact that Barakov, the engineer, always had access to the chief administration, to Schweide himself in fact, but especially to his deputy, Feldner, who, unlike his taciturn boss, was a gossip, made it possible for Barakov, and through him Valko, to be always abreast of the industrial plans of the administration.

Even the most careful observer would have been hard put to it to discover the connection between a routine meeting between Barakov and Feldner and the sudden appearance in the Krasnodon streets some hours later of a modest, quiet girl with a sun-bronzed face and irregular features.

The simple girl, Olga Ivantsova, might sell tomatoes at one house, call at another just to pay a visit; and after a while all the happy plans of the German administration would be dashed to the ground in some curious fashion.

Olga Ivantsova was doing duty as Valko's courier.

Barakov learned from Feldner not only about industrial measures. The officers of the local gendarmerie drank day and night at *Leutnant* Schweide's house and everything they carelessly chattered about among themselves *Herr* Feldner would just as carelessly let out to Barakov.

Lyutikov had spent more than one sleepless night pondering on ways and means of rescuing Shulga and the other prisoners, but for a long time they had even failed to make contact with anyone inside the prison. This was finally achieved with the help of Ivan Turkenich.

Turkenich came from a highly-respected Krasnodon family well known to Lyutikov. The head of the family, Vasily Ignatyevich, was an old miner now living on an invalid's pension; Feona Ivanovna, his wife, was a daughter of what had once been a Ukrainian family from Voronezh Gubernia, but its members had become wholly Russified. In 1921, the year of the harvest failure, they had emigrated to the Donbas. Vanya was still a babe in arms then and Feona Ivanovna had carried him the whole journey, while her little daughter walked behind, holding to her skirt.

Their poverty while on the road had been so great that an old well-to-do childless couple in Millerovo, who had given them shelter for a night, pressed Feona Ivanovna to leave the boy to be brought up by them. The parents wavered for a time, then rebelled at the thought, then quarrelled about it and wept and in the end kept their little boy themselves.

They arrived in the Sorokin mining district and settled there. Later, when Vanya was in the senior class at school and took part in the performances of the dramatic circle, his parents loved to tell their visitors how the Millerovo couple had wanted to keep their little boy and how they had refused to part with him.

When the Germans broke through on the Southern Front, Lieutenant Turkenich, who was in command of an anti-tank battery in the Kalach-on-Don sector, had orders to fight to the last. He beat back the German tank attacks until all his gun crews had been put out of action and he himself lay wounded on the ground. With the scattered remnants of other units and batteries he was taken prisoner and because his wounds had made it impossible for him to walk, a German officer had shot him but failed to kill him. A Cossack widow nursed him back to comparative health in two weeks and he turned up at his home with his chest bandaged under his shirt.

Ivan Turkenich managed to establish contact with the prisoners through Anatoly Kovalyov and Vasya Pirozhok, two of his old friends from the Gorky School.

It would have been difficult to find friends whose physical appearance and character differed so much. Kovalyov was a man of amazing strength, stocky as an oak in the steppe, slow-moving and kindly to the point of naïveté. When still a lad, he had decided to become a famous weight-lifter although the girl he was courting chaffed him about it. She maintained that in the sporting world the chess-player was at the top of the ladder and the weight-lifter at the bottom. Only amoebas were lower than weight-lifters. He led a very regular life, did not drink or smoke and even in the winter went about without cap or overcoat. He had a dip in the ice-hole every morning and trained with his weights every day.

Vasya Pirozhok, on the other hand, was lean, lively and quick-tempered. He had dark roving eyes, was fond of the girls and popular with them. He was also pugnacious and the only sport which interested him was boxing. He was inclined to be adventuresome.

Turkenich had sent his younger married sister to Pirozhok for some gramophone records, and she had brought Pirozhok back with her. Pirozhok had thought fit to bring along his bosom-friend Kovalyov as well.

To the great indignation of the Krasnodon townsfolk—

especially the young people who had known Kovalyov and Pirozhok personally—the two friends were soon afterwards seen on the vacant ground near the park with a swastika on their arms in company with members of the police exercising in their new profession under the supervision of a German sergeant with blue shoulder-straps.

Their work was to keep order in the town. They had to take their turn of duty in the Town Council, the *Direktion*, the district agricultural commandant's office, at the labour exchange and in the market-place and undertake night patrol in various parts of the town. The police arm-band was the insignia of reliability in the company of the German gendarmerie soldiers and Vasya Pirozhok had soon learned not only the cell in which Shulga was confined, but had managed to get through to him and let him know that his friends were working on how to free him.

To free him! Both cunning and bribes were useless for this purpose. The only way Shulga and the others could be freed was by making a raid on the prison. An operation of this sort was now within the strength of the district underground organization. It was gradually gaining reinforcements in the shape of Red Army officers from among the patients of the hospital who had been saved by the efforts of Sergei Tyulenin, his sister Nadya and Nurse Lusha.

With the appearance of Turkenich, the youth group which Lyutikov had organized to work with the district underground committee gained a true fighting leader: an officer.

In the event of military operations, the district underground committee would transform itself into a Central Army Command and, as leaders of the district committee, Barakov and Lyutikov would become detachment commander and commissar respectively. They wanted the young people to build up their organization along the same lines.

During those August days Barakov and Lyutikov were busy organizing an armed detachment for the raid on the prison. Ivan Turkenich and Oleg had received instructions from them to select a group of young people who were also to participate in the operation. To this end they had called on Zemnukhov, Sergei Tyulenin, Lyuba Shevtsova as well as Yevgeny Stakhovich, because he had already had experience of fighting.

Ulya was anxious to get on with the task assigned to her and was fully aware that it was important for her to see Oleg at the earliest opportunity; yet she was so unused to deceiving her parents and had been so burdened with household duties that she had been unable to get to him until the day after her conversation with Victor and Anatoly, and then only towards evening. When she arrived Oleg was not at home.

General Baron von Wentzel and his staff had left for the east. Nikolai Nikolayevich opened the door for Ulya and recognized her at once; but she felt he was not very pleased to see her nor was he even friendly, and this considering that they had experienced so much together and had not seen one another for so long.

Grandma Vera and Yelena Nikolayevna were not at home either. Sitting on chairs facing one another Marina and Olga Ivantsova were winding wool. As Ulya came in, Marina dropped the ball of wool, rushed towards her with a cry of pleasure and embraced her.

"Ulya! Where've you been all this time? Curse these Germans!" she cried overjoyed, tears filling her eyes. "See, I'm unravelling my cardigan to make a little suit for the boy. They're sure to take the cardigan, I thought, but they might not take the clothes from him!"

Speaking rapidly she began to talk of their journey together, the slaughter of the children at the pontoon bridge, the death of the orphanage matron, and how the German soldiers had stolen their silk articles of clothing.

Olga continued to hold the wool outstretched on her firm arms which were almost black with sunburn. Her face bore a mysterious, Ulya thought a worried, expression as she sat there in complete silence staring before her with unblinking eyes.

Ulya did not find it necessary to tell them the purpose of her call. She merely gave them the news that Victor's father had been arrested. Without altering her position Olga exchanged a quick glance with Nikolai Nikolayevich. It suddenly struck Ulya that Nikolai Nikolayevich had not meant to be unfriendly, but that he had been alarmed about something of which she had no knowledge. And she, too, was seized with a vague sense of alarm.

With the same mysterious expression on her face Olga said, with a wry smile, that she had arranged to meet her sister near the park and that immediately she had done so they would return together. As soon as she had made the announcement to no one in particular, she left the house.

Marina had continued to talk, oblivious of what was happening round her.

Shortly afterwards Olga returned with Nina.

"Somebody mentioned you just now at a gathering. Would you like to come and I'll introduce you?" Nina said to Ulya, without smiling.

Without speaking she conducted Ulya through several streets and yards to somewhere in the centre of the town. She did not once look at Ulya. There was a far-away, angry look in her wide-open, brown eyes.

"Nina, what's happened?" Ulya asked softly.

"They'll probably tell you in a minute. I can't say anything."

"You know, Victor Petrov's father's been arrested," Ulya said again.

"Has he? That was to be expected," Nina said, banishing the subject with a gesture of the hand.

They entered a house like any other in that part of the town. Ulya had never been here before.

On a wooden, double bedstead an old man lay propped up on well-shaken pillows; his head had sunk deep into them, so that only the high brow, fleshy nose and thick, fair eyelashes were visible. He was fully dressed. A thin, elderly, large-boned woman sat on a chair by the bed sewing. Two pretty young women, with large bare feet, sat idly on a bench by the window; they regarded Ulya with curiosity.

Ulya greeted them, and Nina quickly took her through to the adjoining room.

Several youths and a girl were seated at a table laid with food, mugs and bottles of vodka. Ulya recognized Oleg, Vanya Zemnukhov and Yevgeny Stakhovich whom she remembered from the days before the war, when he had made a speech to the young people of Pervomaisky. Two of the youths were strangers to her. The girl was Lyuba Shevtsova—Lyuba the Actress—whom Ulya had seen at the gate of her house on that memorable day; the circumstances of their encounter had remained so vivid in her memory that she was startled to see her here. In a flash, however, she understood everything and Lyuba's behaviour that day now appeared to her in its true light.

Nina left the room as soon as she had taken Ulya inside. Oleg stood up to meet Ulya, blushed slightly and looked round for a seat for her. Then he smiled broadly, and the smile warmed her heart, preparing her for the mysterious, alarming news she was to learn.

On the night Victor's father was arrested almost every Party member in the town and district, who had been unable to evacuate, had also been arrested, together with Soviet administrative workers, people who had taken an active part in one or other aspect of social work, many teachers and engineers, leading mine workers and some of the wounded army men in hiding in the town.

The frightful news had been spreading through the town since the morning. But only Lyutikov and Barakov knew what damage to the underground organization had been done by this operation of the German gendarmerie, which was not caused by somebody's carelessness but had been carried out by them as a precautionary measure. Many people who had intended to take part in the raid against the prison guard had been caught in the close-meshed drag-net of the police.

Olga and Nina Ivantsova had come running to Oleg's home. The pallor on their haggard, sunburnt faces immediately became reflected in his. They related that, according to Kondratovich, Uncle Andrei had been arrested during the night.

Valko's hide-out, the address of which was known only to Kondratovich, had suddenly been searched. It later transpired that they had been hunting not for Valko but for the landlady's husband who had been evacuated. But Valko had been identified at once by Ignat Fomin, who had been in charge of the affair which had taken place in one of the Little Shanghais. From what the landlady said, Valko had remained calm until Fomin hit him in the face. Valko had then flown in a rage and knocked Fomin down and then had been overpowered by gendarmerie soldiers.

Oleg and Nina had hurried off to Turkenich, leaving Olga with Oleg's people. Either Vasya Pirozhok or Kovalyov had to be contacted at all cost. Turkenich had sent his sister to their homes but she came back with news which was completely mystifying and alarming. According to their parents. both Pirozhok and Kovalyov had left their homes early the previous night; yet shortly after their departure the policeman Fomin, who worked with them, had arrived and wanted to know where they were. He had been very rude at not finding them at home and had returned later in the night and had said over and over again: "They'll catch it for this!"

Kovalyov and Vasya finally returned home before dawn completely drunk, which was all the more amazing since Kovalyov had never been accustomed to drink. They told their parents that they had been drinking all night in a pot-house, and, brushing aside what their parents told them about Fomin's threats, went to bed. The police arrived in the morning and arrested them.

Through Nina, Oleg reported all this to Polina Sokolova so that she could pass it on to Lyutikov at the earliest opportunity. Then Oleg and Nina had a consultation with Sergei Tyulenin, Lyuba, Vanya Zemnukhov and Stakhovich. The meeting was now taking place in Turkenich's home.

When Ulya entered an argument was in progress between Stakhovich and Vanya Zemnukhov and Ulya was immediately drawn into it.

"I can't see the logic of all this," Stakhovich said. "We were getting ready to free Ostapchuk; we had even hurried forward the preparations, had collected arms, mobilized the fellows, and then, just when Uncle Andrei is arrested, making the matter all the more urgent, we're told to go on waiting and waiting."

Stakhovich's prestige with the young people seemed to be considerable. Troubled, Vanya asked in his husky bass:

"What d'you suggest then?"

"I suggest we attack the prison not later than tomorrow night. If, instead of talking, we'd started to act this morning, we could have carried out the raid tonight," Stakhovich said.

He went on to develop his idea. Ulya noticed that he had changed considerably since she had heard him make his speech at the Pervomaisky Komsomol meeting before the war. Even then he had made full use of bookish words like "logic" and "objectively" and "analyse," but he had not been so self-confident. Now he spoke calmly, without gestures; his long, thin hands were clenched on the table before him and his head, with the fair hair brushed back naturally, was held erect on his shoulders.

It was clear that his suggestion had startled them and no one seemed ready to give an immediate reply.

"You're playing on our emotions, that's what you're doing," Vanya said finally in a shy but firm tone of voice. "It's no good playing hide-and-seek. We've never discussed it but I believe that you know as well as the rest of us that we haven't been preparing the fellows for a serious business like this on our own initiative, so as long as we have no fresh instructions, we've no right to lift a finger. Not only might we fail to free them but we might lose more people into the bargain. After all we're not little boys!" he suddenly added angrily.

"Well, for all I know I'm not being trusted and not being told everything," Stakhovich said, pursing his lips haughtily. "So far I haven't had a single clear, militant directive. We just wait and wait and we'll go on waiting until they really murder the prisoners, if they haven't been murdered already!" he said harshly.

"We feel just as bad as you do about the people there," Vanya said with resentment. "But you can't really believe that by ourselves we'd be strong enough?"

"Are there any staunch, loyal fellows in Pervomaisky?" Stakhovich suddenly asked Ulya, looking her straight in the eye with a patronizing expression on his face.

"Yes, of course," Ulya said.

Without a word Stakhovich turned and looked at Vanya.

Oleg sat on his chair, his head sunk between his shoulders; his large eyes looked seriously and closely at Stakhovich, then at Vanya. Then he gazed straight in front of him plunged deep in thought, and it was as though he had drawn a veil over his eyes.

Sergei sat silent, his eyes downcast. Turkenich kept out of the argument but his eyes studied Stakhovich all the time.

Lyuba moved and sat down by Ulya.

"D'you recognize me?" she whispered. "You remember my father?"

"Yes, it happened right before my eyes." In a few whispered words Ulya gave her details of Grigory Shevtsov's end.

"Oh, how much more can we endure!" Lyuba said. "You know, I hate those fascists and their police so much that I could cut them to pieces with my own hands!" she said, an unaffected, savage expression in her eyes.

"Yes . . . yes," Ulya said softly. "Sometimes I feel such a thirst for revenge that I'm afraid of myself. I'm frightened that I might do something rash."

"You like Stakhovich?" Lyuba whispered in her ear.

Ulya shrugged her shoulders.

"He's giving himself airs; but he's right. There are plenty of lads," Lyuba said with Sergei Levashov in her mind.

"It's not just a matter of people; who's going to lead us?" Ulya whispered in reply.

As though Oleg had heard her words he said at that moment:

"There's no shortage of lads; people with c-courage can always be found, but it's a m-matter of organization." He spoke in a youthful ringing voice with a more pronounced stutter than usual and everybody turned towards him. "We're not really an organization, are we? We just c-come together and talk!" he went on with an artless expression. "There's the Party, you know. How can we go ahead and do anything without the Party—brushing it aside, so to speak?"

"You should have told us that at the outset; now it looks as though I'm against the Party," Stakhovich said, an expression of both embarrassment and annoyance forming on his face. "Up to now we've had dealings only with you and Turkenich, and not with the Party. You might at least tell us why you've called us together!"

"This is why," Turkenich said in such a quiet calm voice that they all switched their eyes to him. "In order to be prepared. How d'you know that they might not in fact call us out tonight?" he asked and looked straight at Stakhovich.

Stakhovich had nothing to say.

"That's the first reason," Turkenich went on. "The second is because we don't know what's become of Kovalyov and Pirozhok. We can't do anything while we're in the dark about that. I'll never allow myself to say anything against either of them, but what if they've got into trouble? How can we take any sort of action when we've no link with the prisoners?"

"I'll volunteer for that," Oleg said quickly. "Parcels are probably being taken to them by their people—it may be possible to get a message to somebody . . . in the bread or in a dish. I'll organize it through Mother."

"Through Mother!" Stakhovich scoffed.

Oleg blushed crimson.

"You evidently don't know the Germans," Stakhovich said contemptuously.

"There's no need to conform to the Germans—you've got to compel them to adapt themselves to us." Oleg could hardly restrain himself and avoided looking at Stakhovich. "W-what d'you think, Sergei?"

"I think we'd better make the attack," Sergei said in some confusion.

"That's it then.... We'll find the fellows to do it, don't you worry!"

Stakhovich instantly brightened up, feeling support.

"And I say that we've neither the organization nor the discipline," Oleg said and stood up, his face flushed.

Just then Nina opened the door and Vasya Pirozhok entered the room. His blood-stained face was covered with bruises, one hand was bandaged. His appearance was so grave and astounding that they all involuntarily half rose from their seats as if to go towards him.

"Where did this happen to you?" Turkenich broke the silence.

"At the police-station." Vasya stood at the door with a look of childlike hurt and embarrassment in his little black eyes.

"And where's Kovalyov? Did you see any of our people there?" They all spoke together.

"We didn't see anybody. They took us into the police chief's office and beat us up," Pirozhok said.

"Now don't pretend to be a silly child. Just tell us all about it," Turkenich said angrily, without raising his voice. "Where's Kovalyov?"

"At home, sleeping it off. What's there to tell?" Pirozhok said, suddenly irritated. "Solikovsky summoned us during the day-time before the arrests and told us to appear with our weapons at his office that evening; he said we'd have to arrest somebody but he didn't say whom. That was the first time he'd given us an assignment; we didn't know, of course, that there would be others besides us or that there were to be large-scale arrests. We went home and thought, 'How can we go out and arrest one of our own people! We'd never forgive ourselves.' And I said to Tolya, 'Let's go and get drunk at Sinyukha's pot-house, and not turn up—afterwards we can say we were drunk.' We thought and thought about what they could do to us. We weren't under suspicion so the worst they could do was to beat us up and chuck us out. That's what they did: locked us up for several hours, questioned us, then knocked us about and kicked us out," Pirozhok said, completely crestfallen.

Serious as the situation was Pirozhok's appearance was so woebegone and at the same time ludicrous because of the foolish schoolboy expression that a furtive smile stole over all their faces.

"And s-some comrades here think they're capable of attacking the German gendarmerie!" Oleg stuttered and a relentless, angry expression filled his eyes.

He was ashamed at the thought that Lyutikov would have to know that in the first serious business entrusted to the young people there had been so much childishness and lack of organization and discipline. And he felt ashamed in the eyes of his comrades because they too felt the same about it. He was annoyed with Stakhovich because of his petty arrogance and conceit yet at the same time he felt that Stakhovich with his military experience was quite right to be dissatisfied with the way Oleg had organized the whole business. Oleg felt the whole failure was due to his own weakness, that it had been all his fault; he was so full of self-condemnation that he despised himself more than Stakhovich.

Chapter 34

WHILE THE YOUNG PEOPLE were deliberating in Turkenich's home, Andrei Valko and Matvei Shulga stood facing *Meister* Brückner and his deputy Balder in the same office in which, some days earlier, Shulga had been made to confront Petrov.

Both no longer young, short in stature and broad of shoulder, they stood side by side like twin oaks in the middle of a meadow. Valko, the leaner, was dark-skinned and sullen; there was an angry glint in the whites of his eyes under the joined eyebrows. Shulga's coal-flecked face, despite its sharp, masculine, heavy features, had something clear and calm about it.

So many people had been arrested that for many days interrogations had been taking place simultaneously in the offices of *Meister* Brückner, *Wachtmeister* Balder and Police Chief Solikovsky. Yet not once had Valko and Shulga been called out. Even the food was now better than when Shulga was alone in the cell. All these days Shulga and Valko had heard the groans and curses on the other side of their cell, the tramp of feet and clatter of arms, people being dragged along the corridor, the clanging of metal basins and pails, the splashing of water when blood was washed off the floors. From a distant cell from time to time came the crying of a child.

Their arms were not bound when at last they were taken out to be questioned, and from this they concluded that an attempt was to be made to bribe and deceive them by mildness and cunning. But to guard against any infringement of *Ordnung* on their part Brückner had in his office, in addition to the interpreter, the four armed soldiers and Fehnbong who had brought them in and who remained standing at their backs, revolver in hand.

The proceedings began with establishing Valko's identity; he gave his real name. He had been a familiar figure in the town. Even Shurka Reiband knew him well and while he was translating Brückner's questions Valko could see in Shurka's black eyes an expression both of fear and lively, almost personal, curiosity.

Brückner then asked Valko whether he had known the man who stood beside him for a long time and who he was. A faint smile appeared on Valko's lips.

"I met him in the cell," he said.

"Who is he?"

"Tell your boss not to act the simpleton," Valko said gruffly to Shurka Reiband. "He knows perfectly well that I only know what this citizen had told me himself."

Meister Brückner remained silent, his eyes round as an owl's and showing clearly that he had no idea how to carry on an interrogation unless the man facing him was bound and being beaten, and that this made things very difficult and tedious for him.

"If he wants the treatment due to his position, let him name the people who were left behind with him to do subversive work," he then said.

Reiband translated.

"I don't know them. What's more, I don't think they succeeded in leaving any behind. I came back here from the Donets, and didn't manage to get evacuated. Anyone can confirm that," Valko said, his dark gypsy eyes looking straight at Reiband and then at Brückner.

Just where the lower part of Brückner's face merged into the neck, fat folds of self-importance began to appear. He stood thus for some moments, then took a cigar without a band from a cigar case on the table, held it between two fingers and offered it to Valko with the question:

"Are you an engineer?"

Valko was an experienced industrial manager; he had been promoted from the ranks of working miners as long ago as the end of the Civil War and in the thirties had graduated from the Industrial Academy. But it would have been absurd to tell this to the German. He feigned not to notice the proffered cigar and simply replied in the affirmative.

"A man of your education and experience could occupy a better, materially more secure position under the New Order if he wanted to," Brückner said, his head sadly inclined. He still held the cigar out to Valko.

Valko said nothing.

"Take it ... take the cigar!" Shurka Reiband hissed, fear in his eyes.

As though he had not heard, Valko continued silently to regard Brückner, an amused expression in his gypsy eyes.

The large, yellow, wrinkled hand holding the cigar began to tremble.

"The entire Donets Coal Basin with all its mines and factories is now under the management of the Eastern Company for the Exploitation of Coal and Metallurgical Enterprises," *Meister* Brückner said and sighed, as though he had found it difficult to pronounce the long name. Then his head inclined still more to the side, and, with a determined movement, he pushed the cigar closer to Valko.

"On behalf of the Company," he said, "I offer you the post of chief engineer to the local management."

When Shurka Reiband heard the words he was horrified. He drew his head down between his shoulders and his translation sounded as though he had an irritation in the throat.

Valko looked at Brückner without saying anything for some moments. Then his dark eyes narrowed.

"I'd accept this proposition," he said, "if good working conditions are provided for me."

He had even found it in him to assume an ingratiating tone. More than anything else he dreaded now that Shulga might not understand the prospects Brückner's startling suggestion offered them. But Shulga made no movement and avoided looking at him; he seemed to have put the correct interpretation on the matter.

"Conditions?" Brückner's face broke into a smile which gave it a brutal expression. "The conditions are the usual ones: I want all the details of your organization, everything, absolutely everything! You let me have them now!" He looked at his watch. "In fifteen minutes from now you'll be a free man, within an hour you'll be sitting in your office in the local administration."

This opened Valko's eyes at once.

"I know nothing about any organization. I'm here only by accident," he said in his normal voice.

"You blackguard!" Brückner yelled in broken Russian, suddenly enraged and, as it were, hurrying to confirm how correctly Valko had understood him. "You're one of the chiefs! We know everything!" And with his self-control suddenly gone he pushed the cigar into Valko's face. The cigar broke and Brückner's closed fist, smelling of some disgusting perfume, pressed against Valko s mouth.

In a second Valko's powerful dark fist swung out and hit *Meister* Brückner squarely between the eyes. Brückner let out a grunt, the broken cigar fell from his hand and he fell flat on the floor with a heavy crash.

For a moment or two there was general stupefaction while Brückner lay flat on the floor quite still, his round, inflated belly sticking out prominently from the heavy body. Then incredible chaos broke out in Brückner's office.

Wachtmeister Balder, short of stature, corpulent and phlegmatic, had stood quietly at the table during the whole proceedings, his watery blue eyes, so full of experience, watching sleepily, his stout, immobile body in the grey uniform heaving and falling like leavened dough, as he drew each leisurely wheezy breath. When he recovered from his consternation, the blood flew to his face and, shaking where he stood, he yelled:

"Hold him!"

Fehnbong, followed by the soldiers, rushed at Valko. But though he had been standing nearest to Valko, he failed to reach him because, in a flash, with one blow Shulga had sent him flying headlong into a far corner, and then hoarsely yelling out the terrifying mysterious words, "Oh! you Siberia of our tsar!", lowered his massive head like an enraged bull and charged the soldiers.

"Good work, Matvei!" Valko shouted enthusiastically, struggling to break away from the soldiers and making for Balder, who stood, purple in the face, his little fat hands stretched out in front of him, shouting:

"Don't fire at them! Hold them, curse them!"

With extraordinary strength and fury Shulga set about him with fists, legs and head, scattering the German soldiers in all directions. Valko rushed at Balder who, with startling nimbleness and energy, ran away from him round the table. Fehnbong again attempted to come to his chief's aid, but Valko, grinding his teeth and snarling, kicked him in the groin and the German collapsed on the floor.

"Good work, Andrei!" Shulga yelled with satisfaction, twisting from side to side like a bull and shaking off the soldiers with each turn. "Through the window, hurry!"

"It's wired up—you follow me!"

"Ugh! Siberia of our tsar!" Shulga roared. With a powerful jerk he broke away from the soldiers, seized Brückner's chair and swung it high over his head. The soldiers making for him fell back. With a savage expression of delight in his black eyes Valko grabbed everything off the table—

inkstand, paper-weights, metal glass-holders—and hurled them at the enemy with all his might and with such a crashing din that Balder threw himself on the floor and covered his bald head with his fat hands, while Shurka Reiband, edging along flat against the wall, crawled under the divan whining miserably.

When Valko and Shulga first hurled themselves into battle, they had been possessed of that last, dying sensation of freedom which comes to strong, courageous people when they realize that their days are numbered. They were having their last fling and the knowledge increased their strength tenfold. But as they fought the thought had suddenly struck them that the enemy was not in the position to kill them, that they had no authorization from their chiefs to do so. This thought filled them with such a feeling of triumph, of complete freedom and impunity, that they were almost invincible.

So they stood shoulder to shoulder with their backs to the wall, blood-stained, terrible and angry, and no one dared approach them.

Then Brückner regained consciousness and tried to set the soldiers on them. Shurka Reiband crawled out from under the divan and made for the door. A few moments later more soldiers burst into the office. All the gendarmerie and police together now threw themselves at the two fearless warriors, threw them to the floor and, giving vent to their rage, began to hit and kick them with fists, boots and knees until long after Valko and Shulga had lost consciousness.

It was the dark, still hour before dawn. The young moon had already set but the clear, bright morning star had not yet risen. It was the hour when nature herself, as though wearied, closes her eyes in deep slumber and the sweetest sleep locks the eyes of human beings, and even in the prisons the fatigued tormentors and their victims are wrapped in sleep.

During this dark, still hour before dawn, the first to awake from the deep, peaceful slumber so far removed from the terrible fate which the future held in store for him was Matvei Shulga. He awoke, turned over on the dark floor and sat up. Almost at the same moment, with an almost inaudible groan that was more like a sigh, it was so soft, Andrei Valko awoke. They sat on the dark floor and brought their swollen, blood-caked faces close to one another.

Not the faintest glimmer of light penetrated into the darkness of the cell, but it seemed to them that they could see each other. Each saw the other as someone strong and splendid.

"What a powerful Cossack you are, Matvei, God preserve your strength!" Valko said, hoarsely. Then he suddenly threw himself back on his hands and burst into loud laughter, just as though they were both free men.

"You're quite a Zaporozhye Cossack too, Andrei, no doubt about it!" And in the still darkness of the night the walls of the prison barracks resounded to their terrible, warrior-like laughter.

They were given nothing to eat in the morning and in the day-time they were not taken out to be questioned. No one was questioned that day. Silence reigned throughout the prison; vague scraps of conversation, like the babbling of a brook along its wooded banks, came to them from the other side of their cell wall. At noon a car drew up at the prison and the soft purr of its engine reached their ears. A few moments later it drove off again. Shulga had learned to distinguish the sounds on the other side of the cell walls and he knew that this was the car which came whenever *Meister* Brückner or his deputy or both of them required to leave the prison.

"They've gone to headquarters," Shulga said gravely, his voice low.

He and Valko exchanged glances. Neither spoke a word but their eyes told one another that both knew their end was near and that they were prepared for it. Evidently, everyone in the prison was aware of it too—so solemn was the complete silence which reigned everywhere.

For several hours they sat without speaking, each alone with his conscience. Already dusk was falling.

"Andrei," Shulga said softly. "I haven't yet told you how I came to be here. Listen."

He had thought a great deal about it all. But now that he was relating it to someone with whom he had ties purer and more inviolable than any in the world, he groaned with agonizing remorse as he once again saw before him the candid features of Liza Rybalova, the friend of his youth, and the lines which hard work had traced on her face, the expression of maternal kindliness with which she had greeted him and parted from him.

With no thought for his own feelings, he told Valko what she had said to him, and his supercilious replies, how much she had wanted him not to leave her home and how she had looked at him, like his mother might have done. Yet he had gone away, putting more trust in false contacts than in the simple, natural promptings of his own heart.

As he spoke Valko's face became more and more gloomy.

"Scraps of paper!" he exclaimed. "You remember what Ivan Protsenko told us? ... You trusted a scrap of paper more than a human being," he said with a man's sorrow in his voice. "Yes, how often this happens to us! We scribble them ourselves and then fail to notice how they get a hold on us."

"That isn't all, Andrei," Shulga said ruefully. "I still have to tell you about Kondratovich." And he went on to narrate how he had felt doubts about Kondratovich, whom he had known since childhood, as soon as he heard the story of Kondratovich's son and learned that Kondratovich had withheld it at the time he had agreed to place his home at the disposal of the underground organization.

Shulga again recalled all this and was appalled at the fact that a simple occurrence which was not rare in the lives of ordinary people could have so blackened Kondratovich in his eyes, and yet a man like Ignat Fomin, who was quite unknown to him and who had so many unpleasant traits, could have impressed him favourably.

Valko had learned all this from Kondratovich himself, and he became gloomier still.

"Appearances!" he said hoarsely. "The habit of judging by appearances. Many of us are so used to seeing people living better than our fathers did in the old days, that we like everyone to conform to a pattern—all clean and neat. Poor old Kondratovich didn't conform to it, so he looked black to you. And that fellow Fomin, blast him, fitted the pattern perfectly. His soul was blacker than the night, but he was clean and neat and that blinded us to his blackness. We ourselves made him look white, promoted him, praised him, made him fit the pattern, and later it fooled us. ... And now you will pay with your life for it."

"That's true, Andrei, that's the sacred truth," Shulga said, and a bright light shone in his eyes, though the topic of their conversation was so grave. "How many days and nights have I sat here, and there has not been an hour in which I have not thought of it all. Andrei! Andrei! I'm just an ordinary fellow and it's not my place to talk about all the labour it's been my lot to shoulder! But as I look back on my life now I can see where I made my mistake and I see that I made it not just today. Here I am, nearly forty-six years old and for the past twenty years I've just been going round and round in one spot, you might say, and in one district! And I've always been somebody's deputy, honestly! First we were called uyezd officials, then they called us district officials," Shulga said with a smile. "All round me so many new men sprang up, and so many of my comrades, district officials like myself, rose high in the world, but I just kept on pulling the same old cart, and grew accustomed to the old rut! I don't know how it began that I became accustomed in this way. Yet to become accustomed to the same old rut means to lag behind."

His voice broke. Deeply moved he grasped his head with both his large hands.

Valko understood that Matvei Shulga was clearing his conscience in the face of death, and that now he must not vindicate him. He listened to him in silence.

"What is to us the dearest thing in the world," Shulga continued, "the thing which makes living, working and dying worth while? Our people, human beings. Is there anything in the world more beautiful than our people? How much work and hardship have they shouldered for the sake of our state, for the cause of our people! In the Civil War they didn't grumble about their two ounces of bread; during the reconstruction years they stood in queues and wore ragged clothes rather than barter away their Soviet heritage for a mess of potage. And now, in the Patriotic War, they are laying down their lives with joy and pride in their hearts; they are accepting every hardship, they are working hard, even the children contribute their share, not to mention the womenfolk. These are our people, people like you and me.

We are part and parcel of them; all the finest, wisest, most gifted and distinguished of our people are part and parcel of them, the ordinary folk. There is no need to tell yout that I've worked all my life for them. ... You know how things are: you're up to your eyes in these affairs, all very important and urgent matters, and you fail to notice that these matters develop in their own way and the people live in their own way. Oh Andrei! When I was about to leave Liza Rybalova's home I saw three lads and a girl there, her son and daughter and two of their comrades, I suppose. ... Andrei! You should have seen their eyes! How they looked at me! One night I awoke in my cell here and had a fit of shuddering. The Komsomols! They were most certainly Komsomols! Why did I ignore them? How could it have happened? Why? And I know why. How many times have the Komsomols come to me: 'Uncle Matvei, give us a talk about the harvest, about the sowing campaign, about the development plan for our district, about the regional congress of Soviets, about all sorts of things.' And what did I reply? 'I'm too busy. You're Komsomols, you can manage that yourselves.' And when there was no getting out of it and I agreed, how hard it used to be to go and talk to them! There might be a report to write for the regional agricultural department, you see, and the regular meeting of the coordination and demarcation commission would be due, or suddenly you had to hurry to the director of the mining department, if only for an hour, because it's his fiftieth birthday, don't you see, and his little boy is one-year-old and he's so proud of it that he's having a sort of birthday and christening party all in one and he'll be offended if you don't come. So, with all this on your hands, there's no time to prepare the talk for the Komsomols. You go and talk impromptu, in a general sort of way, you string a lot of big words together, tongue-twisters you can hardly pronounce yourself, to say nothing of the youngsters. What a shameful business it was!" Shulga said suddenly, and his broad face reddened and he hid it in the palm of his hand. "They expect to learn something from you about how to manage their lives and all you do is to talk in general terms. Who is the prime educator of our young people? The teacher. Teacher! What meaning there is in that word! You and I went to the parish church school, you left school five years before I did, but you probably remember our teacher, Nikolai Petrovich. He went on teaching in our mining village for fifteen years and then died of consumption. I still remember him telling us how the universe came to be—the sun and the earth and the stars; he was probably the first person to shake our belief in God and to open our eyes to the world.... Teacher! Somebody! He holds first place in our country where every child goes to school. The future of our children, of our people, is in the hands of the teacher, in his heart of gold. Everybody should take their hat off to the teacher when he sees him fifty yards away in the street! And me? I remember with shame how each year when the question of school repairs or heating came up, the school directors would waylay me at the door of the offices and implore me to arrange for supplies of wood, coal, bricks and lime. I laughed them off: none of my business, let the district department of education attend to it. And, you know, I didn't consider it a disgraceful thing to do. My reasoning was simple: the plan for coal has been fulfilled, for grain overfulfilled; the ploughing is finished, meat has been delivered to the state, wool has been delivered, a message of greeting has been sent to the secretary of the regional committee—there is nothing to reproach me for! Isn't it true? I saw all that too late, but all the same, I feel easier in my mind now that I do see it. What sort of a man am I?" Shulga said with a shy, good-natured, guilty smile. "I'm of the very flesh and blood of the people, I come from their very midst, I am their son and their servant. As far back as '17, the moment I heard Leonid Rybalov, I understood that there's no greater happiness than to serve the people, and that's when I became a Communist. You remember our underground and our partisan life in those years? How we, children of illiterate parents, found the courage and spirit to stand up to the German invader and the White Guards and to overcome them? At that time we thought that that would be the hardest part—to overcome them; after that it would be easier. But the hardest part was ahead of us. Do you remember the peasant-aid committees, the surplus-appropriation system, the kulak gangs and Makhno, then, suddenly,

379

the New Economic Policy! Learn to buy and sell. What? Well, we began to buy and sell. We learned!"

"And do you remember how we restored the pits?" Valko suddenly said with extraordinary animation. "As soon as I was demobilized they made me director of that ancient mine that's now exhausted. What a job that was! Oh Lord! We had no administrative experience whatsoever, specialists who sabotaged, machinery that didn't work, no electricity, banks that refused credit, nothing to pay the workers' wages with, and Lenin sending telegrams: send coal, save Moscow and Petrograd! Those telegrams were like a holy invocation to me. I saw Lenin as I see you now, at the Second Congress of Soviets in the October Revolution. I was still a soldier then, fresh from the front. I remember I went up to him and touched him, because I couldn't quite believe that he was a man just like me. ... Oh well. I sent the coal!"

"Yes, that's how it was all right," Shulga said in a happy mood. "The troubles we uyezd and district officials carried on our backs in those years! And the knocks we had to take! Has anybody been cursed more than the district official since Soviet power took over? Of all the Soviet officials at that time and now probably no one's been on the carpet as often as we have!" Matvei Shulga said, his face beaming radiantly.

"Well, as regards that, I'd say our industrial managers came a close second!" Valko said, laughing.

"Yes, that's true, bad as I've made myself out to be," Shulga said in a voice full of emotion, "I still think the district official deserves a monument. The plan... the plan— I could talk of nothing else. You just try it: day in and day out, year after year, like a clock, millions of acres of land to plough and sow, corn to harvest and thresh, state deliveries to make and everything to be worked out in terms of workdays. Then the milling to do, beetroot, sunflower, wool, meat storage, expansion of livestock, servicing and repair of tractors and the rest of our wonderful farm machinery!... You see, everybody wants nice things to wear and plenty to eat and sugar in his tea; so our friend the district official must run round like a squirrel in a wheel-cage to satisfy the needs of man. It's the district official, you might say, who carries the whole Patriotic War on his back as far as food's concerned and raw materials...."

"And the business manager?!" Valko asked, at once exasperated and enraptured. "If anybody deserves a monument then he does. He's the one who carried the five-year plans on his back—the first as well as the second—and the whole Patriotic War, too! Isn't that true? What does your farming plan amount to compared with the industrial plan, eh? What's the tempo in agriculture beside the tempo in industry? The factories we've learned to build! As clean and precise as watches! And our mines! Take our 1B. A jewel-box! Look at the capitalists, they're used to having everything at their disposal. While we, with our rate and scale of progress, we're always feeling the pinch: shortage of workers, shortage of building material, lagging transport, a thousand and one troubles, great and small, yet we keep moving ahead all the time. No, he's a titan, is our business manager."

"Yes, that's what he is all right!" Shulga said, his face cheerful and happy. "I remember how I was once nominated for the resolutions commission at a collective farmers' conference in Moscow. A discussion began about us district officials. There was one young fellow, one of those Red professors, as we used to call them, and he got on his high horse about us. We were backward, he said, we hadn't read Hegel, and he even said something about not washing every day. Well, he was told something like this: 'If you went and served an apprenticeship with a district official you'd grow in wisdom....' Ha-ha-ha!" Shulga laughed gaily. "They used to regard me as something of an expert on rural matters and even more, they sent me to one village after another to help the peasants get rid of the kulaks and set up collective farms. Yes, they were great times—who could ever forget them? The whole nation was on the move. We hardly slept in those days. There were many waverers among the peasants, but just before the war even the most backward among them could see the rich fruit we had reaped in those years.... And we really were beginning to live well before the war!"

"And you remember how things were coming to life in the pits?" Valko said, his gypsy eyes aglow. "I didn't get home for months at a time, used to sleep at the pit. My God, when you look round now you just can't believe your eyes: could we really have created all this ourselves? And honestly, there are times when I think that it must have been some relative of mine who did things here and not me at all. I close my eyes now and I can see the whole of our Donbas, the whole of our country under construction and all our nights of feverish activity...."

"Yes, in the whole history of mankind no one has had to bear so many burdens, but you see that we haven't given way under them. And I find myself asking just what manner of people we are," Shulga said with an open childlike expression on his face.

"Our enemies think we're afraid to die, the fools!" Valko said with a smile. "We Bolsheviks are accustomed to facing death. Enemies of all shades and colour killed us Bolsheviks! The tsarist hangmen and gendarmes killed us and the White Guards killed us and so did the Makhno and Antonov gangs and the interventionists of all the nations of the world, the kulaks shot us, but we're still alive because of the people's devotion. Let the German fascists kill us if they like, all the same they, and not we, will lie in the dust. Isn't that true, Matvei?"

"That's the mighty, sacred truth, Andrei!... I shall for ever and always be proud that I, a simple working man, was destined by fate to follow life's road in our Party, which has opened up the way to a happy life for all people."

"That's true, Matvei, this has been our great fortune!" Valko said with emotion rare in a stern nature like his. "And another great good fortune has fallen to my lot: in the hour of death to have a comrade like you, Matvei, by my side."

"I thank you sincerely for the great honour. I immediately recognized you as a man of fine thoughts and feelings, Andrei."

"May God grant happiness to all the people we are leaving behind on earth!" Valko said. He spoke softly, with solemn meaning.

Thus Andrei Valko and Matvei Shulga unburdened their consciences in the last hour before their end.

Chapter 35

Soon after noon *Meister* Brückner and *Wachtmeister* Balder
left for the district gendarmerie in the town of Rovenki,
some seventeen miles from Krasnodon. Peter Fehnbong,
Rottenführer of the SS unit attached to the Krasnodon
Gendarmerie Station, knew they were taking with them
the dossiers appertaining to the interrogations and were to
be instructed as to what was to be done with the prisoners.
He already knew by experience what the instructions would
be and so did his chiefs, because, before their departure,
they had ordered Fehnbong and his SS men to cordon off the
park area and keep people away from it. A small group of
gendarmerie soldiers under Sergeant Edward Bolman had been
dispatched to the park to dig a pit large enough to hold six-
ty-eight people standing close to one another.

Peter Fehnbong knew that his chiefs would not return
before late in the evening. He had therefore sent his soldiers off to the park with the junior *Rottenführer* and had
himself stayed behind in the prison lodge.

He had had a great deal of work to do in the last few
months and had never had a chance to be alone. This had
deprived him of the opportunity not only of washing himself
from head to foot but even of changing his underwear, for
he was afraid someone might see what he carried on his body
underneath his clothing.

As soon as Brückner and Balder had driven off and the SS
men and gendarmerie soldiers had marched away to the park
and all was quiet in the prison, Fehnbong went to the cook
in the prison kitchen and asked for a saucepan of hot water
and a basin so that he could have a wash. He could always
get cold water from the water-butt at the entrance to the
gatehouse.

For the first time after many days of heat, there was a
cold wind driving heavy, low-hanging rain-clouds across
the sky. It was dull like an autumn day and in these mining
areas all nature was looking its worst, and the unsheltered
little town with its uniform houses and coal-dust was no
exception. It was light enough inside the gatehouse for Peter
Fehnbong to see to wash. But as he not only wanted to guard
against being caught unawares but also did not want to be

seen through the window, he dropped the black-out curtain over it and switched on the light.

Since the outbreak of war he had become accustomed to living as he did and his foul-smelling body no longer warned him. All the same he felt an indescribable pleasure at being able at long last to throw off everything and stand quite naked for a while, free of all the weight on his body. He was plump by nature and had put on more weight with the passing years. He sweated a great deal under his black uniform. His underwear, which had not been changed for several months, had become greasy and stinking from the sour sweat which had saturated it and had turned a yellowish-black from dye off his uniform.

Peter Fehnbong took off his underclothes and stood naked, his body, unwashed for so long, still its natural white, with a bushy growth of fair curly hair on the chest and legs, and a little down on the back. The removal of the underclothing revealed that he wore curious strappings on his body. It was not exactly penance chains, but rather something in the nature of the long cartridge-belt which Chinese soldiers carried in olden days. It consisted of a long belt of several small pockets, each with a button to fasten it, and Fehnbong had it wound round his shoulders and chest and fastened above the waistline. Grimy white tapes tied in a bow held it close to his sides. Most of the small pockets were stuffed full and only a few were empty.

Peter Fehnbong untied the tapes and removed the belt which had been strapped to his fat body so long that dark weals of the unhealthy colour associated with bedsores crossed each other on the white skin of his back and chest and just above the waistline. He laid the belt, which was truly very long and heavy, neatly and tenderly on the table and at once fell to scratching himself furiously. Fiercely and angrily he scratched the whole of his body with his short, blunt fingers; he scratched his chest, his belly and legs, then attacked his back, first over one shoulder and then over the other; then he stretched his right hand to the left arm-pit and scratched with his thumb, grunting and groaning with satisfaction.

When the itch had been somewhat allayed he carefully unbuttoned an inside pocket of his jacket and produced a small leather bag like a tobacco pouch and tipped about thirty gold teeth on to the table. He was about to distribute them among two or three of the empty pockets in the belt but now that he had the good fortune to be alone, he could not resist the pleasure of feasting his eyes on the contents of the other bulging pockets. It had been so long since he had seen it all. So, neatly opening button after button, he proceeded to spread the contents of the pockets on the table in separate small heaps, which quickly covered the whole table. It was indeed a sight worth seeing!

Here was the coin of many lands—American dollars, English shillings, French and Belgian francs, coins from Austria, Czechoslovakia, Norway, Rumania, Italy. They were sorted according to the country of origin, gold coins with gold, silver with silver, bank-notes with bank-notes, and among the paper money was even a neat pile of Soviet "blue-backs," hundred-ruble notes, from which he did not actually expect any material gain but which he felt he must keep because his cupidity had by now become a mania for collecting. Here also were small heaps of gold trinkets: rings, scarf-pins, brooches with precious stones or without, and, in separate piles, precious stones and gold teeth.

The fly-specked electric bulb cast its wan light over the money and valuables spread out on the table. Fehnbong, naked, bald and hairy-chested, still wearing his light-rimmed spectacles, sat on a stool in front of it all, scratching himself from time to time, charmed by the sight before him and enormously pleased with himself.

There was a great deal of money and a profusion of small objects, yet he could have picked up any coin or trinket and said exactly where and when, under what circumstances and from whom, he had obtained or stolen it; for from the moment he had reached the conclusion that he ought to indulge in this sort of thing to avoid being left behind among the fools of this world, he had been living for this alone, and everything else had only a shadowy existence for him.

He had taken gold teeth not only from the dead but from the living; but he much preferred them from the dead because it was less trouble. And when he caught sight of gold teeth among a batch of prisoners, he found himself wishing that all the tedious process of questioning could be speeded up and that these people could be killed as quickly as possible.

The money, teeth and trinkets represented such a vast number of robbed, tortured and murdered men, women and children that a trace of uneasiness did cloud the delightful excitement and self-satisfaction he felt every time he looked at it all. However, the uneasiness did not spring from within Peter Fehnbong himself, but from some imaginary very well dressed gentleman who was clean-shaven, wore an expensive soft hat and a ring on his fat finger, who was correct in every detail and fully disapproved of Peter Fehnbong.

This gentleman was extremely wealthy, richer than Peter Fehnbong with all his treasures. Even so, he claimed the right to disapprove of Peter Fehnbong. He disapproved of him because of his method of acquiring wealth. He considered this method dirty in some way. And Peter Fehnbong was involved in a perpetual argument with this gentleman, a good-natured argument to be sure, because the only one who ever spoke was Peter Fehnbong and because he argued from the lofty, secure heights of the modern businessman with experience of life.

"Aha!" Peter Fehnbong would say, "when all's said and done I don't intend doing this sort of thing all my life. I shall eventually become a conventional industrialist or merchant or just a shopkeeper, if you like; but I have to have capital to start with! Yes, I know perfectly well what you think of yourself and about me. Your line of reasoning runs something like this: 'I'm a gentleman; all my enterprises are open for anyone to see; everyone knows the origin of my prosperity. I've a family, children; I'm clean in my habits, I'm well dressed and courteous to people and I can hold my head up anywhere. If I converse with a woman who is on her feet, I also remain standing. I read newspapers and books; I'm a member of two charity organizations and during the war I made substantial contributions towards equipping hospitals. I like music, flowers and moonlight on the sea. But Peter Fehnbong kills people for their money and valuables, which he then appropriates for himself. He doesn't even shrink from wrenching out gold teeth and he hides all this on his body so that no one shall see it. He's forced to go about without washing for months at a time and he stinks, so I've a right to censure him....' Ah yes, permit me, my most esteemed, most respectable friend, to remind you that I'm forty-five, I've been a sailor, I've visited all the countries of the world and have seen absolutely everything that goes on there! Are you familiar with the picture that I, a sailor who has visited distant lands, have had the fortune to observe time and again: how in South Africa, India and Indo-China millions of people die of hunger every year in full view, you might say, of the most respectable individuals? But why go so far from home? In nearly all the capitals of the world, even during the blessed years of pre-war prosperity, you could have seen whole town boroughs populated by unemployed, slowly dying in full view of the most respectable individuals, and at times even outside the portals of ancient cathedrals. It's very difficult to accept the idea that they do so for some personal whim, as it were. And who doesn't know that some most respectable people, gentlemen in every way, feel no shame in throwing millions of their healthy working men and women out of their factories and on to the streets, when it suits them to do so? And when these men and women refuse to accept the situation with a good grace, large numbers of them are annually starved in prisons or simply killed in the streets and squares, killed quite legally with the assistance of police and soldiers!

"I've mentioned several methods, and I could name more, by which millions of people are put to death every year—and not only men in good health but women and children and old folk as well—put to death strictly for the sake of adding to your wealth. I'm not now speaking of wars with their particularly large slaughter of people which are waged in the interests of increasing your wealth. My most esteemed, most respectable friend, why play hide-and-seek? Let's be frank: if we want other people to work for us, then we must kill off a certain number of them every year in one way or another! What worries you about me is only the fact that I'm on the threshold of the mincing-machine, I'm only an unskilled labourer in these matters and the nature of my occupation compels me to go without washing and to carry about a foul smell. Yet you must admit that you'd never manage without people like me and that, as time goes on, you'll have ever greater need of me. We're chips off the same block. I'm your counterpart. You are just another like me if you turn yourself inside out and show people what you're really like. The time will come when I too shall wash and be neat and clean, a simple shopkeeper, if you like, from whom you'll be able to buy really top-grade sausages for your table."

So went the argument on principles which Peter Fehnbong engaged in with the imaginary gentleman with the clean-shaven, respectable appearance, and neatly pressed trousers. This time too he came out best in the argument, as he always did, and his mood reached the heights of happiness. He tucked the little heaps of money and valuables away into their respective pockets which he deftly buttoned. Then he began to wash himself, snorting and grunting with the pleasure of it and splashing soapy water all over the floor which, however, did not worry him in the least: soldiers would come and mop it up.

He was not exactly clean after the wash but he felt more comfortable. Again he wound the belt round his body and tied it firmly, put on clean underclothes, stowed away the dirty ones and donned his black uniform. Then he lifted a corner of the black-out paper and looked out into the pris-on-yard, but there was nothing to be seen because it was already dark. Experience which was now almost instinct told him that his chiefs should arrive any moment. He went out into the yard and remained standing near the lodge for some moments for his eyes to get accustomed to the dark but he found it impossible. The cold wind had driven heavy dark clouds over the town and the whole Donets steppe; they, too, were almost invisible and they seemed to rustle as they raced across the sky, as though the fleecy wet edges were brushing against each other.

Then Peter Fehnbong heard the soft purring of the car-engine and soon distinguished two fiery points, the masked headlights of the car as it rolled down the hill. The head-lights faintly outlined a wing of the building which had formerly housed the district executive committee, but was now used by the German district agricultural commandant's offices. The chiefs were returning from the district gendarmerie. Peter Fehnbong crossed the yard and passed through the back door of the prison building, which was guarded by a gendarmerie soldier who recognized the *Rottenführer* and presented arms in salute.

The prisoners in their cells also heard the soft purring of the engine as the car drew up to the prison. Suddenly the unusual silence which had reigned in the prison throughout the day was disturbed by footsteps in the corridor, the grinding of keys in locks, the banging of doors, increased noise from the cells and that all too familiar crying of a small child in a distant cell which tore at the heart-strings. Suddenly the crying rose to a shrill, harrowing scream—the child was screaming with all its might, with all the strength it had, so that the noise became a hoarse strident screeching.

Matvei Shulga and Valko heard the child's shrieking and the bustling noises in the cells which came nearer and nearer to their own. Sometimes they thought they heard the voice of a woman speaking with raised voice or shouting, but each time the voice fell into subdued weeping, or so it seemed to them. A key rattled in a lock, the gendarmes left the cell which confined the woman and child and went to the next, where the hullabaloo broke out afresh. Even then through all the clatter they seemed to hear the extraordinarily sad and tender voice of the woman as she talked persuasively to the little child, and the quieter voice of the child as it were soothing itself: "A-a, a-a, a-a."

When the gendarmes entered the cell next to Valko's and Shulga's the meaning of the bursts of noise in each cell the gendarmes entered became clear: they were binding the prisoners' wrists.

The last hour had come.

There were many people in the next cell and the gendarmes spent rather a long time there. At last they came out, locked the cell, but made no immediate move to visit Valko and Shulga. They stood in the corridor, exchanging hurried remarks, then someone ran along the corridor towards the exit. For a time all was quiet except for the muttering voices of the gendarmes. Then they heard the footsteps of several people approaching the cell, exclamations of satisfaction in German and then Fehnbong appeared, followed by several gendarmes with electric torches and revolvers cocked for action. Five more soldiers stood in the doorway. The gendarmes were evidently afraid that these two would as usual put up a fight. But Matvei Shulga and Valko did not so much as laugh at them; their minds were already far from such earthly things. They quietly allowed their hands to be bound behind their backs and when Fehnbong signed to them to sit down and have their feet hobbled they allowed the thongs to be wound round their ankles so that they could only take the shortest steps and could not possibly escape.

They were then left to themselves and sat for a time in silence in the cell, while the Germans finished binding the rest of the prisoners.

Then the rapid, regular tramp of feet was heard down the corridor, growing louder and louder until the sound echoed loudly. The soldiers halted, marked time, turned at the command with a clumping of boots and thud of rifle-butts. Cell doors clanged open and the prisoners began to be led into the corridor.

Shulga and Valko had been in the darkness for so long that they involuntarily blinked, though the light was dim from the small globes in the ceiling. They looked closely at their neighbours and at others standing farther up and down the rows which stretched from one end of the corridor to the other.

Near them stood a tall elderly man, his underclothes stained with blood, his bare feet hobbled like their own. Shulga and Valko involuntarily fell back when they saw that the man was Petrov. His flesh was so cut about and lacerated that his clothing stuck to his body as though it consisted of one continuous wound. Every movement he made must have caused untold agony to this strong man. There was a knife or bayonet wound on one of his cheeks. It had been laid open to the bone, and the wound was festering. He recognized them and bowed his head before them.

Almost all the prisoners were staring with an expression of suffering, horror and amazement towards the exit door at the far end of the corridor, where a sight met the eyes of Shulga and Valko which made them tremble with pity and anger. A young woman stood there with exhaustion written in her strong, determined features. She wore a dark-red dress and carried a small child in her arms. Cords bound her arms and the body of the child so that the child was tightly and for all eternity trussed to its mother's body. The child was less than a year old and its delicate little head with the sparse fair hair curling a little at the back lay on the mother's shoulder with closed eyes. It was not dead, only sleeping.

Shulga suddenly had a vision of his wife and children and tears filled his eyes. He was afraid that the gendarmes, and his own countrymen too, might see the tears and misunderstand the sort of man he was, so he was glad when at last Fehnbong had counted the prisoners and they were led out into the yard between two files of soldiers.

The night was so black that people standing side by side were unable to see each other. They were lined up four abreast in a column, surrounded and taken through the gate and along the road up the hill. Electric torches flashed ahead of them, at their backs and on both sides, their beams playing on the road and the column of prisoners. A steady, cold wind blew monotonously over the town and whirled round them in damp streams of air; above them they heard the wet rustling of the clouds, racing across the sky so low overhead that they seemed within reach of their hands. They gulped the air greedily. The column moved at a slow pace and in complete silence. At its head Fehnbong turned round from time to time and flashed the large torch hanging from his wrist over the column, which again and again picked out in the darkness the woman with her child lashed to her body. She was walking in the front row and the wind blowing at her side fluttered the dark-red dress.

Shulga and Valko were walking next to each other, their shoulders touching. Shulga no longer had tears in his eyes. With every step they took there receded from their minds everything that was personal and even important and precious—everything that had troubled and secretly agitated them up to the last minute and had seemed loth to let them depart from this life. The wings of greatness encircled them. An indefinable, lucid serenity embraced their minds. With their faces set against the wind and the low rustling clouds overhead they walked forward silently, calmly to meet their death.

The column halted at the entrance to the park. Fehnbong produced a sheet of paper from an inside pocket of his jacket. By the light of a torch it was scrutinized by him, then by Sergeant of Gendarmerie Edward Bolman and the junior *Rottenführer* in charge of the SS men on patrol in the park. Then the sergeant counted the people in the column briefly flashing his torch on each of them.

Slowly the creaking gate was opened. The column was re-formed two abreast and led down the central avenue running between the Lenin Club and the Gorky School, which now housed the *Direktion* of the combined enterprises formerly attached to the Krasnodon Coal Trust. After passing the school Fehnbong and Bolman turned off into a side alley and the column followed after them.

The trees bowed before the wind, which tossed the leaves in one direction, and the noise of the rustling and tapping of foliage ceaselessly, monotonously filled the darkness all round.

They were taken to a neglected corner of the park rarely visited even on finer days, which adjoined the open space with the solitary stone building of the German police training-school. There a deep trench had been dug in the middle of an oblong-shaped clearing. The people caught the scent of damp, freshly-turned earth, though they had not yet actually seen the long trench.

The column was divided in two, and each section was taken along one side of the trench. Valko and Shulga were separated. People began to stumble over the clods of earth; when they fell they were forced to get up with blows from rifle-butts.

Suddenly the beams of dozens of torches shone down the length of the trench and the mounds of earth on either side, into the exhausted faces of the people, on to the cold, shining steel of the German soldiers' bayonets which made a solid wall round the clearing. *Meister* Brückner and *Wacht-meister* Balder stood with groundsheets thrown over their shoulders under the trees at the far end of the trench and in full sight of all the people standing along it. Behind, and a little to the side, stood the grey bulky figure of Burgomaster Vasily Statsenko, face flushed and eyes bulging.

Meister Brückner gave a sign with his hand. Fehnbong

raised his torch above his head and gave a quiet order in his husky, effeminate voice. The soldiers stepped forward and, with bayonets fixed, prodded the people towards the pit. Fettered hand and foot, stumbling and falling they silently clambered to the top of the mound. All that could be heard was the heavy breathing of the soldiers and the rustling of the wind-lashed foliage.

Moving heavily, within the limit allowed by his hobbled feet, Matvei Shulga, too, clambered up the mound of loose earth. He could see by the light of the flashing torches how the people dropped into the pit; some were leaping, others stumbling silently or with cries of protest or distress.

Meister Brückner and *Wachtmeister* Balder stood motionless under the trees. Statsenko was bowing to the people as they were pushed into the pit. He had been drinking.

Shulga again caught a glimpse of the woman with the child bound to her body. The infant neither saw nor heard what was taking place; it was still sleeping, nestled against the warmth of its mother's body, its head resting on her shoulder. She lowered herself to the ground and, using only her legs, as her arms were bound, she wriggled and slid down into the trench in an effort not to waken the child. Shulga never saw her again.

"Comrades," he began in a hoarse, powerful voice which drowned all other sounds. "My magnificent comrades! Eternal remembrance and glory be yours! Long live—" A bayonet was plunged between his ribs from behind. Summoning all his mighty strength he did not fall, but leapt, into the deep trench and his voice thundered out from it:

"Long live the great Communist Party, which has shown the people the road to justice!"

"Death to the enemy!" Andrei Valko thundered from Shulga's side: fate had decreed that they should meet once more — in the grave.

The people packed the trench so closely that they were unable to turn. The moment of final mental stress had come: each prepared himself for a hail of lead bullets. But no such death had been chosen for them. Avalanches of earth showered down on their heads and shoulders, into the necks of their clothing, into mouth and eyes, and they realized they were being buried alive.

Raising his voice Shulga intoned:

Arise! ye starvelings from your slumbers!
Arise! ye criminals of want. . . .

Valko's deep voice joined in. More and more voices caught up the anthem, first from those nearest, then from people farther down the trench until the slowly, rolling waves of the *Internationale* rose from under the ground to the dark, cloudy sky above the outside world.

In that dark and dreadful hour, the door of a small house on Derevyannaya Street opened softly and Maria Borts and Valya left the porch accompanied by someone short in stature, warmly wrapped up, carrying a walking-stick and a knapsack over his shoulder.

Maria and Valya each took one of his arms and, with the wind tearing at their skirts, led him down the street and out into the steppe.

After a short distance the man halted.

"It's dark; you'd better go back," he said, almost in a whisper.

Maria embraced him and so they stood for a time.

"Good-bye, Masha," he said with a helpless gesture.

Father and daughter proceeded arm-in-arm, while Maria remained standing where she was. Valya was to accompany her father until daybreak. After that he, with his poor eyesight, was to manage as best he could to find his way to the town of Stalino, where he intended to live in concealment with some of his wife's near relations.

Maria listened to their footsteps for some moments. Then their steps became inaudible. A cold, complete darkness surrounded her, but darker, colder still were the thoughts in her mind. Her whole existence, her work, her family and children, her dreams, her love, had collapsed, had been shattered, and before her lay emptiness.

Unable to move, she stood there while the whistling wind fluttered her dress round her and the rustling sound of the clouds close overhead came to her.

Suddenly she felt she was losing her mind. . . . She listened intently. No, it was not her imagination, she could hear it again. Singing! They were singing the *Internationale*! It was impossible to say where the singing came from. It mingled with the howling of the wind and the rustling of the clouds and was carried with them out into the darkened world.

It seemed to Maria that her heart stopped beating, and her body shook with trembling. As though from under the ground the words reached her:

> *Now away with all your superstitions!*
> *Servile masses, arise, arise!*
> *We'll change forthwith the old conditions*
> *And spurn the dust to win the prize. . . .*

Part
TWO

Chapter 1

"I, OLEG KOSHEVOI, on entering the ranks of the Young
Guard take this solemn oath before my comrades-in-arms,
before my long-suffering land, before the whole of my people: I swear that I shall unquestioningly carry out all the
tasks entrusted to me by the Organization; hold in deepest
secrecy all that concerns my work in the Young Guard. I
swear to avenge without mercy the burning and ravaging of
our towns and villages, the shedding of the blood of our
people, the death of our heroes martyred in the mines. And
should my life be needed for this vengeance, I shall lay down
my life without a moment's hesitation. If under torture or
in cowardice I violate this sacred pledge, then may my name
and kinsfolk be cursed for all time and may stern punishment be inflicted upon me by my comrades. Blood for Blood,
Death for Death!"

"I, Ulyana Gromova, on entering the ranks of the Young
Guard take this solemn oath before my comrades-in-arms,
before my long-suffering land, before the whole of my people: I swear—"

"I, Ivan Turkenich, on entering the ranks of the Young
Guard take this solemn oath before my comrades-in-arms,
before my long-suffering land, before the whole of my people: I swear—"

"I, Ivan Zemnukhov, take this solemn oath—"
"I, Sergei Tyulenin, take this solemn oath—"
"I, Lyubov Shevtsova, take this solemn oath —"

. . . .

This Sergei Levashov seemed to have understood nothing
at all when for the first time he had come to Lyuba and
tapped on the window, and she had run out to him and they

had sat up talking all night. Who knows what he had imagined.

However, the first difficulty in this trip had been caused by him. They were old comrades and Lyuba could not very well leave without first telling him. Being so much of a tomboy, she had always been popular with the little boys in her street and had quickly found a willing messenger among them to take word to Sergei Levashov who, before Uncle Andrei's arrest, had been advised by him to take a lorry-driver's job at the *Direktion* garage.

Sergei arrived late in the evening, straight from work. He was dressed in the same clothes he had worn on the day of his arrival from Stalino. The Germans supplied no working clothes, not even to the miners. He was very dirty, tired and sullen.

It would not have been like him to question her about her journey or her destination, but it was obvious that his mind was occupied with nothing else. He had remained moodily silent the whole evening; she had been quite exasperated and could finally stand it no longer and had flared up at him. What did he think she was, his wife, or sweetheart? He was not to start imagining things, it only tormented her and, with all the demands life made on her now, she had no room for thoughts of love. They were simply comrades and she was under no obligation to render an account to him: she was going where she had to go, on family business.

She had seen that he did not quite believe her, that he was simply jealous, and she derived some satisfaction from it.

She had needed a good night's rest, but he had just sat there, making no move to leave. He was the persistent sort and might have remained sitting there all night. In the end Lyuba had thrust him out. He was likely to be in this dismal mood during the whole of her absence, and she felt sorry for him. She took him through the garden as far as the gate and for a moment took his arm and clung to him. Then she ran back into the house, undressed quickly and got into bed by her mother's side.

Her mother was a problem too, of course. Lyuba knew how distressing it would be for her mother to be left alone, helpless as she always was in the face of adversity. She nestled close to her and whispered all sorts of tales into her ear, and her mother never thought to doubt. Finally Lyuba fell asleep.

She rose with the early dawn and, humming to herself, began to get ready for the trip. To save her best dress, she decided to wear simple clothes, which were, at the same time, brightly coloured and would attract attention. Her smartest dress, one of plain blue crepe de Chine, went into her small case together with a pair of pale blue shoes, some lace underwear and sheer silk stockings. Then, standing in her shift and knickers and humming a tune under her breath, she spent two hours waving her hair between two small simple mirrors in which she could see her head from all sides only by constantly twisting and turning. To ease the strain of the posture she kept shifting the weight from one widely planted firm bare foot, with its creamy skin and strong little toes, to the other. Then she put on her suspender-belt, brushed a hand over her pink soles, pulled on a pair of flesh-coloured chiffon-lisle stockings and beige-coloured shoes and then pulled carefully over her head the cool, rustling frock with the pattern of green spots and cherries and goodness knows how many other splashes of bright colour. While she dressed she chewed some food, still humming her wordless song.

She was a little nervous, but instead of disheartening her that gave her courage. She was, after all, pleased because at last the time had come for her to go into action and she would no longer have to waste her efforts to no purpose.

One of the small green vans bringing supplies of food from Voroshilovgrad to the officials of the German administration had stopped outside the Shevtsovs' home one morning two days previously. The driver, a gendarmerie soldier, had said a word to the soldier seated by his side with a tommy-gun on his knees, then leapt down and entered the house. Lyuba had gone to see what he wanted and had found him in the dining-room already looking about. He had quickly turned round to her and before he had had time to open his mouth, she had guessed from something indefinable in his appearance and attitude that he was Russian. And then he did, in fact, say in the purest Russian:

"Could I have some water for the car?"

A Russian in the uniform of the German gendarmerie— he couldn't have done worse than to pick this address!

"Clear out. D'you hear?" Lyuba had replied, her round blue eyes looking calmly straight at him.

Without a moment's thought she had known immediately what to say to this Russian in German Army uniform. If he now tried to harm her she would run screaming out into the street and rouse the whole neighbourhood shrieking that she had told the soldier to get water from the stream and that he had started to beat her for it. But this strange army chauffeur had made no move whatever, he had just smiled and said:

"You're not doing your job very well. It may land you in trouble." He had quickly looked round to see whether anyone had followed him, then said curtly, "Varvara Naumovna asked me to say that she's missing you very much."

Lyuba had turned pale and took an instinctive step towards him. But he anticipated her question and placed a slim, grimy finger to his lips.

He followed her out into the passage. She stood there holding a pail of water before her with both hands and looking searchingly into his eyes. Without glancing at her, he took the pail and went out to the van.

Lyuba had purposely remained behind and watched him through the crack of the door. She had hoped to draw him out when he returned the pail. But after pouring the water into the radiator the chauffeur simply hurled the pail into the front garden, quickly resumed his seat, slammed the door and drove the van off.

So Lyuba had to go to Voroshilovgrad. But she was now subject to Young Guard discipline and could not, of course, leave without telling Oleg. True, some time earlier she had carefully dropped him a hint that she knew people in Voroshilovgrad who might become of some use. Now she told him that here was a good opportunity to meet them. Oleg, however, had not at once given her permission to go but asked her to wait a little.

Great had been her amazement therefore when, only a couple of hours after she had spoken to him, Nina Ivantsova turned up at her home to say that permission had been granted. Nina moreover had said:

"When you get there report about the death of our people, their names, and how they were buried alive in the park.

Then tell them that, in spite of it all, things are getting on well here—the people in charge ask you to say that. And tell them about the Young Guard."

Unable to restrain herself, Lyuba asked:

"How does Kashuk know that it's in order to talk about all this where I'm going?"

During her underground work in Stalino Nina had learned to be guarded. So she merely shrugged her shoulders. However, the thought then struck her that Lyuba might indeed hesitate to make the report as she had been instructed, so she said casually:

"The older comrades probably know to whom you're going."

Lyuba wondered why she had not thought of this simple explanation herself.

Like the other members of the Young Guard, with the exception of Volodya Osmukhin, Lyuba Shevtsova had no idea, nor did she try to find out, who Oleg Koshevoi's contact was among the adult members of the Krasnodon underground. But Filipp Petrovich Lyutikov was fully aware for what purpose Lyuba had been left behind in Krasnodon and who her contacts were in Voroshilovgrad.

The day was cold and clouds were scurrying low across the sky over the steppe. But Lyuba was insensible to the cold wind which was whipping the colour into her cheeks and fluttering her bright frock as she stood on the unsheltered Voroshilovgrad Highway, her small case in one hand and a light dust-coat thrown over her free arm.

Lorries rattled noisily past her over the highway and from them the German soldiers and corporals shouted invitations to her, and guffawed loudly, occasionally making vulgar gestures. She screwed up her eyes contemptuously and paid no attention. But when she saw a long, low pastel-coloured car approaching with a German officer in the front seat beside the driver, she raised a hand with studied casualness.

Displaying the faded back of his army jacket, the officer quickly turned his head round to the rear seat which seemed to be occupied by a senior officer and then, with brake squealing, the car came to a stop.

"*Setzen Sie sich! Schneller!*" the officer said, opening the door a little; the corners of his mouth curled in a faint smile. Then he slammed the door shut, reached over and opened the rear door.

Holding her case and coat in front of her, Lyuba ducked her head and quickly slipped inside; the door slammed behind her. The car leapt forward, humming against the wind.

Lyuba found herself seated beside a lean, dried-up colonel with a sallow, clean-shaven face and drooping jowls; he wore a high, faded army cap. They looked each other in the eye, each with a totally different brand of impudence; the colonel because he had power; Lyuba because she felt far from sure of herself. The young officer in the front seat turned and also looked at her.

"*Wohin befehlen Sie zu fahren?*" the colonel asked with the smile of a savage aboriginal.

"I don't understand what you're saying!" Lyuba simpered. "Speak Russian or, better still, don't talk at all."

"Where ... where—" the colonel said in Russian, his hand gesticulating vaguely into the distance.

"Now he's talking sense, praise the Lord!" Lyuba said. "To Voroshilovgrad, er ... Lugansk, I mean, of course.... *Ferstehte?* That's it!"

As soon as she started speaking she ceased to feel afraid and at once slipped into the natural, easy manner which caused everybody, including the German colonel, to accept whatever she did or said as something completely in the natural order of things.

"Say, what's the time? The time, time. What a blockhead!" Lyuba said and tapped her own wrist.

The colonel stretched out an arm and bent his elbow mechanically, showing Lyuba the square watch strapped to his bony wrist with its down of fine ash-coloured hair.

After all, it was always possible to make oneself understood where there was a will to do so, and without necessarily knowing any languages.

And who might she be? Oh, an actress. No, not attached to a theatre. She danced and sang. Of course she had any number of places in Voroshilovgrad where she could stay. Being the daughter of a well-known industrialist, a Gorlovka mineowner, she was acquainted with many respectable people there. Soviet rule had deprived her poor father of everything and he had died in Siberia leaving a wife and four children—

all of them girls and all of them very attractive. Yes, she was the youngest. No, she couldn't accept his hospitality, it might tarnish her good name, she just wasn't that sort at all. Her address? He should have it without fail, but for the moment she was not certain where she was going to stay. With his permission she'd arrange with his lieutenant how they could meet again.

"Your chances seem to be better than mine, Rudolph!"

"In that case, *Herr Oberst*, I shall put in a word on your behalf!"

Was it far to the front? At the front matters had reached a point where they couldn't possibly interest a pretty girl. Anyway, she could sleep quite peacefully. We'd be taking Stalingrad before long. We'd already broken through to the Caucasus—didn't that please her? Who had told her that the Upper Don was not so far from the front? Oh, those German officers! It seemed then that he wasn't the only chatterbox among them.... They said that all pretty Russian girls were spies. ... Was that true? All right then, the reason for it was that there were Hungarians on that sector of the front. They were better, of course, than those stinking Rumanians and Macaronis, but you couldn't rely on any of them. The front had been extended in an intolerable fashion and Stalingrad was swallowing up a vast number of people. "And what a job to keep all these people supplied with everything necessary—just try yourself! Give me your little hand and I'll show you it all in the lines on your palm. This long one here leads to Stalingrad and this broken one to Mozdok—you've got a most unstable character! Now imagine all this multiplied a million times and you'll understand that a German Army quartermaster has to have nerves of steel...." But she mustn't think that all he was concerned with was the soldiers' trousers—he could manage to find something nice for an attractive little girl too, for those legs, say, or for this bit ... she knew what he meant, didn't she? She wouldn't refuse a little chocolate, would she? And he could recommend a sip of wine for this hellish dust! Oh, it was quite natural that a young girl shouldn't drink, but this was French wine! "Rudolph, stop the car."

The car came to a halt about two hundred yards from a large Cossack hamlet extending down both sides of the road and they all climbed out. A dusty approach led from the spot to a country road skirting the edge of a narrow valley, with willow-trees growing at the bottom of the leeward slope which was thickly overgrown with sun-scorched grass. The lieutenant told the driver to take the car along the road to the valley and running ahead of the officers, Lyuba followed the car. The wind snatched at her frock and she had to hold it down with both hands. Her shoes sank deep into the fine dry soil and were soon filled with it.

The lieutenant whose face Lyuba had scarcely glimpsed as he had had the faded back of his uniform to her in the car, helped the driver to bring a soft leather suitcase and a heavy, finely woven hamper.

They settled on thick dried grass in a sheltered spot on the slope. Although they pressed her to, Lyuba drank no wine; but there was such an assortment of good things spread out on the table-cloth before her that it would have been stupid of her, an actress and the daughter of an industrialist, to turn up her nose at them, so she ate her fill.

She was very much bothered by the earth in her shoes. She settled the question as to whether or not the daughter of an industrialist would behave in such a way, by taking off her shoes, shaking out the fine earth and flicking her hand across the soles of her stockinged feet. Nor did she put the shoes on again. She remained sitting in her stockinged feet in order to rest them. It was probably quite all right—at least the German officers seemed to think so.

She was very anxious to find out whether there were many divisions on the sector of the front which lay closest to Krasnodon and skirted the northern part of Rostov Region; from German officers who had been billeted in her home she had learned that part of Rostov Region was still in Soviet hands. And to the great displeasure of the colonel, whose mood was lyrical rather than business-like, she persisted in expressing fear that the front might be broken at this point and she would once again fall into Bolshevik slavery.

In the end the colonel seemed quite offended by such lack of confidence in German arms—*verdammt noch mal!*— and he satisfied her curiosity.

While they were thus engaged on their repast, they became aware of the sound of feet marching out of step. It was from the direction of the Cossack hamlet and was coming nearer. At first they paid no attention to it when they heard it in the distance, but it increased in volume until it filled the whole neighbourhood and seemed to come from an endless column of people. Thick clouds of dust over the highway which were rolled away by the wind became visible even from this spot on the slope of the valley. Isolated exclamations could soon be distinguished, rough male voices, doleful female voices, which seemed to be bewailing the dead.

The colonel, the lieutenant and Lyuba stood up and looked over the edge of the slope. Soviet prisoners of war, escorted by Rumanian troops and officers, were marching along the highway in an endless column from the direction of the hamlet. Cossack girls and women of all ages were running by the side of the column shouting and lamenting, at times breaking through the file of Rumanian soldiers and pushing a piece of bread, a few tomatoes or eggs, sometimes a whole white loaf or even a bundle, into the grimy, emaciated arms stretched out to them from the column.

What tattered remains of army trousers and tunics the prisoners still had on them, when they were not half-naked, were covered with mud and dust. Most of them were barefoot or had only bast shoes which were so worn that they no longer resembled footwear. Their beards had grown and they were so thin that their clothing seemed to be hanging on living skeletons. And it was terrible to see hopeful smiles on those faces turned to the shouting women who ran by the side of the column and were forever being driven off by the soldiers with fists and rifle-butts.

Only a moment had passed since Lyuba had come up the slope yet in a flash, without knowing when and how, she was standing with white rolls and other articles of food that she had snatched up from the table-cloth in her hands and, oblivious of all else, was darting just as she was, in stockinged feet, over the churned-up powdery soil to the highway, and breaking through to the column. She thrust the rolls and other food into the dirty hands stretched out to her. A Rumanian sergeant-major tried to seize her but she wriggled from his grasp; blows from heavy fists rained down on her, but she ducked and protected her head first with one elbow, then the other.

"Go on, beat me how you like, you scum," she yelled, "anywhere but on my head!"

Powerful hands soon thrust her away from the column. She suddenly found herself by the side of the road watching the German lieutenant, slapping the face of the Rumanian sergeant-major with the back of his hand, while before the enraged colonel, who looked like a lean snarling dog, an officer in the lettuce-green uniform of the Rumanian Occupation Army was standing to attention and mumbling incoherently in the language of the ancient Romans.

Lyuba had calmed down and was her old self again by the time she had put on her beige shoes again and the German officers' car was again whisking her off to Voroshilovgrad. The most astonishing thing was that the Germans accepted even this exploit of Lyuba's as the most natural thing in the world.

They passed the German control post without let or hindrance and entered the town.

Turning round, the lieutenant asked Lyuba where she would like to be put down. With complete mastery of herself once more, she waved him on straight down the street. Then she asked for the car to stop in front of a block of flats which looked to her fit for the daughter of a mine-owner.

Carrying her coat over her arm and accompanied by the lieutenant with her case, she went up to the entrance of the totally unfamiliar building. She debated with herself for a moment as to whether to get rid of the lieutenant or to knock in his presence on the door of the first flat they came to. She regarded him hesitatingly. He put quite the wrong interpretation on her glance, put his free arm round her and drew her close. Without feeling particularly angry she gave him a resounding slap on his pink cheek and ran up the stairs. The lieutenant accepted this, too, as something quite in keeping and with what might be called a wry smile proceeded humbly to carry Lyuba's suitcase up for her.

She had reached the first floor and was pounding her small fist on the nearest door in a peremptory manner, as though she were arriving home after a lengthy absence. The door was opened by a tall, slim lady with a pained, proud expression on her face, which still showed traces if not of former beauty then of meticulous care for her complexion. Lyuba was definitely in luck!

"*Danke schöhn, Herr Leutnant!*" she said very bravely, parading, with a frightful accent, her entire German vocabulary. She put out a hand for the suitcase.

The lady who had opened the door regarded the German lieutenant and the German girl in the gaudy frock with an expression of horror she could not conceal.

"*Moment!*" The lieutenant put down the case, rapidly pulled a note-pad from the map-case dangling by a strap from his shoulder, wrote something with a stub of pencil and handed the sheet to Lyuba.

It was an address, but she had no time either to read it or to consider what a mine-owner's daughter would have done in her place. She quickly pushed the sheet of note-paper into the front of her blouse, nodded casually at the lieutenant who saluted in reply, and entered the hall of the flat. Lyuba heard the lady barring the door with a multitude of locks, bolts and chains.

"Mummy! Who was that?" came a girl's voice from another room.

"Keep quiet! Wait a minute!" said the lady.

Carrying her case in one hand and her coat in the other Lyuba went into the room.

"I've been sent to get lodgings here. D'you mind?" she said, throwing a friendly glance at the girl and looking round the room which was large and well-furnished, but somewhat neglected. It could have been the home of a doctor or engineer or professor, but it seemed obvious that the person for whom it had been so well furnished was no longer living there.

"It would be interesting to know who sent you," the girl said, quietly surprised. "The Germans or who?"

The girl had evidently only just come in. She still wore her brown beret, her cheeks were still flushed from the wind. The girl was round and fat and about fourteen, with plump cheeks like a mushroom into which someone had stuck two lively, hazel eyes.

"Tamara, dear!" the lady sternly said. "This does not concern us in the least."

"But why doesn't it, Mummy, if she's been sent to lodge with us? I was only just interested."

"Forgive me, are you German?" the lady asked, in some confusion.

"No, I'm Russian ... an actress," Lyuba replied, not altogether confidently.

There was a brief pause, during which the girl finally made up her mind about Lyuba.

"All the Russian actresses evacuated long ago!" she declared and swept out of the room, indignantly.

So it seemed that Lyuba was to drink to the dregs all the bitterness which poisons the joy of living of the conqueror in occupied territory. Yet Lyuba saw her advantage in having a foothold in this flat in precisely the capacity in which they had accepted her.

"I shall not stay long. I'll find myself something permanent," she said. All the same she very much wanted relations in this house to be more friendly towards her. "Honestly, I'll soon find something. Where can I change?"

Half an hour later the Russian actress, dressed in a blue crepe de Chine dress and pale blue shoes with the dust-coat over her arm walked to the railway crossing in the hollow which divides the town in two, then up the unpaved stony road to the top of the hill towards the Kamenny Brod. She had come to town on tour and was looking for permanent lodgings.

Chapter 2

IVAN PROTSENKO was a cautious man and preferred as far as possible not to make use of the contact addresses given him, including those in Voroshilovgrad. But it was absolutely essential for him to go there now that Yakovenko, the first of the territory's secretaries to be killed, had met his death. Being a bold man Protsenko took the risk of using an old acquaintanceship, of going to a friend of his wife, a lonely quiet woman who had been unfortunate in private life. Her name was Masha Shubina. Because she loved her native Voroshilovgrad she refused to leave her work in the drawing office of the Locomotive Works on the two occasions when people were evacuated. Despite everyone and everything she had been confident that the town would never fall and that she could be useful.

On his wife's advice, Protsenko had decided to make his way to Masha Shubina; he had reached this decision the night he and his wife were in hiding in Marfa Kornienko's cellar. Katya would not be able to accompany him because they had worked in Voroshilovgrad for many years and would be too conspicuous if seen together now. All things considered, it was better for Katya to remain behind and keep in contact with the partisan groups and the underground organization of the area. While still in the cellar they had decided that she would stay at Marfa's house in the guise of a relation and, if possible, find a teaching post in a neighbouring village.

Once they had made their decision they realized that this would be the first time in their life together that they were forced to separate, and at a time, moreover, when they most likely would never see one another again.

For a long time they had sat quietly with their arms round each other. And it had suddenly struck them how good it was just to sit close together quietly in this dark damp cellar. Their relationship was no longer one that required a constant outward demonstration of feelings. Theirs was one of those numerous relationships whose basis is lasting and firm because of their common interests, because the wife as well as the husband has interesting work, because they have children. Their feelings lay deep inside them concealed just as heat is concealed in ash. They would suddenly well up in times of trial, when together they experienced shock, or grief, or happiness. How vivid then was the memory of their first meetings in the gardens in Lugansk, of the overpowering scent of acacia in the whole town, the starry sky at night which filled their youth, the irrepressible dreams of youth, the joy of their first physical experience, the happiness when their first child was born; and then the first sour fruits of their seeming incompatibility of temperament which, after all, were such wonderful fruits! Only unstable characters part company when they taste sour fruits; strong characters grow together for all time.

Love requires in equal measure the stern tests furnished by life and the vivid memories of how love began. The first bind people together; the second keep people young. Great is the unifying power of the common road, when one remains responsive to the emotion which can be expressed in the words: "And do you remember?" It is not really remembrance. It is the eternal light of youth, the call to travel farther along the road of life into the future. Fortunate is he who has kept this alive in his heart.

It was this happy feeling that Protsenko and Katya had experienced as they sat in the darkness of Marfa Kornienko's cellar. They had been silent, but in their hearts rang the word: "Remember? ... Do you remember? ..."

One day in particular had remained vividly in their memory and that was the day when they had reached the final understanding. They had been meeting for months past and she had been fully aware of how things stood. She had known because of his desperate words and actions, but she somehow could not allow him to make a declaration, nor could she give her promise.

One evening he persuaded her to meet him the following day in the yard of his hostel—he was taking a course at the regional Party school. The mere fact that she had agreed to meet him there had been a great victory for him: it meant that she was no longer embarrassed in the presence of his comrades, for at that hour, immediately after a lecture, the yard was always crowded with students.

A game of *gorodki** had been in progress in the middle of the crowded yard when she arrived. He had been one of the players. He was happy and flushed and wore a Ukrainian shirt with unbuttoned collar, which hung loose without its cord. He had come running to greet her and had said: "Will you wait a little—we shan't be long now." All the students had looked in their direction, some stepping aside to make way for her to watch the game. But her eyes had been on him all the time.

She had always felt a little disappointed because he was rather short. Now she seemed to see the whole of him for the first time, to see how strong he was, how cunningly and trickily he played. With one throw of the stick he could shatter the most intricate figures. She had felt he was doing it because of her presence. He endlessly cracked jokes amicably at his opponents' expense.

* A game something like skittles, but more complicated and played with a long, heavy stick instead of a ball.

Lenin Street had just been asphalted for the first time. It had been a hot day and they had strolled happily over the soft asphalt. He still wore his Ukrainian shirt, but its cord was now tied round his waist, his fair hair lay in waves on his head. He had talked and talked. From the tray of a passing vendor he had bought some dried dates and he had carried them in front of him in a piece of newspaper. The dates had been warm and sweet and she alone ate them because he never stopped talking. She recalled most vividly that there had been no rubbish bins anywhere along this wonderful asphalted street, nowhere to drop the date stones and she had kept them in her mouth hoping to get rid of them as soon as they turned into a more secluded street.

Suddenly he had stopped talking, had looked at her so that she had blushed and had said:

"I'm going to take you in my arms and kiss you right here in the street in front of everybody!"

She had become suddenly shrewish and with a coy glance at him from under her eyelashes had replied:

"Just you try, I'll spit all my date stones at you!"

"Are there many of them?" he had asked quite seriously.

"About a dozen!"

"Let's go to the gardens. Let's run," he had cried before she could stop to think, and catching hold of her hand and regardless of the public, they had raced off to the gardens.

"Remember? Do you remember that night in the gardens?"

And now in the dark cellar, just as on that starlit night in the Lugansk gardens, Katya had trustingly buried her hot face somewhere between his strong, restful shoulder and neck and the cheek with its soft beard.

Daybreak had found them still sitting so; they had not even dozed. Protsenko had drawn his wife still closer for a moment, then raised his face and relaxed the pressure of his arms.

"It's time, my darling!... Come now, my love!"

But she still did not raise her head from his shoulder and they remained sitting until it was bright daylight outside.

Protsenko dispatched Kornei Tikhonovich and his grandson to the Mityakinskaya base to find out how the detachment was making out. For a long time he instructed the old man about how to carry out operations in small groups and how to organize the peasants, Cossacks and former prisoners of war who had settled in the villages into new partisan groups.

While Marfa was giving them food, an old man who was a distant relative of Marfa's had managed somehow to get through the barricade of children and get to the table simultaneously with the food. Always inquisitive, Protsenko immediately pounced on him to discover how a simple old villager regarded the present situation. He happened to be the same worldly-wise old man who had driven the horse for Koshevoi and his relatives. A passing German supply officer had after all taken his little dun-coloured horse from him and Grandpa had returned to his kinsfolk in the village. He had seen at a glance that Protsenko was a man above the average and had begun to expound his views at large.

"All right now, look, it's like this...'. Their troops were marching by here for more than three days, it was a mighty big force that came marching through here! The Reds won't be coming back again ... no. They say fighting's started the other side of the Volga now, at Kuibyshev, and Moscow's encircled and Leningrad's taken! Hitler says he'll take Moscow by starving it out."

"You'll never make me believe that you've been taken in by all that rubbish!" Protsenko had said, and there had been a mischievous sparkle in his eyes. "See here, my old friend, you and I are just about the same size—will you let me have some clothes and shoes? I'll leave you what I'm wearing."

"Aha! So that's what it is, eh?" Grandpa had exclaimed catching on at once. "I'll bring you clothes at once."

So it came about that Protsenko presented himself at Masha Shubina's room in the Kamenny Brod, Voroshilovgrad, in the old man's clothes. A fair-sized beard hid his far from aged features and he had a knapsack on his back.

He experienced a strange feeling as he made his way through the streets of his native town in this disguise. Not only had he been born here, but he had worked in Voroshilovgrad for many years. Many of the office buildings, institutions, clubs and dwellings had been built in his time and, in some instances, due to his efforts. He recalled how the very square he was now passing through had been planned during the sessions of the presidium of the Town Soviet and how he, personally, had supervised its lay-out and the planting of the shrubbery. Despite all his personal efforts to organize the public utilities of his home-town, there had still been constant criticism in the town Party committee of the insufficiently clean streets and yards, and not without justification.

Bombs had destroyed a number of buildings and, in the heat of the defensive battles, this disfiguring of the town had not been so obvious. But even that was not the point; in the past few weeks the town had been so much neglected that it seemed that the new masters themselves did not believe they were settled there for ever. The streets had not been watered or swept; the flowers in the squares were withered; the lawns were full of weeds; paper and cigarette ends lay everywhere in the thick red dust.

The town had been regarded as one of the seats of the coalfields. In former days a greater flow of goods had come into it than into many other districts in the country; the streets had been alive with colourful crowds of well-dressed people. One could feel that this was a southern town: there was always plenty of fruit to be had and a profusion of flowers, and always hosts of pigeons. Now, the crowds had been thinned and looked plain and grey; people were careless in their dress which was dull, giving an impression that they were deliberately neglectful of their appearance. One had the feeling that they had even given up washing themselves. A superficial colourfulness was lent to the street scene by the uniforms, shoulder-straps and badges of the enemy soldiers and officers—Germans and Italians with a sprinkling of Rumanians and Hungarians. Theirs was the only talk heard and their cars alone were seen racing along the streets, blaring their horns and raising whirlwinds of dust. Never before had Protsenko experienced such a profound, personal compassion and love for the town and the people in it. He felt that it was the home from which he had been driven out and that he had secretly returned to it to find the new tenants stealing his property, laying their filthy hands on all that had been precious to him, humiliating his relatives, and all he could do was watch it all, powerless to do anything to prevent them.

His wife's friend too bore the general stamp of this dejection and neglect. She was dressed in a worn dark frock; her fair hair was knotted carelessly; on her feet were slovenly house shoes; and it was obvious that she had gone to bed with unwashed feet for a long time.

"Masha, how can you let yourself go like this!" Protsenko blurted out.

She looked down at herself with an apathetic air.

"Have I? I hadn't noticed. Everyone goes about like this. It's better, too: the Germans don't accost one.... Anyway, there's no water in the town."

She fell silent and Protsenko only then noticed how thin she had grown and how empty and uninviting the room looked. He thought that she was probably starving and had long since sold everything she owned.

"Well, look here, let's have a bite to eat then.... A certain little woman made all sorts of good things for me, a wise little woman she was!" he said, a little awkwardly, fumbling in the knapsack.

"Oh God, but that's not the point!" She buried her face in her hands. "Take me with you!" she cried passionately. "Take me with you to Katya, I'll work for you with all the strength I have. I'm willing to be your servant; anything rather than this vile humiliation day after day, this slow death without work, without any purpose in life!"

She still used the formal mode of address although she had known him since his marriage to Katya who was a childhood friend of hers. In former days too he had suspected that she could not find it in her to address him in the familiar way because she was unable to rid herself of a feeling that he, being in a prominent position, was something rather distant from her, a rank-and-file draughtswoman.

A deep line appeared on his broad forehead and a stern, worried expression showed in his lively blue eyes.

"I'm going to talk to you frankly, maybe roughly," he began, without looking at her. "Masha! If this were just a matter between you and me, then I could take you with me to Katya and conceal both of you and go into hiding myself," he said with a harsh bitter smile on his lips. "But I'm a servant of the state and what I want now is that you, too, should begin to serve our country to the best of your ability. So, not only shall I not take you away from here, but I want to throw you right into the thick of it. Tell me frankly: do you agree? Have you the strength?"

"I'm willing to do anything rather than go on living the life I'm living now!"

"That's no answer!" Protsenko said sternly. "I'm not offering you a way out to save your soul. What I'm asking is, are you willing to serve your people and the state?"

"I am," she said quietly.

He quickly leaned across the table and took her hand.

"I need to get in touch with our people here but there have been arrests and I'm not sure now which contacts I can rely on. You'll have to summon up your courage and the cunning of the devil and sound out the contact addresses I'm going to give you. Will you do that?"

"Yes," she said.

"If you come to grief and they torture you over a slow fire, will you give us away?"

She paused before replying as though consulting her conscience.

"No," she said.

"Then listen...."

Leaning closer to her in the dim light of the little oil-lamp, so that her eye fell on the fresh scar over his temple, he gave her the address of a contact in the Kamenny Brod which he thought might be more reliable than any of the others. He was in particular need of this contact because, through it, he would be able to get in touch with the Ukrainian Partisan Headquarters and learn what was happening not only in the region but also on the Soviet side of the front and everywhere else.

Masha expressed her readiness to go there immediately and this combination of naïve self-sacrifice and lack of experience touched him deeply. A sly little twinkle skipped from one eye to the other.

"Now how could that be done?" he reproached her, good-naturedly and gently. "This requires neat work—like a job in a fashion store. You'll go quite openly in broad daylight. I'll show you the ropes.... Another thing, I must see to my rear defences. Whose house is this?"

Masha rented a room in a small house owned by an old

worker at the locomotive works. It was built of stone and a corridor which ran through the middle provided it with an exit to the yard as well as to the street. The yard had a low stone wall around it. A room and a kitchen lay on one side of the corridor; the other half consisted of two small rooms, one of which Masha occupied. The old man had many children; however, none of them any longer lived with him. His sons were either in the Red Army or had evacuated; his daughters were married and lived in other towns. According to Masha her landlord was a staid sort of man, a book-worm, a bit unsociable, in fact, but very honest.

"I'll pass you off as an uncle from the country, my mother's brother—she was Ukrainian too. I'll tell him I wrote for you to come because I found life too difficult all alone."

"Well, you'd better introduce your uncle to the land-lord, then. Let's see just how unsociable he is!" Protsenko said with a grin.

"But what work is there worth mentioning and what's there to work on?" the "unsociable" fellow muttered gloomi-ly, his large bulging eyes occasionally resting on Protsenko's beard and the scar over the right temple. "Twice now we've packed off all the factory equipment and the Germans have bombed us several times. We used to build locomotives and then tanks and guns. Now we repair primus stoves and cigarette lighters. Some crates have been left behind with gear from the shops, and a little rummaging might produce a good lot of equipment. But you need a proper works man-ager to do that. The present manager there now—" His thin arm with its horny palm shifted disparagingly. "They're an irresponsible lot, these people! They're small fry, and thieves at that. You wouldn't believe it, but three differ-ent factory-owners came rushing in and all of them after the same factory. Krupp's representative came, because the works used to belong to Hartmanns, and Krupp bought up their shares. Then the railway administration and lastly a power company, which would have grabbed the power station, but our people blew it up, of course, before the evacuation. They wandered about through the works and then decided they'd divide it into three sections. It was comic and tragic. A devastated factory, and there they were marking it out with stakes, like peasants in tsarist times marking out their strips of land. They rooted about like pigs and even dug holes in the communication roads inside the factory.... They divided the place up, marked it out and then each shipped the remains of the equipment to their own works in Germany. They sold up the smaller bits and pieces right and left, as though they were traders in a second-hand market. Our workers just laugh: talk about bosses! In the past few years our workers, you know, have grown accustomed to high-speed work and as for working for these masters, well, just to look at them makes you sick! On the whole, we're laughing, but only because we want to hide our tears...."

In the light of the smoking candle the four people looked like cave-dwellers: Protsenko with his long beard, Masha who had become very quiet, the "unsociable" fellow, and a bent, old woman. Their weird shadows came together and separated and then sprang up tall against the walls and ceiling. The "unsociable" man was close on seventy; he was short in stature and thin, but his head was large and he found it difficult to keep erect. He spoke gloomily in a monotonous tone of voice, and he slurred over the mumbled words. Protsenko found it pleasant to listen to him, not only because the old fellow talked sense and spoke truthfully, but also because it pleased him to hear a town worker giving a peasant he had chanced to meet such a clear and detailed account of industrial affairs under the Germans. He was unable to repress his desire to present his own ideas in turn:

"In the village where I come from they think this way: he's got no intention whatever of developing our industry in the Ukraine—all his industry's in Germany—but what he needs from us is grain and coal. He regards the Ukraine as his colony and we're his slaves." Protsenko seemed to detect surprise in the look which the "unsociable" man gave him, and he laughed. "There's nothing surprising in the fact that our farming people reason in this fashion. They have grown up." The sly twinkle again hopped from one eye to the other.

"Yes, that's right enough," the "unsociable" man said, not at all surprised at Protsenko's argument. "All right then—a colony. So it follows that they're pushing on with the development of farming in the villages, is that it?"

Protsenko laughed softly. "We sow the winter wheat straight into the stubble of the winter and spring wheat, and we work the soil with choppers. Judge for yourself!"

"Exactly," the "unsociable" man said, again showing no surprise. "They've no idea how to manage anything.... They've made a habit of living by robbery and with that kind of 'culture'—God forgive me—they hope to conquer the world, the stupid brutes," he said in a voice free of rancour.

"Oho, Grandpa, you can give a farmer like me a handicap of a hundred points and still win," Protsenko thought and the thought pleased him.

"Did anyone see you come in here with your niece?" the "unsociable" man asked without any change in the tone of his voice.

"Not that I know of. But why should I worry? I've got papers for everything."

"That's all very well," the "unsociable" man said evasively. "But the regulation here is that I have to report your arrival to the police. If you're not staying for long we can overlook the matter—I'm telling you straight, Ivan Fyodorovich, I recognized you at once because, you see, you visited the works quite a lot; and the wrong sort of fellow might recognize you at an awkward moment."

His wife was certainly right in saying always that Protsenko was born under a lucky star.

Early the next day Masha called at the contact address and returned with a stranger who, to Protsenko's great astonishment, greeted the "unsociable" man as though they had parted only the previous evening. From him Protsenko learned that the "unsociable" man had been left behind to work underground. He also learned how far the Germans had penetrated into the country: this was at the time when the great Battle of Stalingrad began.

Protsenko spent the next few days taking stock of the conditions in the town and the region as a whole; part of his time he was engaged in establishing contacts. Then one day, in the midst of all these activities, the same man who had put him in touch with the town underground organization brought Lyuba the Actress along to him.

Protsenko listened to everything Lyuba could tell him of the circumstances in which the people confined in the Krasnodon prison had met their death, and then sat gloomily for some time incapable of saying anything at all. He was painfully grieved about Shulga and Valko. "What truly great Cossacks they were!" he mused. And suddenly he pictured his wife sitting and waiting—quite alone....

"Y-e-s," he said. "It's harsh, this underground existence of ours! There's never been a harsher one...." He began to pace up and down, talking to Lyuba, but what he said was more of a soliloquy. "People compare our underground with that at the time of the intervention, under the White Guards, but what comparison can there be? The terror under these butchers makes the White Guards seem like schoolboys; they're annihilating people by the million nowadays. But we have an advantage which didn't exist at that time: our underground fighters and partisans are supported by the full might of our Party and our state and the strength of our Red Army. The awareness of our partisans is greater, their organization's better and the technical equipment's on a higher level, better arms and communications that is. This must be made clear to the people.... The enemy's weak spot is that he's dull-witted; they do everything by order, according to a time-table; they live and operate among our people in complete darkness and understand nothing... that's got to be made use of!" he said coming to a halt and facing Lyuba, then resuming his pacing from one corner of the room to the other. "All this has to be explained to the people, so that they stop being afraid of them and learn to deceive them. The people must be organized—they themselves will supply the forces: small underground groups that could operate in the pits and in the villages must be formed everywhere. People shouldn't go hiding in the forests. Damn it, we're living in the Donbas. We've got to get inside the pits, the villages, even inside the German institutions themselves—into the labour exchange, the Town Council and the *Direktion*, into the Agricultural Commandant's offices, the police, even the Gestapo itself! We've got to disrupt everything we can by wrecking, sabotage and ruthless terror from within! Small groups of local people—workers and villagers and the youngsters—five to a group, everywhere, in every nook and cranny, y-e-s, until the Germans' teeth are chattering in terror of us!" He said this with an expression of vengeance that was transmitted to Lyuba and she found herself breathing heavily. Then Protsenko recalled what she had related to him "on the instructions of the older comrades."

"So that means things are going well with you people? It's the same elsewhere, too. And there are bound to be casualties in an affair like this.... What's your name?" he asked, once again halting and facing her. "Lyuba?... Oh yes, a fine girl like you would have a name like that! So it's Lyuba!" A merry twinkle again danced in his eyes. "Well then, tell me what it is you want?"

With instant clarity, the picture flashed through Lyuba's mind of the scene in the room where the seven of them had stood together in line. Outside the window, low dark clouds had raced across the sky. As each in turn had stepped forward the colour had drained from the cheeks, the voice pronouncing the oath had risen to a high ringing note which concealed the awful tremor in it. The words had been written by Oleg and Vanya Zemnukhov and had been approved by all of them, but when they pronounced the words, the oath seemed suddenly to be something outside them, something above them, more inflexible and inviolable than any law. Lyuba recalled all this and because of the agitation that again seized her, she went pale and against the pallor her childlike, blue eyes, with the cruel, steely glint stood out forcefully.

"We need advice and help," she said.

"Who's 'we'?"

"The Young Guard. Our commander is Ivan Turkenich, a Red Army lieutenant who was cut off from his unit when he was wounded. Our commissar is Oleg Koshevoi, pupil of the Gorky School. Thirty of us have taken an oath of loyalty. We're organized in fives, just as you said, that was Oleg's suggestion."

"The adult comrades probably advised him to do that," Protsenko said, understanding everything in a flash. "All the same, your Oleg's a smart lad!"

Now extraordinarily animated, Protsenko sat up to the table, got Lyuba to sit down opposite him, and asked her to name all the members of their Young Guard headquarters and tell him something about each of them.

When she came to Stakhovich his brows contracted in a frown.

"Wait a minute," he said touching her hand. "What's his first name?"

"Yevgeny."

"Has he been with you all the time or did he arrive from outside?"

Lyuba related how he had turned up in Krasnodon and what he had had to say about himself.

"You be careful in your dealings with this lad. Do some checking-up." Protsenko told Lyuba of the strange circumstances of Stakhovich's disappearance from the detachment. "If only he hasn't been in the hands of the Germans—" he added slowly.

Lyuba's face clouded over, her anxiety all the greater because she had no great liking for Stakhovich. For a time she regarded Protsenko in silence. Then her features relaxed, her eyes lit up and she said in a quiet voice:

"No, it can't be. Probably he was just frightened and went off."

"Why d'you think that?"

"The fellows have known him a long time. He's a Komsomol. He's full of his own importance, but he'd never do anything like that. His family are all good people: the father's an old miner, the brothers are Party members and in the army now.... No, it can't be!"

Protsenko was struck by her extraordinarily clear reasoning.

"Clever girl!" he said, but the sadness in his eyes puzzled her. "There was a time when we thought along those lines too. You see, it's like this," he went on in the simple way one would talk to a child. "There are still lots of people in the world who change their ideas as they change their clothes and sometimes they use them as a mask—the fascists are training such people by the million all over the world—and there are people who are simply faint-hearted and can be broken easily...."

"No, it can't be," Lyuba said, having Stakhovich in mind.

"I hope to God you're right! But, once he has been a coward, it may happen again."

"I'll tell Oleg about it," she said briefly.

"You've understood everything I've told you?"

Lyuba nodded.

"Go ahead then and act accordingly.... Are you in touch with the man who brought you here? Hold on to him."

"Thank you," Lyuba said and looked at him with eyes that held their former sprightliness.

They both got up.

"Take our militant Bolshevik greetings to the comrades of the Young Guard." Tenderly he took her head between his small, capable hands and kissed first one eye, then the other. Then he gently pushed her from him. "Be off, now," he said.

Chapter 3

DURING THE FEW DAYS she was in Voroshilovgrad Lyuba remained under the orders of the person who had taken her to see Protsenko. This person considered it extremely useful that she had come to be on good terms with a German quartermaster colonel and his adjutant and that she had found lodgings in an apartment where she was accepted as someone that she actually was not.

There was no need for her to learn a new code as it was the one she had learned before leaving the wireless school. But she was to take a transmitter with her because it had been found very difficult to operate one in Voroshilovgrad.

The same person taught her to change her location at frequent intervals in order to evade detection by means of cross-bearings. She herself was not to stay in Krasnodon all the time but come to Voroshilovgrad occasionally, and also go to other places; in addition to maintaining the connections she already had, she was to establish new connections among enemy officers—German, Rumanian, Italian and Hungarian.

She even succeeded in coming to an understanding with the people in the apartment where she was living that she would lodge with them whenever she happened to be in

Voroshilovgrad, because the other places she had been offered were not to her liking. The girl with the face like a mushroom continued to treat Lyuba with the greatest disdain, but the mother realized that Lyuba was a less offensive person to have in the house than German officials.

There was nothing for it now but for Lyuba to resort to a passing German car again. But this time she did not signal approaching passenger cars; she was more interested now in soldiers on lorries. Soldiers were more pleasant and less inquisitive, for in addition to her personal things her case now contained a little gadget.

In the end she managed to get a lift on a hospital service van. True, she found that in addition to five or six men of the medical corps the van also carried a senior and several junior medical officers, but all of them were a bit tipsy and Lyuba had long ago discovered that tipsy officers were easier to hoodwink than sober ones.

It transpired that they were taking a consignment of alcohol to a field hospital, large quantities of it in big flat containers. And Lyuba suddenly thought how good it would be to get hold of some of it, for alcohol opens all locks and doors and anything could be obtained in exchange for it.

The upshot of it was that Lyuba persuaded the senior medical officer not to drive through the darkness with his big, heavy van, but to park it for the night at the place of a good friend of hers in Krasnodon where she was going to fulfil an engagement. She gave her mother the fright of her life when she entered the home with a crowd of tipsy German officers and soldiers.

The Germans went on drinking throughout the night and since Lyuba had passed herself off as an actress she had to dance for them. She skated on thin ice, flirting indiscriminately with officers and other ranks, but again outwitted all of them; the officers paid court to Lyuba, the jealous soldiers intervened and finally the senior medical officer kicked one of the hospital orderlies in the belly.

While they were enjoying themselves in this fashion Lyuba suddenly heard a shrill, prolonged police whistle in the street. A policeman was whistling somewhere in the vicinity of the Gorky Club. He was blowing his whistle with all his might without once removing it from his mouth to take breath.

Lyuba did not immediately realize that it was an alarm signal, but the whistling grew louder and nearer to the house. The noise was heard of a pair of clumping feet suddenly rushing to the window and as quickly disappearing: somebody was racing down the street towards the Little Shanghais which were plastered along the edge of the ravine. Shortly afterwards the heavy boots of the policeman, blowing the whistle with all his might, clattered past the window.

Lyuba and those of the Germans who could still stand on their legs dashed out on to the porch. The night was dark, still and warm. The penetrating sound of the whistle drifted away into the distance, a dancing cone of light from an electric torch marked the line of progress of the policeman racing down the street. And as if in reply came the whistling of others on point-duty in the market-place, from the open space beyond the ravine, from the gendarmerie, even from as far away as the second level crossing, which was a long distance from them.

In profound silence and rocking slightly, because the alcohol had dissolved in them that most important backbone which keeps the human being in the vertical position, the German Army medical men remained standing on the porch for some time. Then the senior officer sent one of the orderlies for a torch and played its beam over the front garden with its neglected flower-beds, the broken remains of its fence, the mutilated lilac bushes. Then he shed its light over the van standing in the yard and everyone went back inside.

At this precise moment Oleg, who had left his pursuer far behind, spotted on the open ground across the ravine the flashing torches of the policemen running from the gendarmerie to cut him off. He immediately realized that he would not be able to conceal himself in the Little Shanghais because the local dogs—alive in this area for the sole reason that none of the Germans wanted to live in clay huts—would certainly betray his presence with their barking. No sooner had he realized this than he swung off to the right into Vosmidomiki district and stood stiffly against the wall of the first house he reached. A minute or so later the policeman in his jack-boots came pounding past so close that his whistling nearly deafened Oleg.

He waited a little and then, taking care not to make his presence known, made his way round the back of the houses in the same street through which he had come and returned to the high part of the town to where he had started.

The excitement which had gripped him when he discovered a policeman on the club porch and which had developed into a sort of uncontrollable merriment as he ran away from him down the street now gave way to a feeling of alarm. Oleg heard the whistling in the neighbourhood of the market-place and the gendarmerie and the second level crossing and realized that his carelessness had placed not only himself, but also Sergei, who was with Valya, and Styopa Safonov with Tosya Mashchenko, in a difficult and dangerous position.

This had been their first attempt to distribute leaflets which Oleg and Vanya Zemnukhov had written, the first step towards informing the population of the existence of the Young Guard.

How much effort it had cost them to side-track Stakhovich's proposal that is was quite possible, in one night, to plaster the whole town with leaflets and so make a big impression in one fell swoop! Oleg had got to know him better and had no doubts about the sincerity of his motives, but why could Stakhovich not understand that the larger the number of people drawn into the affair, the greater the risk of failure? And it was annoying, too, that Sergei Tyulenin, as usual, was inclined to favour the most extreme measures. Turkenich and Vanya Zemnukhov had agreed with Oleg's proposal to put up leaflets in one district only and then, after a few days, in a second, and later in a third, and so lay a false train for the police each time.

Oleg had suggested that it was most important for them to work in pairs—one to hold and separate the leaflets, the other to apply the adhesive liquid and for one to paste up the leaflet while the other concealed paste-pot and leaflets. Moreover, a boy and a girl should go out together, so that if the policemen caught them out after curfew, the love motive could be suggested to explain why they were strolling about at such an unreasonable hour.

Instead of using flour and water paste, they decided to use liquid honey. Paste would have to be cooked somewhere and that in itself might provide a pointer for the police, apart from the fact that paste leaves marks on the clothing. In addition, pots and brushes would be required for paste and these would be awkward to carry about. Honey could be taken in a small bottle with a stopper and a little at a time poured straight from the mouth of the bottle on to the back of the leaflet.

Oleg had worked out an additional plan, a very simple one, for distributing leaflets in broad daylight in places where large numbers of people assembled: for instance at the cinema, in the market and by the labour exchange.

For their first night operation they had chosen the district round 1B Pit and also the adjacent Vosmidomiki district and the market-place. Sergei and Valya were to cover the market-place, Styopa Safonov and Tosya Vosmidomiki district while Oleg undertook to do the 1B Pit district.

He had very much wanted to go with Nina, of course, but said he would take his pretty Aunt Marina.

It had been decided that Turkenich was to stay at home so that on this first attempt, in view of their complete lack of experience, each pair on completing their part of the work could immediately report developments to the commander.

However, after they had separated Oleg somehow caught himself thinking things over: what right had he to involve the mother of a three-year-old child in a dangerous business like this without consulting Nikolai Nikolayevich, the child's father? It was wrong, of course, to disturb an arrangement he himself had insisted upon, but by that time Oleg had been possessed by boyish recklessness and had decided to go out alone.

Towards evening, while movement in the town was still unrestricted, Oleg had left the house with several leaflets in the inside pocket of his jacket and a bottle of honey in a trouser pocket. He had followed the street where Osmukhin and Zemnukhov lived and reached the ravine where it lay across the road leading to No. 5 Pit. This was the same ravine which further along to the right separated Vosmidomiki district from the open space with the gendarmerie. The ravine was quite uninhabited at this point. Oleg had followed it to the right and just before reaching the Little Shanghais he had turned into one of the hollows running down into the ravine and made his way through it and then up towards the long broken range of hills along which ran the Voroshilovgrad Highway and which dominated this part of the town.

By concealing himself among the hills he had almost reached the place where the Voroshilovgrad Highway crossed the road leading from the centre of the town to Pervomaisky. Here he had thrown himself down and waited for the darkness. Peering through the sun-scorched tufts of tall grass, he had obtained a good view of the cross-roads, the outskirts of Pervomaisky beyond the highway, the immense tip at the head of the destroyed 1B Pit, the Gorky Club farther down the road where Lyuba Shevtsova lived, Vosmidomiki district and the open space with the Voroshilov School and the gendarmerie.

The police patrol box, which Oleg had most to fear, stood at the cross-roads and was manned by two policemen. One of them was always at the cross-roads and if he did take a short walk to while away the time he preferred to go along the highway. The other patrolled the road from the cross-roads past 1B Pit towards the Gorky Club and along the street where Lyuba Shevtsova lived as far as the Little Shanghais.

The police patrol box nearest to this one was in the market area and was also in charge of two policemen. One of them spent all his time in the market-place itself while the second walked the beat from the market-place to the point where the Little Shanghais merged with the Shanghai.

Night had descended. It was black but so still that the slightest rustle was audible. Now Oleg could rely on nothing but his hearing.

His task was to paste up several leaflets at the entrance to 1B Pit and on the building of the Gorky Club. (They had decided not to stick any leaflets on houses where people lived, as this would cause trouble for the tenants.) Stealthily Oleg had walked down the hills to the first of the prefabricated houses. This was at the end of the street where Lyuba Shevtsova lived. Across an open space and exactly opposite him was the gatehouse of 1B Pit.

He had heard the patrolman and the policeman on duty at the gate talking to one another. For a moment he had even seen their faces as they bent over the flame of a cigarette lighter. He had been compelled to wait until the patrolman had passed down the street; otherwise he might have been caught in the open square. But the policemen had remained together for a long time engaged in low-voiced conversation.

At last the patrolman had walked off, his torch lighting up the road from time to time. Oleg had stood behind the house and listened to his footsteps. As soon as they had receded in the distance he had walked out on to the street. The heavy footsteps had still been audible. The patrolman had continued to flash his torch on the road occasionally and Oleg had watched him passing the Gorky Club. Then he had disappeared from sight, for just beyond the Shevtsovs' home the road wound its way down into the ravine. Flashes of soft deflected light in the distance showed that the policeman was still lighting his way from time to time.

In common with all the large pits which had been blown up at the time of the retreat, 1B Pit was not in production. However, an administrative office, staffed by members of a German mining battalion, had been established at the pit on the instructions of *Leutnant* Schweide. Every morning a number of miners who had either failed, or been unable, to evacuate arrived for work on its "restoration," the term used in official documents to describe the process of cleaning up the mess in the yard; in effect, several dozen people lazily pushed wooden wheelbarrows about the yard, shifting scrap and rubbish from one place to another.

On this night, silence reigned and everything at the pit lay in darkness.

Oleg had pasted a leaflet on the stone wall of the pit yard, another on the gatehouse, a third on the notice-board over all sorts of announcements and orders. He had not been able to spend much of his time there. He had run no risk of the old watchman catching him—he was always sound asleep at night—but at any moment the returning patrolman might pass on the pit side of the street and flash his torch on the gatehouse. So far his footsteps had not been audible and there had been no sign of his flashing torch. Presumably he had been held up in the Little Shanghais.

Oleg had crossed the open space and approached the club which, though very spacious, was the coldest and most uncomfortable building in the town; it was quite unsuitable as a dwelling and therefore stood empty. It faced a road which from early morning was constantly used by people going to the market from Vosmidomiki district, Pervomaisky and from the neighbouring farms. It was also the main route for traffic proceeding to Voroshilovgrad and Kamensk.

Oleg had just begun pasting leaflets along the front of the building when he had caught the sound of the policeman's footsteps coming down the street from the ravine. He had slipped round the building and hid himself against the back wall. The policeman's footsteps had grown louder and louder, had reached the building and then suddenly stopped. Rigid as a statue Oleg had waited for the policeman to pass the building: one minute had passed, then another; five minutes had gone by, but there had still been no sound of footsteps.

What if a torch had been switched on and the policeman had played its light over the front of the building, had seen the leaflets, and was even now standing there reading them? He would naturally try scraping them off, then and there, and he would discover that they had only just been pasted up, in which case he would most certainly come walking round the building flashing his torch; whoever had pasted up those leaflets could not possibly be hiding anywhere but behind the building!

Oleg had held his breath and listened but all he could hear was the pounding of his own heart. He had felt an almost irresistible urge to leave the wall and start running, but had realized that that would only have caused trouble. No, the only thing to be done was to find out where on earth that policeman had got to!

Oleg had craned his neck from the corner where he stood: he had heard nothing to arouse his suspicions. Pressing close to the wall he had softly made his way towards the street lifting his feet high with each step and putting them down carefully. Several times he had stopped to listen but everything had been still. He had reached the other corner of the building; pressing one hand against the wall he had clung to the edge with the other and craned his neck round it. Suddenly a rain-weathered piece of old mortar had broken loose from beneath his hand and fallen to the ground with what seemed to Oleg a terrifying crash. At the same instant he had spotted the glow of a cigarette low on the steps of the porch and knew at once that the policeman had simply sat down for a rest and a smoke. The glowing tip had immediately leapt up, there had been a noise from the porch steps and Oleg had pushed off from the corner of the building and started to race down the street towards the ravine. A shrill whistle had pierced the still air. Within a fraction of a second Oleg had been caught in the cone of light from the torch. But in the same instant he had leapt and hurled himself clear of it.

In justice to Oleg it must be said that from the first moment of this sudden emergency, he had done nothing precipitate. He might have outwitted the policeman within a minute in Vosmidomiki district and concealed himself in Lyuba's or the Ivantsovas' home, but he had no right to place them in danger; he could have made a feint of making for the market-place and then have darted into the Shanghai where the devil himself could not have found him, but that might have endangered Sergei and Valya. Oleg had consequently raced towards the Little Shanghais. But since circumstances had compelled him after all to swing into Vosmidomiki district, he still had avoided placing Styopa Safonov and Tosya in danger by not penetrating deeply into the district. He had then retraced his steps back to the hills, to the cross-roads, where he faced the risk of being caught by the man on point-duty.

He felt a gnawing anxiety for his friends and alarm at the possibility that the whole operation had been a failure. Yet the boyish, mischievous feeling filled him again as he listened to the furious barking of the dogs in the Little Shanghais. He could imagine the patrolman pursuing him meeting the policemen running out from the gendarmerie and discussing the disappearance of the intruder and raking the neighbourhood with their torches.

In the market-place the whistling had ceased. Oleg had again reached the top of the hill and, watching from there, he could tell by the flashing torches that the policemen who had tried to intercept him were now crossing the open space on their way back to the gendarmerie while his pursuer, the patrolman, had remained standing at the far end of the street flashing his torch on a house there.

Had the policeman seen the leaflets on the club building? ...Of course he hadn't! If he had he wouldn't have sat down on the steps for a smoke. Now they could turn the whole of Vosmidomiki district inside out in a search for him—Oleg!

He now felt easier in his mind.

It was not yet dawn when Oleg gave the agreed signal, three soft taps, on Turkenich's window and the door was noiselessly opened for him. They tiptoed through the kitchen, through a room in which people were sleeping, into Vanya's room which he had to himself. A tiny oil-lamp burned high up on the edge of the wardrobe and it was clear that Vanya had not been to bed. He showed no pleasure at all when he saw Oleg, and his face was stern and pale.

"Anyb-b-body get c-caught?" Oleg asked stuttering badly and turning pale.

"No, everybody's all right now," Turkenich replied, avoiding his eyes. "Sit down." He indicated a stool and himself sat on the bed: he had obviously spent the night pacing the room or sitting on the bed.

"Well? Was it a success then?" Oleg asked.

"Yes," Turkenich said, still not looking at him. "They've all been here—Sergei and Valya, Styopa and Tosya.... You went alone, then?" Turkenich raised his eyes to Oleg and dropped them again.

"How d-did you know?" Oleg asked with the expression of a guilty schoolboy.

"We got worried about you," Vanya replied evasively. "In the end I could stand it no longer and went round to Nikolai Nikolayevich's and found Marina at home.... All the chaps wanted to wait for you here but I talked them out of it. I said if you'd been caught, then it would only make matters worse if they surprised the lot of us assembled here in the middle of the night. And you know yourself what a hard day they have before them tomorrow—there's the market and the labour exchange...."

With a growing sense of guilt which he could not fully explain to himself, Oleg briefly related how he had hurried across to the club from the pit and what had taken place there. In spite of everything, he grew animated as he recalled all the circumstances of the affair.

"And when everything turned out all right in the end, I'm sorry, but I felt a bit mischievous and on the way back I clapped two more leaflets on the Voroshilov School...." He looked at Turkenich and grinned broadly.

Turkenich heard him out in silence. Then he stood up, pushed his hands into his pockets and for some moments regarded Oleg seated before him on the stool.

"Now I'm going to tell you something, only don't get angry about it." Turkenich's voice remained calm. "This is the first time you've been out on a job of this kind— and it will be the last. Understand?"

"N-no, I d-do not," Oleg said. "It was a success and this kind of thing never runs smoothly. This isn't j-just a stroll. It's a battle in which there is an op-p-ponent!"

"It is not a matter of the opponent," Turkenich said. "It's just that this isn't the time for boyish pranks and neither you nor I can indulge in them. Yes, although I'm older than you, I still include myself in this. I respect you, you know that, and that's why I'm talking to you like this. You're a good fellow and strong and you probably know more than I do—but you behave like a kid.... It was all I could do to prevent the fellows from going out to your assistance. I talked them out of it, but I very nearly went off myself," Turkenich said with a wry smile. "Perhaps you think the five of us here were on tenterhooks just because of you? Oh no, we were worried about the whole business. The time's come, old chap, to get used to the idea that you're no longer you and I'm no longer me. I've been kicking myself all night for having let you go. Can we really risk our lives now without reason, for mere trifles? No, chum, we've no right to do that! And you'll have to forgive me but I'm going to get my decision passed at headquarters. In a word, it will be decided that you and I are banned from taking part in operations without special instructions to the contrary."

With a grave childlike expression in his eyes Oleg looked at him and said nothing. Turkenich softened towards him.

"Look, chum, when I said that maybe you know more than I do, it wasn't just a slip of the tongue," he said and there was a guilty note in his voice. "It's a matter of education. I spent my childhood running about barefoot in the streets like Sergei, and although I've done some studying, I only acquired real knowledge when I was an adult. After all, you see, your mother's a teacher and your stepfather's politically educated, while my old people—well, you know yourself...." With a kindly expression on his face Turkenich nodded towards the door leading to the other room. "Now the time has come to put all that knowledge of yours to good use, you understand? Teasing policemen is nothing to write home about. That's not what the youngsters expect from you. And speaking really seriously,"—Turkenich pointed significantly over his shoulder with a thumb— "those youngsters truly rely on you."

"Oh, you're a sly one, all right!" Oleg said in surprise, looking happily at Turkenich. "And you're right, you are certainly quite right!" He wagged his head. "You go ahead and get a decision from headquarters, in that case."

They both laughed.

"All the same, you have to be congratulated on yous success—I almost forgot," Turkenich said and shook hand with Oleg.

Oleg reached his home at daybreak. And just about the same time Lyuba, who intended to pay him a call, was seeing off her Germans. She had not slept all night yet could not help laughing at the sight of the vanload of drunken Germans driven by a drunken driver performing arabesques along the street.

Lyuba's mother rounded on her like a fishwife, but when her daughter showed her the four large containers of alcohol she had pilfered from the van during the night, her mother, simple though she was, could see that Lyuba had acted for some calculated purpose of her own.

Chapter 4

"FELLOW-COUNTRYMEN! People of Krasnodon! Miners! Collective Farmers!

"The Germans are liars! Moscow was, is and always will be ours. Hitler is lying about the war coming to an end. The war is only now flaring up. The Red Army will return to the Donbas.

"Hitler is driving us off to Germany so that by working in his factories we shall become the murderers of our fathers and husbands, sons and daughters.

"Do not go to Germany if you want soon to embrace your husband, son or brother here on your native soil, in your own home!

"The Germans torture and torment us and kill the best of our people in order to intimidate us and bring us to our knees.

"Kill the accursed invaders! Better to die fighting than to live in slavery!

"The Motherland is in peril. But she has strength enough to rout the enemy. In its leaflets the Young Guard will tell you the whole truth, no matter how bitter it may be for Russia. Truth will be victorious!

"Read our leaflets, hide them, pass on their contents from house to house, from village to village.

"Death to the German invaders!

"The Young Guard"

Where could it have come from, the little leaflet — the page torn from a school exercise book — pasted on the fringe of the crowded market square on the notice-board on both sides of which the district newspaper, *Sotsialisticheskaya Rodina*, had been formerly displayed and on which German yellow and black posters were now hung?

It was a Sunday. People from villages and Cossack hamlets had been arriving at the market-place since daybreak. Some carried purses, others carried home-made carpet-bags; a woman might be seen carrying a single hen wrapped in a piece of cloth; others who had harvested a good crop of vegetables or still had flour from last year's harvest trundled their goods along on a barrow. Oxen were now a thing of the past, not to mention horses! The Germans had taken them all.

And those barrows—they will be remembered by our people for many, many years to come! They were not the one-wheeled barrows used for carting clay; these had two large wheels and were used for carting all kinds of things; they were pushed along with both hands by means of a crossbar. Thousands and thousands of people used them when they crossed the Donbas from one end of it to the other, in heat and dust, in rain and mud, in frost and snow, sometimes taking goods to market but more often seeking shelter or a grave.

Since early morning people from near-by villages had been bringing to market their vegetables and grain, their fowl, fruit and honey. And the townspeople too had come early with a shawl, perhaps, or a hat; a skirt, a pair of shoes; or nails, an axe, salt, perhaps, even, a length of calico or madapollam or an old-fashioned lace-trimmed dress, an heirloom from Grandma's chest.

Only a complete fool or gambler or downright rogue goes to the market for profit in times like these; it is distress and want which drive people there. German marks were in circulation on Ukrainian soil but who could tell whether they were genuine or would retain their value and, to put it candidly, who had any? No, Grandfather's way was better than that; how often had it helped them out when times were hard: I'll give you this if you'll give me that.... And so, since early dawn, the market-place was crowded with people passing and repassing one another a thousand times.

And everyone's eyes fell on the notice-board, standing on the fringe of the market-place as it had done for many years past. German posters were pinned on it as they had been for weeks. One of them carried a fan-shaped array of photographs: a parade of German troops in Moscow; German officers swimming in the Neva by the Peter and Paul Fortress; German officers arm-in-arm with our girls on the banks of the Volga in Stalingrad. And it was over this poster that they saw the white leaflet neatly written in ink soaked from the lead of an indelible pencil.

At first only one person showed any curiosity about it, then he was joined by two more and still others, until there was a small group—mostly women, old men and youngsters—crowding round and all of them craning their necks to read the leaflet. A crowd of people straining their eyes to read a hand-written leaflet on white paper—who would walk past them indifferently, and on market day!

A huge crowd now surged round the board with the leaflet. Those in front stood in silence, but did not walk away, for an irresistible force compelled them to read the leaflet over and over again. And those in the rear endeavoured to push through to get nearer and became noisy and angry and loudly demanded to know what was written on it. No one replied and no one could get nearer, yet the huge, still growing crowd already knew what this leaflet, this page torn from a school exercise book, had to say to them: "It's not true that German troops are parading in Red Square! It's not true that German officers are bathing by the Peter and Paul Fortress! It's not true that they're strolling with our girls down the streets of Stalingrad! It's not true that the Red Army is no more, that the front lines are manned by Mongols in the pay of the British! It's all lies! What is true is that some of our own people are still in the town, people who know the truth and they are fearlessly telling the population that which alone is the truth."

An incredibly tall man wearing a policeman's arm-band and check trousers pushed into high cow-hide boots and a check jacket under which dangled a heavy holster with a yellow lanyard, joined the crowd. His narrow head with its old-fashioned peaked cap towered above them and, as the people looked over their shoulder and recognized Ignat Fomin, they made way for him with a momentary expression of fear or flattery.

Pushing his cap low over his eyes and dodging behind people to avoid being recognized by Fomin, Sergei Tyulenin scrutinized the crowd. He was searching for Vasya Pirozhok. When he caught sight of him he winked in the direction of Fomin, but Pirozhok who knew what was expected of him was already pushing along after Fomin towards the notice-board.

Despite the fact that Pirozhok and Kovalyov had been

kicked out of the German police force, they had remained on a friendly footing with all the policemen who, for their part, did not at all take a serious view of what Pirozhok and Kovalyov had done. Fomin glanced round, recognized Pirozhok and did not speak to him. Together they made their way to the leaflet. Fomin tried to scrape it off with a finger-nail but the leaflet was stuck firmly to the German poster and would not come away. He dug a hole in the poster, and stripped off the leaflet together with a piece of the German poster and crumpling it up pushed it into his jacket pocket.

"What are you crowding round for? What's there to gape at? Clear off!" he hissed, turning his face, yellow as a eunuch's, to the crowd, while his small grey eyes glared from the maze of wrinkles surrounding them. Gliding and writhing round Fomin like a black serpent, Pirozhok also yelled in a high-pitched boyish voice:

"You hear? Keep moving, ladies and gentlemen, it'll be better if you do!"

Fomin spread his long legs apart and stood towering over the crowd. Immediately Pirozhok was close at his side. The crowd broke up and began to run off in all directions. Pirozhok ran ahead.

Morosely Fomin strode about the market in his heavy leather boots. People stopped their bartering to stare at his back with expressions of fear, surprise or gloating: stuck on the back of Fomin's check jacket was a leaflet on which was printed in large letters;

"You are selling our people to the Germans for a slice of sausage, a mouthful of vodka, a packet of cheap tobacco. But you will pay with your treacherous life. Beware!"

No one stopped him and he walked all the way across the market-place to the police-station with this sinister warning on his back.

Sergei's light curly head and Pirozhok's dark one bobbed up and disappeared here and there among the market crowds as they moved about among the circling bodies, like comets in their mysterious orbits. They were not alone: the fair head of Tosya Mashchenko, a quiet, neatly dressed girl with clever eyes, would at times suddenly emerge from an eddy of people. And if Tosya Mashchenko was about, then for sure somewhere in close proximity there would be her satellite, the fair-headed Styopa Safonov. Sergei's bright, piercing eyes crossed in the crowd with the dark velvety eyes of Vitka Lukyanchenko, their eyes met, then turned away. Valya Borts, too, with her golden plaits circled round the stalls and tables for a long time; she carried a basket on her arm covered with a coarse towel, but no one saw just what she bought or sold.

People would find leaflets in their handbags or inside an empty sack, or even on a bench under a head of cabbage or under a greyish-yellow, dark-green or speckled water-melon. Sometimes it was not a leaflet but just a narrow strip of paper with printed lettering saying perhaps: "Down with Hitler's 200 grammes! Long live the Soviet kilogramme!" And people's hearts would beat faster.

Sergei had passed up and down the rows of stalls several times and had dived into the surging crowd selling old clothes where articles were exchanged from hand to hand when suddenly he found himself face to face with Natalya Alexeyevna, the surgeon at the municipal hospital. In her dusty games slippers and holding a pair of small, well-worn lady's shoes in her childlike, dumpy hands, she was one of a row of women vendors. She looked confused when she recognized Sergei.

"Good-morning!" he said, also feeling embarrassed, and pulled off his cap.

For a moment her eyes assumed the direct, ruthless, business-like expression he knew so well. Then, with a nimble movement of her dumpy hands she wrapped up the shoes and said:

"Fine! You're just the person I need."

Sergei and Valya should have left the market together and gone on to the labour exchange. From there the first party of young people being driven off to Germany was to begin the walk to the Verkhneduvannaya station. Suddenly Valya saw Sergei with a plump little person, looking in the distance like a girl wearing a grown-up hair-style, emerge from the crowd in the market-place, make for the Li Fan-cha huts and disappear behind them. Pride would not allow Valya to follow them. Her full upper lip quivered slightly and a cold look came into her eyes. Carrying her basket in which, under the potatoes, lay several leaflets required for the place she still had to visit, she walked off haughtily to the labour exchange.

The small open space in front of the white single-storey labour exchange building on the hill was cordoned off by German soldiers. The young people who that day were to leave their native town, their mothers, fathers and other relations with bundles and cases, and people who had assembled out of curiosity, crowded outside the cordon on the hill-side.

The last few days had been dull and grey. A wind had blown up in the morning and was now with fierce monotony driving dark rain-clouds over the sky too fast for the rain to fall. It tugged at the multi-coloured skirts of the women and girls on the hill-side and whirled thick clouds of dust along the road past the district executive committee and the house of the Mad Squire.

Motionless and silent, stunned with grief, this host of women, girls and youths presented a mournful sight. Where there was any conversation at all it was in half-tones or a whisper. They were afraid even to weep aloud: the mother would merely brush her tears away with her hand; the daughter would suddenly press a handkerchief to her eyes.

Valya stopped on the fringe of the crowd; from there she could see the neighbourhood of 1B Pit and part of the railway branch line.

More and more people arrived from various parts of the town. Nearly all the young people who had distributed leaflets in the market-place had also made their way to the spot. Valya suddenly caught sight of Sergei—he was walking along the railway embankment, his head lowered to prevent the wind from blowing off his cap. For a moment he was out of sight and then again appeared round the bend of the hill. He came across the open hill-side, scrutinizing the crowd and recognized Valya when still a long way off. Her full upper lip quivered proudly. She refused to look at him and did not ask any questions.

"That was Natalya Alexeyevna," he began softly. He had known she would be angry. He bent to her ear and whispered:

"A whole gang of chaps in Krasnodon mining settlement....
Working on their own.... Tell Oleg...."

Valya was the link from the Young Guard headquarters.
She nodded. Just then they caught sight of Ulya Gromova
coming along the road from the Vosmidomiki with a strange
girl in a beret and coat. Fighting against the wind and
turning their faces away from the dust Ulya and the girl
were carrying a suitcase between them.

"If I will have to go there would you come with me?"
Sergei whispered. Valya nodded.

At last it dawned on *Oberleutnant* Sprick, director of
the labour exchange, that the young people would remain
outside the cordon where they stood with their relatives,
if they were not hurried. Accompanied by his clerk, he
came out on the porch, clean-shaven and in full uniform,
instead of wearing the leather shorts he habitually wore
in hot weather in his office and in the streets. He shouted
that all those about to leave were to get their documents;
the clerk repeated the instruction in Ukrainian.

The German soldiers did not allow parents, relatives
or friends to pass the cordon. The farewells began. Mothers
and daughters no longer restrained their feelings and wept
aloud. The young men kept a hold on themselves but it
was dreadful to watch their faces as their mothers, grand-
mothers and sisters clung to them, and their aged fathers,
who had spent years in the pits and had more than once
faced death, looked downcast and flicked the tears from
their moustaches.

"It's time," Sergei said sternly, trying to hide his agitation from Valya.

Scarcely able to restrain her tears and unaware that
she had heard what he said, Valya mechanically made her
way through the crowd. Mechanically, too, she felt under
the potatoes and took out a folded leaflet and slipped it
into a coat or jacket pocket or under the handle of a suitcase or into a basket.

Close to the cordon a sudden rush of people away from
the labour exchange pressed Valya back. There were not a
few youths, girls and young women among the people who
had come to say farewell and one of these had accidentally
passed through the cordon while seeing off a sister or brother

and was now unable to get out. This had so amused the German soldiers that they had begun to grab the lads and girls nearest to them and drag them inside the cordon. There were screams, weeping and pleading. One woman became hysterical. Terror-stricken, the young people rushed away from the cordon.

Sergei appeared from somewhere with anger and pain written on his face, seized Valya by the arm and pulled her out of the crowd. Suddenly they found themselves face to face with Nina Ivantsova.

"Thank God! Otherwise those monsters would have—" She seized them both by the arm with her own which was large and womanly. "At Kashuk's tonight at five. Warn Zemnukhov and Stakhovich," she whispered to Valya. "Have you seen Ulya?" She darted away in search of her. Like Valya, she also was a link for the headquarters.

For some moments Valya and Sergei remained standing close together. Neither had the slightest wish to leave the other. Sergei looked as though he was about to say something very important, all the same he said nothing.

"I'll run along now," Valya said gently, but made no move for a few moments; then she smiled at him, looked about, felt ashamed and ran off down the hill-side with her basket over her arm.

Ulya was standing close to the cordon waiting for Valentina Filatova to reappear from the labour exchange building. The German soldier who had let Valentina with her case pass inside the cordon had been about to grab Ulya by the arm, but she had looked coldly and disdainfully at him; their eyes had met for a second and in his there had for a moment been something like a human expression. He had let Ulya go, turned away and suddenly and angrily yelled at a fair-haired young woman whose head was bare and who was unwilling to part with her son, a lad of about sixteen. Finally she tore herself away from her son and then it turned out that it was she who was to be taken away and not her son. The youth wept like a child as he watched her enter the building with her bundle in her hand and smile to him for the last time from the threshold.

Ulya and Valentina had sat all night with their arms round each other in the Filatovs' small front room with

its profusion of autumn flowers. Valentina's aged mother
had come in now and again to pat their hair or kiss them
or to sort over the articles in her daughter's case or to sit
quietly in the arm-chair in the corner. Now that Valentina
was to go from her she was to be left quite alone.

Weak from much weeping but quieter, Valentina had
shuddered at rare intervals in Ulya's embrace. The latter
had been terrifyingly aware of the inevitability of what
was about to happen. She was softened and more adult now
and she had silently stroked the girl's fair head with a
feeling that was both childlike and maternal.

The light from the small oil-lamp had been just enough
to reveal the faces and hands of the two girls and the old
mother sitting in the dark room.

If only she had never seen it all! The way Valentina
had parted with her mother, the endless walk with the case
against the whistling wind, the last embrace by the cordon
of German soldiers!

But it had all truly happened. That sort of thing would
continue to go on.... With her face expressing sombre
strength, Ulya stood close to the chain of German soldiers,
her eyes fixed on the door of the labour exchange.

The lads, girls and young women who had passed through
the line of soldiers had been instructed by a fat corporal
to leave their bundles and cases in the yard against the
wall and had been told that their belongings would be
put on a lorry. Then they passed inside. Under the supervision of the *Oberleutnant* Nemchinova handed each of them
a card, which, for the entire journey, was the only document certifying their identity to show to representatives
of the German authorities. The card was not inscribed with
the name and surname of its owner. It bore nothing but
a number and the name of a town. As they received their
cards they left the building and the corporal put them in
their place in the ranks forming up across the open space.

Then Valentina Filatova appeared in the door, looked
round for her friend and stepped towards her, but the corporal caught her by the arm as she passed and pushed her
towards the ranks. She was placed at the far end of the
third or fourth line and the two friends lost sight of each
other.

The bitterness of this senseless separation gave people the right to display their affection. The women in the crowd tried to break through the cordon shouting last words of farewell or words of advice to their children. But the young people in those ranks, mostly girls, seemed already to belong to a different world: they replied in half-tones or with just a wave of a kerchief or did not respond, while the tears streamed down their faces and they kept their eyes fixed on the faces dear to them.

Finally *Oberleutnant* Sprick came out of the building with a large yellow packet in his hand. The crowd grew quiet. All eyes were turned to him.

"*Still gestanden!*" the *Oberleutnant* ordered.

"*Still gestanden!*" the corporal repeated in a terrifying voice.

The column stood rigidly still. *Oberleutnant* Sprick walked down the rank, four deep, facing him. He prodded each nearest him with his thick, stubby finger. There were over two hundred people in the column.

The *Oberleutnant* handed his packet to the stout corporal and waved his arm. A group of soldiers rushed forward to clear the crowd blocking the road. At an order from the corporal the column turned slowly and haltingly, as though unwilling, and began to move down the road under escort, the stout corporal at their head.

Pressed back by the soldiers, the crowd straggled along on both sides of the column. The weeping, wailing and shouting that followed it rose into a long-drawn-out lament and was carried away by the wind.

Ulya walked mostly on her toes, straining to pick out Valentina in the column. At last she saw her; she was searching for her friend along the sides of the road and her staring eyes were full of torment at not seeing Ulya at this last minute.

"Here I am, Valentina dear, I'm here with you!" Ulya shouted, as the throng pressed her back. But Valentina neither saw nor heard her and still looked about, anguish in her eyes. Ulya was being forced farther and farther away from the column, but several times she glimpsed Valentina's face, and then the column was beyond the house of the Mad

Squire, descending to the second level crossing, and no more of Valentina was seen.

"Ulya!" cried Nina Ivantsova, who suddenly appeared at Ulya's side. "I've been looking everywhere for you. Five o'clock tonight at Kashuk's ... Lyuba's here."

Ulya seemed not to be listening and her dark eyes, filled with horror, stared at Nina.

Chapter 5

OLEG TURNED a little pale as he pulled the notebook from the inside pocket of his jacket, and searched its pages closely. He dropped into a chair at the table, on which stood bottles of vodka, mugs and plates with nothing to eat on them. The others also fell silent and with serious expressions on their faces sat down, some at the table, some on the divan. They all silently looked at Oleg.

Only yesterday they had just been school-friends, carefree and full of fun. But since the day they had taken the oath, they had put away from them their former existence. It was as though they had broken their former irresponsible bond of friendship in order to enter into a new, loftier relationship, to form a friendship based on common ideas, on organization; a friendship sealed with the blood, which each of them had sworn to shed for the liberation of their native soil.

The large room in the Koshevois' apartment, similar to the rooms in all the standard houses, with its unpainted window-sills covered with ripening tomatoes, its walnut divan made up as Oleg's bed, with the bed on which Yelena Nikolayevna slept and its many well-shaken pillows under a lace-embroidered cover, still reminded them of their own carefree lives under the parental roof and yet at the same time it was now a conspiratorial centre.

Oleg was no longer Oleg, but Kashuk. This was the name of his stepfather, who, in his youth, had been a well-known Ukrainian partisan and, the year before his death, chief of the land department in Kanevo. Oleg had made it his nickname because it linked with his first, heroic notions of partisan struggle and with all the hardy training his stepfather had given him in the form of work in the fields, hunting, tending horses and rowing boats on the Dnieper.

He opened his notebook at the page where he had written down the agenda in a code of his own, and called on Lyuba Shevtsova to speak.

Lyuba rose from her seat on the divan and screwed up her eyes. She saw in her mind's eye the details of her recent trip to Voroshilovgrad, with its many incredible difficulties, dangers, encounters, adventures; even two evenings would be insufficient to recount it all.

Only yesterday she had been standing at the cross-roads with her case which had become too heavy for her, and now here she was among her friends again.

As she and Oleg had agreed beforehand, Lyuba began by telling the members of the Young Guard headquarters everything that Protsenko had said about Stakhovich. She did not of course mention Protsenko's name although she had at once recognized him; she said that she had casually met someone who had been in Stakhovich's detachment.

Lyuba was a frank, fearless girl, even cruel in her own way towards someone she did not like. And she did not withhold the suggestion the certain person had offered that Stakhovich might have been in the hands of the Germans.

The members of the Young Guard headquarters did not dare to look at Stakhovich while she related all this. Meanwhile he sat at the table, outwardly calm, his lean arms resting on it, staring straight ahead of him. There was a firm expression on his face. But when Lyuba came to her final words, a sudden change came to his face.

He relaxed, his lips and hands were no longer tight, he opened his eyes wide, and with a hurt, surprised look in them regarded each of his comrades in turn. At that moment he looked like a little boy.

"He ... he said that?... He could really think that?" he repeated several times looking Lyuba straight in the eye, with the same injured childlike expression.

No one spoke, and he buried his face in his hand and sat still for a time. Then he moved the hand from his face and said softly:

"A suspicion has fallen on me of a kind that I— Why didn't he tell you that we'd been hunted for a week and had been told to split up into groups?" he said flashing a look at Lyuba and then looking candidly at each of the others. "When I lay in the bushes there I thought: they are attempting the break-through to save their lives and most if not all of them will perish and I, perhaps, will be killed with them; but I can save myself and be useful. That's what I thought, then.... Now I can see, of course, that it was only an excuse. The firing was so ... it was terrifying," he said simply. "Still, I don't consider I committed such a grave crime. They, too, were saving their own lives.... It was already dark, and I thought: I'm a good swimmer, the Germans possibly won't notice me alone. When they all rushed off I stayed lying there for a little, the firing there had stopped, and then it flared up again in another place and it was very heavy. I thought: now's the time, and I swam on my back with just my nose showing—I'm a good swimmer—I swam to the middle and then down with the current. That's how I saved myself! But to be under such suspicion— Can it be possible? After all, that fellow was saved, too, wasn't he? I thought: since I'm a good swimmer I'll make use of it. I swam on my back. That's how I was saved!"

Stakhovich sat with dishevelled hair and looked like a small boy.

"Assuming then ... that you saved yourself," Vanya Zemnukhov said. "But why did you tell us that you'd been sent here by the headquarters of the partisan detachment?"

"Because they really did want to send me.... I thought: since I'm still alive, the position remains the same! After all, I wasn't just saving my skin. I wanted to fight the invaders and that's what I still want to do. I've had experience, I helped to organize the detachment and I have been under fire, that's why I said what I did!"

They had all felt so despondent that after Stakhovich's explanation they experienced a certain relief. All the same, it was a thoroughly unpleasant business. Why should it all have happened?

They all clearly felt that Stakhovich was telling the truth. But they also had a feeling that he had behaved badly and that he had told his story in an unpleasant way;

it was all annoying and puzzling and they did not know how to deal with him.

Indeed, Stakhovich was not an outsider. Nor was he a careerist or at all self-seeking. He was just the type of youngster who from early childhood had been in close contact with important people and had been spoilt through his constantly adopting certain outward manifestations of their power, at a period in his life when he was as yet unable to understand the true meaning and purpose of popular power, or the fact that the right to wield this power had been earned by these people through stubborn labour and by training their characters.

He had been a gifted lad to whom everything came easy. While still at school he had been noticed by important people for the simple reason that his Communist brothers were important people. Having moved among such people all his life, he had acquired the habit of talking to his school-friends about them as equals; and finding it easy to express in writing or in conversation not his own thoughts, which he was unable to develop at the time, but the thoughts of others, which he frequently heard expressed, he was considered by the district Komsomol leaders to be an active Komsomol, although as yet he had done nothing spectacular in his life to prove it. Rank-and-file Komsomols did not know him personally. They only saw him at all their meetings sitting on the platform or up on the speakers' rostrum and had come to regard him as some district, or even regional, official. While he did not understand the true meaning of the work performed by the people among whom he lived and moved, he knew all the details of their private and official relationships: who were rivals, and who supported whom. He had formed for himself a false idea of the art of using power, which he believed to be not to serve the people but to be a matter of skilful manoeuvring between one set of individuals and another, with a view to gaining the greatest support for oneself.

He imitated the mock-condescending manner these people used towards each other, their somewhat rough frankness and independence of judgement, without being aware of how immense and hard was the life which lay at the back of it. And instead of expressing his feelings with the lively directness of young people, he was always deliberately reserved, spoke in an affected, soft tone of voice, particularly when speaking to strangers over the telephone, and, in general, knew how to emphasize his superiority in his relations with his comrades.

Thus, from his earliest years he had become accustomed to regarding himself as someone above the ordinary run of people, for whom the ordinary rules of communal living were not binding.

Why indeed should he die instead of saving himself like the others, like the partisan Lyuba had met? And what right had that fellow to put him under such a suspicion when not he, Stakhovich, but the other more responsible people were to blame for the position the detachment had found itself in?

While the young people were sitting silently, hesitating about the position, Stakhovich even cheered up as a result of these arguments. Suddenly Sergei's harsh voice broke the silence:

"Firing flared up again in another place, but he lay on his back and swam away! Yet the firing flared up again because the detachment had gone over the top for a breakthrough, and there every man was of account. It means that they all went forward to save his life, doesn't it?"

Vanya Turkenich, the commander, had avoided looking at any of them, maintaining his soldierly bearing. There was an uncommonly open and resolute expression on his face, as he spoke up:

"A soldier must carry out orders. You ran away while fighting was in progress. Briefly, you deserted under fire. At the front people are shot for that or demoted to the penal battalion. People atone for their guilt with their blood."

"I'm not afraid to shed my blood," Stakhovich said; the colour drained from his face.

"You're just a swanker, so there!" Lyuba said.

They all looked at Oleg: what did he think of it all? Oleg very calmly said:

"Vanya Turkenich has said it all; it cannot be put better. And judging by Stakhovich's behaviour it's clear that he does not recognize discipline at all. Can a person like that belong to the headquarters of our detachment?"

When Oleg had spoken, everything they had all been thinking burst forth. The boys rounded passionately on Stakhovich. They had all taken the oath together. How could Stakhovich have done so with such an act on his conscience? Why could he not have made a clean breast of it? What sort of comrade was he that he could desecrate such a solemn occasion? Of course, they could not for another minute keep such a comrade at headquarters. The girls, Lyuba and Ulya, said nothing at all because they despised him so much and it was this that hurt him more than anything else.

He was utterly crestfallen and looked humiliated and endeavoured to look into someone's eyes while he repeated again and again:

"Why don't you believe me? Put me to any kind of test...."

It was at this point that Oleg showed that he was no longer Oleg, but Kashuk.

"You see it yourself, don't you, that you can't remain at headquarters?" he asked.

And Stakhovich had to admit that, of course, that was correct.

"It's important for you to understand this yourself," Oleg went on. "We'll give you an assignment all right, and not just one. We'll put you to the test. You'll still lead your group of five, and you'll have plenty of opportunity of restoring your good name."

"He comes from such a fine family. It's a shame, that's what it is!" Lyuba said.

The vote was taken to exclude Yevgeny Stakhovich from the headquarters of the Young Guard. He sat with his head bent. Then he rose and, overcoming his feelings, said:

"This hurts me very much—you can understand. But I know you couldn't act otherwise. I'm not taking offence. I swear—" His lips quivered and he ran from the room.

They remained gravely silent for some minutes. This, their first disappointment in a comrade, had not been easy for them. And it had been hard to be so merciless.

Then Oleg grinned broadly and, with a slight stutter, said:

"H-he'll recover all right, you m-mark my words!"

Vanya Turkenich's soft voice supported his assurance.

"D'you imagine such things don't happen at the front? The young soldier turns coward at first, but what a fine soldier he develops into!"

Lyuba felt it was time to give the details of her meeting with Protsenko. To be sure, she said nothing about how she had come to meet him—there were some aspects of her work which she was not at liberty to divulge—but, pacing the room, she described vividly how he had received her and what he had said. There was great animation when Lyuba related how the representative of the Partisan Headquarters had commended them and praised Oleg and kissed Lyuba when she left. He must, most certainly, be really pleased with them.

Excited, happy, and even a little surprised at seeing themselves in this new light, they began to shake hands and congratulated each other.

"Just think, Vanya—just imagine!" Oleg said to Zemnukhov, happiness shining on his face. "The Young Guard is a reality—recognized even by the regional leadership!"

Lyuba put her arm round Ulya with whom she had become good friends since the gathering in Turkenich's home. She had not yet had a chance to greet her and now she gave her a sisterly kiss.

Oleg then consulted his notebook again and Vanya Zemnukhov, who at their last meeting had been made the organizer of the groups of five, proposed that they should appoint leaders for other groups of five, for the organization would grow.

"Let's start with Pervomaisky, shall we?" he said looking merrily at Ulya through his professorial spectacles.

Ulya rose and stood with her arms straight down by her sides and all their faces unconsciously reflected the splendid, selfless, happy feeling which maidenly beauty never fails to summon up in clean minds. Ulya, however, did not notice the general admiration.

"We, that is Tolya Popov and I, nominate Vitya Petrov and Maya Peglivanova," she said. Suddenly she noticed that Lyuba was watching her with a worried look. "And Lyuba could take on Vosmidomiki district—we'll be neighbours then," she added. Her deep voice was calm and she spoke easily.

"What an idea!... Really!" Lyuba blushed and flapped her little white hands; what sort of an organizer, indeed, was she!

They all supported Ulya and then Lyuba at once calmed down: in a flash she saw herself the organizer in Vosmidomiki district, and she very much liked the idea.

Vanya Turkenich found the time had come to put forward the proposal he and Oleg had agreed upon during the night. He reported all that had happened to Oleg and told how it could have been a menace not only to Oleg but to the whole organization. He suggested that a decision be taken which would once and for all ban Oleg from taking part in operations without permission from headquarters.

"I don't think there's any need for further explanations," he said. "This ban should, of course, also apply to me."

"H-he's right," Oleg said.

So the decision was taken and it was unanimous. Sergei then rose from his chair, utterly confused.

"I've got two announcements to make," he said gloomily and puffed out his thick lips. They all found it so amusing that it was some time before they gave him a chance to speak.

"First of all I want to say something about this Ignat Fomin. Are we really going to put up with the swine?" he burst out, his face dark with anger. "That Judas betrayed Ostapchuk and Uncle Andrei and we don't yet know how many of our miners he's got on his black conscience! What do I suggest? I suggest that we kill him," Sergei said. "You can give that job to me because I'll kill him anyway," he added, and it was immediately clear to them that Sergei would really do it.

Oleg's face became very grave. Deep, long wrinkles lined his forehead. All the headquarters members were still.

"What about it? He's right," Vanya Turkenich said in a quiet, calm voice. "Ignat Fomin's a foul traitor who denounces our people. He must be hanged. Hanged where the people can see him. With a notice round his neck saying why he's been hanged. As a lesson to others. What about it?" There was a note of cruelty in his voice which was unexpected, coming from him. "They wouldn't show us any mercy! Give me and Tyulenin the job."

They all felt a little easier about it, when they heard Turkenich supporting Tyulenin. Deep as was their hatred of traitors, it was difficult for them to take that step. But now that Turkenich, a Red Army officer and their senior comrade had added his opinion, it meant that so it had to be.

"We must, of course, get permission from our older comrades," Oleg said. "In view of that we must be ready with our own general opinion. I shall first put to the vote Tyulenin's proposal concerning Fomin, and then the question as to who shall be entrusted with the task," he explained.

"The question is sufficiently clear," Vanya Zemnukhov said.

"Yes, the question's quite clear, but all the same I'm going to put the question of Fomin to a separate vote," Oleg insisted with a kind of sullen doggedness.

They could all see why Oleg insisted on this. They had taken an oath. Each of them had to decide again according to his conscience. In the gravest silence they voted for the execution of Fomin and charged Turkenich and Tyulenin to carry it out.

"That was a correct decision! That's what they deserve, the swine!" Sergei said with a passionate light in his eyes. "Now for my second announcement."

Natalya Alexeyevna, the hospital surgeon with the small dumpy hands and the ruthless, efficient expression in her eyes, had told Sergei that some young people in a small settlement, also called Krasnodon, about ten miles from the town, had formed a resistance group. Natalya Alexeyevna herself was not a member of the group but she had learned of its existence from Antonina Yeliseyenko, a teacher and her mother's neighbour who actually lived in Krasnodon settlement; she had promised Antonina Yeliseyenko that she would help her establish contact with the town.

On Sergei's suggestion, it was decided to put Valya Borts in touch with this group. The decision was made in her absence, because the Ivantsova girls and Valya, all of them liaison workers, did not attend the meetings at headquarters. Actually they were, at that moment, sitting in the shed in the yard with Marina, keeping a look-out for the headquarters.

The members of the Young Guard headquarters had made use of the opportunity provided by the absence for a few days of Yelena Nikolayevna and Nikolai Nikolayevich, who had gone into the countryside to visit Marina's relatives in order to exchange a few articles for bread. Grandma Vera had allowed the young people to imagine that she thought they were assembled for a party, and she had taken Aunt Marina with her little boy to the shed.

While the young people had been deliberating, it had grown dark, and Grandma Vera entered the room. Looking over the top of her spectacles, with the broken side piece that had been tied to the frame with black cotton, she saw that the bottle of vodka on the table had not been touched and the mugs had not been used.

"You might perhaps like some tea, I've just made some," she said, much to the embarrassment of the conspirators. "And I've persuaded Marina to sleep in the shed with the boy, the air's fresher there."

Grandma fetched Valya, Nina and Olga, brought in the teapot and produced some sweets from the very bottom of a concealed drawer—not of the sideboard but of the chest of drawers; then she closed the shutters, lit the oil-lamp and left the room.

And now indeed, as they sat round the smoking oil-lamp, its small, flickering flame picking out from the gloom only a few details of the faces, clothing, and articles in general, they really began to look like conspirators. Their voices grew hushed and mysterious.

"Would you like to listen to Moscow?" Oleg asked softly.

They all took the remark for a joke. Lyuba alone gave a slight start.

"How, Moscow?" she asked.

"On one condition: no questions!"

Oleg went out into the yard and returned almost at once.

"Be patient for a little," he said and disappeared into the darkness of Nikolai Nikolayevich's room.

The young people sat in silence not knowing whether to believe it or not. But would people joke about things of that sort at a time like this!

"Nina, come and help me!" Oleg called. She went to him.

Then suddenly from Uncle Kolya's room came the soft, so familiar but now half-forgotten, hissing and light crackling, then snatches of music: somewhere people were dancing. German marches kept breaking through. The steady voice of an elderly person announced in English the world's casualty figures; someone talked endlessly in German, rapidly and angrily as though afraid he would not be allowed to finish.

And then, crystal-clear above the faint crackling in the air that seemed to come in waves into the room, from the vastnesses of space, came the familiar voice of the announcer Levitan, solemn and matter of fact, low and velvety but not at all ponderous, announcing easily:

"From the Soviet Information Bureau. Evening communiqué for September 7...."

"Write it down, take it down!" Vanya Zemnukhov whispered excitedly and searched for his own pencil. "We'll put it out tomorrow!"

Then coming to them a thousand miles through space from free territory the same free, easy voice announced:

"...During the course of September 7, our forces engaged the enemy in fierce battles west and south-west of Stalingrad and also in the neighbourhood of Novorossiisk and Mozdok. There was no important change in the position on the other fronts...."

It was as though the echoes from the great battle had entered the room.

Leaning forward taut as bow-strings, their eyes large and dark in the light of the oil-lamp and faces like those seen on icons, they listened in complete silence to the voice from land that was free.

Leaning against the door, unnoticed by anyone, stood Grandma Vera, her lean and wrinkled face so much resembling that of Dante Alighieri.

Chapter 6

ELECTRICITY was supplied only for the German offices. Nikolai Nikolayevich had made use of the fact that the transmission line to the *Direktion* and the Commandant's office did not pass along the street, but between his yard and that of his neighbour, with a post right by Korostylev's house. He kept his receiving set under the floor boards beneath the chest of drawers in his room, and whenever it was to be used, the lead for it was taken through the hinged ventilation pane of the window, connected to a length of flex wound round a long pole and clipped on to a hook at the top of the pole by means of which the pole could be suspended close to the transmission post from the electricity mains.

The communiqué of the Soviet Information Bureau! They had to have a printing outfit whatever it might cost them to get it.

Volodya Osmukhin, Zhora Arutyuniants and Tolya the Thunderer had managed to find only scraps of type when they had dug it up in the park. Probably the people who had buried it had had no packing materials handy, had simply put the type into the hole and covered it with soil. The German soldiers digging pits for lorries and AA guns had at first not bothered to find out what it was and scattered the type along with the soil. But later they had realized their mistake and reported the matter to their superiors. Most of the type was then probably taken away, but some of it still remained at the bottom of the pit. In the course of a few days' patient digging the lads had found scraps of type over a radius of several yards from the spot indicated in the plan and had carefully collected every letter. The type was not suited to Lyutikov's requirements and he had given Volodya permission to use it for Young Guard purposes.

Zemnukhov's older brother Alexander, who was now in the army, was a printer by trade and had for a long time worked at the print-shop of the local newspaper, *Sotsialisticheskaya Rodina*, where Vanya had frequently visited him. Under Vanya's supervision Volodya now set to work to build a small printing-press. He made the metal parts for it secretly in the machine-shop where he worked, while Zhora undertook to provide a wooden crate to keep everything in and also to make some type cases.

Zhora's father was a cabinet-maker. Contrary to Zhora's expectations neither his father nor even his mother, woman of character though she was, had taken to arms after the arrival of the Germans. But Zhora had no doubt that he would be able gradually to draw them into his own activities. After mature deliberation he had reached the conclusion that his mother, being a woman who was rather too energetic, would have to be brought in later and that he had better start with his father. His father was a quiet middle-aged man shorter by a head than his son. The lad took after his mother in every way: character, build and the colour of his hair which was jet-black. The father was highly displeased at the idea of the underground workers sending him such a punctilious order through the medium of his adolescent son, but he proceeded, without his wife's knowledge, to make both the crate and the type cases. He was not in a position to know, of course, that Zhora and Volodya as group leaders, each of five other youngsters, were important people in their own right.

The friendship between these two lads was by now so great that they could not for a single day exist without seeing each other. Relations between Lyudmila Osmukhina and Zhora, however, remained as tense and formal as before.

It was undoubtedly a case of incompatibility of temperament. Both were very well read, but Zhora liked scientific and political reading, while Lyudmila was chiefly interested in books which dealt with human passions, and it should be stated here that Lyudmila was older than the lad. To be sure, whenever Zhora tried to look into the vague future, he was flattered to think that Lyudmila would have complete command of three foreign languages; still, he considered that sort of training insufficiently profound and was, perhaps, rather tactless in his efforts to make of her a civil engineer.

From the moment they met, Lyudmila's clear, flashing eyes and Zhora's, which were black and determined would cross like steel blades. And all the time they were together, for the most part not alone, they would attack each other with sharp rejoinders, supercilious and stinging on Lyudmila's part, pointedly restrained and didactic on the part of Zhora.

At last the day came when Zhora called his friends together in his room: Volodya Osmukhin, Tolya the Thunderer, and Vanya Zemnukhov, who was the oldest of them all and their leader and who now, more as the author of most of the Young Guard's leaflets and slogans than as the poet, naturally took a greater interest in printing than the rest. And there was the complete printing-press. With a wheezing and coughing that sounded as though it was coming out of a barrel, Tolya Orlov paraded several times round the room with it to demonstrate that, in an emergency, the apparatus could be carried about by one person.

They already had a flat brush and a roller, and in place of printer's ink Zhora's father, who had painted and varnished wood all his life, had produced what he called "an original mixture." They set to work at once to sort the letters into their cases, while short-sighted Vanya Zemnukhov, to whom all letters looked like o, seated himself on Zhora's bed saying he failed to see how this one letter o could possibly make all the letters of the alphabet.

Just at that moment there was a tap on the curtained window but they did not get into a panic: no German or policeman had ever yet come to this distant end of the suburb. Actually Oleg and Turkenich had arrived; eager to print something as soon as possible on their printing-press, they had found it impossible to remain sitting at home.

But it later transpired that they were not really such simpletons. Turkenich quietly called Zhora aside and together they went out into the garden, while Oleg unconcernedly began to help Volodya and Tolya.

Turkenich and Zhora went to the far end of the garden fence and lay down in the grass. Frequent clouds overshadowed the sun which, with the approach of autumn, had lost much of its warmth; both the grass and the ground were still wet after the recent rain. Turkenich leaned over to Zhora and whispered a few words. Zhora's reply, given with complete assurance, was what he had expected:

"Quite right! It is just, and it will teach the other blackguards a lesson! Of course, I agree."

Oleg and Vanya Turkenich obtained the permission of the underground district Party committee and now they had a job before them which required a degree of subtlety. Young people had to be found who would undertake the job out of a sense of justice and discipline; but they required to have, in addition, a high moral sense of duty which was so combined with will-power, that their hands would not tremble.

Turkenich and Tyulenin had first of all considered Sergei Levashov who was a purposeful lad and had had a great deal of experience. Then they thought of Kovalyov: fearless, well-intentioned, of powerful physique—they needed someone like him. Tyulenin suggested Pirozhok but Turkenich turned him down because Pirozhok was inclined to be reckless. Tyulenin would not entertain the idea of his own pal, Vitka Lukyanchenko; he wanted to spare him from the unpleasant job. Finally they settled on Zhora. They were not mistaken in him.

"But haven't you yet settled who is to be on the tribunal?" Zhora asked. "There'll be no need to make it a lengthy investigation, but it's important that the accused himself should see that he is given a trial before being executed."

"We shall form the tribunal," Turkenich said.

"We shall pass judgement on him in the name of the people. for now we are the legal representatives of the people here." Zhora's determined black eyes shone brightly.

"Stout-hearted lad," Turkenich mused. Aloud he said, "We still need one person more."

Zhora pondered over the question. Volodya crossed his mind but Volodya was too sensitive for a job of this kind.

"I've got Radik Yurkin in my group. You know him, from our school. I think he'll suit."

"He's only a kid. He'll take it too much to heart."

"Nothing of the kind! Kids don't feel such things. It's adult folk like us who are always taking things too much to heart," Zhora declared, "but kids are not like us, they're harder. He's a terrific lad, and always as cool as a cucumber."

One day while Zhora's father was doing some carpentering job for them in the lean-to shed, Zhora caught his mother watching through the keyhole, and he had been forced to tell her that he, Zhora, was fully capable of standing on his own feet and that his comrades were quite grown-up too, and she needn't be surprised if they all got married the next day.

Zhora and Vanya Turkenich had returned just in time: the type had been sorted out and Volodya was already busy setting a stick of several lines. Zhora quickly dipped the brush into the "original mixture," Volodya slapped down the paper and put the roller over it. The printed text had a mourning edge round it caused by the metal plate, which Volodya, being inexperienced, had not ground down sufficiently in the machine-shop where he worked. In addition, the letters were not all the same size, but they would have to put up with that. The most important thing was that before them lay a page of print, and what Volodya Osmukhin had set up was there for all to read:

"Don't sneak out with Vanya don't get on our nerves all the same we know the secret of your heart nananana."

Volodya explained that he dedicated these few lines to Zhora and that he had been trying to select words containing the letter *n*; that accounted for the *nananana* because there seemed to be more of the letter *n* in their "fount" than of anything else. The reason there were no punctuation marks was that he had forgotten they had to be set up like the letters.

Oleg suddenly became excited.

"You know that two Pervomaisky girls are asking to be admitted to the Komsomol?" he asked, looking at each of them in turn.

"And I have a chap in my group who wants to join the Komsomol," Zhora Arutyuniants said. The chap was the same Radik Yurkin who, so far, was the only member Zhora Arutyuniants had in his "group of five."

"We can use the 'Young Guard' press to print temporary Komsomol membership cards," Oleg exclaimed. "Don't you see—now that we're an officially recognized organization, we've a right to enrol members into the Komsomol."

The man with the eyes like a python, deep-set among the numerous fleshy wrinkles, was as good as dead, despite the fact that his long body and the narrow head in the old-fashioned peaked cap was still walking about from place to place, and his arms and legs were moving.

Whether on duty by day or prowling about by night, vengeance followed on his heels. It watched him through his window, when with his wife he was gloating over the trinkets and rags stolen from the family of his latest victim. Vengeance knew of each of his crimes and kept a reckoning of them. Vengeance pursued him in the guise of a lad, who was little more than a boy, nimble as a cat and had eyes that could see in the dark. If Fomin had known how merciless was this vengeance, this barefoot lad, he would even then have ceased all movement which showed outward signs of life.

Fomin was a dead man because every one of his deeds and actions were no longer prompted by the simple thirst for personal gain and vengeance but, behind the veneer of officialdom and a fine appearance, by an infinitely all-embracing hatred towards the life he had to live, towards all people, even towards the Germans.

This malignant hatred had always devastated Fomin's mind, but never had his hatred been so terrible and hopeless as now, because the last mental support of his existence, foul though it was, had crumbled. For though the crimes he had been committing were so great, he had always hoped that he would achieve such a position of power, that all the people would go in fear of him and out of fear would respect him and bow before him. Then, surrounded by respect of the kind that rich people enjoyed in times gone by, he would reach the safe harbour of prosperity and independence.

But it had turned out otherwise; for far from having acquired for himself the recognized security of property, he now had no hope of ever doing so. He stole the belongings of the people he arrested and killed, and the Germans, though they turned a blind eye to it, despised him for the mercenary, dependent, ignorant blackguard and thief that he was. He knew that the Germans only needed his services for so long as he would continue to do what they wanted in order to consolidate their domination, and that as soon as this domination was assured and law and order, *Ordnung*, had been established, they would throw him out or even do away with him.

True enough, there were many who dreaded him, but even they despised and shunned him, as did everyone else. And while he had no proper standing, while he was without the respect of the people, no amount of trinkets and rags brought home to his wife could give him the slightest satisfaction. He and his wife lived worse than animals, for even animals do enjoy the sunshine and their food, and have the joy of procreation.

In common with all the police, Ignat Fomin's duties included patrolling the streets and guarding office buildings as well as assisting in arrests and raids on people's homes.

This particular night he was on duty at the *Direktion* which occupied the premises of the Gorky School in the park.

A gusty wind sighed in the branches of the trees and moaned round the slender tree-trunks, driving moist leaves along the avenues. A fine misty rain was falling, the low sky was dark and overcast, but a trace of the moon and stars was felt behind the mist. The small clumps of trees made dark, greyish patches, their damp outlines merging with the sky, melting into it.

Standing opposite each other in the wide avenue, the brick school building and the abandoned wooden summer theatre loomed out in the darkness like huge boulders.

Tightly buttoned up in a long black overcoat with upturned collar, Fomin was striding up and down the avenue between the two buildings, never passing beyond them, as though he were attached to a chain. From time to time, he would halt at the wooden arch of the park entrance and lean against the gate post. He was standing thus peering in the darkness towards the houses in Sadovaya Street, when suddenly a powerful hand gripped his throat from behind so that not even a gurgle escaped and forced him over backwards until something in his spine cracked and he fell to the ground. That same instant he felt several pairs of hands on his body. One hand still held him by the throat, and a second pressed on his nose like an iron vice, and a third thrust a gag into his convulsively gaping mouth and with something like a rough towel securely bound the lower part of his face.

When he had recovered slightly he found he was bound hand and foot, lying on his back under the wooden arch of the park gates, the grey sky and vague, hanging mistiness forming a canopy overhead.

Several dark human shapes whose faces he could not distinguish stood motionless on either side of him.

One of them, his slim silhouette outlined sharply in the night, looked at the arch and said quietly:

"This will suit us perfectly."

Using his sharp elbows and knees skilfully a small, skinny lad climbed the arch and fumbled about for a time in the centre of it. Then suddenly, high above him, Fomin saw the thick rope noose swinging to and fro against the diffused greyish light of the sky.

"Tie it in a double clove hitch," ordered one of the boys on the ground, the black peak of his cap pointing towards the sky.

Fomin heard the voice, and he suddenly saw again his living-room in Shanghai district, the pots of indoor plants, the thick-set figure of a man sitting at the table with blue coal-marks in the skin of his face, and this boy. Ignat Fomin's long frame began to writhe violently like a worm over the wet cold ground; as he writhed and squirmed, he moved from the place where they had placed him, but someone in a bulky coat like a sailor's pea-jacket, incredibly broad-shouldered and squat, with powerful arms, shifted Fomin back with his foot to his former place.

Fomin recognized Kovalyov who had been with him in the police force but had been thrown out. Besides him, Fomin also recognized one of the chauffeurs of the *Direktion*, another powerful broad-shouldered chap. Fomin had seen him earlier that day in the garage, where he had gone to have a smoke before going on duty. It was strange that in his present position Fomin should immediately have thought that this driver was probably the main culprit in the numerous mysterious break-downs *Direktion* lorries had suffered. The German administration had complained about them and the matter should be reported. Just at that moment he heard a voice above him pronouncing softly and solemnly with a slight Armenian accent:

"In the name of the Union of Soviet Socialist Republics—"

Fomin instantly lay still and raised his eyes to the sky, again saw the thick rope noose hanging over him in the misty, grey sky and the skinny lad perched on top of the arch, gripping it with his legs and gazing down. Then the voice with the Armenian accent stopped speaking. Fomin was seized with such panic that he began to writhe wildly. Several powerful arms grasped him and lifted him on to his feet. The lad on the arch ripped off the towel which bound his jaws and placed the noose round his neck.

Fomin tried to force the gag from his mouth, made a few convulsive movements in the air and hung suspended with his feet just unable to reach the ground, his long black overcoat buttoned closely round him. Vanya Turkenich turned him round to face Sadovaya Street and using a safety pin attached a piece of paper to his chest, explaining the crime for which Ignat Fomin had been executed.

The lads then dispersed, each going his own way, with the exception of little Radik Yurkin who went off to spend the night in Zhora's home in the suburbs.

"How d'you feel?" Zhora asked in a terrible whisper, his black eyes glittering in the dark.

Radik was shivering.

"I'm sleepy, I can't keep my eyes open ... I'm used to going to bed very early," he replied and looked up at Zhora with meek eyes.

Sergei Tyulenin stood under the trees in the park, sunk deep in thought. Here, at long last, the oath which he had taken the day he learned that Fomin had betrayed to the Germans the big, kindly man he had seen in his home, had been fulfilled. Sergei had not only insisted that the sentence should be carried out. He had also devoted all his physical and mental powers to the task. And now the deed had been done. His mind was filled with a sense of satisfaction and the excitement of success, the last, belated flames of vengeance and a terrible weariness and longing to wach himself clean in hot water, an extraordinary desire to have a grand, friendly talk about something altogether remote, something simple and clean like the whispering of the leaves, the murmuring of a brook, the light of the sun on closed, weary eyes....

His greatest happiness now would have been to be at Valya's side. But he would never dare to visit her at night, especially with her mother and young sister in the house. Besides, Valya was not in the town; she had gone to the small settlement of Krasnodon.

And so it came about that on this strange, misty night, when a fine rain drifted through the air without ceasing, Sergei Tyulenin, shivering in his damp shirt, his feet spattered with mud and blue with the cold, rapped on the window of Vanya Zemnukhov's home.

They sat in the kitchen by the light of an oil-lamp, with the windows blacked out. The fire crackled, a large family kettle was heating on the stove, for Vanya had decided to wash down his friend with hot water. With his legs tucked under him, Sergei Tyulenin sat as close as possible to the fire. Gusts of wind blew against the window, showering it with fine raindrops; the steady sound of them and the buffeting of the wind, which even there, in the kitchen, made the oil-lamp flicker, reminded the two friends of the sorry plight of any solitary wayfarer out in the steppe and of how good it was to be together in the warm little kitchen.

Vanya, in his spectacles and with nothing on his feet, said in his muffled bass:

"That's how I picture him, in his tiny peasant cottage with the snow-storm howling outside, no one with him but Nurse Arina. The snow-storm rages outside and the nurse sits by the spinning-wheel, and the spinning-wheel hums, the fire crackles in the stove. I can distinctly feel it all, I come from the countryside myself and my mama, you know, can't read or write. She also comes from the countryside. Just like yours.... I can still remember our little cottage; I can remember lying on the stove when I was six and my brother Sasha coming home from school and learning a poem.... And then I can remember them driving the ewes from the flock, and I mounted the ram and kicked the heels of my bast shoes into its sides to urge him on, but he threw me."

Vanya suddenly felt confused and fell silent. In a few moments, however, he began again:

"He was always immensely happy, of course, when one of his friends came to visit him.... And I can just picture Pushchin coming to see him, for instance. He would hear the horse bells. 'Who's that?' he would think. 'Is it the gendarmes coming for him?' But it would be his friend Pushchin.... Then I can imagine him sitting alone with the nurse; they were somewhere in a snow-bound village far away, without any light; in those days they used splinters for lighting. Do you remember *Storm-Clouds Darken the Sky*? You must. This is the bit that particularly moves me."

Vanya got up and for some reason stood in front of Sergei, as he began to recite:

> *Let us drink, dear old companion,*
> *You who shared my sorry start;*
> *Get the mug and drown our troubles;*
> *That's the way to cheer the heart.*
>
> *Sing the ballad of the titmouse*
> *Who beyond the seas was gone,*
> *Or the song about the maiden*
> *Fetching water just at dawn.* *

Sergei sat quite still, pressed close to the stove, his full lips protruding; his eyes as they watched Vanya held an expression that was stern, yet tender. The lid of the kettle on the stove began to bob up and down and the water merrily bubbled and hissed.

"Enough of poetry!" Vanya said, awaking to the present. "Get your things off! I'm going to give you a first-class wash, old chap!" he said gaily. "No, come on, strip them all off! I've got a bast scrubber ready for you."

While Sergei undressed, Vanya took the kettle from the stove, produced a wash-basin and put it on a stool, together with a well-used piece of evil-smelling, household soap.

* A. Pushkin, *Winter Evening*. From *The Works Of Alexander Pushkin*. Nonesuch Press, London. (Printed in U.S.A.)

"In our village in Tambov Province, there was once an old man who'd been an attendant in the Sandunov Baths in Moscow all his life," Vanya said, seating himself on another stool with his long legs spread out. "You know what being a bath attendant is like, don't you? Well, just imagine you were at a bath-house. Imagine yourself a grand gentleman or that you were too lazy to wash yourself, well then, you just hired an attendant to do the job; he was always a bewhiskered old devil, and he'd give you a scrub-down, you see? The old fellow I knew used to say that he'd scrubbed no less than a million and a half people altogether during his life. And you know, he was really proud of it—of having made all those people clean! Well, you know yourself what people are like, a week later they were all dirty again!"

Sergei grinned, tossed aside his last garment, poured some more hot water into the bowl and blissfully dipped his rough curly head into it.

"Your wardrobe's nothing to be proud of," Vanya said, hanging up the damp clothing over the stove. "Worse than mine, even.... But I see you know all the rules. Here— pour it into the refuse pail, and take some more. Don't worry about splashing—I'll mop the floor afterwards."

His face suddenly broke into a rough, resigned grin; exaggerating his customary stoop, dangling his arms in front of him as though his long, slim hands were suddenly heavy and benumbed, he said in the gruffest bass he could muster:

"Please turn round now, Your Grace, I'll do your back."

Looking at his friend out of the corner of his eye, Sergei silently soaped the scrubber and chuckled. He handed the scrubber to Vanya and, resting his hands on the stool, presented his sunburnt, lean and muscular back with the prominent backbone to Vanya.

Because his eyesight was poor Vanya went about the job of scrubbing Sergei's back rather clumsily. In a surprisingly lordly accent, Sergei cried out querulously:

"What's wrong with you, my good man? Weak or just lazy? I am not at all pleased with you, my man...."

"Well, I get little enough food, Your Grace. Judge for yourself!" Vanya replied gravely excusing himself.

Just then the kitchen door opened. Vanya, in his horn-rimmed spectacles and sleeves rolled up, and Sergei, naked and with soap on his back both spun round: in the door-way, in vest and underpants stood Vanya's father; he was tall and lean and his arms hung down in precisely the same fashion as Vanya had only just been mimicking. He gazed at them from faded eyes. He stood there for some moments, then silently turned round and left the room, closing the door behind him. They listened to his steps shuffling down the passage to the living-room.

"The storm has passed," Vanya said calmly. But he did not scrub Sergei's back with the same enthusiasm as before. "What about a tip, Your Grace?"

"God will reward you," Sergei replied, not sure that it was the correct thing to say to a bath attendant, and sighed.

"Yes ... I don't know how things are with you, but we'll be having trouble with our mothers and fathers," Vanya said gravely when Sergei, clean, rosy and combed, was again sitting at the small table by the stove.

But Sergei was not afraid of any difficulties with parents. He regarded Vanya with his thoughts elsewhere.

"Could you let me have a scrap of paper and a pencil? I'm going in a minute, but I've got to make a note of something first," he said.

And while Vanya pretended to be busy tidying the kitchen, this is what Sergei Tyulenin wrote:

"Valya, I never thought I should have taken it so much to heart that you have gone away alone. I keep wondering whether everything is all right. Don't let's ever separate again, let's do everything together. Valya, if I am killed I ask you one thing: come to my grave and remember me with a soft, kind word."

Barefoot in the icy drizzle he once again followed the roundabout route through the Little Shanghais, fighting his way through ravines and pot-holes, against the moaning gusts of wind; again he ran through the park and along Derevyannay Street in order to hand the note at daybreak to Valya's little sister Lyusia.

Chapter 7

VALYA AND NATALYA ALEXEYEVNA had taken the road across the steppe early one dull morning. In her canvas gym shoes Natalya nimbly stepped out on the glistening wet surface of the road, in her customary businesslike way, but Valya's pleasure in the walk was spoiled by the thoughts of her mother.

The first task she was carrying out alone was fraught with danger to herself, but what about Mama?

The way her mother had looked at her when she had announced quite casually that she was just going on a visit to Natalya Alexeyevna for a few days! At a time like this, when Mother was so lonely without Father in the house, what a cruelly heavy weight her daughter's selfishness must have hung round her mother's heart!... And supposing she already suspected something!

"Tosya Yeliseyenko to whom I shall introduce you is a teacher," Natalya was saying. "She's a neighbour of my mother's or, rather, she and her mother share a two-room flat with my mother. She's got a strong, independent character; she's much older than you, and I'll tell you frankly she'll be a bit embarrassed at my bringing a pretty girl along instead of a bearded underground fighter." Natalya Alexeyevna was always greatly concerned about the precise meaning of what she said and not at all concerned about their effect on the listener. "I know Sergei well. He's a very serious boy and in a way I trust him more than I do myself. If Sergei tells me that you're from the district underground organization, that's good enough for me. And I want to help you. If Tosya isn't sufficiently frank with you, then go to Kolya Sumskoi, who, I'm sure, is the most important man there, judging by Tosya's attitude to him. Tosya's mother and mine are being made to believe they're in love, but, although I have been too busy with other things to organize my own personal affairs, I know quite a bit about the affairs of young people in general. I happen to know that Kolya Sumskoi is in love with Lida Androsova, and she's a terrible flirt," Natalya said disapprovingly, "but undoubtedly she's also a member of their organization," she added moved by her strong sense of fair play. "Should you find it necessary for Kolya Sumskoi to get in personal touch with the district organization then I shall use my position as doctor at the district labour exchange, and prescribe two days' sick-leave for him; he works at a small pit somewhere. To be precise, he turns windlass...."

"And the Germans believe your certificates?" Valya asked.

"The Germans!" Natalya exclaimed. "They not only believe my certificates, they've a blind faith in any piece of paper with an official stamp on it. The management of that pit is Russian and it's all right. There's a sergeant or corporal of the technical corps attached to the director, just like everywhere else. But he's a complete blockhead. We, Russians, seem so alike to them that they can't keep account of who is at work and who is absent."

Things turned out exactly as Natalya Alexeyevna had predicted. Devoid of all greenery Krasnodon mining settlement was a straggling, unsheltered sort of place, with its large barrack-like buildings, immense black tips and idle pit-head pile-drivers. Valya was destined to spend two whole days in these inhospitable surroundings and, moreover, among people who were difficult to convince that behind her long, dark eyelashes and golden plaits stood the powerful authority of the Young Guard.

Natalya's mother lived in the older, most densely populated part of the settlement, which had been formed by the gradual merging of a number of farmsteads. There the little houses even boasted small gardens. But the bushes in the gardens had already turned yellow. As a result of the recent rains a cream-like mud, almost waist-deep, had formed in the streets and would, no doubt, remain there until the winter came.

During these days a Rumanian formation passed uninterruptedly through the settlement in the direction of Stalingrad; its guns and wagons, pulled by struggling, emaciated horses, stood for hours on end in the mud, while the drivers cursed them in Russian that echoed through the whole mining settlement, their voices like steppe bagpipes.

Tosya Yeliseyenko, a plump attractive Ukrainian girl of twenty-three, with black, passionate eyes, told Valya outright that in her opinion the district centre of the underground was guilty of underrating a mining settlement like Krasnodon. Why had no leader yet visited Krasnodon mining settlement? Why had they not complied with their request that a responsible person be sent in to instruct them on the work to be done?

Valya thought it right to explain that she represented only the Young Guard youth organization which was working under the guidance of the underground district Party committee.

"Then why hasn't one of the members of the Young Guard headquarters come to see us?" Tosya said with a hostile gleam in her eyes. "We've got a youth organization too, you know," she added proudly.

"I'm an authorized messenger from the headquarters," Valya said equally proudly and quivered her upper lip slightly. "To send a member of the headquarters to an organization which has so far shown no signs that it is doing any work at all would have been rash and not at all in line with conspiratorial work, if you understand anything at all about it."

"Shown no signs of doing any work!" Tosya exclaimed angrily. "A fine headquarters, I must say, that is unaware of the work of its organizations! I'm not fool enough to talk about our activities to somebody we don't know."

It is possible that these two proud, nice-looking girls might never have reached agreement but for the assistance of Kolya Sumskoi.

True, when Valya mentioned his name Tosya swore she'd never heard of him. But Valya coldly and pointedly told her that the Young Guard was quite aware of Sumskoi's leading position in the organization and that if Tosya refused to take her to him, she would seek him out for herself.

"It'd be interesting to know how you'd seek him out," Tosya said, a little alarmed.

"Possibly through Lida Androsova."

"There's no reason why Lida Androsova should not treat you just as I do."

"So much the worse.... I shall go out and look for him

myself and as I don't know his address I may accidentally get him into trouble."

Tosya Yeliseyenko was forced to give in.

Once they reached Kolya Sumskoi everything was plain sailing. He lived in a roomy country cottage on the very edge of the mining settlement; beyond the house was the open steppe. His father had at one time been a pit carter, but their mode of life had always had a rural background.

Sumskoi had a swarthy complexion and an intelligent face full of his grandfather's Ukrainian courage and a mixture of cunning and directness which was his greatest charm. He screwed up his eyes, listened patiently to Valya's haughty and Tosya's passionate explanations, then without a word beckoned them out of the cottage. Climbing a ladder which was resting against the wall, he reached the loft and invited the girls to follow him. With a loud fluttering several pigeons flew out of it and rose into the sky, others settled on his head and shoulders while others tried to perch on his hands. He finally held out his hand to a beautifully shaped tumbler pigeon as pure-white as only a dove can be.

A youth of truly Herculean build was sitting in the loft. At the sight of a strange girl he became dreadfully embarrassed and quickly concealed something under the hay; Sumskoi signed to him that everything was all right. The Hercules grinned, pushed the hay aside and Valya saw a wireless receiver.

"Volodya Zhdanov ... meet Valya the Unknown," Sumskoi said without smiling. "Well, here we are, three of us: Tosya, Volodya and I, the sinner in hell. We're the leading trinity of our organization," he explained, covered with cooing pigeons, nestling close to him and occasionally flapping their wings.

While they were discussing whether Sumskoi would be able to go back to the town with Valya, she felt the Hercules looking at her and found his look disturbing. She knew of another warrior lad like this one—Kovalyov of the Young Guard who, because of his physical strength and kind heart, was called the Little Tsar in the outlying districts. But this one here was of extraordinarily imposing proportions, both the face and the body; his neck seemed to be cast in bronze and he gave a sensation of strength, both calm and beautiful. Then for some odd reason Valya suddenly thought of little Sergei Tyulenin, skinny and barefoot, and her heart began to ache with such tender happiness that she fell silent.

They all four stepped to the edge of the loft and Kolya Sumskoi suddenly caught hold of the tumbler pigeon perched on his arm, lowered it and then swung it upwards with all his strength into the dull, drizzling sky. The other pigeons flew off his shoulder and through the sloping skylight everybody watched the tumbler pigeon soaring high and soon disappearing in the sky like a phantom.

Clapping her hands, Tosya Yeliseyenko jumped up and down and squealed with such delight that they all looked round and laughed. This exhibition of high spirits and the challenging expression in her eyes clearly said, "I know you think I am unkind but use your eyes and see what I am really like."

The next morning found Valya and Kolya Sumskoi out in the steppe making their way to the town. During the night the dense clouds had rolled away, the sun had risen in a clear sky, its warmth had soon dried everything. The steppe lay vast all round them, nothing but faded grasses, yet beautiful in its early autumn colouring of molten copper. The long threads of fine cobwebs stretched in all directions. German transport planes, all flying in the direction of Stalingrad, filled the steppe with their roar, then everything grew quiet again.

When they had covered about half the distance, Valya and Sumskoi lay down to rest in the sun on the hill-side. Sumskoi lit a cigarette.

Suddenly they heard singing coming clearly to them across the steppe; it was a song so familiar that it met an immediate response in both their hearts: *Darkly Still the Hills Are Sleeping*—a song popular with all the people of the Donets steppe. But where was it coming from—out here, and in this morning? Valya and Kolya raised themselves on their elbows and mentally repeated the words of the song as it came nearer and nearer to them. Two voices, male and female, were singing it; they were very young voices singing with great gusto as though shouting a challenge to the whole world round them:

Darkly still the hills are sleeping
While the early light is seeping
And the morning sun comes peeping
Through the drifting haze.

Fields and groves will soon be waking
Green the dress they will be taking—
For the steppe a lad is making
From the forest's maze....

Quickly, Valya wriggled to the crest of the hill, peeped cautiously over the top, then stood up and burst out laughing: coming down the road towards her were Volodya Osmukhin hand in hand with his sister Lyudmila singing, or rather yelling the song.

Valya jumped up and raced headlong like a child down the hill to meet them. Not greatly surprised, Sumskoi followed at a more leisurely pace.

"Where are you off to?"

"To Grandpa in the village to get some grain from him. Who's that traipsing after you?"

"One of our comrades from the settlement. Kolya Sumskoi."

"Allow me to introduce another sympathizer—my dear sister Lyudmila. She opened her heart to me just now, here in the steppe," Volodya said.

"Judge for yourself, Valya, aren't they pigs! They all know me perfectly well, yet my own brother conceals everything from me. And I could see what was going on! I even caught him with the type of the printing-press and some smelly stuff he was washing them in; he'd finished washing part of them. And today... Valya! D'you know what happened today?" she suddenly exclaimed with a swift glance at Sumskoi, who had just come up.

"Wait a moment," Volodya interrupted gravely. "My mates in the shop have seen it with their own eyes, and they told me all about it: they were passing by the park as usual and suddenly they saw somebody hanging by the neck in the gateway, somebody in a black overcoat, and he had a notice pinned to his chest. At first they thought the Germans had hanged one of our chaps. They went closer and saw it was Fomin! You know the bastard, that policeman swine. And the notice said: 'This is what we shall do with all who betray our people.' No more, just that.... You see?" he said lowering his voice to a whisper. "They made a good job of it!" he suddenly exclaimed. "For two solid hours he hung there in broad daylight! You see it was on his own beat, and there wasn't another policeman anywhere near. Masses of people saw him and that's all they're talking about in the town today."

Neither Volodya nor Valya knew anything of the Young Guard headquarters' decision to execute Fomin, nor could they even have assumed that anything of the sort would happen. Volodya was certain that the Bolshevik underground organization must have done the work. But suddenly the colour drained from Valya's face and she paled beneath the golden sunburn: she knew one person who was capable of doing such a thing.

"You don't happen to know whether, on our side, everything went off all right? Whether anyone was caught?" she asked almost unable to keep her lips from quivering.

"Brilliant!" Volodya exclaimed. "Nobody knows anything and everything is all right. But there's hell to pay at home.... My mother's sure that I must have hanged the son of a bitch and she's prophesying that I'll be hanged, too. So I gave Lyudmila a nudge and I said, 'You know that Mother's a bit deaf and she's got a temperature and, anyway, it's time to go to Grandpa.'"

"Kolya, let's go," Valya said suddenly to Sumskoi.

For the rest of the way Valya almost outstripped Sumskoi. He could find no explanation at all for the change that had come over her. At last her heels were clicking up the porch steps of her home and Sumskoi followed her into the dining-room, feeling a little embarrassed.

There, Maria Borts, plump in her dark tight-fitting dress and pale little Lyusia with her light-golden hair falling to her shoulders sat facing each other, silent and tense, like visitors at a formal birthday celebration.

When her elder daughter entered the room Maria Borts quickly rose, was about to say something, but choked it back and, after looking doubtfully from Valya to Sumskoi, fiercely kissed her daughter. Only then did Valya realize that her mother must have been experiencing the same agonies as Volodya's mother: she suspected her own daughter, Valya Borts, of having been involved in the execution of Fomin and that for that reason she had been absent for the past two days.

Forgetting all about Sumskoi who was standing, ill at ease, in the doorway, Valya regarded her mother with an expression, which seemed to say, "What can I tell you, Mother?"

At that moment little Lyusia went to Valya and, without a word, held a note out to her. Absent-mindedly Valya flicked it open and recognized the handwriting before she had even read it. Her face, sunburnt and dust-covered from the road, suddenly became radiant with the happy smile of a child. She looked swiftly over her shoulder at Sumskoi and her neck and ears flushed scarlet. She grasped her mother's hand and pulled her into the other room.

"Mother!" she began. "Mother! It's all nonsense what you're thinking. But can't you see, can't you understand what it is that we're living for now, me and my comrades? Don't you see that there's no other way for us to live? Mama darling!" Valya, happy and flushed, gazed into her mother's face.

Maria Borts, whose face was usually glowing with health, suddenly went white. She felt even inspired.

"My daughter! May God bless you!" said Maria, who all her life, at school and out of it, had engaged in active anti-religious teaching. "May God bless you!" she said, and burst into tears.

Chapter 8

IT IS HARD for parents who are unaware of the thoughts and feelings of their children and yet see them drawn into clandestine, mysterious, and dangerous activities without having the power to enter into the world of their activities or to put a stop to them.

Vanya had sensed the approaching storm during breakfast, when he saw his father's grim expression and noticed that he would not look at him. The storm had broken when his sister Nina returned from the well with the water and brought back the rumour of Fomin's execution and what people were saying about it.

His father's face underwent a change, the muscles becoming taut in his lean cheeks.

"The chances are that we can get the most authoritative"—he liked using big words—"information about the affair here, at home," he had said venomously, without looking at his son. "Why don't you speak up? Tell us about it. You're more closely in touch with things, so to speak, aren't you?" He spoke very quietly.

"More closely in touch with whom? The police?" Vanya's face grew pale.

"What did Tyulenin come for last night? After curfew?"

"Who observes the curfew anyway? As if Nina never goes out to meet someone in prohibited hours! He came for a chat, and not for the first time."

"Don't lie!" the father yelled and crashed his scraggy fist down on the table. "It's prison for this! You can stick your own neck out if you like, but why must you drag us, your parents, into it?"

"That's not what's in your mind, Father," Yanya said quietly and got up, ignoring the way his father thumped again on the table, shouting, "Yes, it is!" "What you want to know," Vanya continued, "is whether I belong to the underground organization, that's what you want to know. Well, I don't. And what Nina said about Fomin was the first I'd heard about it. He deserved it, anyway, the swine, that's all I can say! And from what Nina says that's what everybody else is thinking. And you think it too. I'll tell you one thing: I'm helping our people all I can. We should all be helping them, and I'm a Komsomol. I said nothing to you or Mother about it because I didn't want to cause you unnecessary worry."

"You hear that, Anastasya?" Almost beside himself with fury the father fixed his faded eyes on his wife. "Listen to him—worrying about us, he is! Have you no shame at all? I've spent all my life working for you.... Have you forgotten how we used to live twelve families in a house—twenty-eight children crawling about on the floor? Your mother and I spent the last ounce of our strength for the sake of you children. Look at her! Alexander went to school, but we didn't let him finish his education; the same with Nina's education; we staked everything on you, and now you put your own head in a noose. Look at your mother! She's cried her eyes out because of you, only you're too blind to see anything."

"And what d'you suggest I should do?"

"Get to work! Nina's working, so can you. She's an accountant and yet she's doing manual labour, but what do you do?"

"Work for whom? For the Germans? So they can kill more of our people? When the Red Army comes back I'll be the first to go to work. My brother, your own son, is in the Red Army, yet you're telling me to go and help the Germans so that they can kill him the sooner, or what?" Vanya said angrily. By now they were standing facing each other.

"And where's your food to come from?" the father shouted. "And will it be any better when the first of the people you're so concerned about hands you over, betrays you to the Germans? What d'you know even about the people in our street? What's going on in their minds? I'll tell you! All they think about is their own skin and personal gain. Only you are wanting to oblige them all!"

"That's not true! Were you self-seeking when you helped to send state property into the safety of the rear?"

"We're not talking about me."

"Oh yes, we are! What makes you think you're better than anyone else?" Vanya said, his head and spectacles at a stubborn angle, the fingers of one hand resting on the table to give him support. "Personal gain! Each for himself! I ask you: How were you looking after yourself in those days when you had your discharge pay in your pocket and knew that you'd stay here and yet you still went on, sick as you were, loading stuff that was not your own? And lay awake at night, worrying over it? Are you perhaps the only person in the world to act like that? That's denying scientific facts, that is!"

His sister Nina, at home because it was Sunday, sat frowning on her bed with averted eyes while the quarrel went on, keeping her thoughts to herself as usual. Her mother, a kindly and weak woman prematurely aged, who had spent her whole life working in the fields or bending over the kitchen stove, was tormented by the over-riding fear that, in his rage, her husband might curse her Vanya and turn him out of the house. Every time the father spoke she tried to propitiate him with a winning smile and a wagging of her head and when the son spoke she still looked at her husband, but with a forced smile and blinking as if asking him to listen to what their son had to say and to forgive him, although they, the old folk, knew there was no rhyme or reason in it.

The father stood in the middle of the room in his long jacket over the frequently washed blouse and an ancient pair of baggy trousers patched at the knees. His gnarled, aged feet were in slippers.

"It's life I'm talking about, not scientific facts!" he shouted, feverishly pressing his fists to his chest and then dropping them helplessly to his sides.

"And if science isn't part of life, what is it?... You're not the only one clamouring for justice—others are, too!" Vanya said with a show of temper unusual for him. "You're just ashamed of what's good in you!"

"I've got nothing to be ashamed of!"

"Then prove that I'm wrong! Just shouting does nothing to convince me—I can submit to you and keep quiet, that's one thing. But I shall continue to do what my conscience dictates."

The father suddenly crumpled up. His faded eyes dimmed.

"There you are, Anastasya," he said in a high-pitched voice. "We have given our son an education.... We've given him an education, and now we're no longer needed. Adieu!"

He waved his arms, turned away and left the room.

Anastasya tripped after him. Nina remained sitting on the bed. She did not speak or raise her head.

Vanya wandered aimlessly from one corner of the room to the other; unable to quieten his conscience he sat down.

He even tried, as he had often done before, to pour out his heart to his brother, in a letter, written in verse:

> *My glorious and loyal friend,*
> *Sasha, my excellent brother....*

No good.

> *My dearest friend, my own dear brother....*

No, it just would not come. He could hardly send a letter to his brother anyway. Then at last Vanya realized what he must do: he must go to Nizhny Alexandrovsky and see Klava.

Yelena Koshevaya was extremely worried because she was quite unable to decide whether she should put a stop to Oleg's activities or help him in them. Like all other mothers, she went about in an agony of fear for him which constantly, from one day to the next, prevented her from sleeping and was wearing her down mentally and physically, lining her face with wrinkles. Sometimes the fear was like that of an animal and she caught herself wanting to break out, to scream aloud, to wrench her son by force from the terrible fate he had prepared for himself.

Yelena possessed some of the traits of her husband, Oleg's stepfather, who had been the only deep and passionate love of her life; she had the same fighting spirit and so she could only sympathize with her son.

Often, however, she felt offended at his attitude: how could he be so secretive and hide things from his mother to whom he had always been so frank, so affectionately polite, so obedient! She felt particularly slighted because her mother, Grandma Vera, was obviously involved in Oleg's plotting and was also hiding things from her daughter; her brother Nikolai Nikolayevich, as far as she could tell, was also in the plot. Even a comparative stranger, Polina Sokolova or Aunt Polina as she was called by the Koshevois, had apparently become closer to Oleg now than his own mother. How, when, and from what had all this come about?

Formerly Yelena and Aunt Polina had been so inseparable that when one of them was mentioned in conversation, the other immediately came to mind. Theirs was the friendship of mature, experienced women, whose work had brought them together and who were bound by a common outlook. But when war broke out Aunt Polina had suddenly become shut up in herself and had stopped visiting the Koshevois. Whenever Yelena, for old friendship's sake, called on her, Aunt Polina seemed ashamed of having a cow and selling milk and afraid that Yelena Nikolayevna might reproach her for having given up working for the good of the motherland in favour of her own personal interests. And Yelena had not even found it possible to discuss the matter with Polina. So their friendship had ceased to flourish of its own accord.

Aunt Polina had resumed her visits to the Koshevois when the Germans came and began to make themselves at home in the town. She came with her heart open and bleeding and Yelena found her old friend in her. Now they met frequently to unburden themselves. It was still Yelena who did most of the talking, while quiet, reticent Aunt Polina watched her with wise, tired eyes. Yet for all Aunt Polina's reticence, Yelena could not help noticing that she had a magic attraction for Oleg. Invariably, as soon as she appeared, he would be hanging about near by and often Yelena would intercept a sudden glance, swift as lightning, between them—the sort of glance people exchange when they have something to tell each other. Indeed, if she had to leave the room for a moment and then returned to it she could sense that her return had caused them to interrupt their own special conversation. And when Polina left and Yelena wanted to see her to the door she would hurriedly say with modesty, "No, don't trouble, Yelena dear, I'll let myself out." But she never said it when Oleg rose to see her to the street.

How had all this come about? What could help a mother's heart to bear it? Who, of all people on earth, could better understand her son, share his thoughts and actions, protect him, with the power of love, in evil times? But the voice of truth assured her that her son was keeping things from her for the first time in his life because he was not sure of her.

Like all young mothers with an only child she was apt

to see only his good points, yet she knew her son very well indeed.

The moment the leaflets began to appear in town with the mysterious signature *The Young Guard*, she had no doubt at all that Oleg was not only involved in that organization, but had a leading part in it. She worried and suffered and was proud of him in turn, but she also considered it impossible to get him to be frank by any artificial means.

Only once had she asked him with a casual air:

"Who are your friends these days?"

With a wiliness which was unusual in him he had pretended to take this as a continuation of a previous conversation about Lena Pozdnysheva and rather nervously he had replied:

"I k-keep c-company with Nina Ivantsova...."

She had for some reason not stood her ground against this ruse and had asked slyly:

"And Lena?"

Without a word he had produced his diary and handed it to her; in it she had read the whole story of his former infatuation for Lena Pozdnysheva and what he now thought of her.

But the morning she had learned from the neighbours of Fomin's execution she had almost screamed aloud. But she had controlled herself and had thrown herself down on her bed. Grandma Vera had come in as unperturbed and mysterious as a mummy, and had put a cold towel on her forehead.

Again like other parents, she had not for a moment suspected her son of being involved in the actual hanging— but this was the sort of world he moved in now, and this was the cruel sort of struggle they were waging! What punishment would he receive? She had still no answer in her mind for him but there must be an end to this terrible secrecy—life could not go on like this!

Meanwhile her son, as always clean, neatly dressed, sunburnt, was in the shed sitting on his bed with his head drawn into his shoulders, one of which was higher than the other. Kolya Sumskoi, swarthy, agile and large-nosed, sat opposite him on a block of wood; they were playing chess.

They were completely absorbed in their game, except

for a few seconds from time to time when they exchanged remarks the drift of which would have led anyone less experienced to believe he was dealing with inveterate criminals.

Sumskoi: "There's a granary at the station.... As soon as the corn from the first threshing was dumped there Kolya Mironov and Palaguta infected it with weevils...."

Silence.

Oleg: "Is all the grain in yet?"

Sumskoi: "They're making us get it in.... But most of it's in stoops and shocks. There's nothing to thresh it with or to cart it away."

Silence.

Oleg: "The shocks must be fired. Your castle is threatened."

Silence.

Oleg: "It's a good thing you've got your own fellows at the state farm. At headquarters we discussed this and decided we must have our own groups on the farms. Have you any arms?"

Sumskoi: "Not much."

Oleg: "You'll need to collect some."

Sumskoi: "Collect some, where?"

Oleg: "In the steppe. And you can steal them from the Germans, they're extremely feckless."

Sumskoi: "Sorry, check!"

Oleg: "You'll pay for that, like the aggressor!"

Sumskoi: "I'm not the aggressor!"

Oleg: "But you're pin-pricking like one of the satellite countries!"

Sumskoi: "My position's more like that of the French, now." Sumskoi smiled.

Silence.

Sumskoi: "Forgive me if I shouldn't be asking, but about that fellow who was hanged, did you people have a hand in it?"

Oleg: "Who can tell?"

"Good," Sumskoi said, clearly satisfied. "I think it would be a good thing to kill more of them, even from ambush. And not so much the underlings as their bosses."

"It's definitely worth while. They're careless enough, too."

"You know, I'll give up, I think," Sumskoi said. "My position's hopeless and it's time I went home."

Oleg carefully put the chess set away, then went to the door, looked out and came back.

"Take the oath."

Only a brief moment after they had been sitting playing chess, they stood facing one another. They were the same height, but Oleg had broader shoulders. They stood with their arms hanging at their sides, the expression in their eyes natural and sincere.

Sumskoi felt in his jacket pocket and produced a small scrap of paper. His face went pale.

"I, Nikolai Sumskoi," he began in a low voice, "on entering the ranks of the Young Guard take this solemn oath before my comrades-in-arms, before my long-suffering land, before the whole of my people: I swear—" He was so excited that there even was a metallic ring in his voice, but fearing that he might be heard in the yard, he went on in a whisper. "...If under torture or in cowardice I violate this sacred pledge, then may my name and kinsfolk be cursed for all time and may stern punishment be inflicted upon me by my comrades. Blood for Blood, Death for Death!"

"I congratulate you. From now on your life's no longer your own, but belongs to the Party and to the whole people!" Oleg said with emotion, and shook hands with him. "You'll get the whole of your Krasnodon group to take the oath now."

The main thing now was to get into the house, undress and get to bed quietly, when his mother was already asleep, or pretending to be. Then there would be no need for him to turn away his gaze to avoid her bright, tortured eyes, nor would he have to pretend that nothing had changed in their lives.

Conscious of his bulk, he tiptoed into the kitchen, softly opened the door of the room and entered it. The shutters were tightly closed as always, the black-out curtain was drawn across the window. The kitchen range had been alight all day and the whole house was unbearably stuffy. The edges and outlines of familiar objects were thrown into relief in the darkness by the light of a wick stuck on the bottom of an old tin so as to raise it a little higher and prevent it from dripping oil on the table-cloth.

For some reason or other his mother, always so neat, was sitting on the bed. The blanket was turned back, but she was still dressed, with her hair up, her small brown hands with their swollen joints folded in her lap. She was gazing at the wick flame.

How still it was in the house! Nikolai Nikolayevich, who spent most of his time now with his colleague engineer Bystrinov, had come home and was in bed asleep; Marina, too, was asleep, and the little nephew with his pouting mouth had probably been in bed a long time. For once Grandma was not snoring in her sleep. Even the ticking of the clock had become inaudible. Only Mama was still awake. Loving Mama!

But the important thing now was not to give way to his feelings.... He had just to tiptoe past her without a word and lie down on his bed and feign sleep at once....

Heavy and tall, the lad tiptoed to his mother, dropped on his knees at her side and buried his face in her lap. He felt her hands against his cheeks, felt the warmth that no one else could give him and smelt the scarcely perceptible virgin scent of jasmin which seemed to come from far away, and something else that was slightly bitter, wormwood or egg-plant leaves ... but what did it matter!

"Dear, loving Mama!" he whispered and looked up at her, a bright light in his eyes. "You understand everything, absolutely everything, my darling Mama!"

"I understand everything," she whispered and bent over him, without looking at him.

He tried to look into her eyes but she kept her eyes hidden in his silky hair, whispering over and over again:

"Always with you ... everywhere. Don't be afraid. Be strong, my soaring eagle ... to the last breath...."

"Don't, please don't .... You must get to sleep, Mama," he whispered. "Would you like me to take your hairpins out for you?"

And just as he did in his childhood, he felt with his fingers and drew one hairpin after another from her hair, while she kept her face hidden and her head on his arm. He drew out every hairpin and let down her plaits, which fell as heavily as apples in an orchard and were long enough to cover her entirely.

Chapter 9

VANYA ZEMNUKHOV needed the permission of the Young Guard headquarters before going to Nizhny Alexandrovsky for a few days.

"It's not just a case of looking up the lass, you know," he told Oleg. "I've been planning for a long time to give her the job of organizing the young people on the Cossack farmsteads," he said, rather sheepishly.

But Oleg turned a deaf ear to all Vanya's pressing motives for the journey.

"Wait a day or two," he said. "There may be another job for you.... No, not here, there," he added quickly, with a broad grin, when he saw the restrained expression on Vanya's face. Vanya always looked like that when he wanted to hide his real feelings.

For the last few days Aunt Polina had persistently asked Oleg to find an intelligent lad to work directly under Lyutikov. He was to act as courier between Krasnodon and Nizhny Alexandrovsky. Oleg had thought of Zemnukhov.

When Aunt Polina had passed on Lyutikov's request she had repeatedly emphasized that the lad must be very sharp-witted and thoroughly reliable—only the most intelligent and most reliable would do.

The day after he had spoken with Oleg, short-sighted Vanya with gym shoes on his bare feet and a handkerchief knotted at the corners on his head, although the sun was not hot, was striding along the country road across the steppe with a poor harvest of standing grain on both sides of him.

He was filled with the importance of his mission and engrossed in the thoughts engendered by his new role. Being engrossed in his own thoughts while on a journey was the state most characteristic of short-sighted Vanya. Thus he walked through the steppe and past numerous villages hardly noticing anything he passed on the way.

A person unfamiliar with the situation—if there could be such a person—happening upon a farming district in German-occupied territory would have been struck by the unusually dismal and strangely contrasting scenes before his eyes. He would have seen hundreds of villages reduced to ashes, where in place of former villages and Cossack farmsteads nothing now remained but the frame of a stove here, a charred beam there, perhaps a lone cat sitting in the sun on a blackened doorstep overgrown with weeds. And he would also encounter Cossack farmsteads where no German had set foot, save for occasional, straggling marauding soldiers.

Then there were villages where German rule had been established in the way the Germans considered would be most profitable and convenient for the state, where downright military plunder, that is to say, pillaging by passing army units, and where every form of violence and bestiality was carried on to a no greater or lesser extent than in the other cases recorded in the history of German military occupation in Russia, where German administration was represented in its purest form, so to speak.

The Cossack village of Nizhny Alexandrovsky was just such a village. Klava Kovalyova and her mother had been given shelter there by relatives on the mother's side.

Klava's Cossack uncle, whose house they now shared, had been just an ordinary collective farmer before the Germans came. He had been neither a brigade-leader on the farm, nor a stable-man, but simply a collective farmer who, with his family, had cultivated the commonly-owned fields and had lived on what he earned and what he could get from his own plot of land.

As soon as the Germans came Ivan Nikanorovich, Klava's uncle, and his family had gone through experiences which were neither greater nor less than history recorded for the ordinary, everyday farming household during German domination. They had been robbed when the advancing German armies had passed through, robbed to the extent that their cattle, fowl and foodstuffs had been clearly evident; in a word they had been very thoroughly robbed, but not quite cleaned out. For nowhere in the world are there peasants so experienced in concealing their possessions in lean times as are the Russian peasants.

After the armies had passed through and the *Neue Ordnung* had been introduced, Ivan Nikanorovich, like everyone else, had been informed that the land at Nizhny Alexandrovsky, which had been given to the collective farmers for their collective use in perpetuity, would now become the property of the German state, in common with all other land. But, said the *Neue Ordnung* through the mouthpiece of the *Reichskommissar* from Kiev, this land, which with so much labour and so many trials had been merged into one single collective farm, would now again be divided into small plots, to be cultivated by each Cossack family individually. But! These measures would not be put into operation until all the Cossacks and peasants had their own farming implements and haulage power. And as, for the time being, they could not have these things, the land would remain in its former state, except that it would now be the property of the German state. To supervise the cultivation of the land, an Elder would be appointed over the Cossack village; he would be a Russian appointed by the Germans. In fact he had already been appointed. The peasant households would be grouped in tens and a Russian Elder appointed by the Germans for each group. They, too, had already been appointed by the Germans. In payment for their work on the land the peasants would receive a certain amount of corn; to encourage the peasants to work well, they were to be given to understand that only those peasants who were now working well would receive a plot of land for individual use at a later date.

Meanwhile, the German state was not yet able to supply machinery and fuel or even horses, to enable the peasants to work well. The farm workers should manage with scythe, sickle and hoe and for haulage they would have to use their own cows. Those who wanted to spare their cows could hardly count on being given a plot of land for their individual use at some date in the future. Despite the fact that this type of labour required a large amount of labour power, the German authorities, far from endeavouring to preserve labour power locally, took all measures to dispatch to Germany the healthiest and ablest of the local population.

As the German state was not at present in a position to estimate how much meat, milk and eggs it would need, it imposed on the hamlet of Nizhny Alexandrovsky an initial levy of one cow from every five households, and in addition, one pig, one hundredweight of potatoes, twenty eggs and seventy-five gallons of milk from every household. But! As more might be required—and more was for ever being required—Cossacks and peasants were not allowed to slaughter any cattle or fowl for their own use. If, however, as an extreme measure they very much required to slaughter a pig, then four households could combine for the purpose, but they would be obliged at the same time to deliver three pigs to the German state.

In order to appropriate all this from the household of Ivan Nikanorovich and his fellow-villagers, an apparatus of the district agricultural *Kommandantur* under its director *Sonderführer* Sanders was established in addition to the Elders over the ten households and the chief Elder of the village. This *Sonderführer*, not unlike *Oberleutnant* Sprick, found the climate rather hot and toured villages and hamlets in a pair of shorts and an army tunic, and when he came in sight the Cossack women would cross themselves and spit as though he was Satan himself. This district agricultural *Kommandantur* was subordinated to the area agricultural *Kommandantur* with its much larger staff. At its head stood *Sonderführer* Glücker who, it is true, wore trousers, but was so high up that he never condescended to tour the villages. Finally, the area agricultural *Kommandantur* was subordinated to the *Landwirtschaftsgruppe* or *Gruppe* "LA" for short, chief of which was Major Stander. *Gruppe* "LA" was on such an immensely high level that no one ever saw it at all. But even the "LA" *Gruppe* was no more than a department of *Wirtschaftskommando* 9 or "WIKDO 9" for short, with *Doktor* Lüde at its head. And *Wirtschaftskommando* 9 was subordinated on the one hand to the *Feldkommandantur* in the town of Voroshilovgrad—to gendarmerie headquarters in other words—and, on the other, to the Chief Directorate of State Properties under the *Reichskommissar* himself, which had its seat in Kiev.

Under the shadow of this weighty hierarchy with its

increasingly weighty ranks of loafers and robbers, speaking in an unintelligible tongue, all of whom nevertheless had to be fed, Ivan Nikanorovich and his fellow-villagers who daily felt on their backs the fruits of their activities, realized that German fascist rule was not only brute rule— that had been obvious from the start—but also an unimportant, stupid, robber state.

By that time Ivan Nikanorovich and his fellow-villagers and all the inhabitants of the neighbouring Cossack hamlets—Gundorovskaya, Davidov and Makarov Yar—began to behave towards the German authorities in the only way that self-respecting Cossacks could and should behave towards stupid authorities: they began to hoodwink them.

The chief way they deceived them was to make a show of working in the fields rather than actually doing so; to scatter to the four winds whatever they did grow, or if the opportunity presented itself, to pilfer it for their own use, and to conceal livestock, fowl and foodstuffs. To facilitate this process of deception, the Cossacks and peasants did their best to get the right people appointed as the Elders over ten households and the village and hamlet Elders. Like all brute forms of government the German authorities found sufficient brutes to appoint as Elders but, as the saying goes, man's life is not eternal. The Elders were here today and gone tomorrow. They just vanished into thin air.

Klava Kovalyova was eighteen and far removed from all these doings. She simply fretted because of the many restrictions on her present way of living, because she had no friends and could not study, and she was worried about her father's fate. She cheered herself up by dreaming about Vanya, dreaming in a very clear and practical way about how all this confusion would some day come to an end and then they could marry and have children and live very happily all together, with their children.

She also lightened her hours by reading books, although it was not easy to get books in Nizhny Alexandrovsky. And so, when she learned that a new teacher had arrived in the hamlet to take the place of the teacher who had evacuated, she decided that there could be nothing shameful in asking her for books, even though the teacher had been appointed by the new district authorities.

The teacher had moved into the room at the school where her predecessor had lived and, according to the local gossip, was even using her furniture and personal belongings. Klava knocked and without waiting for an answer pushed the door open with her plump, strong hand. She went into the room which lay on the shady side of the building and had the curtains at the window drawn. She peered into the room to see whether its occupant was at home. The teacher was half-turned away from Klava bending over the window-sill, dusting it with a feather mop. She turned her head, raised one of her thick eyebrows, suddenly started back and leaned against the window-sill. Then she straightened up and scrutinized Klava again.

"Are you, perhaps—"

She did not finish. A guilty smile appeared on her face and she stepped forward to meet Klava. She was a slender, fair woman in a simple dress with finely drawn lips and direct, even stern, grey eyes. The frank radiant smile that came to her lips every now and then lent a surprising charm to her features.

"The cupboard where the school books were kept was smashed by the Germans who were billeted in the building. Pages from the books are to be seen in the most unsuitable place, but some books are still intact. Let's have a look," she said, articulating her phrases as correctly and purely as only the good Russian teacher does. "Are you a local girl?"

"I suppose I am, yes," Klava replied, hesitantly.

"Why the reservation?"

Klava faltered. The teacher looked straight at her.

"Let's sit down," she said.

Klava remained standing.

"I've seen you in Krasnodon," the teacher said.

Klava gave her a sidelong glance, but made no reply.

"I thought you'd gone away," the teacher continued with her radiant smile.

"I didn't go away anywhere."

"Then you were just seeing someone off!"

"How d'you know?" Again Klava, frightened and curious, gave her a sidelong glance.

"I just happen to know. But don't worry. You're probably thinking, 'She's been sent here by the Germans and—'"

"I'm not thinking anything."

"Yes, you are!" The teacher laughed and her face turned a little red. "Who were you seeing off?"

"My father."

"No, it wasn't your father."

"Yes, it was."

"All right, and who is your father, then?"

"A Trust employee," Klava said, and blushed to the roots of her hair.

"Do sit down and stop being shy." The teacher caressingly put out a hand to touch Klava, who sat down.

"So your friend's gone?"

"What friend?" Klava's heart began to thump.

"Don't be secretive, I know all about it." The teacher's eyes quite lost their stern expression, and sparkled with kind, mischievous laughter.

"I shan't tell you, even if you kill me!" Klava thought, suddenly furious. "I don't know what you're talking about, and I don't like it!" she said aloud and stood up.

No longer able to control herself, the teacher laughed outright greatly pleased, clasping and unclasping her sunburnt hands and wagging her fair head from side to side. Suddenly she rose and with an impetuous movement put her arm round Klava's shoulder.

"My dear.... Forgive me. You wear your heart on your sleeve, you know," she said and drew her a little closer. "I'm only joking, you needn't be afraid of me. I'm just a Russian teacher, we have to live, and even under the Germans we are not compelled to teach what is bad."

There was a loud knock on the door.

"It's Marfa!" she said softly and happily.

A tall, strong-boned woman in a gleaming white shawl entered the room. Her bare, darkly sunburnt legs were covered in dust and she carried a bundle of clothing under her arm.

"Good-evening," she said with an inquiring glance at Klava. "We live near enough, yet I could not come to see you for a very long time," she said to the teacher in a loud voice, displaying her strong teeth.

"What's your name?"

"Klava."

"Klava," the teacher said, "I'll take you to the classroom and you can find yourself some books. Only don't go away, I shan't be long." They left the room together.

Katya Protsenko, for it was she, returned a few minutes later.

"What is it? What's the news?" she asked excitedly.

Marfa was sitting, her eyes covered with her large, toil-worn hand. There were deep lines of distress at the corners of her still youthful mouth.

"I don't know whether to laugh or cry," she began in Ukrainian, removing her hand from her eyes. "A young fellow came over from Pogorely farmstead and said that my Gordei Kornienko's been taken prisoner. Katya, tell me what to do!" She raised her head and continued in Russian: "There are prisoners working at the Pogorely Forestry Station, under guard. About sixty of them, cutting timber for the army. My Gordei's there. They live in barracks, and they are not allowed out. He's starving and he's all swollen. Tell me, what should I do? Should I go there?"

"How did he send word to you?"

"Some people who are not prisoners work there and he was able to whisper a word to one of the villagers. The Germans don't know that he's from these parts."

Katya regarded her in silence for some moments. This was a case where advice could not be given. Marfa might live for weeks at the Pogorely farmstead worrying herself sick and still not see her husband. At best they might get a glimpse of each other from a distance but that would only add unbearable mental anguish to her husband's physical sufferings. And it would be impossible even to get food to him: it was not difficult to imagine what sort of prisoner-of-war barracks it was!

"You'll have to decide for yourself."

"Would you go?" Marfa asked.

"I'd go, yes," Katya said and sighed. "And you'll go—but all to no purpose."

"And I say, it'll be to no purpose. So I'm not going," Marfa said. She covered her eyes with her hand.

"Does Kornei Tikhonovich know?"

"He says, if he were given permission to take his detachment out he'd be able to free him...."

A worried, sad expression came to Katya's face. She knew that the partisan group under Kornei Tikhonovich's command must not be used for any subsidiary purpose of this kind.

Important German communication lines were now running through Voroshilovgrad Region. Everything, literally everything at the disposal of Ivan Protsenko, everything that he had newly created, was now directed towards assisting the victory of the great battle for Stalingrad hundreds of miles from the Donbas.

All the partisan detachments in the region, split up into several small groups, were now operating along all the highways, country roads and the three railway lines running to the east and to the south. And yet the forces were still small. Ivan Protsenko, whose whereabouts were now known only to his wife, Marfa Kornienko and Krotova, the liaison courier, had, therefore, switched the activities of all the underground district committees in the region to wrecking operations on all the roads.

Katya knew all this only too well, because all the countless threads of their communications were held in a bunch in her small, capable hands and were passed on as one thread of information to Ivan Protsenko. That was why she made no reply when Marfa brought her Kornei Tikhonovich's suggestion, although she realized that Marfa's only motive in coming to her was to bring her secret hope.

Katya had no direct contact with her husband but kept in touch with him through Marfa, or rather, through Marfa's home; however, she did not inquire about him: she realized that since Marfa had nothing to say about him, then there was nothing to report.

Meanwhile Klava stood by the cupboard examining what books there were left. They were books she had read as a child and this encounter with her childhood friends made her melancholy. She felt sad as she looked at the black, empty school desks. The rays of the evening sun came slanting through the window and in their soft, strong light was a sad, mellow smile of farewell. Life seemed so overwhelmingly sad to Klava now, that she forgot to be tortured with curiosity about how it was the teacher knew her.

"Have you found anything?" The teacher was looking straight at Klava, her lips were firmly compressed but there was sadness deep in her grey eyes. "So you see life is sometimes cruel," she said. "Yet when we are young, we hurry along, not realizing that what we are given then has to last us all our lives.... If I could become again what you are now, I would know that truth, yet I can't even explain it to you. You must introduce me to your friend if he comes here."

Little could Katya guess that at that very moment Vanya Zemnukhov was entering the village; coming, moreover, with a message for her.

The message which he handed her was in code, a report of the work of the Krasnodon District Underground Committee. For her part Katya informed him verbally of her husband's instruction that the Krasnodon underground organization should become a partisan fighting detachment and that wrecking operations on all roads should be intensified.

"Tell them that at the front the position is not at all bad. It may be that very soon now we shall all have to go into action with rifles," Katya said. And she looked searchingly at the awkward youth before her, as though wishing to know what was hidden behind the spectacles.

Vanya sat, hunched up and silent, constantly pushing back his hair with his hand. Could she only have known what fire burned in his heart!

Soon, however, they were deep in conversation.

"How cruelly things can turn out for people at times!" Katya said, when she had heard from Vanya the gloomy report of the death of Matvei Shulga and Valko. "Ostapchuk, as you call him, had all his family in occupied territory and they may also have been tortured to death by now or else the poor woman and her children are among strangers, still nourishing a hope that he'll come one day and rescue her and the children; yet he is no longer among the living.... A woman's just been to see me." And Katya told Vanya about Marfa and her husband. "They're so close to each other, yet they have no chance of meeting. They'll drive him off further into the rear, where he'll slowly die.... Can there be any punishment hard enough for these fiends!" She clenched her strong, small hand.

"Pogorely—that's not far from us. One of our fellows lives there," Vanya said, recalling Vitya Petrov. A vague idea crept into his mind though as yet he was not quite aware of it. "Are there many prisoners? Have they got many guards?" he asked.

"Can you remember if any capable organizers are still in Krasnodon?" she asked suddenly, following up her own train of thoughts.

Vanya named those he knew.

"What about army men who've been cut off or have remained there for other reasons?"

"There are plenty of them." Vanya remembered the wounded soldiers who had been concealed in private homes; he knew from Sergei that Natalya Alexeyevna was still secretly giving them medical care.

"Tell the people who've sent you here to get in touch with them and get their cooperation.... You'll need them very soon yourselves. They'll be wanted to command you young people. You're good youngsters, but they're more experienced than you," Katya said.

Vanya unfolded his plan to set up a secret meeting-place at Klava's home, so that the Young Guard could keep in touch with the young people of the village; he asked her to help Klava in this.

"It's better that Klava shouldn't know who I am," Katya said with a smile. "We'll just be friends."

"But how do you come to know us?" Vanya asked, unable to restrain his curiosity.

"That's a thing I shall never tell you—it would be very embarrassing for you," she said, and a sly look suddenly came over her face.

"What were all those secrets between you and her?" There was a note of jealousy in Klava's voice as she asked Vanya the question. They were sitting in pitch darkness in the living-room of Ivan Nikanorovich's home. Klava's mother had for a long time now, and particularly since the events at the pontoon bridge, come to look upon Vanya as a member of the family and was sleeping peacefully in the stiflingly hot feather bed, customary among Cossacks, which had been tossed and fluffed up like a balloon.

"Can you keep a secret?" Vanya whispered into Klava's ear.

"What a question...."

"Swear!"

"I swear!"

"She said that one of our Krasnodon folk is in hiding somewhere near by and asked me to tell his family. After that, we talked about trifles.... Klava!" he went on softly, solemnly and took her hand, "we've formed an organization of young people to keep up the struggle against the invaders, do you want to join?"

"Are you in it?"

"Of course."

"Then naturally I'll join!" She put her warm lips to his ear. "I'm yours, aren't I?"

"You must take the oath in my presence. Oleg and I wrote it and I know it by heart and you'll have to learn it, too."

"I'll learn it—you know I'm all yours...."

"You'll have to organize the young people here and at the near-by farmsteads."

"I'll organize them all for you."

"And don't be flippant about it. If things go wrong your life'll be in danger."

"Yours too?"

"Mine too."

"I don't mind dying with you."

"But I think it would be better for us to stay alive, don't you?"

"Of course, much better."

"Listen, they've given me a shake-down with the fellows. I must go now, or it won't look so good!"

"Why must you go there? I'm yours, don't you understand? Absolutely all yours," whispered Klava's warm lips close to his ear.

Chapter 10

By the end of September the Pervomaisky Young Guard, which also took in Vosmidomiki district and the area round 1B Pit, had grown into one of the largest underground youth groups. All the most alert of the former pupils from the senior classes of the Pervomaisky school had been drawn into it.

The Pervomaisky youngsters had set up their own wireless receiver and were secretly publishing the communiqués of the Soviet Information Bureau, which they printed in Indian ink on pages torn from school exercise books.

The trouble that wireless receiver had caused them! Several useless old wrecks of wireless sets had been found lying about in all kinds of homes and had been quietly smuggled away. Boris Glavan (known as Aleko in the group), a Moldavian whose parents, refugees from Bessarabia, had settled in Krasnodon, undertook to make a workable wireless receiver out of them. On the way home, however, he had been arrested in the street by a policeman and several valves and various radio parts were found on him.

In the police-station Glavan refused to speak anything but Rumanian and kept shouting that the police were depriving his whole family of their livelihood, because he required all the material found on him to make cigarette lighters, swearing that he would lodge a complaint with the Rumanian Army Command. There were always several Rumanian officers billeted in Krasnodon. A search in Glavan's home disclosed several completed lighters and others in the process of manufacture; he actually did earn a living making them. The police released this national of an allied power, but relieved him of the radio parts. All the same, he managed to construct a wireless receiver out of what he had by him.

The Pervomaisky youth maintained their own contacts with the outlying farmsteads through Lilya Ivanikhina, who had taken a teacher's post on the Sukhodol farmstead when she had recovered from her experiences in German captivity. These farmsteads became the chief suppliers of weapons, which they collected out in the steppe—sometimes making very extensive journeys for the purpose into the area of the Donets battles; they also filched arms from the German and Rumanian soldiers and officers when they made a halt in the villages. Once all the members of the Pervomaisky organizatio i had armed themselves, the weapons were turned over for safe keeping to Sergei Tyulenin, who added them to the general store, the whereabouts of which was known only to Sergei himself and a very few other people.

Just as the leading spirits in the Young Guard were Oleg Koshevoi and Ivan Turkenich, in the settlement of Krasnodon Kolya Sumskoi and Tosya Yeliseyenko, so, in Pervomaisky, they were Ulya Gromova and Anatoly Popov.

Anatoly Popov had been appointed commander of the Pervomaisky group by the Young Guard headquarters. With the organizational skill he had acquired in the Komsomol and his naturally serious outlook, he brought to everything the Pervomaisky youth undertook to do a spirit of conscientious discipline and resolute boldness based on extremely harmonious work on the part of all the young people.

Ulya Gromova, on the other hand, was the initiator of every form of activity and the author of most of the Pervomaisky appeals and leaflets. Only now was it apparent how much tremendous moral prestige she had accumulated among her friends and comrades since the time when she had gone to school with them as equals, had rambled in the steppe, had sung and danced, recited poetry and led the Young Pioneers—this tall, slender lass with the heavy black plaits and the eyes which were sometimes aflame with a clear, strong light, sometimes full of a mysterious strength, the girl who was more inclined to be silent than boisterous, was more equable than passionate, yet was capable of being both at one and the same time.

Youth is apt to pass judgement on ostentation and sincerity, liveliness and tedium, the spurious and the momentous at first glance, from a word or a gesture, rather than by close observation and experience. Ulya at this time had no special friends: she was equally attentive, kind and exacting to all of them. But the girls had only to exchange a word or two with her for them to realize that Ulya was not like she seemed, and that behind her outward appearance lay a world of sensations and thought, of appraisals of people and attitudes towards them, and that this world could reveal itself with startling intensity, particularly if one happened to incur its moral censure. From natures like Ulya's, even equability is accepted as a distinction, but how much greater was the distinction when such a nature revealed the heart, if only for a brief moment!

She was equable in her attitude to the lads, as well. Not only could no single one of them declare that she was more friendly with him than with the rest, but not one of them in his heart ever dared to entertain the possibility for himself. By the way she looked at them, by every movement she made, each lad understood that he was not dealing with a proudly exaggerated personality, and even less with a girl of emotional poverty, but with someone who had an untrammelled, hidden world of genuine passions which had as yet found no one upon whom to lavish themselves in full, pure measure, and which could not expend themselves sparingly, drop by drop. And so Ulya found herself surrounded by the unperceived, tender, generous adoration of the young men, an adoration which only comes the way of exceptionally strong, pure-minded young women.

Precisely for this reason Ulya naturally, freely and imperceptibly to herself influenced the minds of her Pervomaisky friends and comrades.

One day the girls had gathered in the home of the Ivanikhina sisters, which had become their usual meeting-place; they were making up packets of bandages for the wounded.

Lyuba had stolen the bandages from the officers and other ranks of the German medical corps who had made a night of it in her mother's home. She had pilfered it quite casually, without attaching great importance to what she was doing. But when Ulya heard of it, she immediately incorporated the bandages into their activities.

"Each of our boys should carry a first-aid packet of bandages. Unlike us, they will have to do some fighting," she said.

Evidently she must have known something which made her add:

"The time will come very soon for all of us to go into action. Then we'll need lots and lots of bandages."

In actual fact, Ulya was merely passing on in her own words what Vanya Zemnukhov had said at a meeting of the

Young Guard headquarters. Where he had got it from she did not know.

Thus they sat, making up the packets and even Shura Dubrovina, a student who had formerly been considered unsociable and something of an individualist, was doing her share. She had joined the Young Guard because of her affection for Maya Peglivanova.

"D'you know, girls, what we look like now?" Sasha Bondareva said. "Like the old women who used to work in the pits and who were pensioned off or taken care of by their children—I've seen them often enough at my grandma's. It's just how they used to come in, one after another, and sit down: one would start knitting, another would have some sewing, a third would play patience, and a fourth would help Grandma peel the potatoes—and nobody would say a word. Not a word from one of them, and then somebody would get up, stretch herself and say, 'How about it, now, let's liven up a bit.' Then they'd all simper and look coy and one of them would say, 'Well, you couldn't call it a sin, could you?' And straight away they'd take up a collection, a few coppers from each, and hey presto! there's a pint bottle on the table—they don't need much, the old dears, do they? They drink a thimbleful all round, then rest a cheek on their hands, like this, and start singing, 'A ring of gold on my finger....' "

"You are a one, Sasha, always digging up something like that!" The girls had a good laugh. "What about singing a song, like those old grannies?"

But just at that moment Nina Ivantsova arrived. Now she only very rarely came just to sit with them; it was almost always as courier from headquarters. But none of the girls knew the whereabouts of the headquarters or who its members were.

The word "headquarters" conjured up in their minds a group of adults in underground session somewhere, possibly in an underground shelter, with all the walls hung with maps, the people themselves heavily armed and able to talk with the front or even to Moscow by radio telephone at any time they liked.

Nina Ivantsova entered the room and at once called Ulya out into the street and the girls immediately gathered that Nina had brought them a new assignment. In a few moments Ulya came back and said that she would have to leave them. She called Maya Peglivanova aside and told her that the girls should take the packets of bandages to their homes and that she herself was to leave seven or eight of them at Ulya's home, because bandages might soon be needed badly.

Less than fifteen minutes later Ulya, with her skirt hitched up, was lifting first one long, slender leg and then the other over the fence, climbing from her own to the Popovs' garden. There in the scorched grass under the shade of the old cherry-tree Anatoly Popov, his Uzbek cap on his corn-coloured hair and dark-haired Victor Petrov, his head bare, were lying flat on their bellies facing each other and examining a map of the district.

They saw Ulya in the distance and, as she came up, went on with their quiet conversation, without raising their eyes from the map. With a casual turn of the wrist Ulya tossed her plaits over her shoulder, pulled her skirt down her legs, sat on the ground, hugging her knees, and also began to study the map.

The job concerning which Anatoly and Victor had already been informed, and for which Ulya had been summoned, was to be the first important test for the Pervomaisky youth: the Young Guard headquarters had charged them with the liberation of the prisoners of war working at the Pogorely Forestry Station.

"Where are the guards quartered?" Anatoly asked.

"On the right-hand side of the road, in the village itself. The barrack is on the left here, near this grove, you remember? There used to be a storehouse there. They just put in some bunks and surrounded the place with barbed wire. There's only one sentry. I think it'd be better not to bother with the guards at all, but just to remove the sentry. ... It's a pity—we ought to strangle the lot of them, really," Victor said with an angry expression on his face.

Victor Petrov had changed a great deal since his father's death. He lay on the grass in a dark velvet jacket chewing a blade of grass, his bold eyes resting gloomily on Anatoly.

"At night the prisoners are locked up, but we can take along Glavan, with his jemmy. He'll do everything without making a noise," he said, as though reluctantly.

Anatoly raised his head and looked at Ulya.

"What do you think?" he asked.

Although Ulya had not heard the beginning of the conversation she was able immediately to grasp why Victor was dissatisfied, because of the habit that had developed in all of them since they began to work together of being able to understand the drift of a conversation after hearing only a few words.

"I can well understand Victor: it would be a good thing to kill off the whole guard. But we're not experienced enough to do things on that scale," she said in her calm, vibrant voice.

"Yes, that's what I think," Anatoly said. "We must do what is simplest, what brings us closest to the goal."

Towards evening the next day the boys made their way singly to the forest near the Pogorely Farm, on the bank of the Donets. There were five of them: Anatoly, Victor, two of their schoolmates—Volodya Ragozin and Zhenya Shepelyov, the youngest of them all—and Boris Glavan. All were armed with revolvers. Victor also carried his father's ancient hunting-knife, which he now always wore on a belt under his velvet jacket. Boris Glavan had a pair of wire-nippers, a jemmy and a screwdriver.

It was a fresh, starry night in early autumn, but there was no moon. The boys lay down at the foot of the steep river-bank, where the whispering undergrowth above them came down to the water's edge. The river, flecked with light, rolled by almost without a sound, save for the soft trickles of water lower down where the bank had subsided, which, either by seeping through the pores of fallen earth or by catching and then letting loose again some fallen twig, gave out a lapping, sucking noise, like a calf at the cow's udder. The low opposite bank was lost in a silvery-grey mist.

They were waiting for midnight when the sentry would be relieved.

Such was the mysterious beauty of this early autumn night, with its silvery-grey mist over the river and the sucking, lapping, almost childlike sounds, that none of the lads could rid himself of a strange feeling: would they really have to leave the river and these sounds and attack a German sentry, struggle with barbed-wire fences and bolted doors? The river and the sounds were so familiar and dear to them while what lay ahead of them, what they had to do was something they were doing for the first time in their lives; not one of them could imagine what it would be like. But they kept their feelings to themselves and whispered about the familiar things.

"Victor, you remember this spot? It's the same surely, isn't it?" Anatoly asked.

"No, it was a little lower down—over there where the bank has subsided and there's a sucking sound. I had to start swimming from the opposite bank and I was so afraid you'd be swept further down, straight into the wirlpool."

"It's a bit late to admit it, but I can tell you I was in a devil of a funk," Anatoly said with a grin. "I'd swallowed about half the river."

"Zhenya Moshkov and I were coming out of the woods and ... oh, hell! I couldn't swim a stroke!" said Volodya Ragozin, a thin, lanky boy whose face was almost hidden under the long peak of a cap, which he wore pushed down over his eyes. "No, if Zhenya Moshkov hadn't dived straight in off the cliff, fully dressed, clothes and all, you'd never have pulled him out," he said to Victor.

"No, of course I wouldn't," Victor admitted. "Has anyone heard anything of Moshkov since?"

"Not a word," Ragozin said. "Except that he's a junior lieutenant, and in the infantry! It's the lowest of the commanding ranks, and they get killed like flies...."

"No, this Donets of yours is too quiet but our Dniester—there's a river for you!" Boris Glavan said, raising himself on one elbow, his teeth gleaming in the darkness. "How fast it runs! What a beauty it is! If you start drowning in the Dniester, you never get saved. And the forests here—what sort of forests are they? We live in the steppe, too, but you ought to see the forests we've got along the Dniester! Black poplars and yews so large your arms don't meet round them and so high they reach the sky...."

"Well, then you should live there," Zhenya Shepelʹov said. "It's really scandalous that people can't live where they want to. All these wars and everything ... If it wasn't for that people would live where they wanted to. If they liked Brazil, it would be there for them. Personally I'd just want to live quietly here in the Donbas. I like it very much here."

"Listen, if you want to live really quietly, come to us when the war is over and live in Soroka—that's our district centre—or better still in our village. It's got a loud-sounding, historical name: Tsar-Grad," Glavan said, chuckling. "Only don't come and take a worrying job—don't for God's sake take a job as an official of the cattle purchasing department, for instance! Come as chairman of the local Red Cross society—you'll have only the barber shops to look after, nothing to do all day, but sip wine! Honest to God it's a job to be envied!" he said laughing merrily.

"Quiet, you with your fooling!" Anatoly said good-naturedly.

And again they listened to the sucking and lapping of the river.

"It's time," Anatoly said.

In a flash the simple natural awareness of nature, of the joy of life, deserted them.

With Victor leading because he knew every bush in the neighbourhood, and carefully avoiding open ground by keeping to the edge of the cutting, they made their way in single file to the grove beyond which stood the barrack, which was still out of sight. There they lay down for a moment to listen: it was astonishingly silent all round. Victor signed to them with his arm and they crawled forward.

At last they were lying at the edge of the grove. There before them loomed the tall black building—an ordinary barn-like structure with a sloping roof, yet there were people herded together in it, and it looked gloomy and horrible. The area round it had already been denuded of trees; to the left of it stood the dark silhouette of the sentry while still further to the left lay the road, and beyond it the first houses of the village which could not be seen from where they lay.

About half an hour remained before the sentry would be relieved, and they spent the time lying with their eyes fixed on the dark, motionless figure of the sentry.

At last they heard footsteps ahead of them to the left and although they could still see nothing they heard two people marching in step turn into the road and come towards them. They were the corporal of the guard and the relieving sentry. The dark shapes approached the sentry on duty who, when he heard them, stood at attention.

A muffled order in German, a faint click of rifles, a clumping of heels on the ground, then two figures detached themselves and again the sound of footsteps came from the gravel road fading away along its hard surface and disappearing into the night.

Anatoly turned his head slightly to Zhenya Shepelyov who, however, had already crawled off into the depths of the grove. His job was to close in on the edge of the farmstead and keep watch by the small house where the guards lived.

The sentry was walking up and down along the barbed-wire fence like a wolf in a cage. Rifle-strap over his shoulder, he was stepping out briskly and they could hear him rubbing his hands together; probably he was feeling chilly after coming from his bed.

Anatoly felt for Victor's hand, which, unexpectedly, was warm, and pressed it.

"Should both of us go?" he whispered, his lips close to Victor's ear.

This was nothing but comradely wavering. It was countered by Victor who firmly shook his head and began to crawl forward.

With bated breath Anatoly, Boris Glavan and Volodya Ragozin watched him and the sentry. Every time Victor made the slightest rustle they felt he had given himself away. But Victor continued to crawl farther away from them until his velvet jacket vanished into its surroundings and he was out of sight and earshot. They kept their eyes riveted on the sentry, for any second now it would happen; but the dark shape continued to march up and down along the fence and nothing at all happened. They felt that a very long time had elapsed and it would soon be daylight,

Just as he used to in the half-forgotten childhood games in his Young Pioneer days, when he tried to outwit the comrade on duty, Victor glided forward pressing close to the ground, but with his body raised from it and using only his unusually supple hands and his feet to propel himself along. Every time the sentry turned to walk towards him he stopped, still as a statue; when the sentry marched in the opposite direction Victor moved forward again, forcing himself to proceed slowly.

His heart was pounding but there was no fear in his heart. Until the moment he had started to crawl, he had been forcing himself to think of his father in order again and again to fill his mind with a desire for revenge. But now he had completely forgotten all that; all his mental powers were concentrated on creeping up to the sentry unnoticed.

He reached the corner of the barbed-wire square enclosing the barrack and lay motionless. The sentry had reached the opposite corner and was turning to come back. Victor reached for his hunting-knife, gripped it between his teeth, then crawled towards him. His eyes had become so used to the darkness that he could see the wire of the fencing, and it seemed to him that the sentry would probably also by now have become accustomed to the darkness and would spot him on the ground as soon as he came close. But when the sentry reached the entrance through the enclosure he halted. The entrance, as Victor knew, was barred by a number of trestle-like structures wound round and round with barbed wire. Tensely he waited, but the sentry pushed his hands into his trouser pockets and, without removing the rifle from his shoulder, remained standing there with his back to the barrack, his head bent a little.

Like his friends, who with palpitating hearts were waiting for him to act, Victor suddenly thought that time was racing by and it would soon be daylight. Without stopping to consider that it would be easier now for the sentry to see him and easier still to hear him, because his own footsteps would no longer drown any other sounds, Victor crawled straight towards him. He was already barely two yards from the sentry who still stood, however, in the same position, his hands in his pockets, rifle slung over his shoulder, his head in the forage-cap bent low, rocking slightly on his heels. Whether Victor made another crawling movement then, or simply leapt up, he could never remember afterwards, but suddenly he was on his feet by the sentry's side, his hunting-knife grasped firmly in his hand. The sentry opened his eyes and quickly turned his head—he was a thin, elderly German with a stubble beard. A frenzied look came into his eyes and before he could remove his hands from his pockets he let out a strange, soft sound, like "Ugh. ..." Victor had plunged the knife with all his might into his neck to the left of the chin. The dagger had entered up to the hilt into the soft flesh above the collar-bone. The German fell and Victor fell over him and was about to strike again, but the German had already jerked convulsively and blood was gushing from his mouth. Victor stood aside, tossed the blood-stained knife to the ground and suddenly began to retch so violently that he had to press his jacket sleeve to his mouth to stifle the sound of it.

Suddenly Anatoly was standing in front of him, thrusting the dagger at him and whispering:

"Put it away, can't leave it here as a clue. ..."

Victor hid the knife, and Ragozin seized his arm and said, "Come on now, to the road!" Victor brought out his revolver, and all three ran out on to the road and there lay down again.

Afraid of getting tangled up with the barbed-wire trestles in the dark, Boris Glavan set to work on the fencing itself and, handling the wire-nippers with professional speed, had soon cut an entry between two of the enclosure posts. Then he and Anatoly rushed to the doors of the barrack. Glavan felt for the fastening which turned out to be an ordinary padlock securing an iron bar. He pushed the jemmy into the hoop of the lock and broke it; they pushed the bar aside and, terribly excited, opened the door.

A stifling, hot stench rushed towards them. Before them and to the left and right of them, people began to rise from their bunks, and a sleepy frightened voice wanted to know what was happening.

"Comrades..." Anatoly began, but because of the great emotion that overwhelmed him he could say no more. Low, happy exclamations broke out here and there but were silenced by the others.

Anatoly took hold of himself. "Make your way through the woods to the river, then follow it in either direction, up or down," he said. "Is Gordei Kornienko here? If so, go home, your wife's waiting. ..." Anatoly went outside and stood at the barrack door.

"Thanks ... brother ... our rescuers ..." Anatoly heard voices saying. As those in front began to stream towards the exit barred by the barbed-wire trestles Glavan quickly seized them and directed them towards the opening he had made in the fence itself. The prisoners were pressing towards it, when someone suddenly stepped up to Anatoly and seized him by the shoulders with both hands, whispering in a frenzy of happiness: "Tolya?... Tolya?..."

Anatoly started and peered into the face of the man holding him. "Zhenya Moshkov," he said, for some reason without surprise in his voice.

"I recognized your voice," Moshkov said.

"Wait, let's go together."

It was nowhere near dawn when the three of them, Anatoly, Victor and Zhenya Moshkov, sat down to rest in the thick undergrowth of a narrow ravine. Moshkov was barefoot and in evil-smelling rags.

It seemed now to be a miracle that they had rescued Moshkov so soon after speaking about him while waiting at the river-bank. Exhausted as he was, Anatoly was happily excited. He kept recalling one after another the details of the operation which had been so successful, praised Victor and Glavan and the other fellows, then returned to the wonder of having rescued Zhenya Moshkov. Victor replied sullenly and in monosyllables while Moshkov said nothing at all. Finally Anatoly, too, fell silent. It was very dark and quiet in the ravine.

All of a sudden there was a glow in the sky farther down the Donets. It came suddenly, filling a large part of the sky, which seemed to hang low over the area of the fire, like a red canopy; even in the ravine it became light.

"Where would that be?" Victor asked quietly.

"That's near Gundorovskaya," Anatoly said after a few moments' hesitation. "That's Sergei's work," he whispered.

"He's burning the stacks of corn. He does it every night now."

"We studied in school, we saw the broad open road of life before us, and now this is what we have to turn our hands to!" Victor blurted out. "And there's no other way out."

"Fellows! I can't believe I'm really free.... Oh, you fellows!" Zhenya Moshkov's voice was hoarse. He buried his face in his hands and threw himself down on the dried grass.

Chapter 11

THERE CAME A TIME when even the homeless became afraid to use the highways and larger secondary roads for lorries, cars and petrol tankers were being blown up by mines more and more frequently. So they trundled their handcarts along country lanes or straight across the open steppe.

Hard on the heels of a rumour about a serious accident somewhere along the highway from Matveyev Kurgan to Novoshakhtinsk in the south came another from the north: a whole petrol convoy had been destroyed between Starobelsk and Belovodsk.

Then suddenly a concrete bridge over the Krepenka on the main highway towards Stalingrad blew sky-high. How this could have happened was quite beyond comprehension for the bridge was in the middle of the large populated centre of Bokovo-Platovo and heavily guarded by the Germans. And a few days later the huge railway bridge near Kamensk on the Voronezh-Rostov railway collapsed into the river. The explosion wrecking this bridge, which had been guarded by a platoon of German tommy-gunners and four machine-guns, had been so powerful that the noise it made during the night had come rolling down as far as Krasnodon.

Oleg suspected that this last explosion was most likely the result of the combined efforts of the Krasnodon and the Kamensk underground Party organizations, because about two weeks before it took place Aunt Polina had brought a further request from Lyutikov for a courier he wished to send to Kamensk.

Oleg had chosen Olga Ivantsova.

For the next two weeks Olga had not been within the orbit of the Young Guard's activities, although Oleg knew from Nina that Olga had several times been home in Krasnodon in that period, only to set off again. Two days after the remarkable explosion she had appeared in Oleg's home once again and modestly resumed her everyday duties as courier to the Young Guard headquarters. Oleg was aware that he was not at liberty to question her about anything but occasionally he caught himself watching her face with curiosity and interest. However, she seemed not to notice it and was as even-tempered, calm and taciturn as always. Her immobile face with its strong irregular features, only rarely lit up by a smile, seemed designed to safeguard secrets.

By this time the Young Guard had three operational groups in action along the roads of the district and far beyond its boundaries.

One of them operated on the road between Krasnodon and Kamensk and concentrated on attacks on German officers' cars. Victor Petrov was the leader of this group.

The second covered the Voroshilovgrad-Likhaya roads and was commanded by the recently rescued Red Army Lieutenant Zhenya Moshkov. Its task was to deal with petrol tankers—kill the drivers and guards and run the petrol off into the ground.

The third group was under Tyulenin and had a roving commission. It held up German lorries carrying arms, food and clothing, and hunted for straying and straggling soldiers—hunted them even in the town itself.

The members of each group would join forces to carry out a job and disperse, singly, immediately it was completed. Each kept his weapon buried in the steppe at a spot of his own choosing.

With Moshkov's liberation from captivity, the Young Guard gained yet another experienced leader. Sturdy and strong as a young oak, he had fully recovered from his gruelling experience and lounged along in leisurely fashion, a knitted scarf wound round his neck which made him look bulky, and in high boots and galoshes both of which he had taken from a policeman with the same size feet whom he had killed in the attack on the Shevyrevka village police-station. Though he looked ill-tempered he was, in fact, kind-hearted. His army service, particularly since the day when at the front he had been admitted to the ranks of the Party, had taught him endurance and self-discipline.

A fitter by trade, he had gone to work in the machine-shop of the *Direktion* No. 10, and, on Lyutikov's suggestion, had been made a member of the Young Guard headquarters.

Up to the present there had been no sign that the Germans were concerned about the existence of any organization like the Young Guard, although it already had a number of considerable operations to its credit.

Just as brooks and rivers are formed as a result of the infinitely small movement of subterranean waters which the eye does not see, so the activities of the Young Guard merged inconspicuously into the deep, hidden, broad movement of millions of people seeking to speed the return of the natural condition in which they were living before the Germans came. And in this abundance of greater and lesser acts and operations directed against the Germans, the enemy failed to see the particular mark of the Young Guard.

The front was so far away now that, to the Germans stationed in Krasnodon, the town seemed almost like a remote civilian province of the German Reich. But for the operations of the partisans along the roads, it might have been thought that the *Neue Ordnung* had been established here for all time.

In the north and the south, in the east and in the west a lull had come on all the war fronts just as though all were listening to the rolling thunder of the great battle at Stalingrad. And throughout September and October, the brief daily communiqués on the fighting in the areas of Stalingrad and Mozdok contained something that was so customary and permanent that it seemed that things would always remain thus.

The stream of prisoners which at one time had flowed from the east through Krasnodon and thence to the west had dwindled away to nothing. But German and Rumanian troop formations, transport, guns and tanks continued to move from the west through the town in an easterly direction: they left the town and did not return, and ever new formations continued to arrive, so that Krasnodon was always full of passing German and Rumanian soldiers and officers, and it seemed that this state of affairs would continue for ever.

For several days the Koshevois' and Korostylevs' home had served as billets simultaneously for a German officer flying "ace," on his way back to the front after recuperating from wounds, and a Rumanian officer with his batman, a merry young fellow who spoke Russian and stole everything he could lay his hands on from the garlic in the garden to the frames of the family photographs.

The Rumanian officer was a short man in a lettuce-green uniform with a tie and gold-braid shoulder-straps. He had a narrow black moustache, small bulging eyes and was very lively, even the tip of his nose was in perpetual motion. He had settled himself in Nikolai Nikolayevich's room, but spent all his days wandering about the town in civilian clothes investigating pits and office buildings and army units.

"Why does your chief go about in civvies?" Nikolai Nikolayevich asked the batman with whom he had established an almost friendly relationship.

The merry batman puffed out his cheeks, then, clapping them with the palms of his hands and expelling the air like a circus clown, said very amiably;

"He's a spy!"

Nikolai Nikolayevich was never able to find his pipe after this conversation.

The German "ace" had made himself comfortable in the large room by pushing Yelena Nikolayevna out into Grandma Vera's room and Oleg into the wood-shed. He was a tall, fair-haired man with bloodshot eyes and numerous decorations won in air battles over France and Kharkov. He was fantastically drunk when they brought him along from the *Kommandantur* and remained several days solely because he went on drinking day and night and was therefore never sober enough to leave. He tried to draw everyone in the house into his drinking-bout, with the exception of the Rumanians whose existence he simply ignored. He was quite unable to remain for a second without someone to talk to. In an atrocious mixture of German and Russian he would explain how he would first beat the Bolsheviks, then the British, then the

Americans, and after that everything would be fine. Towards the end of his stay, however, he fell into the depths of gloom.

"Stalingrad!... Ha!" he said lifting his red index finger. "Bolshevik shoot ... puff! Me *kaputt!*" And tears of despondency welled up to his reddened eyelids.

Before his departure he sobered up just enough to go out and fire his Mauser at the chickens in the yards. He had nowhere to put them so he tied them together by their legs and they remained lying near the porch while he collected his belongings.

The Rumanian batman beckoned Oleg over, puffed out his cheeks, deflated them in the manner of a clown and pointed at the dead chickens.

"Civilization!" he said amiably.

Oleg was never able to find his penknife after that.

Under the New Order, Krasnodon witnessed the birth of an elite very much like that of, say, Heidelberg or Baden-Baden—a whole hierarchy of rank and position. At the top of the hierarchy stood *Hauptwachtmeister* Brückner, *Wachtmeister* Balder and *Leutnant* Schweide, the chief of the *Direktion*. The latter was accustomed to working in the clean atmosphere of German enterprises, which were standardized and where everything was provided for. He failed to notice how the perplexity he had once voiced to Barakov concerning the state of affairs in the enterprises under his control was now all that was left of his plan of management. If indeed there were no workers or machinery, no tools, transport or timber, no pits to speak of, then there could be no coal. He could carry out his duties conscientiously only to the extent of checking regularly to see that the Russian stable-boys fed the German horses of the *Direktion* with oats every morning, and signing papers. The rest of his time he devoted with far greater energy to his personal domestic fowl-house, his piggery and cattle-shed and to arranging parties for the officials of the German administration.

A little lower down in the hierarchy came Schweide's deputy, Feldner, *Oberleutnant* Sprick and *Sonderführer* Sanders in his shorts. Still further down stood Police Chief Solikovsky and Burgomaster Statsenko, who was drunk all day long. Every morning Statsenko, puffed up with his own importance and armed with an umbrella, would pick his way neatly through the mud towards the municipal offices in order to return equally staidly in the evening, just as though he were really carrying the burdens of office. At the very bottom of the hierarchy came N.C.O. Fehnbong and his soldiers—it was they who did all the work.

How lacking in comfort and unfortunate was the little mining town when the October rains came down in torrents! There was mud everywhere, no fuel or light, all the fences gone, trees and bushes in the front gardens hacked down, windows broken in the empty houses, from which everything had been stolen by passing soldiers and, in the case of furniture, by the officials of the German administration to use in their own flats. The people could not recognize each other when they met, they had become so emaciated, worn-out and impoverished. At times the most uninitiated person would suddenly stop dead in the middle of the street or wake up at night and think to himself: "Surely, surely this can't be true? It must be a nightmare. A hallucination? Or have I gone out of my mind?"

And only the sudden and mysterious appearance on a wall or telegraph-pole of a rain-soaked little leaflet which burned the mind with the flaming word "Stalingrad!", or the rumbling thunder of yet another explosion somewhere along a road, constantly told people: "No, this is no dream, this is no hallucination—it's the truth! And the battle goes on!"

There had been several days of heavy autumnal rain and driving wind when Lyuba arrived from Voroshilovgrad in a grey low-sprung German car. A young lieutenant jumped out first, held the door open for her and saluted as, suitcase in her hand, she ran up the porch steps of her home, without once looking round.

This time her mother, Yevfrosinya Mironovna, was unable to restrain herself and, when they were getting ready for bed, said to her:

"You really should be more careful, Lyuba dear. You know what people are saying? 'She's too chummy with the Germans....'"

"Is that what they're saying? That's good, Mama darling,

suits me very well indeed," Lyuba said, smiling, and she rolled herself up in a ball and fell asleep.

The following morning Vanya Zemnukhov, who had heard of her arrival, all but ran on his long legs across the large vacant plot which lay between his street and Vosmidomiki district. Covered in mud to the knees and shivering from the soaking rain, he burst into the Shevtsovs' large living-room without even knocking at the door.

Lyuba was alone in the house. One hand held a small mirror in front of her and the other was first patting her uncombed locks, then smoothing down the waist of her simple green house frock, as she paced barefoot to and fro across the room saying something to herself on these lines:

"Oh you little darling Lyuba! I simply don't understand why the boys love you so much. Just what's so nice about you? Ugh! Your mouth's too big, your eyes are too small, your face is plain, your figure ... well, your figure isn't so bad.... No, it's definitely not bad. And yet, if we analyse it— It'd be different if you were running after them, but there's nothing like that.... Ugh, the idea! Running after boys! No, I just don't understand it at all."

Shaking her curls, she inclined her head first to one side, then to the other and began tap-dancing diagonally across the room with a loud patter of her bare feet, singing:

> Lyuba, my little Lyuba,
> My darling little Lyuba....

Vanya, unruffled and cool, watched her, then decided it was time to cough.

Far from confused, Lyuba assumed a provocative expression, slowly lowered the mirror, turned to Vanya, screwed up her blue eyes, then burst into a peal of laughter.

"I can see quite clearly what's in store for Sergei Levashov," Vanya said in his deep bass. "He'll have to go to the queen and steal her slippers for you."*

* In N. Gogol's fairy-tale *Christmas Eve*, Vakula the Blacksmith must produce a pair of the queen's shoes in order to win the heart of his beloved.

"You know, Vanya, it's quite a surprise to me but I love you even more than that Sergei fellow!" Lyuba said but she blushed a little.

"My eyesight's so bad that, frankly, all girls look alike to me. I distinguish them by their voices and I like girls with deep voices like a deacon's. You know, yours is more like a little bell!" Vanya said calmly. "Who's at home?"

"No one. Mama's gone to the Ivantsovas'."

"Let's sit down. And put that mirror away because it gets on my nerves. Now listen to me! Have you been too busy to remember that the twenty-fifth anniversary of the Revolution is not far off?"

"Of course I remember," Lyuba said, though, if the truth were known, she had forgotten all about it.

Vanya bent over and whispered something in her ear.

"Oh good! Good lads! What a wonderful idea!" And she gave him a hearty kiss on his lips so that he nearly lost his spectacles, he was so taken aback.

"...Mama! Have you ever had to dye any of your clothes?"

Lyuba's mother looked at her, puzzled.

"What I mean is, have you ever had a white blouse that you wanted to turn into a blue one?"

"Yes, I've had to do that, dear, at some time or other."

"And did you ever have to dye one red too?"

"The colour wouldn't make any difference."

"Teach me, Mama dear, I might want to dye something one day."

"...Tell me, Aunt, have you ever had to dye any clothing to make it a different colour?" Volodya Osmukhin asked his aunt Marusya who lived with her children in a small house, not far from the Osmukhins.

"Of course, my boy."

"You couldn't possibly dye two or three pillow-cases red for me, could you?"

"But, Volodya dear, sometimes the colour isn't fast and then you'd get red on your cheeks and ears."

"I'm not going to sleep on them. I'll have them on the bed just during the day. It'll look nice...."

"...Dad, I've come to the conclusion that you're extremely good at colouring wood and even metals. D'you think you could dye a sheet red for me? It's those underground people again, you see, they said: 'Give us one red sheet.' Well, what could I say!" Zhora Arutyuniants said to his father.

"I could dye it. But... a sheet! What would Mother say about it?" was his father's cautious reply.

"Why don't you once and for all settle the question as to who wears the trousers in the house—you or Mama? After all! One thing's clear: I must have a red sheet...."

After Valya Borts had received Sergei's note she never once mentioned it to him, nor did he question her about it. But from that day on they were inseparable. From break of day they pined for each other and it was usually Sergei who first put in an appearance. The lean curly-headed young fellow had come to be a familiar sight as he walked along Derevyannaya Street, barefoot even during the cold, rainy October days. Maria Andreyevna, and especially little Lyusia, had taken a great liking to him although he rarely spoke in their presence.

"Why don't you like wearing shoes?" Lyusia asked him one day.

"Easier to dance in bare feet," he replied, grinning.

Nevertheless, the next time he came he was wearing shoes—it was just that he had never found time to mend them.

One day during the period when the Young Guards were displaying a sudden interest in the dyeing of material, the turn of Sergei and Valya had come to go out with leaflets— for the fourth time. They were to take them to a film show in the summer theatre.

The summer theatre, formerly the Lenin Club, consisted of a long high timber building equipped with a bleak, gaping stage which, when films were shown, was hidden behind the screen. People sat on long unpainted benches sunk in the ground and standing on an inclined plane sloping down from the back rows. Since Krasnodon's occupation by the Germans, German films were shown there, mostly war documentaries; from time to time there were performances by touring variety troupes. The seats were not numbered and there was a uniform price of admission. The choice depended upon the energy and enterprise of the audience.

As always, Valya made for the back rows in the upper half of the hall while Sergei remained near the front, not far from the entrance. Immediately the lights went out and while the clamour for seats was still in progress they showered the leaflets in a fan-shaped arc over the heads of the audience.

Amid shouting and cries the leaflets were snatched up everywhere and Sergei and Valya made for the agreed meeting-place near the fourth pillar from the stage. As usual there were more people than seats and they took up their position among those standing in the aisle. When the dust-flecked, bluish beam of light shone out from the projecting booth on to the screen, Sergei nudged Valya's elbow and his eyes drew her attention to the left of the screen where a huge Nazi flag—dark red with the black swastika on a white field—hung suspended over the stage, stirring faintly in the draught from the hall.

"I'll get up there; when it's finished go out with the crowd and start talking at the box office. If anybody comes to clean the hall try and delay them for five minutes or so," Sergei whispered into Valya's ear.

She nodded, without replying.

The name of the film appeared in German on the screen and in white letters below it the Russian sub-title; *Her First Adventure.*

"We'll meet at your home afterwards?" Sergei whispered again, rather bashfully.

She nodded.

The screen had hardly darkened before the start of the final part when Sergei moved away from Valya and disappeared. He vanished leaving no trace, as only Sergei knew how to vanish. No movement had been noticed among the people standing in the aisles. She was curious about just how he would do it. Slowly she made her way nearer to the exit, keeping her eyes on the small door to the right of the screen, through which only Sergei could sneak unobtrusively on to the stage. The show came to an end and the people thronged noisily towards the exit. The lights came on before Valya had seen anything of Sergei. She left the theatre with the crowd and then waited under the trees opposite the exit.

It was cold and damp in the dark park. The few leaves left on the trees were wet and when they moved it sounded as though they were sighing. By now the last of the audience were already coming out. Valya ran quickly across to the box office, bent down and pretended to look for something on the ground in the square of feeble light coming through the open door of the hall.

"You haven't found a small leather purse anywhere here, have you?"

"How could I, my dear? The people have only just stopped crowding out!" replied the elderly woman in the box office.

Valya stooped down and began to grope about here and there in the trampled mud.

"It must be here somewhere.... I pulled my handkerchief out, when I came by here, and a few steps farther on I noticed my purse had gone."

The woman also began to look about for it.

Sergei, meanwhile, had reached the stage—not through the door, however, but by climbing over the rails of the orchestra pit and crossing the stage. He was tugging with all his might to bring the flag down from its fixture on the beam above him but it was too well secured. He took hold of it higher up, and leapt into the air, using his full weight. The flag came away and Sergei nearly fell with it into the orchestra pit.

In the dim light of the deserted hall, with its door wide open to the park, he stood on the stage and began in a leisurely way to fold the big flag several times until it was small enough to tuck down the front of his shirt.

The watchman outside, after closing the door to the projection-room, moved from the darkness into the beam of light from the hall and joined the ticket-woman and Valya, who were still searching for the purse.

"Mind that light there! You ought to know what you can get for it when it's left on!" he shouted angrily. "Swich it off now, we're locking up."

Valya ran to him and seized his coat lapel.

"Oh, please, ple-e-ease, just another second!" she pleaded.

"I've lost my purse, we shan't be able to see! Oh, please ... just another second!" she reiterated, firmly retaining her grip on his jacket.

"Where will you find it now!" the watchman said, softening a little and involuntarily searching round with his eyes.

At that instant an incredibly pot-bellied lad, his cap pulled low over his eyes, darted out of the empty theatre on incongruously spindly legs, leapt high into the air, waggled his legs and vanished into the darkness with a plaintive sound like: "Me-eo-ow...."

Valya managed to say hypocritically, "Pity about that purse!", and then felt such a desire to burst out laughing that she covered her face with her hands, and choking, half ran from the theatre.

Chapter 12

NOTHING STOOD in the way of Oleg's activity once he had explained things to his mother: the whole household was now involved in it, his relatives had all become his helpmates with his mother taking the lead.

No one could say how it was that something valuable from the experience of the older generations had become welded in the heart of this sixteen-year-old youth, something unnoticeably taken from books, something from the tales his father told him, and particularly all that had been impressed upon him by his immediate mentor, Filipp Lyutikov. No one could tell how it had become fused in his heart with the experiences he and his comrades had shared in connection with their first set-backs and their first accomplished designs. But as the work of the Young Guard developed, Oleg acquired increasing influence over his comrades and more and more recognized the fact himself.

He was so sociable, vivacious and direct that it was entirely against his nature to entertain any thought of dominating his comrades or to fail to pay attention to them. But he grew to realize more and more that the success or failure of their enterprises largely depended on whether he, among his friends, was able to foresee everything or whether he made mistakes.

He was always enthusiastically active, always cheerful and, at the same time, reliable, prudent and exacting. In matters which affected him alone, one could still see the schoolboy—he wanted to go alone and paste up the leaflets, burn down corn stoops, steal rifles and waylay Germans. But he was already fully conscious of the share of responsibility for everyone and everything which he now carried, and so he curbed himself.

He was very friendly with a girl older than himself, the strangely frank, fearless, silent and romantic lass, with the dark hair falling in heavy curls to her shapely, firm shoulders, with the beautiful, dark-brown arms and the provocative, passionate expression in the highly arched brows and the large brown eyes. Nina Ivantsova could interpret Oleg's every glance and gesture and carried out his instructions without question, fearlessly and to the letter.

Always busy preparing leaflets or writing out provisional Komsomol membership cards or studying maps, they could spend hours of silence in each other's company, and never feel bored. And when they had occasion to talk, they soared high above the world of everyday things: everything created by the greatness of the human mind that could be understood by young people swept by in their imaginations. At times and for no reason at all both would feel so merry that they did nothing but burst into peals of laughter, Oleg boyishly unrestrained and rubbing together the tips of his fingers and the girl softly, with trusting gaiety and then suddenly becoming womanly, even a little mysterious as though she were hiding something from him.

One day he very shyly asked her permission to recite some verses to her.

"Whose—your own?" she asked, surprised.

"You just listen...."

He began to recite, stuttering badly at first but becoming master of himself after the first few lines:

> *A battle song, my Love, let's sing!...*
> *Oh, do not grieve nor let your courage wane,*
> *For our eagles, scarlet red of feather,*
> *Will soon come soaring back to us again!*

Come soaring back and break the cruel tether
And shatter dungeon and the prisoners' chain.
Your tears, my Love, tomorrow's sunny weather
Will drive away and then you'll smile again.

Your tears will dry—we shall be free together
And sing as though it were the First of May—
And none of us can then be doubtful whether
We may exact revenge!—Not far the day!

"I've not quite finished the end," Oleg said, feeling embarrassed again. "It will be all about us joining the army together.... Would you like to?"

"You've written it for me? Haven't you?" she said gazing at him with shining eyes. "I knew at once that it was yours. Why didn't you tell me that you wrote poetry?"

"Probably because I was shy," he said grinning broadly, and pleased because she liked his verses. "I've been writing for a long time. I don't show them to anyone. Vanya more than anyone else makes me feel awkward about them. You know, he really writes well! Mine are just ... I feel the metre's never sustained in mine and I find it difficult to get the rhythm." He was happy because Nina liked his verses.

Indeed, it so happened that Oleg entered the happiest period of his life, the blossoming of all his youthful faculties, when things were most difficult for him.

On November 6th, the eve of the October celebrations, the Koshevois' home became the meeting-place of the entire Young Guard headquarters with the couriers, Valya Borts and Nina and Olya Ivantsova, in attendance. Oleg had decided to mark this day by solemnly enrolling Radik Yurkin in the ranks of the Komsomol.

Radik Yurkin was no longer the small boy with the calm, meek eyes who had told Zhora Arutyuniants that he was "used to going to bed very early." After participating in Fomin's execution he had become a member of Tyulenin's operational group and went on night raids against German lorries. He looked pretty confident sitting on the chair by the door looking through the window on the opposite side of the room while Oleg made the introductory speech and Tyulenin followed him with an outline of Radik's character. Now and again he felt curious to know what these people were like who were to decide his fate, and he would calmly look, through his long grey lashes, at the headquarters members seated round the large dining-table which was laid as though for a dinner-party. But then two of the girls, one fair and the other dark, smiled at him so caressingly, and both were so charming to look at that Radik suddenly felt unusually embarrassed and turned his eyes away.

"Are th-there any questions to ask Comrade Radik Yurkin?" Oleg wanted to know.

There were none.

"Let him run over his life-story for us," Vanya Turkenich said.

"Tell us the s-story of your life."

Radik Yurkin stood up and in a ringing voice as though answering a question in the class-room began.

"I was born in the town of Krasnodon in 1928. I went to the Gorky School...." With that he had come to the end of the story of his life. He felt that it did not amount to much and, a little less confidently, added:

"Since the Germans came I haven't been to school...."

There were no comments.

"Have you ever done any social tasks?" Vanya Zemnukhov asked.

"No," Radik Yurkin said with a deep, boyish sigh.

"You know what the duties of a Komsomol are?" Vanya asked, staring at the table through his horn-rimmed glasses.

"The duty of the Komsomol is to fight the German fascist invaders until there's not a single one of them left," was Radik Yurkin's very pointed reply.

"Well, I think the lad has a fair understanding of politics," Turkenich said.

"I move we accept him!" said Lyuba who had been on tenterhooks for fear things might not go well with Radik Yurkin.

"Quite right!" said the other headquarters members.

"All in favour of enrolling Comrade Radik Yurkin as a member of the Komsomol?" Oleg said, raising a hand himself and grinning from ear to ear.

They all raised a hand.

"P-passed unanimously," Oleg said and rose from his chair. "Come over here, please."

Radik turned a little pale. Turkenich and Ulya Gromova looked gravely at him and moved aside to let him pass. He walked up to the table.

"Radik!" Oleg began, solemnly. "On the instructions of the Young Guard headquarters I hereby hand you a temporary Komsomol membership card. Guard it as you would guard your honour. You'll pay your dues to your own group. As soon as the Red Army returns, the district committee of the Komsomol will exchange this temporary card for a permanent one."

Radik put out a thin sunburnt hand and took the card. It was the same size as the proper one, cut out of cartridge paper of the kind used for plans and maps, and folded in half. Across the top on the outside, printed in irregular letters, ran the inscription: "Death to the German invaders!" And a little lower: "All-Union Lenin Young Communist League"; still lower and in slightly larger type: "Temporary Komsomol Membership Card." Inside on the left page were Radik's name, surname and patronymic and the year of his birth; below that, the date of joining: November 6, 1942, and lower down: "Issued by the Young Guard Komsomol Organization in the town of Krasnodon. Secretary: *Kashuk*." The right-hand page was laid out in squares for entering payment of membership dues.

"I'll sew it into my jacket and then I'll always have it on me," Radik said so softly he could hardly be heard. He put the card into the inside pocket of his jacket.

"You may go now," Oleg said.

Everyone congratulated him and shook his hand.

Radik Yurkin went out into Sadovaya Street. It was not raining, there was a strong, cold wind. It was almost dusk. That night he had to lead a group of three boys in an operation, in honour of the October Revolution anniversary. Conscious of the membership card he carried, Radik walked down the street towards his home with a stern but happy expression on his face. He reached the approach to the second level crossing and, as he passed the building of the District Soviet which now housed the agricultural *Komman-*

dantur, he pulled back his lower lip, took a deep breath and emitted a piercing whistle, just to let the Germans know of his existence.

Not only Radik, but almost the whole organization was to join in the important job that night in honour of the anniversary.

"Don't forget now, as soon as you're free come straight to my place," Oleg had said. "Except the Pervomaisky comrades!"

These last had planned to have a celebration party in the Ivanikhinas' home that night.

Oleg, Turkenich, Vanya Zemnukhov and the couriers, Nina and Olya, had remained behind in the room. Oleg suddenly began to look worried.

"C-come on, g-girls ... it's t-time," he urged them. He stepped over to the door of Nikolai Nikolayevich's room and knocked. "Aunt Marina! T-time!"

Marina came out of the room in her coat, tying her kerchief round her head; Nikolai Nikolayevich followed. Then Grandma Vera and Yelena Nikolayevna came from their room.

Olya and Nina put on their coats and, with Marina, left the house. They were to keep watch in the neighbouring streets.

It was dangerous to attempt such a thing at such an hour, when people in their homes were not yet asleep and pedestrians were still about in the streets, but how could they let such an opportunity slip?

It was growing darker. Grandma Vera dropped the blackout curtain and lit the lamp. Oleg went out to Marina in the yard. She stepped away from the wall.

"No one about," she whispered.

Nikolai Nikolayevich stuck his head through the ventilation window, looked around and then handed Oleg the end of the flex. Oleg connected it to the pole, then hooked the pole over the mains cable, close to the post so that pole and post merged into one in the darkness.

Oleg, Turkenich and Vanya Zemnukhov seated themselves round the desk in Nikolai Nikolayevich's room with their pencils ready; Grandma Vera sat up straight, with an unfathomable expression on her face, and Yelena Nikolayevna, leaning forward and looking innocent and a little frightened, sat with her on the bed, their eyes glued to the wireless set.

Only Nikolai Nikolayevich's steady, skilful fingers could select the required wave-length so quickly and noiselessly. Straightaway he had tuned into the ovation. Atmospherics made it difficult to hear the voice which was saying:

"Comrades! We are today celebrating the 25th anniversary of the victory of the Soviet Revolution in our country. Twenty-five years have elapsed since the Soviet system was established in our country. We are now on the threshold of the next, the 26th, year of the Soviet state...."

Turkenich, outwardly calm and serious, and Vanya, whose spectacles were almost touching the paper, were quickly taking down the words. It was not very difficult, because Stalin spoke unhurriedly. Now and again he fell silent and they could hear him pouring water into a glass and putting the glass down. All the same, at first it required all their attention not to miss anything. But later they became used to the rhythm of the speech, and then the realization of the unusualness, almost the impossibility of what they were sharing in came home to them.

No one, who has not sat by oil-lamp in an unheated room or a dug-out, with the cold, autumn storms raging outside and people everywhere crushed, humiliated, wretched, who has not, with fingers stiff with cold, tuned the secret radio set to a wave-length from the unoccupied part of his homeland, will ever understand the emotions of these people as they listened to that speech from Moscow.

"...The cannibal Hitler says, 'We shall destroy Russia so that she will never be able to rise again.' That appears to be clear, although rather stupid."

The laughter coming to them from the great hall immediately brought a smile to their faces and Grandma Vera even had to press a hand to her mouth.

"...We have no such aim as to destroy Germany, for it is impossible to destroy Germany, just as it is impossible to destroy Russia. But the Hitlerite state can and should be destroyed, and our first task, in fact, is to destroy the Hitlerite state and its inspirers."

The storm of applause called forth an urge in them to give vent to their feelings, too, in the form of noisy movements, but they were unable to do that, and merely exchanged glances.

Everything that lay dormant in the patriotic emotions of these people, from the sixteen-year-old boy to the aged woman, was coming back to them now, wrapped in the simple, direct language of facts and figures.

It was they, the simple people to whose lot had fallen such incredible sufferings and torments, who now spoke to the whole world:

"The Hitlerite scoundrels ... outrage and slaughter the civilian population of the occupied territories of our country: men and women, children and old folk, our brothers and sisters.... Only villains and scoundrels, devoid of all honour and fallen to the level of beasts, can permit themselves commit such enormities against innocent, unarmed people. ... We know who are the men guilty of these outrages, the builders of the 'New Order in Europe,' all those newly-baked governor-generals or just ordinary governors, commandants and sub-commandants. Their names are known to tens of thousands of tormented people. Let these butchers know that they will not escape responsibility for their crimes or elude the avenging hand of the tormented nations...."

It was their hope and vengeance that was speaking.

This was a breath of the vast world outside their little town now trampled in the mud by the boots of enemy soldiers; a mighty shudder from their native land; the heartbeat of Moscow at night, which had burst into their room and filled their hearts with happiness in the knowledge that this was the world they really belonged to....

A burst of applause drowned each of the tributes made in the speech.

"Glory to our men and women partisans!..."

"You hear that?" Oleg exclaimed, looking at them all with shining, happy eyes.

Nikolai Nikolayevich switched the radio off and a terrible silence filled the room. Everything had gone in a flash. A faint ringing came from the open ventilation window. The autumn wind whistled outside. They were alone in the dimly lit room and hundreds of miles of grief lay between them and the world, which had so recently made itself heard.

Chapter 13

THE NIGHT was so dark that people coming right up against one another failed to see each other. A wet cold wind lashed the streets and whirled round corners; it rattled over the roofs, whined down the chimneys, whistled in the telephone wires and made a humming noise in the telegraph-poles.

One had to know the town like they did to be able to find the way through the darkness and thick mud to the gatehouse.

As a rule, the section of the road, lying between the Voroshilovgrad Highway and the Gorky Club, was patrolled every night by the policeman on duty. But he had evidently found shelter somewhere from the cold and the mud.

The gatehouse was of stone and it was not so much a gatehouse as a crenellated tower like those on a castle. There was a small office at ground level and the gateway leading to the coal-pit itself. A high stone wall ran to right and left of the tower.

Sergei Levashov, who was broad-shouldered, and Lyuba who, though light as a feather, had good, strong legs, seemed to be specially made for the job they both had to do. Sergei thrust a knee forward and held out his hands. Although Lyuba could not see them her small hands straightaway grasped his, and she chuckled softly. She put her overshoe-clad foot on his knee and the next instant was standing on his shoulders, grasping the top of the wall while he retained a firm hold on her ankles to prevent her from falling. Her dress fluttered round his head like a flag. She leaned over the top of the wall clinging to the farther edge, so that the weight of her body rested on her folded arms. She would not have had enough strength in her arms to pull Sergei to the top, but in her present position she was anchored securely enough for Sergei to grasp her firmly by the waist, pull himself up by using his knees, pressed against the wall, and then, with a swift, powerful movement, to transfer first one hand, then the other to the top of the wall. Lyuba made room for him and in another moment he was at her side.

The top of the thick wall sloped and was very wet and slippery, but Sergei stood firmly with his forehead and hands against the wall of the tower. Lyuba climbed up his back on to his shoulders unaided. The crenellated tower was now level with her breast and she found it easy to clamber over the top. The wind tore at her dress and jacket and made her feel that any minute she would be blown off the tower. But the most difficult part was now over.

She took a cloth bundle from her bodice, felt for the cord which ran through the hem and, holding the bundle tightly to keep the wind out, fastened the cloth to the flagstaff. She let go of the bundle and the wind snatched at it with such ferocity that Lyuba's heart began to beat rapidly with excitement. She pulled out a second, smaller cloth and tied it to the base of the flagstaff, so that it hung suspended below the tower and inside the pit territory. Then she lowered herself down to the wall again, using Sergei's back as before, and sat down, dangling her legs, hesitating to jump down into the mud. Sergei dropped to the ground, stretched his arms out and called up to her softly. She could not see him, could only guess where he was by the sound of his voice. Suddenly her heart sank. She stretched out her arms, screwed her eyes up tightly and jumped. She landed straight in his arms and put her own round his neck. He held her thus for a moment. But she freed herself, jumped to the ground and, her breath on his face, whispered excitedly:

"Sergei! Let's get the guitar, eh?"

"Let's! And I'll get a change, you've made a mess of me with those overshoes of yours," he said, delighted.

"No, you won't; they'll accept us just as we are!" She laughed gaily.

Valya and Sergei Tyulenin had been allotted the centre of the town which was, of course, the most dangerous area: German sentries were stationed at the building of the District Soviet and the labour exchange; a policeman guarded the *Direktion* and the gendarmerie headquarters lay just at the foot of the hill. But they were favoured by the darkness and the wind. Sergei had chosen the deserted house of the Mad Squire and, while Valya kept watch on the side facing the District Soviet, Sergei climbed the rickety ladder, leading up to the loft, which was old enough to have been placed there during the lifetime of the Mad Squire himself. The job was done in fifteen minutes.

Valya was feeling very cold and she was glad that everything was over so quickly. But Sergei laughingly put his face close to hers and said:

"I've got a spare one. Let's hoist it on the *Direktion.*"

"What about the policeman there?"

"What about the fire-escape there?"

The fire-escape ladder was, in fact, at the rear of the building, out of sight from the main entrance.

"Let's go then," she said.

In the inky darkness they climbed down to the railway siding and walked for a long time along the sleepers. Valya thought they must be near Verkhneduvannaya, but she was wrong. Sergei could see in the dark like a cat.

"Here we are," he said. "Only follow close behind me, because if you go off down that hill you'll run slap into the police training-school."

In the park the wind howled among the trees, and the bare branches knocked together and showered cold drops over them. Sergei led her swiftly and surely through lane after lane, until the rattling of the school roof told her they had not far to go.

Sergei began to climb the iron staircase, she could hear it rattling a little as he went up, then the faint noise ceased and he was gone. He seemed to be away a very long time. Valya waited alone in the darkness at the foot of the fire-escape.... What a cheerless, horrible night it was with the awful soughing of the leafless branches. How weak and helpless they were—she and her Mama, and little Lyusia—in this dark, terrible world! And her father? Suppose, even now, he was wandering about somewhere, without shelter. Half-blind!... Valya had a vision of the vast expanses of the Donets steppe, the mines now blown up, the rain-soaked little towns and villages—all without lighting, and with gendarmes everywhere.... Suddenly it seemed to her that Sergei would never come down from the rattling roof and her courage deserted her. But then she felt the staircase shaking and her face at once assumed its cold, independent expression.

"Are you there?" He smiled in the darkness.

She sensed that he was holding a hand out to her and she

put out her own. His was ice-cold. What had he not endured, thin, in boots with holes in them in which he had been walking about for so many hours that they were probably full of water, and in his old, threadbare, unbuttoned jacket? She took his face between her hands; it was also as cold as ice.

"You're quite frozen," she said pressing her hands to his cheeks.

He stood still and they did not move for some moments. Only the bare branches knocked against each other overhead. Then he whispered:

"No more circling around tonight.... Let's get away somewhere, through the fence...."

She withdrew her hands from his face.

They approached Oleg's home from the neighbouring house. Sergei suddenly seized Valya's arm and they flattened themselves against the wall. Puzzled by this, Valya put her ear close to his lips.

"Two people coming this way. They heard us and have stopped too," he whispered.

"You imagined it!"

"No, they're still there."

"Let's make for the backyard!"

No sooner had they passed the side of the house than he again held her back: the other two did exactly the same on the opposite side of the house.

"You're imagining things."

"No, they're there."

The Koshevois' door opened, someone came out and bumped into the two people Sergei and Valya were dodging.

"Lyuba? Why don't you come in?" Yelena Nikolayevna's soft voice said.

"Sh-h-h...."

"Friends!" Sergei said, seizing Valya by the hand and pulling her along.

They heard Lyuba laugh softly in the darkness; she and Levashov with his guitar stepped forward and, choking with laughter, the four of them entered the Koshevois' kitchen arm in arm. They were all so wet, muddy and happy that Grandma Vera raised her long, thin arms in their bright-coloured sleeves and cried:

"Goodness gracious! Where *have* you been?"

Never in their lives had they enjoyed such a party as this one by the light of a smoking lamp, in an unheated room, in a town where for over three months the Germans had held sway.

It was extraordinary how all twelve young people managed to find room on one divan. Pressing close to each other, their heads bent, they took turns to read the speech aloud and their faces unconsciously mirrored what some of them had experienced that day sitting by the radio and others had experienced during the night tramping through the mud. Their faces also reflected the tender affection which some among them had for each other and which communicated itself to the remainder as though by an electric current; and the extraordinarily happy feeling of community which arises in young hearts when together they come in contact with a great human idea, and particularly the idea which expresses what is most important, at the moment, in their lives; their faces so shone with friendship and bright youth and confidence in the future that, in their company, Yelena Nikolayevna felt young and happy. And only Grandma Vera sat quite still, her thin face propped on her brown hand, and gazed at the youngsters from the heights of her many years with a sort of fear and sudden compassion.

After reading the speech the young people remained sitting still, thinking. A sly look appeared on Grandma Vera's face.

"Just look at you!" she said. "How can you sit like this on such a wonderful holiday! Look at the table—the drinks are not just a decoration! They're there to be drunk!"

"Oh Granny, you're the best person in the world!... Let's gather round the table, come on now!" Oleg called.

The main thing now was not to make too much noise and they found it great fun saying "hush" in unison every time anyone raised his voice. Nevertheless they decided to take turns keeping watch outside and it became a joke to chase out for guard duty anyone who was getting too friendly with his or her neighbour, or had become too merry.

In his normal state, tow-headed Styopa Safonov could talk about anything on earth, but if he had occasion to sip wine, there was only one topic for him—his favourite.

Little beads of sweat covered his freckled snub nose and he began to tell Nina Ivantsova, who sat next to him, all about the flamingo. He was immediately hushed and sent out on guard duty. He came back indoors just when the table was being moved aside and Sergei Levashov had picked up his guitar.

Sergei played in the debonair way that was particularly common among Russian craftsmen, the whole attitude, and especially the face, expressing complete indifference to what is going on: he does not watch the dancers or the audience; and, of course, he does not look at his instrument; in fact he looks at nothing in particular, but his hands by themselves produce something that makes one want to dance.

Sergei took up his guitar and played a Boston two-step that had been fashionable just before the war. Styopa Safonov rushed at Nina and they began to whirl round. Lyuba the Actress was of course better than the rest, but the best among the men was Ivan Turkenich; tall, graceful and gallant, he was the real officer. Lyuba danced first with him, then with Oleg who, at school, had been considered one of the best dancers.

Styopa Safonov kept his hold on Nina, who had grown very silent, almost wooden in fact; he took her through all the dances and explained to her in great detail the differences in the plumage of the male and female flamingo and how many eggs the female laid.

Suddenly Nina's face flushed up and she looked quite ugly as she said:

"Styopa, it's awkward dancing with you, you're so short and you keep treading on my toes and you never stop talking nonsense."

With that she broke loose and ran off.

Styopa was about to make a bee-line for Valya, but just then she moved off with Turkenich. He caught Olga Ivantsova. She was a quiet, serious girl and was more taciturn than her sister, so he was able to tell her about the strange habits of the flamingo with impunity. Still, he did not forget easily when he had been offended, consequently his eyes continued to search round for Nina. She was dancing with Oleg, who was calmly and confidently whirling her large, strong figure this way and that; there was an involuntary smile on her lips, there was happiness in her eyes and she looked most attractive.

Grandma Vera could stand it no longer and called out:

"What kind of dancing d'you call that? What next will they think of in those foreign parts! Sergei, give us a Gopak! Come on!"

Without even raising his eyebrows, Sergei switched over to a Gopak. In two bounds Oleg was across the room and had seized Grandma by the waist; she showed no trace of confusion but, with startling agility, set off with him, stamping the floor with her shoes. The way in which the dark hem of her skirt circled smoothly an inch or two from the floor showed that Grandma was an excellent dancer, yet it was her hands, rather than her feet, and particularly the expression on her face, that revealed her abandon and skill.

In nothing is the national character so manifested as it is in songs and dances. Oleg, with sly mischief not expressed on the mouth or even in the eyes, but somewhere in the quivering corners of his eyebrows, Oleg with the collar of his Ukrainian shirt unbuttoned and beads of sweat on his forehead, with his large head and shoulders held easily and almost motionless, threw himself into the squatting postures of the Gopak with such dashing, devil-may-care enthusiasm that the born Ukrainian in him, as in his grandmother, was immediately obvious.

Marina, black-eyed and beautiful with her snow-white teeth, and with all her beads which she wore for the sake of the party, could restrain herself no longer and with a stamp of her feet and her arms flung out as though releasing something precious, burst into a whirlwind dance round Oleg. But Nikolai Nikolayevich caught her, Oleg had Grandma's waist once more and, stamping and tripping, the two couples set off together again.

Suddenly Grandma flopped on to the divan and fanned her flushed face with a handkerchief, crying, "Oh! My old bones are no good for this!"

They all grew lively and clapped their hands. Now they had all stopped dancing, yet Levashov, blind and deaf to everything round him, continued to play the Gopak as though nothing else mattered to him, that is, until he suddenly broke off in the middle of a bar, the palm of his hand silencing the strings.

"The Ukraine has come out on top!" Lyuba cried. "Now, Sergei! Give us one of ours!"

Hardly had he touched the strings than she was off in a Russian dance, with such a pattering of feet and stamping of heels that none of them could watch anything but her feet. With her head proudly erect on her shoulders, she sailed round the floor and marked time in step before Sergei Tyulenin, then stamped her feet for the last time and withdrew, inviting him to take her place.

With the detached facial expression typical of Russian working folk, whether playing an instrument or dancing, Sergei casually approached Lyuba, his old, patched shoes tapping the floor. He took a turn round the room and came back to Lyuba, and then withdrew with a stamp of the heels. Lyuba whipped out her kerchief and seemed to float through the air as she followed him round, her heels clicking, and made a full circle round the room, and the art she brought to her dancing was not ostentatious, but subtly expressed in her still, erect head and the way she occasionally conferred on the spectators a careless, humorous turn of the head, in which, however, only her nose seemed to participate. Sergei slid over the floor after her, his legs performing miracles of skill, his face wearing the same indifferent expression and his arms hanging easily yet expressing as much devotion to the task in hand as did his legs, by their casual and somewhat comical endeavours.

Lyuba quickened her pace to keep time with the heightened rhythm of the guitar and whirled round to face Sergei, who continued to pursue her with such desperation, with such a frenzy of unrequited love that as he stamped his shoes lumps of mud flew off them in all directions.

The remarkable thing about his dancing was the perfect sense of time, the daring—a daring that was closely concealed. As for Lyuba, the devil alone knew what she did with her firm and shapely legs; her face became more and more flushed, her curls rippled and tossed and looked like purest gold, and as they all beheld her their eyes seemed to say, "That's our Lyuba! There goes our actress!" Only Levashov, who was in love with Lyuba, did not watch her; his face still had an expression of inspired indifference to what was going on, while his strong nervous fingers continued to tremble swiftly across the strings of his guitar.

Sergei, with an expansive, desperate flourish as though flinging his cap to the floor now made straight for Lyuba, his palms slapping his knees and the soles of his shoes in time to the music, and drove her into the midst of the spectators where both came to a halt with a final stamp of their heels. They all laughed merrily and roundly applauded. With a sad note in her voice Lyuba suddenly said:

"That was it—our Russian dance...."

She danced no more after that, but sat beside Sergei Levashov with one of her small, white hands resting on his shoulder.

That same day the Young Guard headquarters, by permission of the underground district Party committee, had given some money to a few families of Red Army men at the front who were most in need.

The Young Guard's funds came not so much from membership dues as from the sale of cigarettes, matches, clothing and a variety of other articles, and particularly alcohol, all of which the boys managed to steal from German lorries.

Volodya Osmukhin had been to see his aunt Litvinova during the afternoon and had handed her a packet of Soviet currency which was in circulation as well as German marks, though its rate of exchange was very low.

"Aunt Marusya, the underground people want you and Kaleria Alexandrovna to have this," he had told her. "Buy something for the children to celebrate our great holiday...."

Like Litvinova, whose neighbour she was, Kaleria Alexandrovna was the wife of a Red Army officer. There were children in both homes and both families were in great distress: the Germans had robbed them of everything they possessed, even most of their furniture, which had been loaded on lorries and carried off.

The two women had decided to celebrate the holiday by preparing a supper-party; they had bought a little home-brewed vodka and baked a cabbage and potato pie.

At about eight o'clock Volodya's mother Yelizaveta Alexeyevna, his sister Lyudmila and Aunt Marusya with her two girls gathered in Kaleria's home, where she lived with her children and her mother. The boys had promised to come later—they explained that they had to see their friends first. The adults had a drink or two and bemoaned the fact that such a holiday as this had to be celebrated secretly. The children sang Soviet songs in hushed voices. The parents shed a few tears. Lyudmila grew very bored. Then the children were sent to bed.

At rather a late hour Zhora Arutyuniants arrived. He was covered in mud and this made him feel dreadfully ill at ease when he emerged into the light, especially when he saw that the other boys were not there yet and that he had to sit beside Lyudmila. He was so put out that he downed the half a glass of home-brew which she handed him and immediately felt tipsy. By the time Anatoly Orlov and Volodya turned up he was in such a black mood that even the arrival of his comrades could not rouse him out of it.

The two new arrivals also had a drink. The adults were engrossed in a conversation of their own; from scraps of the conversation the boys exchanged with each other Lyudmila soon realized that they were not really just on a visit.

"Where?" Volodya whispered to Zhora, leaning across Tolya the Thunderer.

"Hospital," Zhora replied sullenly. "And you?"

"Our school—" With a sparkle of boldness and cunning in his narrowed, black eyes, Volodya bent closer to Zhora and excitedly whispered something in his ear.

"What? Not a fake?" Zhora had momentarily dropped his melancholy mood.

"No, the real thing," Volodya said. "Pity about the school but what's the use of worrying? We'll build a new one!"

"If you must make appointments, then you should stay at home," Lyudmila said to Volodya, offended for being excluded from these secrets. "All day long there's been a stream of fellows and girls wanting to know: 'Is Volodya in? Is Volodya in?'"

Volodya laughed, and passed the question off with a joke.

Tolya the Thunderer, all raw-boned limbs and bristling hair, suddenly rose from his chair and announced in a voice that was not quite steady:

"My congratulations to all on the occasion of the twenty-fifth anniversary of the Great October Revolution!"

He had found the courage to do so, because he was drunk. His face was quite flushed, his eyes had grown cunning, and he fell to teasing Volodya about a girl called Fimochka.

With his dark Armenian eyes staring sullenly at the table in front of him, Zhora suddenly said to no one in particular:

"It's not contemporary of course but I can well understand Pechorin*.... It may of course not be in keeping with the spirit of our society.... But in different circumstances they might deserve precisely such an attitude." He fell silent, then added gloomily: "Women—"

Lyudmila demonstratively rose from her chair, went over to Tolya the Thunderer and, kissing him tenderly on the ear, said, "Tolya, my dear, you're getting very drunk, aren't you?"

In general, the situation seemed to be deteriorating, and so with the abruptness and common sense typical of her, Yelizaveta Alexeyevna suddenly announced it was time to go.

Aunt Marusya, accustomed as she was to rising early because of the house work and the children, woke up at dawn, pushed her feet into slippers, slipped into her dress and quickly lit the kitchen stove. She put on the kettle, and, with her thoughts far away, crossed over to the window, which looked out on to vacant land. To the left lay the Children's Hospital and the Voroshilov School; on the hill to the right loomed the building of the District Soviet and the house of the Mad Squire. Suddenly she let out a stifled shriek.... Beneath the bleak low sky and the fleeing, tattered clouds a red flag fluttered in the wind on the roof of the Voroshilov School. The wind tore at it so fiercely that the flag stood out like a quivering rectangle, only to droop, a second later, so that it hung in folds, its edges curling and uncurling in the breeze.

A still larger flag floated over the house of the Mad Squire. A large group of German soldiers and several civilians stood at the foot of a wooden ladder leaning against the house and regarded the flag. Two soldiers were actually on the ladder,

* Pechorin—the principal figure in Lermontov's *A Hero of Our Time*, a sketch of 19th-century Russian life in the Caucasus.

one of them level with the roof, the other a few steps lower down; they looked at the flag, then exchanged a few words with the people on the ground, then looked at the flag again. For some reason or other no one climbed any higher to take the flag down and it fluttered there magnificently for all to see from the highest point in the town.

Aunt Marusya kicked off her slippers, beside herself with excitement, stepped into her shoes and, her hair uncombed, without a kerchief on her head, ran next door to the neighbours.

She found Kaleria Alexandrovna in her underclothes, her swollen legs bare, kneeling on the window-sill and gazing at the flags with an ecstatic expression in her face. Tears streamed down her dark, sunken cheeks.

"Marusya!" she said. "Marusya! They've done it for us Soviet people! They remember us, our people haven't forgotten us! Oh, Marusya! I ... my congratulations on this great day!"

They rushed into each other's arms.

Chapter 14

THERE WERE red flags flying not only over the house of the Mad Squire and the Voroshilov School. They fluttered above the *Direktion* and the building of what was once the district cooperative; over pits No. 12, No. 7-10; over 1B and 2B pits; and over all the pits in Pervomaisky and the Krasnodon mining settlement.

People streamed in from all parts of the town to look at the flags. Dense crowds gathered at the buildings and pit gates. Gendarmes and policemen ran their feet off dispersing the crowds but no one could be got to take the flags down, for at the foot of each flag was a piece of white cloth with the black inscription: "Mined."

N.C.O. Fehnbong had climbed the roof of the Voroshilov School and discovered a wire leading from the flag into the darkness of a window; and he had indeed found a mine under the eaves, which had not even been camouflaged.

Not one of the gendarmes or the SS men knew how to deal with mines. *Hauptwachtmeister* Brückner sent his car to gendarmerie headquarters in Rovenki for sappers. But there were no sappers in Rovenki and the car raced off to Voroshilovgrad.

At two o'clock in the afternoon sappers arrived from Voroshilovgrad and removed the fuse from the mine in the school loft. No mines were found anywhere else.

The news of Krasnodon's red banners in honour of the October Revolution travelled to all the towns and villages of the Donets Basin and the disgraceful lapse of the German gendarmerie could not be concealed from Major-General Klehr, regional *Feldkommandant* in Yuzovka. *Meister* Brückner received instructions to track down and arrest the underground organization at any cost. If he failed to do so, he would lose the silver flashes on his shoulder-straps and be reduced to the ranks.

Meister Brückner had not the vaguest ideas about the organization he was to arrest and so he behaved just as any gendarme and Gestapo agent would have behaved in such a case; he cast his drag-net, as Sergei Levashov had once called the process, and dozens of innocent people were arrested throughout the town and the district. But although his drag-net was of fine mesh he failed to catch a single member of the district Party organization which had issued the instructions to hang out the flags, or a single member of the Young Guard. The Germans had no reason at all for supposing that the organization which had actually done the work consisted of mere boys and girls.

And indeed it was difficult to suppose such a thing when we remember that on the night when the most frightful arrests were made, Styopa Safonov, most prominent of all the underground fighters, was sitting with his head on one side, licking a pencil and making the following entry in his diary:

"Senka came at five o'clock; invited me to come with him to his house in Golubyatniki district saying there would be some nice girls there. We went and sat around for a bit. Two or three of the girls were all right but the rest not up to much."

During the second half of November the Young Guard received information from contacts in the farmsteads that the Germans were driving a herd of some fifteen hundred head of cattle from Rostov Region to the rear. The herd had already been ferried to the right bank of the Donets at a point near Kamensk and was now being driven along between the river and the big highway between Kamensk and Gundorovskaya. In addition to the Ukrainian drovers from the Don, with the herd was a guard of about a dozen elderly German soldiers from an administrative unit, who had been armed with rifles.

On the night this news was received, Tyulenin's, Petrov's and Moshkov's operational groups armed themselves with rifles and tommy-guns and gathered in a wooded ravine on the bank of a stream which flowed into the Northern Donets. They were within sight of a wooden bridge over which the road crossed the stream. Scouts brought back a report that the herd had halted for the night among the shocks of corn, some of which the drovers and soldiers had knocked down to provide food for the cattle.

There was a heavy cold rain, with snow, which melted and formed a muddy, soggy pea soup underfoot. The boys' boots were heavy with the lumps of mud collected on their march across the steppe. They pressed close together to warm each other and cracked jokes—"How d'you like this health resort?"

At the first gleam of dawn it was so heavy, overcast and sleepy and the daylight took so long to come, that it seemed to be thinking: "Is it worth while getting up in such disgusting weather or shall I turn round and go back to bed?" But its sense of duty overcame these lazy early-morning reflections and dawn came to the land of the Donets. The mixture of rain, snow and fog reduced visibility to about three hundred paces.

On the orders of Turkenich, who was in command of all three groups, the boys, with rifles at the ready in their cold-stiff hands, took up positions on the right bank of the stream, on which side the Germans would appear on the bridge.

Oleg was also taking part in this operation and he lay hidden near the bend a little further away from the bridge. With him was Stakhovich who had been taken along to be tested in action. He had taken part in many Young Guard activities since his exclusion from the headquarters, and had almost re-established his good name—not a difficult task, since in the eyes of most of the Young Guard he had never lost it.

Because of a soft streak in human nature, to be found sometimes also in individuals with strong principles, people are very loth to change an attitude to a man which has become a habit, part of their life. They even consider it awkward to do so. And this, even though irrefutable facts have shown the person to be in no way what he had seemed. "He'll mend his ways! We all have our faults," is what people say in such cases.

Not only the rank-and-file members of the Young Guard who knew nothing about Stakhovich, but also most of those who were in close touch with the Young Guard headquarters treated him as though nothing had happened.

Oleg and Stakhovich lay silently on the fallen leaves in the undergrowth and looked about over the bare, wet, slightly undulating terrain. They were straining their eyes to penetrate as far as possible the misty curtain of pouring rain and drifting snow, when suddenly they heard a discordant lowing from hundreds of cattle, growing in volume till it became a cacophony of sound, as though the devil himself were playing the bagpipes.

"They're thirsty," Oleg softly said. "They'll water them in the stream. That will suit us nicely."

"Look! Over there, look!" Stakhovich whispered excitedly.

In front and to the left of them red heads emerged from the mist—first one, then another, a third ... ten, twenty, and then countless heads with strange, thin horns growing straight upwards, thin sharp points inclining towards each other. Their heads were like ordinary cows' heads but cows, even hornless ones, have clearly defined prominences or bulges between their ears from which the horns develop. These creatures, however, whose bodies were as yet invisible owing to the dense mist close to the ground, had their horns growing straight out of the smooth top of their heads. These beasts were like chimeras as they came into view from out of the mist.

They were probably not the leading animals of the herd but part of its extreme left flank; from behind and far beyond them came a mighty bellowing and one could sense the powerful movement of animal bodies knocking against each other and the thudding of thousands of hoofs, which shook the ground.

Just then Oleg and Stakhovich heard the sound of lively conversation in German somewhere ahead of them on the right-hand side of the road. One could tell by their voices that the Germans had rested well and were in good humour. They were stepping out merrily, their boots squelching in the mud.

Oleg and Stakhovich bent low and hurried to the place where the boys were lying.

Turkenich was standing under the clayey cliff which overhung the stream, not more than ten yards from the bridge. His tommy-gun rested lightly in the crook of his left arm, his head protruded a little from the tufts of scorched, damp grass, as he looked into the distance along the road. At his feet, very angry, sat red-haired Zhenya Moshkov with a muffler round his neck. He too held a tommy-gun in his left arm and was watching the bridge. The rest of the boys lay one below the other in a diagonal along the sloping bank. Sergei was first in the line and Victor was at the end; both armed with tommy-guns.

Oleg and Stakhovich threw themselves on the ground between Moshkov and Sergei Tyulenin.

The carefree, leisurely talk of the elderly German soldiers seemed now to be just overhead. Turkenich dropped on to one knee and released the safety catch of his gun; Moshkov laid himself flat, straightened his damp, padded jacket under him and got his gun ready.

Oleg watched the bridge with a naïve, childlike expression on his face. Suddenly there was a tramp of boots on the bridge and a group of German soldiers in mud-splashed greatcoats, some with rifles carelessly carried by the strap and others with them slung across the shoulder were seen on it.

Among the first few was a tall lance-corporal with a florid, fair *Landsknecht* moustache; he was saying something turning back now and then so those behind would hear him. He looked round him turning his face towards the boys lying along the bank, and the soldiers, with the natural curiosity of people passing an unfamiliar spot, also looked along the stream to right and left of the bridge. But as they did not expect to see any partisans in these parts, they did not see any.

At that moment Turkenich's tommy-gun let fly, its sharp, ear-splitting rattle making a continuous sound; next Moshkov opened fire and then the rest sent over a hail of sporadic shots from their rifles.

Everything had happened so suddenly and so differently from what Oleg had imagined it would be that he had no time to fire; for the first second he had regarded it all with childlike surprise, then something prompted him to fire as well, but by that time it was all over. Not a single soldier could now be seen on the bridge; most of them had fallen and two, who had only just stepped on it, had doubled back to the road. Sergei, followed by Moshkov and Stakhovich, jumped up the bank and shot them.

Turkenich and several of the others sprang to the bridge. One of the soldiers was still writhing and they finished him off. They then dragged all the soldiers by their legs into the bushes so that they could not be seen from the highway, and carried off their rifles. The herd of cattle had lined the stream for a long distance and the animals were slaking their thirst in the stream, some with their forelegs, or even all their legs, in the water; some of them had straggled across to the opposite bank. They drank with their damp nostrils widely dilated, with a powerful sucking sound as though several pumps were at work.

In the gigantic herd there was a confusion of ordinary draught cattle, of red, grey and dappled, of very ponderous, low-chested, thick-horned bulls looking as though cast in metal, as they stood firmly on their strong, cloven hoofs; cows of all breeds, graceful heifers, animals just about to calve, their flanks distended, udders full and the teats swollen and red, for they had not been milked; strange-looking dull-red cows with horns growing straight from their smooth crowns, keeping somewhat aloof from the rest of the herd; black and white Friesians and red and white Holstein cattle, looking so respectable with the white patches that they seemed to be wearing caps and aprons.

The drovers were aged gaffers who during their lives had, as it were, acquired the slow-moving habits of their herds or, perhaps, had simply become used to the vicissitudes of life in war-time; for they had paid no attention to the firing close at hand and had seated themselves in a circle on the wet ground behind the drinking cattle and had lit their pipes. However, they stood up at once when they saw armed people approaching them.

The boys politely raised their caps and offered them a greeting.

"Good-morning, Comrade Gentlemen!" replied an old fellow, a thick-set, dumpy chap with splay feet and wearing a sleeveless jacket of untanned sheepskin over his linen shirt. The fact that he held a plaited hunting-crop instead of a *batıg*, the long drover's whip, which the others carried, showed that he was the leader. Clearly anxious to allay the fears of his companions, he turned to them and said:

"It's all right—they're partisans!"

"Excuse us, good people," Oleg said, again raising his cap and putting it on again. "We've finished off the German guard and now we're asking you to help us disperse the cattle in the steppe, so that the Germans don't get them."

There was silence for some moments. Then:

"Hm.... Disperse them, eh!" said one bright, little old fellow. "They're our own cattle, from the Don. Why should we scatter them in these foreign parts?"

"All right! Then you'll drive them back again, eh?" Oleg said with a broad grin.

"No, we can't do that, the way things are," ruefully agreed the little old gaffer.

"If we disperse them our own people will pick them up."

"Ay-ya-yai, such a powerful herd!" suddenly cried the little old man in desperation mixed with pleasure and seized his head in both hands, a gesture which showed clearly what these old people must be enduring, forced as they were to drive this immense herd away from their native soil and to foreign, German land. The boys felt sorry for both the cattle and the old men. However, there was no time to be lost.

"Give me your whip, Grandpa!" Oleg said, and taking the drover's whip from the hands of the little old man walked down to the herd.

As the cows and oxen quenched their thirst they gradually crossed to the other side of the stream where some of them straggled away, their nostrils close to the bare wet ground, in search of scraps of withered grass. Others stood dejectedly with their hind parts turned towards the rain or looking round as though wondering: "Where are those drovers, what are we to do now?"

With extraordinary confidence, as though now he was in his element, Oleg calmly made a way for himself among the cattle, elbowing one aside, slapping the back or neck of another one, or driving them off with a crack of the whip. He crossed the river and cut his way into the thick of the herd. The old fellow in the sleeveless sheepskin jacket came to assist him with his hunting-crop. He was followed by the other old men and all the boys.

Yelling and cracking their whips they finally managed to split the herd in two, losing a great deal of time over the job.

"No, this's no good," said the gaffer in the sheepskin jacket. "Fire into them with your tommy-guns; they're lost to us anyway."

"Ay-ya-yai!" Oleg winced as though in pain, and almost simultaneously his face involuntarily took on a fierce expression; he took the gun from his shoulder and fired a burst into the herd.

Several animals fell to the ground; others, wounded, rushed off into the steppe bellowing frantically. Scenting the smell of powder and blood one half of the herd began to stampede fanwise out over the steppe, and the ground hummed with the sound of their hoofs. Sergei and Zhenya Moshkov each fired a round into the second half of the herd and it also moved off.

The boys followed after them and whenever a dozen or more of the animals crowded together they fired into them. The steppe resounded with the noise of rifle-fire, the lowing and bellowing of cattle, the thunder of hoofs, the cracking of whips and the dreadful plaintive shouts of human beings. Sometimes a heifer was hit while running, stopped in its tracks, its forelegs crumpling under it, and fell heavily forward on its muzzle. Wounded cows lowed piteously, raised their beautiful heads and lowered them again helplessly. The whole area was covered with carcasses, red through the mist against the black earth.

Long after the boys had separated and each had gone singly on his way they encountered cows and oxen roaming here and there over the steppe.

Some time later a column of smoke rose into the sky over the steppe. Sergei Tyulenin acting on Turkenich's instructions had set fire to the wooden bridge which by a miracle had until then escaped damage.

Oleg and Turkenich had gone off together.

"Did you notice those cows with the horns growing straight up from their heads and the points almost touching on top?" Oleg asked excitedly. "They're from the eastern part of the Salsk steppe and maybe even from as far as Astrakhan. They're Indian cattle. They've come down to us from the days of the Golden Horde."

"How d'you know?" Turkenich asked sceptically.

"My stepfather always used to take me with him on business trips when I was a child and he knew a lot about that sort of thing."

"Stakhovich showed his mettle a bit today, didn't he?" Turkenich said.

"Ye-es ..." Oleg replied uncertainly. "The journeys we used to make, my stepfather and I! Just imagine, the Dnieper and the sun and the immense herds of cattle in the steppe.... Who'd have thought then that I ... that we—" Oleg again wrinkled his forehead as though in pain, put his thoughts behind him with a gesture of the hand and spoke no more until he reached his home.

Chapter 15

Since the Germans had succeeded in deceiving the people and so driving off to Germany the first party of townsfolk, everyone had become alive to the danger and had fought shy of registering at the labour exchange. Consequently the Germans were now seizing them in the streets and in their homes much as Negroes were hunted down in the jungle in the days of slavery.

Nove Zhittya, the news sheet published in Voroshilovgrad by Department 7 of the *Feldkommandantur*, printed in every issue so-called letters from deported children to their parents alleging that they were living in freedom and abundance in Germany and that they were getting high wages.

Occasionally, too, letters came to Krasnodon from the young people, some of whom were working in East Prussia on the lowest-grade jobs like farm-labouring and domestic service. The letters arrived free of censorship marks and, in them, much could be read between the lines, though they only told sparingly of the external circumstances in which they were living. Most of the parents received no letters at all.

The woman at the post-office explained to Ulya that all letters arriving from Germany were examined at the post-office by a specially appointed Russian-speaking German from the gendarmerie. He intercepted them one after another, kept them locked up in a drawer of his desk and when they had grown into a large pile he burned them.

Acting on the instructions of the Young Guard headquarters, Ulya Gromova had taken charge of all the work directed against the recruitment and deportation of young people; she wrote and distributed leaflets, found jobs in the town for young people who were in danger of being deported or, with Natalya Alexeyevna's assistance, secured their release, on the pretext of illness, and sometimes found refuge in the farms for those who had registered and escaped.

Ulya did all this not only because she had been entrusted with the work, but also because of a sort of inner compulsion: she probably felt a little to blame for having failed to save Valentina from the dreadful fate. This feeling of guilt persecuted Ulya the more because neither she nor Valentina's mother had had any news from her.

One night, early in December, the Pervomaisky lads, assisted by the woman at the post-office, stole all the undelivered letters from the censor's drawer. The sack containing them was now lying in front of Ulya.

With the coming of the cold weather she had moved back into the house and lived with the rest of the family; but like most of the Young Guard, she kept her membership of the organization secret from her relatives.

She had experienced some trying moments when her parents, worried for her safety, had tried to find a job for her. Her bed-ridden mother had stared at her in a bewildered way with her wild-bird black eyes, and then fallen to weeping. And for the first time in many years old Matvei Maximovich had shouted at his daughter. He had gone purple in the face up to his bald pate, and for all his huge bony frame and terrifying fists, there had been something pathetic in the sight of the thinning curls round his bald head and his inability to influence his daughter.

Ulya had told them that if they ever again reproached her with being a burden for them she would leave the house. Matvei Maximovich and Matryona Savelyevna had been completely bewildered, because Ulya was their favourite. For the first time it became quite obvious that old Matvei Maximovich had lost his authority over his daughter, while his wife was too ill to assert hers.

Because Ulya concealed her activities, she was particularly careful to carry out her duties about the house, and whenever she went out for any length of time, she would refer to the fact that life was so humiliating and poor now that she must cheer herself up in the company of her friends. Ever more frequently she felt her mother gazing at her long and sorrowfully, as though she were looking into her soul. Her father seemed to shrink into himself and had less and less to say when she was present.

The situation was different in Anatoly's home. When his father left for the front he had become the head of the household, for both his mother Taisya Prokofievna and his little sister idolized him and he had it all his own way. And now, here was Ulya sitting with the sack of letters in front of her, not in her own home but in Anatoly's. He had gone away for the day to see Lilya Ivanikhina in Sukhodol. Her slim fingers removed the letters from the envelopes slit open by the censor, and she cast a rapid glance over their contents and then placed them on the table.

Her eyes quickly scanned the names and surnames, the messages to parents and sisters with the conventional greetings, so touching in their artlessness. There were so many of them that even her cursory examination of them took up a great deal of time. But among them, there was no letter from Valentina....

Ulya bent forward in her chair, dropped her hands in her lap and stared into space with a helpless expression on her face. It was quite still in the house. Taisya Prokofievna and the little girl had gone to sleep. The small flame of the oil-lamp, with the tiny curl of sooty smoke at its hazy tip, now toppled over, now stretched upward again, moved by Ulya's breathing. Above her the old pendulum clock counted the seconds with its rusty-sounding "tick ... tock ... tick ... tock." The Popovs' house, like Ulya's, stood alone among the farmsteads and the sensation that their lives were lived in complete isolation from the lives of other people had become ingrained in Ulya since childhood and was particularly strong during the autumn and winter nights. The Popovs' house was solidly built and the thin whining of the wind outside, which had a wintry note in it already, came only faintly through the shutters at the windows.

Ulya felt herself utterly alone in this world of mysterious, unpleasant sounds and with the now toppling, now rising, little flame of the oil-lamp....

Why was the world so arranged that people were never able to give their hearts completely to another? How was it that although her feelings and Valentina's had always been in fullest harmony since earliest childhood—how was it that she, Ulya, did not forsake her home with all its every-day worries, did not renounce everything she had become accustomed to in life, renounce parents and comrades, and devote all her efforts to saving Valentina? To be suddenly at her side, to be drying her tears and throwing open the road to freedom for her? "Because that would not be possible. Because you have given your heart to something greater than Valentina alone—you have given your heart to the liberation of your native land," replied an inner voice. "No, no," she said to herself, "don't try to find excuses. You did nothing about it even before it was too late, because you could not find it in your heart to do so. You turned out to be like all the rest."

"But why couldn't I do it now?" Ulya thought. She gave herself up to childlike dreaming: she would find courageous people, ready to do her bidding; they would overcome all obstacles and fool the German Commandant and there, in that horrible country, she would find Valentina and would say to her, "I've done everything in my power, I haven't spared myself to save you and now you're free." Oh, if all this were only possible! But it was not possible, there were no such people, she herself would be too weak. A friend could do it—a boy, if Valentina only had one.

But then, had she herself, Ulya, a friend like that? If she were even now in Valentina's position, who was there to do all that for her? No, she had no such friend. Probably there were no such friends in the whole world.

Was there anyone in the world whom she could come to love? What would he be like? She could not picture him but he lived in her heart: tall and strong, and fair in everything, and courageous and with kind eyes. An inexpressible yearning for love surged into her heart. To close the eyes, to forget everything and give all of oneself.... Her dark eyes reflected the light of the hazy-golden flame of the oil-lamp and now shone with the happiness, now dimmed with the misery of her emotions....

Suddenly Ulya heard the faintest little moan like someone softly calling. A shiver passed over her, the finely chiselled nostrils quivered.... But it was only Anatoly's sister moaning in her sleep. The heap of letters lay in front of Ulya on the table. Delicate wisps of smoke curled up from the tongue of the flame. Faintly from outside the shutters came the soft whine of the wind and the pendulum continued to count the seconds: "tick ... tock ... tick ... tock...."

A blush came to Ulya's cheeks. She was unable, even to herself, to account for this feeling of shame: was it because she had neglected her work because of her dreaming? Or was there something yet to be told in her dreaming, something of which she was ashamed? Angry with herself, she began to examine the letters carefully, searching out those which might be utilized.

"If you could only have read them! It's horrible!" she said, when she confronted Oleg and Turkenich. "Natalya Alexeyevna says that altogether the Germans have deported about 800 people from the town. And a secret register's been made of another 1,500, with their addresses and everything. Something on a really large scale must be done, like attacking them when they're escorting a party of people away, or maybe killing that fellow Sprick!"

"We could kill him but they'll only send someone in his place," Oleg said.

"We must destroy the register. And I know how: we'll burn down the whole labour exchange!" she said suddenly, her face vindictive.

This, the most fantastic feat, accomplished by the Young Guard, was carried out by Sergei Tyulenin and Lyuba Shevtsova with the assistance of Vitya Lukyanchenko.

There was already a touch of winter in the air; there were pretty hard frosts at night and the clods of earth and furrows left by the lorries became frozen solid and only thawed out a little by midday when the sun had become warm.

The appointed meeting-place was the Lukyanchenkos' kitchen garden. From there they set out along the railway siding, then straight across the hill-side, ignoring the road. Sergei and Vitya carried a tin of petrol and several incendiary bottles. They were both armed. Lyuba's entire equipment consisted of a bottle of honey and a copy of *Nove Zhittya*.

The night was so still that the slightest sound could be heard. If a foot tripped or there was a careless movement so that the petrol tin made a metallic sound, it would be enough to give them away. And it was so dark that for all their excellent knowledge of the locality they were unable sometimes to determine their whereabouts. They would take a step and listen, then another step and listen again.

They took a long time to get there. It seemed an eternity to them. Strange as it might appear, when they heard the tramp of the sentry at the labour exchange they became less afraid. The sound of his steps would come clear and distinct through the night, then suddenly cease for a few moments while he stopped to listen or, perhaps, simply to rest near the porch.

The long front of the building with its porch faced the agricultural *Kommandantur*. They could not yet see the building, but they could tell by the sentry's footsteps that they had reached the left side of it. They skirted it in order to get at the building from its long rear wall. Vitya Lukyanchenko remained behind some twenty yards from the building. Sergei and Lyuba stealthily moved up to one of the windows. Lyuba smeared honey over the whole of one of the lower oblong panes and then stuck a sheet of the newspaper over it. Sergei pressed against the glass. It splintered but did not fall and he was able to lift all of it away. This work required patience. They treated the pane in the adjoining frame in the same manner.

Then they took a rest. The sentry seemed to feel the cold and was stamping his feet on the porch. They had to wait because they were afraid that from the porch he might hear Lyuba's footsteps inside the building. It seemed ages before he started to walk up and down again. Then Sergei bent over a little and held his hands together. Lyuba gripped the window-frame, put one foot on to Sergei's hands and swung the other leg over the sill. She then held on to the inside wall and straddled the window-sill, feeling all the time that the frame was cutting her thighs. But this was not the time to notice such trifles. She lowered her leg inside, carefully trying to reach the floor. At last she was there, inside the building.

Sergei passed her the petrol tin.

She was rather a long time inside. Sergei was very much afraid that she might knock into a chair or table in the dark.

When she finally reappeared at the window she smelt strongly of petrol. She smiled at Sergei, threw her leg over the window-sill, then put out a hand and her head. Sergei took her under the arms and helped her out of the window.

Then Sergei was alone at the window, with the strong smell of petrol in his nostrils. He stood there until he was sure that Lyuba and Vitya were at a safe distance. Then he pulled one of the incendiary bottles from inside his shirt and hurled it into the gaping window. The flash was so powerful that it momentarily blinded him. He did not throw the rest of the bottles, but raced back over the hill to the railway.

The sentry yelled and fired after him. Sergei heard one of the bullets whistle past very high over his head. The whole locality was intermittently illumined by a strangely pallid light, then again fell back into the darkness. Then suddenly a column of flames shot up and it became as light as day.

That night Ulya had gone to bed without undressing. Softly, in order not to wake anyone, she had gone to the window from time to time and lifted a corner of the blackout. But everything was dark outside. She was anxious about Sergei and Lyuba and sometimes she felt that she had planned the affair to no purpose. Slowly the night dragged on and on. She became very tired and dozed off.

Suddenly she woke up and, knocking a chair over with a crash, rushed to the door. Her mother awoke and asked something in a sleepy frightened voice. Without replying, Ulya darted out into the yard as she was, in her thin dress.

Over the town, beyond the hill, there was a red glare, in the distance shots could be heard, and Ulya thought she also heard shouts. The light from the flames showed up the roofs of houses and sheds even in this remote part of the town.

The sight of the red glare did not make Ulya feel what she had expected to feel. The glow in the sky, the light it threw on the buildings, the shouting and firing and her mother's terrified voice combined and caused a vague feeling of alarm in Ulya's heart. She felt alarmed for the safety of Lyuba and Sergei; and in particular concerning the effect the whole affair might have on the whole of the organization at a time when efforts were being made to track them down. She also felt alarm lest, in the midst of all this terrible, enforced work of destruction she might lose something supreme and good, something that was yet alive in the world and that she was feeling in her own heart. It was the first time that Ulya had experienced this feeling.

Chapter 16

ON NOVEMBER 22, 1942 dozens of secret radio sets in all the districts of Voroshilovgrad Region picked up the late-night communiqué of the Soviet Information Bureau which reported that Soviet forces had cut the two railway lines supplying the German front at Stalingrad and had taken a tremendous number of prisoners. Then the entire, unseen underground work which, little by little, Ivan Protsenko had been organizing and directing day in and day out suddenly rose to the surface and began to assume the proportions of a popular movement directed against the New Order.

Every day brought fresh news that the Soviet troops were developing their successes at Stalingrad. And all that had been but a vague gleam in the mind of each Soviet citizen, some sort of expectation or hope, suddenly filled the heart to overflowing with the thought: "They're coming!"

Early in the morning of November 30th, Aunt Polina delivered Lyutikov's milk as usual. Filipp Petrovich had in no way altered the daily routine he had established on the day he first went to work at the central workshops. It was a Monday morning. Polina found him dressed in an old suit, shiny from continuous contact with metal and lubricating oil; Filipp Petrovich was about to go to work. The suit was one he had always worn in working hours, even before the occupation. When he arrived at the works office he still covered the suit with blue dungarees as always. The only difference, however, was that in former days the dungarees were kept in a cupboard in the office, but nowadays he carried them home with him in a bundle under his arm. At the moment it was lying on a stool in the kitchen while Lyutikov finished his breakfast.

He judged from the look on Polina's face that she again had news for him, good news. Together they went into his room with a little joke for Pelagea Ilyinichna's benefit, which was not really necessary, for in all the months he had lived in her home she had loyally never once given any indication that she had noticed anything.

"Here, I've taken this down specially for you ... it only came through last night," she said excitedly; from her bodice she produced a scrap of paper covered with fine writing and handed it to him.

The morning before she had brought him the previous night's communiqué of the Soviet Information Bureau about the large-scale offensive launched by Soviet troops in the Velikiye Luki and Rzhev sectors of the Central Front. The news now was that the Soviet troops had reached the eastern bank of the Don.

For some moments Lyutikov gazed intently at the sheet of paper, then raised his stern eyes to Polina and said:

"*Kaputt* ... Hitler *kaputt*. ..."

He had used the same words which, according to eyewitness reports, the German soldiers used when they surrendered. But he said the words very seriously and then embraced Polina. Tears of happiness filled her eyes.

"Shall we duplicate it?" she asked.

Lately they had almost ceased putting out their own leaflets, but had, instead, distributed the printed Soviet Information Bureau communiqués that were dropped to them at stipulated places by Soviet aircraft. The previous night's communiqué was so important, however, that Lyutikov decided to publish it in leaflet form.

"Combine the two communiqués. We'll paste them up tonight," he said. He took his lighter from his pocket, set light to the scrap of paper over an ash-tray, rubbed the ash, and, pushing open the ventilation window, blew the ash out into the back garden. As the frosty air blew on his face, his eyes rested on the frost which lay on the leaves of the sun-flowers and pumpkins in the kitchen garden.

"Has there been a hard frost?" he asked, a note of anxiety in his voice.

"About the same as yesterday. The puddles are frozen solid and it's not thawing yet."

Lyutikov wrinkled his forehead, and stood for a moment at the window, engrossed in his own thoughts. Polina waited for further instructions, but he seemed to have forgotten her presence.

"I'm going now," she said quietly.

"Yes, yes," he responded as if coming down to earth, and heaved such a deep sigh that Polina thought perhaps he was unwell.

Lyutikov was, indeed, not well. He was suffering from gout and shortness of breath, but he had been unwell for a long time and it was not that which had caused him to become so engrossed in thought. Lyutikov knew that for people in their position trouble always comes from the least expected quarters.

Lyutikov's position as the leader of the underground organization was advantageous in so far as he had no direct dealings with the German administration and was therefore able to operate against it without being held responsible. It was Barakov who was responsible to the German administration. And for just this reason, in all matters affecting production, Barakov, on Lyutikov's instruction, was doing everything he could to appear in the eyes of the German administration and of the workers as a director doing his best for the Germans. He did everything, that is, with the exception of one thing: Barakov was not to notice anything that Lyutikov was doing against the Germans.

Outwardly the situation was something like this: an energetic, capable Barakov was doing everything in his power to build everything up, and everyone saw that; an insignificant, modest Lyutikov was pulling everything down again—and not a soul saw that! Things at a standstill? No, things were moving on the whole, but moving at a slower rate than was required. The reasons? The reasons were all the same: "No workers, no machinery, no tools, no transport; when there's nothing, then there's nothing you can be blamed for."

According to the division of labour that existed between Barakov and Lyutikov, the former, after politely accepting a heap of orders and instructions from the management, would warn Lyutikov about them and then develop frenzied activity in order to carry all these orders and instructions into effect. Lyutikov would frustrate them.

Barakov's feverish endeavours to restore production were completely fruitless. But they served admirably to cover the other, most fruitful activity he engaged in as organizer and leader of the partisan raids and subversive acts along the roads which passed through Krasnodon and the adjoining districts.

After Valko's death, Lyutikov had himself organized the sabotage in all coal-mining and other enterprises of the town and district, above all in the Central Electro-Mechanical Shops, because it was on these, more than on anything else, that the restoration of the equipment of the pits and other enterprises depended.

There was a large number of them throughout the district and in the absence of an adequate number of people they could trust, the German administration had no effective control over them. Everywhere there took place what from time immemorial has popularly been known as "swinging the lead": instead of working, people were "swinging the lead," and there were those among them who voluntarily and on their own initiative assumed the role of "Lead-Swingers-in-Chief."

For example, Nikolai Nikolayevich's mate, Victor Bystrinov, had a position in the *Direktion* similar to that of a book-keeper or clerk. Not only did he himself do nothing in the *Direktion*, but he also formed a group of people who did nothing in the pits and, being an engineer by training and calling, he taught them what they had to do to get all the rest of the workers in the pits to do nothing.

For some time now old Kondratovich had been in the habit of calling on him. Since the death of his comrades, Shevtsov, Valko and Shulga, he had been as solitary as a tall, wizened oak on a bare hill-side. The old fellow was positive that the Germans had not touched him because of his son, who dealt in beer and spirits and was on friendly terms with the policemen and the lower ranks of the gendarmerie.

Incidentally, in one of his rare moments of frankness, the son had asserted that German rule was less to his advantage than Soviet rule.

"The people have become terribly poor. Nobody's got any money!" he had admitted with something like grief in his voice.

"Just you wait, the boys'll be home soon from the front and you'll be in heaven then. No trouble or worry there!" the old man had replied calmly, in his deep, hoarse voice.

Kondratovich was still doing no work and spent days on end loafing about the smaller pits and the homes of miners, unconsciously becoming a repository of all the evil, the stupidities and the blunders of the German administration at the mines. As an old, skilled workman of vast experience he despised the German administrators and his contempt for them grew in proportion to his increasing conviction that they were worthless administrators.

"You young engineering comrades can judge for yourselves," he said to Bystrinov and Nikolai Nikolayevich. "They've got everything under their thumb and what d'they get? Two tons a day from the whole district! This is capitalism, while we're used to working for ourselves, you might say. But they've got a century and a half of experience behind them, and we've had twenty-five years and could teach them a thing or two! Then there's their world fame as managers and financiers, organizing robbery on a global scale! Disgusting, that's what I call it!" growled the old man in his monstrously deep voice, and spat.

"Upstarts, that's what they are! And they'll get nowhere with their 20th-century robberies either: they were beaten in 1914 and they'll be beaten this time! Always keen on grabbing, but no creative imagination. Petty-minded rabble on the crest of a wave.... They're a complete failure at running industry and the whole world can see it!" Bystrinov said with an angry sneer.

The aged workman and the two young engineers were able each day, without any special effort, to lay their plans to bring to nought what little effort Schweide made to obtain coal.

In this and like manner the activity of scores of people underpropped the activity of the underground district Party committee.

It was more difficult and dangerous for Lyutikov to do all this in the shops where he worked himself. The rule he observed was this: he would carry out implicitly all the instructions of a minor order which in themselves were not of decisive importance in the production process, and he would dilly-dally interminably with the fulfilling of large orders. Since the earliest days of their work under German management, several presses and the pumping equipment of a number of large pits had been undergoing repairs, but so far nothing at all had been repaired or restored.

However, Director Barakov could not be placed in a position where none of the measures he took showed any results. Some of the jobs were, therefore, brought to completion, or nearly so, for an unforeseen break-down would bring everything to a standstill. An electric motor, for instance, would fall out of commission over and over again—a few grains of sand did the trick. While it was being repaired the engine would fail: the cylinder would be overheated and the cooling water turned on. Lyutikov had people in every shop to do these small acts of diversion; officially these people were under the supervision of their own departmental foremen, but in actual fact they only did what Lyutikov told them.

Barakov had lately taken on a large number of new workers from among former servicemen. Two Red Army officers were operating hammers in the forge. Both were Communists and at night became partisan group commanders and engaged in large-scale wrecking activities on the roads. Quite unnecessary trips, allegedly for tools and stores, to workshops in other districts were frequently made to serve as cover for the absence from work of various people. Workers outside the underground organization were also sent on official trips of this sort, in order not to arouse their suspicions. The workers would thus be convinced that it was impossible to obtain either tools or equipment, and the management would see that director and departmental foremen were doing their best. The work failed to progress and there thus appeared to be a legitimate reason for the failure.

The workshops had become the centre of the Krasnodon underground organization; forces unknown to anyone were concentrated at one spot, always ready to hand; it was simple and easy to get in touch with them. But in that very fact lay dangers.

Barakov worked boldly, with self-restraint and in an organized fashion. Being a military man and engineer, he was attentive to details.

"You know, I've organized everything to a T," he said to Lyutikov at an opportune moment. "And why should we proceed on the assumption that we're more stupid than they are?" he said. "So, being wiser, we have to outwit them. And outwit them we shall!"

Lyutikov dropped his massive chin on his chest, which gave his face a still more drooping appearance; this was always a sign that he was displeased about something.

"You make it appear too easy," he said. "They are Germans, fascists. True, they're not wiser than you and not more cunning than you. But they need not worry about whether you're right or wrong. When they see things going wrong, they'll wring your neck without thinking twice about it. Then they'll put a scoundrel in your place which would mean either the end of all of us, or else, having to run away. And we haven't the right to run away. No, my friend, we're skating on thin ice. Maybe you are already being careful, but now you should be three times as careful."

These were the thoughts in Lyutikov's mind as he lay tossing heavily on the bed in the darkness of his room and sleep refused to come. He also often thought that time was running out....

As the delays in filling orders increased and the technical hitches, break-downs and accidents accumulated, Barakov's standing with the German administration became ever more ambiguous. But a still greater danger arose from the fact that in the course of time an ever-widening circle of people in the workshops, among whom there were numerous experienced workers, came more and more to the conclusion, and could not fail to do so, that someone in this enterprise was deliberately throwing a spanner into the works.

Barakov who was always seen with Germans and spoke their language, and was exacting as far as the work was concerned, was looked upon by the workers as being on the Germans' side. They shunned him and as far as the shops were concerned he could hardly come under suspicion. Suspicion could only fall on Lyutikov. All the same there were very few people in Krasnodon indeed who believed that Lyutikov was genuinely working for the Germans. He was the type of Russian worker who used to be regarded as the conscience of the working class. Everyone knew him and trusted him—and the people make no mistakes.

He had several dozen workers under him in the shop. No matter how little he said, and how modestly he behaved, the workers at the bench could not fail to notice that his instructions, issued as it were in passing, a little absent-mindedly and uncertainly in the face of difficulties, ran counter to the interests of production.

His wrecking activity was composed of trifles, each of which, taken separately, was not noticeable. But as time went on the trifles piled up and became something on a large scale and Lyutikov himself became more noticeable. By far the greater number of the workers round him were people he could trust and he guessed that there were also quite a few people, whose attitude was like that of his landlady, Pelagea Ilyinichna. They saw everything, sided with him but did not reveal anything either to him or to anyone else or even to themselves. But it does not take many scoundrels to get one given away; when the occasion arises one single coward is enough.

The most important work entrusted to the workshops was the restoration of Krasnodon's large pumping-station, which supplied water not only to a group of pits, but also to the central part of the town and the central workshops themselves. About two months previously, Barakov had been charged with the work and had passed it on to Lyutikov.

The task was a simple one but, like all the rest, went against the grain. However, the pumping-station was required very urgently. *Herr* Feldner had several times arrived in person to check on the progress of the work and was very angry because progress was slow. Even when the pumping-station was ready, Lyutikov would not start it up, saying it had to be tested first. Its system of water-pipes and conduits had been filled. The early-morning frosts had come early this year and were getting still harder.

When it was almost time to knock off one Saturday, Lyutikov arrived to take over at the pumping-station. He nagged endlessly about leaking tanks and leaking pipes and with great care tightened nuts and stopcocks. The foreman followed after him, saw that everything was in good working order and said nothing. Outside in the road the workers were awaiting events.

At last, Lyutikov and the foreman came out to the workers. Lyutikov took a tobacco pouch from his waistcoat pocket and a few carefully cut slips of the newspaper *Nove Zhittya*, and without saying anything offered the workers his home-grown rough-cut tobacco. Eager hands accepted the tobacco, because even home-grown tobacco was a rare thing by this time. Their usual smoke now was a foul mixture, half of which was hay, generally known as "my grandma's mattress."

They stood silently round the pumping-station smoking. From time to time they threw a questioning glance at Lyutikov and the foreman. Lyutikov finally dropped his stub on the ground and pressed his boot on it.

"Well, that seems to be the lot for today. Time to knock off now," he said. "It's obvious we can't hand over the job now, it's too late. We'll wait till Monday."

He felt they were all looking at him perplexedly; it was freezing hard even now, though it was early in the evening.

"The water should be drawn off," said the foreman uncertainly.

"It's not winter yet, is it?" Lyutikov said sternly.

He had not the slightest desire to meet the foreman's

glance, but it so happened that he did. And he realized then that the foreman understood everything. And judging by the sudden awkward silence everyone else probably understood. With great self-control Lyutikov said casually, "Let's go then," and in profound silence they all walked away from the pumping-station.

Lyutikov recalled all this as he looked through the small ventilation window at the thick layer of frost on the leaves of the sunflowers and pumpkins, which the bitter cold had blackened.

As he had expected the whole team of workmen was there, waiting for him at the pumping-station. There was no need to tell him that the pipes had swollen and burst, that the whole works was now quite useless and everything had to be started from scratch again.

"Pity. But who could have expected it! A hard frost like that!" Lyutikov said. "Never mind, don't let's be down-hearted. We'll have to change the pipes. There aren't any others, of course, but let's do our best to find some."

They all looked nervously at him. He knew that they all respected him for his courage and were frightened at what he had done, but were still more frightened by his cool manner. Yes, the people Lyutikov worked with were all right. But for how long could he continue tempting Providence?

By tacit agreement, Barakov and Lyutikov never met in their leisure hours. This was to prevent anyone having even an inkling of their friendship or even of the possibility of their having any dealings with each other than those in connection with their work. When there was urgent need to have a talk, Barakov would call Lyutikov to his office and never fail to call in other department foremen before and after he had gone.

It was essential now for them to have a talk.

Lyutikov walked into his own small office in the shop, tossed his rolled-up dungarees on to a chair, removed his cap and overcoat, smoothed his grey hair, ran a comb through his clipped, bristling moustache and went to Barakov.

The works offices were in a small brick building in the yard.

Unlike the majority of the Krasnodon offices and homes

inside which the temperature had dropped with the advent of the cold weather to below that on the streets, the works offices were as warm as any of the houses and offices in which the Germans lived or worked. Barakov was sitting in his warm office in a loose serge jacket with a wide turn-down collar over a neatly pressed blue shirt with a brightly coloured necktie. He had grown thinner and was well-tanned, which made him look younger than usual. He had let his hair grow and had a wavy quiff on his forehead. The quiff, the dimple in his chin, the clear, direct, bold look in his large eyes and the tightly compressed thick lips which signified strength, made a two-fold impression on people in the existing circumstances.

Barakov was sitting in his office doing literally nothing at all. He was very glad to see Lyutikov.

"You know already?" Filipp Petrovich asked, sitting down opposite him, and breathing heavily.

"Good riddance!" A faint smile played round Barakov's thick lips.

"No, I mean about the communiqué."

"I know about that, too." Barakov had his own radio.

"Well—and how's all that going to affect us in the Ukraine?" Lyutikov asked in Ukrainian, grinning. He was Russian, but having grown up in the Donbas, he sometimes took this sort of liberty.

"This is how," Barakov replied, also in Ukrainian. We'll prepare a general rising." He made a wide circular movement with both arms, and it was quite clear to Lyutikov just what Barakov's preparations would be. "As soon as our troops approach the town—" he moved his hand across the table and closed his hand.

"Exactly." Lyutikov was pleased with his colleague.

"I'll have the whole plan here for you tomorrow. It's not the children who are holding things up, but the lack of drumsticks and sweets...." It so happened that all the phrases Barakov used went into rhyme and this made him laugh. What he was in fact saying was that there would be no shortage of willing people but not enough rifles and ammunition.

"I'll tell the lads to get busy. They'll produce them. It's not a question of the pumping-station," Lyutikov went on, suddenly raising the subject uppermost in his mind. "It's not that. It's just— Well, you know what I mean."

Barakov frowned hard.

"D'you know what I suggest? I suggest I should fire you," he said firmly. "I'll complain that you're to blame for the freeze-up in the pumping-station and fire you."

Lyutikov thought for a moment: this might indeed offer a solution.

"No," he said, after a brief pause. "I would have nowhere to hide. And even if I had, we mustn't do it. They'll understand everything immediately, you'd be in for it and the others as well. To lose the hold we have at the present—no, it just wouldn't do," he said decisively. "No, we'll wait and see how things turn out at the front. If our troops move rapidly we'll start working for the Germans with such enthusiasm and drive that even if anyone had been suspecting us he would realize at once that he'd been mistaken, because we would be doing our best just when things were going badly for them at the front! All the same our own people would reap the benefit from our work!"

For a moment Barakov was struck by the extraordinary simplicity of this move.

"But if the front comes very close, they'll put us on repairing armaments," he said.

"If the front comes very close we'll chuck everything to hell and join the partisans!"

"Tough old fellow," thought Barakov, pleased.

"We must set up a second centre of leadership," Lyutikov said. "Outside the works, without you and me. A sort of reserve." He very much wanted to add something comforting, a half-joking remark like: "We shall never need it, of course, but better safe than sorry," and so on; but then he felt that neither he nor Barakov needed anything of the sort.

"We've got some experienced people now and if anything happens they'll manage quite well without us. Isn't that so?" he added.

"Yes, that's true."

"We must call a meeting of the district Party committee. The last time we called a meeting was before the Germans came. Where's our inner-Party democracy I'd like to know?" Lyutikov looked severely at Barakov and winked.

Barakov laughed. They had not indeed called a meeting of the district Party committee because as things stood in Krasnodon, it was almost impossible to call it. But the most important matters were decided by them only after consultations with the other leading people of the district.

On his way back through the workshop to his own small office, Lyutikov encountered Moshkov, Volodya Osmukhin and Tolya Orlov, who worked at the adjoining benches. He walked across to the fitters' benches, which ran down half the length of the wall and pretended to check the jobs. The boys, who had just been smoking and having a chat, made a show of filing away at something.

As Lyutikov passed his bench, Moshkov looked up at him with a nasty grin and muttered:

"Well, did he sack you?"

Lyutikov guessed that Moshkov already knew about the pumping-station and was referring to Barakov. Like the other lads, Moshkov did not know the truth about Barakov and considered him a stooge of the Germans.

"Don't talk about it." Lyutikov shook his head slowly just as though he really had been on the carpet. "How's it going?" he asked Osmukhin, bending over as though to examine the job in the vice, then mumbled softly through his prickly moustache:

"Tell Oleg I want to see him tonight. Same place."

This was yet another vulnerable point in the Krasnodon Young Guard underground organization.

Chapter 17

THE RED ARMY'S SUCCESSES became ever more apparent not only at Stalingrad and along the Don but also in the Northern Caucasus and the Velikiye Luki area and to keep pace with them, the Young Guard's activities assumed ever wider proportions and became increasingly daring.

By now the Young Guard was a large, growing organization with branches throughout the district and over a hundred members. It had an even larger army of helpers.

In developing its activities, the organization went on to acquire new members and could not fail to do so, for that was its job. True, the young people began to feel they were becoming rather conspicuous, as compared with the days when they had first launched their activities. But what could they do? To a certain extent this was unavoidable.

Yet the more wide-spread the Young Guard's activities became, the closer was the "drag-net" of the Gestapo and the police drawn round them.

At one of the headquarters meetings Ulya suddenly said: "Who among us knows the Morse code?"

No one asked for what it was required; neither did anyone treat the question as a joke. Perhaps for the first time since they had begun to work together the members of the headquarters entertained the thought that they might, indeed, be arrested. But it was only a fleeting thought for they could see no danger threatening them for the time being.

It was just at this period that Oleg was summoned for a private talk with Lyutikov.

They had not seen each other since their first meeting and found that each had changed a great deal. There was more grey in Lyutikov's hair and he seemed to have become stouter and bulkier. One could sense that this was not a sign of good health. He rose and paced the room briskly several times during their conversation. Oleg listened to his breathing and it seemed to him that Lyutikov found it difficult to carry his heavy body. Only his eyes still held the same stern expression and showed no trace of fatigue.

Lyutikov noticed that Oleg had developed and even grown physically. He was now a grown lad, passing through the best years of his life. The features of the face with its high cheek-bones seemed to have become stronger, more clearly defined; only his large eyes and something in the line of his full lips now and again revealed the former schoolboy expression, particularly when he smiled. At this meeting he was in more of a pensive mood, however, sitting stoop-shouldered with his head drawn down between his shoulders and with long wrinkles on his forehead.

Returning several times to the subject, Lyutikov questioned him closely and in detail regarding all the Young Guard operational groups, the old ones and those newly formed; he demanded to know the names and traits of character of the members. One felt that he was not so much interested now in the external aspect of the matter, about which he was kept well informed by Aunt Polina, as in the internal state of the organization and especially in Oleg's views about his organization and what he personally thought about the state of affairs inside it.

Lyutikov wanted to know what proportion of the members knew each other, how liaison was maintained between the headquarters and the groups, what links existed between the numerous groups themselves, and how they coordinated their work. He referred to what they called operation "Cattle Dispersal" and spent some time questioning Oleg about what technical method the headquarters used in order to send word to the groups about any impending action, how the group leaders had notified the boys and in what manner they had met together. He was also interested in the more ordinary measures, such as pasting up leaflets, and also more from the viewpoint of liaison and leadership.

Let us repeat here that it was a feature of Lyutikov's conversation with people that he always gave them a chance to say all they had to say and was never in a hurry to express his own opinion. He never tried to ingratiate himself with the person he was talking to, and conversed naturally, as an equal, with young and old alike.

Oleg was conscious of this. Lyutikov spoke with him as though he was a political leader and listened to his opinions. At any other time such an attitude would have filled Oleg's heart with pride and happiness. But now he felt that Lyutikov was not quite pleased with the Young Guard. He had questioned him and had then suddenly stood up and begun to pace the room, which was so unlike him. Then he had stopped asking questions, and did nothing but pace up and down. Oleg had become silent too. At length Lyutikov dropped heavily into a chair opposite Oleg and raised his stern eyes to him.

"You've matured a lot. The organization has grown up and you've grown up yourselves," he began. "That's good. You're being very useful to us. You've made yourselves felt among the people and the time'll come when they'll thank you for it. But I'll tell you this: there's something wrong somewhere. ... Don't accept another member into your organization without my permission. You've got enough. The time has now come when even the laziest and most timid will help us without necessarily being in the organization. You follow me?"

"I understand," Oleg said softly.

"Your liaison ..." Lyutikov paused. "The arrangements are amateurish. There's too much dashing round to each other, to each other's homes. Particularly to your home and to Turkenich's. That's dangerous. If I, for instance, were someone living in your street, I would notice it and begin to wonder: 'Why are those lads and girls everlastingly running to his house, day after day and even at night when no one's supposed to be out? What do they come for?' That's what I'd be thinking if I lived in your street. Don't forget that the Germans are looking for you and they're bound to notice all this coming and going in the long run. You people are young, I dare say you sometimes get together for purposes other than political, don't you? Say, just for a bit of fun?" Lyutikov asked with a good-natured smile.

Oleg was slightly confused, then he grinned and nodded.

"It won't do. You'll have to be bored for a bit. When our troops come, we'll all have a good time," Lyutikov said gravely. "And fewer meetings of your headquarters. It's time now for military affairs. You've got a commander, a commissar. Work now as you would at the front in battle conditions. And your liaison arrangements must reach the same level as your organization. It would be a good thing if you could think of a place where each of you could go freely, without anyone seeing anything unusual in it. What's happening in the Gorky Club these days?"

"It's empty," Oleg said. He recalled the night he had pasted leaflets on the wall of the club and nearly been caught by the policeman. "It was so long ago!" he thought. "It's fit neither for offices nor to live in, so it's standing empty," he explained.

"All right then, ask the administration for permission and make a regular club out of it."

Oleg remained silent for some moments and frowned. "I don't understand," he said.

"There's nothing to understand: a club for the young people, for the whole population. Organize the fellows and girls who are not at all interested in politics but only want a good time, who are feeling bored; get some of them together to form an inaugurating group with you, then ask the Burgomaster for permission to take the building over as a club. Tell him you feel there ought to be cultural facilities for the population in the spirit of the New Order. Suggest that the young people should have dances to keep them from gossiping and getting harmful ideas into their heads! That scoundrel doesn't decide anything by himself, of course, but he'll ask his superiors. They may allow you to do it; they're stifled with boredom themselves," Lyutikov said.

Oleg's shrewdness, considerable for his years and extremely practical rather than petty and worldly, helped him to see at once that he would be able to plant the members of the headquarters in the club and through them keep in contact with the leaders of the groups. But this possibility of being drawn unwittingly into this misanthropic world, of even indirectly participating in the loathsome affairs of that alien world, was against Oleg's conscience. To countenance in person the foulest morals or even indirectly to further them.... No, anything but that! He bowed his head in silence, unable to look at Lyutikov.

"I thought as much," Lyutikov said calmly. "You did not understand! If you had understood, it would have been a big thing for me and the whole organization." He rose and took a few ponderous steps across the room. "The little boy's afraid ... he might get himself dirty. The pure don't get themselves besmirched! And what does their blasted propaganda amount to, anyway? Even if they fix up one of their loud speakers in the club—what of it? We hear them everywhere. It's got to be done so that the club will be under our control. Our propaganda will not be loud, but it'll carry more weight than theirs. I can tell you frankly that we'll also be having a bit of a hand in your affairs. You won't notice it much and you'll just have to forgive us for that. But your programme must be a neutral one. That part of it could well be organized by people like Moshkov, Zemnukhov or Osmukhin, or better still Lyuba Shevtsova. They're the sort you should turn loose on it. "

Old Lyutikov went on for a long time persuading his young comrade, even after Oleg had finally agreed with him. Oleg was already unhappy because he had allowed false sentiments to prevail over him.

"The reason I'm saying all this is that your comrades will say exactly the same thing to you as you've just said to me. And I want you to know what to reply to them," he said. And so he went on priming Oleg.

Once the support of the management of 1B Pit had been secured, Vanya Zemnukhov, Moshkov and two girls who were in no way connected with the Young Guard went to see Burgomaster Statsenko. They truly represented the group of young people that had been brought together to organize the new club.

Statsenko, drunk as usual, received them in the unheated, dirty premises of the Town Council. He laid his small hands with the swollen fingers on the green baize cloth in front of him and fixed his eyes on Vanya Zemnukhov who was modest, courteous and eloquent, and who, through his horn-rimmed spectacles, looked not at the Burgomaster but at the green baize cloth.

"False rumours alleging that the German army is suffering defeat at Stalingrad are beginning to seep through the town. This has resulted in a certain"—Vanya's slim fingers motioned vaguely in the air—"a certain unsteadiness in the outlook of our young people. With the support of Mr. Paul," —he named the mining battalion commissioner at 1B Pit— "and of the gentleman in charge of the Town Council's education department, of which you have no doubt been informed, and, finally, on behalf of all the young people loyal to the New Order, we would ask you in person, Mr. Statsenko, knowing your kindness—"

"For my part, ladies and gentlemen — My dear boys!" Statsenko suddenly exclaimed affectionately. "The Town Council—" His eyes filled with tears.

Statsenko, the gentlemen and the dear boys were fully aware that the Town Council could decide nothing itself because all decisions were made by the senior *Wachtmeister* of the gendarmerie. But Statsenko was all in favour, because he himself was "stifled with boredom," as Lyutikov had correctly guessed. The *Hauptwachtmeister*'s permission was therefore obtained, and December 19, 1942 witnessed the first variety show at the Gorky Club.

The building was unheated, there were twice as many spectators, sitting and standing about in overcoats, army coats and fur jackets, as the club was intended to hold, and the steam condensing on the ceiling soon began to drip on to them.

The front rows were occupied by *Hauptwachtmeister* Brückner, *Wachtmeister* Balder, *Leutnant* Schweide, his deputy Feldner, *Sonderführer* Sanders and the entire staff of the agricultural *Kommandantur*; *Oberleutnant* Sprick with Nemchinova; Burgomaster Statsenko; Chief of Police Solikovsky with his wife and Kuleshov, the examining judge recently appointed to assist him, a courteous quiet man with a round, freckled face, blue eyes and thin ginger eyebrows, wearing a long black overcoat and a Cossack hat with gold braid across the red crown. Present also were *Herren* Paul, Jühner, Becker, Bloschke, Schwartz and several lance-corporals of the mining battalion; translator Shurka Reiband, the *Hauptwachtmeister*'s cook and the chief cook of *Leutnant* Schweide.

Then came rows of policemen, German and Rumanian soldiers from units on their way to the front and gendarmerie soldiers, their uniforms sharply contrasting with the drab clothes, shabby caps and head scarves of the local people who filled what remained of the hall. Fehnbong was not present; he had too much work to do and, in any case, was not fond of amusements.

In front of the "eminent guests" hung the old, heavy curtain adorned with the arms of the U.S.S.R. and the hammer and sickle emblem. When the curtain was rung up it revealed at the back of the stage a huge coloured portrait of the Führer, painted by local artists. Despite some disproportions, the face was very much a copy of the original.

The performance opened with an old-fashioned vaudeville sketch with Vanya Turkenich in the role of the bride's old father. Faithful to tradition and to its artistic principles, he was made up to look like Danilych, the old gardener. The Krasnodon townsfolk greeted the appearance of their favourite with great applause and remained enthusiastic throughout his performance. The Germans did not laugh, because *Hauptwachtmeister* Brückner kept a straight face. When the sketch came to an end, however, *Meister* Brückner brought his palms together once or twice, and then the Germans applauded too.

Then the string orchestra with Vitya Petrov and Sergei Levashov, the town's two best guitarists, in star roles, played the waltz *Autumn Dream* and *Shall I Go Down to the River.*

Then the club manager and compère Stakhovich, slim and self-possessed in his dark suit and well-polished boots, took the centre of the stage.

"Lyubov Shevtsova, actress from the Lugansk Regional Theatre!"

The audience clapped.

Lyuba appeared in the blue crepe de Chine dress and shoes to match and sang a few sad ballads followed by a number of gay songs, accompanied by Valya Borts on a piano which badly needed tuning. She was a great success and the audience called her back to the curtain several times. She whirled out on to the stage again, this time in her gaudy dress and beige shoes, and with a mouth organ, and began to dance intricate steps, her shapely legs twinkling rapidly. The Germans roared with delight and gave her an ovation.

Then Stakhovich came from the wings again.

"Parodies of gypsy romances. Vladimir Osmukhin, accompanied on the guitar by Sergei Levashov!"

Using his arms to good effect and sticking out his neck affectedly, Volodya appeared and began forthwith to dance wildly round the stage, singing, *Mother Mine, How Lonely I Am.* With a gloomy face, Sergei Levashov, playing his guitar, trailed after him like a Mephistopheles. The audience laughed, including the Germans.

Volodya gave an encore. Turning his head about in the unnatural way he had, he proceeded to sing, with his face chiefly in the direction of the Führer's portrait:

> *Oh tell me, tell me, tramp,*
> *What kin are you, whence you come?*
> *Soon now the sun will shine warmer,*
> *And your reward will be what you deserve,*
> *Ah yes! you'll slumber deep and long.*

The audience rose from their seats, shouting enthusiastically, and Volodya took an endless number of curtain calls.

The show ended with an acrobatic turn by a troupe led by Kovalyov.

While the concert was in progress at the club, Oleg and Nina took down the late night communiqué, which brought news of a large-scale Soviet offensive in the Middle Don sector and of the recapture of Novaya Kalitva, Kantemirovka and Boguchar, places which had been taken by the Germans just before their break-through in the south in July.

Oleg and Nina spent the whole night making copies of the communiqué. Towards dawn they suddenly heard the roar of aircraft engines overhead. Startled by a peculiar note in it, they rushed out into the yard. Above them they clearly distinguished in the clear frosty air Soviet bombers passing over the town. They flew over unhurriedly, filling the air with the resonant sound of their engines, and dropped their bombs somewhere near Voroshilovgrad. The rumble of the detonations was heard even in Krasnodon. No enemy fighters troubled the Soviet bombers and the AA batteries opened up somewhat belatedly, for by then the bombers were again returning over Krasnodon at the same unhurried pace.

Chapter 18

DURING the historic months of November and December 1942, the Soviet people, particularly those deep in the rear of the Germans, were not able fully to appreciate the events which world history engraved in the memory of the people with the single, symbolic word: "Stalingrad."

Stalingrad was not merely the historically unequalled defence of a narrow strip of the Volga embankment in a city destroyed to its foundation against an enemy, which had concentrated a tremendous number of superbly-equipped troops of every branch of the Armed Forces on a scale never seen before even in the greatest battles in the history of mankind.

Stalingrad was a remarkable demonstration of brilliant

generalship by army leaders trained under the new, Soviet system. In the infinitely short period of less than six weeks, fulfilling a unified, purposeful design in three stages, each of which was a masterpiece of military art, executed as it was on the unbounded expanses of the steppes between the Volga and the Don, the Soviet troops encircled 22 divisions and routed another 36. And only another month was required to annihilate or take prisoner the encircled enemy.

Stalingrad was the finest testimony to the organizing talent of people reared under the new, the Soviet system. In order to understand this, one needs only to imagine the vast masses of manpower and military equipment set in motion under this unified plan, this unified will, the reserves of men and materials accumulated and newly-created for the purpose of carrying out this plan, the organizing efforts and material resources required to move all this mass to the front, to keep it supplied with food, clothing, ammunition and fuel, and, finally, the educational and instructional work of epoch-making importance, that was needed to ensure that hundreds of thousands of leaders and commanders, from sergeants to marshals, all with military experience and political understanding, would be available to lead this operation and transform it into a purposeful movement of millions of armed people.

Stalingrad was the supreme indicator of the superiority of the new society's economy, with its unified plan, over the old society with its anarchy. No state of the old type could have tackled and solved the economic problems behind an offensive on this scale a year and a half after it had been deeply penetrated by a hostile army of many millions, armed and equipped by the industry and agriculture of most of the countries of Europe, and after suffering inconceivable material destruction and devastation.

Stalingrad was the expression of the spiritual power and the historical intellect of a people freed from the chains of capital. And thus it has entered history.

Like other Soviet people, Ivan Protsenko could not be aware of the real scale of the events which he witnessed and in which he was playing a part. But he was in touch by radio, as well as through people, with the Ukrainian Partisan Headquarters and the Army Council of the South-Western

Front, which was to be the first to advance into Ukrainian territory; and so he knew more of the nature and the scale of the offensive than other Soviet people who were fighting the enemy in Voroshilovgrad Region.

Ivan Protsenko remained in Voroshilovgrad no longer than was necessary to mobilize into activity the four underground district Party committees in the town. By the time the news arrived that the Soviet troops had broken through the German front on the Middle Don, he had changed his whereabouts several times and by the end of November he was operating mainly in the northern districts of the region.

No one had prompted Ivan Protsenko to operate at this time precisely there, in those northern districts. But he had realized by ordinary common sense and intuition that his presence was more important in the area where the approaching Soviet forces were nearest and where, sooner than anywhere else, military coordination could be effected between the partisan detachments and the regular Soviet Army.

The hour was approaching which Ivan Protsenko had so long awaited, when it would be possible once more to merge the small partisan groups into detachments capable of large-scale operations.

His base was now in one of the villages in Belovodsk District, in the home of some relations of Marfa Kornienko, which was also the hide-out of Marfa's husband, Guards Sergeant Gordei Kornienko, who was recently liberated from enemy captivity. Kornienko had set up a partisan group in the village which, in addition to its normal duties, guarded Ivan Protsenko against all eventualities. All the Belovodsk District partisan groups were under the command of the director of the state farm, where the pupils of the Gorky School at Krasnodon had worked during the summer months; he was the man who had given Maria Andreyevna Borts his last lorry for the purpose of evacuating the children. Ivan Protsenko instructed him to bring together all the Belovodsk District groups and form a detachment of about 200 men.

Before the world had been informed of the mighty new offensive launched by the Soviet troops in the Middle Don area, Ivan Protsenko's radio operator received a coded message about a deep break-through in the German front from the north-east on the Novaya Kalitva-Monastyrshchina sector, and from the east in the area of Bokovskoye on the Chir River. Instructions for Ivan Protsenko were received at the same time: he was to throw all available partisan forces into an operation to break the enemy's lines of communication with Kantemirovka and Markovka in the north and with Millerovo, Glubokaya, Kamensk and Likhaya in the east. This was an order from the Army Council at the front.

"Our time has come!" Protsenko said triumphantly and embraced the radio operator.

They kissed like brothers. Then he gave the operator a gentle shove and hurried out of the hut without his overcoat.

It was a clear, starlit, frosty night. There had been a heavy fall of snow during the past few days and the village roofs and distant hills slumbered under a blanket of snow. Protsenko was not conscious of the cold as he stood with heaving chest greedily gulping down the icy air, the tears falling unrestrained and turning to ice on his cheeks.

It took him about an hour to reach his home. He took along with him the radio operator and his equipment. Gordei Kornienko, the Herculean Guardsman, had not long since returned from operations, during which the police posts at several farmsteads had been wiped out, and was sleeping heavily. But he quickly shook off his sleep when Ivan Protsenko touched his shoulder and began to tell him the news.

"At Monastyrshchina!" he exclaimed, and his eyes lit up. "I'm from that front! That's where I was taken prisoner! They'll be here in a few days now, you mark my words!" The old soldier groaned with emotion and began to dress hurriedly.

Gordei Kornienko had been put in charge of all the northern partisan groups and he was to go into action immediately in the Markovka-Kantemirovka area. Ivan Protsenko, the radio operator, and two partisans were to reach the village of Gorodishchi, the operational base of the statefarm director and his detachment: Ivan Protsenko realized that the time had now come for him to be permanently with the detachment.

His wife's friend, Masha Shubina, whom he had taken with him from Voroshilovgrad, had served as his permanent courier during all the days of travelling from one place to another. As he had expected, she had turned out to be one of those steadfast, devoted creatures who, in their everyday life, are so completely retiring that only the keen eye of the born organizer can select them from the mass of other people. But once selected, they disclose such a superhuman capacity for work and, together with it, such absolute self-effacement that all the practical fulfilment of the assignments of their chiefs and leaders falls on their shoulders. Without the help of people like these even the most important tasks would remain tasks that were never transformed into action.

Masha Shubina was so busy that she had forgotten how to distinguish day from night. If the people she worked with were to try to imagine what was most characteristic in her life and work, they would have been struck by the fact that no one could recall that she ever slept. If she did sleep, then it was so little and, above all, so imperceptibly that it seemed she never slept at all.

The heart of this woman was aflame with a magnificent enthusiasm for work. The only personal happiness that warmed her heart was the happiness of knowing that she was not alone. True, she was not able to maintain personal contact with her friend, Katya; her only contact with her was through Marfa Kornienko. But Masha knew that her best and only real friend was somewhere near at hand and that they both worked for a common cause. And Masha was selflessly devoted with all her heart to Ivan Protsenko, because he had noticed her among the many, and had trusted her. In return for this trust, she was prepared to lay down her life for him.

Engrossed in the tremendous nature of the events now unfolding, the development of which he had helped to promote to the best of his ability, Ivan Protsenko was giving Masha his last-minute instructions:

"At Marfa's you'll meet the commander of the Mityakinskaya detachment. His operational area lies along the roads to Glubokaya and to Kamensk. Tell him to get started right away and operate day and night without allowing the enemy any breathing-space. And tell Marfa to instruct Katya to throw up the teaching job and come here."

"To this house?" Masha asked in order to make sure.

"Yes, to this house. And after that, lose no more time than you can help to get to Xenia Krotova. Will you find your way?"

"Yes."

When Ivan Protsenko had introduced Masha to her duties, he had given her an address: Dr. Valentina Krotova, First-Aid Post, Village Uspenka. Valentina's sister, Xenia, was working now as courier between Protsenko's wife, Katya, and all the district Party committees south of the Donets.

"Tell Xenia: the field of operations is to be along the roads to Likhaya, Shakhty, Novocherkassk, Rostov and Taganrog," Ivan Protsenko continued. "Operations to be carried on day and night without any breathing-space for the enemy. In all areas where the front comes close, inhabited localities are to be captured and the enemy drawn against ourselves. Katya's main contact address is now eliminated. From now on it's to be at Marfa's home. The new password is—" He whispered it into Masha's ear. "You won't forget it, will you?"

"No."

He thought for a moment, then said:

"That's all."

"Is it?" She raised her face and looked at him. The real meaning of her question was: "What about me?" But her eyes remained expressionless.

Ivan Protsenko had a good memory, and so he made a mental check to see whether he had omitted anything and remembered that he had given no instructions as to what Masha was to do.

"Yes.... When you get to Xenia, you'll place yourself at her disposal. You'll both act as liaison with Marfa. Tell them I said you're not to be sent anywhere else."

Masha dropped her eyes. She saw herself going off alone, putting an ever increasing distance between herself and all these places where any day now the Soviet Army would arrive. Yes, in a few days' time, in the place where she was standing with Ivan Protsenko, not a single enemy soldier would be left, and that bright world for which they had been waiting so long, for which they had not spared their lives, would come into its own once more.

"Well then, Masha," Protsenko said, "neither of us has any time to spare. Thank you for everything...."

He embraced her firmly and kissed her on the lips. For a moment she remained still in his arms, unable to make any reply.

When she left the cottage, she was wearing clothes like those of the poorest women in the rear of the German advance and carried a haversack slung over her shoulder. Ivan Protsenko did not see her off at the door. It was still long before dawn. The snow crunched under her feet as, with a youthful expression in her middle-aged features, she set out on her long and lonely road, an inconspicuous woman with an iron will.

Ivan Protsenko and his small group left some time later, as the bleak, wintry dawn began to filter through the pale mist. Sky and earth showed no signs of life; not a sound could be heard, not even the rustling of wind. As far as the eye could see there was nothing but white emptiness, with here and there along the valleys, or on the slopes of hillocks, clumps of bushes appearing as faint, grey patches. Everything lay under a thick blanket of snow, and there was an air of discomfort, poverty and cold desolation which seemed to have come to stay for ever. Ivan Protsenko strode out across this limitless waste, the thunder of victory beating in his swelling heart.

Not more than five days after that still morning when Ivan Protsenko had set out to join his detachment, a partisan, wearing a German hood lined with artificial fur, brought Protsenko's wife Katya late at night to the place where he was waiting for her in a deserted cottage outside Gorodishchi. Earth and sky trembled monstrously with the thunder from the gigantic battles that were being fought across the vast expanses of the land. And Ivan Protsenko, black from gun-powder, sat and looked into the beautiful face of his wife.

There was confusion and ferment and a shimmering light all round. By night the flare of Very lights and even bursts of gun-fire could be seen for tens of miles around. There was a rumbling in the air and on the ground. Somewhere gigantic tank and air battles were in progress. Knowing that a tank corps, which had recently been awarded the Guards insignia, was breaking through to meet them, some of the men in Ivan Protsenko's detachment could not rid themselves of the illusion that they could actually hear the grinding of the armour of the clashing masses of tanks. High overhead aircraft, Soviet and enemy, plotted white spirals which hung motionless for hours in the frosty air.

Rear elements of German army units were crawling in disorder along the main roads in a westerly and south-westerly direction, while the countless country roads were held by Protsenko's men. As often happens at times of heavy defeat, when the victor is still forcing the pace of advance, all German arms still capable of offering resistance were engrossed in repelling the main peril which threatened them. They could not cope with partisans at such a time.

There were German garrisons in all inhabited localities, large or small, and especially in those along the Kamysh-naya, Derkul and Yevsug rivers flowing into the Northern Donets. Permanent fortifications had been built earlier at all of them and now new ones were hurriedly being added. Fierce and prolonged fighting developed for each of these fortified points, even those among them which had been by-passed by the advancing Soviet forces and were at their mercy. The German garrisons fought to the last man, for they had received Hitler's order not to withdraw and not to surrender. The scattered remnants of German units routed or captured earlier, and now fleeing along the country roads in oddly-assorted groups of soldiers and officers, were the prey of the partisans.

The gathering speed of the Soviet advance could be judged from the fact that the German rear airfields, which for several months had been almost idle, had now become active within a period of only five days and were targets for the entire might of the Soviet Air Force. The Germans speedily withdrew their long-range bombers to bases deep in the rear.

They were alone in the deserted hut. Katya, her face still glowing from the frost outside, had thrown off her peasant sheepskin coat. Protsenko's face was heavy from lack of sleep, but the impish twinkle skipped from one eye to the other, as he said in Ukrainian:

"We're doing everything we've been advised to do by the political department of the Guards tank corps and we're doing it well!" He laughed. "Katya, I've sent for you because you're the only one I could really trust with this business. Can you guess what it is?"

She could still feel his first impulsive embrace and his kisses on her eyes which were moist and still radiant because they were looking at him. But he could talk of nothing but the most important thing now occupying his mind. And she guessed at once why he had summoned her. In fact, there had been no need for her to guess, she had known the moment she saw him. In a few hours she would have to leave him again, and go—she knew where. She could not have explained how she knew. She just loved him. So Katya only nodded in reply and then again looked at him with the moist, radiant eyes which were so beautiful with her slightly severe, sharply defined, weather-beaten face.

He leapt to his feet, made sure that the door was bolted, then drew from his map-case several sheets of tissue-paper, each the size of a quarter of a page of foolscap.

"Look." He carefully spread the leaves out on the table. "I've coded the text, as you can see. But you can't put a map into code."

Both sides of each sheet of paper were written all over with a finely sharpened pencil in such small handwriting that it was difficult to imagine how any human hand could have written it. And on one of the sheets was a finely-drawn map of Voroshilovgrad Region marked with squares, small circles and triangles. The meticulous labour that had been put into this job could be seen from the fact that the largest of the marks was no bigger than an aphid, and the smallest the size of a pin-head. All this represented information, carefully collected over the past five months, thoroughly checked and then supplemented with the latest data, which concerned the disposition of the main lines of defence, fortified points and gun emplacements, the airfields, AA batteries, lorry parks and repair shops; the numerical strengths of troop concentrations, the strength of the garrisons and details of their armaments, and much more besides.

"Tell them that in Voroshilovgrad and along the Don there will be many modifications as compared with my information, modifications in favour of the enemy. North of the Donets everything will be as I have given it. Tell them also that the Mius River is being strongly fortified. They'll draw their own conclusions, it's not for me to teach them. I can tell you this: if they're fortifying the Mius, it means that Hitler no longer believes they'll be able to hold Rostov. You understand?"

Protsenko laughed loudly and merrily, just as he used to laugh in the family circle, especially with the children, in those rare moments when he was completely at his ease. For a brief minute both forgot what lay ahead of them. Protsenko took her face between his hands, held it away a little and, with eyes full of tenderness, whispered over and over again:

"Ah, my dearest one, my love.... Oh, yes!" he exclaimed, "I haven't told you the most important news: our troops have entered the Ukraine. Look."

From his case he took a large army map glued together from several pieces and spread it on the table. The first thing Katya's eyes fell on was a number of inhabited localities, ringed heavily in blue and red pencil, which the Soviet troops had already occupied in outlying parts north-east of Voroshilovgrad Region. Katya's heart beat fast, for some of these places were quite close to Gorodishchi.

Ivan Protsenko and his wife had their meeting at a time when the second and third stage of the great Stalingrad Operation had not yet been carried out and the second ring of encirclement had not quite closed round the German army groups at Stalingrad. But information had come through, during the night, that the German reinforcements being rushed to the Kotelnikovo area to relieve the pressure on the Stalingrad grouping had been routed and news had arrived of a Soviet offensive in the Northern Caucasus.

"Our troops have cut the railway from Likhaya to Stalingrad at two points, Chernyshevskaya here and Tatsinskaya," Ivan Protsenko gaily said. "But the Germans still hold Morozovsky. Just here, along the Kalitva River, almost all the inhabited points are in our hands. We've crossed the Millerovo-Voronezh railway line up to this point, north of Kantemirovka, but the Germans still hold Millerovo. And they've strongly fortified it. But it looks as though our forces have bypassed it—see how far the tanks have broken through." He ran his finger along the Kamyshnaya River to a point west of Millerovo and looked up at Katya.

She was looking intently at the map where it showed where the Soviet troops were nearest to Gorodishchi and in the expression of her eyes there was something hawk-like. Protsenko knew why she was so intent on these areas, and he made no comment. Katya raised her eyes from the map and for a time gazed into space. She now wore her usual, intelligent, pensive, somewhat sad expression. Protsenko sighed and placed the sheet of tissue-paper with the map on it on top of the large army map.

"Look at this, you've got to remember it all, because you'll not be able to look at it again, once you're on your way," he said. "Hide the sheets of paper somewhere on you, where you can get at them quickly in case of trouble and ... well, swallow them. And get your mind fixed on your new identity. A refugee, I'd say; a teacher fleeing from Chir; fleeing from the Reds. That's what you'll tell the Germans and the policemen. As for the local people, tell them that you're from Chir, on your way to relatives in Starobelsk, you couldn't make ends meet on your own. The decent folk will be sorry for you and give you shelter, and the bad ones will find nothing to pick on," Protsenko said in a soft, flat tone of voice, without looking at his wife. "Remember: there's no front, not in the sense we speak of it. Our tanks are advancing here and there. Make a detour round all German strongpoints, so that you're not seen. But you may come across stray Germans anywhere and you'll have to be particularly careful of them. When you reach approximately this line, here, stop and wait for our troops. Look, I've entered nothing on the map here because we have no information about this area and you'll not be able to ask anyone—it would be dangerous. Find some lonely old woman or other, and stay with her. If the fighting comes close, get down into the cellar with her and sit tight...."

There was no real need for him to tell Katya all this but he very much wanted to help her, if only with advice. How gladly would he have gone in her stead!

"As soon as you've started off, I'll let them know you're on your way. If you are not met, make yourself known to the first sensible Red Army man you encounter and ask him to take you to the political department of the tank corps." A mischievous twinkle suddenly showed in his eyes, as he continued: "And when you get to the political department, mind you don't forget, in relief at being safe, that you've got a husband. Ask them to let me know you've arrived safely."

"You can bet I'll ask them, only I'll say, 'Either you push on fast and rescue my husband or else let me hurry back to him alone,'" Katya said and laughed.

Protsenko suddenly seemed at a loss.

"I had wanted to avoid the subject, but evidently it can't be avoided," he said. His face had become grave. "No matter how quickly our forces advance, I shall not be waiting for them. Our job is to retreat as the Germans retreat. Our troops will come here, but we'll go with the retreating Germans. We're going to stick fast to these Germans. Until the last of them leaves our Voroshilovgrad territory, I shall go on fighting them. Otherwise what would our underground fighters and our partisans from Starobelsk, Voroshilovgrad, Krasnodon, Rubezhansk and Krasniye Luchi think of me? And it would be nothing less than foolhardy for you to come back to me here; there'd be no need at all for that. Listen to me." He leaned towards her, placed his strong hand on her slim fingers and pressed them lightly. "Don't remain with the corps, there's nothing for you to do there. Ask to be sent to the Army Council at the front. You'll see Comrade Khrushchov there, ask him to let you pay a visit to the children. There's nothing to be ashamed of in that, you've earned it. As for the children, we don't even know where they are, whether they're in Saratov or somewhere else; whether they're still alive and in good health."

Katya looked at him and made no reply. The thunder of distant night fighting shook the lonely little cottage.

Protsenko's heart was full to overflowing with love and compassion for her, his comrade, his beloved wife. Only he knew how tender and gentle his Katya really was, with what superhuman strength of character she overcame all the dangers, privations and humiliations, how she steeled herself to face the death of her closest comrades. He very much wanted to get his Katya away so that she could be where people were free and there was light and warmth, and the children. But Katya was thinking on different lines.

She could not take her eyes off her husband's face; she freed her hand and began gently to pass it over his fair hair which, during recent months, had receded still further from the temples, making his forehead appear higher still. She tenderly stroked his soft fair hair as she said to him:

"Don't speak. Don't say anything. I know it all myself. Let them make use of me as they see fit, because I shan't ask to be sent anywhere. As long as you're over here I shall always be as close to you as they will allow."

He would have raised some objection, but suddenly his features relaxed. He seized both her hands and buried his face in them.

After some moments he lifted his blue eyes to hers:

"Katya," he said very softly.

"Yes, it's time," she said and stood up.

Chapter 19

HER ESCORT was an old man from the near-by village. Everybody called him Old Foma and he was huge like a grizzly bear. At the beginning of the journey Katya and Old Foma were still able to exchange a few words and she discovered that his name was Kornienko, and he was one of that numerous clan from among the early Ukrainian settlers in these parts, and, like the rest, was a distant relative of Gordei Kornienko.

Later conversation was no longer possible.

They walked all night, using the country roads or tramping the open steppe. The snow on the ground was not deep and walking was easy. From time to time there were beams from headlights over the horizon to the north or south, for over there lay the highways. Though they were so far away, the travellers could hear the engines of the cars on them. German units routed in the Millerovo area were withdrawing to the south, while in the north others were retreating from the area of Barannikovka, the first village recaptured by the Soviet forces in Voroshilovgrad Region.

Katya and Old Foma were proceeding towards the east, but were frequently compelled to make detours round villages and fortified places in the steppe. The road seemed interminable to Katya, but they were all the same getting nearer to the fighting lines: the heavy gun-fire became increasingly loud and the flashes of light from the bursting shells became more clearly defined. Towards morning a fine, dry snow began to fall, muffling all sounds and blotting everything from sight.

Katya, the canvas knapsack slung on her back now sprinkled with snow, strode along in the ragged felt boots of the typical refugee. She had a strange sensation that everything—the huge figure of Old Foma in his fur cap with loosely dangling ear-flaps; the shuffling of their footsteps; and the fine snow whirling down before her eyes—was unreal and ghostly. Her mind was in a state of drowsiness, she was half-dreaming.

Suddenly she felt hard ground under her feet. Old Foma halted. Katya put her face up to his and with a sudden jolt realized that this was the spot where they were to separate.

Old Foma looked at her with a caressing, anxious expression, then his weathered, dark hand pointed along the country road they had now reached. Katya looked in the direction he indicated. It was already growing light. The old fellow placed his large hands on her shoulders, drew her close so that his beard and moustache tickled her cheek and ear, and then whispered:

"Only about 500 yards. You understand?"

"Good-bye, then," she whispered.

She walked a few steps, then looked back. Foma Kornienko was still standing on the road. She realized that he would remain there until she was out of sight. Fifty yards further on she could still make out the huge old fellow standing there covered in snow and looking so much like Santa Claus. But when she turned round for the third time, Old Foma had disappeared from sight.

This was the last village where Katya could count on assistance: once beyond it, she would have to rely entirely on herself. The small village was situated behind high fortifications to the east of it, which formed part of the defence line which the Germans had hurriedly thrown up in this area. Protsenko had told Katya that all the most comfortable houses in the village had been occupied by the officers and staffs of the small detachments manning the fortifications. He had warned his wife that the situation might become complicated for her if the village turned out to be full of army units forced out of the defence positions along the Kamyshnaya River. The course of this river, which flowed into the Derkul, a tributary of the Donets, ran from north to south near the boundary of Rostov Region and almost parallel with the Kantemirovka-Millerovo railway. Katya was to make her way to one of the villages on the Kamyshnaya and wait there for the arrival of the Soviet troops.

She could now make out the silhouette of the first cottage looming through the gossamer of falling snow; carefully keeping the roofs in sight she turned off the road and cut across the field in order to approach the village from the back. She had been told that hers was the third cottage. It was almost daylight when she approached the tiny hut. She listened at the closed window-shutter. Everything was quiet inside. She did not knock but scraped the glass, as she had been instructed.

For a considerable time there was no reply. Her heart beat fast. After some moments she heard a low voice inside, the voice of a youngster. She scraped again. A pair of small feet pattered over the earthen floor, then the door opened and Katya went inside.

It was pitch dark inside the cottage.

"Where're you from?" a child's voice asked quietly in Ukrainian.

Katya said the agreed phrase.

"You hear that, Mama?" the boy said.

"Quiet..." whispered a woman's voice. "Don't you know any

Russian? Can't you hear she's Russian? Come in, please, and sit on the bed. Show the way, Sashko."

The boy's cold fingers grasped Katya's hand, warm from her mittens, and drew her across the room. Then the woman's hand grasped her and the lad dropped her hand.

"Wait a bit," Katya said. "I'll take off my jacket."

But a woman's hand took Katya's hand from the boy's and drew her to the bed.

"Sit down as you are. It's cold here. Did you notice any German patrols?" asked the woman.

"No."

Katya dropped her knapsack, removed the shawl from her head and shook the snow off. Then she unbuttoned her sheepskin jacket, took it by the lapels and shook it. Only then did she sit down on the bed by the side of the woman. The boy silently climbed up beside his mother and Katya sensed with her mother instinct, rather than saw, that the boy nestled close to the warmth of his mother.

"Are there many Germans in the village?" Katya asked.

"Not really very many. Most of them don't sleep in the village now, but in the cellars farther away."

"Cellars," the boy chuckled. "You mean in the trenches!"

"It's the same thing. They say they'll be getting reinforcements now, because they're going to hold the front here."

"Tell me, please, are you Galina Alexeyevna?" Katya asked her.

"Just call me Galya, I'm not an old woman. Galya Kornienko."

Katya had been told that she would find herself with yet another Kornienko.

"Are you going across to our people?" the boy asked in a quiet voice.

"Yes. It can be done, can't it?"

The boy did not answer immediately. Then he said enigmatically:

"People have done it...."

"Recently?"

The boy did not reply.

"What shall I call you?" asked the woman.

"I'm Vera on my passport."

591

"Then Vera it is; the people here are reliable, they'll trust you. And if anyone doesn't he'll not say anything. There might be a scoundrel among them who would betray you, but who would dare to, now?" the woman said and laughed softly. "They all know that our troops will soon come. Take your things off now, and lie on the bed. "I'll cover you up so you'll be warm. My boy and I sleep together, it's warmer that way."

"I can't drive you out of your bed! No, no," Katya said animatedly. "I can lie on a bench or on the floor, anyway I shan't sleep."

"You'll sleep! It's time for us to be up."

It really was very cold in the cottage, one could feel it had not once been heated since the beginning of winter. Katya was used to the idea of cottages having no heating now the Germans were here. The villagers cooked their meals, a simple skilly or cereal pudding or potatoes, on whatever they could get hold of, chips of wood or straw.

Katya took off her sheepskin jacket and felt boots and lay down. The woman covered her with a warm quilt and spread the sheepskin jacket on top of it. Katya was asleep in no time.

She was awakened by a loud, terrifying crash, which she had not so much heard through her sleep as felt with her whole body. Still in a daze, she raised herself up in the bed and in that instant several more explosions filled the air with their mighty sound and concussion. She heard the loud roar of engines; one after another the planes swept low over the village, and then soared at an incredibly steep angle into the sky. Katya did not actually realize the fact, but she nevertheless heard by the sound of them that they were Ilyushins.

"They're ours!" she exclaimed.

"Yes, they're ours," the boy said tersely, sitting on the bench by the window.

"Sashko, put your clothes on, you too, Vera, don't just sit there! Ours! Of course they're ours! But if they bomb the place you'll never get up from that bed!" Galya said. She was standing in the middle of the room with a wormwood broom in her hands. Although it was cold indoors, she stood barefoot on the earthen floor and her arms were bare. The boy too was sitting only half-dressed.

"They won't drop anything here," he said, conscious of his superiority over the women. "They're bombing the fortifications." He looked a puny lad with his serious, grown-up eyes, sitting there with his bare legs crossed under the bench.

"Our Ilyushins, and in this horrible weather!" Katya said in a worried tone.

"No, that's left from last night," the boy said, seeing her look at the frosted window-pane. "The weather's fine now. There's no sun, but it's stopped snowing."

Having dealt with children of his age all her life as teacher, Katya felt that the boy was interested in her and wanted her to take notice of him. Yet the lad also had such a natural sense of his own dignity, that not by a single gesture or by any intonation of his voice would he in any way reveal anything that might be interpreted as lack of modesty on his part.

Katya listened to the furious pounding of AA machine-guns somewhere outside the village. Wrought up though she was, she could not help noticing that the Germans had not yet any AA artillery in the vicinity, which meant that this line of fortifications had only recently acquired the importance of a serious defence line.

"If only our people would come quicker!" Galya said. "We haven't even a cellar. When our troops were retreating we used to go into the neighbours' cellar during German air raids, or else out into the open field. We used to lie flat among the tall weeds or in the ditches, press our hands over our ears and just wait...."

More bomb crashes, one, then another, and a third, shook the little cottage and again the Soviet planes swooped over the village, then rose at a steep angle into the sky.

"Oh, you darlings!" Galya cried and crouched on the floor, her hands over her ears.

This woman, crouching down on her heels at the sound of planes, was the housekeeper of the chief partisan contact centre of the district. Through her home passed the main stream of Red Army soldiers who had escaped from captivity or extricated themselves from enemy encirclement. Katya knew that Galya's husband had been killed very early in the war, and that two of her younger children had died of dysentery during the occupation. There was something very simple and very human in her involuntary effort to get down to a lower level, to take shelter from danger, if only by covering her ears to shut out the noise. Katya rushed towards her and put her arms round her.

"Don't be frightened, don't be frightened," she said with feeling.

"I'm not frightened, I'm only doing what's expected of a woman." Galya raised her calm face to Katya, and smiled.

Katya spent the whole day in the cottage. It required all the restraint she could muster to wait until darkness fell; she was so anxious to go out to meet the Soviet troops. Throughout the whole day, the Soviet bombers with their fighter escort worked on the defences outside the village. There were not many of them, judging by all the signs, just two groups of three. They came over two or three times, and after dropping their bombs, flew off to refuel and take on more bombs and then returned. They worked in this way from the early morning, when they had wakened Katya, until nightfall.

High over the village there were air battles all day long between the Soviet fighter-planes and Messerschmidts. From time to time Soviet bombers droned past at a very high altitude on their way to attack more distant German defence positions. Most likely they were bombing targets along the Derkul River which flowed into the Donets not far from the base of the Mityakinskaya detachment, where, in a cave in the clay pit, Protsenko's Gazik was concealed.

Several times during the day, German assault planes shot past to drop bombs somewhere not far off, possibly the other side of the Kamyshnaya River. The rumble of heavy gun-fire came continuously from the same direction.

Once there was sporadic artillery fire in the area just beyond the German fortifications, which was the route that Katya would now have to take. The firing appeared to come from some distance, then came nearer, and just as it was at its height suddenly ceased. Towards the evening, this firing flared up again and shells burst on the outskirts of the village. For several minutes the German guns replied so furiously that it became impossible to carry on a conversation in the cottage.

Katya and Galya exchanged meaning glances. But little Sashko continued to gaze into space, an enigmatic expression on his face

The dogfights in the air and the bursts of artillery kept the local people inside their cottages and cellars, and saved Katya from chance visitors. The German troops were obviously fully occupied with their most immediate task. There seemed to be no life in the village save in the little cottage, inhabited by two women and one small boy.

The shorter the period of time became, which separated Katya from the decisive and, perhaps, fatal moment when she would have to take the road again, the more difficult she found it to control her feelings. She asked Galya for details of the route she would have to take and whether there was anyone who could show her the way, but Galya merely said:

"Don't alarm yourself, have a good rest. You'll have plenty of time to worry later."

Presumably Galya knew nothing herself and was simply sorry for her, and this only served to increase Katya's agitation. Yet if anyone had entered the cottage at that moment and had talked with Katya, he would never have guessed what she was experiencing.

Dusk was falling. The Soviet bombers had completed their last raid and the AA machine-guns were still. Silence descended all round and only far away beyond the vast expanses everything continued its mysterious working, fighting and suffering.

Little Sashko uncrossed his legs under the bench—he had finally put on his felt boots some time during the day—went to the door and silently began to struggle into his little patched sheepskin jacket, the fur of which had once been white, but was now very dirty.

"It's time now, Vera," Galya said. "Right this very moment. The devils are all having a rest. Some of our people may come now, and it's better that you should not be seen."

It was difficult to see her expression in the twilight, her voice sounded flat.

"Where's the boy off to?" Katya asked, a vague feeling of alarm gripping her.

"Never mind, never mind," Galya said hurriedly. She darted here and there about the cottage, helping her son and Katya to get their coats on.

For a moment Katya looked with a motherly expression at Sashko's pale little face. So this was the famous guide, who for the five long months of German occupation had been escorting people through the depths of the enemy's fortifications; who had safely conducted hundreds, possibly thousands of Soviet people through them, singly, in groups, in whole detachments! The boy was now no longer even looking in Katya's direction. He was putting on his sheepskin jacket and all his movements seemed to say: "You've had plenty of time to look at me, yet you never once guessed. And now, you'd better not hinder me."

"You wait a bit now; I'll take a look round to make sure and tell you." Galya helped her to get her arms, encumbered by the bulky sleeves of her jacket, into the straps of the knapsack, and straightened it on her back. "Let's say good-bye now, there may not be time later. God grant you a very safe journey."

They kissed, then Galya went outside. Katya felt no surprise that the mother had not caressed her son, had not even said good-bye to him. Katya was no longer surprised at anything. She was aware that the words, "They're used to it," did not apply here. She herself would have been unable to refrain from kissing and fussing over her son, if it had been her destiny to dispatch him on such a mortally dangerous business. At the same time, she could not help admitting that Galya was behaving more correctly. Little Sashko would probably have declined to accept her caresses, would, perhaps, even have given them a hostile reception, because maternal caresses could now only have softened him.

Alone with him, Katya felt awkward. She felt that anything she might say would sound false. Yet she could not refrain from saying in a very matter-of-fact tone of voice:

"Don't come far, just show me where to get through those fortifications. I know the road after that."

Sashko made no reply, nor did he look at her. Just then Galya opened the door a crack and whispered:

"No one about, come out now."

It was a cloudy, still night, not very cold or dark; there

was probably a moon in the sky behind the wintry haze, and the snow made it lighter.

Sashko, in felt boots, with no mittens, and wearing a crumpled old peaked cap too big for him, instead of a fur cap, set off across the fields without looking about him. Evidently he knew that his mother would make no mistake; once she said there was no one about, then there really was no one about.

The broken range of hills which they had to cross stretched from north to south forming a watershed between the Derkul and the Kamyshnaya, its tributary. The village lay in a hollow between two low ridges running off from the hills towards the Derkul and gradually sloping down and merging into the steppe. Sashko cut straight across the fields away from the village in order to cross one of these ridges. Katya could see now why he took this direction: low as the ridge was, once they had crossed it they would be out of sight of the village. As soon as they were over the ridge, Sashko swung round and walked parallel with it towards the east and then they were heading straight for the line of hills with the German fortifications.

Not once since they had left the cottage had Sashko looked over his shoulder to see whether his companion was following. She walked after him submissively. They continued their way through the sparse stubble sticking out through the covering of snow, over low ground like that where the village lay. As during the previous night, they could clearly hear the bustling noises of the German troops in retreat along the roads somewhere to the north and south of them. The sound of gun-fire became less frequent, except somewhere to the south-east, near Millerovo, where it was louder and heavier. In the far distance, probably beyond the Kamyshnaya River, German flares hung suspended like lamps in the sky. They were so far away that their ghostly light could only just be seen and was not strong enough to dispel the semi-darkness around them. If such a lamp had hung above one of the hills ahead of them Sashko and Katya would have been as visible as on the palm of a hand.

Their feet sank noiselessly into the soft snow and the only sound was the faint shuffle of their felt boots against the stubble. Then there was no longer any stubble. Sashko looked back and motioned to Katya to come closer. When she reached him, he squatted on his heels and signed to her to do the same. She simply sat down in the snow in her sheepskin jacket. Sashko quickly pointed first to her and then at himself, and traced a line in the snow pointing towards the east. He wriggled his hands out of the long sleeves of his jacket and rapidly scraped snow into a heap across the line he had just drawn. Katya understood that he was sketching the course of their journey and the obstacle they would have to surmount. He then took a handful of snow first from one point of the little ridge, then from another, making as it were two passes across the ridge; with his knuckle he marked out the strong points on each side of the passes and drew a line first through one pass, then the other.

Katya understood him to be indicating two possible routes. She had to smile as she recalled Suvorov's maxim that every soldier should have a clear understanding of his own manoeuvres. As far as this ten-year-old Suvorov was concerned, she was his only soldier. She nodded her head to indicate that she had understood "her own manoeuvres," and they set off again.

They now made a detour in a north-easterly direction and reached some thick barbed-wire entanglements. The boy motioned to Katya to lie flat, and set off alone along the barbed wire. He soon disappeared from sight.

The lines of barbed wire ahead of Katya were drawn in about a dozen closely-spaced rows. They seemed to have been there a long time, because the wire was rusty to her touch. There was no trace of the work of the Soviet bombers in these parts and it seemed likely that the Germans had drawn the barbed wire against the partisans, because it protected the hill from the rear and lay a long distance from the main fortifications.

For a long time Katya had not experienced such an agony of suspense. Time passed, yet Sashko did not return. An hour passed, then another and there was still no sign of the boy. But Katya was not anxious for him: he was a true young soldier and could be depended upon.

She had lain motionless for so long that she began to shiver. She turned over from one side to the other, and finally could stand it no longer and sat up. No, the little

Suvorov could reprimand her, but he had left her for so long that she would at least try and investigate her whereabouts. The boy had walked away upright, he had not crawled, so surely she could stretch her legs a little too as long as she did not stand upright.

She had barely covered fifty paces when she saw something that sent a thrill of happy surprise through her: ahead of her was a fresh irregular shell-hole. The shell must have burst quite recently and turned up the black soil, scattering it over the snow. It was clearly definitely a shell-hole and not a bomb-crater, as was evident from the way the thrown-up soil had fallen mainly on one side of the hole, the side from which Sashko and Katya had come. Sashko had evidently also noted it, for the tracks in the snow showed that he had walked round the hole before proceeding on his way.

Katya's eyes searched the stretch of snow for more shell-holes, but there were none, at least not in her immediate vicinity. An indescribable, peculiar excitement gripped her; this could only be a shell-hole made by a Soviet Army shell. Moreover, it had not been made with a heavy long-range gun, but by one of medium calibre, which indicated that the Soviet troops were shelling from a range not far distant! This was most likely the mark, or, rather, one of the marks left by the heavy firing all three of them had heard in Galya's cottage early the previous evening.

Our troops are near! They're in the closest proximity! What words could describe the feelings of this woman who had spent five months away from her children in ceaseless terrible fighting, carrying in her heart the ever present dream of the moment when the Man in the Army Greatcoat, bespattered with blood, would enter his own enemy-desecrated land again and open his arms in a brotherly embrace! How her tortured spirit rushed out to him, this Man in the Army Greatcoat who at this moment was closer to her than husband or brother!

She heard the soft shuffle of felt boots in the snow and Sashko came up to her. At first it even escaped her attention that the front of his sheepskin jacket, his knees and felt boots were covered with earth rather than snow. He had pushed his hands into the jacket sleeves; probably he had had to crawl for a long time and had become very cold. She peered anxiously into his face. What news had he for her? The boy's face, under the huge peaked cap that covered his ears, was undismayed. He simply pulled his hands out of his sleeves and made a negative gesture, meaning, "We can't get through here."

She was overcome by the gesture. The boy glanced at the shell-hole, then at Katya and their eyes met; the boy suddenly smiled. Presumably the sight of the hole in the ground had earlier made the same impression on him as it had on her. He knew what must be going on in her mind and his smile seemed to say, "Never mind, we can't get through here, but we'll get through somewhere else."

Their relationship entered a new phase: now they understood each other. They still said nothing to each other, but they had become fast friends.

She pictured him crawling along somewhere over there, supporting himself on his bare, thin hands pressed to the frozen ground. But the boy refused to allow himself a moment's respite. He beckoned Katya to follow and set off in the opposite direction along their earlier tracks.

It would have been difficult to define Katya's feeling concerning the boy. It was a feeling of comradeship, trust, subordination and respect. At the same time it was a maternal feeling—all those feelings rolled into one.

She did not question him about what prevented them from getting through here; not for a moment did she doubt that he had turned back, not to take her home but to make a detour and conduct her to the second pass and so through the fortifications. She did not offer him her mittens to warm his hands because she knew he would not accept them.

After a time they turned north, then north-east, and again reached the barbed wire which belted the base of a different hill. Sashko went off alone and Katya again had to wait interminably for him. Finally he reappeared, his peaked cap over his ears, his hands tucked into the sleeves and with still more earth smeared all over him. Katya, sitting in the snow, waited for him to come up. He brought his face close to hers, winked and grinned.

In spite of her decision, she tried to press her mittens on him, but he refused them.

As often happens, what she had expected to be most difficult turned out to be not only easy, but unnoticeable. She was simply unaware of the fact that they were passing between two fortified positions. Of all her experiences during the journey this was the most straightforward; but why this was so she understood only afterwards. She could not remember how long they had walked, and then crawled. She only remembered that the whole vicinity had been turned inside out as a result of the daylight raids of the Ilyushin bombers; and she remembered it because when they reached the open fields she found that her sheepskin coat, felt boots and mittens were just as much smeared with earth as Sashko's.

For some time they pressed onwards over the clean snow of the open, slightly undulating fields. Finally Sashko halted, turned round and waited for Katya to catch up with him.

"There's a road over there. Can you see it?" he whispered, and pointed into the distance.

He gave her directions how she could reach the country road which ran from the village they had left to the farmstead, where the next stage of her journey began. She had now reached the zone where, according to Protsenko's map, there were few German defence positions but which, as he had put it, was likely to be in a devil of a mess because of the Germans' helter-skelter retreat through it. There was a possibility that retreating German detachments may have set up temporary defence positions in the zone and be fighting rearguard actions. Bands of fleeing Germans or single straggling soldiers might be lurking anywhere, while any one of the inhabited places might unexpectedly prove to have become part of a German forward defence line. Protsenko had regarded this part of the journey as the most dangerous.

But if one disregarded the still persisting bustle of the retreat along the surfaced roads and the ceaseless sound of gun-fire from the direction of Millerovo in the south-east, there was nothing in the area to indicate the state of affairs Protsenko had described.

"Good luck to you," Sashko said, dropping his hand.

At this point her maternal feeling for him overshadowed everything else. She wanted to take him up in her arms, press him to her heart and hold him there for ever, sheltering him against the whole world. But, of course, to do so would have spoilt their relations completely.

"Good-bye. Thank you very much," she said, removing a mitten and shaking hands with him.

"Good luck," he repeated.

"Oh, I almost forgot," Katya said, a little smile on her lips. "Why was it not possible to get through at the other pass?"

Sashko looked stern as he dropped his eyes to the ground.

"The Fritzes were burying their dead. They'd dug an enormous pit just there!"

As Katya walked away she repeatedly turned to look back in order to keep the boy in sight for as long as she could. But not once did Sashko look back, and soon he had vanished into the darkness.

At this point Katya experienced the greatest shock, which she was to remember all her life. She had gone about two hundred yards and felt that she should be striking the road at any moment when suddenly, as she reached the top of a hillock, she saw before her a gigantic tank with the long barrel of its gun swung obliquely across her path. Something strange and dark crowned with what looked like a ball rising above the turret immediately caught her eye and then moved suddenly and turned out to be a tankman in a helmet, standing in the open hatch.

He levelled a tommy-gun at Katya so quickly that she felt he must have been waiting with it trained on her.

"Halt!"

The word was spoken quietly, but at the same time loudly, the tone used was peremptory but polite because he was addressing a woman. But the most important thing was that he had said the word in the purest Russian.

Katya by now had no strength to reply and the tears rushed to her eyes.

Chapter 20

THE TWO TANKS (Katya had not immediately noticed the other standing behind a rise across the road) formed the advance patrol of a forward tank detachment. The tankman who had halted her was the commander of the tank and also officer in command of the advance patrol, a fact which no one would ever have guessed since he was in ordinary overalls. Katya learned all this later.

The officer ordered her to approach, then leapt down from the tank, followed by a second member of the crew. While he questioned her as to her identity, she studied his face.

He was still quite young, and tired to death; he had not slept for so long that his eyelids drooped and he clearly found difficulty in keeping his eyes open.

Katya explained who she was and why she was on the road. The expression of his face gave no clue as to whether he believed her story or not, but Katya did not notice it. She only saw the young face, so utterly weary, and the swollen eyelids, and the tears again and again welled up in her eyes.

A motor cycle swung down the road out of the darkness and came to a stop by the tank.

"What's happened?" asked the rider in a natural tone of voice.

Something in the question made it clear to Katya that she was the cause of his being summoned. Five months' work behind the enemy's lines had developed in her a habit of noticing trifles, to which, in ordinary times, people would attach no significance. Yet even if they had summoned him by radio he could not have arrived so quickly; how, then, had he been summoned?

By this time the commander of the second tank had come up to them, threw a cursory glance at Katya, and with the first commander and the motor cyclist moved a few paces away and conferred together for a few moments. The motor cyclist then rode away into the darkness.

The tank commanders approached Katya again and with some diffidence the senior of them asked Katya for her documents. Katya said she had no right to present her documents to anyone but the Supreme Command.

They remained silent for some moments, then the second commander, who was younger even than the other, asked in a bass:

"Where did you get through? Are the Germans well dug in?"

Katya told them all she knew of the fortifications and explained how she had been taken through them by a ten-year-old boy. She also reported the burying of the German dead and that she had seen a shell-hole made by a Soviet shell.

"Aha! So that's where it fell! You hear that?" exclaimed the younger commander, looking at the other with a boyish grin.

Only then did Katya realize that the gun-fire she had heard sometimes nearer, sometimes farther in the distance, while in Galya's cottage, and later, just before dark, had come from Soviet advance tanks attacking enemy fortifications.

Relations between Katya and the tank commanders became more friendly after that. She even plucked up the courage to ask the commander of the patrol how he had summoned the motor cyclist. He told her that it had been done with a signal from a lamp in the rear of the tank hatch.

While they were talking a motor cycle with a side-car raced up to them. The rider even saluted Katya, and she felt he not only accepted her as a friend but as an important person.

From the moment she took her seat in the side-car, an entirely new sensation came over Katya and it remained with her for some days after reaching the Soviet troops. She guessed she had happened on a tank detachment which had broken through to territory still held by the Germans. But she no longer attached any importance to the forces of the enemy. Both the enemy and the whole existence she had led for the past five months, and, in addition, the hardships of the journey, were not merely left behind, but seemed suddenly to recede far away into the background of her mind.

A great moral boundary divided her from the surroundings of her immediate past. She now moved in a world of people with feelings, experiences, thought processes and opinions like her own. And this world was so immense that in comparison with the other world where she had up till then been living it seemed to her simply infinite. She could travel on this motor cycle for a whole day, for a whole year even, and everywhere it would be her kind of world, where there was no need to hide, to tell lies, to make unnatural moral and physical efforts. Katya had become herself again for ever and always.

A freezing wind stung her face but she felt she could have burst into song.

The motor cycle tore along with her not for a day or even an hour but, in fact, for no longer than two minutes. The rider braked slightly as they drove through rough snow over a small bridge spanning a stream which had probably dried up during the summer. Katya saw about a dozen tanks on the gentle slopes running down to the bed of the stream, and several lorries standing parked in line along a road beyond. Tommy-gunners of what was known as the motorized infantry stood or sat round the lorries, just ordinary tommy-gunners in winter caps and quilted jackets.

Here Katya was already expected. The motor cycle drove down from the bridge and came to a stop. Two tankmen in overalls came up and grasping her under the arms helped her to climb out of the side-car.

"Excuse me, Comrade..." An elderly tankman saluted and addressed her by the name of the teacher from Chir, indicated in her forged identity papers. "Excuse me, but this is a formality we have to comply with...."

He carefully examined her document by the light of a pocket torch, and promptly handed it back to her.

"Everything in order, Comrade Captain!" he reported to the other tankman, who had a fresh scar running down from the forehead over the bridge of the nose and across the left cheek.

"You're probably frozen!" the captain said, and by the intonation of his voice, gentle, kind and smooth and his unassuming, but at the same time courageous and authoritative bearing Katya guessed he was the officer commanding the tank detachment. "And there's no time for you to warm up, we're advancing. However, if you're not too particular—" With an awkward movement of his heavy hand he produced from his side a flask slung by a strap from his shoulder and removed the stopper.

Katya took the flask in both hands and took a long swig at it.

"Thanks."

"Have another!"

"No, thank you."

"We have orders to get you to corps headquarters, and to get you there in a tank," the captain said, smiling. "Although we've crushed the enemy forces along the road, it's the sort of zone where the devil only knows what might happen!"

"How did you know my name?" Katya asked, the mouthful of diluted spirits burning like fire inside her.

"You're expected."

This meant Protsenko, her own Ivan, had made all the arrangements. She began to feel hot.

Once more she had to relate all she knew about the defences outside the village. She suspected that the tanks were about to move off to storm those heights. And, just as she was being helped on to the turret and down into the coldness of one of the tanks, the hugeness of which she had not fully appreciated until she had come close to it, the tanks started to roar with terrifying eloquence and the tommy-gunners rushed to their lorries.

The crew of the tank in which she was to complete her journey consisted of four men. Each of them had his place. Katya was seated at the commander's feet on the floor of the action deck. It was cramped in the tank. The only one of the crew not wounded was the driver.

The tank commander had a head wound. The bandage round his head, with the thick layer of cotton wool, made it impossible for him to put on his helmet and he was wearing an ordinary soldier's cap. He was also wounded in the arm, which was in a sling, and he instinctively took great care not to knock it against anything, and he frowned from time to time when the tank jolted.

He and his crew were very loth to leave their comrades and at first their attitude was cold towards Katya, since she was to blame for their being sent into the rear. It transpired that only the commander and driver belonged to the original crew of the tank; the others had been transferred, with violent opposition on their part, from other tanks to which the two fit men from this crew had been assigned. At the very moment Katya had been brought to the tank a slight argument had been in progress between the tank commander and the captain—in the most correct language, to be sure. But both had dreadful expressions on their faces. However, the captain with a fresh, unhealed scar across his face had insisted on having his own way. He had made use of the opportunity offered by Katya's journey to get the wounded men away from his detachment.

When the tank got under way and the men found that they had a young woman travelling with them, they changed their attitude towards her. Besides, they soon discovered that Katya had just come through the very defences which the detachment was about to capture and brightened up. All of them were young chaps, perhaps five or seven years younger than Katya.

The commander at this juncture ordered a Second Front to be opened—this was what they called the tins of American corned pork. Like a shot the gunner-radio operator opened a Second Front and cut some gigantic slices of bread, while, with his left hand, the commander offered Katya his flask. She declined the drink but made good work of the corned pork and bread. The tankmen took turns to have a swig from the commander's flask, and the friendliest relations were established inside the tank.

They were travelling at top speed and Katya was being jolted from side to side, when suddenly the gunner standing in the open hatch above them stopped down, and with his lips close to the commander's ear, said:

"Do you hear it, Comrade Senior Lieutenant?"

"They've started, have they?" said the commander hoarsely and his foot lightly touched the driver's shoulder. The driver stopped the tank and in the resulting silence they heard rapid artillery fire. The sound, which filled the night air, came from the direction from which Katya had arrived.

"Ha-ha! Fritz hasn't any flares!" the turret gunner said with satisfaction, leaning out through the hatch again. "Our chaps are giving it them, I can see the shells bursting."

"Let's have a look!"

The senior lieutenant exchanged places with the gunner and carefully pushed his bandaged head through the hatch. While he watched, the tankmen, forgetting Katya's presence, advanced various suppositions regarding the progress of the attack and again expressed annoyance at not being in their own tanks.

The commander carefully pulled his bandaged head back into the tank with a sickly look on his face. However, he remembered Katya's presence and at once put a stop to the whole conversation. Yet Katya could tell by the expression in his face how bitter he felt about not being able to take part in the battle. He had to give every member of the crew a turn at the hatch to see what was happening, before they proceeded on their way.

They were all a little glum after that. Katya, however, was a resourceful woman and at once began to ask them questions about military affairs. It was very difficult to carry on a conversation because of the grinding noise the engines made. They had to shout continuously. They soon warmed to their reminiscences and although their tales were contradictory at times, Katya, for the first time, gained an approximate picture of the military operations in the area in which she now found herself.

Soviet tank units had crossed a long section of the Voronezh-Rostov railway between Rossosh and Millerovo; they had dislodged the Germans from their defensive positions along the Kamyshnaya River; and further to the north they had advanced as far as the upper reaches of the Derkul near the village of Novo-Markovka. Retreating German units had hastily turned the watershed between the Kamyshnaya and the Derkul into a forward defence area, which included the heights where Katya had succeeded in getting through. The new line ran through Limarevka, Belovodsk and Gorodishchi—all places where Protsenko's partisan detachments were operating—and thence to a point on the Donets itself, near the base of the Mityakinskaya partisan detachment. Katya knew all these places well and could now form an estimate of the full might of the Red Army's thrust. At the same time she saw all the difficulties the Soviet troops would have tô face along the road: the fortifications along the banks of the Derkul, Yevsug, Aidar and Borovaya rivers; the railway 'line between Starobelsk and Stanichno-Luganskaya; and, finally, the Donets River itself.

The leading tank detachment, which Katya had encountered, had been separated for two days now from its unit which was following at a distance of about ten miles. Moving in a westerly direction, it had wiped out the enemy's defence positions all along its route and had captured a number of farmsteads and villages, among them the very village which Katya, according to Protsenko's instructions, was to make for.

The tank in which Katya was travelling had been in the advance patrol during the day and had taken part in the attack on the heights which she knew. The patrol had stumbled on the strong points, had opened fire from heavy guns and machine-guns and had thereby drawn on itself all the fire of the enemy. The tank had been damaged, the commander wounded in the head and arm.

They were thus moving away now from the battle area and this was so irrevocably established that gradually all of them, with the exception of Katya and the driver, became overcome by the fatigue and a longing for sleep, which assails soldiers withdrawn for a rest after a stretch of hard fighting. Katya felt great tenderness and compassion for them.

They had passed several inhabited localities when suddenly the driver turned towards Katya and shouted:

"Here they come—our chaps!"

They had kept to the road the whole time, but now the driver swung the tank into the fields and stopped.

It was a dark night, its silence broken only by the sound of near and distant fighting, so familiar to the ears of fighting men. And in this silence, growing nearer and louder, came the drone and grinding of a metallic mass moving towards them. The driver flashed out a signal from his dimmed headlights; the commander and the gunner clambered down to the ground; Katya stood erect in the turret.

Several motor cyclists raced past, followed by tanks and armoured cars approaching along the road and over the steppe. They filled the night air with a thundering roar and Katya clapped her mittened hands to the shawl over her ears. Grinding along, with sharp noises from their exhausts, the tanks crawled past; massive and cumbersome with their dark guns bristling from them, they produced a mighty, terrifying impression, intensified by the darkness.

A small armoured car stopped near their solitary tank. Two military men in greatcoats extricated themselves. For some moments they conversed in loud voices with the tank commander, and from time to time glanced at Katya standing in the turret. Then they climbed back into their car and drove off over the steppe to overtake the stream of tanks.

Tanks alternated with lorries full of motorized infantry. Tommy-gunners looked from the smoothly rolling vehicles at the solitary tank in the steppe from which a woman looked out with mittened hands pressed to her ears.

Katya was stunned by the movement of this heavy mass of armour and the large numbers of people seemingly fused into one with the metal. And it was probably during these moments that a new sensation was added to her feeling of inner liberation; a sensation which remained with her for a long time. She felt that it was not really she who was seeing and experiencing all this, but some other person. She was seeing herself from outside as one sees oneself in a dream. It was her first awareness that she had become unaccustomed to this world which was bursting in on her mind with such incredible force. And for a long time she was unable to find herself in this overpowering kaleidoscope of faces, events, conversations and, finally, human concepts among which were some entirely new to her and others which she had not applied for a long time.

The greater then was her longing to see her husband, to feel his nearness. Her anxiety for him bordered on suffering. Love and anguish made her heart ache, the more so, since she had long forgotten how to find relief in weeping.

The Red Army, when Katya encountered it, was aware that it was now a victorious army.

In the eighteen months of war, this victorious army had not become impoverished in equipment. In fact, as Katya saw it now, it possessed a might of armaments which exceeded the enemy's might even during those never-to-be-forgotten days of humiliation when the enemy was armed and equipped with everything the finest workshops of enslaved Europe could give it, and was sweeping all before it as it rolled inexorably over the burning Donets steppe. But the people with whom fate had now joined Katya staggered her far more than all that. Yes, the people she had rubbed shoulders with, and came into contact with, at every change of the kaleidoscope, were indeed people of a new type. Not only could they control their powerful, new equipment, they seemed, mentally, to have entered upon a new and higher stage in the history of mankind.

Katya was painfully aware that these people were so far in advance of her that she would never be able to catch up with them.

The tank with this marvellous, mixed crew commanded by a senior lieutenant wounded in the head and arm, brought Katya to the headquarters of the tank brigade, which they had encountered en route. It was not really a headquarters, just the brigade commander with an operational group of officers. They had installed themselves in a hamlet which had suffered badly in a skirmish with the enemy only the morning before. The young colonel, with eyes like coals of fire and a face dull from lack of sleep, like those of his staff officers, received her in the only undamaged little house. He apologized for not being able to give her a better reception, but he had only come over for a minute himself, and would have to leave almost at once. He nevertheless suggested that Katya should break her journey and get some sleep.

"Our second echelon is due here soon, someone will be found to see to your wants and look after you," he said.

The small cottage was warmly heated. The officers induced Katya to take off her sheepskin coat and warm herself.

The hamlet had been badly knocked about but there were still very many villagers about, most of them women, children and old folk. The Soviet Army people—tankmen at that—were a novelty and a joy to them. Crowds of people gathered round the soldiers, and especially round the officers. Signallers were already running telephone wires to the small cottage, as well as to the neighbouring half-destroyed houses, in preparation for the staff and its establishments.

Katya had a cup of tea—real tea it was. And half an hour later the closed jeep of the commander was carrying her swiftly towards corps headquarters in the company now of a sergeant armed with a tommy-gun. The faces of the senior tank lieutenant with the bandaged head, of the dull-faced colonel with the fiery eyes and of dozens of others faded from Katya's memory.

The morning came with a bitterly hard frost and mists shrouded everything from view. Somewhere beyond the mists the sun was rising and Katya was travelling straight towards it.

They were driving along a surfaced road when they began to meet troop units marching in the opposite direction. If Katya had not been in the jeep which, as it was, had continually to slither down into the steppe and proceed on its way over the thin covering of snow, Katya would have taken a long time to reach her destination. Soon the car forded the shallow, muddy waters of the Kamyshnaya, which meandered along, a mixture of snow, ice and sand, ground down by the tanks and guns which constantly crossed it, probably, at numerous points.

The mists had lifted a little and the sun, into which one could look without blinking, hung low over the horizon. Along both banks of the stream Katya saw the German fortifications, now captured by the Soviet troops. Everywhere the ground had been churned up by shells, tanks, and the tractors moving heavy guns to new forward positions.

On the other side of the river it became even more difficult to proceed because of the masses of troops moving to the south-west and the marching in the opposite direction of captured enemy soldiers. These were escorted in small groups and also in large contingents. Unshaven and dirty, they straggled along in their shabby overcoats through the mud on the road or across the steppe, crushed by the shame of defeat and captivity. The area through which they were being taken bore the marks of the destruction they themselves had wrought. The fertile steppe, which for centuries had brought forth corn, now lay ravaged, the villages were burnt down and destroyed. Here and there the carcasses of burnt-out tanks or mangled lorries, the jutting barrels of disabled guns, swastika-bearing aircraft wings lay blackened on the ground. The frozen, distorted bodies of the enemy dead lay about on the steppe and on the road. There had been no one and no time to carry them away; tanks and heavy guns rolled over them, flattening them into a horrifying mass.

The men marching in the advancing columns or seated in the tanks and lorries, tired men inspired by the heroic, heavy trials of battles lasting for some ten days, battles from which they were emerging victorious, these men no longer paid attention to the enemy dead. Katya alone brought herself to look at them from time to time with fastidious indifference.

The battle, one of the greatest in history, and one of the links in the great defeat of Hitler's forces at Stalingrad, assumed ever greater proportions and intensity as it moved towards the south-west. Here and there in the dispersing mist air battles flared up, heavy guns thundered over the vast expanses of the steppe and everywhere the eye could see there was the same picture of gigantic movements of the troops and equipment, the food and shells which go hand in hand with large-scale military operations.

Towards noon, when it would have been quite clear but for the smoke from fires which mingled everywhere with the dispersing mists, Katya arrived at the headquarters of the Guards tank corps. Again this was not a headquarters proper, but the temporary command post of the corps commander established in a brick-built railway station, north of Millerovo, which had miraculously escaped destruction. The adjacent small village had been blown to smithereens. But, as in all newly-liberated places, what first struck the eye was the astounding combination of continuing military operations and the Soviet civilian life which was already falling back into position.

The first person Katya saw among the men at the command post was a man the sight of whom at once awakened memories of pre-war life, of her husband, and her family, of her work as a teacher and later as a modest official at the education department.

"Andrei Yefimovich! My dear!" Involuntarily the cry escaped her lips, and she rushed to him and threw her arms about him.

He was one of the leaders of the Ukrainian Partisan Headquartes, who more than five months previously had given Protsenko his instructions before he took up his underground activities.

"Now you must embrace us all!" said a lean, youthful general, looking at her from steady grey eyes behind long lashes.

Katya looked at the tanned, roughened face of the carefully-shaved general, whose hair was greying at the temples and she suddenly felt embarrassed. She covered her face with her hands and lowered her head in the warm, dark peasant shawl. So she stood, her face in her hands, in a sheepskin jacket and felt boots contrasting with the smart appearance of the army men.

"See now, you've embarrassed her! Don't you know how to treat women?" Andrei Yefimovich said, smiling. The officers laughed.

"I'm sorry," the general said, and his hand lightly touched her shoulder. She took her hands from her face; her eyes shone.

"It's all right," she said, as he began to help her out of her jacket.

Like most of the Soviet officers of the day, the corps commander was still young for his rank and duties. In spite of his position, he was unaffectedly calm, precise in his movements, reliable and business-like and full of a restrained, rough humour, yet, at the same time, courteous. And all the military people with him bore the stamp of the same calm, business-like, courteous bearing and a certain general neatness.

While Protsenko's report was being decoded, the general carefully laid the sheet of tissue-paper with the infinitely small map of Voroshilovgrad Region on top of a large army map spread out on the table, just as Protsenko had previously done in front of Katya (it was hard to imagine that it had only been two nights ago!). The general's slim fingers smoothed out the tissue-paper.

"Now that is the kind of work I understand!" he exclaimed with obvious pleasure. "What the devil! Just look, Andrei Yefimovich, they're fortifying the Mius again!"

Andrei Yefimovich bent over the map. The numerous wrinkles on his strong face deepened, making him look older than he was. The other officers also crowded round the slip of tissue-paper lying on the map.

"Not that we'll have any dealings with them along the Mius, but you know what it means?" the general said with a merry glance at Andrei Yefimovich. "They're not such fools as not to realize they'll have to withdraw from the North Caucasus and the Kuban!"

The general laughed. Katya flushed with pleasure, for

the general's words so closely coincided with her husband's forecast.

"Let's see, now, what is new for us here." The general took up the large lens lying on the map and began to scrutinize the marks and little circles placed on the minute map by Protsenko's steady hand. "This we already know ... hm, this we know about, too ... hm ... well...." He comprehended Protsenko's symbols without any reference to the explanatory notes, which had not yet been decoded. "Well, it means that our Vasily Prokhorovich isn't so bad after all, yet you're always saying, 'The intelligence work's no good,'" concluded the general, with thinly disguised irony, addressing the corps Chief of Staff, a heavy-set colonel with a black moustache, who was at his side.

An officer who was completely bald and very short of stature and whose pale, lively eyes were full of an indescribable guile anticipated the colonel's reply:

"That information, Comrade Corps Commander, came to us from precisely the same source," he said, unabashed. He actually was Vasily Prokhorovich, Chief of Intelligence of the corps headquarters.

"Oho! and I thought you'd found it out yourself!" said the general, disappointed.

The officers laughed. Vasily Prokhorovich, however, attached no importance either to the general's mocking remark or his service colleagues' laughter. He was evidently accustomed to it.

"No, you just pay attention to the data at this spot, along the Derkul, Comrade General," he said, unruffled. "They're behind the times. We already know more about this area."

Katya felt that Vasily Prokhorovich's rejoinder somehow detracted from the importance of the information Protsenko had collected, for the sake of which she had made the long journey.

"The comrade who handed me this report," she began sharply, "asked me to warn you that he would be sending you fresh information on the retreat of the enemy; and I expect that at this very moment he is dispatching it. This map, with the explanations to it, gives an over-all picture of the situation in the region."

"True," said the general. "It'll be needed more by Comrade Vatutin and Comrade Khrushchov. We'll make use of the information in it that concerns us directly."

It was late at night before Katya found an opportunity to have a private talk with Andrei Yefimovich.

They were not sitting, but standing in the warm, empty room lit by captured German night-lights, and Katya was saying:

"How on earth d'you come to be here, Andrei Yefimovich?"

"Why should that surprise you? We are back on Ukrainian territory, after all. We haven't much of it yet, but what we have is ours! The government's returning to our native land and establishing Soviet order." Andrei Yefimovich smiled and his strong, finely-wrinkled face immediately looked younger. "As you know, our troops have joined forces with the Ukrainian partisans, indeed, could they manage without us?" He looked down at Katya, his eyes sparkling, then again became grave. "I wanted you to have a rest and talk things over tomorrow. But you're a very brave person!" He said it a little shame-facedly, but his eyes looked straight into Katya's. "We'll be wanting to send you back, straight to Voroshilovgrad. We need a great deal of information that only you can obtain for us." He paused, then went on softly, questioningly: "Of course, if you're very tired—"

But Katya did not let him finish. Her heart was welling over with pride and thankfulness.

"Thank you," she whispered. "Thank you, Andrei Yefimovich! And don't say any more. You couldn't have said anything that would have given me greater happiness," she said agitatedly and her sunburnt, sharp-featured face, framed with her fair hair, became very beautiful. "I want to ask only one thing of you: let me go tomorrow, don't send me to the political department at the front; I don't need a rest!"

Andrei Yefimovich thought for a moment, then shook his head and smiled.

"We're not in such a hurry," he said. "We'll tidy up a bit and consolidate the lines we've taken. The Derkul and the Donets, in particular, will be no walk-over. Millerovo and Kamensk are holding us up. And you'll have plenty to tell the political department. So, we're in no particular hurry. You can set out in two or three days' time."

"But why not tomorrow?" exclaimed Katya, her heart aching with longing and love.

Three days later towards nightfall Katya was again in Galya's cottage, wearing the same sheepskin jacket and dark shawl and carrying the same documents identifying her as a teacher from Chir.

Soviet troops were now stationed in the little village, but the hills to the north and south were still held by the enemy. The line of German defence positions ran along the watershed between the Kamyshnaya and the Derkul, then deep into the west along the Derkul.

During the night little Sashko, as reliable and silent as before, conducted Katya back along the road which earlier she had travelled with old Foma as her guide, and she reached the hut where a few days previously Protsenko had set her off on her journey.

There one of the numerous Kornienkos told her that her husband had been informed of her return, and that he was safe and sound himself, but would not be able to arrange a meeting with her.

Katya then began the journey to Marfa Kornienko; unaccompanied, she walked day and night with never more than two or three hours' rest in twenty-four; when she reached her destination she learned the shattering news that Masha Shubina had been killed.

The Germans had discovered the contact address at the first-aid station in Uspenka village. Warned by one of their own people in the police, the Krotova sisters had managed to get away and give the alarm to the underground organizations they were in touch with. But the news of the catastrophe did not reach Marfa Kornienko until after Masha had set out for Uspenka. Attempts to intercept Masha on the road had failed. She fell into the hands of the gendarmes and was tortured there, in Uspenka. From the same contact in the police it was later learned that Masha Shubina had to the very end denied all connection with the underground and betrayed no one.

This was dreadful news indeed! But Katya had no right now to give way to grief: she would need all the strength she had.

Two days later she was already in Voroshilovgrad.

Chapter 21

EVEN THE MOST uninformed people in German-occupied territory, people who understood nothing of military affairs realized by now that this was to be the end of the Hitlerites.

The clearest indication of this, in places as far distant from the front as Krasnodon, was the flight of the Hitlerites' junior partners in pillage—the Hungarian and Italian mercenaries and the remnants of Antonescu's army.

Rumanian officers and men, without any motor transport and artillery, were in flight along all the roads. Day and night they dragged past, in their box-wagons, drawn by emaciated horses, or made their way on foot, their hands pushed into the sleeves of their tattered greatcoats, in forage-caps or tall goatskin hats, their frost-bitten faces wrapped in towels or women's woollen underclothes.

One of these box-wagons halted at the gate to the Koshevois' home; a not unfamiliar officer leapt down from it and ran into the house, followed by a batman carrying the officer's large suitcase and his own smaller one, his face averted to hide a frost-bitten ear.

The officer's cheek was swollen with a gumboil and he no longer wore gilt shoulder-straps. He rushed into the kitchen and at once began warming his hands at the stove.

"Well, how's things?" Nikolai Nikolayevich asked him.

The officer's face assumed the expression which always accompanied the motion of wrinkling the tip of his nose, which, however, he could not wrinkle now because it was frost-bitten. He suddenly grimaced in an imitation of Hitler's face, most successfully, too, thanks to his little moustache and the demented expression in his eyes. Then he rose on his toes and made a feint of running. There was no smile on his face, for he was not, in fact, joking.

"We go home to the wife!" the batman said good-naturedly with a cautious glance at the officer and a wink for Nikolai Nikolayevich.

They warmed themselves, had a bite to eat and had hardly left the house with their cases when Grandma, moved by intuition, turned back the blankets on Yelena Nikolayevna's bed and saw that both sheets had vanished.

So infuriated that some of her youth returned to her, Grandma rushed after the guests and at the gate stormed at them in such a fashion that the officer realized that he might at any moment become the centre of a howling mob of women. He ordered the batman to open his case. One of the sheets was indeed inside. Grandma seized it shouting:

"Where's the other one?"

The batman fiercely rolled his eyes in the direction of his master, but he had snatched up his suitcase and was climbing into the wagon. So he actually carried off the sheet to Rumania, unless, of course, a Ukrainian or Moldavian partisan availed himself of it after dispatching to the other world this descendant of the ancient Romans and his batman.

Sometimes an element of surprise brings more success to the most risky undertakings than to those which are carefully prepared. More often, however, the most important affairs come to grief because of one false step.

In the evening of December 30, Sergei, Valya and a group of comrades were on their way to the club when they saw a German lorry piled up with sacks parked in front of a house, without any guards or driver.

Sergei and Valya climbed on the lorry, felt the sacks and came to the conclusion that they were full of New Year presents. Snow had fallen during the previous night, there was a hard frost and the snow made everything light. People were still about in the streets; the youngsters, nevertheless, took a chance and dropped several of the sacks from the lorry and dragged them into adjacent yards and sheds.

Club director Zhenya Moshkov and Vanya Zemnukhov, its arts manager, suggested that as soon as the club emptied for the night the sacks should be transferred to it, for there were all kinds of places for concealing things in the basement.

German soldiers crowded round the lorry and swore drunkenly, especially a corporal in a coat with a dogskin collar and *ersatz* felt boots, while the woman of the house stood without her coat protesting her innocence. The Germans could see that she had nothing to do with the affair. In the end the Germans climbed on to the lorry, the woman ran back into the house, and swinging down towards the ravine, the lorry was driven off to the gendarmerie station.

The youngsters then dragged the sacks to the club and concealed them in the basement.

In the morning, Vanya Zemnukhov and Moshkov met at the club and decided that part of the presents, especially the cigarettes, should be sold at once in the market-place as it was New Year's Eve: the organization needed money. Stakhovich happened to be in the club, too, and he supported the suggestion.

Under-the-counter trading in German goods was nothing unusual in the market-place. The German soldiers did it more than anyone else; they traded cigarettes, tobacco, candles and petrol for vodka, warm clothing and food. German articles were resold from hand to hand and the policemen turned a blind eye to it. And Moshkov already had a whole gang of boys who willingly undertook the sale of cigarettes in return for a percentage of the proceeds.

But on this particular day the policemen, after searching since early morning through the houses near the spot where the loss had been discovered and finding no trace of the New Year presents, were on the look-out for these traders. And one of the small boys was caught with cigarettes on him by Police Chief Solikovsky himself.

When questioned the boy said that he had bartered some bread to an old man in exchange for the cigarettes. The boy was given a thrashing with a whip. But he was one of those boys who had been thrashed more than once in his life, and moreover had learned not to split on his comrades; the beaten, tearful lad was thrown into a prison cell and kept there until nightfall.

In the course of other business, *Meister* Brückner had been informed by the police chief of the arrest of a boy in possession of German cigarettes and had connected this with various other thefts from lorries. He decided he would question the boy himself.

Late in the evening the boy, who had fallen asleep in the cell, was awakened and taken to *Meister* Brückner's room, where he was immediately confronted with two gendarmes, the chief of police and a translator.

Snuffling, the boy repeated his story.

The *Meister* flared up, seized the boy by the ear and himself dragged him along the corridor.

The boy found himself in a cell in which stood two blood-stained trestle-beds; ropes dangled from the ceiling, and ramrods, bradawls, lashes made of twisted electric cable and an axe lay on a long, whitewood trestle-table. There was a fire in the iron stove. In a corner stood a pail of water. Gutters, like those in public baths, ran along two sides of the room.

A fat, bald German gendarme with large red hands covered with fair hair sat smoking on a stool by the table. He wore a black uniform and light horn-rimmed spectacles.

The little boy looked at him, trembled with fright and said Moshkov, Zemnukhov and Stakhovich had given him the cigarettes in the club.

On the same day a Pervomaisky girl by the name of Vyrikova ran across a friend, Lyadskaya, in the market-place; they had shared the same desk at school, but had lost sight of each other at the beginning of the war when Lyadskaya's father was transferred to a job in Krasnodon settlement.

Theirs was not so much a friendship. Both had been brought up with an eye to the main chance, and such upbringing does not make for friendship. But they understood each other, had common interests and each profited from the relationship. From early childhood both had acquired ideas about the world from their parents and the people their parents associated with, which led to their believing that all people really live for personal gain and that the aim and purpose of life was to strive not to be the loser but to prosper at the expense of others.

At school Vyrikova and Lyadskaya had performed various social duties and they had habitually and freely employed all the terms, which covered contemporary social and moral concepts. But they were convinced that their duties and all the phrases they used and even the knowledge they imbibed at school had been conceived by people for the express purpose of concealing their striving for personal gain and the use they made of other people to further their own interests.

They displayed no particular exuberance on meeting, but were very pleased all the same to have met each other. They amicably shook each other's stiff hands—little Vyrikova in a cap with ear-flaps with her short pigtails sticking out in front over the thick coat-collar and Lyadskaya, tall, large-boned and red-haired, with painted finger-nails. They drew aside from the milling crowd in the market for a quiet chat.

„Germans! Talk about deliverers!" Lyadskaya said. "'Culture ... culture,' but all they can think about is how to fill their bellies and have a good time for nothing. No, I must say I expected more of them than that. Where are you working?"

"In what used to be the cattle procurement office." Vyrikova's face took on an injured, angry expression. At last she was able to talk to someone who could criticize the Germans from the correct angle. "I get only bread, 200 marks and nothing else. They're fools! Can't appreciate anyone who volunteered to work for them. I'm very disillusioned," Vyrikova said.

"I could see at once there was no advantage in it. So I didn't go," Lyadskaya said. "At first I didn't live too badly. There were a few of us all of a mind, and I used to do the travelling to the villages to trade for things. One of them had it in for me though, and she reported that I was not registered at the labour exchange. Much good it did her! I knew one of the officials, an oldish fellow from the labour exchange, but he was so funny. He wasn't even a German, but was from the Lorraine or somewhere like that. I kept company with him for a while and in the end he used to bring me drinks and cigarettes. Then he fell ill and they sent another fellow; a regular bone-head he was! He had me working at the pit in no time. No joke, you know, turning a windlass handle all day! That's why I'm here now, to see if they'll offer me something better at the exchange. Have you got any pull there?"

Vyrikova pouted.

"A fat lot of good that would be to me! But I'll tell you this: it's more worth while to stick to the army fellows! They're here temporarily, sooner or later they will have to go and you're under no obligation to them; and they're not so stingy. They know they may get killed any day, and they don't grudge themselves a good time. You should call in some time."

"How can I? It's fifteen miles to come to town and then all that way to your Pervomaisky!"

"My Pervomaisky! It's not so long since it was yours too. Try and come anyway, you'll be able to tell me about your new job. I'll have something to show you, might even have something to give you, you know what I mean. Try and come!" With a casual air, Vyrikova offered her a small stiff hand.

In the evening a neighbour who had been that day to the labour exchange handed Vyrikova a note. It was from Lyadskaya who wrote: "Your bone-heads at the labour exchange are worse than ours in the settlement," and added that her plans had not worked out and she was going home "brokenhearted."

On New Year's Eve searches were carried out in selected houses in Pervomaisky as well as elsewhere throughout the town. In Vyrikova's home they found Lyadskaya's note which she had carelessly pushed among some old school exercise books. Examining Judge Kuleshov who carried out the search had no trouble in eliciting her friend's name from Vyrikova who, in her terror, added fancifully-embroidered information about Lyadskaya's "anti-German" sentiments.

Kuleshov told Vyrikova to report at the police-station after the holiday. He took the note with him.

Sergei Tyulenin was the first to get the news of the arrest of Moshkov, Zemnukhov and Stakhovich. He told his sisters Nadya and Dasha, warned his friend, Vitka Lukyanchenko, then rushed off to see Oleg. There he found Valya and the Ivantsova sisters who met in Oleg's home every morning to receive the assignments for the day.

During the previous night Oleg and Nikolai Nikolayevich had written down the communiqué of the Soviet Information Bureau on the results of the six weeks' Red Army offensive in the Stalingrad area and on the double encirclement of the huge German forces at the approaches to Stalingrad.

Laughing as they grasped his hands, the girls pounced on Sergei to tell him about it. And despite his toughness, Sergei's lips trembled as he broke his terrible news to them.

For some moments Oleg sat quite still. The colour had drained from his face, the long fingers of his large hands were locked together and there were deep lines on his forehead.

At last he stood up, a business-like expression on his face.

"Listen girls," he said softly, "find Turkenich and Ulya. Then go round to all people in close touch with Young Guard headquarters, tell them to hide everything and to destroy what they can't hide. Tell them we'll let them know within two hours what to do after that. Warn their relatives. Don't forget Lyuba's mother," he said (Lyuba was in Voroshilovgrad). "I'll have to be away for a little while now."

Sergei also put on his quilted jacket and a cap, which was all he wore on his head despite the cold.

"Where are you going?" Oleg asked.

Valya blushed, suddenly thinking that Sergei was getting ready to accompany her home.

"I'm going to keep a look-out in the street while you all get ready," he said.

And then it struck them all for the first time that what had happened to Vanya, Moshkov and Stakhovich might happen to them at any moment, even now.

The girls, after deciding among themselves which homes each of them would visit, went out of the house.

As Valya was passing through the yard Sergei stopped her.

"Be careful now. If you don't find us here, go to Natalya Alexeyevna in the hospital. I'll find you there, then. I won't go away anywhere without you."

Valya silently nodded and ran off to Turkenich.

Trying hard to walk at his usual pace, Oleg went to Aunt Polina, who lived in a street near the labour exchange.

When he entered she was peacefully occupied, peeling potatoes and tossing them into a saucepan, steaming on the stove. The calm, reserved woman suddenly paled when Oleg told her of the arrest of his comrades. The knife dropped from her hand and for a few seconds she was struck dumb. Then she got herself under control.

Being New Year's Day, no one was at work. Lyutikov would, indeed, be home, but it was not a good thing to go there in broad daylight, after having been there in the morning with the milk. But there could be no delay; many things might be decided not only in a few hours, but even in a few minutes.

Though Aunt Polina was conversant with all the affairs of the Young Guard, she asked Oleg whether any of the arrested knew of the connection Oleg and Turkenich had with the district Party committee. Of course, all the arrested knew of the connection, but none of them knew with whom personally. Moshkov himself was in touch with the district Party committee, but he could be trusted under any circumstances. Zemnukhov was in contact with the district Party committee only through Aunt Polina. She knew Vanya so well that no thought of personal danger to herself crossed her mind.

It was unfortunate that Stakhovich knew so much about the Young Guard. Oleg described him as being honest, but weak.

Aunt Polina left Oleg in her home and instructed him what to say to anyone asking for her.

One can well imagine how slowly that hour passed for Oleg! Luckily no one came to the house. He could hear the neighbours pottering about on the other side of the wall, and that was all.

At long last Aunt Polina came back. The cold had returned the colour to her cheeks and Lyutikov had evidently found the right words to instil hope in her heart.

"Listen now." She removed her shawl and in her unbuttoned coat sat down opposite Oleg. "He said I was to tell you not to lose heart. And he instructed you all to leave the town and leave at once; this applies to all the members of the Young Guard headquarters and everyone in close touch with it or with the arrested people. Leave two or three reliable people in charge of the organization, put their leader in touch with me and then leave. If any of you can find a hide-out in a village or town at some distance from here, then let him go into hiding. He advises the headquarters members and the people in close touch with them to go to the northern districts, the other side of the Donets; there they may be able to get through the lines or else wait until the Red Army arrives. Wait, that's not all," she said, anticipating a question from Oleg. "He gave me an address for you. Now listen attentively," a stony expression had come into her face. "This address you may pass on to Turkenich alone. And you're the only two who may make use of it. It is to be given to no one else, definitely no one else, no matter how dear the other lads and girls may be to you.

Understand me?" Aunt Polina spoke in a quiet voice and watched his face closely. He knew whom she meant.

He sat hunched up and motionless for some moments, his brow, like an adult's, furrowed with long wrinkles.

"Must we go to this address whatever happens, Turkenich and myself?" he asked softly.

"No, of course not. But it's an absolutely reliable address. You'll not only be kept in concealment there, but given something to do."

In Oleg's face she could read the agonizing struggle going on in his mind. But the question he asked then was not at all what Aunt Polina had expected:

"And the fellows in prison? How can we go away without even making an attempt to get them out?"

"You can't be the people to assist them now," she replied, with sudden severity. "The district Party committee will do everything it can. And the young people you're going to leave here will also be of help. Who is it you're leaving in charge?"

"Anatoly Popov will be here," Oleg said after a moment's thought. "If anything happens to him, there's Kolya Sumskoi. Do you know him?"

They sat in silence for some minutes. He would have to be on his way now.

"Where are you thinking of going?" she asked softly. She spoke now simply as someone who was very fond of him and all his family. He could feel how profoundly upset she was.

Oleg's face became so gloomy and sad that she regretted having asked the question. Then with an agonizing effort he said slowly:

"Aunt Polina, you know why I can't make use of that address."

Yes, she knew: Nina! He could not go away without Nina.

"We're going to try to get through the lines together," said Oleg. "Good-bye."

They embraced.

While Oleg was out, Turkenich arrived at his home and, shortly afterwards, Styopa Safonov and Sergei Levashov, though they had not been summoned. Then Zhora Arutyuniants came, but without Osmukhin. New Year's Day was

Volodya Osmukhin's eighteenth birthday; his sister Lyudmila had presented him with a pair of warm woollen socks she had knitted for him and then they had gone out into the country to visit their grandfather.

Turkenich sent the lads outside to keep watch all round the house, then he and Sergei went into consultation without waiting for Ulya who had a long way to come.

What was to be their next step? This was the only question to which they now had to find the answer and find it at once. They realized that it concerned not only the fate of their arrested comrades but the fate of the whole organization. Should they wait and see how things turned out? They might be arrested at any moment. Hide? They had nowhere to hide, everyone knew them.

Valya came back, then Ulya arrived with Olya Ivantsova and Nina, who had run into them on the way. Nina reported that the club was now guarded by German gendarmes and policemen, no one was allowed to enter and everybody in the neighbourhood knew of the arrest of the club leaders and that the German New Year gifts had been discovered in the basement of the club.

Turkenich and Nina expressed the view that this was the only reason why the lads had been arrested. Grave as this was, it did not mean the catastrophic end of the whole organization.

"The chaps won't betray us," Turkenich said with the confidence characteristic of him.

At this point Oleg came in and, without a word, sat down at the table with a profoundly thoughtful expression on his face. Then he called Turkenich into his grandma's room. He gave him the address Aunt Polina had given him. They conferred a little, then returned to Sergei and the girls who were waiting for them in deep silence. All of them, filled with suffering and hope, looked inquiringly at Oleg.

When Oleg began to speak there was an almost ruthless expression on his face.

"We have t-to give up all hope of any kind of safe way out for us," he said, looking at them frankly and boldly. "However m-much it may hurt and hard as it may b-be, we must give up any idea of being able to stay here until the arrival of the Red Army, of helping it from the rear, of doing the things we had planned even for tomorrow. Otherwise it's the end of us and the end of all our people as well," he went on, hardly able to keep his self-control. They all listened to him, pale and rigid. "The Germans have been hunting for us for several months now. They know that we exist. They've blundered right into the centre of our organization. Even if they know nothing apart from those presents, and find out nothing more," he emphasized, "they'll pounce on all who had anything to do with the club and dozens of innocent people as well. What's to be done?" He paused, then went on: "We must go away. We must leave the town. Yes, we've got to disperse. Not all of us, of course. The fellows in Krasnodon settlement are hardly affected by this set-back. The same with the Pervomaisky comrades. They can go on working." Suddenly he looked very seriously at Ulya. "With the exception of Ulya. Because as a member of our headquarters she may be caught any moment. We've fought our battle honourably," he went on. "And we can separate in the knowledge that we've done our duty. We've lost three of our comrades, including one of the very finest, Vanya Zemnukhov. But we must go our ways without any feelings of despondency or despair. We have done everything we could."

He had finished. The others neither wanted nor were able to say anything more.

For five months they had worked harmoniously side by side. Five months under German rule, and each day, because of the weight of physical and moral torment and exertion put into it, was far more than an ordinary day of the week. Five long months—how they had rushed past! And how they had all changed in that time! How much they had learned of what is grand and what is terrible, good and bad. How much of the bright, splendid efforts of their minds had been put into the common cause and into each other. Only now did it become apparent to them just what this Young Guard organization had been to them, how much they themselves were indebted to it. And now they had to abandon it.

The girls, Valya, Nina, Olya, wept quietly. Ulya seemed outwardly calm, but a terrible, powerful light shone in her eyes. Sergei's head was bowed over the table, as his finger-nail traced a pattern on the cloth. Turkenich's clear eyes stared straight ahead; the stern, wilful lines round his finely-moulded mouth had deepened.

"Any other op-pinions?" Oleg asked.

There were none. But then Ulya spoke up:

"I don't see any need for me to go away now. We in Pervomaisky had very little to do with the club. I'll wait a bit, I may be able to do some more work. I'll be careful."

"You must go away," Oleg said and again gave her a very serious look.

Sergei had been silent throughout; now he said:

"She's certainly got to go away!"

"I'll be careful," Ulya said again.

With heavy hearts, and avoiding each other's eyes, they decided to leave behind three members of the headquarters: Anatoly Popov, Sumskoi and Ulya if she did not go away. If Lyuba were to return, and it was found that she could stay, then she would make the fourth. They passed a resolution: everyone was to leave as soon as possible. Oleg said that he and the liaison girls would remain until everyone had been warned and contact had been established with Popov and Sumskoi. But no member of the Young Guard headquarters, and no one in close touch with it, was to spend the night at home.

They called in Zhora, Sergei Levashov and Styopa Safonov and informed them of the decisions the headquarters had taken.

The farewells began. Ulya went up to Oleg. They embraced.

"Th-thank you," said Oleg. "Thank you for what you've been and for what you are."

She gently passed a hand over his hair.

But when the girls began to say good-bye to Ulya it was too much for Oleg and he went outside into the yard. Sergei Tyulenin followed him. They stood without their coats out in the frost and blinding sunlight of the year 1943.

"Is everything quite clear?" Oleg asked in a dull voice.

Sergei nodded. "Everything. So Stakhovich may not hold out. Is that so?"

"Yes. And it wouldn't be very nice to mention it; it's wrong not to trust, when you don't know. They are most likely torturing him already, and we're still free."

They were silent for some moments.

"Where d'you expect to go?"

"I'm going to try and get through the lines."

"So am I. Let's go together, eh?"

"Of course. Only Nina and Olya will be with me."

"I think Valya'll come with us too," Sergei Tyulenin said.

Meanwhile Sergei Levashov, a sullen and awkward look on his face, had begun to take his farewell of Turkenich.

"Wait, what're you up to?" Turkenich asked watching his face closely.

"I'm staying for a bit," Levashov replied sullenly.

"It's not wise," Turkenich said quietly. "You'll not be able to help her or protect her. And they'll pick you up while you're waiting for her. She's a smart girl; she'll get away or else fool them."

"I'm not leaving," said Levashov.

"You'll come through the lines to join up!" Turkenich said, sharply. "I'm not replaced yet, I'm giving you an order!"

Levashov made no reply.

"Well, Comrade Commissar, you're going through the lines. That's final, isn't it?" Turkenich asked Oleg as the latter re-entered the room. Oleg's refusal to make use of the address which had been given to both of them annoyed him but he knew that nothing would make Oleg change his mind. When he heard that Oleg's group was to consist of five people he shook his head:

"That's rather a lot. Well, it seems that we'll all be in the ranks of the Red Army until we meet again here!"

They shook hands and were about to embrace, but Turkenich suddenly broke away, flung out both his arms and rushed out of the house. Sergei Levashov embraced Oleg and then followed Turkenich.

Styopa Safonov had relatives in Kamensk; he decided to go to them to await the arrival of the Red Army. In Zhora's mind a struggle was taking place which he was unable to share with anyone. But he knew that he must not stay, and would probably have to go to his uncle in Novocherkassk, the same uncle he and Vanya Zemnukhov had failed to reach on a previous occasion. As Zhora's mind went back to that journey with Vanya, the tears rushed to his eyes and he went into the street.

For several minutes after that five of them stayed in the room: Oleg, Sergei Tyulenin and the liaison girls. They decided that Sergei had better not go home and that Olya would warn his people through Vitya Lukyanchenko. Valya, Nina and Olya then left to inform the people concerned of the decisions reached, while Sergei put on his overcoat and went outside to keep watch; he understood that Oleg needed to be alone with the family.

Oleg's people already knew of the arrest of Zemnukhov and the others and knew that in the meetings taking place in the dining-room and in Grandma's room the young people were discussing the matter.

The rifles kept in the house, the leaflets and the red material for flags Yelena Nikolayevna and Nikolai Nikolayevich had already hidden or burnt. Nikolai Nikolayevich had buried the wireless set in the cellar under the kitchen floor, smoothed the earth and placed the barrel of sauerkraut over the spot.

All this had been done and now the family was gathered in Nikolai Nikolayevich's room, responding as usual, but absent-mindedly, to the chatter and playfulness of Marina's three-year-old son, and waiting like people doomed to know what the conferences would bring forth.

The door closed behind the last comrade and Oleg entered the room. They all turned to him. The marks of mental struggle and activity had left his face, but with them had gone the childlike expression which so frequently had been seen. His face wore the stamp of grief.

"Mother," he began. "And you, Grandma, Kolya, Marina." The child scampered up and clung to his leg, with a cry of joy. Oleg laid his large hand on the boy's head. "I have to say good-bye to all of you. Help me to get some things together. After that let's sit together for a little while, the way we did on that other occasion ... so long ago!" The ghost of a smile, distant and tender, touched his eyes and lips.

They stood up and pressed round him.

... They are busy, these hands of the mother! Busily they flutter like birds across the flimsiest of dainty little garments before ever there is a being to clothe, when as yet it is but knocking with sharp heart-moving tender thrusts in its mother's body. Busily they flutter as they swaddle the child for its first airing; they flutter as they array him for his first day at school. And again, for the first parting from home, for the journey to distant parts, a lifetime of partings and reunions, rare moments of happiness, eternal heart-aches. Fluttering busily while he is still there, while there is hope; fluttering when hope is gone, arraying the child for the grave.

Something was found for everyone to do. There were papers to sort out with Nikolai Nikolayevich. The diary had to be burnt. Someone stitched his Komsomol card and a few blank temporary membership cards into his jacket. He had to take a change of underwear—it needed mending. Then everything was packed into the knapsack: food, soap, tooth-brush, a needle with some cotton, black and white. An old fur cap with ear-flaps was found for Sergei Tyulenin. And more food in another knapsack for Sergei to carry—after all, there would be five of them.

But they did not manage to sit together for a little while as they had before. Sergei kept coming in and going out again. Then Valya, Nina and Olya came back. Night had already come. They had now to say good-bye.

There were no tears. Grandma Vera looked them over, fastened a button here, straightened a knapsack there. Fitfully she pressed each of them closely, then pushed them from her; but Oleg she held for a long time, her pointed chin pressed on his cap.

Oleg took his mother's arm; they went into the next room.

"Forgive me, Mother," he said to her.

Oleg's mother ran out into the yard and the frost stung her face and legs. She could no longer see the young people. she only heard their boots crunching through the snow, the sound had already faded and then it was gone. But she remained a long time standing under the dark, starry sky.

Dawn came and Yelena Nikolayevna had not closed her eyes. She heard a knock on the door. Quickly slipping into her dress she called, "Who's there?"

There were four of them: Police Chief Solikovsky, N.C.O. Fehnbong and two soldiers. They asked for Oleg. Yelena

Nikolayevna said he had gone out to the villages to barter some articles˙for food.

They searched the house and arrested everyone in it, even Grandma Vera, Marina and the little boy. Grandma hardly had time to warn the neighbours to keep an eye on the house.

At the prison they were placed in different cells. Marina and the boy were put in a cell with a large number of women totally unconnected with the Young Guard. But among them were Maria Borts and Sergei Tyulenin's sister, Fenya, who had lived with her children in a home of her own. Marina heard from her that Fenya's old mother Alexandra Vasilyevna and even her crippled old father with his crutch had also been arrested; Sergei's sisters, Nadya and Dasha, had managed to get away into time.

Chapter 22

VANYA ZEMNUKHOV had been arrested at dawn. He had planned a visit to Nizhny Alexandrovsky to see Klava and had risen when it was still dark. He had taken a crust of bread with him, put on his overcoat and cap with ear-flaps and had gone out into the street.

Below the greyish-pink mist melting into the pale clear sky, the bright yellow dawn crept along the horizon, a smooth strip, extraordinarily clear and strong. Little yellow and pink patches of mist, puffy and ethereal, hung over the town.

Vanya saw nothing of all this; he had put his glasses away in an inside pocket, because they would only become steamed over. But he remembered from his childhood the appearance of nature on just such a clear frosty morning as this, and a happy expression was on his face. With this same cheerful appearance, he met the four people approaching the house, until he looked closely and saw they were German gendarmes with Kuleshov, the new examining judge at the police-station.

By the time they had come close to him and Vanya recognized them for what they were, Kuleshov was already addressing him and Vanya realized that they had come for him. And, as was always the case with him at a decisive moment in his life, Vanya became infinitely calm and cool-headed and Kuleshov's question did not fluster him.

"Yes, that's me," he said.

"Well, you're in for it now," Kuleshov said.

"I'll let my people know," Vanya said. But he knew very well they would not allow him to enter the house. He swung round and tapped on the nearest window, not on the pane, however, but with his fist on the wood in the middle of the window-frame.

Kuleshov and one of the gendarmes immediately gripped his arms, while Kuleshov rapidly ran his hands over Vanya's overcoat pockets and, through the overcoat, down his trouser pockets.

The small ventilation pane opened, and Vanya's sister looked out; he was unable to see the expression on her face.

"Tell Mama and Papa I've been called to the police-station, and they're not to worry. I shan't be long," he said.

Kuleshov snorted, shook his head and accompanied by a gendarme went on to the porch; they had to make a search. The German sergeant and the other soldier led Vanya off past the line of houses along the narrow well-trodden path in the snow which still lay smooth on this little-used street. Not wishing to wade through snow the sergeant and the soldier released their hold on Vanya and followed close behind him.

They pushed him into a small dark cell as he was, in overcoat, fur cap and worn shoes, with trodden-down heels. The walls were covered with hoarfrost, the floor was slimy. The door clanged shut and was locked behind him. He was alone.

The morning light struggled weakly through a narrow chink below the ceiling. There was neither bench nor bunk in the cell. An acrid stench came from a bucket in a corner.

His mind was in turmoil of speculation why he had been arrested, whether they had come to know anything of his activities, or only suspected something, or had acted on someone's treachery; thoughts of Klava, his parents and his comrades rushed in on him. Then, with a characteristic effort of will as though he were saying to himself, "Steady, Vanya, just keep calm," he forced himself to concentrate on the sole thought that was now important for him: "Patience now! Wait and see how things turn out."

Vanya's hands were stiff from the cold. He pushed them into his overcoat pockets, and leaned against the wall, with his fur-capped head bowed on his chest. With his usual patience he stood for a long time; how long he did not know, perhaps several hours.

The heavy steps of one, and sometimes several people were constantly heard along the whole length of the corridor. Cell doors slammed. The sound of voices, far away and nearer to hand, penetrated to his cell.

Several people came to a halt outside his cell and a hoarse voice said:

"In this one? Send him to the *Meister!*"

The man moved further down and a key scraped in the lock.

Vanya stood away from the wall and turned his head. A German soldier entered, not his former escort. He carried a key and was probably guarding the cells in this corridor. With him came a policeman whose face was familiar to Vanya, because they had all made a point of knowing the faces of all the policeman. He took Vanya to the waiting-room of *Meister* Brückner's office. There Vanya saw one of the urchins he and his friends had sent to the market to sell cigarettes. Another policeman was guarding him.

The boy, who was looking pinched and dirty, regarded Vanya for a moment, then shrugged his shoulders, sniffed and turned away.

Vanya felt somewhat relieved. But all the same, he would have to deny everything; if he even admitted that he had stolen German New Year gifts in order to supplement his earnings a little, he would be ordered to reveal his accomplices. No, there was no use in thinking that this affair could turn out favourably for him.

A German clerk emerged from the *Meister*'s office and, standing aside, held the door open.

"Go on, go on," said the policeman hurriedly, a frightened look on his face, and pushed Vanya towards the door. The other policeman seized the urchin by the scruff of the neck and propelled him towards the door. They entered the office almost simultaneously. The door closed behind them. Vanya removed his cap.

There were several people in the office. Vanya recognized *Meister* Brückner seated behind the table, leaning back in his chair. The thick folds of his neck overlapped the collar of his uniform. His round owlish eyes looked straight at Vanya.

"Step closer! How quiet you are now," Solikovsky said with a rasping voice which seemed to have been scratched by prickly undergrowth. He was standing to one side before the *Meister*'s table, a horsewhip gripped in his huge fist.

The long arm of Examining Judge Kuleshov standing opposite him shot out and grabbed the urchin's elbow, pulling him with a jerk closer to the table.

"Is that him?" he asked grinning, with a wink towards Vanya.

"Yes," breathed the urchin, then sniffed and stood rooted to the ground.

Pleased, Kuleshov looked at the *Meister*, then at Solikovsky. Behind the table the interpreter inclined his head courteously towards the *Meister* explaining what was taking place. Vanya recognized Shurka Reiband. Like everyone else in Krasnodon, Vanya knew him well.

"Hear that?" Solikovsky stared at Vanya from narrowed eyes which were almost hidden by the big cheek-bones and seemed to be peering over a mountain-top. "Tell the *Herr Meister* who was working with you. Hurry up now!"

"I don't know what you're talking about," Vanya said in his deep bass, looking him straight in the face.

"Would you believe it, eh?" Solikovsky turned to Kuleshov, shocked and indignant. "That's the sort of upbringing they got under the Soviet regime!"

Hearing Zemnukhov's reply, the boy looked at him with a scared expression and huddled himself as though against the cold.

"Aren't you ashamed of yourself? You should be sorry for the kid, he's suffering because of you," Kuleshov said, softly reproachful. "Just look at this—what d'you call this?"

Vanya followed Kuleshov's glance. Against the wall lay an open sack of gifts, some of which were strewn over the floor.

"I don't know what this can possibly have to do with me. I've never seen this boy before," Vanya said. He was growing calmer with every passing minute.

Meister Brückner who had listened to Shurka Reiband's translation of everything that had been said, was obviously getting sick of it all; with a swift glance at Reiband, he muttered something. Kuleshov respectfully held his tongue. Solikovsky drew himself up, his hands along his trouser seams.

"The *Herr Meister* requires you to tell him how many times you have raided lorries, for what purpose, who assisted you, what else you have done—he wants to know everything," Shurka Reiband said coldly, looking past Vanya.

"How can I make raids on lorries? I can't even see you standing there! You know that very well!" said Vanya.

"Answer the *Herr Meister*'s question."

But the *Herr Meister* was evidently quite clear on the matter; with a flock of his fingers, he said:

"To Fehnbong!"

In a flash the scene had changed. Solikovsky's huge fists grasped Vanya by the collar; shaking him savagely he dragged him to the waiting-room, then swung him round to face him and struck him fiercely across both cheeks with his riding-crop. Scarlet weals appeared on Vanya's face. One blow had caught the corner of the left eye, and it was closing fast. The policeman who had brought him in seized him by the collar and, together with Solikovsky, began to drag and kick him along the corridor.

N.C.O. Fehnbong and two SS men were sitting in the room, to which they had dragged him; their faces were weary and they were smoking.

"If, you scoundrel, you don't tell me this minute who the others were—" Solikovsky said, hissing in a terrifying way, his enormous hand clutching Vanya's face and tearing at it with the steely finger-nails.

The soldiers had finished smoking. Their boots stubbed out the cigarette ends, and then, with unhurried practised movements, they began to rip off first Vanya's overcoat, then the rest of his clothes; then they thrust him, naked, on to the blood-stained trestle-bed.

Fehnbong's red, hairy hand as unhurriedly selected two electric-cable lashes from the table; he passed one to Solikovsky and, keeping the other for himself, tried it out with a sweeping stroke through the air. They took turns at lashing

Vanya, dragging the lash across his body with each stroke, while the soldiers held him down by the legs and head. The blood began to flow after the first strokes.

The moment they began to lash him Vanya made a vow not to answer a single question, not to utter a single groan.

And so he remained silent all the time. Occasionally they paused from their task and Solikovsky asked:

"Have you come to your senses yet?"

Vanya made no reply, nor did he raise his face, and then the beating started again.

Half an hour earlier, Moshkov had been beaten in the same manner on the same trestle-bed. Like Vanya, Moshkov had denied that he had taken part in the theft of the gifts.

Stakhovich, whose home lay far away on the outskirts of the town, had been arrested later.

Like all young people of his stamp, whose main driving force in life is vanity, Stakhovich was quite capable of being steadfast to a greater or lesser degree, was capable even of performing great heroic deeds, provided he had an audience, particularly an audience of people in his own circle, or of people who influenced him morally. But when alone and faced with danger or difficulty he was a coward.

He had lost his head the moment he was arrested. But he was endowed with that resourceful turn of mind which in a flash finds dozens, hundreds of moral justifications to lighten his position.

When confronted with the young urchin, Stakhovich at once realized that the affair of the New Year gifts was the only evidence they had against him and his comrades who, so he assumed, could not have escaped arrest; in a flash he had decided to transform the affair into criminal proceedings, to admit frankly that there had been three of them, to cry bitter tears about his terrible poverty and hunger, and then to promise to expiate his sins through honest labour. And the sincerity with which he went through this performance in front of *Meister* Brückner and the rest made clear to them at once the sort of a chap they were dealing with. They started forthwith to knock him about in the office, demanding to know the names of his accomplices, for having spent the evening in the club how could they, these three, have carried out the raid on the lorry themselves?

Luckily for him, it was then time for *Meister* Brückner and *Wachtmeister* Balder to have their dinner and he was left in peace until the evening.

At the evening session they treated him kindly at first and said they would let him go as soon as he had named the people who had carried out the theft of the gifts. He repeated that he and the two others had done it. Then he was put into Fehnbong's hands and tortured until Tyulenin's name had been wrung from him. He said he had not been able to make out the rest of the faces in the dark.

The miserable fellow did not know that by betraying Tyulenin, he had thrown himself into an abyss of misery, that he would have to endure still more horrible tortures, because the people who had their clutches on him knew that they must break him altogether, now that he had shown weakness.

They tortured him, poured water over him and tortured him again. And before morning came, when he had lost all human appearance, he begged for mercy: he had not deserved all the suffering, he was only a tool, there were people who had given him orders to carry out, so let them be taken to account for it! And he betrayed the entire Young Guard headquarters, and its liaison workers. Ulya Gromova was the only name he did not betray, for some unknown reason. For a hundredth part of a minute he had remembered her magnificent black eyes, and did not name her.

One day during this period, Lyadskaya was brought in from the Krasnodon mining settlement and taken to the gendarmerie where she was confronted with Vyrikova. Each blamed the other for her misfortunes and, with the imperturbable Balder and delighted Kuleshov as audience, began to brawl like fishwives and betray each other.

"You grovelling snake, it was you who was Pioneer leader!" bawled Lyadskaya, so red in the face with temper that the freckles on her face were no longer apparent.

"...You! All Pervomaisky knows you used to collect for the Osoaviakhim!*" yelled Vyrikova, clenching her fists, even her sharp pigtails joining in the fray.

They almost came to blows, but they were separated and put under arrest for the day. Then they were taken separ-

* Voluntary Society for Air and Chemical Defence.

ately before *Wachtmeister* Balder once more. Dealing with Vyrikova first (and later with Lyadskaya, in similar fashion) Kuleshov took her by the hand and hissed, "Don't try and make yourself out an angel! Name the members of the organization!"

First Vyrikova, and later Lyadskaya, burst into tears, and swore that far from being members of the organization, they had hated the Bolsheviks all their lives, just as the Bolsheviks had hated them, and they gave the names of all the Komsomols and active youngsters still in Pervomaisky and the Krasnodon mining settlement. They knew all about their own school-friends, of course, where they lived, what views they held, which of them had done social work of any kind. Each of them named roughly twenty people, and with that rendered a fairly comprehensive list of all the young people connected with the Young Guard.

Fiercely rolling his eyes, *Wachtmeister* Balder told each that he did not believe what they had said about not being in the organization themselves; just like the criminals they had named, they ought to be subjected to dreadful torture. However, he felt sorry for them and there was a way out of the situation....

Vyrikova and Lyadskaya were released from prison simultaneously, neither of them knowing but each assuming that the other was not leaving the scene with clean hands. Each of them was to receive a monthly salary of twenty-three marks. They parted with a wooden handshake, as though nothing at all had taken place between them.

"Got off cheaply," Vyrikova said. "Come round some time."

"Cheap's the word. I'll be seeing you," Lyadskaya said.

Then they went their different ways.

Chapter 23

THERE WAS A STRANGELY METHODICAL SEQUENCE in the way the arrests were made. The news of them travelled through the whole town like wildfire. First the parents of the Young Guard headquarters members who had left the town were arrested; then the parents of Arutyuniants, Safonov and Levashov, of those of the boys, that is, who had been in close touch with headquarters, but had also left the town.

Then suddenly Tosya Mashchenko and certain other rank-and-file members of the Young Guard were arrested. But why them in particular, and not others?

None of those who were still free could possibly suspect that the ebb and flow of arrests was the result of the gruesome elements of Stakhovich's confessions. As soon as he had betrayed someone, they allowed him a rest. Then they began to torture him again, and he betrayed more names to them.

Yet none of the workers of the underground organization led by Lyutikov and Barakov were affected in any way although several days had gone by since the arrest of Moshkov, Zemnukhov and Stakhovich. In the central workshops everything went on in the same old way.

Volodya Osmukhin had spent the first three days of the New Year with his grandfather in the country and on January 4, went back to work. When he had arrived home on the previous night, his mother had given him the news of the arrests and the instructions from the Young Guard headquarters that he was to leave the town. He refused to go.

"The chaps won't talk," he told his mother; it would be senseless to keep anything secret from her now.

There was more than one reason why Volodya did not want to go away. He felt sorry about leaving his mother and sister, especially when he recalled that they had not evacuated because he had been ill. But the chief reason was that Volodya, not having been present at the conference in Oleg's home, not only failed to see the danger threatening him, but even felt in his heart that the headquarters' members had been in rather a hurry. The three arrested had been among Volodya's closest friends and he had confidence in them. And the spirit of daring in him gave birth to a series of plans for their liberation, each of which was more fantastic than the preceding one.

Volodya had hardly set foot into the workshop when Lyutikov, under some pretext or other, called him into his office.

The Osmukhins were very old friends of his; he knew Volodya better than he knew anyone else of the young people and was very fond of him. And not only his experience and reasoning, but also his heart told the old fellow how terrible was the danger threatening his young friend and pupil. He suggested to Volodya that he leave the town at once. He did not even want to hear Volodya's explanations, he was harsh and inexorable; he was not giving advice but issuing an order.

But it was too late. Before Volodya had time to consider when and where to go, he was arrested, at the bench in his own workshop.

The butchers who were torturing Stakhovich were endeavouring not only to wring from him the names of all the members of the Young Guard, but to get him to supply them also with the threads which would lead them to the Communist underground organization in the town. There were many facts, as well as their own common sense, to suggest to senior and junior ranks of the gendarmerie, that the young people were working under the leadership of adults and that the centre of the Krasnodon conspiracy was therefore in the Bolsheviks' underground organization.

But Stakhovich truly had no idea how Oleg maintained contact with the district Party committee. All he could say was that there had been contact. When they tried to find out from him which of the adults had been the most frequent visitors at the home of the Koshevois, he cast about in his mind and finally settled on Sokolova. It was true that he had encountered Aunt Polina there more often than anyone else; not only during the earlier period when he had still been a member of the Young Guard headquarters, but later, too, whenever he called on Oleg on matters concerning the organization. At the time, he had not connected her presence there with the activity of the Young Guard. But now he recalled that Oleg had occasionally gone off into a corner with her and that there had been whispered conversations between them. And so he gave them her name.

From Sokolova the thread led directly to heavy, silent, enigmatic Lyutikov. And the fact that prisoners Moshkov and Osmukhin had worked in the machine-shop under Lyutikov now appeared to *Meister* Brückner as something more than mere coincidence. They unearthed all the evidence from his past, and brought to light all the true circumstances of the wreckings and break-downs in the central work-shops.

At dawn on January 5, Aunt Polina delivered Lyutikov's milk as usual, and took away hidden in her blouse a leaflet which he had written over the signature of the Young Guard. There was not a word in the leaflet about the arrest of the young people. Lyutikov intended the leaflet to show that the enemy had missed the target, that the Young Guard was alive and active.

When he returned from work in the evening, he found his wife Yevdokia Fedotovna and his daughter Raya sitting in the kitchen with Pelagea Ilyinichna. They had come to town from the farm where they lived to pay him a visit. What happiness this was for him! He discarded his working clothes, put on a fresh white shirt, a dark blue tie with a grey stripe and the best suit, that Pelagea Ilyinichna had cleaned for him. Thus, arrayed in his holiday clothes, calm, eventempered and gentle, he spent the evening in the company of those dearest to him, joking with them as though nothing at all had happened.

Did Lyutikov know that he was in mortal danger? No, nor could he have known. But he always entertained the possibility, was always ready for it and, of late, he had felt that the danger was increasing.

Schweide, usually sparing of words, had with increasing frequency made attacks on Barakov and in a fit of uncontrollable fury had accused him of sabotage. What guarantee was there that he had not blundered on the right track?

Several days previously four cart-loads of coal had been dispatched to near-by villages under the pretext of bartering the coal for grain. The removal of the coal from the grounds of the central workshops in itself constituted an unprecedented violation of the New Order; but Lyutikov and Barakov had had no other way out of the situation and they had no right to wait any longer: hidden under the coal had been rifles for the Krasnodon partisan group which was to join forces with the Mityakinskaya detachment. What guarantee was there that this daring venture had come off unnoticed?

The enemy had arrested one member of the Young Guard

after another. Who could tell what hidden wires had tripped up whole groups of the organization at a time?

Old Lyutikov knew and felt all this. But for him there could be no grounds for, or possibility of retreat. His mighty spirit was not here: it was marching across rivers and steppes, over ice and through the snow, marching with the Great Army of Liberation. And no matter what he spoke about to his wife and daughter, he always returned to the subject of the gigantic offensive launched by the Soviet forces. How could he leave his post on the basis of mere suppositions, just at a time when he was required to exert himself to the utmost! Within a very few weeks, perhaps days, he would be able, at last, to cast off the oppressive yoke of pretence and disclose to people his true face!... Well, and if fate decreed that he was not to live to see that happy day, there were still people who would carry on the work to its conclusion, without him. Ever since the memorable talk in Barakov's office a second, "reserve" district Party committee had been in existence consisting of reliable people in possession now of all the secret addresses and contacts.

Lyutikov sat in his holiday clothes, cheerful and perhaps a little more gentle and talkative than was his custom. His daughter looked at her father with merry laughter in her eyes. But his wife, who had traversed the long journey of life with him, had come to know even the slightest changes of mood, and from time to time threw a worried, searching glance at him which seemed to say, "All these festive garments, all this merriment, I don't like it."

Catching a moment when his wife had gone out to the kitchen to chat with Pelagea Ilyinichna, Lyutikov, nevertheless, told his daughter of the arrests in the Young Guard organization. Raya was only just thirteen; she had heard stories about the existence of the Young Guard, had a shrewd idea of her father's work and dreamed of being able to help him but she dared not ask about it.

"Don't stay too long, you hear? I'm not going to let you stay the night. You'll go straight across the steppe from here, no one'll see you in the dark," Lyutikov said, lowering his voice. "Tell Mama that's the best way. You can't explain things to her, you know that," he said with a humorous little smile.

"Are you in danger?" Raya asked and turned pale.

"Nothing definite. People like us are always in danger and I'm used to it. I've devoted my whole life to it. I'd like you to be the same," he said softly.

The girl became thoughtful, then wound her slender arms round his neck and pressed her face close to his. The mother came in and looked at them, surprised. Lyutikov, joking and bantering, started to send them off on their way. They had seen a good deal of each other since the Germans came and Yevdokia Fedotovna had become used to her husband becoming gruff when family matters stood in the way of his work. Since she could not tell whether he was right or not she always gave in, even though it hurt at times.

Now it seemed to her that she was seeing her husband with new eyes as he stood before her, the well preserved, neatly pressed jacket sitting well on his large frame; she suddenly kissed his freshly-shaven, nevertheless prickly face, even kissed him somewhere on the tie and then she rested her head close to his chest. His heavy jowls twitched, he gently moved her from him and then said a few bantering words. There were tears in his daughter's eyes; she turned away and tugged at her mother's sleeve.

That night Aunt Polina was arrested. Lyutikov and Barakov were arrested the following morning, January 6, at their place of work. Several dozen people were also taken away from the works. Just as Lyutikov had prophesied, evidence was of no importance to the enemy: most of those arrested had no connection whatever with the organization.

Tolya the Thunderer was not arrested when Volodya was taken, and he was again left alone at the time of the mass arrests in the works. He was on tenterhooks for the rest of the day, and when he knocked off he went immediately to the Osmukhins'. They had already heard the news.

"What on earth are you still doing here? You'll be done for! Go right away, quickly!" exclaimed Yelizaveta Alexeyevna in a burst of maternal despair.

"I'm not going," Tolya said quietly. "Why should I?" He flourished his cap.

No, he could not possibly go, as long as Volodya was in prison.

645

They persuaded him to stay the night, but he went off again. He went to Vitya Lukyanchenko to talk things over about doing something to free the boys from prison. It was dark when he went, and as usual he skirted round the police patrol boxes. How lonely he felt in his own town with no Volodya, no Zemnukhov, Moshkov or Zhora Arutyuniants or any of the others. Despair and vengeance were confused in his mind.

Early next morning there was a loud knock at the Osmukhins' door. With the fearless decision typical of her, Yelizaveta Alexeyevna opened the door without asking who was there. She almost started back at the sight of Tolya Orlov again, so completely frozen, so haggard, his eyes so filled with a burning flame that he was almost unrecognizable.

"Read this," he said, offering a crumpled sheet of paper to Yelizaveta Alexeyevna and Lyudmila.

He was in a fever of excitement and as they started reading, he said:

"I can tell you the whole truth now and I've got to tell you. Vitya was handed this by a soldier he once helped to find a hide-out, while his wounds were healing. Vitya and I spent the whole night pasting them all over the town. It's instructions from the district Party committee and dozens of people were out last night pasting them up and by now the whole town and all the farms and villages are all reading it!" It all came out in an uncontrollable rush of words because Tolya felt all the time that he was not telling them what was most important.

But Yelizaveta Alexeyevna and Lyudmila were not even listening; they were reading:

"Citizens of Krasnodon! Miners, collective armers, office workers! Soviet men and women! Brothers and sisters!

"The enemy has been crushed by the mighty Red Army and is fleeing! In his impotent, bestial rage he is seizing upon innocent people and subjecting them to inhuman tortures. Let these monsters bear in mind: we are still here! They will pay with their fiendish lives for every drop of Soviet blood they spill. Let the enemy tremble in fear of our revenge! Show no mercy! Exterminate the enemy! Blood for blood! Death for death!

"Our Army is coming! Our Army is coming! They are on the way!

"The Krasnodon Underground District Committee of the Communist Party of the Soviet Union (Bolsheviks)."

Chapter 24

FOR THE FIRST FEW NIGHTS after the arrests began Ulya had stayed away from home. But, as Oleg had predicted, the arrests had not affected either Pervomaisky or the Krasnodon mining settlement, so Ulya returned home.

After so many nights spent away from home, Ulya woke up in her own bed once more and driven by an inner urge to cast oppressive thoughts off her mind, she zealously plunged into domestic affairs, scrubbed the floor and prepared the breakfast. Her mother, cheered by her presence, even rose from her bed and sat up to the table for breakfast. Father was grumpy and silent. All the days Ulya had been away, only occasionally calling for an hour or two to visit her parents or to fetch something, Matvei Maximovich and Matryona Savelyevna had been able to talk of nothing but the arrests. But they had talked of them without daring to look into each other's eyes.

At breakfast Ulya tried to talk of irrelevant matters and, in her awkward fashion, her mother supported her, but it all sounded so forced that both fell silent. Lost in thought, Ulya could hardly remember clearing the table and washing up. Her father went about his business.

Dressed in her dark blue house frock with the white polkadots which she loved so much, Ulya stood at the window with her back to her mother. Her heavy wavy plaits hung loosely over her back to the supple, firm waist; bright sunshine shone through the window, melting the ice on it and glistening on the stray locks of hair at the girl's temples.

Ulya stood at the window looking out over the steppe and sang to herself. She had not sung once since the Germans had come. Her mother was propped up on the bed, darning something. She was so surprised to hear her daughter singing that she even put down her darning. In a smooth, deep voice, her daughter was singing something quite unfamiliar to her;

> ...*You fought and died for the Homeland*
> *Your glory will never die....*

Matryona Savelyevna had never even heard the words. There was something very heavy and sad in her daughter's singing.

> ...*Relentless the rising avenger*
> *And stronger than you and I....*

Ulya broke off and remained standing there gazing far over the steppe.

"What was that you were singing?" her mother asked.

"Just singing, without thinking ... something I happened to remember," Ulya replied without turning round.

The door flew open and, puffing and panting, Ulya's elder sister rushed into the room; plumper than Ulya, rosy-cheeked and fair, she took after her father, but at the moment her face was as white as a sheet.

"The gendarmes are at the Popovs'!" she said in a breathless whisper, as though she might be heard over at the Popovs' house.

Ulya turned round.

"Are they? They're the kind of people you want to keep away from," Ulya said calmly, without any change in her expression. She went to the door, unhurriedly put on her coat and covered her hair with a shawl. But she already heard the tramp of heavy boots coming up the porch steps; she stepped back against the flowered curtain which concealed the family's winter coats, and turned to face the door.

That was the picture her mother retained of her for the rest of her life—the strong, clear-cut profile against the flowered curtain, the quivering nostrils, the long lashes half-closed, as though trying to put out the flame that blazed in her eyes, the white shawl, not yet tied, and falling loosely on the shoulders.

Police Chief Solikovsky, N.C.O. Fehnbong and a soldier armed with a rifle entered the room.

"There she is, the little beauty!" Solikovsky cried. "You

were too late, eh," he said, glancing at the graceful figure in the coat and the loosely hanging shawl.

"Please, kind people, kind friends," pleaded the mother, trying to rise from her bed. Ulya swiftly flashed angry eyes at her; the mother was cut short and said no more. Her jaw began to tremble.

The search began. The father pushed at the door, but the soldier kept him outside.

At the same time, a search was taking place in Anatoly's home. It was made by Examining Judge Kuleshov.

Capless, with his coat unbuttoned, Anatoly stood in the middle of the room, a German soldier holding his arms behind his back. One of the policemen took a step towards Taisya Prokofievna and shouted:

"You heard what I said! Get a rope!"

Tall Taisya Prokofievna, flushed with anger, screamed back at him:

"Are you mad, that I should get you a rope to tie my own boy up with?"

"Give him the rope, Mama, to stop his yelling," Anatoly said, his nostrils dilated. "There's only six of them—how could they manage me if I'm not tied up?"

Taisya Prokofievna burst into tears, fetched a rope from the passage and hurled it on the floor at her son's feet.

Ulya was thrown into the large communal cell in which were Marina and her little boy, Maria Borts and Tyulenin's sister, Fenya, as well as a member of the Young Guard who had belonged to Stakhovich's group of five; she was a sallow, puffy-faced, full-bosomed girl by the name of Anna Sopova. She had already been so badly beaten that she could hardly lie down. All the other prisoners had been removed from the cell, and during the day it had been filled with Pervomaisky girls, including Maya Peglivanova, Sasha Bondareva, Shura Dubrovina, the cousins Lilya and Tonya Ivanikhina and several others.

The cell contained no seats or bunks. The women and girls had to stand or sit on the floor. The cell was so crowded that the temperature in it rose above freezing, and the ceiling dripped ceaselessly.

The adjoining cell, also a large one, had apparently been reserved for the boys. New people kept arriving all the time.

Ulya tapped out in Morse: "Who is in there?" Back came the answer: "Who wants to know?" Ulya gave her name; Anatoly replied. Most of the boys from Pervomaisky were next door. Victor Petrov, Borya Glavan, Ragozin, Zhenya Shepelyov, and Vasya Bondarev, who had been arrested at the same time as his sister Sasha. Since it had had to happen, the fact that the Pervomaisky boys were next door to them gave some comfort to the girls.

"I'm terribly frightened of the tortures," frankly confessed Tonya Ivanikhina, a long-legged girl with large childlike features. She stood gazing down at a group of girls sitting on the floor against the wall. "I'll die first before I tell them anything, of course, but I'm so frightened. . . ."

"No need to be frightened. Our troops aren't far off and we might yet manage to escape from here!" Sasha Bondareva said.

"The trouble with you girls is that you don't know the first thing about dialectics ...." Maya suddenly began and everybody burst out laughing because it had sounded very incongruous here in prison. Maya remained unruffled. "Of course! There's no pain that one can't get used to!"

Towards evening all was silent in the prison. A dim little globe in a wire net dangled by its short flex from the ceiling, leaving the corners of the cell in darkness. Now and again a peremptory shout in German somewhere far away brought the sound of feet running past the cell door. At times several feet marched in step along the corridor to the accompaniment of clanking weapons. Once they all leapt to their feet when a horrible, animal-like scream struck their ears—the more horrible for being the scream of a man.

Ulya tapped out against the wall:

"Was that from your cell?"

Came the answer:

"No. From the Big ones'...." This had been their code name for adult underground workers.

Then someone was taken away from the cell next door and the girls could hear it. Immediately afterwards came a tapping:

Ulya ... Ulya...."

She acknowledged.

"This is Victor.... Tolya's been taken away...."

Ulya suddenly visualized Anatoly's face, his eyes always serious with the peculiar gift of suddenly becoming radiant and giving out strength. She trembled as she thought of what faced him. But just then a key turned in the lock, the cell door opened and a languid voice said:

"Gromova!..."

This was what remained in her memory of subsequent events:

For some time she was left standing in Solikovsky's waiting-room. Someone was being beaten in the inside office. On a sofa in the waiting-room sat Solikovsky's wife, yawning with impatience as she waited for her husband. Her wavy hair was the colour of tow. She had a bundle on her lap and by her side was a sleepy-eyed little girl, with hair like her mother's, stuffing an apple pie. The door opened and Vanya Zemnukhov was led out, his face swollen beyond recognition. He almost knocked against Ulya as he passed, and she almost cried out.

Next she was standing with Solikovsky in front of *Meister* Brückner who asked her a question which, judging by his indifferent attitude, he was not asking for the first time. Shurka Reiband, with whom she had danced in the club in pre-war days and who had tried to flirt with her, now pretended not to know her and interpreted the question. But she did not listen to what he said, because during the period before her arrest she had decided on what she would say, if she were arrested. With a cold expression on her face, she said:

"I shall not answer your questions, because I deny your right to sit in judgement on me. You can do with me what you like, but you will not hear another word from me."

Within the past few days *Meister* Brückner had most likely heard similar statements many times; he did not get angry, but flicked his fingers, and said:

"Take her to Fehnbong!"

It was not the pain of being tortured that was so terrible—she knew how to bear every kind of pain, she did not even remember being knocked about—no, the worst part had been when they rushed at her to tear off her clothing, and having to strip herself in front of them in order to avoid being handled by them.

As she was led back to the cell Anatoly Popov was carried past her. His fair head hung backwards, his hands dragged along the floor; blood was trickling from the corner of his mouth.

Nevertheless, Ulya remembered that she must control her feelings when she re-entered the cell, and possibly she succeeded in doing so. She entered the cell and the police escort shouted:

"Antonina Ivanikhina!..."

Ulya passed Tonya in the doorway. Tonya's timid terror-stricken eyes rested on her for a moment, then the door closed behind Ulya. Just at that moment the prison resounded to the piercing scream of a child. It was the voice of a little girl, not Tonya.

"They've taken my youngest," Maria Borts cried out. Like a tigress, she rushed to the door, and battered at it, screaming: "Lyusia! They've taken you, my little Lyusia! Let her go! Let her go!"

Marina's little boy woke up and started to cry.

Chapter 25

MEANWHILE LYUBA HAD BEEN SEEN IN VOROSHILOVGRAD, then in Kamensk and in Rovenki, and, on one occasion, even in besieged Millerovo. Her circle of acquaintances among the enemy officers had grown rapidly. Her pockets were stuffed with biscuits, sweets and chocolate which she had been given and she good-naturedly offered them to all she met.

With desperate courage and a carefree attitude she circled about at the edge of an abyss, a guileless smile on her lips, her blue eyes, which sometimes had something cruel about them, narrowed.

During her last stay in Voroshilovgrad, she again contacted the person who was her immediate chief. He told her that the Germans were on a rampage in the town. He was changing his living-quarters almost daily. His eyes were blood-shot from lack of sleep, he was dirty and unshaven, but in high spirits because of the news from the front. He needed information on the German reserves in the immediate vicinity, on the state of their supply lines, about individual German units—in short, a heap of information.

Lyuba had had to get in touch with the quartermaster colonel once more, and there was one occasion when it looked as though she would be unable to extricate herself unscathed. The whole of the quartermaster's department including its chief, the colonel with the flabby face and drooping jowls, was leaving Voroshilovgrad in unprecedented haste. Consequently, not only the colonel, who was becoming increasingly glassy-eyed with every drink he had, but the other officers as well were in a desperate humour.

Lyuba managed to escape only because there were so many of them. They got in each other's way and quarrelled about her. In the end, she had found herself back in the house where the chubby-faced girl was living; she even succeeded in taking with her the tin of lovely jam presented by the lieutenant, who still lived in hopes concerning Lyuba.

She undressed and lay down on the bed in the cold, high-ceilinged room. Suddenly there was an angry hammering on the front door. Lyuba raised her head. In the room next to hers there were movements from the girl and her mother. The door was being pounded as though someone was trying to break it down. Lyuba threw back the blankets and, in her brassière and stockings, which she had kept on because of the cold, pushed her feet into her shoes and slipped on her dress. It was pitch dark in the room. From the hall came the landlady's frightened voice asking who it was. Several rough voices replied. The Germans had come. Lyuba imagined it was the drunken officers coming to see her, and she completely lost her head.

Before she had time to decide on any course of action, the tramp of heavy, thick-soled boots reached her door, and three men entered, one of whom shone his torch on her.

"*Licht!*" somebody shouted, and Lyuba recognized the lieutenant's voice.

Yes, it was the lieutenant with two gendarmes. He peered at Lyuba by the light of the candle which the landlady had handed him from behind the door; his face was convulsed with rage. He passed the light to the gendarme and struck Lyuba heavily across the face. Then he scattered Lyuba's toilet articles in all directions, searching for something.

A mouth-organ, lying under a handkerchief, fell to the floor, Angrily he stepped on it and crushed it with his heel.

Then he left, leaving the gendarmes to search the whole flat. Lyuba realized that he had not brought the gendarmes, but that they had traced her through him: somewhere something had been discovered. What it was she could not know.

The lady of the house and the chubby-faced girl had dressed and, shivering with the cold, were watching the search; or rather the lady was watching, while the girl could not take her eyes off Lyuba, out of burning interest and curiosity. At the last moment, Lyuba impetuously pressed the girl to her heart and kissed her rosy cheeks.

Lyuba was taken to the Voroshilovgrad Gendarmerie. An official examined her papers and asked her, through an interpreter, whether she was, in fact, Lyubov Shevtsova and in what town she lived. A young chap was present while she was being questioned. He sat in a corner and Lyuba did not see his face. He was twitching nervously all the time. Lyuba's case was taken from her with all her clothes and personal articles, apart from a few trifles, the tin of jam and a gaily-coloured scarf, which she sometimes wore round her neck and which she requested to be given back so that she could wrap up in it the trifles they had left her.

In her sole remaining frock, the brightly-coloured crepe de Chine, and carrying the little bundle with her toilet accessories and the tin of jam, she made her appearance at the cell where the Pervomaisky girls were gaoled. She arrived in the day-time, when the interrogations were in progress.

The policeman opened the cell door, pushed her inside and said:

"Accept your Voroshilovgrad actress!"

Her cheeks glowing from the frost outside, Lyuba cast her sparkling, screwed-up eyes round the cell to see who was there. She saw Ulya, Marina with her little boy, Sasha Bondareva—all her friends. She dropped her arms, the bundle still in one hand, and the colour drained from her face.

By the time Lyuba was brought to the Krasnodon prison, it was already overcrowded with both adults and Young Guard members with their relatives; so much so, in fact, that there were people with children living, as it were, in the corridor.

Room would still have to be found for a group of prisoners from the Krasnodon mining settlement.

The wave of arrests continued through the town, following, as before, the ebb and flow of the confessions drawn from Stakhovich. Reduced to the state of a tortured animal, he would buy respite for himself by betraying his comrades, yet each new betrayal brought the prospect of increasing tortures. Now he would recall the whole story of Kovalyov and Pirozhok; then he would remember that Tyulenin had a friend, he did not know his name, but he could describe him, and he recalled that his home was in Shanghai district.

Then suddenly Stakhovich recalled that Osmukhin had a friend by the name of Tolya Orlov. And presently an already tortured Volodya confronted a courageous Tolya the Thunderer in *Wachtmeister* Balder's office.

"No, I've never seen him before," Tolya said softly.

"No, I don't know him at all," Volodya said.

Stakhovich recalled the Zemnukhov's beloved friend lived in Nizhny Alexandrovsky, and a day or two later a totally unrecognizable Zemnukhov and Klava, with a cast in her eye, confronted each other before *Meister* Brückner. In less than a whisper Klava said:

"No.... We went to the same school, but I haven't seen him since the outbreak of war. I've been living in the country."

Zemnukhov said nothing.

The whole group from the Krasnodon mining settlement was kept in the local prison. They had been betrayed by Lyadskaya, but she could not have known what role each of the members had played in the organization. She did know, however, that Lida Androsova was in love with Kolya Sumskoi.

Lida Androsova, a pretty girl with a pointed chin and face that made one think of a fox cub, was beaten with rifle-straps in an attempt to force from her information about Sumskoi's activities in the organization. As they beat her, she counted aloud the strokes, but refused to disclose anything.

The adults were isolated from the young people in order to prevent them influencing them, and strict watch was kept to see that no contact existed between them.

But there is a limit even to what hangmen can do in their brutality. None of the battle-steeled Bolsheviks, nor any of the arrested Young Guards ever admitted their membership of the organization or testified against their comrades. This staunchness, unexampled in history, of nearly one hundred young lads and girls, mere children, gradually made them stand out from the innocently arrested and from their parents and relatives. In order to make things easier for themselves, the Germans gradually began to release all who had been arrested by chance and those of the relatives who had been imprisoned as hostages. Thus, the relatives of Koshevoi, Tyulenin, Arutyuniants and several more, including Maria Borts, were released. Little Lyusia had been released a day earlier than her mother, and it was not until Maria arrived home, that, in tears, she was able to prove that her maternal ear had not deceived her, and her youngest child had really been imprisoned. The only people now left in the hands of the butchers were a group of adult underground fighters, including their leaders Lyutikov and Barakov, and the members of the Young Guard.

From early morning until late at night, their relatives crowded outside the prison, grasping the arms of policemen, of German soldiers, as they went in and out, pleading with them to give them news of the prisoners or to take parcels in to them. They were driven away, but gathered round again, their number increased by passers-by and the curious. At times the cries of the prisoners being flogged were heard through the plank walls, and inside the prison a gramophone played all day long, to drown the sound of them. The town was in a fever of excitement and there was not a single inhabitant who did not spend some part of the day near the prison. Finally *Meister* Brückner was compelled to allow parcels to be taken in for the prisoners, and in this manner it was found possible to send word in to Lyutikov and Barakov that the district Party committee they had left outside was functioning and that it was exploring ways and means of liberating "Big ones" and "Little ones" alike.

By now the young folk had spent about two weeks in the prison and, unnatural as their life was in the outrageously brutal conditions of imprisonment under German occupation, gradually their own peculiar prison regime became established, which included the most monstrous violence against their bodies and minds, and, at the same time, all the human relations: love and friendship and even their old ways of amusing themselves.

"Would you like some jam, girls?" Lyuba said, squatting on the floor in the middle of the cell and untying her bundle. "The lout! Smashed my mouth-organ! What shall I do without my mouth-organ, here?"

"Just you wait, they'll play a tune on your back that'll kill all desire for a mouth-organ!" Shura Dubrovina said heatedly.

"You don't know your Lyuba! D'you think I'll just whimper or say nothing when they beat me? I'm going to swear and yell at them. Like this: 'Oh-oh-oh! You fools! What're you beating Lyuba for?'" she squealed. The girls laughed.

"But honestly, girls, what have we to complain about? It's much harder for our parents. The poor things don't even know what's happened to us. And who knows what's in store for them yet!" Lilya Ivanikhina said.

Round-faced, fair-haired Lilya had probably become hardened to a great many things in concentration camps; she never complained, she cared for everyone, and was the good fairy of the whole cell.

In the evening, Lyuba was summoned to *Meister* Brückner for questioning. It was evidently an unusual occasion because all the heads of the gendarmerie and police were present. They did not beat her. In fact they were somewhat gentle. Completely self-possessed and in ignorance of what they knew about her, Lyuba behaved as she always had with all the Germans: she was coquettish and giggled and displayed complete ignorance of what they might be wanting from her. They hinted that it would be very much to her advantage to hand over the wireless transmitter and, together with it, the code.

This was a mere shot in the dark, because they had no direct evidence. But they had no doubt that she did possess such articles. Information to the effect that she was a member of the organization had given them sufficient reason for guessing at the nature of her trips to the various towns, and for her close relations with Germans. That a number of secret transmitters were at work in the region had been established by the German counter-intelligence. And the young fellow who had been present when Lyuba was being questioned in the Voroshilovgrad Gendarmerie had previously been in the company of Borya Dubinsky, a friend of hers at the wireless school, and he had confirmed that she had been a student at the secret wireless courses.

Lyuba was told to consider whether it might not be better to confess, and then she was allowed to return to the cell.

Her mother had sent her a shopping-bag of provisions. Lyuba sat down on the floor, with the bag between her knees and, taking from it now a rusk, now an egg, swayed her head from side to side and sang:

> *Lyuba, Lyuba, Lyubushka dear,*
> *I cannot feed you much longer, I fear....*

To the policeman who had brought the shopping-bag in to her she had said;

"Tell Mama that Lyuba is alive and well, but would like more *borshch*!"

She turned to the others and shouted:

"Come on, girls, fall to!"

In the end she was handed over to Fehnbong after all and was beaten very harshly. She kept her word: her curses resounded throughout the prison and across the large open space outside:

"You lout! You bald-headed fool! You son of a bitch!" were among the least offensive of the names she bestowed on Fehnbong.

The next time Fehnbong, in the presence of *Meister* Brückner and Solikovsky, flogged her with the twisted cable. Lyuba bit her lip hard, but was unable to choke back her tears. She came back to the cell and silently lay on her stomach on the floor, her face buried in her arms to keep it out of sight.

With the other girls huddled close round her, Ulya sat in a corner of the cell wearing a brightly-coloured jumper, sent in to her from home, which suited her dark eyes and black hair. There was a mysterious light in her eyes as she told them the story of *The Secret of St. Magdalen Monastery.* Every day now she narrated them an instalment of some entertaining story. They had already listened to *The Gadfly*, *The House of Ice* and *Queen Margot*.

The door to the corridor had been opened in order to air the cell. A Russian policeman sat on a stool opposite the door and also listened to *The Secret of St. Magdalen Monastery*.

Lyuba had recovered a little and she sat up and gave half an ear to the story. She looked at Maya Peglivanova who had lain prone for many days without moving. Vyrikova had disclosed that Maya had at one time been secretary of the Komsomol group at school and Maya was undergoing more torture than the others. As Lyuba looked at Maya, an insatiable feeling of vengeance against the torturers stirred in her, seeking an outlet.

"Sasha ... Sasha ..." she called softly to Sasha Bondareva, who was in the group sitting round Ulya. "The boys've become very quiet for some reason."

"Yes!"

"They're not down-hearted, d'you think?"

"Well, you know, they're being made to suffer more than us," Sasha said and sighed.

Sasha with her rough, boyish ways and voice had only in prison suddenly begun to reveal gentle, girlish traits and she seemed to be ashamed of them and of their having shown themselves so late.

"Let's liven them up a bit," Lyuba said, becoming more cheerful. "Let's draw a cartoon of them."

From her bundle she quickly produced a piece of paper and a blue and red pencil. Then both lay side by side flat on their stomachs and with much whispering began to plan the cartoon. Then, snatching the pencil from each other, and with much giggling, they drew a picture of a thin, emaciated young fellow, almost doubled up, with hanging head and a huge nose that almost touched the floor. They coloured him blue and left the face white but gave him a red nose. Beneath the picture they wrote:

> *What's wrong, dear boys, what's wrong*
> *That your faces are so long?*

Ulya had come to the end of her instalment. The girls rose, stretched themselves, then wandered off to their own corners; several of them went over to Lyuba and Sasha. The cartoon was passed from hand to hand. The girls laughed:

"You've been wasting your talents!"

"How can we get it to them?"

Lyuba took the sheet of paper and went to the door.

"Davidov! Pass the boys' portrait in to them!" she said to the policeman, provocatively.

"Where d'you get the pencil and paper? By God, I'll tell the chief to make a search!" he said and scowled at her.

Shurka Reiband was passing along the corridor and he saw Lyuba standing in the doorway.

"Hello, Lyuba! How soon's the trip to Voroshilovgrad with me?" he said, fooling with her.

"With you? No fear! All right then, I'll come if you'll give this to the boys—it's a portrait we've drawn of them!"

Reiband glanced at the cartoon, his lean face grinned, then he offered the paper to Davidov.

"Go on, no harm in it," he said carelessly, and passed on down the corridor.

Davidov was aware of Reiband's good standing with the chief, and being a toady like the rest of the policemen he took the piece of paper without a word, opened the boys' cell door a chink and tossed it inside. A burst of merriment came from the cell, followed, after a few moments, by tapping on the wall:

"You girls only think that. All our residents are behaving properly.... This is Vasya Bondarev. Greetings to my little sister."

From the bundle she used as a pillow, Sasha produced an empty jar in which her mother had sent her milk, and ran over to the wall and began to tap:

"Can you hear me, Vasya?"

Then she placed the bottom of the jar against the wall, put her lips to the opening and began to sing *Suliko*, her brother's favourite song.

But after a very few notes, the words of the song brought such memories of the past that her voice faltered. Lilya went up to her, stroked her hand and said in a gentle, soothing voice:

"Don't, my dear! Steady!"

"I hate myself when tears flow," Sasha said with a nervous smile.

"Stakhovich!" Solikovsky's hoarse voice came echoing along the corridor.

"It's starting again," Ulya said.

The policeman slammed the cell door and turned the key.

"We'd better not listen," Lilya said. "Ulya dear, you know my favourite—recite from *The Demon*, please, like you did before, remember?"

Ulya raised a hand and began:

> *Oh! what is life, its misery, its grief,*
> *Its momentary acts of ill?*
> *Is there no hope? Is there not the belief,*
> *Though judged, there may be pardon still?*
> *Not such is mine! My woe will never quit,*
> *Assuaged my grief shall never be.*
> *Alas! There never will be end to it,*
> *As never there will be to me!*
> *It twines around—it makes my heart its own,*
> *A snake with which no force can cope,*
> *It ceaseless presses on my thought like stone,*
> *A sepulchre of shatter'd hope!...*

How the lines throbbed in the girls' hearts! How clearly they seemed to say to them: "This is about you! Your scarcely awakened passions, your perished hopes!"

Ulya went on to recite the lines which tell of the angel carrying away Tamara's sinful spirit. Tonya Ivanikhina said:

"You see! The angel came after all and saved her. How good that is!"

"No!" Ulya said, the same steadfast look in her eyes as when she had been reciting. "No! I'd have flown off with the Demon.... Just think, he revolted against God himself!"

"That's right! There's no one who can break our people!" Lyuba suddenly said, her eyes aflame. "Is there another people like it, anywhere in the world? With a spirit like ours? Able to endure so much? Maybe we'll die, I'm not afraid. I'm not at all afraid," she said with a vehemence which shook

---

* *The Demon.* Ibid.

her body. "But I don't want to at all ... I'd like to settle accounts with them, those degenerates out there! And sing songs.... No doubt, during all this time lots of good songs have been composed in our unoccupied lands! Just think. we've spent six months under the Germans, like being in the grave: no singing, no laughter, nothing but moaning, blood, tears," Lyuba said forcefully.

"We'll have a song right now, to hell with the lot of them!" Sasha Bondareva exclaimed and beating time with her thin, brown hand, she sang:

> *Onward marched the serried forces*
> *Through the lowlands, o'er the heights....**

Rising from their places, the girls took up the song and crowded round Sasha. The song, sung in unison, rolled through the prison building. The girls heard the boys next door join in with them.

The cell door opened noisily, the policeman stuck an angry, frightened face inside and hissed:

"Have you all gone crazy? Silence!"

> *Ever will their deeds be cited,*
> *Never lose their high renown;*
> *For the Partisan Red Fighters*
> *Then broke through and took the town....*

The policeman slammed the door and hurried away.

Shortly afterwards there were heavy footsteps in the corridor. *Meister* Brückner stood in the doorway—tall, with the tight drooping paunch and the yellow face and dark bags under the eyes, the rolls of fat on his neck overlapping his collar. Smoke curled upwards from the cigar in his hand.

"*Platz nehmen! Ruhe!*" came his voice, bursting from him with a sharp deafening report as though fired from a toy pistol.

> *...Of the days at Volochayev,*
> *Of the night the city fell*
> *There'll be memories undying*
> *As of glorious tales to tell...*

sang the girls.

* *Song of the Partisans.* Tr. by Marion Bergman in *The Russian-American Song and Dance Book.* A. S. Barnes & Co. New York, U.S.A.

Gendarmes and policemen burst into the cell. A scuffle started next door in the boys' cell. The girls found themselves flung against the wall on the floor.

Lyuba alone remained standing in the middle of the cell, her small hands on her hips, her eyes full of hatred staring straight in front of her. She began stamping her heels in a dance-step, and advanced straight towards Brückner.

"Oh! You pest!" he yelled at her panting. His large hand seized her arm, twisted it and dragged her out into the corridor.

Lyuba snarled, ducked her head, and bit hard into the yellow flesh of his hand.

"*Verdammt noch mal!*" Brückner roared and began to thump Lyuba's head with his other fist. But she continued to bite his hand.

With great difficulty the soldiers tore her away from him and then, assisted by Brückner himself, shaking his fist in the air, they dragged her along the corridor.

Soldiers held her down, while *Meister* Brückner and Fehnbong flogged her with lengths of twisted electric cable on weals on her back that had only just begun to heal. Biting her lips savagely, Lyuba did not utter a sound. Suddenly from somewhere high above the prison, she caught the sound of aircraft engines. She recognized the sound and her heart filled with exultation.

"Ah, you sons of bitches! Go on, beat me, beat me! Our comrades up there are making themselves heard!" she screamed.

The roar of a diving plane burst into the room. Brückner and Fehnbong stopped torturing her. Someone quickly switched off the light. The soldiers released Lyuba.

"Ah! You cowards! You scoundrels! Your hour has come, you outrageous monsters! Aha-a!" Lyuba screamed, too weak to turn over, her legs flailing angrily on the blood-stained trestle-bed.

The blast from an explosion shook the prison building. The plane was bombing the town.

That day marked the turning-point in the prison life of the members of the Young Guard, who ceased to conceal their membership of the organization and entered into open battle against their torturers. They were rude to them and derided them; they sang revolutionary songs in their cells, they danced and created an uproar every time someone was dragged from the cell to be tortured.

And the tortures to which they were now subjected were of a kind the human mind could not possibly imagine, tortures that were inconceivable to all human reason and conscience.

Chapter 26

OLEG, who was the best informed regarding the movement of the front, led his group almost due north with a view to crossing the frozen Northern Donets somewhere in the Gundorovskaya area and reaching Glubokaya, a station on the Voronezh-Rostov railway.

With their minds filled with thoughts of families and comrades, they walked all night and hardly exchanged a word.

Skirting Gundorovskaya, they crossed the Donets unhindered early in the morning. Then, proceeding along a smooth army road which had been laid over the old country lane, they continued their way in the direction of Dubovoi farmstead, while their eyes searched the steppe for some human habitation where they might warm themselves and have some food.

There was no wind, the sun was high and it began to get warmer. Around them the undulating steppe glistened pure and white. The thin snow covering the road began to thaw, the edge of the ditches could be seen through the snow; wisps of steam curled from the ground and there was an earthy smell in the air.

Now and again they saw scattered groups of German infantry and artillery, army service and supply units which, after having eluded the great Stalingrad encirclement, had been crushed in subsequent fighting. They caught sight of them not only on the army road but also on near-by country roads and others more distant, which they could see particularly well each time their road topped a hill. The Germans they met were quite unlike those who, five and a half months previously, had driven through these parts on thousands of lorries. Now their greatcoats were tattered, their heads and feet wrapped up against the cold; their hands and unshaven faces were as black as if they had come straight out of a chimney.

On one occasion the young people watched a group of Italian soldiers ahead of them, as they proceeded along a road running from east to west, which crossed the military road on which they were tramping.

Several Italians carried rifles reversed on their shoulders, holding them by the barrels like sticks, but most of them were without rifles. An officer in a summer cloak, wearing something that was neither a forage-cap nor a peaked army cap, had tied it down with a pair of child's leggings. He was riding bareback on an ass and his huge boots almost touched the ground. This denizen of a warmer, southern clime caught in the snows of Russia, with the drips from his nose frozen to his upper lip, was such an amusing and symbolic spectacle that the youngsters looked at each other and burst out laughing.

Many civilians, whom the war had uprooted from their homes, were seen on the roads, so the group of two youths and three girls with knapsacks on their backs attracted no attention as they proceeded on their way.

All this put them in a lighter mood. With the carefree courage of youth, which has no real conception of danger, they already saw themselves on the other side of the front lines.

Nina strode along in her felt boots, her head protected by a cap with ear-flaps from under which the heavy waves of her hair fell to the collar of her warm coat. The walking had brought the colour to her cheeks. Oleg constantly looked at her and, when their eyes met, they smiled. As for Sergei and Valya, at one point they had begun to pelt each other with snowballs and, as they chased each other, had left their comrades far behind. Olya, the oldest of the group, who wore dark clothing and was quiet and uncommunicative, behaved like a condescending mother to the two couples.

They spent a day and a night at Dubovoi farmstead and made careful inquiries about the state of affairs along the front. A war invalid with one arm missing, who had settled in the neighbourhood after being separated from his unit, advised them to make for Dyachkino village further to the north.

In this village and the adjacent farmsteads they spent a few days moving about among the confusion of German Army bases and the villagers hiding in their cellars. They were now in the immediate vicinity of the battle lines; the booming of gun-fire was incessant and at night they could see the flashes from the gun muzzles. The German bases were bombed all the time and it was obvious that the front was giving way under the pressure of the Soviet Army, because everything German in this area was on the move, streaming to the west.

Every soldier gave them a sidelong glance, and the villagers were afraid to let them in, without knowing what sort of people they were. Merely to wander about in this area or even remain here was dangerous, and for a group of five to attempt to cross the lines was out of the question. At one of the farmsteads the peasant woman, after looking at them in a definitely hostile manner, suddenly dressed warmly during the night and went out. Oleg was awake and roused his comrades, and they left the farm and made for the open steppe. Overcome with a desire to sleep and with nowhere to lay their heads, they found it very hard to battle against the wind which had been blowing since the previous day. They had never felt so helpless and abandoned. Then Olya, the oldest among them, did at last speak up.

"Don't be offended at what I'm going to say," she began. She kept her eyes averted from them and pressed a sleeve against her cheek, to shield it from the wind. "It's impossible for a large group like us to get across the battle lines. And it would probably be very difficult for a woman or a girl to cross them at all...." She glanced at Oleg and Sergei, expecting them to object, but they said nothing, because what she said was true. "We girls must give the boys a free hand," she said firmly. Nina and Valya realized that she was speaking about them. "Nina may want to object, but your mother put you into my care; we'll go to Fokino village, a student-friend of mine lives there, she'll put us up, and we can wait there."

For the first time Oleg could find nothing to say. Sergei and Valya also remained silent.

"Why should I object? No, I don't object," Nina said, almost in tears.

The five of them stood there for some moments without saying a word, sad at heart and reluctant to take the final step.

"Olya's right," Oleg said at last. "Why let the girls take the risk, when there's a simpler way out for them. And it's true, we'll find it easier that way. You g-get along on your way th-then," he said, suddenly stuttering. He embraced Olya.

Then he walked over to Nina, and the rest turned away. Impetuously she threw her arms round him and began to rain kisses on his face. He embraced her, and kissed her on her lips.

"You r-remember how I pestered you once to let me k-kiss you on the cheek, you r-remember how I said, 'Just on the cheek, you know, only the cheek'? So this is when we were destined to kiss. Y-you remember?" he whispered, a boyish, happy expression on his face.

"I remember, I remember everything, I remember more than you think ... I shall always remember you ... I shall wait for you," she whispered.

He kissed her again and moved away from her.

After they had walked a few steps, Olya and Nina waved back at the lads and then no more could be seen or heard of them; only a fine snow was covering the thin layer of ice.

"How about you two?" Oleg asked turning to Valya and Sergei.

"We'll try it together, all the same," said Sergei guiltily. "We'll proceed parallel with the front and maybe we'll manage to nip across somewhere. And you?"

"I'm going to try it here, somewhere. Here, I at least know the neighbourhood, now," Oleg replied.

Again there was a moment's painful silence.

"Don't make such a long face, old fellow! It's nothing to be ashamed of.... W-well?" Oleg said. He knew exactly what was going on in Sergei's mind.

Valya embraced Oleg impetuously. Sergei was not inclined to display tenderness. He shook hands with Oleg, gave him a gentle shove on the shoulder and set off, without looking round. Valya ran to catch up with him.

That was on January 7.

They, too, found they were unable to get across the front. They walked from village to village and finally reached Kamensk. They passed themselves off as brother and sister, separated from their family in the battle area along the Middle Don. People felt sorry for them and gave them a bed in a corner, on the earthen floor. And like brother and sister in misfortune, they slept in each other's arms. In the morning they would get up and continue on their way. Valya wanted to try crossing the front just anywhere, but Sergei was a realist and was against crossing the front at all.

In the end, the girl realized that her companion had no intention of trying to cross the enemy lines so long as she was with him: Sergei alone could get through anywhere, but he was obviously afraid to expose her to the risk.

"You know, if I were alone I could easily find a corner in some village and wait until the front runs through it," she said to him at last.

But he would not hear of it.

But the girl outwitted him, all the same. In all the work they had done together he had always been the leader and she had subordinated herself to him. But in personal affairs, she had always had the upper hand, and the lad had never noticed how much he had been in her leading-strings. So now she told him that he could get in with a Red Army unit, tell them of the Young Guards enduring torture in Krasnodon, and, together with the unit, save the young people and help her out as well.

"I'll wait for you somewhere in the neighbourhood," she said.

The day had been exhausting, and she slept soundly that night. When she awoke just before dawn, Sergei had gone. He had not wanted to awaken her to say good-bye.

So Valya now found herself alone.

All her life, Yelena Nikolayevna never forgot the bitterly cold night of January 11. The whole family was asleep when someone tapped softly at the window facing the street. Yelena Nikolayevna heard it at once, and knew in a flash that it was her son.

Oleg dropped heavily on to a chair. His cheeks were frost-bitten, he was too weary to remove his cap. Everyone was awake by now. Grandma lit a candle and placed it under the table so that its light would not be seen from the street: the police had been calling on them several times each day. The light shone up into Oleg's face as he sat in his frosted cap. There were black patches on his cheek-bones. He had grown thin.

He had made several futile attempts to get across the front. But he had been unfamiliar with the modern system of armament and location of groups and detachments. Moreover, he was too large and his clothing too dark for him to crawl unnoticed over the snow. He had been constantly tortured by thoughts of the fate which hung over his comrades in the town. Finally, he had persuaded himself that so much time had now elapsed that he could make his way unseen back to the town.

"Any news of Zemnukhov?" he asked.

"Still the same...." his mother replied, avoiding his eyes.

She helped him out of his coat and removed his cap. There was nothing in the house with which to warm some tea for him, and the family exchanged glances, fearing that at any moment the lad would be arrested there, in the home.

"How's Ulya?" he asked.

There was no immediate reply.

"Ulya's been arrested," his mother said in a low voice.

"And Lyuba?"

"Lyuba, too...."

The expression on his face changed. He was silent for some moments. Then he asked:

"What about Krasnodon settlement?"

This slow torture could not be allowed to go on.

"It'd be easier to tell you who hasn't yet been arrested," Nikolai Nikolayevich said.

He went on to tell of the arrest of a large group of workers, including Lyutikov and Barakov, in the central workshops. No one in Krasnodon now had any doubt that the last two were reliable comrades, who had been left in the rear of the Germans to carry out special assignments.

Oleg hung his head. He asked no more questions.

After debating the situation, they decided to send Oleg to Marina's relations in the country immediately, that very night. Nikolai Nikolayevich volunteered to accompany him.

They walked along the Rovenki road across the deserted steppe. The stars shed a soft bluish light on the snow and they could see a long way over the vast expanses.

Although Oleg had scarcely rested at all after many days of wandering, often without food and shelter, and in spite of the shock of the news he had heard at home, he was completely master of himself. As they proceeded on their way, he asked Nikolai Nikolayevich for the details of the collapse of the Young Guard and the arrest of Lyutikov and Barakov. He also told Nikolai Nikolayevich of his own misadventures.

The road had been rising almost imperceptibly. They had reached the highest point, where it dipped abruptly; about fifty yards ahead of them lay the shadowy outskirts of a large village.

"We're heading straight for the village. We must make a detour," Nikolai Nikolayevich said.

They swung off the road and skirted the left side of the village, keeping at a distance of about fifty yards from the nearest houses. The snow was deep only in the drifts.

They were about to cross one of the smaller side roads leading to the village, when several grey figures rushed across their path from the nearest house, shouting hoarsely in German.

Without a word, Nikolai Nikolayevich and Oleg made off down the road away from them.

Oleg was too weak to run and felt that he was being overtaken. He mustered every ounce of his remaining strength, but slipped and fell. The men threw themselves on him, and twisted his arms behind his back. Two of them raced after Nikolai Nikolayevich and fired several revolver shots. But they returned laughing after some minutes, and swore at not having caught him.

Oleg was taken to a large house, at one time probably the seat of the Village Soviet, but now the office of the village Elder. Several gendarmerie soldiers were lying asleep on straw spread out on the floor. Oleg realized that he and Nikolai Nikolayevich had come straight up against a gendarmerie station. On the table stood a field telephone sheathed in a dark leather case.

A corporal turned up the wick of the lamp and, shouting angrily, began to search Oleg. Finding nothing to arouse suspicion, he pulled off Oleg's jacket and felt over it inch by inch. His large fingers were flat and spatulate and performed their work deftly and methodically. They rooted out Oleg's Komsomol card and the lad knew then that it was all up with him.

With his hand covering the Komsomol card and the blank temporary cards lying on the table, the corporal spoke a few words into the telephone in a strained voice, then replaced the receiver and said something to the soldier who had brought Oleg in.

On the evening of the following day, escorted by the corporal and a soldier who acted as driver, Oleg was taken by sleigh to the town of Rovenki and handed over to the gendarme on duty at the police and gendarmerie headquarters.

Alone, in complete darkness, Oleg sat in the cell with his arms hugging his knees. If it had been possible to see his face, it would have been found to be calm and stern. He did not think of Nina, of his mother, of the stupid way he had been caught; he had had plenty of time for such thoughts, while sitting in the office of the village Elder and during the sleigh ride. He did not speculate on what lay ahead: he knew it only too well. He was calm and stern, because he was drawing the line which marked the end of his short-lived existence.

"All right, I may be only sixteen, but it's not my fault that my road through life has turned out to be so short.... What's there to be scared of? Death? Torture? I can face that. Of course, I should have liked to die in such a way that my memory would live on in people's hearts. But suppose I do die in obscurity—millions are dying like that now, people like myself, full of strength and love of life. Have I anything to reproach myself for? I told no lies and never chose the easy road. Sometimes I've been flippant—maybe weak, too, out of the kindness of my heart. Oleg, my friend, that's no crime when you're sixteen! I haven't even tasted all the happiness that was my due. All the same, I'm happy!

Happy that I did not crawl to anybody like a worm, but fought instead. Mama always called me her 'soaring eaglet'.... I shall not betray her faith in me or the trust of my comrades. Let my death be as pure as my life has been—I'm not ashamed to say that to myself. You'll die honourably, Oleg, old chap...."

The lines on his face were smoothed out; he lay down on the frozen, slimy floor, his cap under his head, and slept soundly.

He awoke when he felt someone standing over him. It was morning.

Almost blotting out the cell door, a thickset old man with freckled face and a large, purple nose, and wearing a Cossack greatcoat with a Polish cap too small for his big, ginger-haired head was standing over him, his rheumy, crazed eyes goggling at him.

Oleg sat up on the floor and looked at him, surprised.

"I've been thinking, what sort of fellow is Koshevoi? So this is what he's like ... the little reptile! The scoundrel! Pity it's the Gestapo that'll teach you—you'd have been better off with me. I only beat in exceptional cases. So that's what you look like! You're as famous as Dubrovsky. You've no doubt read your Pushkin. Ugh, you little reptile! Pity I haven't got you in my clutches." The old man bent over him, screwed up one crazed, watery eye and, with his vodka-laden breath close to Oleg's face, whispered mysteriously, "You're wondering why I've come so early, aren't you?" He winked intimately, confidentially. "Today I'm dispatching a party up there." He pointed a swollen finger skywards. "I've come with the barber to shave them, because I always shave them first," he whispered. Then he straightened up, heaved a sigh and lifting a thumb said, "Cultured, we are! But you're headed for the Gestapo and I don't envy you. *Au revoir!*" He touched the peak of his cap with his aged, swollen hand and went out. The door was slammed shut behind him.

When Oleg was transferred to a common cell, full of people from distant places and completely unknown to him, he learned that the old man was Orlov, chief of the Rovenki Police, formerly a Denikin officer and now a ruthless butcher and torturer.

Two or three hours later, he was taken away to be questioned. Only Gestapo officials had dealings with him. The interpreter was a German corporal.

There were numerous German gendarmerie officers in the room where he was taken. They all looked at him with unconcealed curiosity and surprise; several of them even stared at him as they might at an important personage. In many respects Oleg's conception of the world was still childish and so he could not possibly have imagined how far the fame of the Young Guard had spread nor how much he himself had become a legendary figure, thanks to Stakhovich's evidence and the fact that the Germans had been unable for so long to capture him. A loose-limbed German, who seemed to be as boneless as a lamprey, questioned him. He had terrible, dark blue semicircles, starting from the corners of his dark, almost black eyelids, running under his eyes and across the cheek-bones, spreading down in large patches on his sunken cheeks. The whole effect was supernatural and made him look like the sort of person one could see only in some horrible nightmare.

To the demand that Oleg reveal the activities of the Young Guard and name its members and supporters, the lad replied:

"I alone am the leader of the Young Guard and I alone am responsible for what its members have done on my instructions. I could give the details of the activities of the Young Guard, if I were being tried by a public court. But it is of no use to the organization for me to relate its activities before people who kill the innocent as well." He paused, glanced calmly at the officers and said: "What's more, you're all as good as dead yourselves."

The German who, in fact, looked like a corpse, nevertheless asked another question.

"You've heard all I have to say," Oleg said and lowered his eyelids.

Oleg was then thrown into the Gestapo torture-chamber and there began for him the terrible existence which was not only beyond human endurance, but about which no human being with a heart could possibly write.

But Oleg endured this existence until the end of the month; he was not killed because of the anticipated arrival of Major-General Klehr, *Feldkommandant* of the region, who wished to question in person the ringleaders of the organization and give orders as to their fate.

Oleg did not know that Filipp Petrovich Lyutikov had also been transferred to the Rovenki Gestapo to be questioned by the *Feldkommandant*. The enemy had failed to discover that Lyutikov was the leader of the Krasnodon Underground Communist Organization, but they felt, and saw with their own eyes, that he was the most important of all the people who had fallen into their hands.

Chapter 27

AUTOMATIC RIFLES, operating from three points, like the corners of a triangle, pounded the hollow which lay between the hills like the saddle of a two-humped camel. The bullets smacked into the slime of snow and mud with a noise that sounded like: "E-e-you... e-e-you." But Sergei had already reached the far side of the saddle, and strong hands gripping his arms were pulling him into the trenches.

"What are you up to?" said a short, round-eyed sergeant in the purest Kursk accent. "Aren't you ashamed of yourself! A Russian lad too, I shouldn't wonder.... Have they been threatening you or promised you something?"

"I'm a friend, one of you," Sergei said, grinning nervously. "I've got documents stitched into my jacket; take me to your commanding officer. I've got important information!"

With the divisional Chief of Staff, Sergei stood before the divisional commander in the only undamaged cottage at a little farmstead near the railway line. At one time the whole farmstead had lain in the shade of acacia-trees, but bombs and shells had cut them down. This was the divisional headquarters; no units passed this way and motor traffic was banned. Except for the ceaseless roar of heavy firing from battles in progress behind the hills, it was very quiet at the farmstead, and inside the cottage.

"I'm not merely judging by his documents, but by what he says. The little fellow knows everything: topography, the position of the heavy guns, even the gun emplacements in squares 27, 28, 17 ..." the Chief of Staff said and named a few more numbers. "Much of it coincides with what we have had from our intelligence; on some points he has given more precise information. Incidentally, they've scarped the river-banks. Remember?" he said. He was a young curly-headed chap with three insignia bars. From time to time he frowned, and drew air through one side of his mouth; a tooth was aching.

The divisional commander examined Sergei's Komsomol card and the crudely printed document, filled in by hand over the signatures of Young Guard Commander Turkenich and Commissar Kashuk, and certifying that Sergei Tyule-nin was a member of the headquarters of the Young Guard underground organization in the town of Krasnodon. He examined the card and document, then returned them, not to the Chief of Staff from whom he had taken them, but to Sergei himself. Then he regarded Sergei from top to toe with candid interest.

"Well," said the divisional commander.

The Chief of Staff winced with pain and drew air through one side of his mouth.

"He has some important information for you alone," he said.

Sergei thereupon told him of the Young Guard and said he imagined the division would no doubt advance immedi-ately to rescue the young people languishing in prison.

The Chief of Staff, after listening to this tactical plan for moving the division to Krasnodon, smiled, but almost at once groaned softly and pressed a hand to his cheek. The di-visional commander did not smile, however, because he apparently did not consider it such a fantastic proposition to move the division towards Krasnodon.

"D'you know Kamensk?" he asked.

"I know it, not from this side, but from the other side. I came here from there...."

"Fedorenko!" The commander shouted in such a loud voice that it echoed in some army utensils somewhere out-side the room.

Apart from the three mentioned there had been no one in the room, yet suddenly, out of the blue, Fedorenko was standing before the commander, clicking his heels to everyone's amusement.

"Here!" he reported.

"First of all, boots for the lad. Next, give him some food. Then let him sleep it off in a warm spot, until I send for him."

"Boots, food, sleep until you send for him."

"In a warm spot...." stressed the commander, raising an admonishing finger. "How's the bath-house?"

"It'll be ready soon, Comrade General!"

"Be off, then!"

Sergeant Fedorenko put a friendly arm round Sergei's shoulder and together they left the cottage.

"The Commander-in-Chief is coming over," the commander said, smiling.

"That's fine!" the Chief of Staff beamed and even forgot his toothache for the moment.

"We'll have to move over into the shelters. See that they're heated, or you'll catch it from Kolobok!" the divisional commander said with a merry laugh.

Meanwhile, the army Commander-in-Chief whom the divisional commander had referred to by the soldiers' nickname, "Kolobok,"* was still sleeping. He was at his command post, which was not in a house or near any human habitation, but in an old German dug-out in a grove. Although the army was advancing very rapidly, the Commander-in-Chief observed the rule never to set up his command post in populated places, but to occupy abandoned German dug-outs at each new position and, if they were all destroyed, to have a new shelter dug for him and his staff, as had been done during the first days of the war. He had begun to adhere to this principle very firmly since, early in the war, a number of his comrades, important military men, had been killed in air raids, because they had considered it unnecessary to dig shelters.

The Commander-in-Chief had not so long ago been in command himself of the division which Sergei Tyulenin had now joined. This was the division which exactly six months previously should have coordinated its operations with those of Ivan Protsenko's partisan detachment. And the officer who was now the army Commander-in-Chief, was the

* Small round loaf. In a folk tale of that name a Kolobok rolled nimbly over hill and dale surmounting all obstacles and outwitting all the ferocious wild animals it encountered.

same general who, as divisional commander six months previously, had personally arranged matters with Protsenko at the offices of the Krasnodon District Party Committee; subsequently he had distinguished himself in the defence first of Voroshilovgrad, then of Kamensk and finally in a skilful rearguard action, during the memorable retreat in July and August 1942.

The Commander-in-Chief possessed a simple, peasant name, passed on to him from his father and grandfather. After the battles mentioned, the name had become prominent among those of other army leaders and was never forgotten by the people of the Northern Donets and Middle Don. And now, after two months' fighting on the South-Western Front, the name had acquired nation-wide fame, side by side with the names of other army leaders who had covered themselves with glory in the epic Battle of Stalingrad. "Kolobok" was his new nickname but he was quite unaware of it.

In some respects the name suited him. He was short, broad of shoulder and chest, and had a round, strong, candid Russian face. For all his heavy outward appearance, he was very light on his feet and lively; he had clever, merry little eyes and all his movements were deft and neat. The name "Kolobok" had not, however, been given him because of his appearance.

Through a chain of circumstances, he was now advancing over the same ground from which he had retreated during July and August. The fighting had been fierce in those days, yet he had fairly easily broken away from the enemy and withdrawn in a direction where the enemy was unable to pick up his trail.

After joining up with the formations which later established the South-Western Front, he and the rest had dug in and bided their time in the trenches until the stunned fury of the enemy had been broken down by their inflexible stubbornness. When the right moment arrived, he and the rest had scrambled out of their dug-outs; he had commanded first the division and later an army that had rolled up hill and down dale on the heels of the enemy. He had taken thousands of prisoners and captured hundreds of guns in the course of his leap-frog advance from the Don to the Chir, then forward from the Chir to the Donets, overtaking the enemy and leaving scattered enemy units in his wake, to be dealt with by others.

It was at this time that the fairy-tale name "Kolobok" arose from the hearts of his soldiers and stuck to him. And forward he rolled like the round fairy-tale loaf.

Sergei made contact with the Soviet forces during the days half-way through January, when a change for the better saw the Soviet forces developing terrific offensive movements along the Voronezh, the South-Western, the Don, the Southern, the North Caucasus, the Volkhov and the Leningrad fronts; these had been followed by the final rout and capture of the German fascist forces, encircled at the approaches to Stalingrad, by the breaking of the more than two-year-old Leningrad blockade and by the liberation in only six weeks of such towns as Voronezh, Kursk, Kharkov, Krasnodar, Rostov, Novocherkassk and Voroshilovgrad. Sergei reached the Soviet forces just when a powerful new tank offensive was getting under way against the German defence positions along the line of the Derkul, Aidar, and Oskol rivers, three of the Donets tributaries; when on the Kamensk-Kantemirovka railway the final resistance of the German garrison in besieged Millerovo was broken down and, with the capture two days earlier of Glubokaya station, the Soviet troops were preparing to cross the Northern Donets.

The army Commander-in-Chief was still asleep when the divisional commander was chatting with Sergei. As with all commanding officers, it was his habit to prepare, or deal with, all important matters overnight, when no one unconnected with such questions could disturb him, and he was free from the daily routine of army life. Now Sergeant-Major Mishin (a man as huge as Peter the Great, who, to the general commanding the army, was what Sergeant Fedorenko was to the general commanding the division) was already examining the war-trophy watch on his wrist—it had been presented to him—and was thinking it must already be time to wake the general.

The Commander-in-Chief never got enough sleep, and this day he had to be up earlier than usual. By a coincidence, frequent enough in war-time, the division, which in July had fought under his command in the defence of Kamensk, now had the task of recapturing the town. There were few of the "old soldiers" left in the division. Its commanding officer, who had only recently become a general, had then been a regimental commander. "Old soldiers" like him could still be found among the officers but there were very few among the other ranks; nine-tenths of the division consisted of replacements assigned to it before the offensive along the Middle Don.

With a final glance at his watch, Sergeant-Major Mishin stepped over to the bunk on which the general was sleeping. It was no more than an ordinary shelf. The general dreaded dampness and always had his bed made on the first floor, as it were, like the upper bunk in a railway sleeper.

As always, Mishin began by violently shaking the general, who was sleeping on his side, with the childlike expression of a healthy man with a clear conscience. This, of course, did not break through his warrior sleep. It was merely the preliminary for what Mishin always did next. He pushed one arm under the general and placing the other round his shoulders, easily and carefully raised his heavy body into an upright position, as one would a child.

The general, who slept in a dressing-gown, was wide awake in a flash; his eyes, as he looked at Mishin, were as clear as though he had not just been sleeping.

"Thank you very much," he said. He leapt down from the shelf with surprising nimbleness, passed a hand over his hair, sat down on a stool and looked round for the barber. Mishin dropped a pair of slippers at his feet.

The barber, in huge leather boots and snow-white apron over his army tunic, was already preparing the lather in that part of the shelter which housed the kitchen. Silent as a ghost, he appeared by the commander's side, tucked a hand-towel into the collar of his dressing-gown and lightly and deftly lathered the general's face, covered with the hard, dark stubble that had grown overnight.

In less than fifteen minutes the general, fully dressed, his single-breasted jacket buttoned to the throat, was sitting heavily at his desk and, while breakfast was being served, glancing rapidly through the papers which his adjutant handed to him one by one, flipping them nimbly from a red-lined leather portfolio. The first paper handed him was a dispatch just received, reporting the capture of Millerovo, but this was no news to the general, who had known that Millerovo would most certainly fall during the night or early in the morning. Then followed various routine matters.

"The devil take it! Of course let them keep the sugar, if they've captured it!... Change Safronov's medal For Courage to the Order of the Red Banner; the divisional staff apparently think that the rank and file can only be recommended for medals, that only officers can be recommended for Orders!... Haven't they shot him yet? That's no tribunal; more like the editorial board of *A Heart-to-Heart Chat.**
He's to be shot immediately, or else they'll all come before a tribunal! Hell. 'Request invitation for transfer....' I'm from the rank and file myself, but I'm damn sure that's not how you say it in Russian. Tell Klepikov, who signed this without reading it, to read it through, to correct the mistakes in blue or red pencil and to bring this paper back to me himself.... Oh no! You're bringing me a lot of rubbish today. All this can wait," the general said and set about his breakfast energetically.

The Commander-in-Chief was still drinking coffee when a general carrying a portfolio came in to see him. He was short, sedate, and neatly turned out, precise and sparing in his movements and his high, pale forehead seemed even higher because his head was bald in front and the hair closely trimmed at the temples. He looked more like a professor than an army man.

"Take a seat," the Commander-in-Chief said.

The Chief of Staff had arrived with more important matters than those the adjutant had put before the Commander-in-Chief. But before raising any of them, he smilingly handed over the latest edition of a Moscow newspaper delivered to the front by plane and distributed that morning to the various Army Commands.

The paper contained the usual list of officers and generals newly decorated or promoted, several of them from his own army.

With the keen, good-natured interest typical of army

---

* *A Heart-to-Heart Chat*—pre-revolutionary journal for children.

people, the Commander-in-Chief rapidly read aloud the list of names and every time he recognized that of someone he had known at the Military Academy or had come to know during the war, he glanced at the Chief of Staff, sometimes with a meaning look, sometimes surprised or doubtful, sometimes beaming like a child, particularly when the matter concerned his own army.

The list contained the name of the officer who was in command of the division, which had once been under Kolobok, to which the present Chief of Staff had once belonged. This divisional commander had been decorated several times already, and this time it was also for past services, only the recommendation had taken some time to pass through the usual channels; only now had the matter reached the press.

"A fine time to let him know—just when he has to capture Kamensk!" the Commander-in-Chief said. "It'll unnerve him!"

"On the contrary, it'll brace him up," the Chief of Staff said with a smile.

"I know, I know all your weaknesses!... I shall see him today and congratulate him.... Send a telegram of congratulations to Chuvyrin. To Kharchenko, too. And something warm and kindly to Kukolev, nothing official, you understand, just something friendly. I'm really glad for his sake. I was beginning to think he would never recover after the Vyazma business," the Commander-in-Chief said. Suddenly *a cunning smile spread over his face. "When are the* shoulder-straps coming?"

"They're on the way!" the Chief of Staff said and smiled again.

An order had quite recently been published that shoulder-straps were to be introduced for soldiers, officers and generals, and the whole army was interested in it.

The divisional commander had merely mentioned to his Chief of Staff that the Commander-in-Chief was due to arrive, but the news had travelled in a flash through the whole division. It had even reached the men who were lying prone in the snow and mud along the low, flat left bank of the Donets, with their eyes fixed on its steep right bank and the buildings of Kamensk, from which several columns of smoke were rising. Silhouetted against the sky above the town, Soviet bombers were dropping their loads on it through the haze.

While the Commander-in-Chief was still driving in his car towards the second echelon of the division where he was met by the commander himself, and again later when together they were walking to divisional headquarters, soldiers and officers singly and in groups continually came in sight along the road as though by accident; everyone wanted not only to see their chief but also to be seen by him. They all stood to attention in a particularly smart fashion, and their faces were eager or smiling.

"Own up, you only crawled into this shelter an hour ago. Devil take it, the walls aren't even sweating!" said the Commander-in-Chief, who had immediately seen through the divisional commander's ruse.

"Two hours ago, to be precise. And we won't leave it now, until we take Kamensk," the divisional commander said, standing respectfully in front of the Commander-in-Chief, while a sly look in his eyes and the calm, confident expression of his mouth seemed to say: "I'm in charge in my own division and I know what you can seriously reprimand me for; but this is only a trifling matter."

The Commander-in-Chief congratulated him on his decoration. Then, seizing an opportune moment, the divisional commander said casually:

"Before we go on to important matters ... there's a village bath-house not far from here which has escaped damage. We're heating the water. I dare say it's long since you had a bath, Comrade General?"

"You don't say?" the general said, seriously. "But is it ready?"

"Fedorenko!"

It transpired that the baths would only be ready by the evening. The divisional commander bestowed a look on Fedorenko which indubitably signified that he would hear more about the affair later.

"By this evening—" The Commander-in-Chief was wondering whether perhaps something could be postponed, something cancelled, perhaps, then he suddenly recalled that on the way over some additional item had been wedged in. "I'll have to leave it for another time," he said.

On the advice of the army Chief of Staff, who was regarded throughout the army as an infallible military authority, the divisional commander had worked out his plan for the capture of Kamensk, and he now began to outline it to the Commander-in-Chief. The latter listened and then began to show signs of dissatisfaction.

"What sort of a triangle is this: the river, the railway, the outskirts of the town—it's all fortified."

"I expressed the same doubts, but Ivan Ivanovich quite correctly pointed out that—"

Ivan Ivanovich was the army Chief of Staff.

"You'll get across there, with nowhere to deploy laterally. They'll go on reducing your numbers as you move up," the Commander-in-Chief said tactfully evading the question of Ivan Ivanovich.

But as the divisional commander saw it, Ivan Ivanovich's expert knowledge served to reinforce his own position and again he said:

"Ivan Ivanovich is of the opinion that they can't possibly expect a frontal attack from this direction; they'll regard it as a diversion, and our intelligence reports confirm that."

"You'll no sooner burst into the town from here than they'll come at you in a flood down the streets and from the station, here...."

"Ivan Ivanovich—"

It struck the Commander-in-Chief that they would get nowhere unless the obstacle in the shape of Ivan Ivanovich was removed.

"Ivan Ivanovich is mistaken," he said.

He then proceeded to express his idea somewhat subtly, with deft, rounded movements of his broad hand and short fingers indicating through an imaginary locality on the map his plan to outflank the town and capture it by a frontal attack from a totally different direction.

The divisional commander recalled the boy, who that morning had crossed the front from the outskirts of the town, from which side the Commander-in-Chief had indicated the direction of the main thrust. Suddenly, without any further effort, his mind clearly grasped the plan for the assault on the town.

Towards nightfall all the important, decisive matters had been settled at divisional headquarters and passed on to the regiments. The commanders turned in to the bath-house, which had curiously escaped damage in what had once been the little village.

At five in the morning the divisional commander and his deputy from the political department toured the regiments to check on their preparedness.

In the dug-out of the regimental commander, Major Kononenko, no one had slept. All night long, from the senior officers to the junior commanders, orders and explanations had been going out concerning the smallest, even personal, aspects of the operation ahead of them, which were, for all that, important and decisive aspects.

In spite of the fact that all the orders and explanations had been given, the divisional commander with his customary method and patience repeated all that had been said the day before and verified every step Major Kononenko had taken.

The major was a young, typical soldier of the worker type. He had a lean, bold, energetic face. His sweater was rolled over the neck of his army jacket, over which he wore a warm padded jacket. He had discarded his army greatcoat, as it restricted his movements. Now he listened with patience, but not very attentively, because he knew it all, to everything the commander had to say, and then reported what he himself had done.

Sergei had been put into this regiment. He had negotiated the whole ladder backwards, from divisional headquarters down to the company commander; he had been supplied with a tommy-gun and two hand-grenades and was assigned to the assault group which was to be the first to break through to the cross-roads near Kamensk.

For the past few days, a mild snow-storm had swept over the open, undulating area, dotted with bushes, which lay round Kamensk. A south wind had then brought mists. The snow, which on the open ground was not deep, had begun to thaw, and roads and fields were now slushy.

All the villages and farmsteads along both banks of the

Donets had been badly damaged by bombs and shells and the troops were quartered in old trenches and dug-outs, under canvas or simply under the open sky, without being able to light fires.

The whole day before the assault the fair-sized town across the river was visible through the haze, with its network of deserted streets, the station water-tower rising above the house-tops, damaged church belfries and a few factory chimneys still standing. German blockhouses could be seen with the naked eye on the outskirts of the town and on the hills outside.

Mixed emotions are experienced by the Soviet citizen in the soldier's greatcoat just before a battle to liberate a populated place such as this. He feels morally elated because he, the Man in the Soldier's Greatcoat, is about to advance and to liberate something that is vital to him. He feels compassion for the town and its people, its mothers and little children hiding away in cold cellars and damp shelters. He feels infuriated against the enemy who, as experience had shown, will resist with doubled and trebled strength because he is conscious of his crimes and the retribution to come. His mind is involuntarily disturbed a little at the thought that there is the danger of death and the task is difficult. And how many are the hearts that quake from a natural feeling of terror!

But not one of the soldiers showed these feelings. All of them were elated and cheerful and exchanged rough jokes.

"Once Kolobok has undertaken the job he'll roll to the right place," they said, just as though not they, but the fabulous Kolobok himself was about to roll to the town.

The assault group, in which Sergei found himself, was under the command of the sergeant he had first met after crossing the front; a short, lively, cheerful fellow, with a network of fine wrinkles all over his face and large, blue eyes that had such a sparkle in them that they seemed to change colour constantly. His name was Kayutkin.

"So you're from Krasnodon?" he asked Sergei, with an expression of pleasure, yet something like incredulity.

"You've been there, perhaps?" asked Sergei.

"I met a friend there, a girl," Kayutkin said, a little sadly. "She was evacuating. I saw her on the road and we got friendly. A really lovely girl.... I was passing through Krasnodon at the time." He paused, then went on: "I was at the defence of Kamensk, too. All the defenders were either killed or taken prisoner. Except me ... and here I am back again. Have you heard these lines?" Gravely he began to recite:

> *Wounded I've been in attack*
> *But survived with scarce a scar.*
> *Thrice surrounded, Fritz said, "Got him!"*
> *Thrice, though, I escaped.*
>
> *At the time it was unpleasant*
> *Under flanking fire or crossing*
> *Under fire both curved and straight,*
> *Yet ever I came unscathed out.*
>
> *Often on my route familiar*
> *Hid by dust of marching columns*
> *They reported I was "routed"*
> *Or "wiped out," they often said.*

"Written about people like me," he said with a grin, and winked at Sergei.

So the day passed and night came. While the divisional commander was again repeating the assignment to Major Kononenko, the soldiers who were to fight in the operation were sleeping. Sergei, too, slept.

At six in the morning they were roused by the orderlies. The men were issued a round of vodka, a billy can of meat soup with a cereal, and a large ration of millet pudding. Then, under cover of the mist, undergrowth and bushes they began to move forward to their assault positions.

The ground turned into a muddy slush of wet snow and clay under their feet. Visibility was down to 200 yards. The heavy guns roared out, just as the last groups reached the Donets bank and lay down on the wet slush.

The firing was measured and systematic, but there were so many guns that the sound of firing and the explosions merged into an unbroken din.

Lying by Kayutkin's side, Sergei saw the red balls of fire, some quite round, others with tails, flying straight overhead and to the right through the haze across the river; he heard the swish of them as they skimmed past, the sharp bursts on the opposite bank and the rumbling of the more distant explosions in the town. All these sounds had an exhilarating effect on him and his comrades.

The Germans only aimed mortar shells at places where they assumed the infantry to be massed. From time to time came a salvo from the six-barrel mortar in the town. Then Kayutkin would say, somewhat apprehensively:

"Oi-oi ... there it goes!"

Suddenly thunderous roars came rolling up from far away, at the back of Sergei. They increased in volume, spread along the horizon. A singing droning sound passed over the heads of the troops lying on the bank and terrific bursts of fire, enveloped in dense black smoke, blanketed the whole of the opposite river-bank.

"The *Katyushas* have opened up," Kayutkin said. He crouched tensely and his wrinkled face looked hard and ruthless. "Now one more from the heavies and the—"

The droning in their rear had not yet died away and the explosions were still continuing on the far side, when Sergei, without hearing whether the order had been given or not, but seeing Kayutkin leap forward and run, jumped up from his shallow trench and raced across the ice on the river.

It seemed to him that they were running across the ice in absolute silence. Actually they were under fire from the far bank and men were felled on the ice. Black smoke and a smell of sulphur rolled in waves through the drifting mists towards the running troops. But the soldiers already felt that everything had been done correctly and that everything would be all right.

Stunned by the sudden silence, Sergei came to himself when at last he lay by Kayutkin's side in a shell-hole of churned-up, steaming earth. Grimacing fiercely, Kayutkin was firing his tommy-gun at something straight in front of him and Sergei saw, not more than fifty feet away, the shaking barrel of a machine-gun protruding from a half-buried trench, and he also began to fire into the trench. The machine-gunner had spotted neither Sergei nor Kayutkin but was firing at something further away; they silenced him immediately.

The town lay far to their right, almost no firing came their way and they were moving farther and farther from the river-bank, into the open steppe. Only some considerable time later did the shells, fired from the town, begin to fall into the steppe, along the whole line of their advance.

Then, from small farmsteads, which Sergei knew well, but which were not visible through the mist, they encountered furious firing from machine-guns and automatic rifles. They dug in and lay still until their light artillery had caught them up and began pounding the farmsteads at almost point-blank range. Finally, groups of soldiers burst into the farmsteads together with the light guns, which were rolled forward by tall cheerful artillery men, all of them a little intoxicated. Straightaway the battalion commander came up, and signallers began to lay telephone wires into the cellar of a damaged brick farm-house.

Thus far, everything had gone well with their advance to the cross-roads, the final goal of their own, minor operation. If they had had tanks, they would long ago have reached the cross-roads; but tanks had not been used this time, because the ice on the Donets would not have supported them.

It was completely dark when the troops began to move forward again. As soon as the enemy opened fire, the battalion commander, who had himself taken charge of the operation, was forced to attack with the groups he had at his disposal, for the main troops were still moving up. The soldiers burst into the hamlet, Kayutkin's group thrusting far down the main street and engaging in battle for the school building.

They drew such fierce return fire from the school that Sergei stopped firing and lowered his head into the slush. A bullet had seared his left arm above the elbow, but glanced past the bone; in the heat of the fighting he had not felt the pain. When he finally brought himself to raise his head, he found he was alone.

The most likely thing to assume, of course, was that his comrades had withdrawn to the outskirts under pressure of the firing and joined the main body. But Sergei was inexperienced and he concluded that his comrades were all killed, and terror gripped him. He crawled behind a house and listened. Two Germans ran past him. He heard German voices to the right, the left and behind him. The firing close by had now ceased, but it had flared up on the outskirts of the hamlet, and finally died away there, too.

Far away above the town flickered an immense red glow, which lit up not the sky but the billows of black smoke which were growing still more dense; from the same direction came a tremendous bombardment.

Wounded and alone, Sergei lay in the icy slush in the middle of a farmstead occupied by the Germans.

Chapter 28

MY FRIEND! My Friend!... I come now to the most grievous pages of my story and involuntarily I think of you....

If you only knew the agitation I felt during those far-off childhood days when you and I went to school in town! It was more than thirty miles from my home to yours, and when I set out from home I was so afraid I should not find you, that you had left already. For we had not seen each other all summer!

The mere possibility of such sorrow filled my heart with indescribable longing when, late at night, my father drove the cart into your village and the tired horse toiled so slowly along the street. Long before we reached your cottage I would jump from the cart. I knew you always slept in the hayloft, and that if I did not find you there, it meant you had gone.... But did you ever go without waiting for me? I know you would rather have been late back to school than have left me behind, alone.... We never closed our eyes all night; we would sit in the hayloft, our bare legs dangling outside, and talk and talk and muffle our laughter in our hands; and the roosting hens would ruffle their wings. The hay smelt sweet, the autumn morning sun would creep up from behind the woods and suddenly light up our faces. Only then did we see how much we had changed during the summer months....

I remember one occasion, standing knee-deep in the river, when you confessed to me that you were in love.... Frankly, I did not like the girl, but I said to you:

"You're in love, not me! I hope you'll be happy!..."

And you laughed and said:

"As a matter of fact, to restrain a chap from taking a wrong step, one might have to break a friendship, but can one give advice in affairs of the heart? How often do one's closest friends, moved by protective instincts, meddle in love affairs, linking people together, separating them, passing on unfavourable comments about the person you love.... If they only knew how much harm they cause, how many precious moments they poison, moments that are lost for ever!"

And again, I remember how that fellow N.—I would rather not name him—came one day and began with a mocking smirk on his face to gossip carelessly about his friends: "So-and-so is head over heels in love with so-and-so, he simply grovels at her feet, but, strictly between ourselves, her finger-nails are always dirty. And so-and-do, you know, got so drunk last night at a party that he vomited—only don't let it go any further. And so-and-so wears second-hand clothes; he pretends to be poor, but actually he's just a miser. I know that for a fact, and he's not above drinking beer at other people's expense ... only don't pass it on...."

You just looked at him and said:

"Listen here, N., you clear out and look sharp about it."

"What d'you mean ... clear out?" N. said, surprised.

"Just clear out.... There's nothing more despicable than a man who has nothing to say about his comrade's face, because he only sees his back. And what can be worse than a fellow who gossips?"

How I admired you for that! I felt the same about it, but perhaps I would have found it difficult to be so harsh....

But best of all I remember the summer when, again far away from you, I realized that there was no other road for me but to join the Komsomol.

And then we met again in the autumn, in the hayloft as we always did, and I felt a certain awkwardness and estrangement on your side, and I experienced something of the kind in my own attitude to you. We sat there silently dangling our bare legs as we did when we were children. You spoke first.

"You may not, perhaps, understand me, possibly you may condemn me for making my decision without talking things over with you first, but while I was alone during the summer I realized that for me there was no other road. You know, I've decided to join the Komsomol."

"But that'll mean new obligations and new friends—what about me, then?" I said, to put our friendship to the test.

"Yes," you said, sadly, "it's bound to be like that. Of course I know it's a matter of one's conscience, but it would be grand if you joined too!"

I could not torment you any longer; we looked at each other and burst out laughing.

There followed perhaps the happiest talk we had ever had, our last, sitting there in the hayloft with the roosting hens, and the sun which came out above the aspens, just as we were pledging that we would never turn aside from the road we had chosen, and would always remain loyal friends....

Friendship! How many people in this world pronounce the word and mean no more than a pleasant chat over a bottle of wine, and a condescending attitude to each other's weaknesses! What has that to do with friendship?

No, we quarrelled at every turn, we did not spare each other's pride. Indeed, we hurt each other's feelings when we disagreed. But, in consequence, our friendship was all the faster, it matured, and became strong as iron.

So often I was unfair to you, but once I realized I had been in the wrong I always admitted it to you. True, all I could bring myself to say was that I had been wrong. And you would say:

"Don't torture yourself, there's no sense in it. Now you realize you were wrong, forget it. Such things happen. It's part of the struggle."

And then, you nursed me better than the kindest hospital nurse, possibly even better than my own mother, because you were a rough, unsentimental fellow.

And now I have to tell how I lost you. It happened so long ago but I somehow imagine it was not in the other war but in this one. I dragged you through the reeds away from the lake, your blood trickled over my hands, the sun burned down mercilessly. At the river's edge behind us, probably no one was left alive—the firing had been so heavy on that narrow strip of bank covered with reeds. I dragged you away, because I refused to believe that you could not live. You lay there, on a bed of reeds; you were conscious, but your lips were very dry, and you said:

"Water, give me some water."

There was no water up there, and we had neither mug nor billy can, nor flask, or I would have gone back to fetch some from the lake. Then you said:

"Take off one of my boots, carefully. They're still water-tight."

I understood your idea. I removed one of your big army boots, which had tramped so many roads, we had been on the march for so many days and never a chance to change our socks; but I took the boot and set off for the lake and crawled to the edge; I was dying of thirst myself. Of course I could not dream of stopping to drink myself, under such a hail of fire; and only by a miracle did I succeed in filling the boot with water and crawling back again.

But when I reached you, you were dead. Your face was very calm. For the first time I saw what a big man you were. No wonder they had always confused us. Tears rushed to my eyes. I was so thirsty I could stand it no longer. I put my lips to your boot, to that crude, bitter cup of our soldierly friendship, and as I wept, I drained it to the dregs.

Conscious neither of cold or fear, worn out, frozen, and hungry as a wolf, Valya roamed along the front from one farmstead to the next, sometimes spending the night in the open steppe. After each advance of the front, the waves of retreating Germans compelled her, too, to approach ever nearer to places that she knew from childhood.

She roamed for a day, two days, a week, without knowing why. Perhaps she still hoped to cross the front, or perhaps she had begun to believe the suggestion she had made to Sergei, just to deceive him. Why, indeed, should Sergei not return with a Red Army unit? He had said, "I shall come back, never fear." And he had always kept his promise.

During the night when fighting broke out inside Kamensk and the immense glare through the columns of black smoke was visible for miles around, Valya had found shelter in a farmstead about ten miles from the town. There were no Germans there, but like most of the villagers, Valya had not slept all night, but had watched the glare in the sky. Something made her wait and wait....

At about eleven in the morning, news arrived in the village that Red Army units had broken into Kamensk, that fighting was in progress in it and that the Germans had already been dislodged from the greater part of it. At any moment now the most terrible kind of enemy, an enemy beaten in battle, would come streaming through the village. Valya again took up her knapsack into which the peasant woman, out of pity, had thrust a crust of bread, and left the village.

She walked aimlessly on and on. It was still thawing, but the direction of the wind had changed and it was getting colder. The mists had lifted and shapeless snow-laden clouds covered the sky. In the middle of the road Valya stopped, and stood for a long time, a thin figure, with the knapsack on her shoulders, the wind lashing the wet locks of hair that escaped from under her beret. Then she slowly turned into a country lane, covered with melted snow and slush, and walked in the direction of Krasnodon.

Meanwhile Sergei, his arm dangling from a blood-stained sleeve, without his gun, was knocking at the window of the last cottage at the far end of the same hamlet.

No, fate had not decreed that he should die this time. He had lain in the wet, muddy snow in the middle of the hamlet at the cross-roads until the Germans had quietened down. It had been too much to hope that the Soviet troops would again break into the hamlet that night. He had to get away, away from the front. He was not in uniform, and he could leave his gun where it was. It was not the first time that he had had to make this way through enemy positions!

It had been dull and misty, just before dawn, when, with his arm hanging loosely, he had crawled laboriously across the railway line. At this hour, the good housewife in the peasant cottage was usually up and lighting an oil-lamp. But now all good housewives were in their cellars with their children.

Sergei had crawled a hundred yards away from the railway line and had then stood up and walked until he had arrived at the farmstead.

A girl with ginger plaits ripped up a piece of old linen and bandaged his arm. Then, with the water she had just brought from the well, she washed the blood from the sleeve of his jacket and rubbed ashes into it. The people in the house were so afraid the Germans might suddenly appear that they gave Sergei no warm food, but merely something to take away with him.

And so, although he had not slept all night, Sergei set out to search for Valya in the farmsteads along the front.

As often happens in the Donets steppe, the weather had again become wintry. Thick snow was falling and showed no signs of thawing. Then it began to freeze hard.

One day, towards the end of January, Sergei's married sister Fenya arrived home from the market and found her door locked.

"Are you alone, Mama?" the eldest son had asked through the door.

Sergei was sitting at the table, one arm resting on it, the other one hanging down. He had always been thin but now his face was drawn, and he sat hunched up; only his eyes, as he looked at his sister, still had their former lively, energetic expression.

Fenya told him of the arrests at the central workshops, and that most of the Young Guards were in prison. From Marina she had already heard of Oleg Koshevoi's arrest. Sergei said not a word; his eyes had a terrible light in them.

"I'm going, don't be afraid," he said, finally.

He had felt Fenya's anxiety for him and her children.

His sister rebandaged his arm and made him change into women's clothes. She made a bundle of his own clothing and, when dusk fell, accompanied him to his home.

After the privations he had experienced in prison, his father had become quite doubled up, and lay in bed now most of the time. His mother did her best to keep on her feet. His sisters were not at home. Both of them, Dasha and his favourite, Nadya, had gone away in the direction of the front.

Sergei wanted to know whether anything had been heard of Valya Borts. The parents of the Young Guards had drawn closer to each other during the events of this period, but Maria Andreyevna had said nothing to Sergei's mother about her daughter.

"And she's not with the others?" he asked, morosely.

No, she was not in the prison; they knew that for a certainty.

Sergei undressed and, for the first time in a month, lay down on a clean bed, his own bed.

The oil-lamp burned on the table. Everything was just as it had always been since his childhood. But his mind was elsewhere. His father, lying in bed in the adjoining room, was shaking the walls with his coughing. Yet, to Sergei, everything seemed unnaturally still in the other room: there was none of his sisters' customary bustling about. Only his little nephew crawled about the floor in Grandpa's room, prattling away to himself.

His mother had gone out into the yard. Sergei heard the young woman from next door go into the old man's room. She had been coming nearly every day, and in the simplicity of their minds, Sergei's parents had never given a thought to the reason why she had become such a constant visitor. Sergei heard her talking to the old man.

The child crawling about the floor picked up something and came crawling into Sergei's room.

"Uncle ... Uncle ..." he lisped.

The woman quickly glanced into the room, and her eyes lighted on Sergei; then she talked a few minutes more to the old man and left the house.

Sergei turned over and tried to sleep.

At last his father and mother were asleep. It was dark and quiet in the house. But Sergei was still awake, tormented with longing....

Suddenly there was a loud knocking on the front door: "Open up!"

Only a second before, the indefatigable life force which had carried him through all his ordeals seemed to have deserted him altogether and left him helpless and broken. But the moment he heard the knocking on the door, his body had become lithe and agile. Leaping silently from the bed and darting to the window, he lifted a corner of the black-out curtain. Everything outside was white and flooded with the serene light of the moon. Not only was the figure, but also the shadow of the German soldier, standing by the window with his tommy-gun at the ready, stamped clearly against the snow.

The mother and father awoke and began to confer in frightened, sleepy tones. Then they lay still, listening to the pounding on the door. Accustomed by now to dressing with one hand, Sergei pulled on his trousers, shirt and boots, but was unable to tie the leather laces of the army boots the division had issued to him; then he went into his parents' room.

"Somebody open the door, but don't make a light," he said softly.

By now, the little cottage seemed about to crumble under the blows at the door.

The mother ran about the room, she had completely lost her head.

The father quietly climbed from the bed, and Sergei felt by the way he silently moved about how difficult it was for him to move at all, how hard it all was for him.

"Nothing for it, we must open the door," the old man said in a strange piping voice.

Sergei knew his father was weeping.

Tapping his crutch, the old man went to the passage and called out:

"Just a minute, I'm coming."

Noiselessly, Sergei slipped behind his father.

The mother padded heavily into the passage, touched the metal fastening and there was just a breath of frosty air. The father opened the outer door and stood aside, holding it open.

Three dark figures appeared in the moonlit rectangle of the door and entered the passage, one after the other. The last closed the door behind him and the beam of a powerful torch lit the passage. The ray of light first fell on the mother, who stood at the far end by the door leading to the lean-to cow-shed. From where he stood in a dark corner, Sergei saw that the hook on it was thrown back and the door was ajar; he realized his mother had done this for him. But the beam of light was now on the father and Sergei, hiding behind him. Sergei had not expected them to use a torch in the passage and had hoped to slip out into the yard, when they had passed through the room beyond.

Two of the men seized his arms. Sergei cried out, the pain in his wounded arm was so great. They dragged him into the room.

"Don't stand there like a statue—light the lamp!" Solikovsky yelled at the mother. Her hands shook so much that she took a long time fumbling. Solikovsky flicked his lighter. An SS man and Fehnbong were holding Sergei.

When the mother saw them she began to weep and threw herself at their feet. Large and ponderous, she clawed the earthen floor with her round, aged hands, as she crawled towards them. The old man stood bent almost double, leaning on his crutch and trembling from head to foot.

Solikovsky carried out a superficial search; the Tyulenins' home had been searched more than once already. The soldier produced a cord from his trouser pocket and they began to twist Sergei's arms behind him.

"He's my only son ... spare him ... take everything— the cow, clothing...."

The Lord only knows what else she said.... Sergei could have wept, he felt so sorry for her; he could say nothing for fear of breaking down.

"Take him away," Fehnbong said to the soldier.

The mother tried to stop him, but he fastidiously pushed her away with his boot.

Pushing Sergei ahead of him, the soldier moved to the door; Fehnbong and Solikovsky followed.

"Good-bye, Mama ... good-bye, Father," said Sergei over his shoulder.

The mother rushed at Fehnbong, and began to drum on his back with arms that were still strong.

"You murderers!" she screamed. "Killing's too good for you ... just you wait till our soldiers come!"

"Oh ... so you want to go there again, all right!" roared Solikovsky, and despite the old man's hoarse, broken pleadings he dragged her out as she was, in the old dressing-gown she always slept in. The old man had hardly time to throw her a shawl and coat.

Chapter 29

SERGEI remained silent when they beat him. Despite the excruciating pain in his wounded arm not a sound escaped his lips when Fehnbong jerked him up to the beam with his arms lashed behind him. Only when Fehnbong prodded his wound with a ramrod did he grit his teeth.

His vitality was astounding. He was thrown into a solitary cell, but at once began tapping on each of the walls to find out who were his neighbours. Standing on tiptoes, he stretched up to examine a chink close to the ceiling to see whether he could widen it, loosen a board and slip out, if only into the prison-yard; he was confident of being able to escape, if he could find a way out of the cell. He sat down and tried to remember the arrangement of the windows in the rooms in which he had been questioned and tortured, whether the door leading from the corridor to the yard was locked. If only his arm was not wounded! He was far from believing that all was lost. The roaring of artillery on the Donets could be heard through the clear frosty night even in the cells.

In the morning he was confronted with Vitya Lukyanchenko.

"No ... I knew he lived near by, but I never saw him," said Vitya Lukyanchenko, and his dark, gentle eyes which alone seemed alive, gazed past Sergei. Sergei said nothing.

Vitya Lukyanchenko was taken away, and a few minutes later Solikovsky brought in Sergei's mother.

They tore the clothing off the old woman, the mother of eleven children, hurled her on the blood-stained trestle-bed and, before the eyes of her own son, began to beat her with lengths of electric cable. Sergei did not turn away, he watched them flogging his mother and remained silent.

Then he was beaten in front of his mother, and he still said nothing. Fehnbong flew into a rage. Snatching an iron crow-bar from the table, he broke Sergei's sound arm at the elbow. Sergei turned white and sweat broke out on his forehead.

"That puts the lid on me," he said.

The same day, they brought to the prison the whole group of people who had been arrested in the Krasnodon mining settlement. Most of them were no longer able to walk; they were dragged in by their arms and pushed into the already overcrowded cells. Kolya Sumskoi was still able to move about, but one of his eyes had been struck by the lash, and was bleeding. Tosya Yeliseyenko, the girl who had once squealed delightedly at the sight of a tumbler pigeon soaring into the sky, could now only lie on her stomach; before being brought in, she had been held down on a red-hot stove.

They had no sooner been brought in than a gendarme entered the cell where the girls were confined and took Lyuba away. All of them, including Lyuba, were certain that she was being led out to be executed. She said good-bye to the girls and was taken away.

But she was not going to be executed. On the instructions of the Regional *Feldkommandant*, Major-General Klehr, they were taking her to Rovenki, where he would question her himself.

It was the day when parcels for the prisoners could be handed in, a still and frosty day. The ring of an axe, the clanging of a pail at the well, even the steps of passers-by were carried far on the still air which sparkled in the sunshine and snow. Yelizaveta Alexeyevna and Lyudmila, who always took parcels to the prison together, made up a bundle of food, took the pillow which Volodya had asked for in his last note, and set out along the path made in the snow, across the large open space towards the long prison building, which, with its white walls and the snow on the roof, tinted a delicate blue on the half that lay in shadow, merged into the surrounding locality.

Mother and daughter had become so thin that they more than ever resembled each other and could easily be taken for sisters. The mother who had always been sharp and abrupt now seemed to be a bundle of nerves.

Because of the sound of the women's voices, as they crowded outside the prison, and because all of them still held their parcels and made no move towards the prison door, Yelizaveta Alexeyevna and Lyudmila felt that something was seriously wrong. Paying no attention to the throng of women, the German sentry stood, as usual, at the porch. A policeman, in a yellow sheepskin jacket, was sitting on the banister of the porch steps. But he was not accepting any parcels.

Yelizaveta Alexeyevna and Lyudmila had no need to look round, to see which of the women were present, for they all met there every day.

Zemnukhov's mother, a little old woman, was standing in front of the porch steps holding a bundle and parcel in front of her.

"Take at least some of the food...." she pleaded.

"There's no need. We'll give him all the food he needs," said the policeman without looking at her.

"He asked me for a sheet."

"He'll get a good bed today."

Yelizaveta Alexeyevna went up to the porch and said in her abrupt tone of voice:

"Why aren't you accepting any parcels?"

The policeman paid no attention to her.

"We're not in a hurry; we'll stay here until somebody comes to give us an answer!" Yelizaveta Alexeyevna said, looking round at the crowd of women.

So they remained standing there, until suddenly they heard the footsteps of numerous feet inside the prison yard and someone unlocking the gate. The women always seized an opportunity of this kind to look into the cell windows facing the yard; sometimes they managed to catch a glimpse of those of their children who were in the cells. The throng of women rushed to the left side of the gate. A squad of soldiers under the command of Sergeant Bohlmann came out of the gates and began to disperse the women.

The women ran off, only to return again. Many of them began to wail.

Yelizaveta Alexeyevna and Lyudmila moved away a short distance and watched it all in silence.

"They'll execute them today," said Lyudmila.

"I only pray to God that they don't break him down before he dies, that he doesn't tremble before these dogs, that he spits in their faces!" Yelizaveta Alexeyevna said, her hoarse voice making a choking sound, her eyes shining with a terrible light.

Meanwhile, their children were undergoing the last, the most horrible ordeals it had been their lot to suffer.

Vanya Zemnukhov stood swaying before *Meister* Brückner, blood was pouring down his face, his head drooped helplessly, but he was doing his best to hold it upright, and finally he succeeded. Then for the first time in all the four weeks of silence, he spoke.

"You can't do it, can you?" he said. "You can't do it! You've seized so many countries ... all the honour and conscience you've rejected ... and yet you can't do it. You're not strong enough!"

And he laughed in their faces.

Late that night, two German soldiers carried Ulya into her cell. Her face was white, her plaits dragged along the floor. They tossed her up against the wall.

She groaned, and turned on to her stomach.

"Lilya dear," she said to the elder of the Ivanikhina girls. "Lift the blouse off my back—it stings me."

Lilya could hardly move herself, but to the very last she tended the others like a nurse; she gently turned back the blood-soaked blouse, then recoiled in horror and began to weep: a five-pointed star blazed in bloody weals on Ulya's back.

Never, until the last of this generation is laid in the grave, will the people of Krasnodon forget that night. The waning moon hung slantwise, unusually bright and clear. One could see for miles around in the open steppe. The frost was cruelly bitter. To the north, over the length of the Donets River there were flashes of light and the thunder of battles great and small rose in intensity and fell alternately.

None of their dear ones slept that night. Even people who were in no way related were awake, for they all knew that the Young Guards would be executed that night. Round their wick lamps, or in complete darkness, they sat in their unheated rooms or plaster huts, and from time to time one of them would go outside and stand a long time in the moonlight listening for the sound of voices, the rumbling of lorries, or the firing of rifles.

In the cells, too, no one slept except those who had been beaten unconscious. The Young Guards who had been the last to be tortured had seen Burgomaster Statsenko arrive at the prison. They all knew that the Burgomaster visited the prison prior to an execution, because his signature was required for the death sentence.

The sound of the majestic roar of battle rolling along the Donets reached the cells.

Half-lying on her side, with her head against the wall, Ulya tapped out a message to the boys in the adjoining cell:

"Boys, d'you hear, can you hear? Be strong.... Our men are coming. No matter what happens, our men are coming...."

The tramp of army boots was heard in the corridor, doors were slammed. The prisoners were led out into the corridor and then taken out to the street through the main doors, instead of by way of the prison-yard. The girls, sitting in their cell in overcoats or warm jackets, began to help one another to put on warm caps and tie their shawls. Anya Sopova lay motionless on the floor, and Lilya got her into a coat. Shura Dubrovina helped her dear friend Maya. Some of the girls scribbled their last notes and tucked them in with their discarded linen.

In her last parcel, Ulya had received fresh underclothing. She now began to make a bundle of her soiled linen but suddenly tears choked her. Unable to force them back, she buried her face in the blood-stained clothes to stifle her sobbing, and sat huddled over them for some minutes.

They were led out to the open space, flooded with moonlight, and loaded into two lorries. First they carried Stakhovich, completely helpless and out of his mind, and tossed him, with a swing, on to the lorry. Many of the Young Guards were unable to walk. They carried out Anatoly Popov, one of whose feet had been hacked off. Zhenya Shepelyov and Ragozin led out Vitya Petrov, whose eyes had been gouged from their sockets. Volodya Osmukhin's right hand had been cut off, but he was still able to walk unaided.

702

Tolya Orlov and Vitya Lukyanchenko carried out Vanya Zemnukhov. Behind them, swaying like a blade of grass, came Sergei Tyulenin.

Girls and youths were placed in different lorries.

Soldiers closed the hinged drop-sides and then climbed over them into the packed lorries. N.C.O. Fehnbong sat beside the driver of the first lorry. Both lorries moved off along the road across the open space and past the children's hospital and the Voroshilov School. The first lorry carried the girls. Ulya, Sasha Bondareva and Lilya began to sing:

> *Tormented by ruthless invaders*
> *A glorious death became yours....*

The other girls joined in. The youths sang, too, in the lorry behind. Their singing carried far into the distance in the still frosty air.

Leaving the last house behind on their left, the lorries swung on to the road, leading to No. 5 Pit.

Pressed hard against the back of the lorry, Sergei greedily drank in the frosty air. The lorries had already passed the road to the newly-built village and would soon cross the ravine. No, Sergei knew now that he was too weak to accomplish his plan. But Anatoly Kovalyov, kneeling on the floor boards in front of him, with his hands tied behind his back, was still strong; that was why his arms had been lashed behind his back. Sergei nudged him with his head. Kovalyov looked round.

"Anatoly, we're coming to the ravine...." Sergei whispered, with a nod of his head towards the side of the lorry.

As he looked over his shoulder, Anatoly struggled with his bound hands. Sergei attacked the knot with his teeth. He was so weak that he several times stopped to lean against the back of the lorry, the sweat standing out on his forehead. But he struggled, as though he were fighting for his own freedom. At last the knot was untied. Anatoly kept his arms behind his back, but moved them about a little.

> *...Relentless the rising avenger,*
> *And stronger than you and I...*

sang the girls and youths.

The lorries had descended to the ravine, the one in front was already about to make the ascent on the other side. Roaring and skidding, the second now also began to climb. Anatoly stood on the back of the lorry; then, in a flash, he had leapt off and was running across the ravine, ploughing up the snow.

For a moment there was general confusion, but the lorries had already climbed the slope, and Anatoly was out of sight. The soldiers hesitated to jump off the lorry for fear the other prisoners might get away, and began to fire at random from the lorry. Fehnbong heard the firing, stopped the lorry and jumped out. Both lorries drew up. Fehnbong's effeminate voice launched into furious cursing.

"He's escaped!... He's escaped!..." Sergei's piping voice cried out, in an indescribable frenzy of triumph. Then he swore roundly, in the most atrocious terms he knew; but coming from Sergei at such a moment the oaths sounded like the most sacred pledges.

The engine house of No. 5 Pit was now coming into view. It was leaning slantwise, as the result of the blast which had wrecked the pit below.

The young people began to sing the *Internationale*.

They were transferred from the lorries into the frozen building of the pit-head bath and kept there for some time, until the arrival of Brückner, Balder and Statsenko. The gendarmes began to undress those of them who had clothing and shoes in good condition.

The Young Guards were given an opportunity to say their last farewells. Klava Kovalyova was able to sit by Vanya's side, place her hand on his forehead and remain with him to the end.

They were taken out in small groups and hurled one by one into the pit shaft. Those who were able to speak had time to say the few words they wished to leave to the world.

Then, apprehensive lest not all of them would perish in the shaft, into which they had hurled, simultaneously, several dozen people, the Germans lowered two coal-wagons on to them. But the groans from the shaft were heard for several days afterwards.

With their wrists bound, Filipp Petrovich Lyutikov and Oleg Koshevoi stood facing *Feldkommandant* Klehr. During the whole time they were under arrest in Rovenki, they had not known that they were in the same prison. But this morning they had been brought together, then bound together, and confronted in the hope that they would disclose the threads of the whole underground organization, not only in the district but throughout the region.

Why had they been tied together? The Germans were afraid of them, except when they were bound. The enemy also wanted to demonstrate that they were aware of the role these two had played in the underground organization.

The grey hair on Lyutikov's head was matted with dried blood; his torn clothing stuck to the wounds on his large body and every movement caused him agonizing pain. But in no way did he give any indication of this. Excruciating torture and starvation had dried up his body, and on his face the strong lines, which had been so distinctive when he was younger and which indicated great mental powers, were more deeply defined. The expression in his eyes was calm and severe, as always.

Oleg's right arm had been broken, and it hung limp at his side. His face had scarcely changed, but the hair at his temples had turned quite grey. His large eyes, under the dark-golden lashes, held a clear expression, clearer than ever before.

So they stood before *Feldkommandant* Klehr—leaders of the people, one old and one young.

Feldkommandant Klehr, hardened to murder because there was nothing else he was capable of doing, subjected them to more frightful tortures, but one might say that they no longer felt anything: their spirit had soared to those boundless heights which only the great creative spirit of man can attain.

Later they were separated, and Lyutikov was taken back to the Krasnodon prison. The investigations into the case of the central workshops had not yet been completed.

The comrades working in the underground were unable, however, to help the prisoners, not only because the prison was heavily guarded but also because the town was full of retreating enemy troops.

Filipp Petrovich Lyutikov, Nikolai Barakov and their comrades met the same fate as the Young Guards: they were hurled down the shaft of No. 5 Pit.

Oleg Koshevoi was shot in Rovenki in the afternoon of January 31st. His body with those of others shot the same day was buried in a common pit.

They tortured Lyuba Shevtsova until February 7th, endeavouring to obtain from her the code and the wireless transmitter. Before she was shot she managed to send her mother a brief note:

"Good-bye, Mama, your daughter Lyuba is going away, into the damp ground."

As they led her out to be shot, she was singing one of her favourite songs:

On the sweeping plains of Moscow....

The SS *Rottenführer* who led her out to her execution wanted her to kneel and be shot in the nape of the neck, but Lyuba refused to go down on her knees and received the bullet in her face.

Chapter 30

WHEN LYUTIKOV gave Aunt Polina the address for Vanya Turkenich and Oleg to use, he took the precaution of instructing her not to tell them who lived there. He knew that Marfa Kornienko, to whom he was sending them, would inform Protsenko or his wife that they would arrive. They would know how to make use of the Young Guard leaders.

The very fact that Lyutikov had decided to pass on this most confidential address to Oleg and Turkenich was an indication of the faith he had in them, of the value he placed on them, of his anxiety for their fate.

But although Aunt Polina did not explain to Oleg where Lyutikov was sending him and Vanya Turkenich, Vanya had guessed at once that this was the way to the partisans.

He and Moshkov had been the only adults, the only mature comrades among the members of the Young Guard. To Vanya Turkenich, as to his comrades, the arrest of their friends had come as a bitter blow. All his mental powers had been concentrated on the problem of how to set them free. But unlike his comrades, Turkenich saw events in their true light. And with him, the idea of helping his friends was a practical one.

The shortest road to the liberation of his comrades was the road to the partisans. Turkenich knew that the Soviet forces had already entered Voroshilovgrad Region and were advancing, and that an armed uprising was in preparation in Krasnodon. He had no doubt whatever that, as a man with military experience, he would be given a detachment or at the least a chance to form a detachment. Without hesitation he made use of the address which Oleg had passed on to him.

He took it for granted that his name was possibly known to all the gendarmerie administrations and police-stations and did not risk taking any documents to establish his identity. He had no papers showing a false name, and there was no way of getting them. He set out on the road to the north without any documents whatever. The initial of his Christian name had been tattooed on his left wrist since childhood; he would, therefore, retain it, but he chose Krapivin for his surname.

He was in a difficult position. Neither his bearing nor his age, even, helped him to look like the sort of person who loafs from place to place behind the German lines without papers, without any occupation, and particularly in the immediate vicinity of the front. The explanations he might be able to give, if he fell into the hands of the Gestapo or the police, such as, that he had fled from the Reds at Olkhov Rog in Rostov Region when their tanks broke through to his farmstead and he had had no time to take his papers— such explanations could do no more than save his life. But they would inevitably doom him to work in the rear with the German troops or to deportation to Germany.

Avoiding all the villages and hamlets where he calculated he might run into the police, Vanya walked day and night. He went over the roads or across the steppe, always choosing the route which afforded the greatest cover. If he felt he was too conspicuous he lay low during the day and walked by night. His feet were nearly frozen, particularly when he had to lie low and had eaten almost nothing. Mental suffering had hardened his spirit; physically he was as hardy as any young Russian worker who had passed through the experiences of the Patriotic War.

So he arrived at Marfa Kornienko's cottage.

Enemy troops were quartered throughout the village, even in her own home, and at all the neighbouring farmsteads—Davidov, Makarov Yar and so on. Strong defence positions had been built along both banks of the Northern Donets. This line of German defence works formed such an effective dividing line between the northern and the southern part of Voroshilovgrad Region that contact between Marfa and Protsenko had become almost impossible. Even if contact had been possible, there was now no need for it. The partisan detachments of the northern districts of Voroshilovgrad Region were operating in close contact with units of the Red Army and were fighting under the command of those units and not under Protsenko. The detachments of the southern districts, which only came within range of the front in the middle of February, were now operating as circumstances permitted. Separated from them by scores of miles, Protsenko was unable to judge of the circumstances and could not guide the operations of the partisan detachments.

The Belovodsk detachment, to which Protsenko was attached, had relinquished its base in Gorodishchi village which was now held by the Germans. It had no permanent base and was operating in the German rear, following instructions from the Soviet Command. Marfa had no contact with Protsenko or her husband. Neither was she in touch with Kornei Tikhonovich or, for that matter, anyone else of the Mityakinskaya detachment, which had also abandoned its base; Mityakinskaya District was in the hands of the Germans, who were building fortifications there. By the time Vanya Turkenich arrived at Marfa's home, Katya Protsenko had been in Voroshilovgrad for some time and all contact with her had ceased.

Only his resourcefulness and daring had made the meeting between Vanya and Marfa possible. Moreover, it was lucky for him that the woman trusted him, trusted his word, though he had no papers; and she had no way of checking what he told her. She had met his calm, very serious look with feigned indifference at first. She had been struck at once by the tired, thin face with the determined wrinkles. She gradually became aware of his military bearing, his unassuming way of behaving and she had suddenly trusted him as only Slav women can trust—immediately and without error. True, she did not immediately let him see that she trusted him, but yet another miracle then happened.

After she had confirmed that she was Marfa Kornienko, Vanya recalled the name of Gordei Kornienko, of whose liberation from the prisoner of war camp he had been told by his namesake Vanya Zemnukhov and the others who had taken part in the operation. He asked Marfa whether he was her relation.

"Well? Supposing he is?" she said, a lively expression suddenly lighting her dark, young eyes.

"It was the boys of our Young Guard who freed him." And he told her how it had come about.

Her husband had more than once told her the story. And now all the womanly, motherly gratitude she had been unable to express to the lads who had freed her husband, was bestowed on Vanya Turkenich, and not in words or gestures. She merely gave him the address of her relatives in Gorodishchi.

"The front is quite near there, and they'll give you all the help you need to get through the lines," she told him.

Vanya nodded. He was not intending to cross the lines, but he wanted to find the partisans who were operating in cooperation with the Soviet forces. He could of course find them more quickly in the area to which Marfa was sending him.

They talked it over not in the village but out in the open steppe behind a barrow. Dusk was falling. Marfa told him she would send someone who would take him across the Donets during the night; then she left him. Modesty and pride forbade him to ask her for food. But Marfa was not the kind to forget such things. A little old man, the same who had exchanged clothing with Ivan Protsenko, brought Vanya some dried bread and a piece of pork fat in his cap. In an ominous whisper, the garrulous old gaffer explained to Vanya that he would not take him across the Donets because the man was not living who would dare to cross the river now, let alone take a partisan with him. But he would show him the way by which it was easiest and quickest to cross.

Vanya Turkenich crossed the Donets. A few days later he had reached Chuginka, a lonely village about seven miles south of Gorodishchi.

Now he found himself in a locality where there were frequent enemy fortifications and he observed large-scale movements of German troops. He had learned from the local people that there was a small police post in Chuginka and that German and Rumanian detachments frequently passed through the village. He was also told that Chuginka was the nearest point to Voloshino village on the Kamyshnaya River, near its confluence with the Derkul. Voloshino had already been recaptured by the Soviet troops and Vanya decided to get into Chuginka at all cost, because some of the villagers there might be in contact with the Soviet forces.

But at this point he was unfortunate: he was captured by the police just outside the village. He was taken to the building of the Village Council where the Russians serving as policemen for the Germans were engaged in a drunken orgy so abominable and degrading as to defy description.

Vanya was stripped to his underclothing; his hands and feet were bound and he was thrown into a cellar, the walls of which were frozen through. He was so exhausted by his journeyings, the ordeals he had come through and the last shock, that in spite of the terrible cold, which caused him to shiver all over, he fell asleep on the evil-smelling litter he discovered after crawling all over the earthen floor in the foul cellar.

He was awakened by a car, back-firing; in his sleep it had seemed to him like rifle shots. Immediately after, he heard the engines of several heavy cars which pulled up in the street outside. The floor thundered overhead shortly afterwards, the cellar door opened and in the light of the winter morning Vanya watched Soviet tommy-gunners in dark padded jackets entering the cellar. A sergeant at their head flashed the beam of his torch on Vanya.

Vanya had been liberated by a Soviet patrol which had broken into the village on three captured German armoured cars. In addition to the police, all of whom had already been captured and bound, there was a company of German soldiers stationed in the village, consisting in all of seven privates, one officer and a cook. The cook had just begun to prepare a meal when the German armoured cars arrived, and had been not a wit perturbed; he had even stood to attention just in case the chiefs were in the cars. Several minutes later, after he had been taken prisoner, he very willingly showed his captors where the company commander was sleeping. With the Soviet tommy-gunners on his heels, he tiptoed along in his monstrous *ersatz*-felt boots, made of straw, winked slyly, put a finger to his lips and said, "Sh-sh...!"

The senior lieutenant in command of the patrol, which for lack of petrol had to return to its unit, suggested that Turkenich should go with them. But Vanya refused the offer. The conversation took place, while the local people were crowding round the armoured cars, making much of the Red Army men and imploring them not to leave the village. And here was a man who would not leave them.... People? There were plenty here! He would find all the people he wanted right here! Arms? Just give them, for a start, the rifles of the captured German company; they would find more themselves! Only, he wanted to be put in touch with the Soviet units on the Kamyshnaya....

That was the beginning of the Ivan Krapivin partisan detachment which later became a byword throughout the region. A week later the detachment had some forty men, equipped with the latest arms, with the exception of artillery. It established its base on what had once been the dairy farm in Alexandrovo village, and it defended a district which covered several villages in the immediate rear of the German front; the Germans completely failed to dislodge the partisans of Ivan Krapivin's detachment from the area which they held until the arrival of the Soviet troops.

Yet Vanya did not succeed in liberating the Young Guard. The front on this sector remained stationary until January 20th; not until February did the Soviet forces cross the Northern Donets along a considerable length of its course; moreover, the earliest crossings had been made by units operating in the more distant, upper reaches of the river, in the Krasny Liman, Izyum and Balakleya area.

Vanya knew nothing of the tragic fate of the majority of his Young Guard comrades. But the longer the advance to

Krasnodon was delayed, the greater was the torment and anguish in his heart, the loftier, purer and nobler became the picture in his mind of those youths and girls with whom he had performed such glorious deeds, to whom the best part of his heart was given.

On one occasion some girls, the milkmaids at the dairy farm, hesitated to carry out one of his instructions, admitting frankly that they were afraid of the German fascists. Krapivin, one time Vanya Turkenich, showed no anger. Instead he said sadly:

"Oh, you girls! Is that behaving like Soviet girls?"

Then, forgetting all else, he began to tell them of Ulya Gromova and Lyuba Shevtsova and their friends. The girls were sincerely impressed. They were ashamed and, at the same time, spellbound by the sudden happy light in his eyes. Vanya abruptly stopped short, waved his arms to dismiss the subject and went off without finishing what he had to say.

Only in February, when Vanya Turkenich's detachment had joined forces with a unit of the Red Army and, with it, had fought its way across the Northern Donets, did Vanya arrive finally in Krasnodon.

The people of Krasnodon were meanwhile experiencing all the evils and horrors which the fleeing German army brought in its wake. Retreating SS units plundered the townsfolk, drove them from their homes, and blew up the pits, factories and all the larger buildings in the town and district.

Lyuba Shevtsova had died one week before the Red Army entered Krasnodon and Voroshilovgrad. On February 15th, Soviet tanks broke through to Krasnodon and immediately afterwards Soviet power was re-established in the town.

For many long and weary days, before the eyes of an immense crowd of people, the miners brought up the bodies of the underground fighters and the Young Guards from No. 5 Pit. During all those days the mothers and wives of the victims remained at the pit-head waiting to receive the mutilated bodies of their children and husbands.

Yelena Nikolayevna had gone to Rovenki while Oleg was

still alive. But she had been unable to do anything for her son and he did not even know that she was near.

And now, in the presence of his mother and all his family, the people of Rovenki brought out from the holes the bodies of Oleg and Lyuba.

It was difficult to recognize the former Yelena Koshevaya in the tiny, aged woman with the dark, sunken cheeks, and eyes that showed the profound suffering that strikes hardest at strong natures. Yet the fact that during the past months she had been helping her son in his work, and particularly his tragic death which had caused her so much pain, had revealed in her spiritual forces which raised her above her own, personal grief. It was as though the veil of humdrum existence which had concealed from her the great world of human effort, struggle and passion had now been lifted. She had now entered this world, following her son's footsteps, and before her lay the great road of service to the people.

During these days the details came to light of yet another German crime: the miners' grave in the park was opened up. When the bodies were exhumed, they were found to be in a standing position. First the heads were revealed, then the shoulders, trunks and hands. Among them were those of Valko, Shulga, Petrov and the woman with the baby in her arms.

The Young Guards and their elder comrades who had been brought to the surface from the shaft of No. 5 Pit, were given two fraternal graves in the park.

The funeral ceremony was attended by all the surviving members of the Krasnodon Underground Organization and the Young Guard: Ivan Turkenich, Valya Borts, Zhora Arutyuniants, Olya and Nina Ivantsova, Radik Yurkin and others.

Turkenich's unit had moved out of Krasnodon towards the River Mius, but he was given leave so that he could bid his last farewell to his friends who had met their death.

Valya Borts made her way home from where she was, near Kamensk, and her mother sent her to stay with friends in Voroshilovgrad. Valya was there to meet the Red Army, when it entered the town.

Sergei Levashov was no longer among the living. He had been killed while attempting to cross the front lines.

Styopa Safonov, too, had met his death. He was in the part of Kamensk that had been captured by the Red Army during the first night of the assault. He had joined one of the Red Army detachments and had been killed in the fighting.

Anatoly Kovalyov, after leaping from the lorry, had been concealed for a time by a worker in the newly-built village. His powerful frame had been so badly cut about that it seemed to be one continuous wound. There was no possibility of bandaging his wounds; they had simply washed him in warm water and wrapped him in a sheet. He remained hidden for several days, but it had been risky to keep him any longer. He left to join his relatives who were living in a part of the Donbas which had not yet been liberated.

Ivan Protsenko and his detachment continued to move just ahead of the retreating Germans, fighting them in their immediate rear, until the Red Army captured Voroshilovgrad. Only there did Protsenko meet his wife Katya for the first time since their separation outside Gorodishchi.

On Protsenko's instructions, a group of partisans, under the guidance of Kornei Tikhonovich, dug out the famous Gazik from the cave in the quarry near Mityakinskaya. They found it undamaged with its tank full and even a spare tin of petrol, immortal as the age which had given it birth.

Ivan Protsenko and Katya drove into Krasnodon in the Gazik and on the way took Gordei Kornienko home to his Marfa. There, too, they listened to Marfa's story of the last days of the Germans in the village.

The day before the Soviet troops had captured the village, Marfa and the old gaffer, who had at one time driven the Koshevois in his cart and had later changed clothing with Protsenko, had gone to the building of the Village Council where policemen and German gendarmes on the run from beyond the Donets had temporarily established themselves. A large number of the villagers had been crowding round the building in the hope of hearing a chance remark as to how far or how near the Red Army was, or simply in order to derive pleasure from the sight of the fleeing fascists.

While Marfa and the old man stood there another police official had driven up on a horse-drawn sleigh. He had leapt out, glanced about wild-eyed, and hurriedly asked the old man:

"Where's the *Herr* Chief?"

The old man had peered at him and said:

"The *Herr* Chief! It appears the comrades are coming!"

The police official had sworn, but had been in too much of a hurry to strike the old man.

The Germans, chewing as they came, had rushed out of the building and, a moment later, had driven hurriedly away on sleighs, a cloud of snow-dust swirling behind them.

The Red Army had arrived in the village the following day.

Ivan Protsenko and Katya arrived in Krasnodon to honour the memory of the underground fighters and Young Guards, who had lost their lives.

Protsenko had other business there, as well: he had to restore the Krasnodon Coal Trust and the pits. Moreover, he wanted to hear at first hand the details of the death of the adult underground workers and the Young Guards and to learn what had become of their butchers.

Statsenko and Solikovsky had managed to escape with their masters, but Examining Judge Kuleshov had been recognized by some of the local people; he had been detained and handed over to the Soviet judicial authorities. Through him the facts became known of Stakhovich's evidence and the part Vyrikova and Lyadskaya had played in the betrayal of the Young Guards.

At the graves of the fallen Communists and Young Guards, their surviving comrades vowed to avenge them. Temporary monuments were erected over the graves in the form of simple wooden obelisks. The obelisk over the grave of the adult underground fighters was inscribed with their names, headed by those of Filipp Petrovich Lyutikov and Barakov, while on the sides of the Young Guard obelisk were inscribed the names of all who had fought in its ranks and given their lives for the Motherland.

Here are the names:

Oleg Koshevoi. Ivan Zemnukhov. Ulyana Gromova. Sergei Tyulenin. Lyubov Shevtsova. Anatoly Popov. Nikolai Sumskoi. Vladimir Osmukhin. Anatoly Orlov. Sergei Levashov. Stepan Safonov. Victor Petrov. Antonina Yeliseyenko.

Victor Lukyanchenko. Klavdia Kovalyova. Maya Peglivanova. Alexandra Bondareva. Vasily Bondarev. Alexandra Dubrovina. Lidia Androsova. Antonina Mashchenko. Yevgeny Moshkov. Lilia Ivanikhina. Antonina Ivanikhina. Boris Glavan. Vladimir Ragozin. Yevgeny Shepelyov. Anna Sopova. Vladimir Zhdanov. Vasily Pirozhok. Semyon Ostapenko. Gennady Lukashev. Angelina Samoshina. Nina Minaeva. Leonid Dadyshev. Alexander Shishchenko. Anatoly Nikolayev. Demyan Fomin. Nina Gerasimova. Georgy Shcherbakov. Nina Startseva. Nadezhda Petlya. Vladimir Kulikov. Yevgenia Kiikova. Nikolai Zhukov. Vladimir Zagoruiko. Yury Vitsenovsky. Mikhail Grigoryev. Vasily Borisov. Nina Kezikova. Antonina Dyachenko. Nikolai Mironov. Vasily Tkachov. Pavel Palaguta. Dmitry Ogurtsov. Victor Subbotin.

1943-1945-1951

CPSIA information can be obtained
at www.ICGtesting.com
Printed in the USA
BVHW032046090521
606892BV00004B/7